BRANDON
HARRUP
CHARLES

BH

SCHOOL TRIP

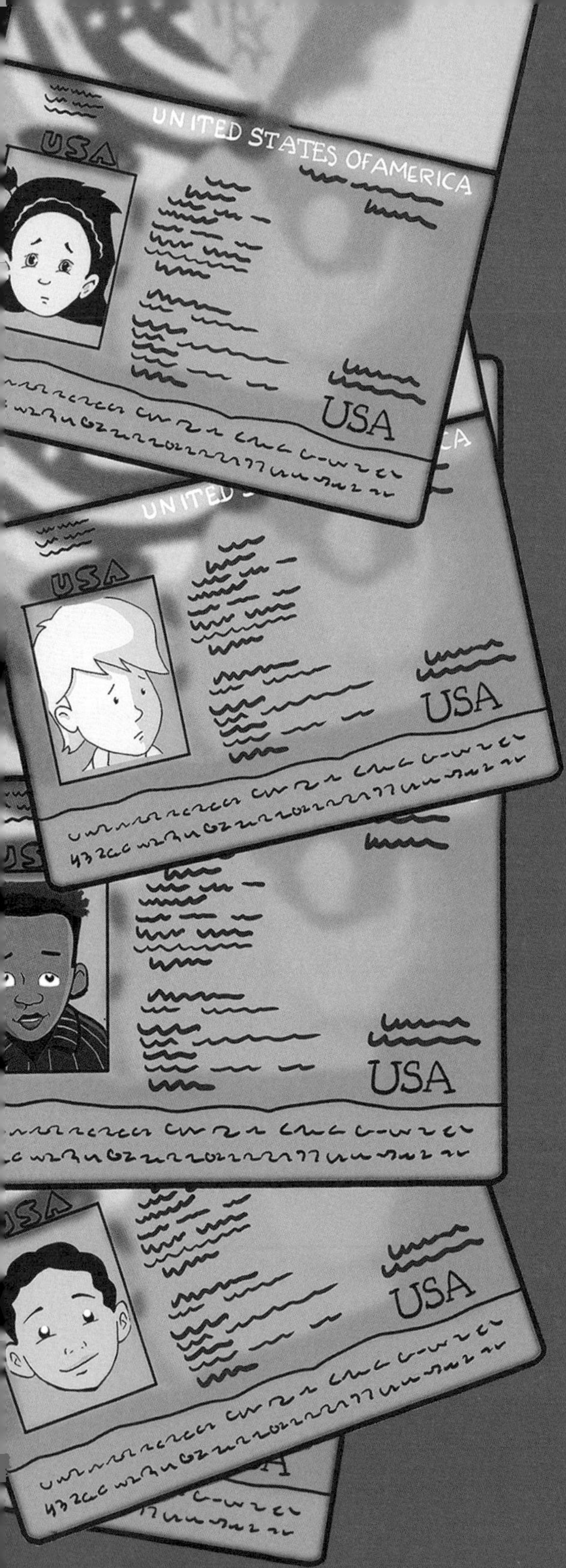

USA
UNITED STATES OF AMERICA
USA
USA
UNITED
USA
USA
USA
USA
USA

JERRY CRAFT

SCHOOL TRIP

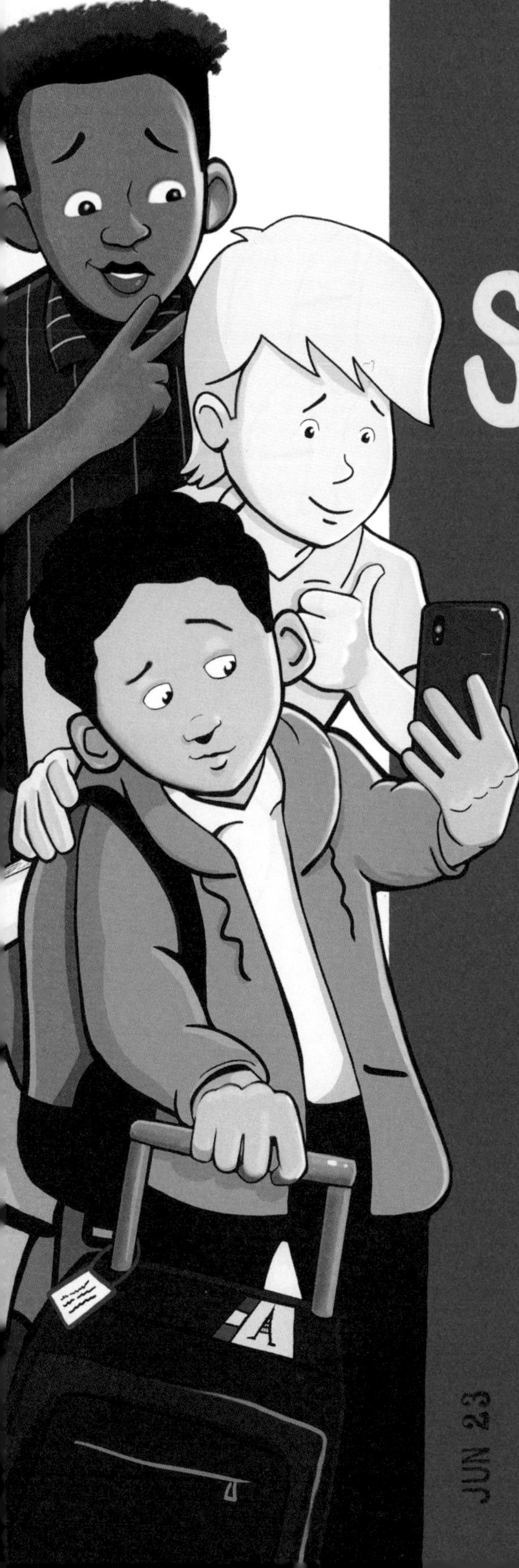

Quill Tree Books
Imprints of HarperCollinsPublishers

HARPER alley

Quill Tree Books and HarperAlley are imprints
of HarperCollins Publishers.

School Trip
Copyright © 2023 by Jerry Craft
All rights reserved. Manufactured in Bosnia and Herzegovina.
No part of this book may be used or reproduced in any manner
whatsoever without written permission except in the case of
brief quotations embodied in critical articles and reviews.
For information address HarperCollins Children's Books,
a division of HarperCollins Publishers,
195 Broadway, New York, NY 10007.
www.harperalley.com

Library of Congress Control Number: 2022946437
ISBN 978-0-06-288553-1 (paperback) - ISBN 978-0-06-288554-8
(hardcover)

22 23 24 25 26   GPS   10 9 8 7 6 5 4 3 2 1
❖
First Edition

Don't be a thumbs-downer!

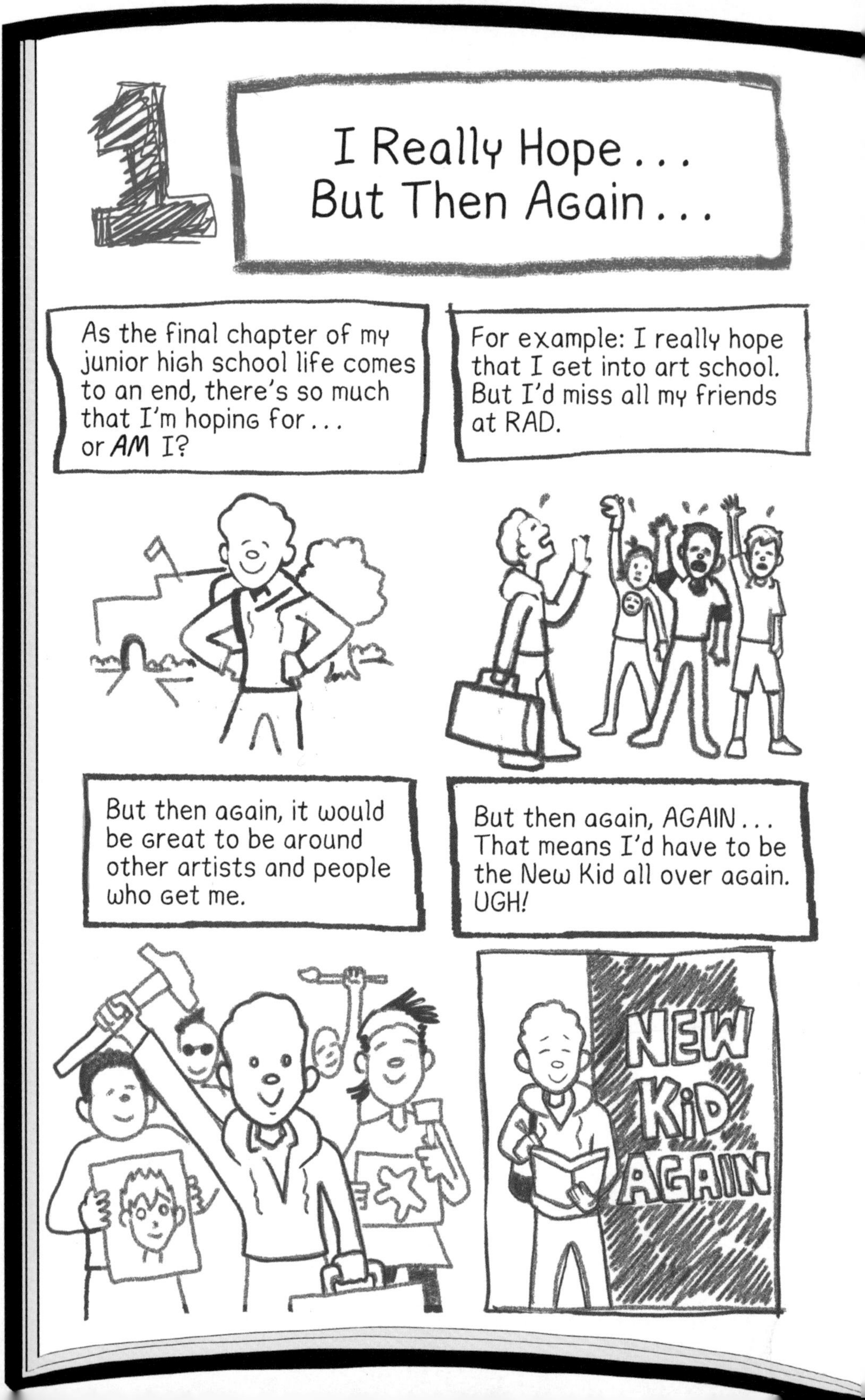
1
I Really Hope . . .
But Then Again . . .
As the final chapter of my junior high school life comes to an end, there's so much that I'm hoping for . . . or AM I?
For example: I really hope that I get into art school. But I'd miss all my friends at RAD.
But then again, it would be great to be around other artists and people who get me.
But then again, AGAIN . . . That means I'd have to be the New Kid all over again. UGH!
NEW KiD AGAIN

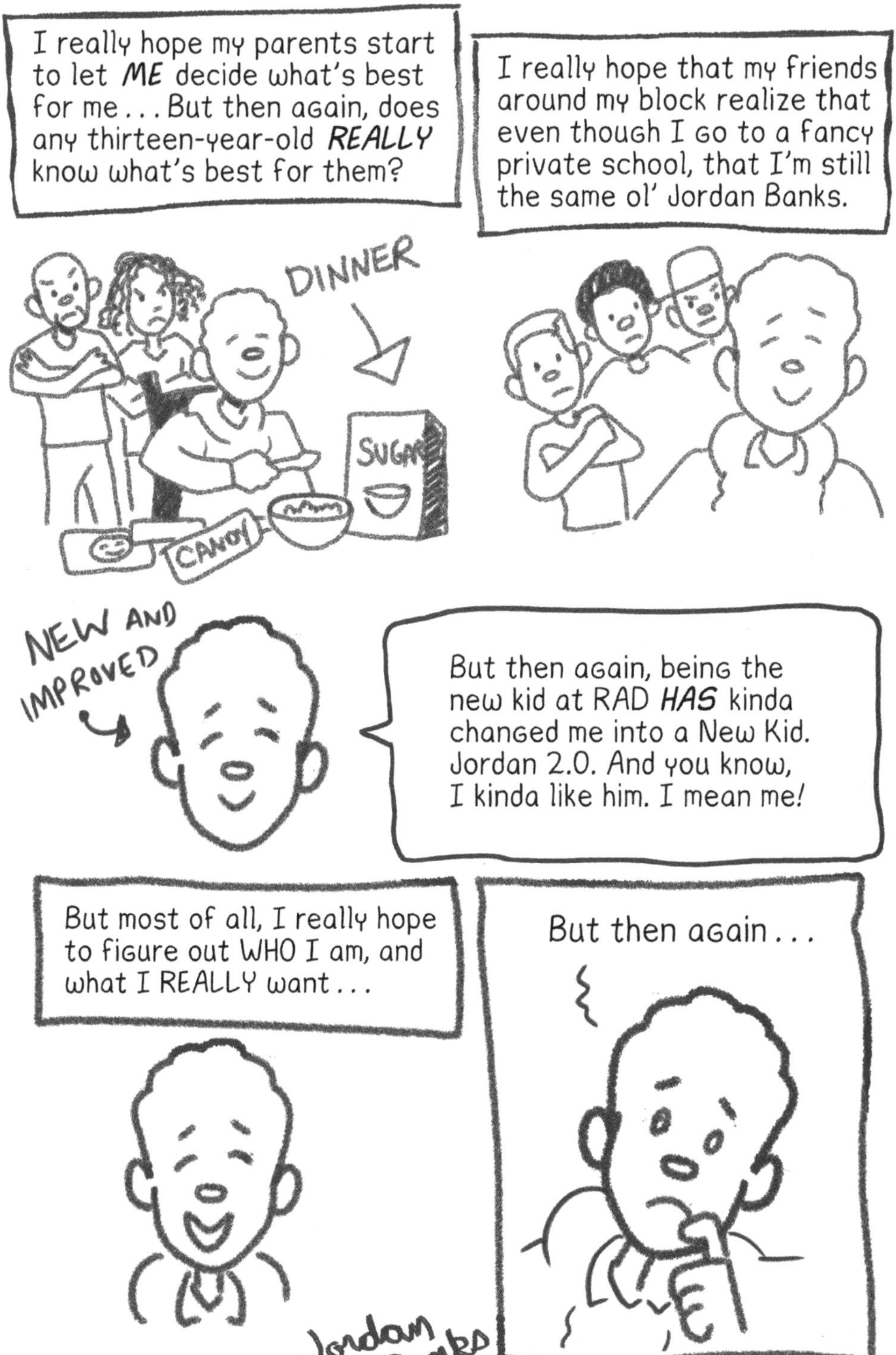

I really hope my parents start to let *ME* decide what's best for me . . . But then again, does any thirteen-year-old *REALLY* know what's best for them?
DINNER
SUGAR
CANDY
I really hope that my friends around my block realize that even though I go to a fancy private school, that I'm still the same ol' Jordan Banks.
NEW AND IMPROVED
But then again, being the new kid at RAD *HAS* kinda changed me into a New Kid. Jordan 2.0. And you know, I kinda like him. I mean me!
But most of all, I really hope to figure out WHO I am, and what I REALLY want . . .
Jordan Banks
But then again . . .

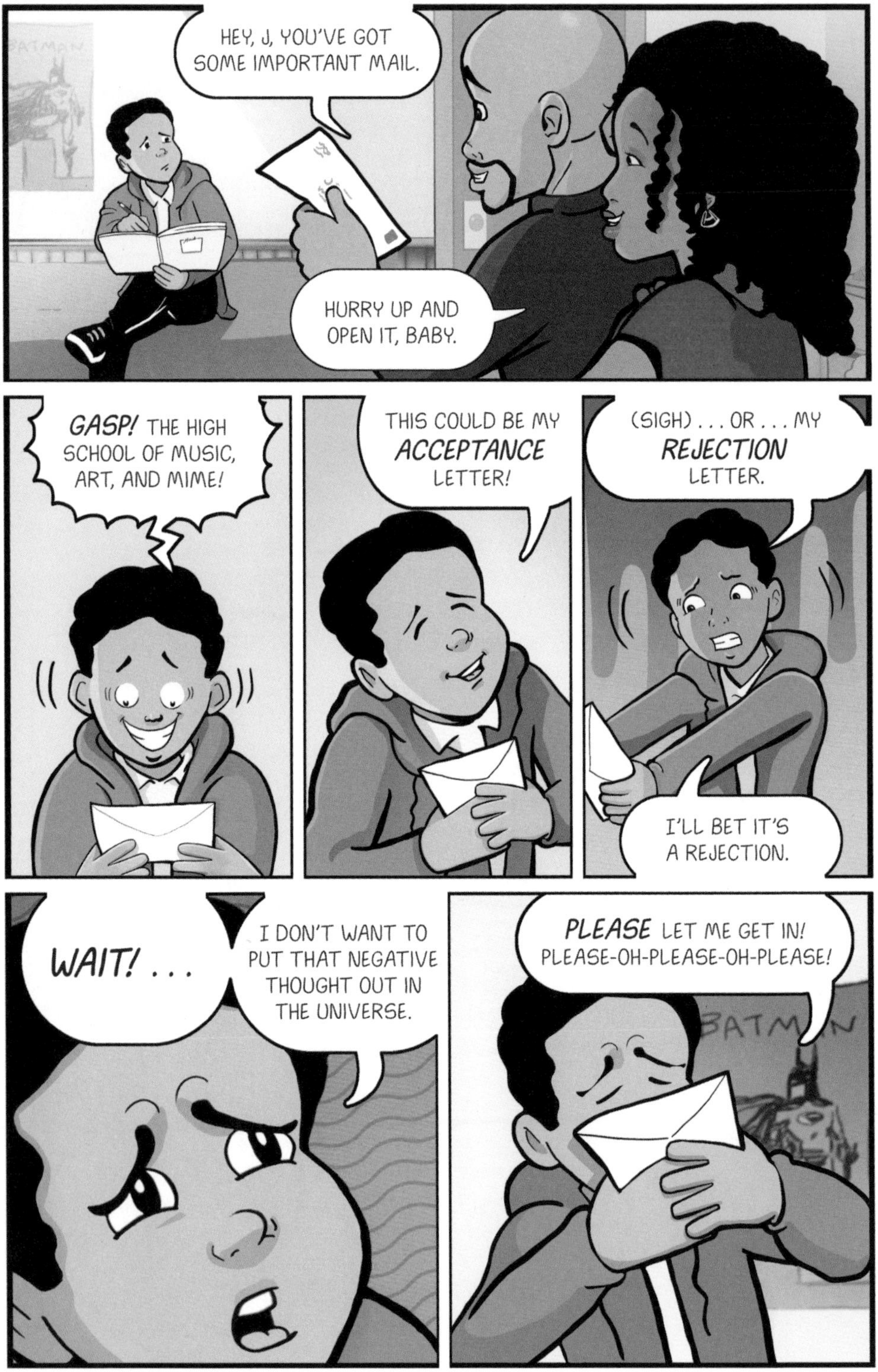
HEY, J, YOU'VE GOT SOME IMPORTANT MAIL.
HURRY UP AND OPEN IT, BABY.
GASP! THE HIGH SCHOOL OF MUSIC, ART, AND MIME!
THIS COULD BE MY ACCEPTANCE LETTER!
(SIGH) . . . OR . . . MY REJECTION LETTER.
I'LL BET IT'S A REJECTION.
WAIT! . . .
I DON'T WANT TO PUT THAT NEGATIVE THOUGHT OUT IN THE UNIVERSE.
PLEASE LET ME GET IN! PLEASE-OH-PLEASE-OH-PLEASE!

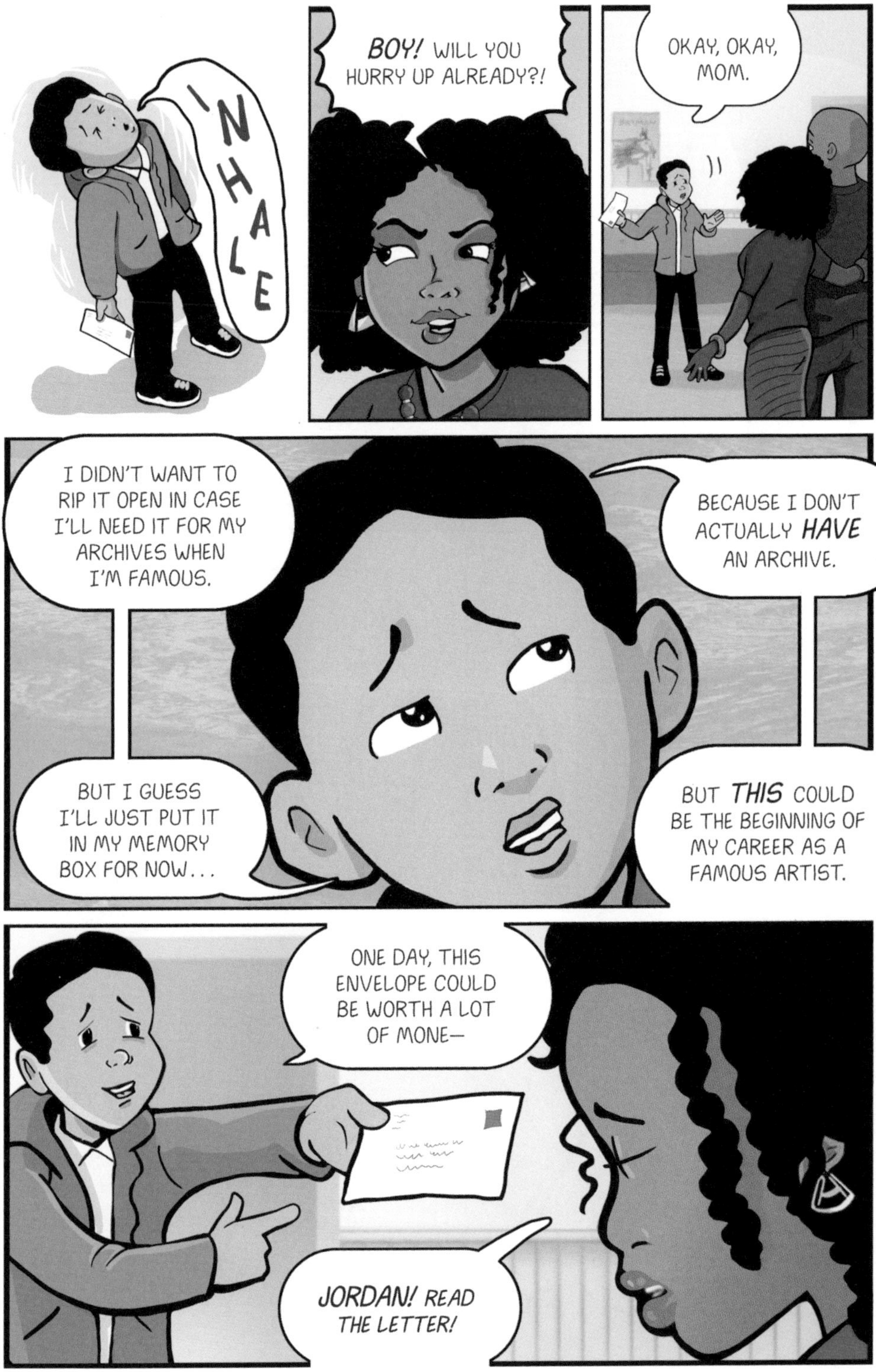
INHALE
BOY! WILL YOU HURRY UP ALREADY?!
OKAY, OKAY, MOM.
I DIDN'T WANT TO RIP IT OPEN IN CASE I'LL NEED IT FOR MY ARCHIVES WHEN I'M FAMOUS.
BUT I GUESS I'LL JUST PUT IT IN MY MEMORY BOX FOR NOW...
BECAUSE I DON'T ACTUALLY HAVE AN ARCHIVE.
BUT THIS COULD BE THE BEGINNING OF MY CAREER AS A FAMOUS ARTIST.
ONE DAY, THIS ENVELOPE COULD BE WORTH A LOT OF MONE—
JORDAN! READ THE LETTER!

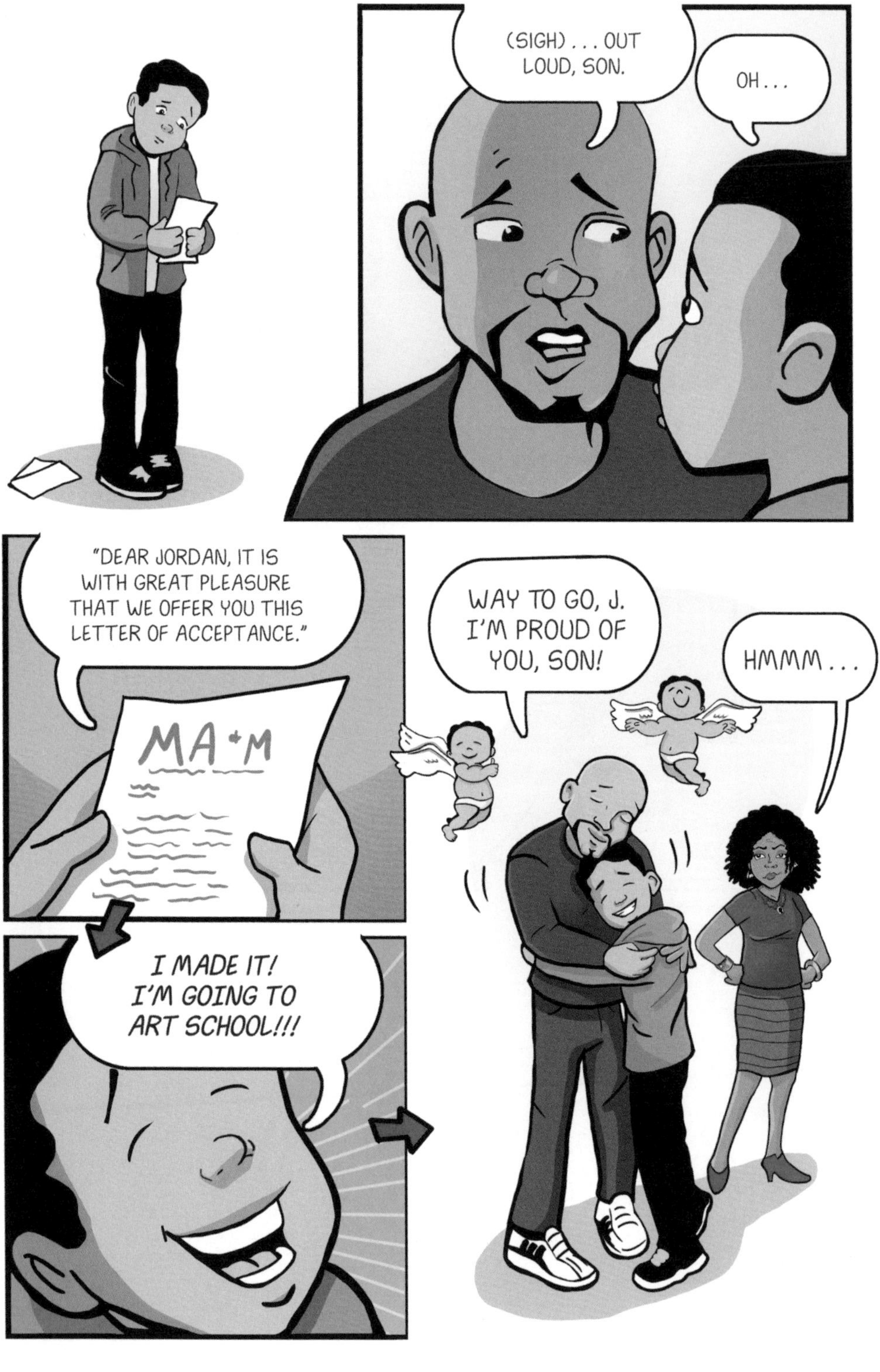
(SIGH) . . . OUT LOUD, SON.
OH . . .
"DEAR JORDAN, IT IS WITH GREAT PLEASURE THAT WE OFFER YOU THIS LETTER OF ACCEPTANCE."
MA+M
I MADE IT! I'M GOING TO ART SCHOOL!!!
WAY TO GO, J. I'M PROUD OF YOU, SON!
HMMM . . .

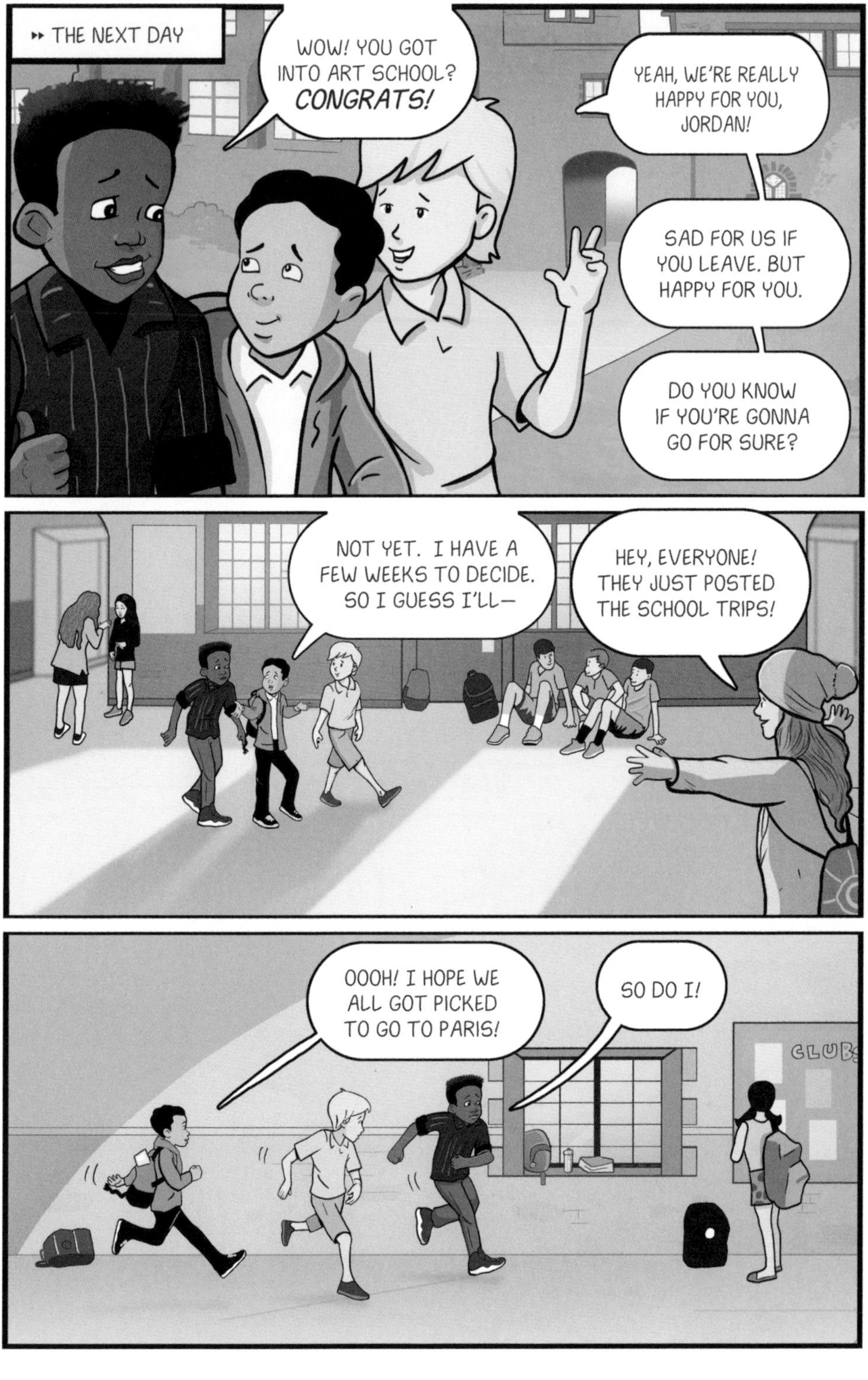
THE NEXT DAY
WOW! YOU GOT INTO ART SCHOOL? *CONGRATS!*
YEAH, WE'RE REALLY HAPPY FOR YOU, JORDAN!
SAD FOR US IF YOU LEAVE. BUT HAPPY FOR YOU.
DO YOU KNOW IF YOU'RE GONNA GO FOR SURE?
NOT YET. I HAVE A FEW WEEKS TO DECIDE. SO I GUESS I'LL—
HEY, EVERYONE! THEY JUST POSTED THE SCHOOL TRIPS!
OOOH! I HOPE WE ALL GOT PICKED TO GO TO PARIS!
SO DO I!
CLUB

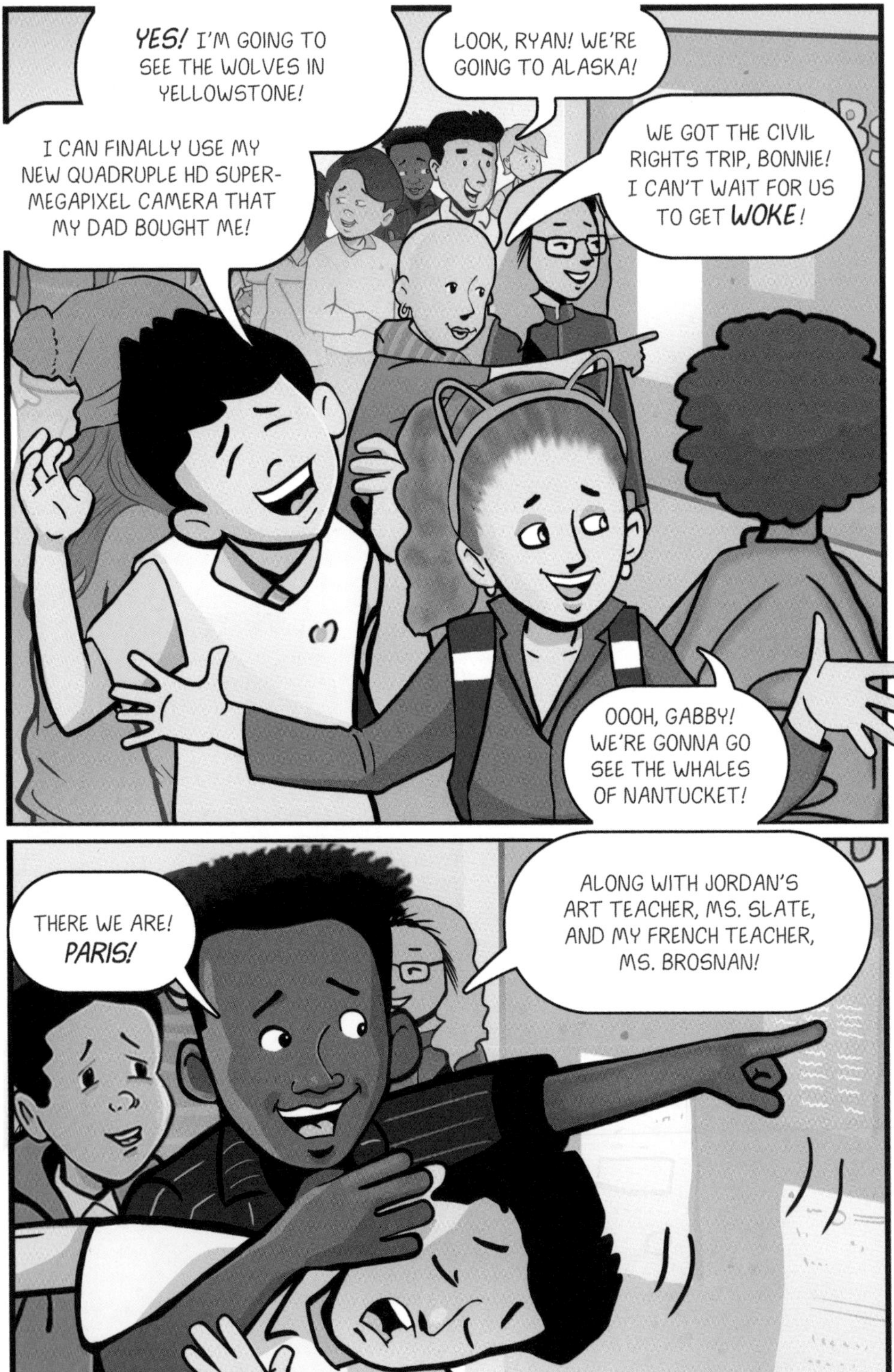
YES! I'M GOING TO SEE THE WOLVES IN YELLOWSTONE!
LOOK, RYAN! WE'RE GOING TO ALASKA!
I CAN FINALLY USE MY NEW QUADRUPLE HD SUPER-MEGAPIXEL CAMERA THAT MY DAD BOUGHT ME!
WE GOT THE CIVIL RIGHTS TRIP, BONNIE! I CAN'T WAIT FOR US TO GET WOKE!
OOOH, GABBY! WE'RE GONNA GO SEE THE WHALES OF NANTUCKET!
THERE WE ARE! PARIS!
ALONG WITH JORDAN'S ART TEACHER, MS. SLATE, AND MY FRENCH TEACHER, MS. BROSNAN!

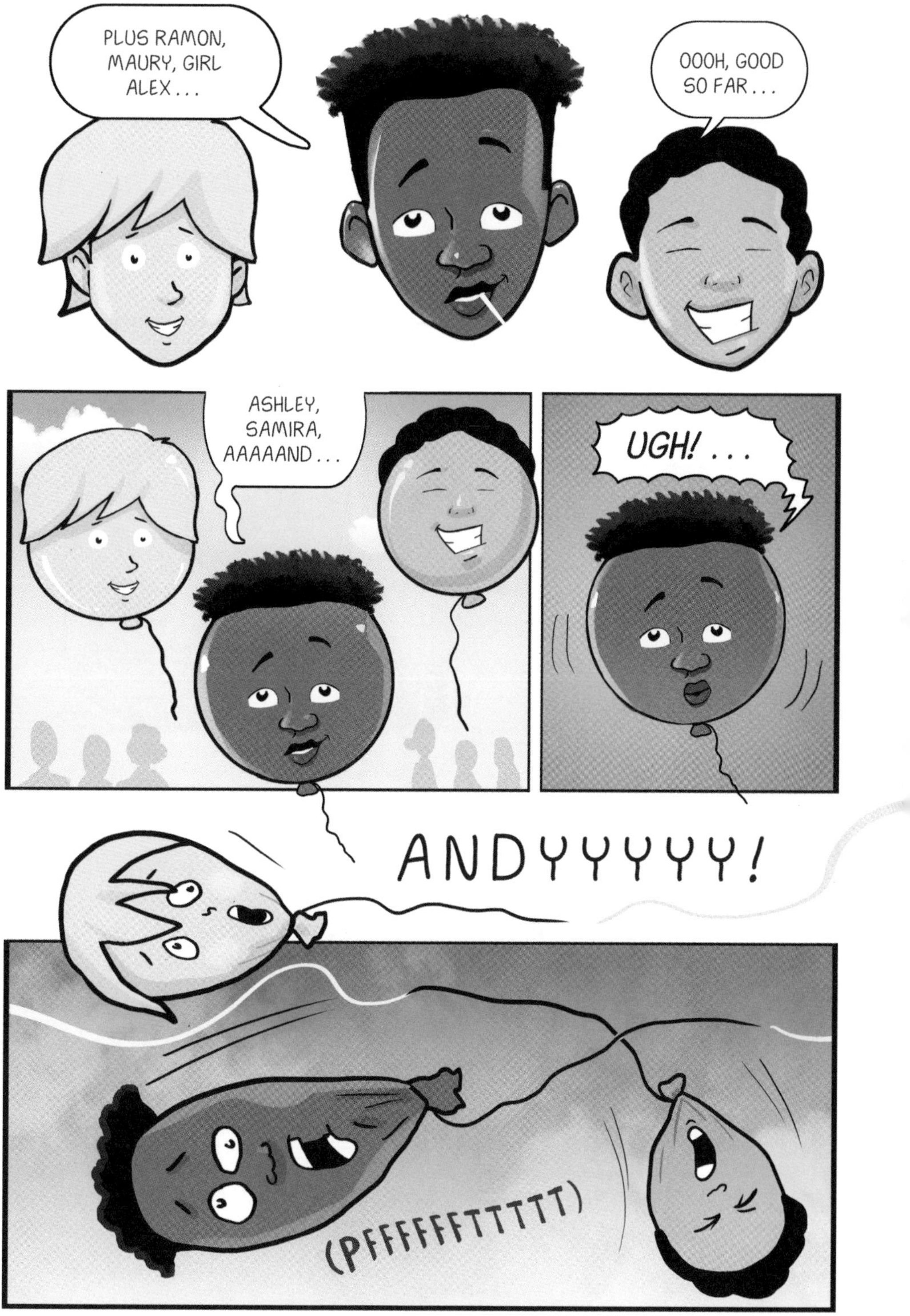
PLUS RAMON, MAURY, GIRL ALEX...
OOOH, GOOD SO FAR...
ASHLEY, SAMIRA, AAAAAND...
UGH! ...
ANDYYYYYY!
(PFFFFFFTTTTT)

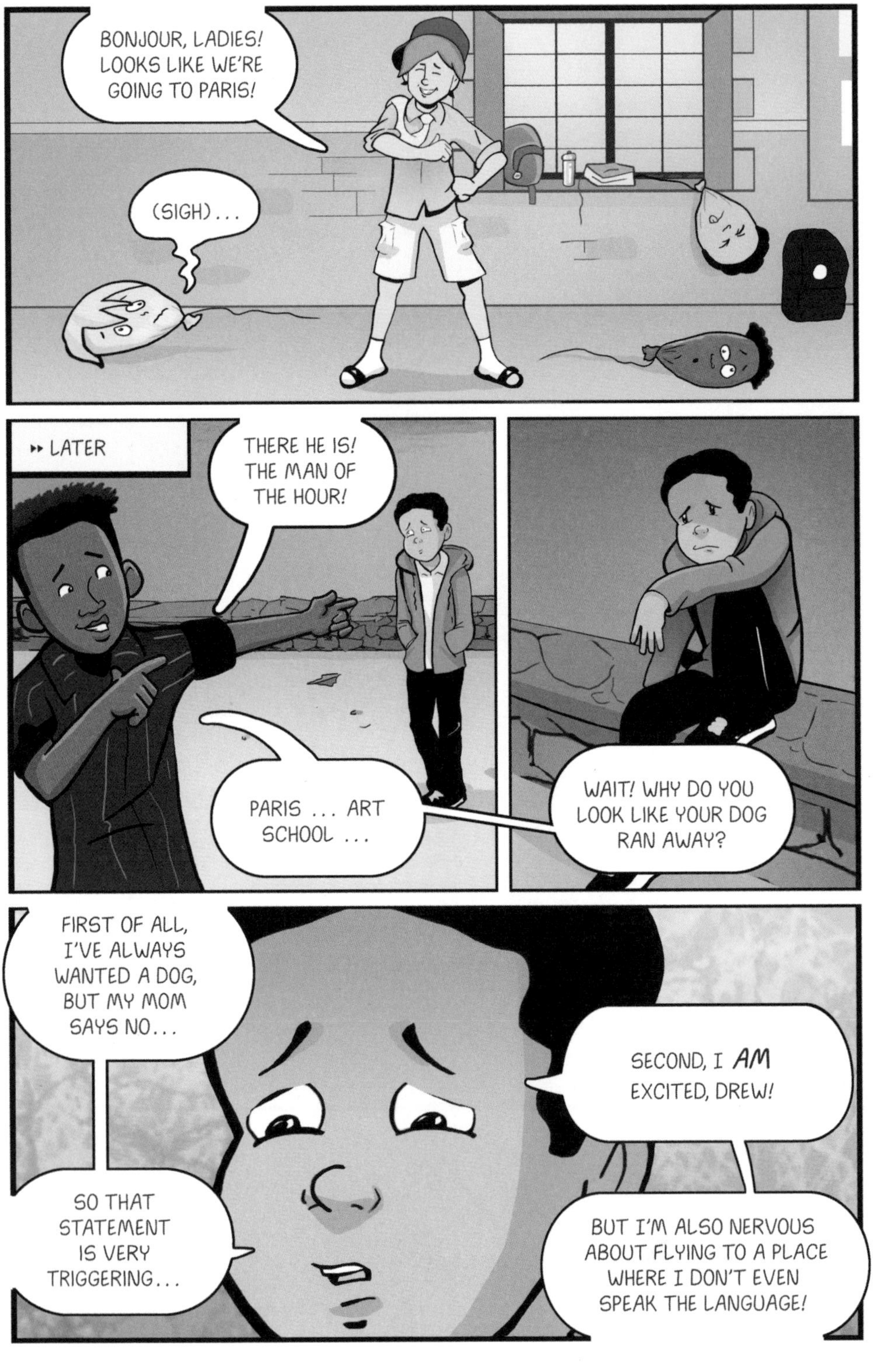
BONJOUR, LADIES! LOOKS LIKE WE'RE GOING TO PARIS!
(SIGH) . . .
LATER
THERE HE IS! THE MAN OF THE HOUR!
WAIT! WHY DO YOU LOOK LIKE YOUR DOG RAN AWAY?
PARIS . . . ART SCHOOL . . .
FIRST OF ALL, I'VE ALWAYS WANTED A DOG, BUT MY MOM SAYS NO . . .
SO THAT STATEMENT IS VERY TRIGGERING . . .
SECOND, I AM EXCITED, DREW!
BUT I'M ALSO NERVOUS ABOUT FLYING TO A PLACE WHERE I DON'T EVEN SPEAK THE LANGUAGE!

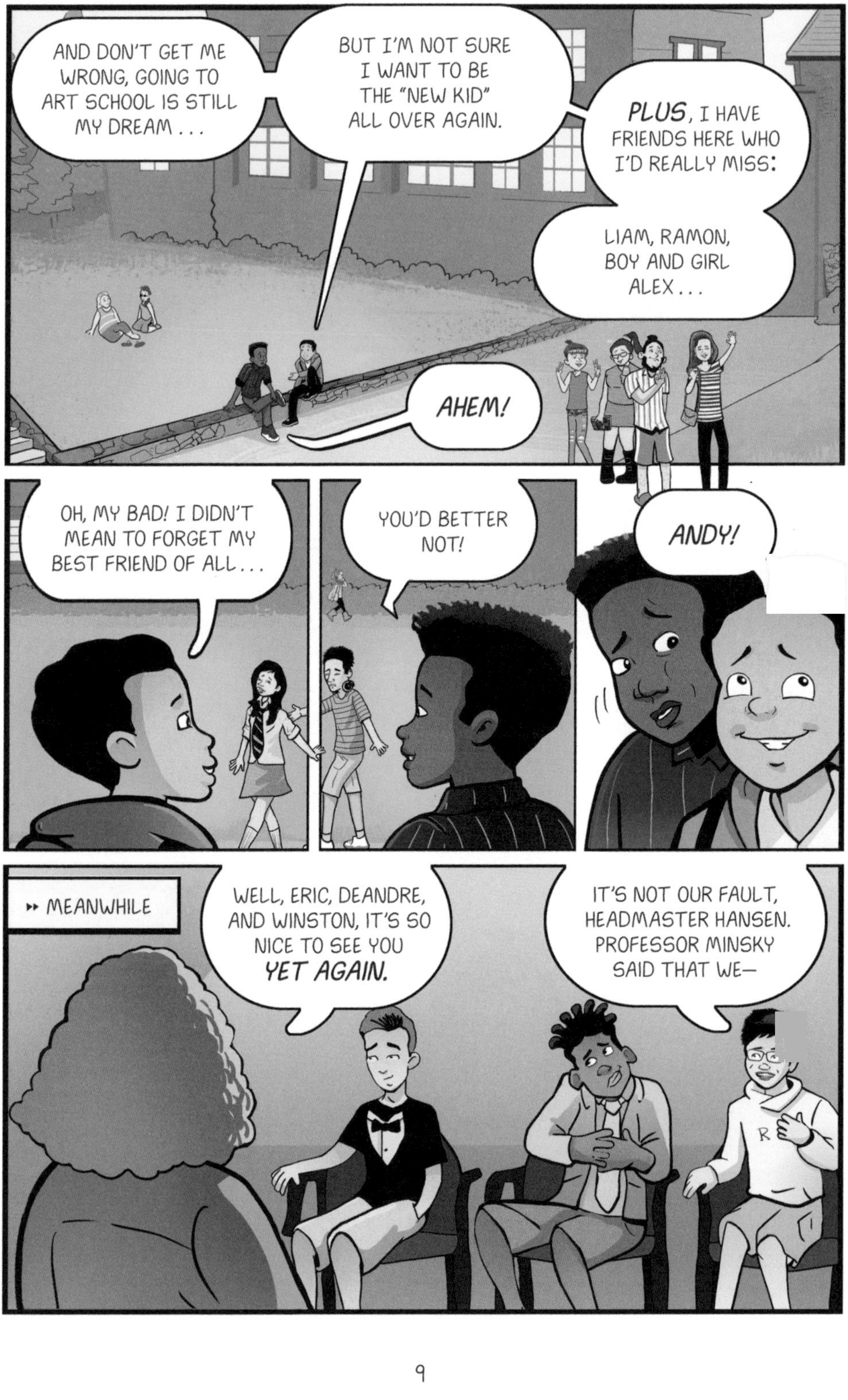
AND DON'T GET ME WRONG, GOING TO ART SCHOOL IS STILL MY DREAM . . .
BUT I'M NOT SURE I WANT TO BE THE "NEW KID" ALL OVER AGAIN.
PLUS, I HAVE FRIENDS HERE WHO I'D REALLY MISS:
LIAM, RAMON, BOY AND GIRL ALEX . . .
AHEM!
OH, MY BAD! I DIDN'T MEAN TO FORGET MY BEST FRIEND OF ALL . . .
YOU'D BETTER NOT!
ANDY!
MEANWHILE
WELL, ERIC, DEANDRE, AND WINSTON, IT'S SO NICE TO SEE YOU YET AGAIN.
IT'S NOT OUR FAULT, HEADMASTER HANSEN. PROFESSOR MINSKY SAID THAT WE—

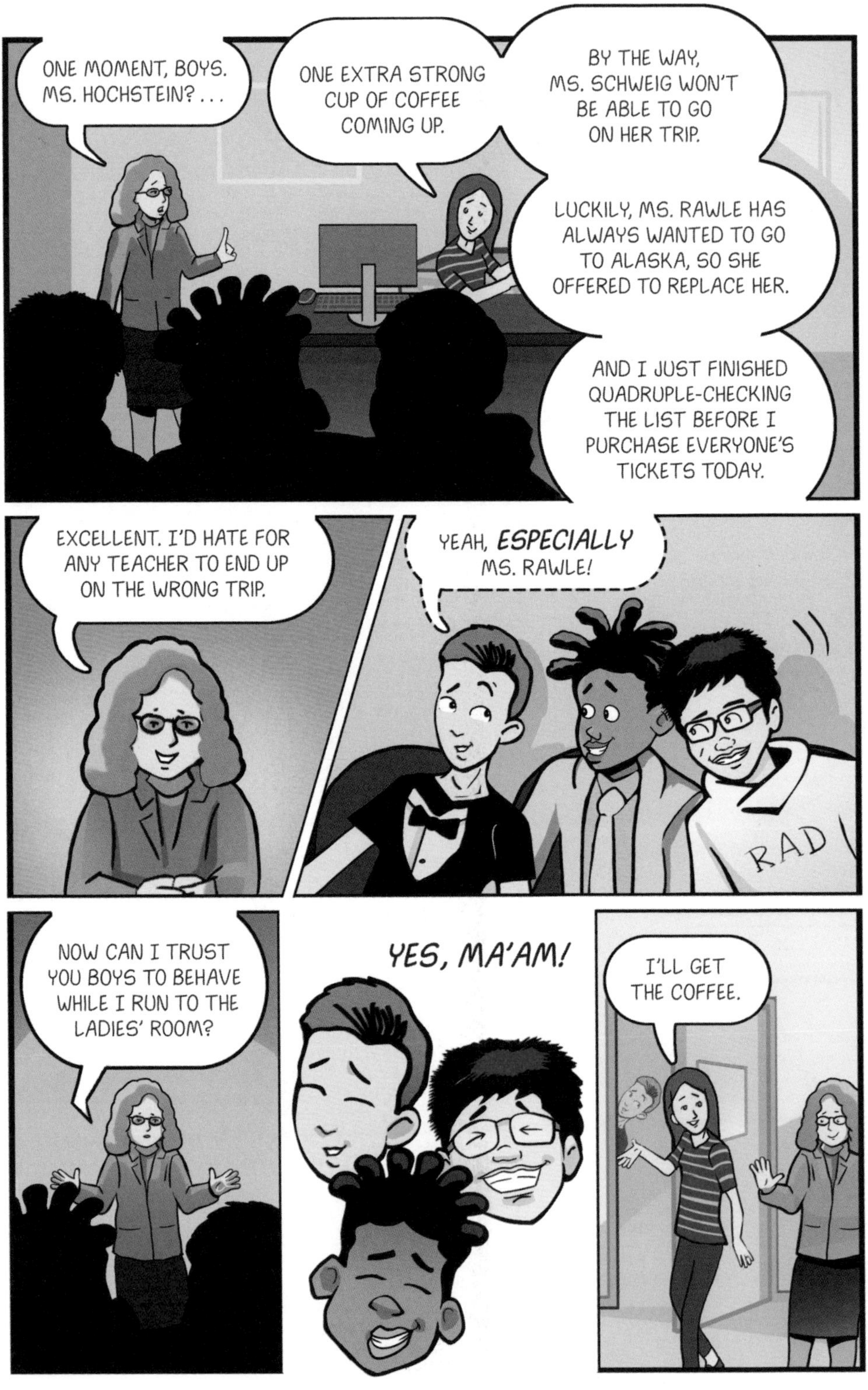
ONE MOMENT, BOYS. MS. HOCHSTEIN? . . .
ONE EXTRA STRONG CUP OF COFFEE COMING UP.
BY THE WAY, MS. SCHWEIG WON'T BE ABLE TO GO ON HER TRIP.
LUCKILY, MS. RAWLE HAS ALWAYS WANTED TO GO TO ALASKA, SO SHE OFFERED TO REPLACE HER.
AND I JUST FINISHED QUADRUPLE-CHECKING THE LIST BEFORE I PURCHASE EVERYONE'S TICKETS TODAY.
EXCELLENT. I'D HATE FOR ANY TEACHER TO END UP ON THE WRONG TRIP.
YEAH, ***ESPECIALLY*** MS. RAWLE!
RAD
NOW CAN I TRUST YOU BOYS TO BEHAVE WHILE I RUN TO THE LADIES' ROOM?
YES, MA'AM!
I'LL GET THE COFFEE.

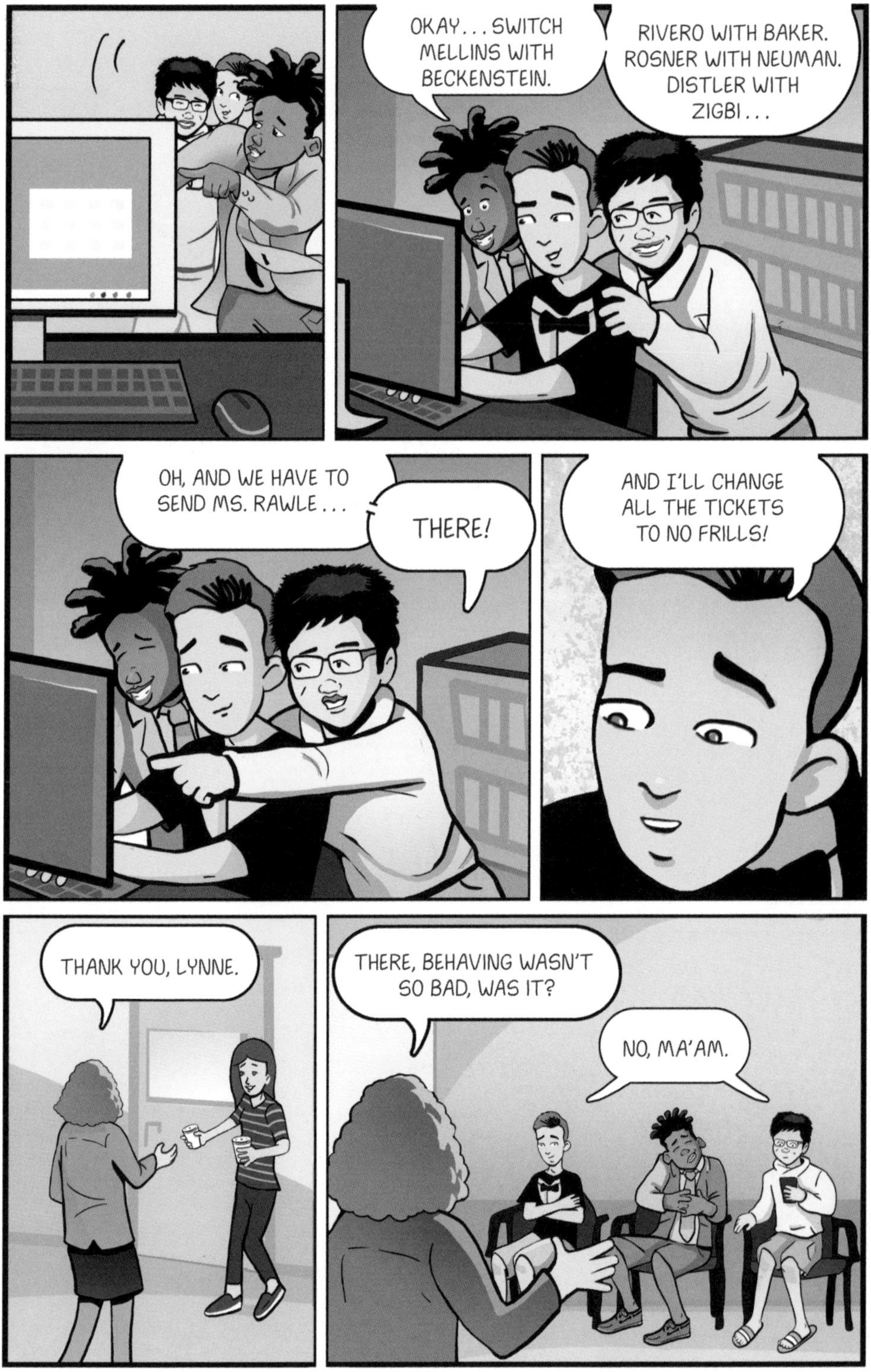
OKAY... SWITCH MELLINS WITH BECKENSTEIN.
RIVERO WITH BAKER. ROSNER WITH NEUMAN. DISTLER WITH ZIGBI...
OH, AND WE HAVE TO SEND MS. RAWLE...
THERE!
AND I'LL CHANGE ALL THE TICKETS TO NO FRILLS!
THANK YOU, LYNNE.
THERE, BEHAVING WASN'T SO BAD, WAS IT?
NO, MA'AM.

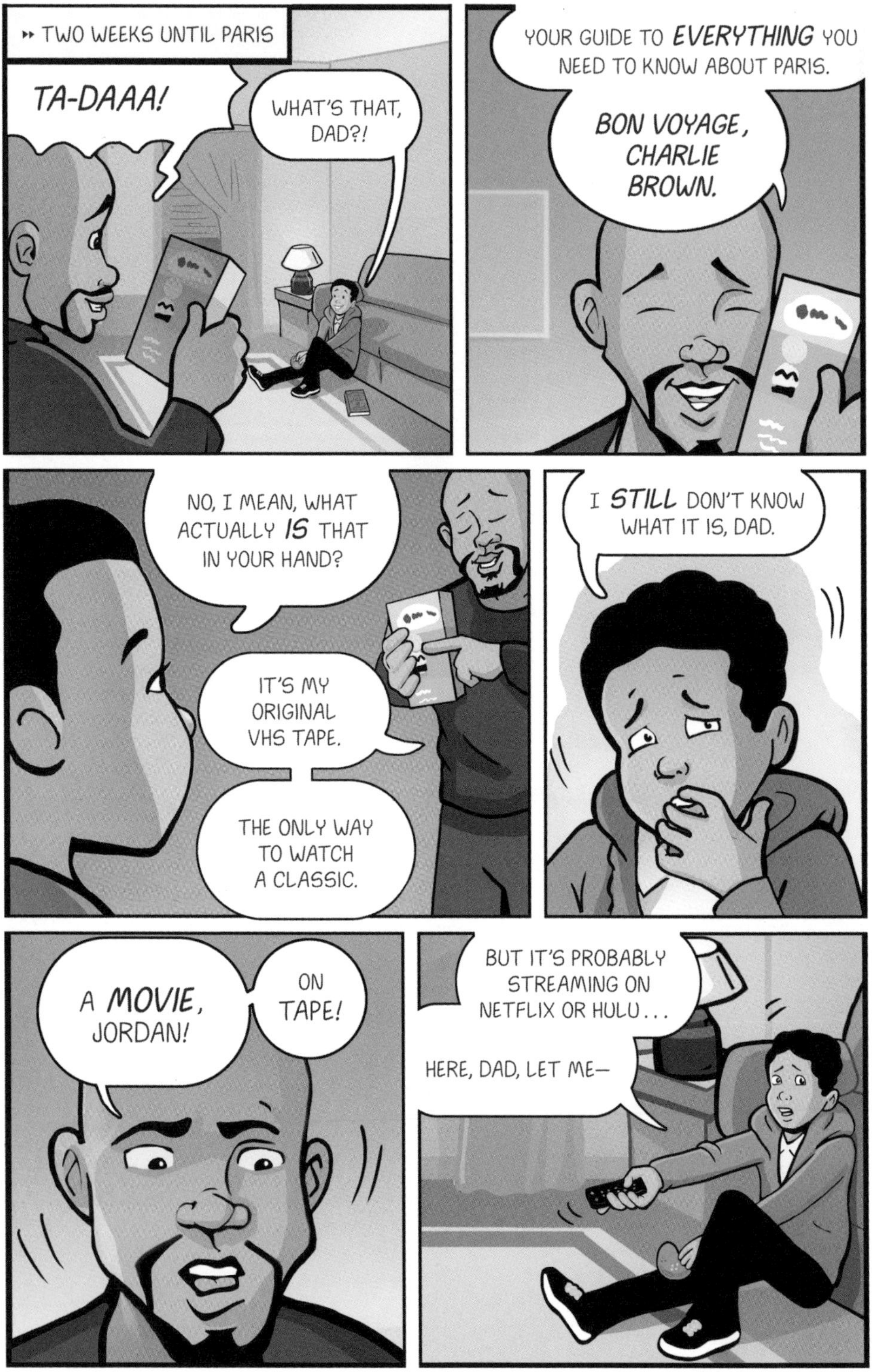
TWO WEEKS UNTIL PARIS
TA-DAAA!
WHAT'S THAT, DAD?!
YOUR GUIDE TO EVERYTHING YOU NEED TO KNOW ABOUT PARIS.
BON VOYAGE, CHARLIE BROWN.
NO, I MEAN, WHAT ACTUALLY IS THAT IN YOUR HAND?
IT'S MY ORIGINAL VHS TAPE.
THE ONLY WAY TO WATCH A CLASSIC.
I STILL DON'T KNOW WHAT IT IS, DAD.
A MOVIE, JORDAN!
ON TAPE!
BUT IT'S PROBABLY STREAMING ON NETFLIX OR HULU . . .
HERE, DAD, LET ME—

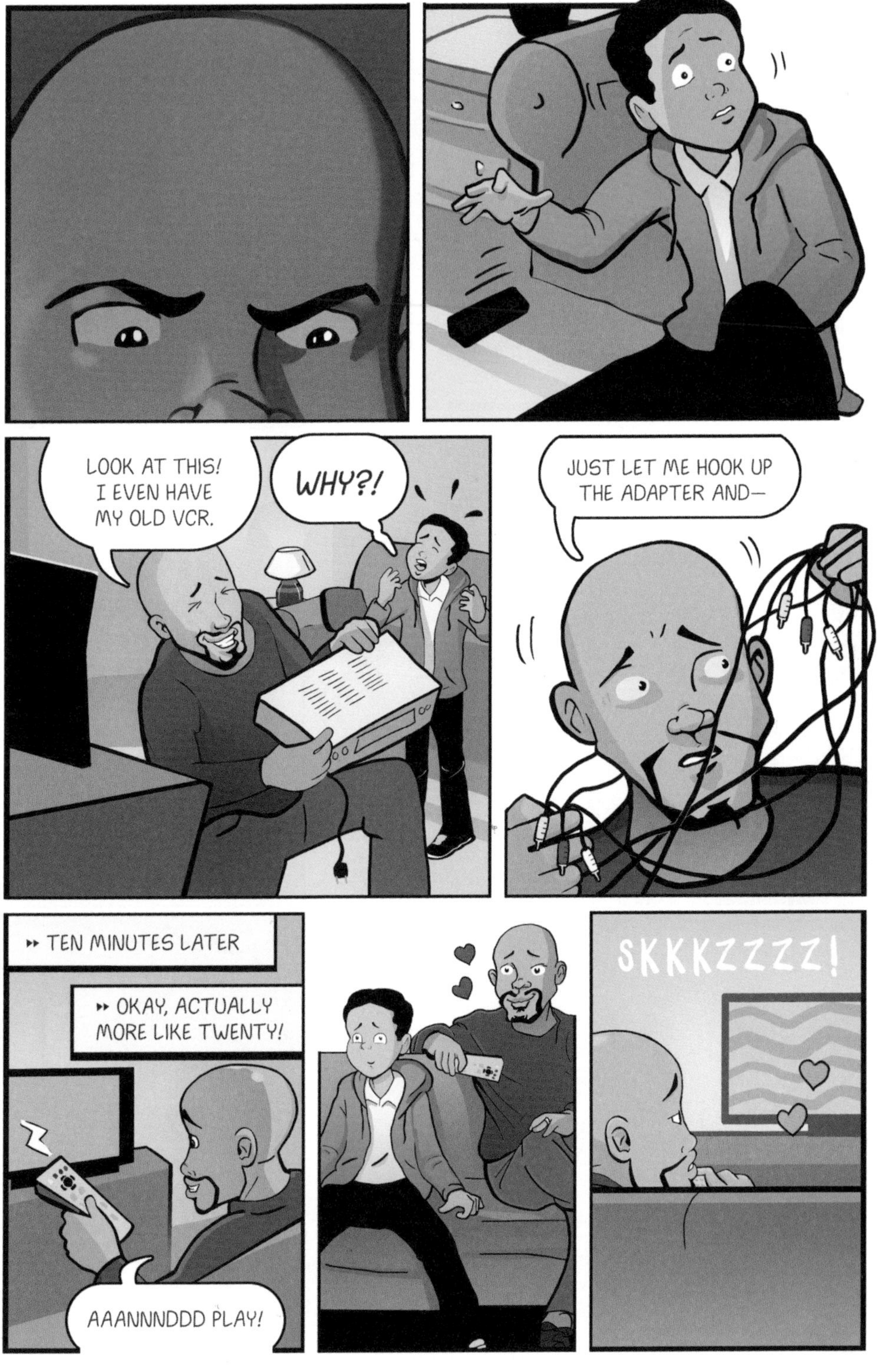
LOOK AT THIS! I EVEN HAVE MY OLD VCR.
WHY?!
JUST LET ME HOOK UP THE ADAPTER AND—
TEN MINUTES LATER
OKAY, ACTUALLY MORE LIKE TWENTY!
AAANNNDDD PLAY!
SKKKZZZZ!

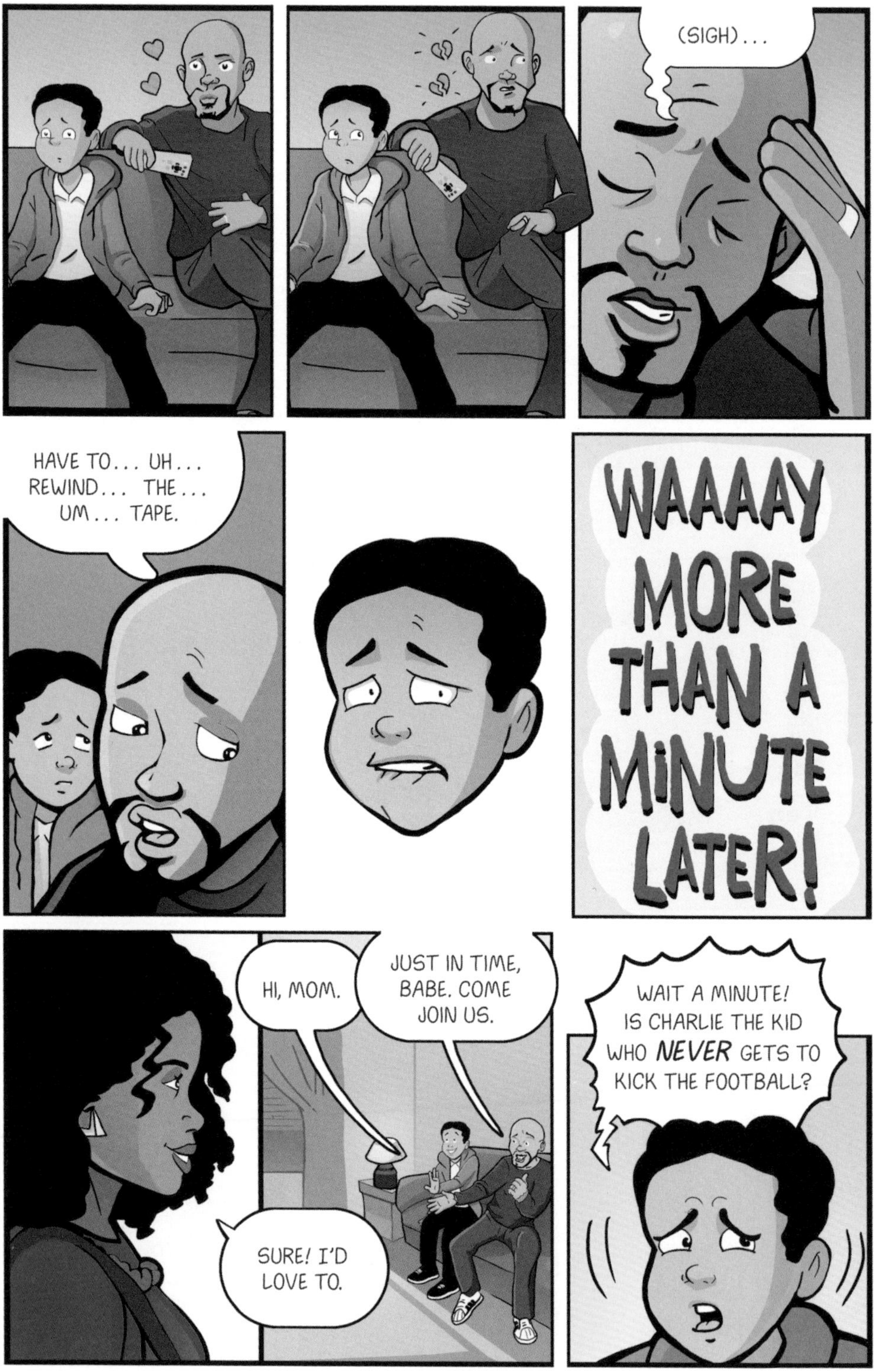
(SIGH)...
HAVE TO... UH... REWIND... THE... UM... TAPE.
WAAAAY MORE THAN A MINUTE LATER!
HI, MOM.
JUST IN TIME, BABE. COME JOIN US.
SURE! I'D LOVE TO.
WAIT A MINUTE! IS CHARLIE THE KID WHO ***NEVER*** GETS TO KICK THE FOOTBALL?

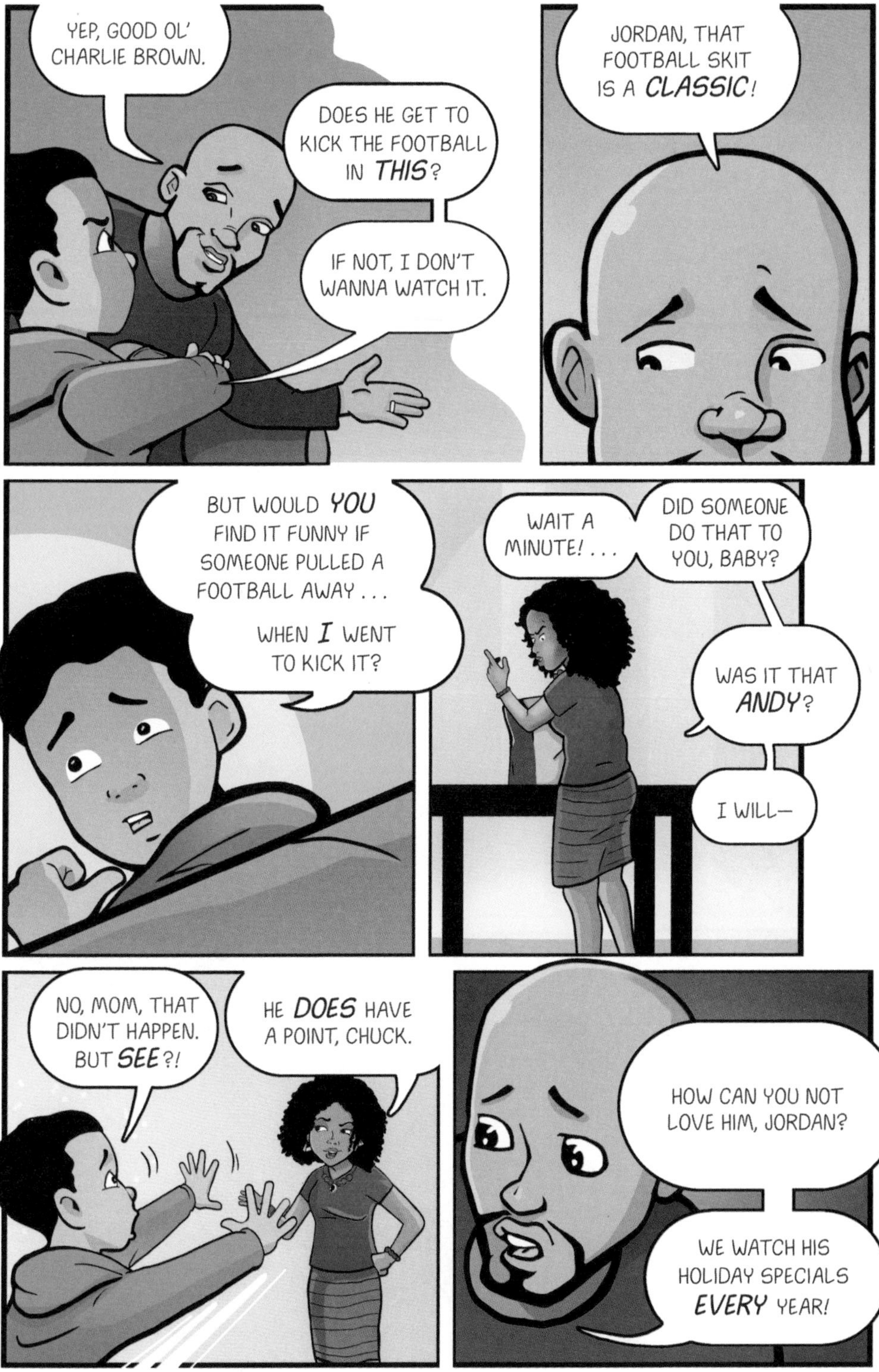
YEP, GOOD OL' CHARLIE BROWN.
DOES HE GET TO KICK THE FOOTBALL IN THIS?
IF NOT, I DON'T WANNA WATCH IT.
JORDAN, THAT FOOTBALL SKIT IS A CLASSIC!
BUT WOULD YOU FIND IT FUNNY IF SOMEONE PULLED A FOOTBALL AWAY . . .
WHEN I WENT TO KICK IT?
WAIT A MINUTE! . . .
DID SOMEONE DO THAT TO YOU, BABY?
WAS IT THAT ANDY?
I WILL—
NO, MOM, THAT DIDN'T HAPPEN. BUT SEE?!
HE DOES HAVE A POINT, CHUCK.
HOW CAN YOU NOT LOVE HIM, JORDAN?
WE WATCH HIS HOLIDAY SPECIALS EVERY YEAR!

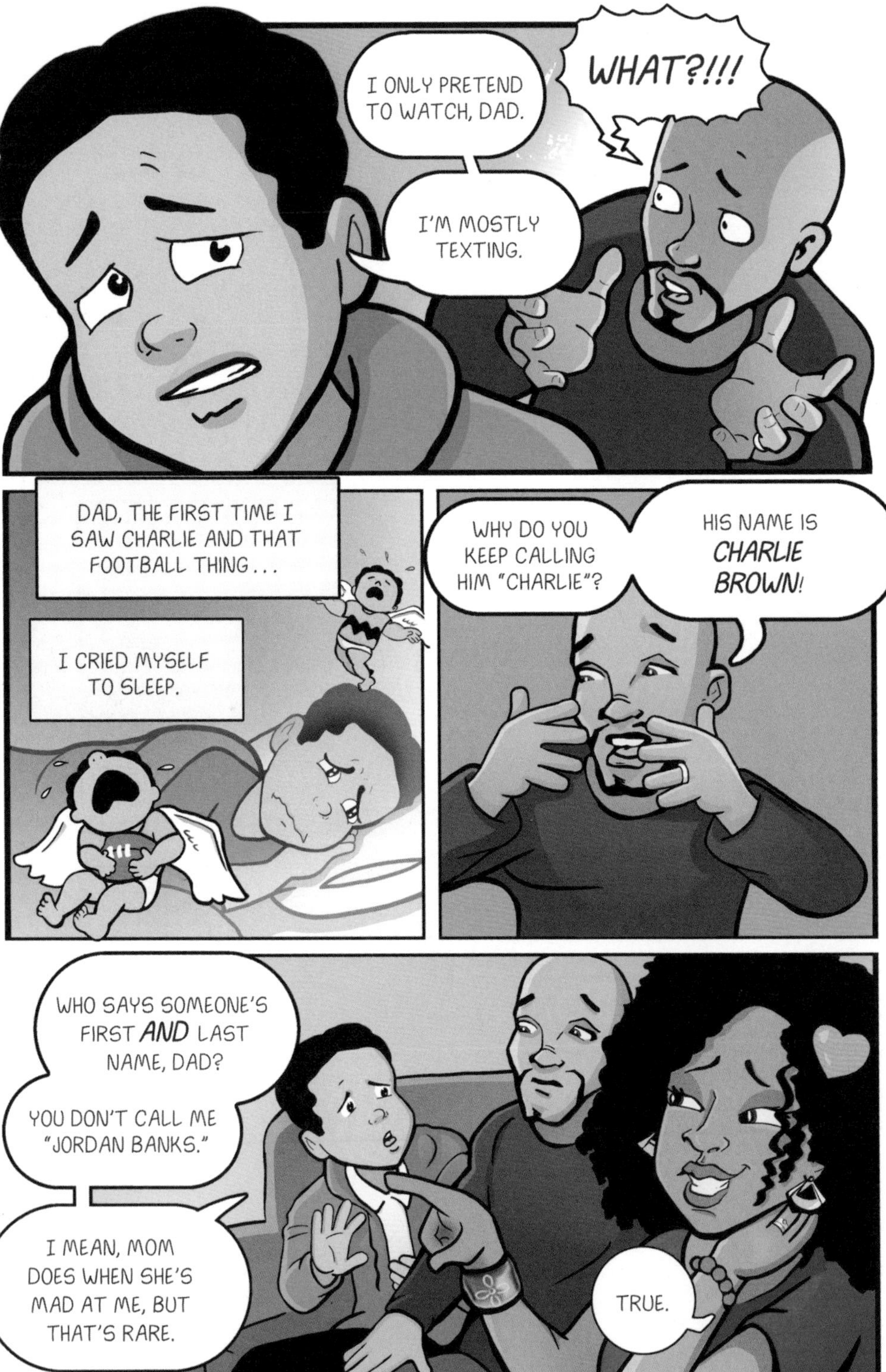
I ONLY PRETEND TO WATCH, DAD.
I'M MOSTLY TEXTING.
WHAT?!!!
DAD, THE FIRST TIME I SAW CHARLIE AND THAT FOOTBALL THING . . .
I CRIED MYSELF TO SLEEP.
WHY DO YOU KEEP CALLING HIM "CHARLIE"?
HIS NAME IS CHARLIE BROWN!
WHO SAYS SOMEONE'S FIRST AND LAST NAME, DAD?
YOU DON'T CALL ME "JORDAN BANKS."
I MEAN, MOM DOES WHEN SHE'S MAD AT ME, BUT THAT'S RARE.
TRUE.

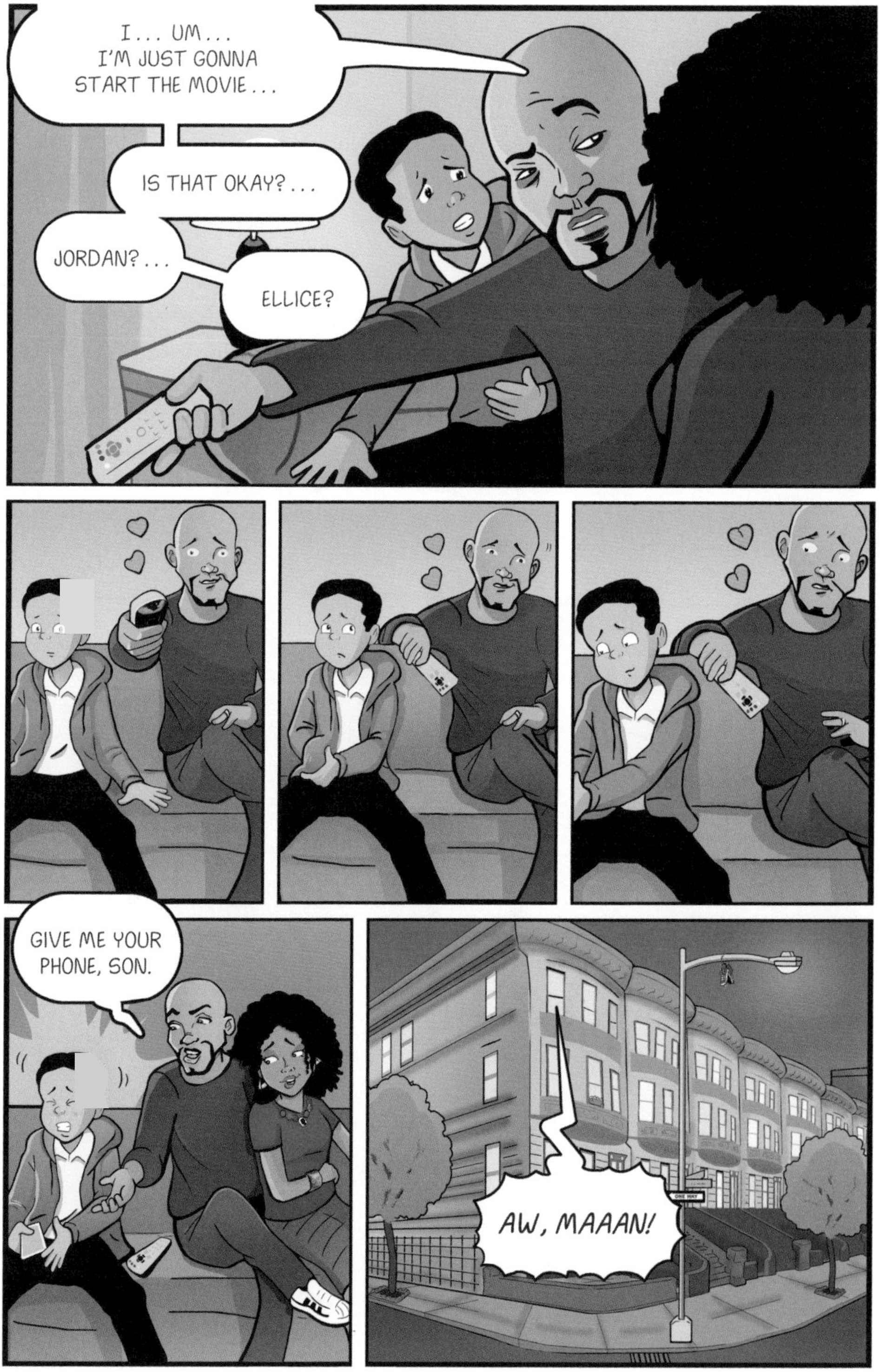
I... UM...
I'M JUST GONNA
START THE MOVIE...
IS THAT OKAY?...
JORDAN?...
ELLICE?
GIVE ME YOUR
PHONE, SON.
ONE WAY
AW, MAAAN!

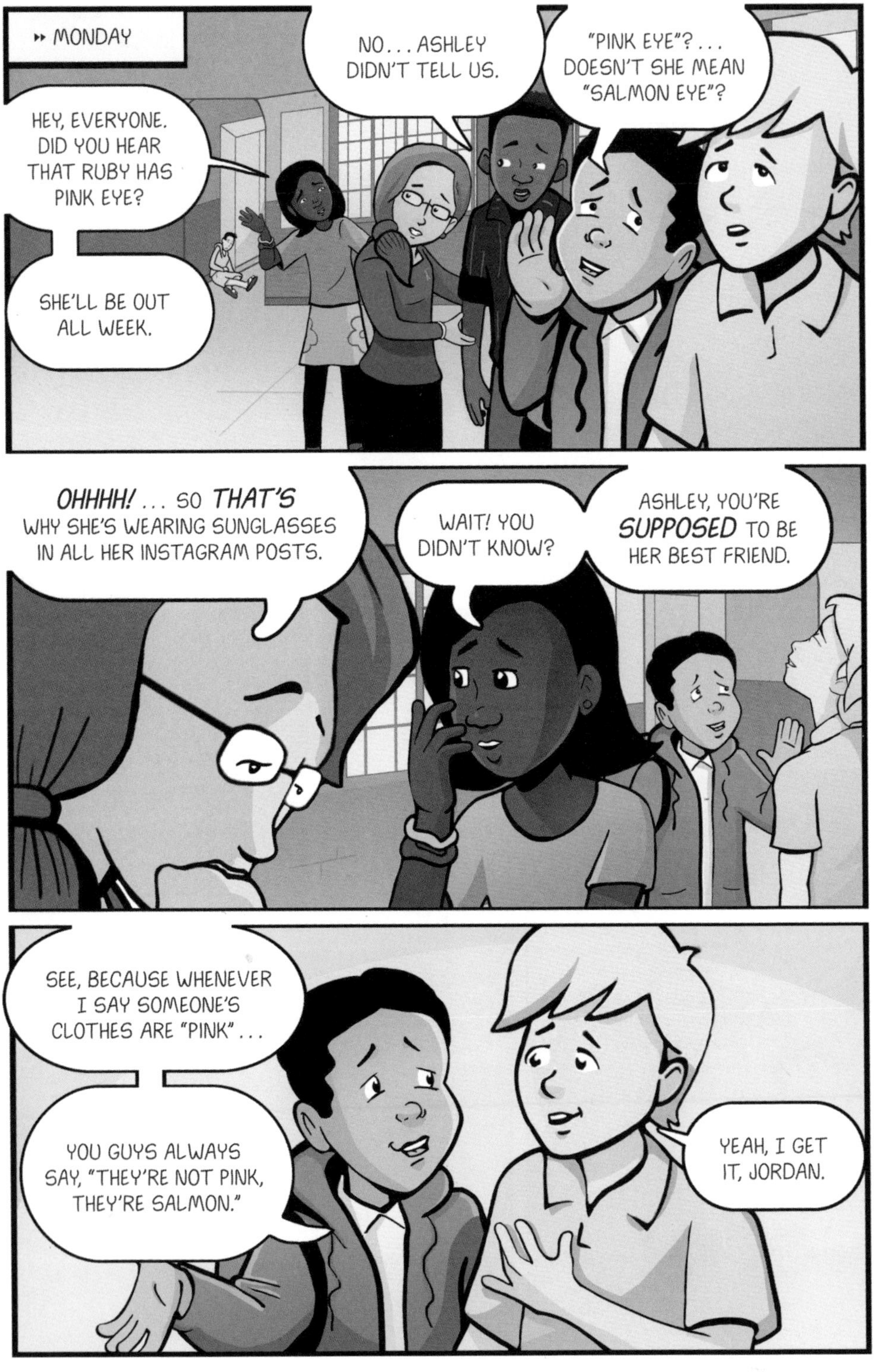
MONDAY
HEY, EVERYONE. DID YOU HEAR THAT RUBY HAS PINK EYE?
SHE'LL BE OUT ALL WEEK.
NO... ASHLEY DIDN'T TELL US.
"PINK EYE"?... DOESN'T SHE MEAN "SALMON EYE"?
OHHHH! ... SO THAT'S WHY SHE'S WEARING SUNGLASSES IN ALL HER INSTAGRAM POSTS.
WAIT! YOU DIDN'T KNOW?
ASHLEY, YOU'RE SUPPOSED TO BE HER BEST FRIEND.
SEE, BECAUSE WHENEVER I SAY SOMEONE'S CLOTHES ARE "PINK"...
YOU GUYS ALWAYS SAY, "THEY'RE NOT PINK, THEY'RE SALMON."
YEAH, I GET IT, JORDAN.

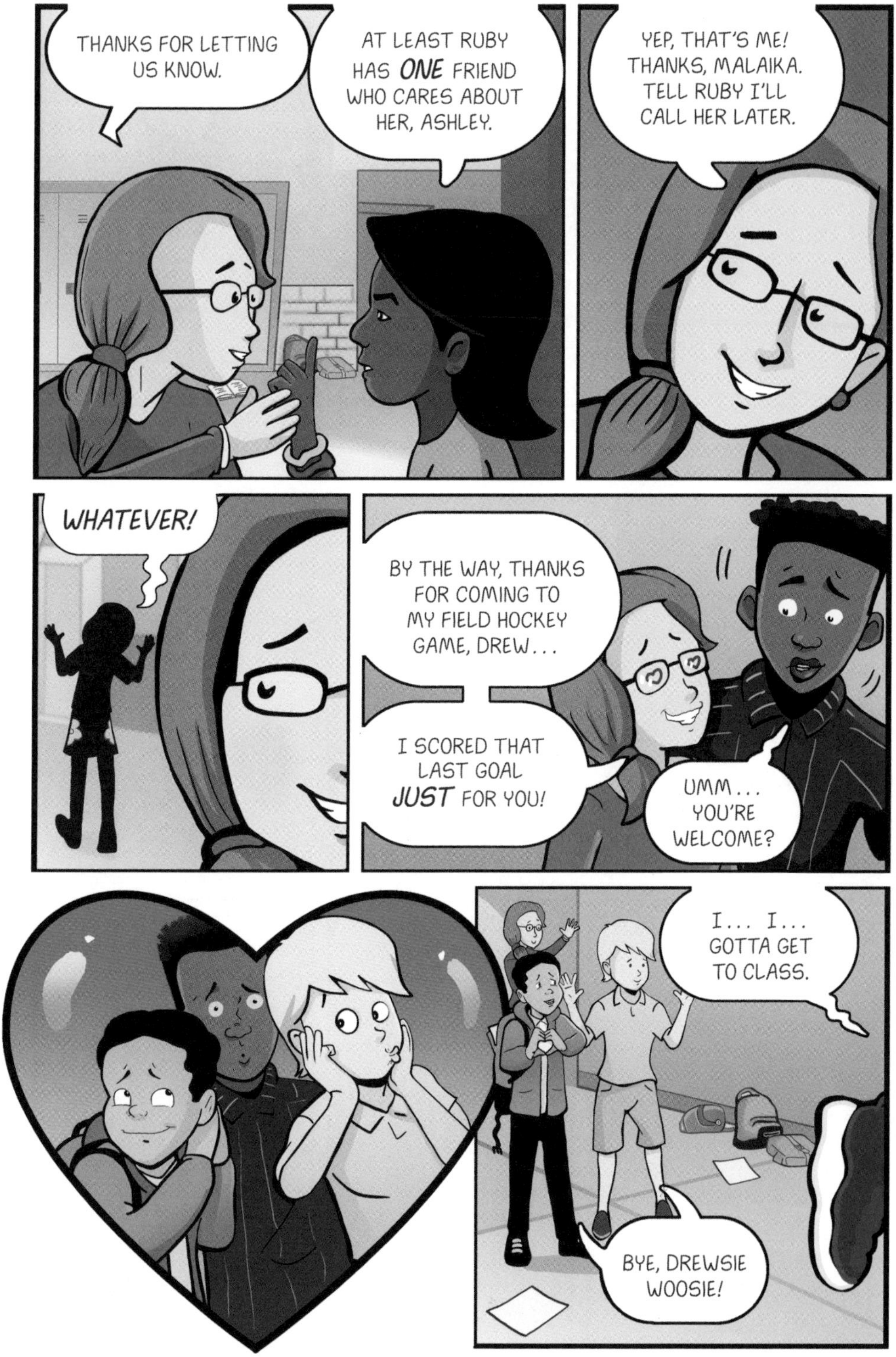
THANKS FOR LETTING US KNOW.
AT LEAST RUBY HAS ONE FRIEND WHO CARES ABOUT HER, ASHLEY.
YEP, THAT'S ME! THANKS, MALAIKA. TELL RUBY I'LL CALL HER LATER.
WHATEVER!
BY THE WAY, THANKS FOR COMING TO MY FIELD HOCKEY GAME, DREW...
I SCORED THAT LAST GOAL JUST FOR YOU!
UMM... YOU'RE WELCOME?
I... I... GOTTA GET TO CLASS.
BYE, DREWSIE WOOSIE!

HI, ALEXANDRA, WANT TO GO TO LUNCH?

TOGETHER?!

SURE! I SAW YOU BY YOURSELF AND I KNOW THAT SOME PEOPLE DON'T LIKE TO BE BY THEMSELVES.

SO I CAME OVER SO YOU WOULDN'T HAVE TO BE... YOU KNOW... BY YOURSELF.

I SPEND MOST OF THE DAY BY MYSELF, ASHLEY. IT'S REALLY NOT A BIG DEAL.

AWW...

WELL, WE CAN HANG OUT ALL DAY IF YOU WANT.

ALL WEEK, EVEN!

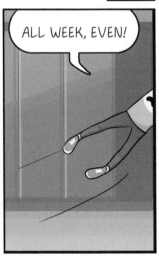

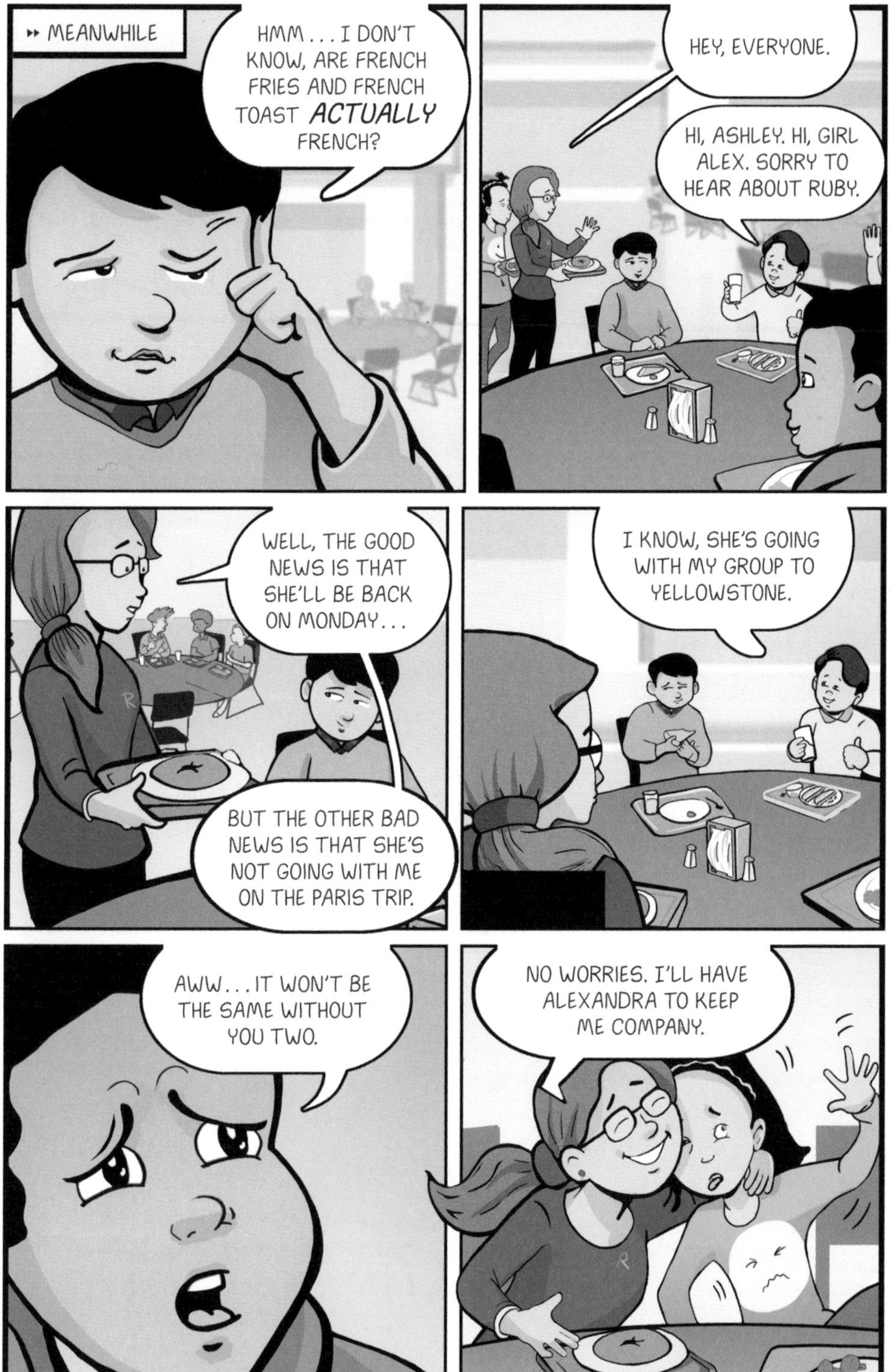

MEANWHILE
HMM . . . I DON'T KNOW, ARE FRENCH FRIES AND FRENCH TOAST ACTUALLY FRENCH?
HEY, EVERYONE.
HI, ASHLEY. HI, GIRL ALEX. SORRY TO HEAR ABOUT RUBY.
WELL, THE GOOD NEWS IS THAT SHE'LL BE BACK ON MONDAY . . .
BUT THE OTHER BAD NEWS IS THAT SHE'S NOT GOING WITH ME ON THE PARIS TRIP.
I KNOW, SHE'S GOING WITH MY GROUP TO YELLOWSTONE.
AWW . . . IT WON'T BE THE SAME WITHOUT YOU TWO.
NO WORRIES. I'LL HAVE ALEXANDRA TO KEEP ME COMPANY.

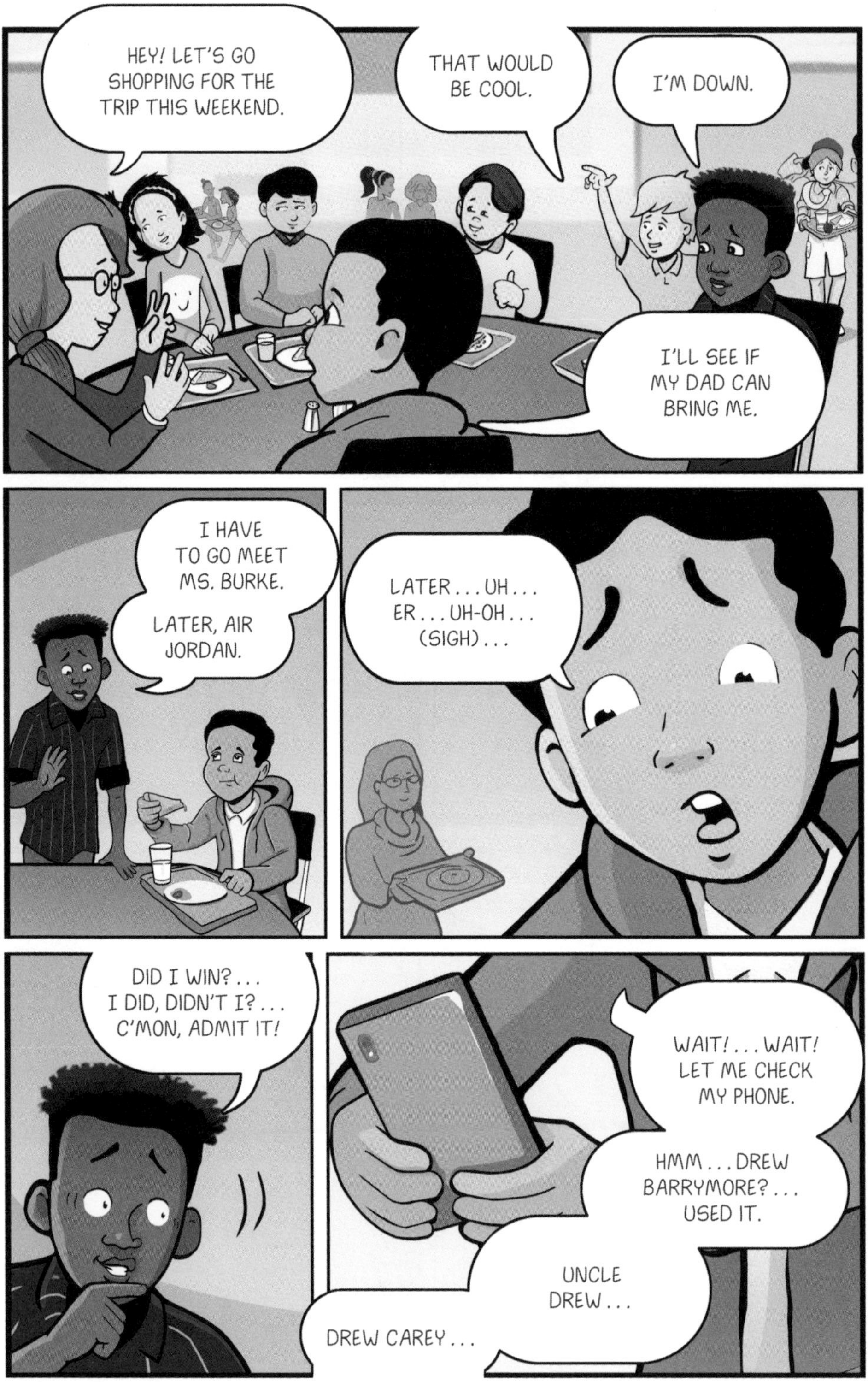
HEY! LET'S GO SHOPPING FOR THE TRIP THIS WEEKEND.
THAT WOULD BE COOL.
I'M DOWN.
I'LL SEE IF MY DAD CAN BRING ME.
I HAVE TO GO MEET MS. BURKE.
LATER, AIR JORDAN.
LATER . . . UH . . . ER . . . UH-OH . . . (SIGH) . . .
DID I WIN? . . . I DID, DIDN'T I? . . . C'MON, ADMIT IT!
WAIT! . . . WAIT! LET ME CHECK MY PHONE.
HMM . . . DREW BARRYMORE? . . . USED IT.
UNCLE DREW . . .
DREW CAREY . . .

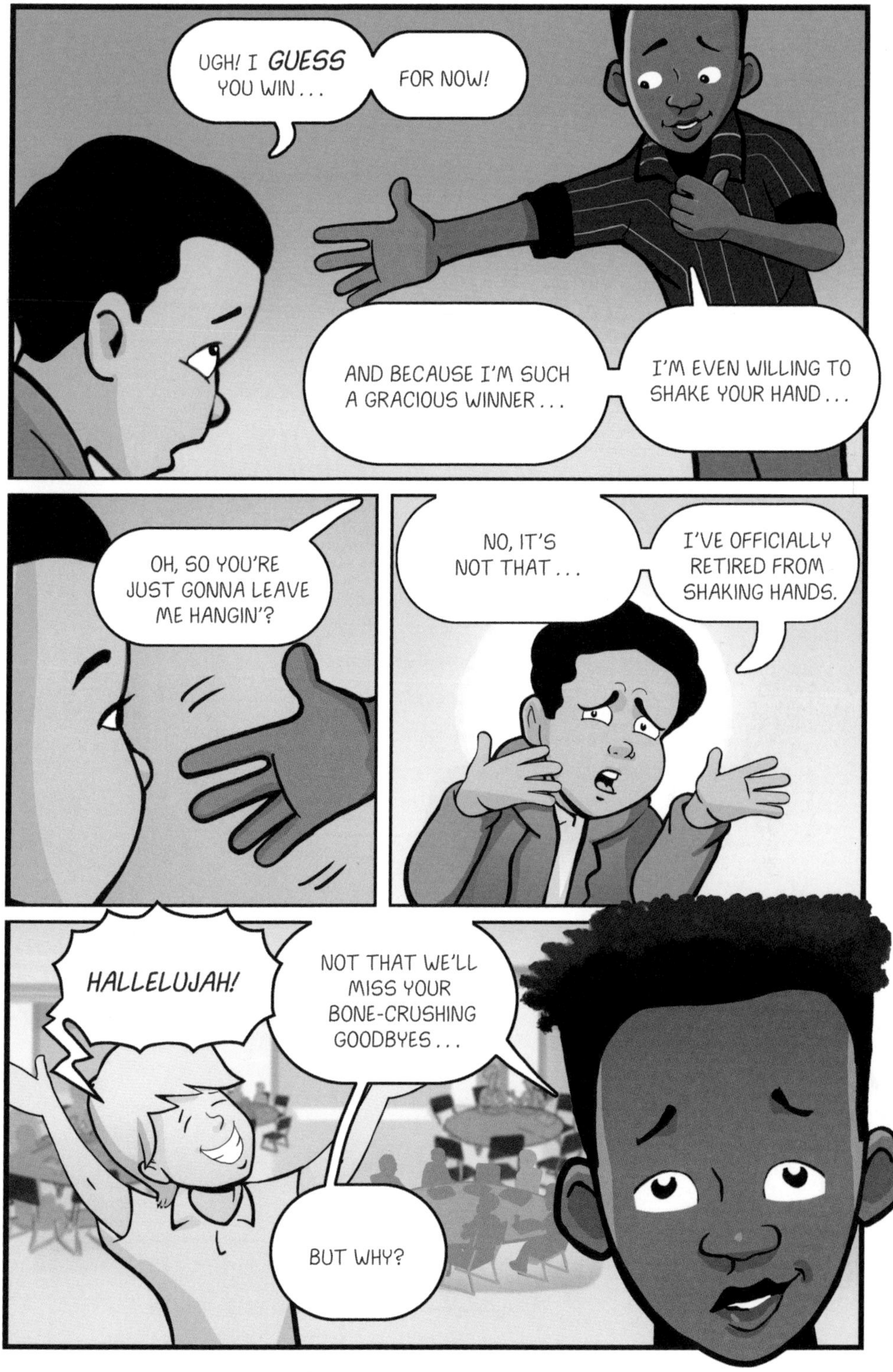
UGH! I GUESS YOU WIN . . .
FOR NOW!
AND BECAUSE I'M SUCH A GRACIOUS WINNER . . .
I'M EVEN WILLING TO SHAKE YOUR HAND . . .
OH, SO YOU'RE JUST GONNA LEAVE ME HANGIN'?
NO, IT'S NOT THAT . . .
I'VE OFFICIALLY RETIRED FROM SHAKING HANDS.
HALLELUJAH!
NOT THAT WE'LL MISS YOUR BONE-CRUSHING GOODBYES . . .
BUT WHY?

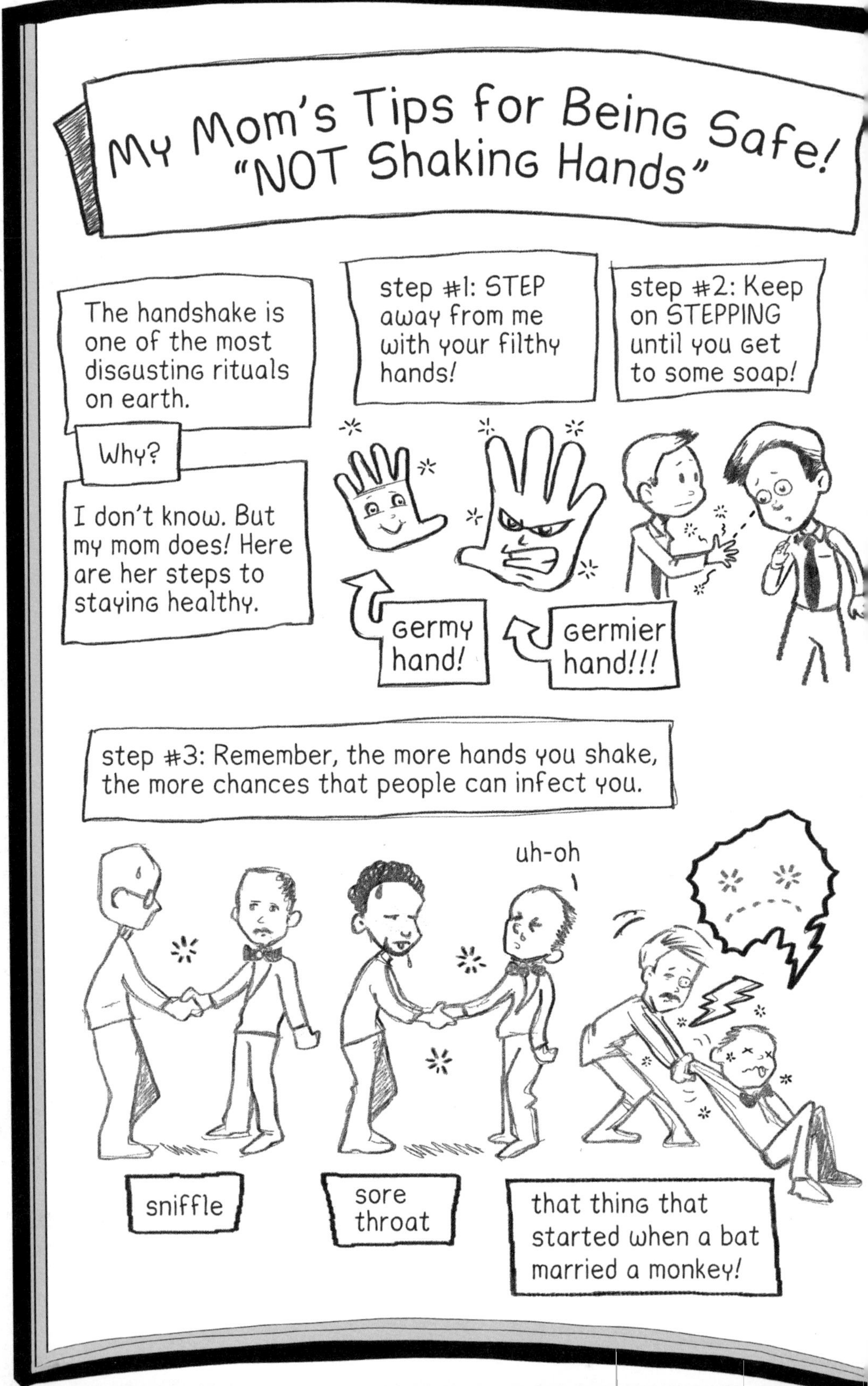
My Mom's Tips for Being Safe!
"NOT Shaking Hands"
The handshake is one of the most disgusting rituals on earth.
Why?
I don't know. But my mom does! Here are her steps to staying healthy.
step #1: STEP away from me with your filthy hands!
step #2: Keep on STEPPING until you get to some soap!
germy hand!
germier hand!!!
step #3: Remember, the more hands you shake, the more chances that people can infect you.
uh-oh
sniffle
sore throat
that thing that started when a bat married a monkey!

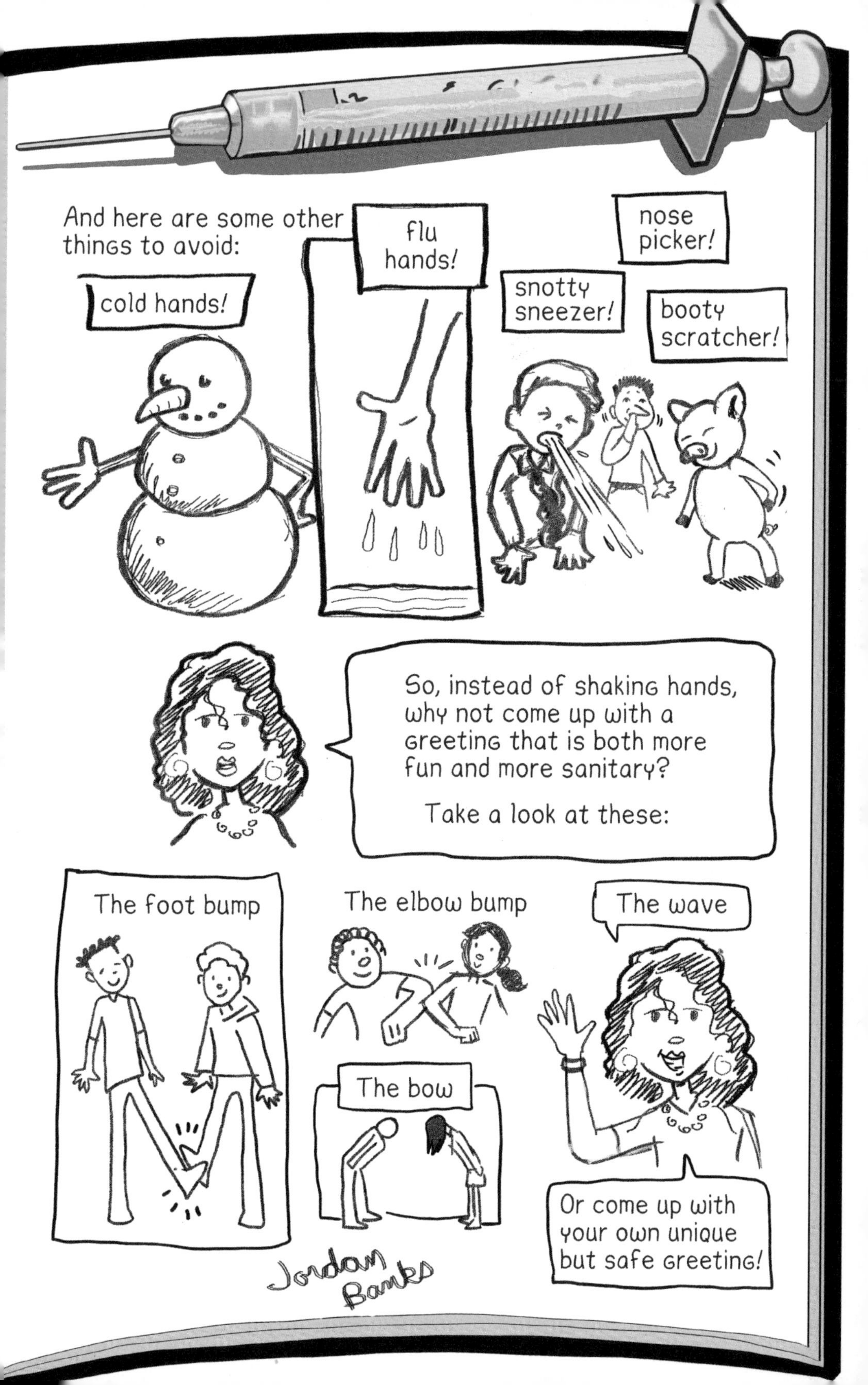

And here are some other things to avoid:
cold hands!
flu hands!
snotty sneezer!
nose picker!
booty scratcher!
So, instead of shaking hands, why not come up with a greeting that is both more fun and more sanitary?
Take a look at these:
The foot bump
The elbow bump
The bow
The wave
Or come up with your own unique but safe greeting!
Jordan Banks

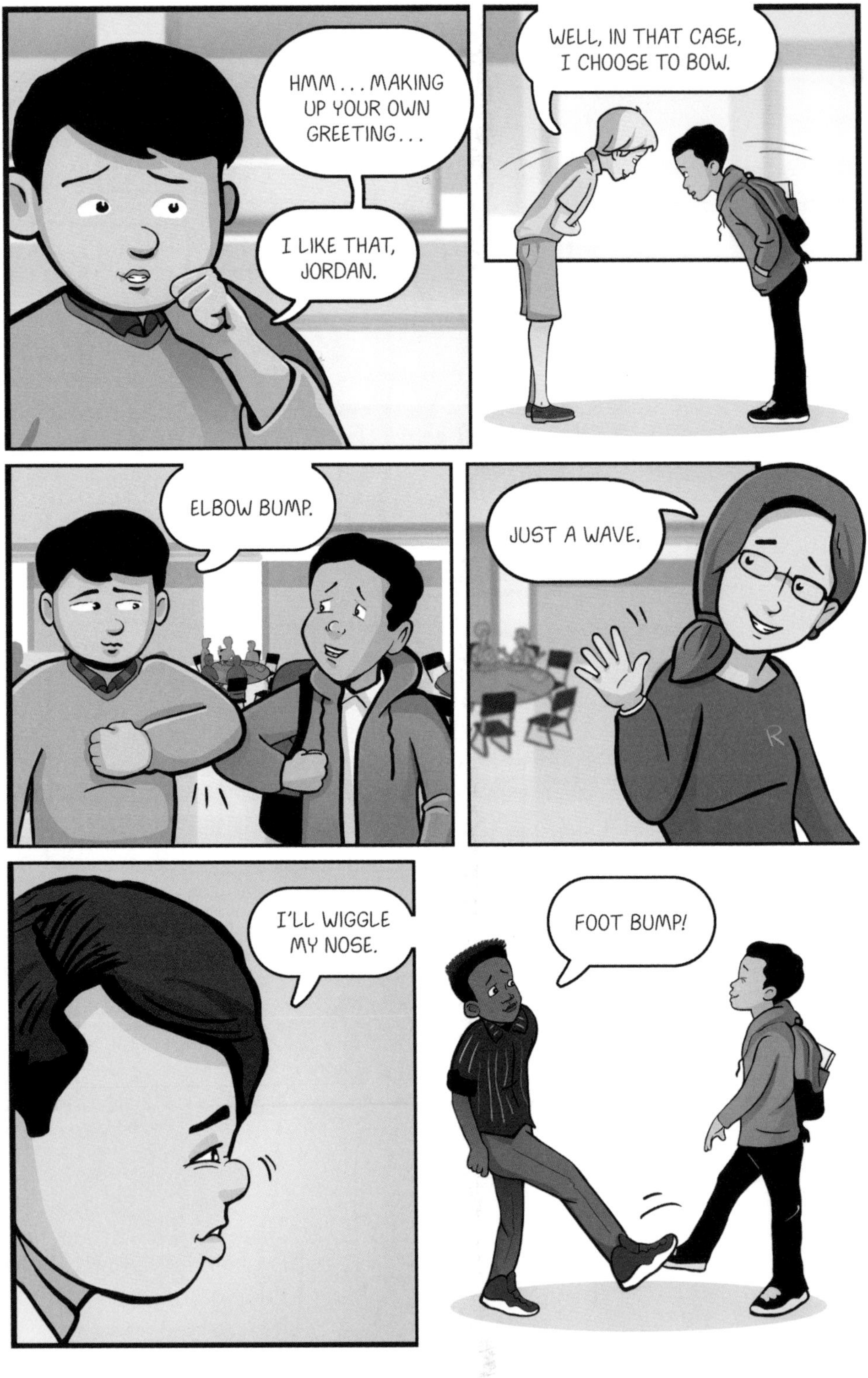
HMM . . . MAKING UP YOUR OWN GREETING . . .
I LIKE THAT, JORDAN.
WELL, IN THAT CASE, I CHOOSE TO BOW.
ELBOW BUMP.
JUST A WAVE.
I'LL WIGGLE MY NOSE.
FOOT BUMP!

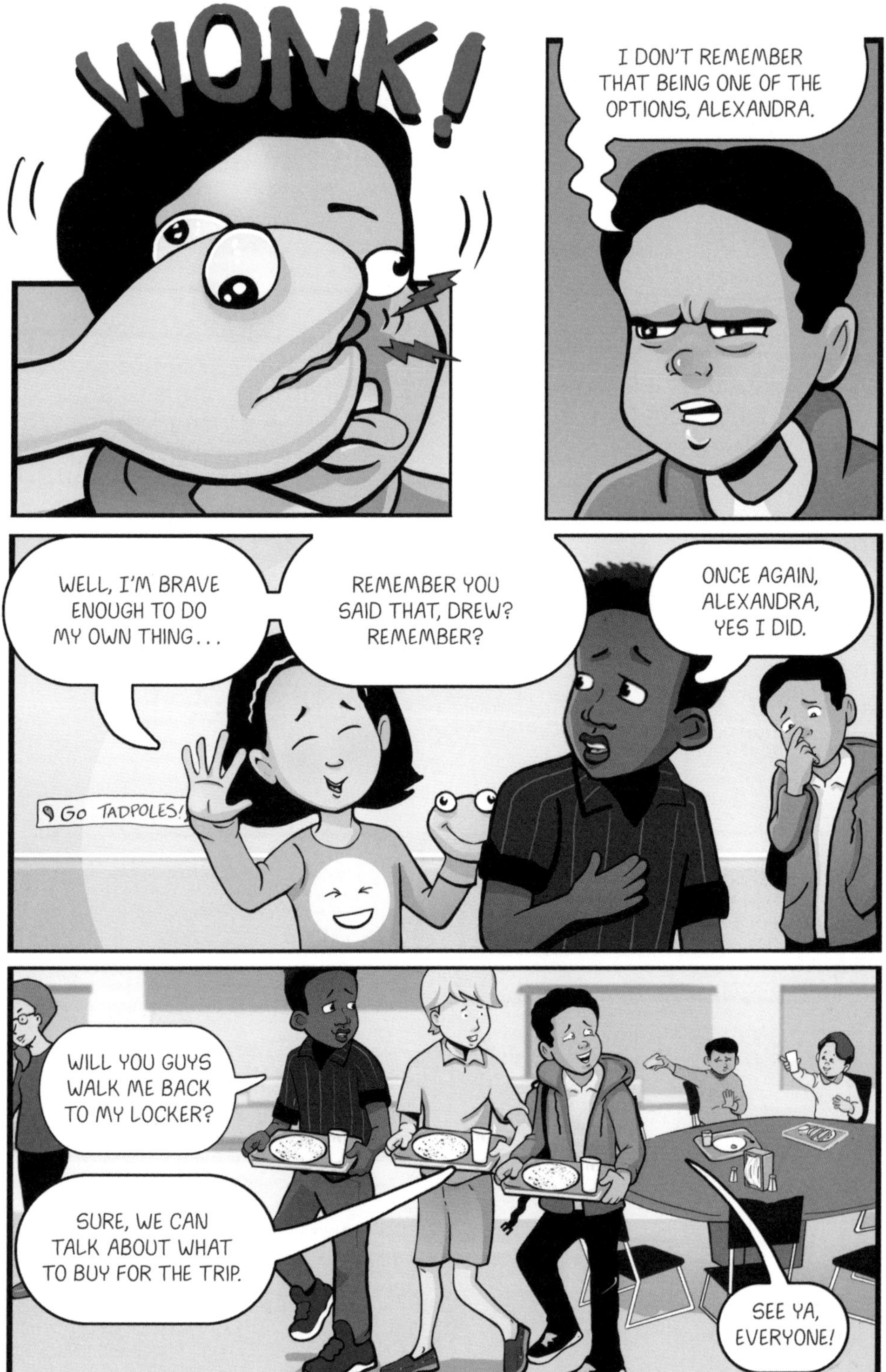
WONK!
I DON'T REMEMBER THAT BEING ONE OF THE OPTIONS, ALEXANDRA.
WELL, I'M BRAVE ENOUGH TO DO MY OWN THING . . .
REMEMBER YOU SAID THAT, DREW? REMEMBER?
ONCE AGAIN, ALEXANDRA, YES I DID.
GO TADPOLES!
WILL YOU GUYS WALK ME BACK TO MY LOCKER?
SURE, WE CAN TALK ABOUT WHAT TO BUY FOR THE TRIP.
SEE YA, EVERYONE!

2 Where's Mall-do?

(Now You Don't See Us . . . Now You DO!)

Now You Don't See Us:
When my dad tries to get a salesperson's attention while we shop.

EXCUSE ME!
BUSY!

Now You Don't See Us:
When my mom goes shopping and she says all the clothes are three sizes too small.

FOREVER SIZE 0

Now You Don't See Us:
When we finally get a salesperson . . .

Only to lose them to someone else. AGAIN!

EXCUSE ME.
YES?

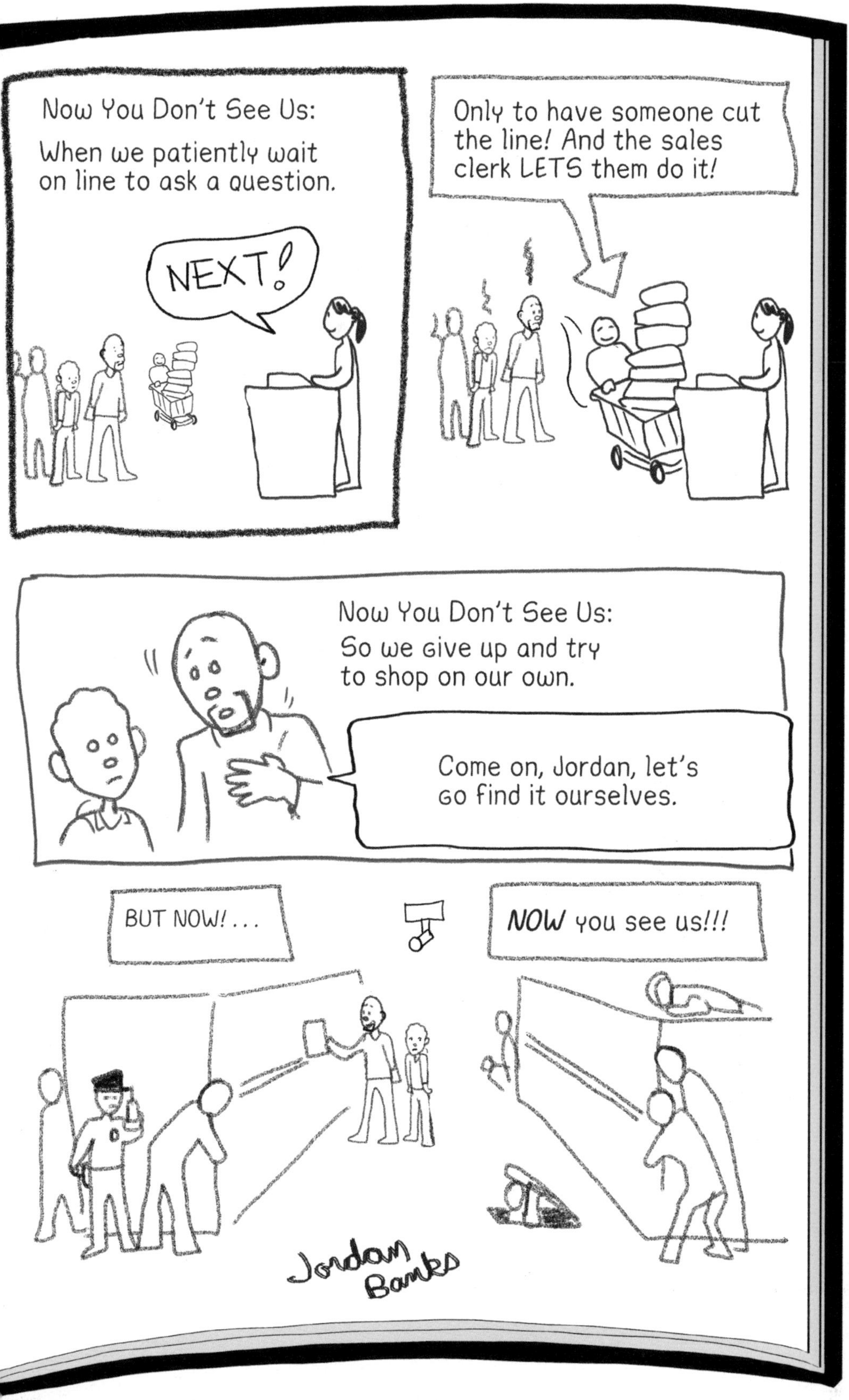
Now You Don't See Us:
When we patiently wait on line to ask a question.
NEXT!
Only to have someone cut the line! And the sales clerk LETS them do it!
Now You Don't See Us:
So we give up and try to shop on our own.
Come on, Jordan, let's go find it ourselves.
BUT NOW! . . .
NOW you see us!!!
Jordan Banks

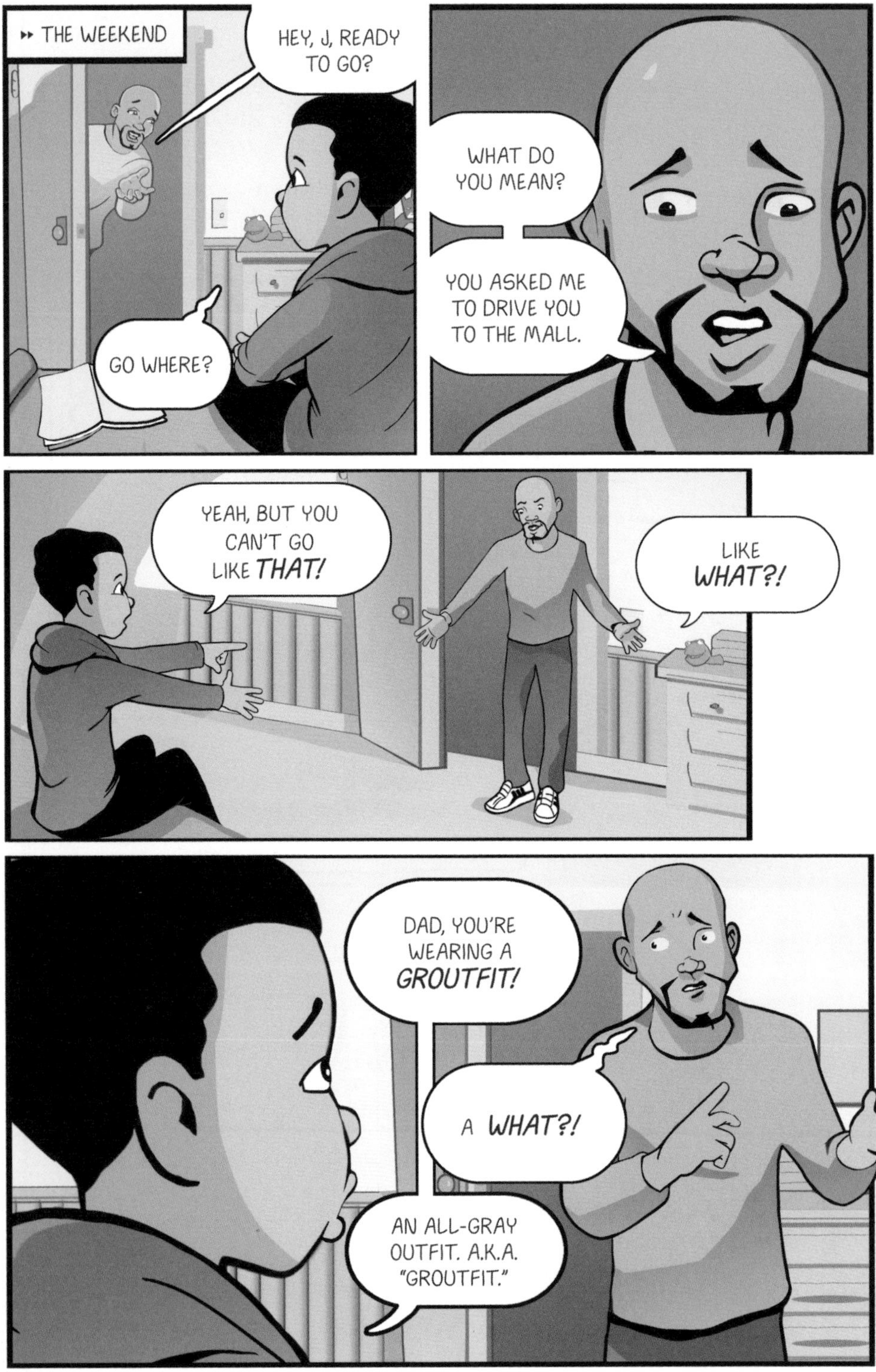
THE WEEKEND
HEY, J, READY TO GO?
GO WHERE?
WHAT DO YOU MEAN?
YOU ASKED ME TO DRIVE YOU TO THE MALL.
YEAH, BUT YOU CAN'T GO LIKE THAT!
LIKE WHAT?!
DAD, YOU'RE WEARING A GROUTFIT!
A WHAT?!
AN ALL-GRAY OUTFIT. A.K.A. "GROUTFIT."

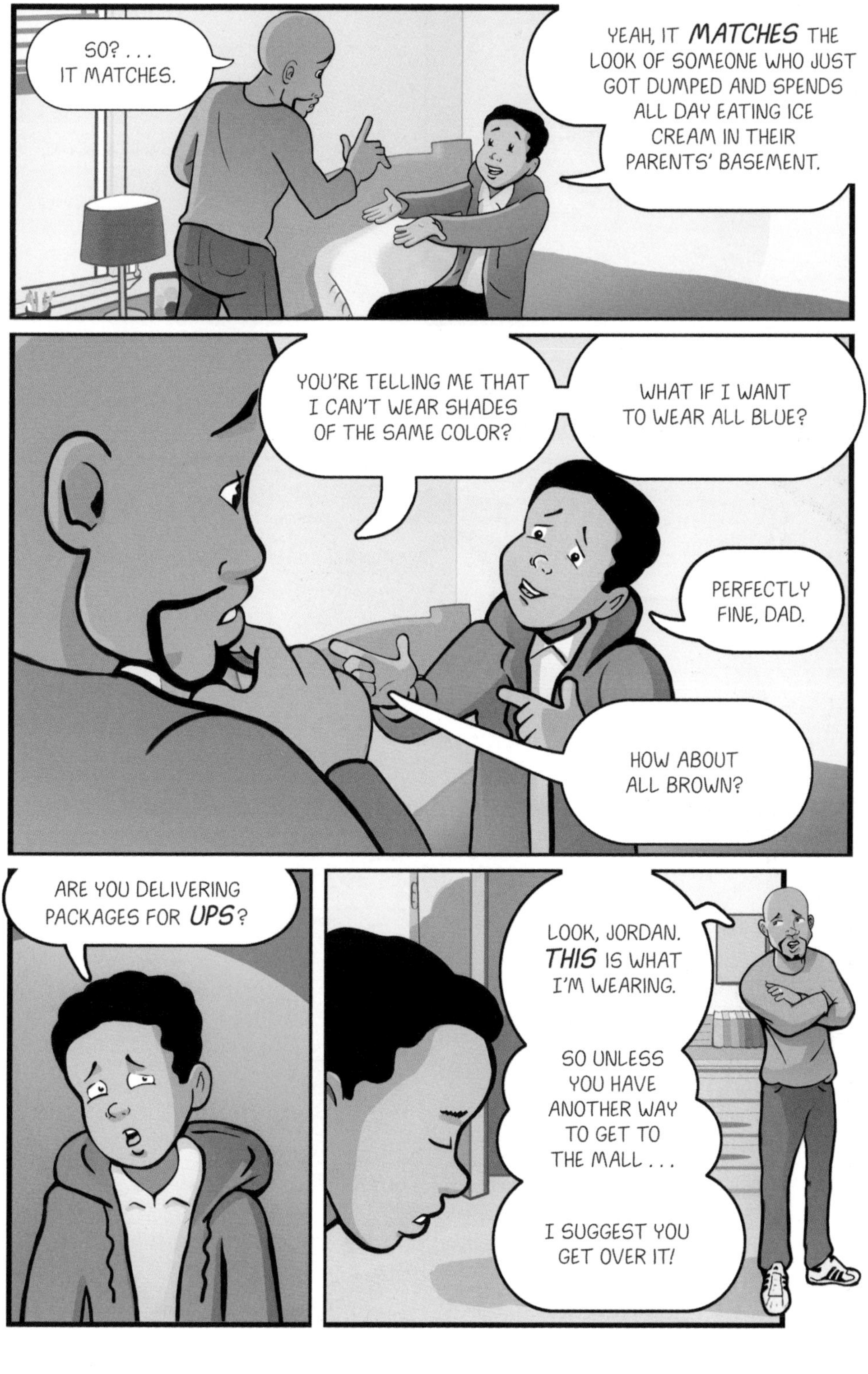
SO? . . .
IT MATCHES.
YEAH, IT MATCHES THE LOOK OF SOMEONE WHO JUST GOT DUMPED AND SPENDS ALL DAY EATING ICE CREAM IN THEIR PARENTS' BASEMENT.
YOU'RE TELLING ME THAT I CAN'T WEAR SHADES OF THE SAME COLOR?
WHAT IF I WANT TO WEAR ALL BLUE?
PERFECTLY FINE, DAD.
HOW ABOUT ALL BROWN?
ARE YOU DELIVERING PACKAGES FOR UPS?
LOOK, JORDAN. THIS IS WHAT I'M WEARING.
SO UNLESS YOU HAVE ANOTHER WAY TO GET TO THE MALL . . .
I SUGGEST YOU GET OVER IT!

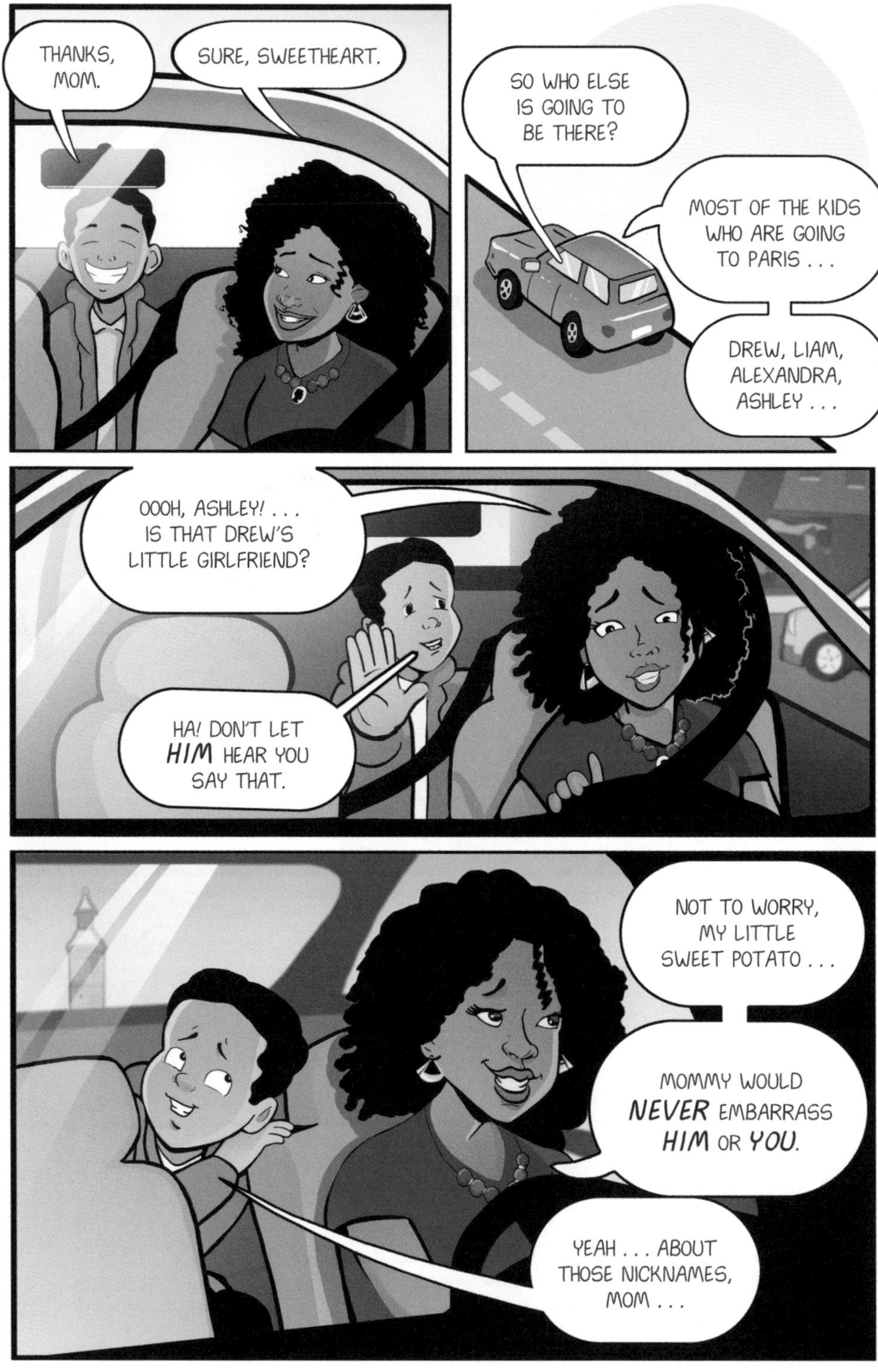
THANKS, MOM.
SURE, SWEETHEART.
SO WHO ELSE IS GOING TO BE THERE?
MOST OF THE KIDS WHO ARE GOING TO PARIS . . .
DREW, LIAM, ALEXANDRA, ASHLEY . . .
OOOH, ASHLEY! . . . IS THAT DREW'S LITTLE GIRLFRIEND?
HA! DON'T LET **HIM** HEAR YOU SAY THAT.
NOT TO WORRY, MY LITTLE SWEET POTATO . . .
MOMMY WOULD **NEVER** EMBARRASS **HIM** OR **YOU**.
YEAH . . . ABOUT THOSE NICKNAMES, MOM . . .

ARE YOU HUNGRY, BABY?

NO! NO! NOT AT ALL, MOM! REALLY!

JORDAN, WHAT IS GOING ON?

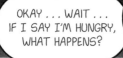

OKAY . . . WAIT . . . IF I SAY I'M HUNGRY, WHAT HAPPENS?

WHAT DO YOU MEAN, "WHAT HAPPENS"? WE STOP AND EAT.

WELLLL . . . WHENEVER I TELL DAD I'M HUNGRY, HE ALWAYS PULLS OUT SOME OLD FRUIT THAT'S BEEN IN HIS BAG FOR, LIKE, A WEEK.

MUSHY APPLES AND SPOTTED BANANAS?

I KNOW, BABY.

THEN IF YOU REFUSE TO EAT HIS MEALY FRUIT, HE ALWAYS SAYS:

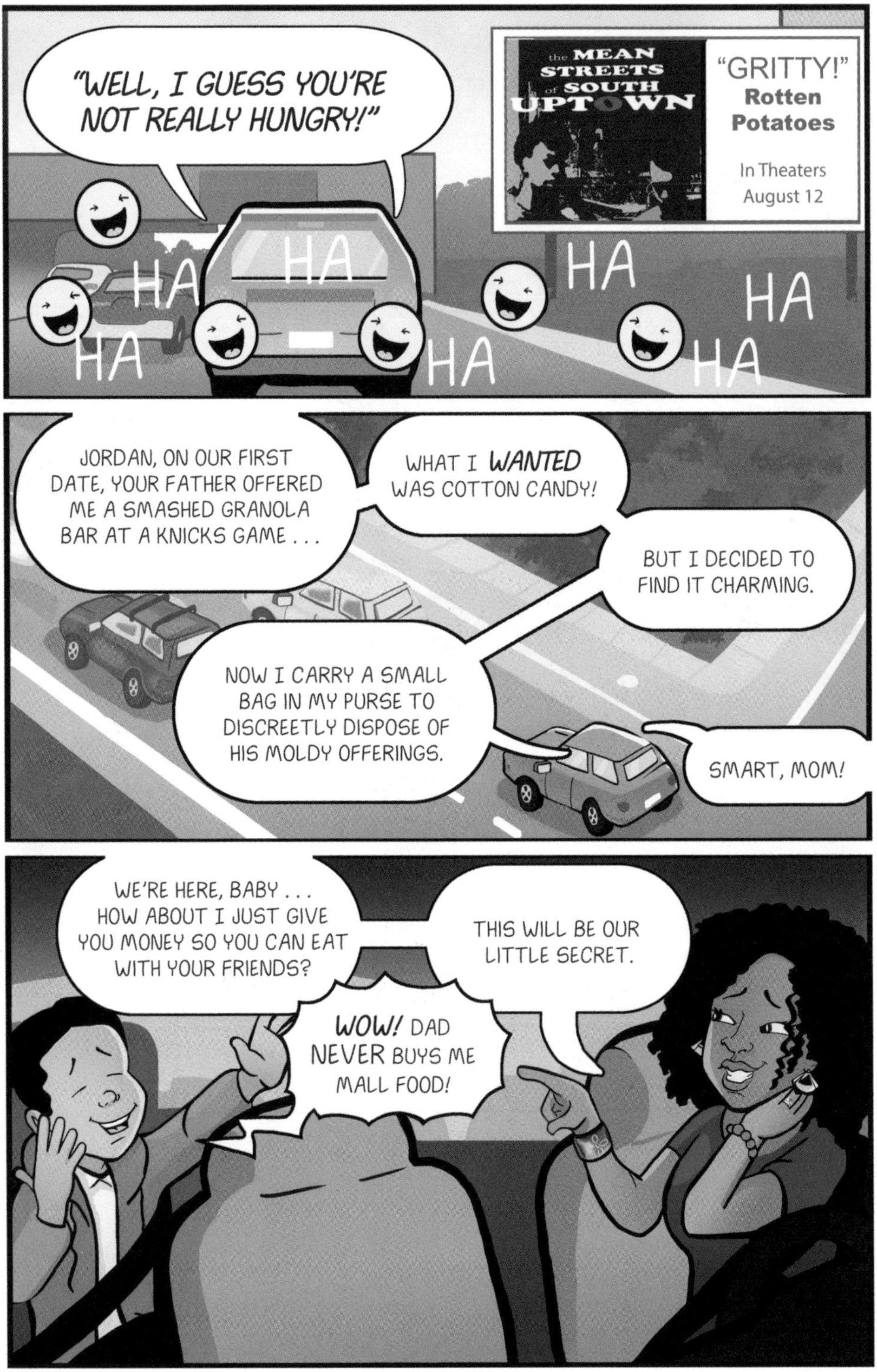
"WELL, I GUESS YOU'RE NOT REALLY HUNGRY!"
the MEAN STREETS of SOUTH UPTOWN
"GRITTY!" Rotten Potatoes
In Theaters August 12
HA HA HA HA HA HA HA
JORDAN, ON OUR FIRST DATE, YOUR FATHER OFFERED ME A SMASHED GRANOLA BAR AT A KNICKS GAME . . .
WHAT I WANTED WAS COTTON CANDY!
BUT I DECIDED TO FIND IT CHARMING.
NOW I CARRY A SMALL BAG IN MY PURSE TO DISCREETLY DISPOSE OF HIS MOLDY OFFERINGS.
SMART, MOM!
WE'RE HERE, BABY . . . HOW ABOUT I JUST GIVE YOU MONEY SO YOU CAN EAT WITH YOUR FRIENDS?
THIS WILL BE OUR LITTLE SECRET.
WOW! DAD NEVER BUYS ME MALL FOOD!

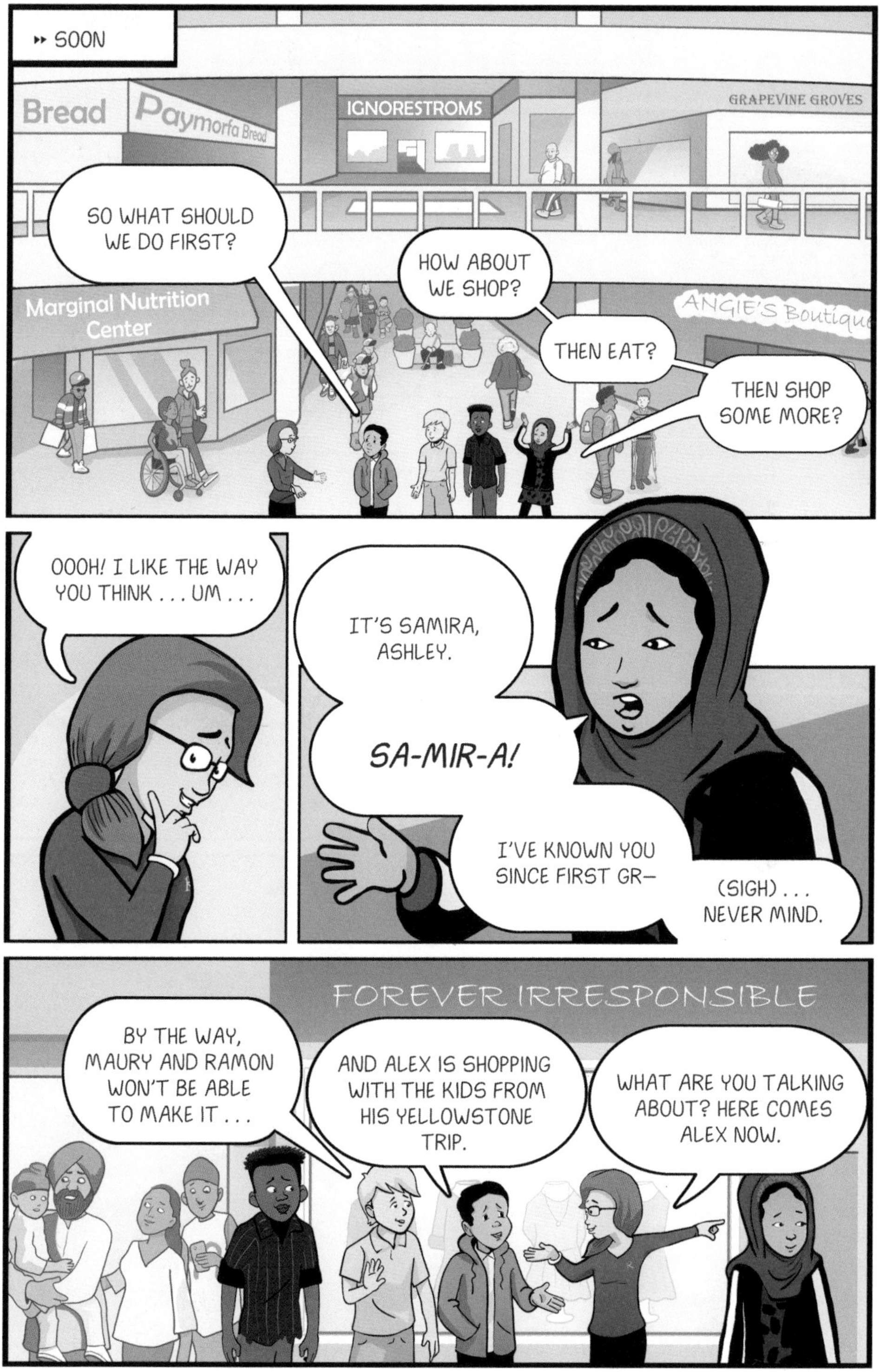
SOON
Bread
Paymorfa Bread
IGNORESTROMS
GRAPEVINE GROVES
Marginal Nutrition Center
ANGIE'S Boutique
SO WHAT SHOULD WE DO FIRST?
HOW ABOUT WE SHOP?
THEN EAT?
THEN SHOP SOME MORE?
OOOH! I LIKE THE WAY YOU THINK . . . UM . . .
IT'S SAMIRA, ASHLEY.
SA-MIR-A!
I'VE KNOWN YOU SINCE FIRST GR—
(SIGH) . . . NEVER MIND.
FOREVER IRRESPONSIBLE
BY THE WAY, MAURY AND RAMON WON'T BE ABLE TO MAKE IT . . .
AND ALEX IS SHOPPING WITH THE KIDS FROM HIS YELLOWSTONE TRIP.
WHAT ARE YOU TALKING ABOUT? HERE COMES ALEX NOW.

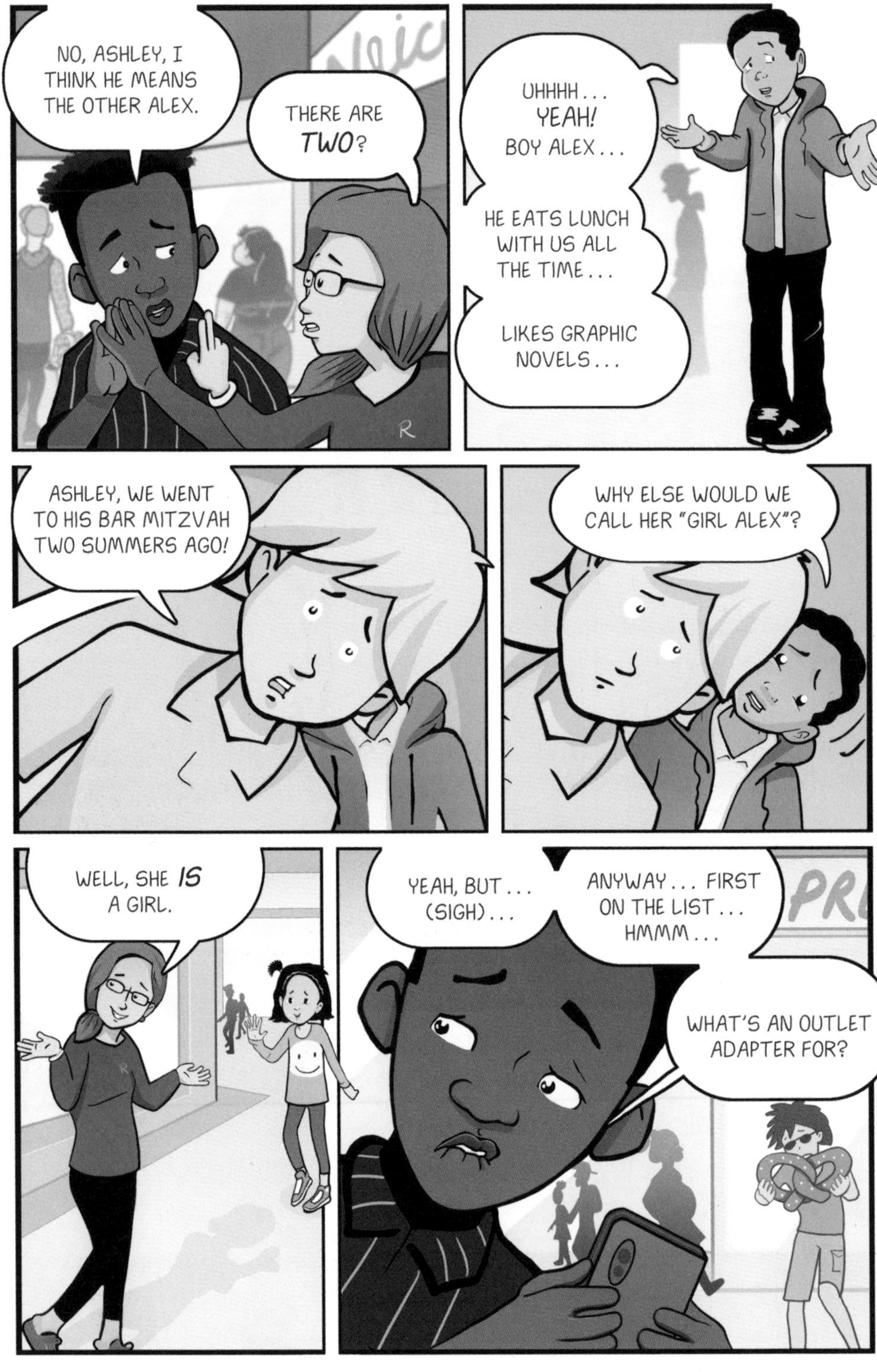
NO, ASHLEY, I THINK HE MEANS THE OTHER ALEX.
THERE ARE TWO?
UHHHH . . . YEAH! BOY ALEX . . .
HE EATS LUNCH WITH US ALL THE TIME . . .
LIKES GRAPHIC NOVELS . . .
R
ASHLEY, WE WENT TO HIS BAR MITZVAH TWO SUMMERS AGO!
WHY ELSE WOULD WE CALL HER "GIRL ALEX"?
WELL, SHE IS A GIRL.
YEAH, BUT . . . (SIGH) . . .
ANYWAY . . . FIRST ON THE LIST . . . HMMM . . .
WHAT'S AN OUTLET ADAPTER FOR?

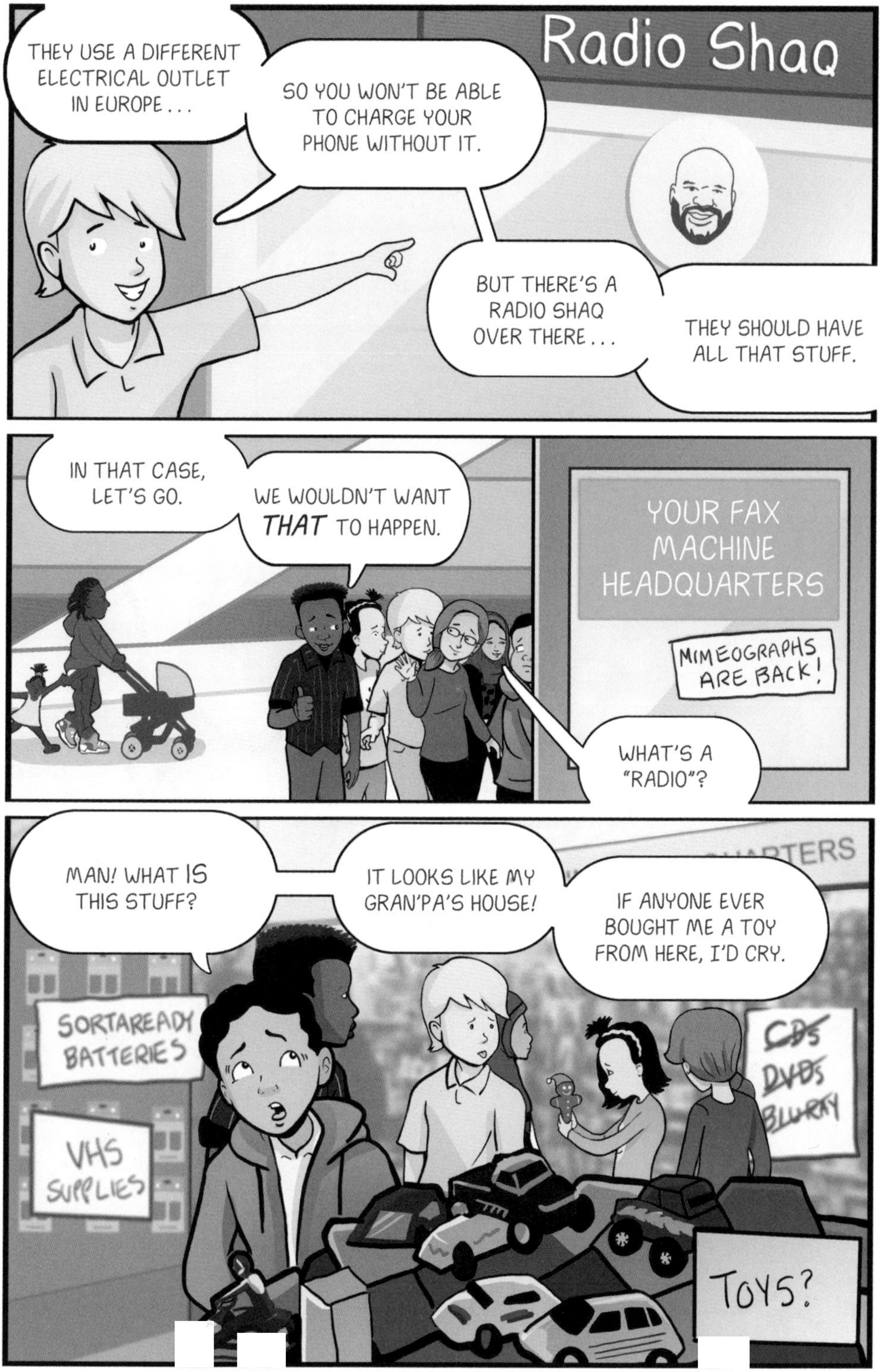
Radio Shaq
THEY USE A DIFFERENT ELECTRICAL OUTLET IN EUROPE . . .
SO YOU WON'T BE ABLE TO CHARGE YOUR PHONE WITHOUT IT.
BUT THERE'S A RADIO SHAQ OVER THERE . . .
THEY SHOULD HAVE ALL THAT STUFF.
IN THAT CASE, LET'S GO.
WE WOULDN'T WANT *THAT* TO HAPPEN.
YOUR FAX MACHINE HEADQUARTERS
MIMEOGRAPHS ARE BACK!
WHAT'S A "RADIO"?
MAN! WHAT IS THIS STUFF?
IT LOOKS LIKE MY GRAN'PA'S HOUSE!
IF ANYONE EVER BOUGHT ME A TOY FROM HERE, I'D CRY.
SORTAREADY BATTERIES
VHS SUPPLIES
CDs DVDs BLURAY
TOYS?

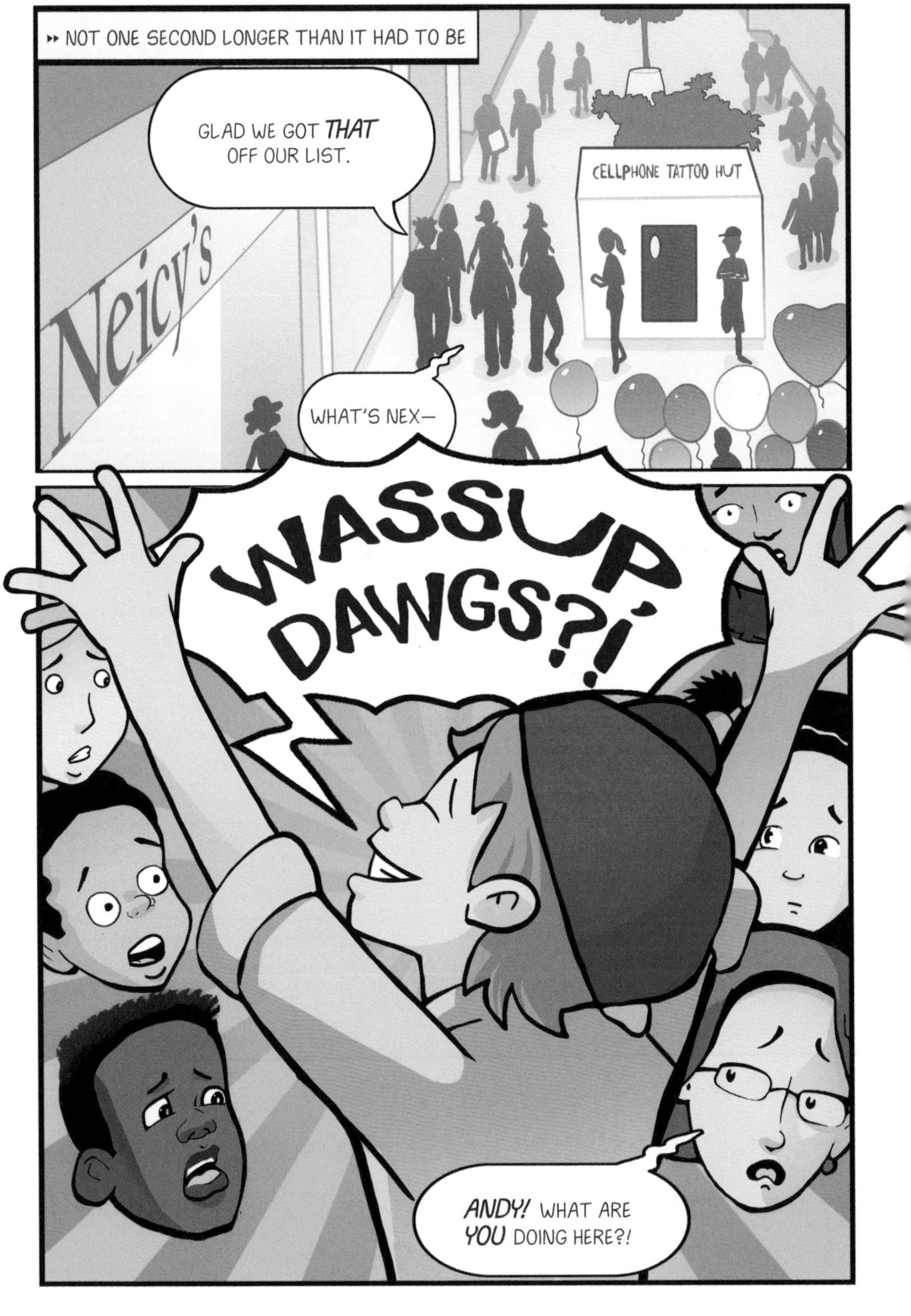
▸▸ NOT ONE SECOND LONGER THAN IT HAD TO BE
GLAD WE GOT THAT OFF OUR LIST.
CELLPHONE TATTOO HUT
Neicy's
WHAT'S NEX—
WASSUP DAWGS?!
ANDY! WHAT ARE YOU DOING HERE?!

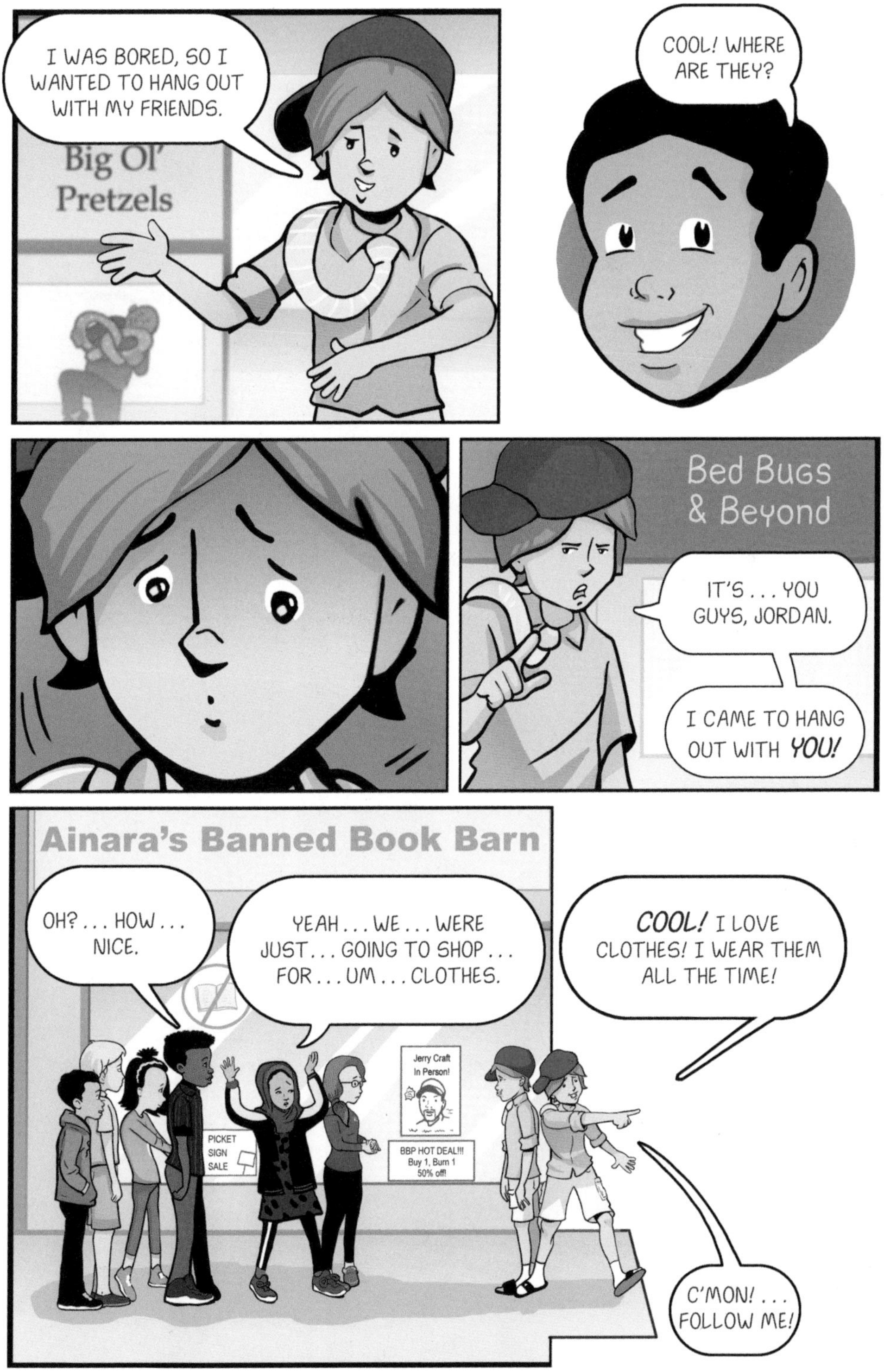
I WAS BORED, SO I WANTED TO HANG OUT WITH MY FRIENDS.
Big Ol' Pretzels
COOL! WHERE ARE THEY?
Bed Bugs & Beyond
IT'S . . . YOU GUYS, JORDAN.
I CAME TO HANG OUT WITH YOU!
Ainara's Banned Book Barn
OH? . . . HOW . . . NICE.
YEAH . . . WE . . . WERE JUST . . . GOING TO SHOP . . . FOR . . . UM . . . CLOTHES.
COOL! I LOVE CLOTHES! I WEAR THEM ALL THE TIME!
PICKET SIGN SALE
Jerry Craft In Person!
BBP HOT DEAL!!! Buy 1, Burn 1 50% off!
C'MON! . . . FOLLOW ME!

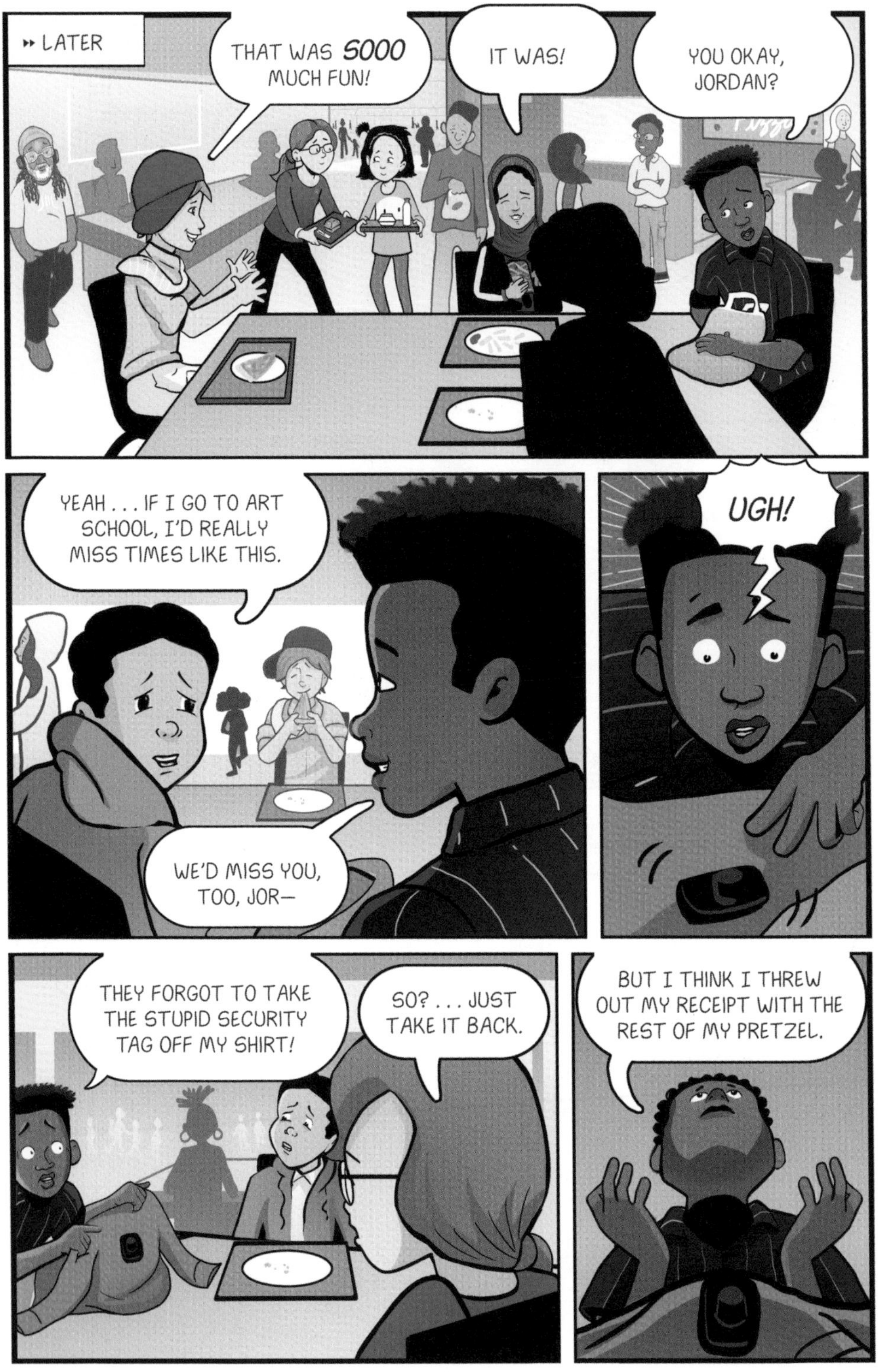
LATER
THAT WAS SOOO MUCH FUN!
IT WAS!
YOU OKAY, JORDAN?
YEAH . . . IF I GO TO ART SCHOOL, I'D REALLY MISS TIMES LIKE THIS.
WE'D MISS YOU, TOO, JOR—
UGH!
THEY FORGOT TO TAKE THE STUPID SECURITY TAG OFF MY SHIRT!
SO? . . . JUST TAKE IT BACK.
BUT I THINK I THREW OUT MY RECEIPT WITH THE REST OF MY PRETZEL.

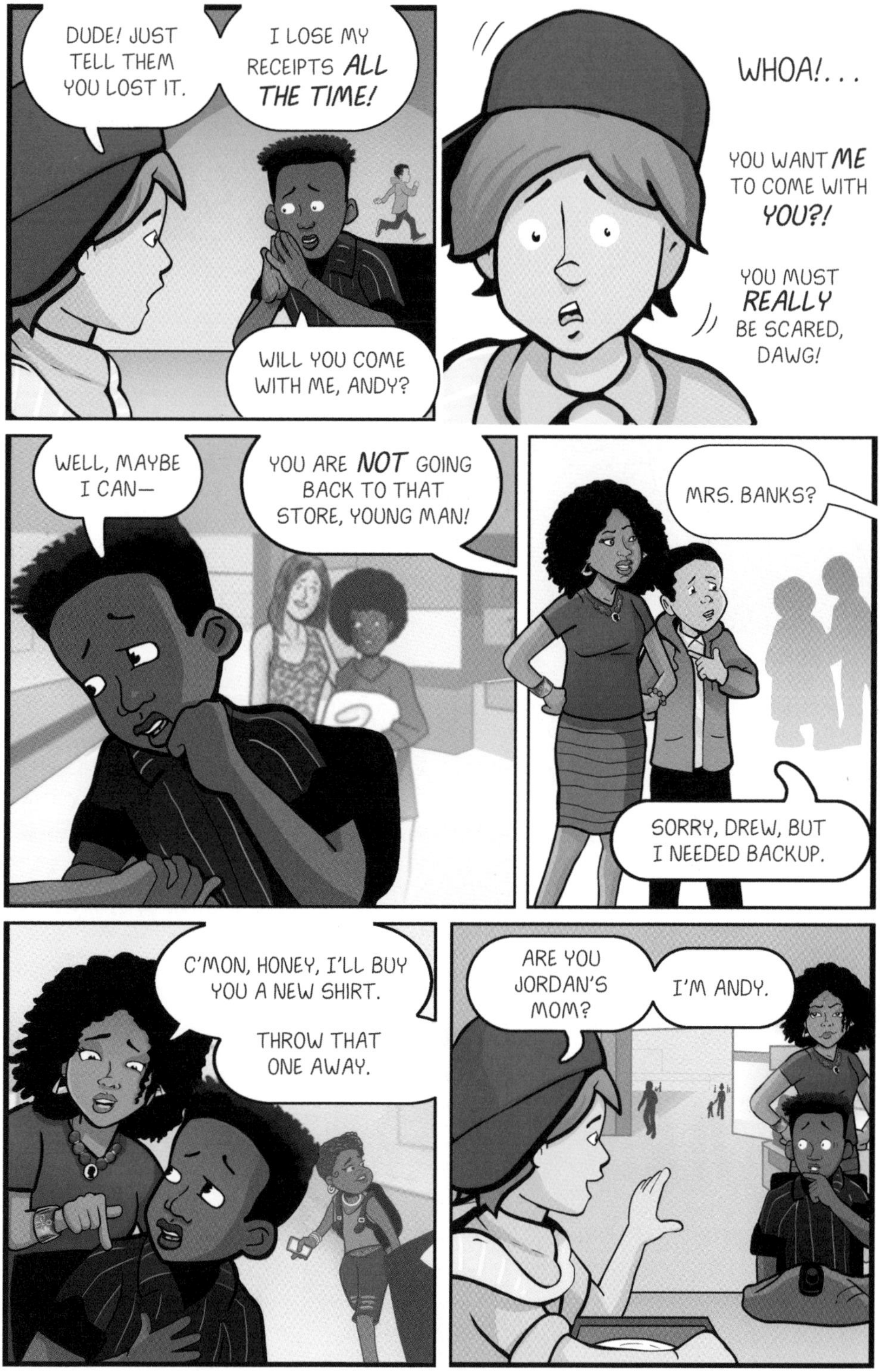
DUDE! JUST TELL THEM YOU LOST IT.
I LOSE MY RECEIPTS ALL THE TIME!
WILL YOU COME WITH ME, ANDY?
WHOA!. . .
YOU WANT ME TO COME WITH YOU?!
YOU MUST REALLY BE SCARED, DAWG!
WELL, MAYBE I CAN—
YOU ARE NOT GOING BACK TO THAT STORE, YOUNG MAN!
MRS. BANKS?
SORRY, DREW, BUT I NEEDED BACKUP.
C'MON, HONEY, I'LL BUY YOU A NEW SHIRT.
THROW THAT ONE AWAY.
ARE YOU JORDAN'S MOM?
I'M ANDY.

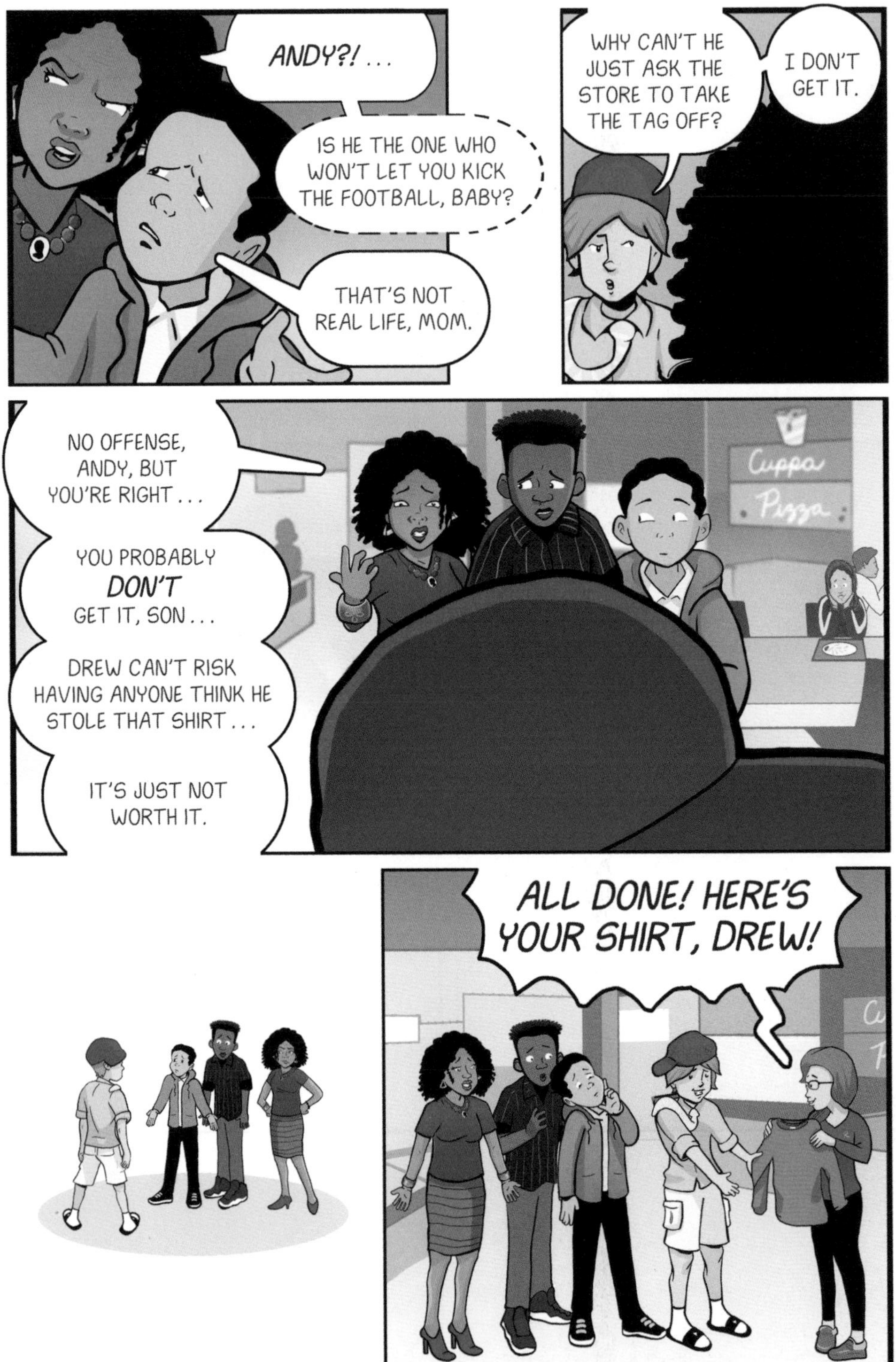
ANDY?! ...
IS HE THE ONE WHO WON'T LET YOU KICK THE FOOTBALL, BABY?
THAT'S NOT REAL LIFE, MOM.
WHY CAN'T HE JUST ASK THE STORE TO TAKE THE TAG OFF?
I DON'T GET IT.
NO OFFENSE, ANDY, BUT YOU'RE RIGHT . . .
YOU PROBABLY DON'T GET IT, SON . . .
DREW CAN'T RISK HAVING ANYONE THINK HE STOLE THAT SHIRT . . .
IT'S JUST NOT WORTH IT.
Cuppa Pizza
ALL DONE! HERE'S YOUR SHIRT, DREW!

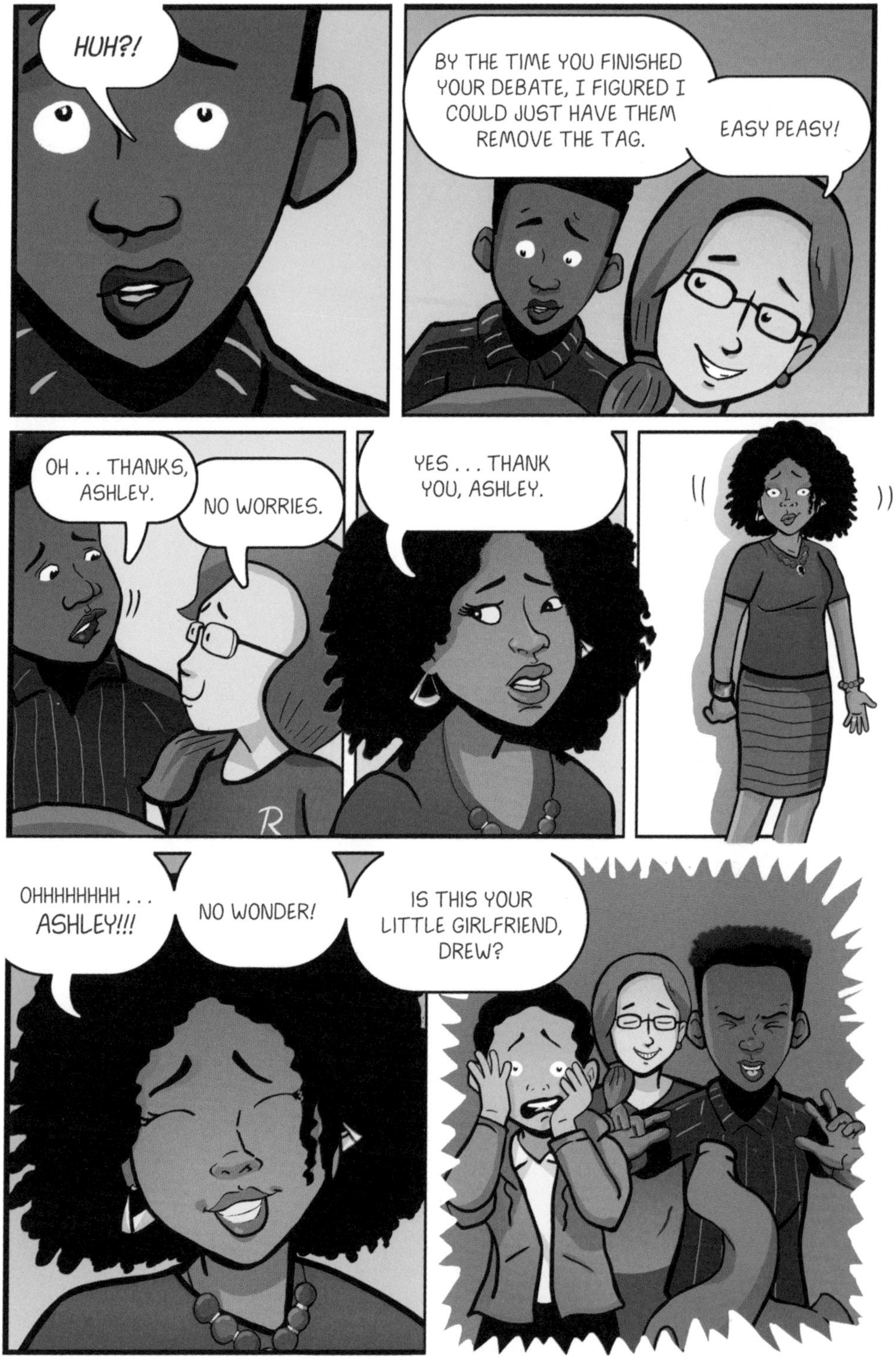
HUH?!
BY THE TIME YOU FINISHED YOUR DEBATE, I FIGURED I COULD JUST HAVE THEM REMOVE THE TAG.
EASY PEASY!
OH . . . THANKS, ASHLEY.
NO WORRIES.
YES . . . THANK YOU, ASHLEY.
OHHHHHHHH . . . ASHLEY!!!
NO WONDER!
IS THIS YOUR LITTLE GIRLFRIEND, DREW?

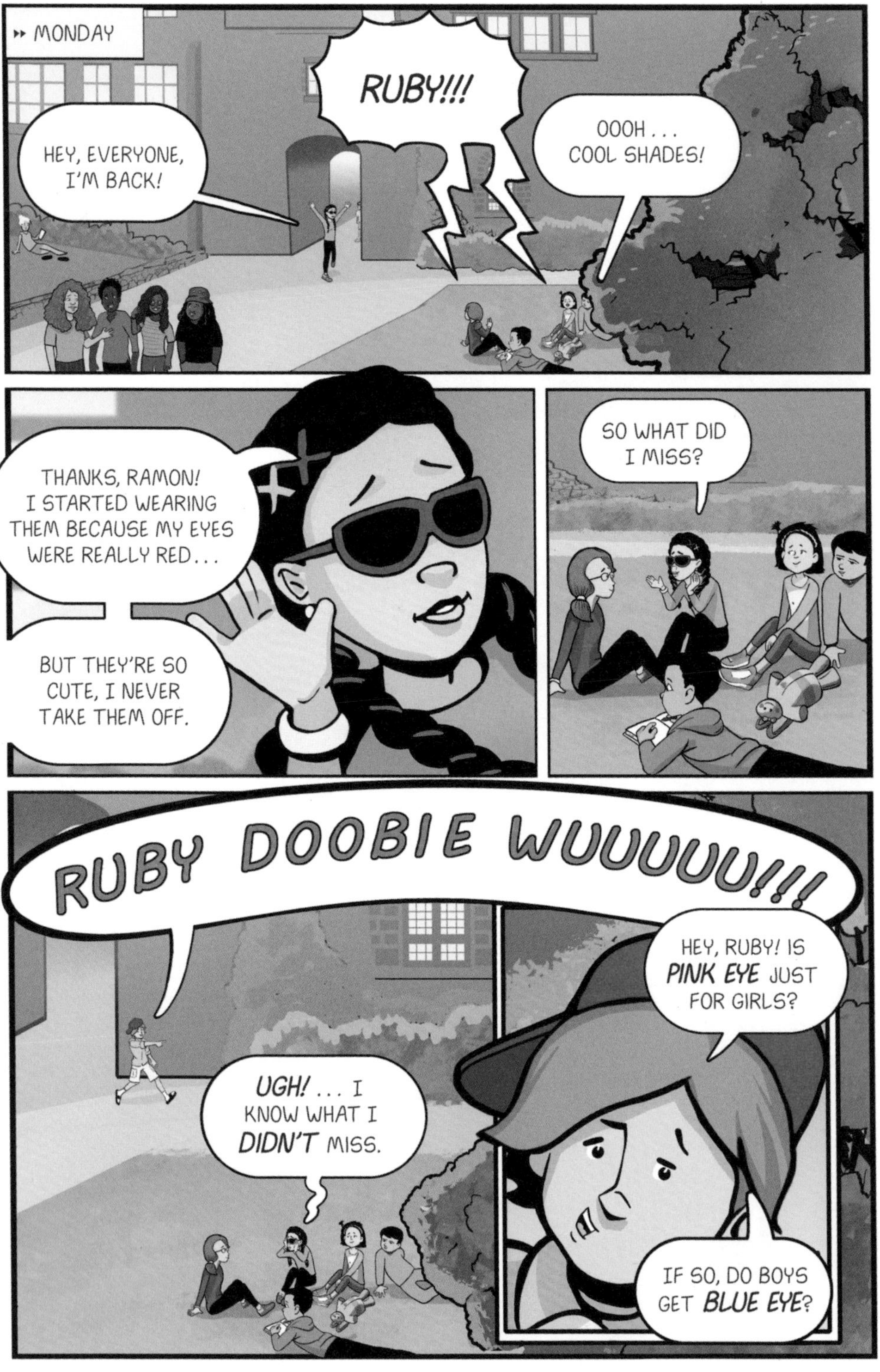
MONDAY
HEY, EVERYONE, I'M BACK!
RUBY!!!
OOOH . . . COOL SHADES!
THANKS, RAMON! I STARTED WEARING THEM BECAUSE MY EYES WERE REALLY RED . . .
BUT THEY'RE SO CUTE, I NEVER TAKE THEM OFF.
SO WHAT DID I MISS?
RUBY DOOBIE WUUUUUU!!!
HEY, RUBY! IS PINK EYE JUST FOR GIRLS?
UGH! . . . I KNOW WHAT I DIDN'T MISS.
IF SO, DO BOYS GET BLUE EYE?

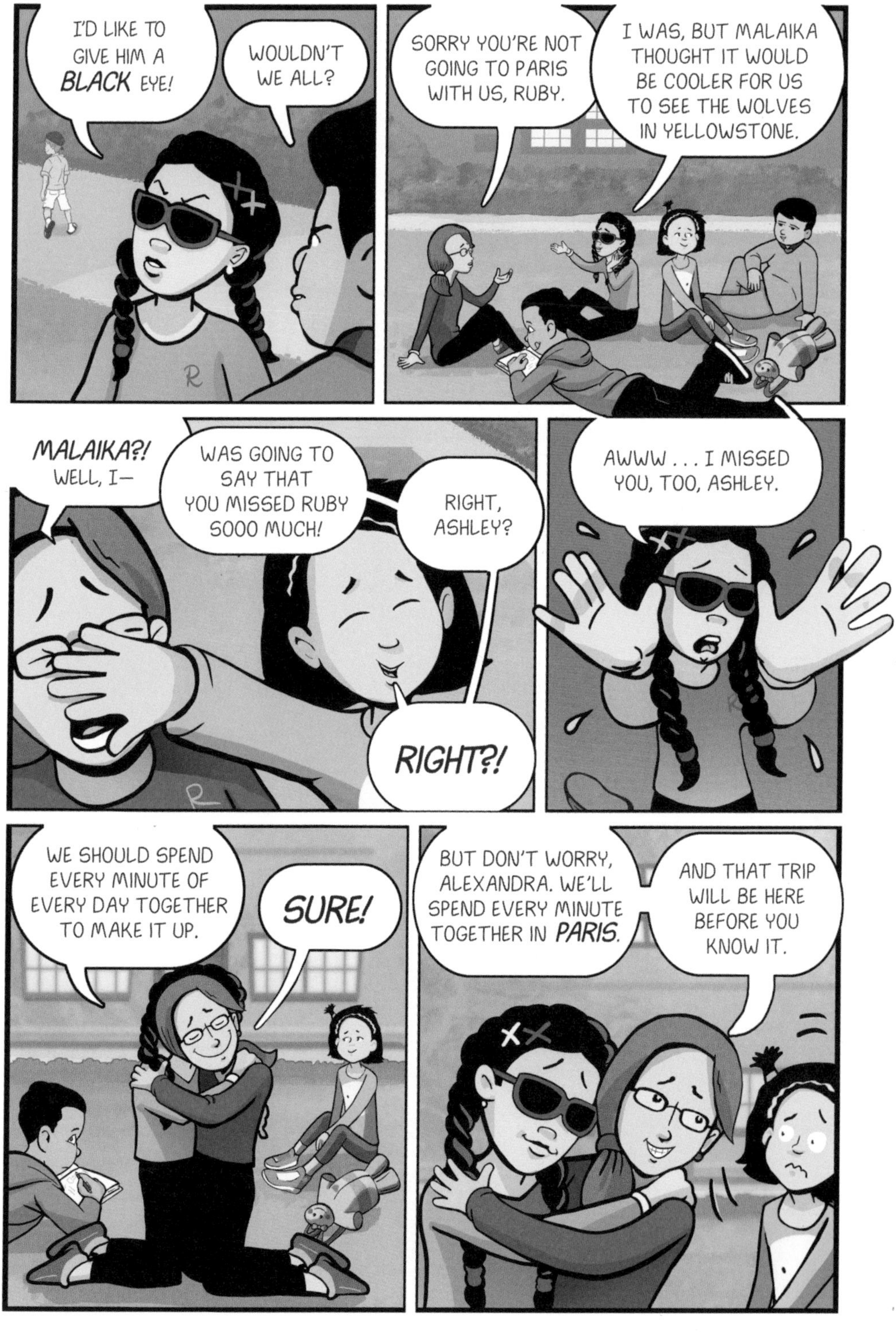
I'D LIKE TO GIVE HIM A *BLACK* EYE!
WOULDN'T WE ALL?
SORRY YOU'RE NOT GOING TO PARIS WITH US, RUBY.
I WAS, BUT MALAIKA THOUGHT IT WOULD BE COOLER FOR US TO SEE THE WOLVES IN YELLOWSTONE.
MALAIKA?! WELL, I—
WAS GOING TO SAY THAT YOU MISSED RUBY SOOO MUCH!
RIGHT, ASHLEY?
RIGHT?!
AWWW . . . I MISSED YOU, TOO, ASHLEY.
WE SHOULD SPEND EVERY MINUTE OF EVERY DAY TOGETHER TO MAKE IT UP.
SURE!
BUT DON'T WORRY, ALEXANDRA. WE'LL SPEND EVERY MINUTE TOGETHER IN *PARIS*.
AND THAT TRIP WILL BE HERE BEFORE YOU KNOW IT.

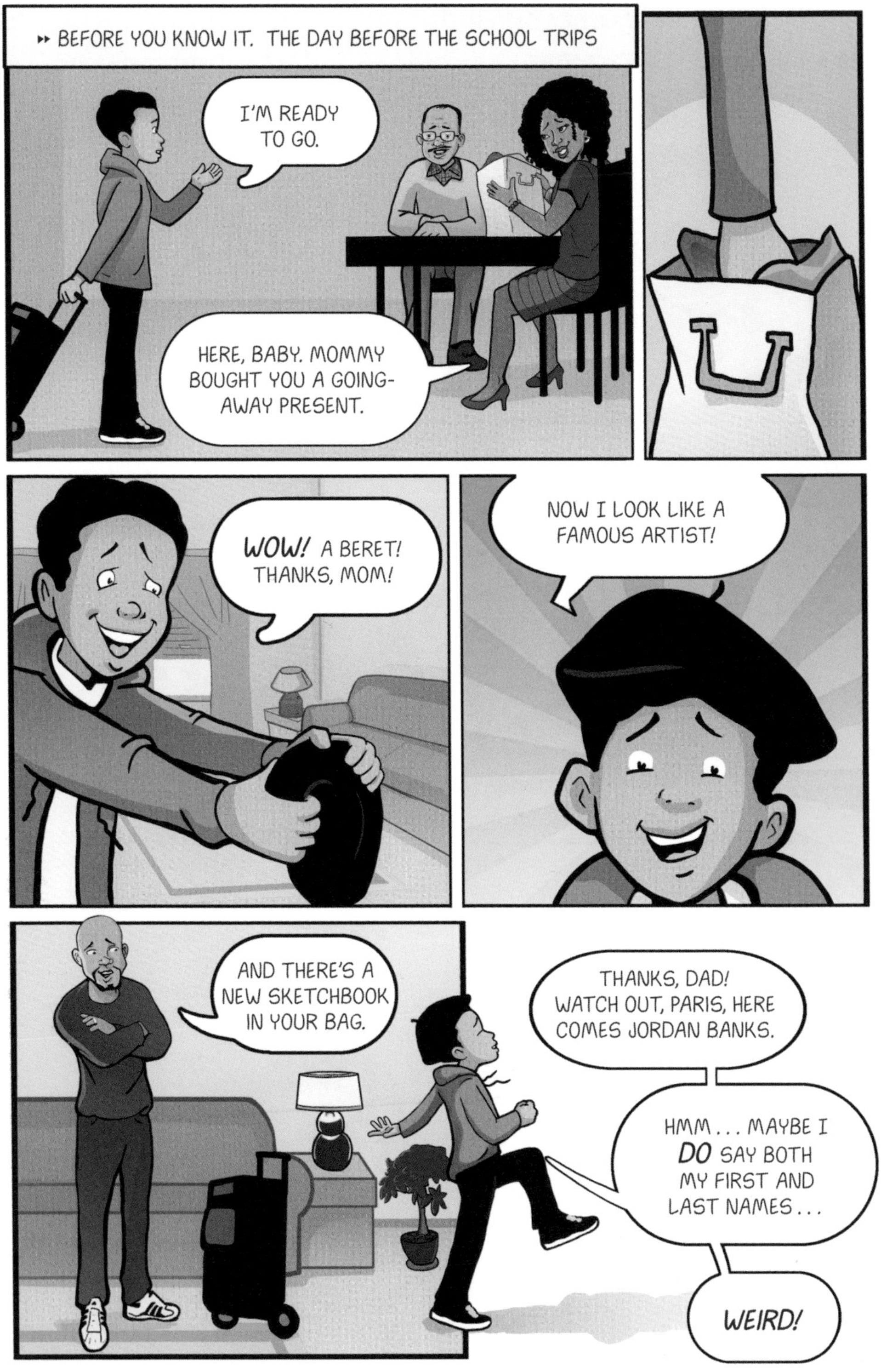
BEFORE YOU KNOW IT. THE DAY BEFORE THE SCHOOL TRIPS
I'M READY TO GO.
HERE, BABY. MOMMY BOUGHT YOU A GOING-AWAY PRESENT.
WOW! A BERET! THANKS, MOM!
NOW I LOOK LIKE A FAMOUS ARTIST!
AND THERE'S A NEW SKETCHBOOK IN YOUR BAG.
THANKS, DAD! WATCH OUT, PARIS, HERE COMES JORDAN BANKS.
HMM . . . MAYBE I DO SAY BOTH MY FIRST AND LAST NAMES . . .
WEIRD!

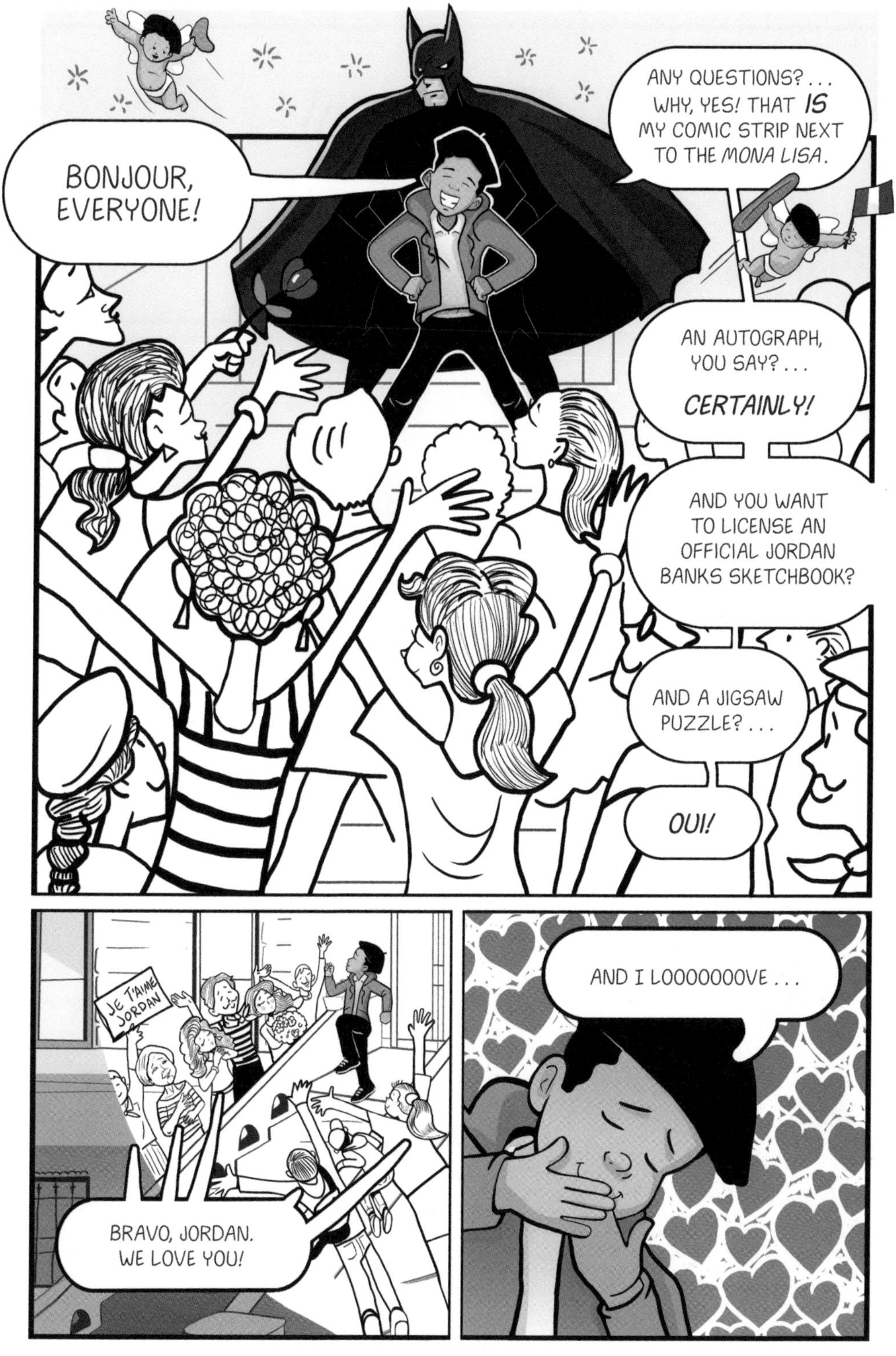
BONJOUR, EVERYONE!
ANY QUESTIONS? . . . WHY, YES! THAT IS MY COMIC STRIP NEXT TO THE MONA LISA.
AN AUTOGRAPH, YOU SAY? . . .
CERTAINLY!
AND YOU WANT TO LICENSE AN OFFICIAL JORDAN BANKS SKETCHBOOK?
AND A JIGSAW PUZZLE? . . .
OUI!
JE T'AIME JORDAN
BRAVO, JORDAN. WE LOVE YOU!
AND I LOOOOOOOVE . . .

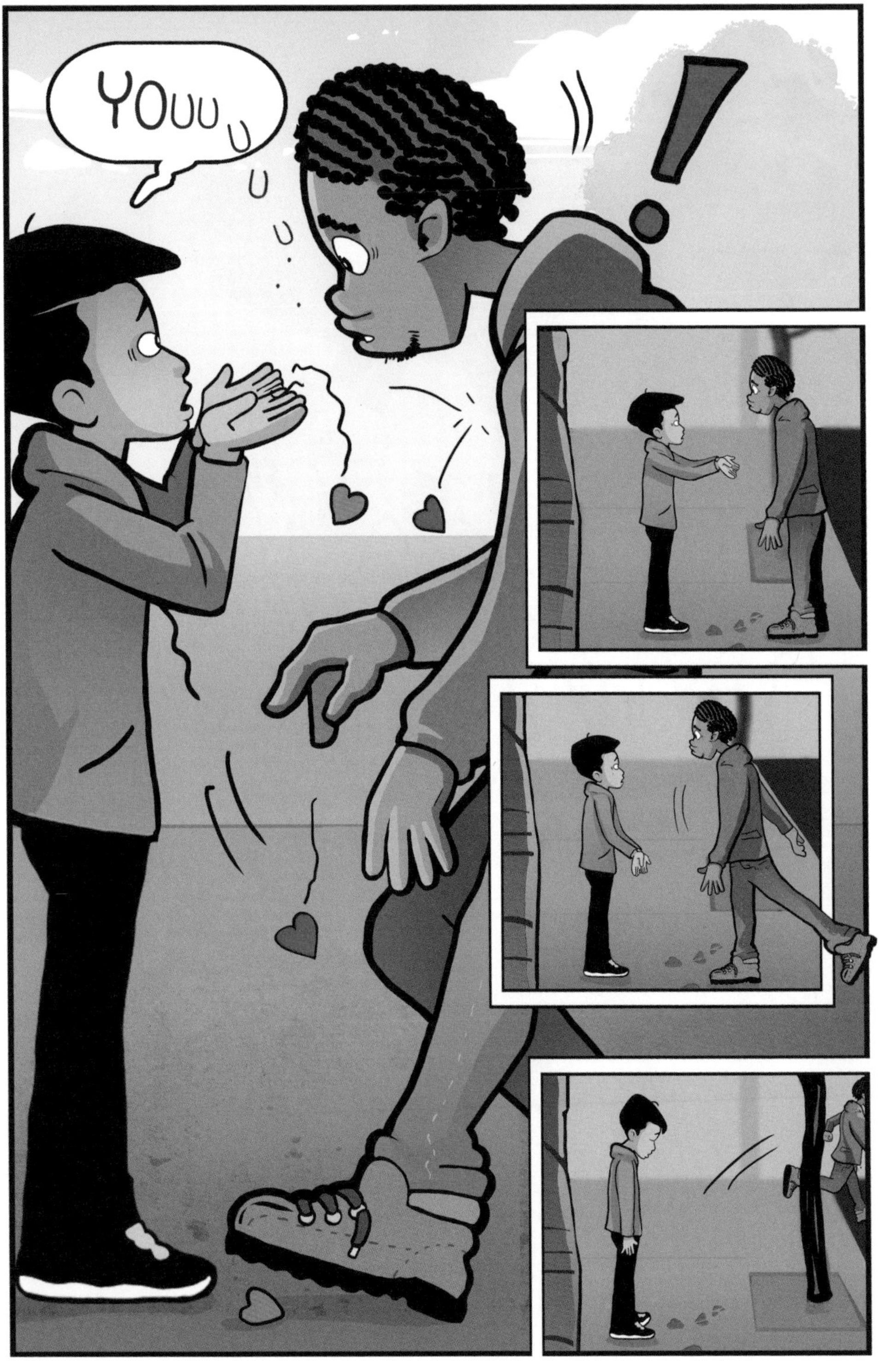
YOUUUUUU
!

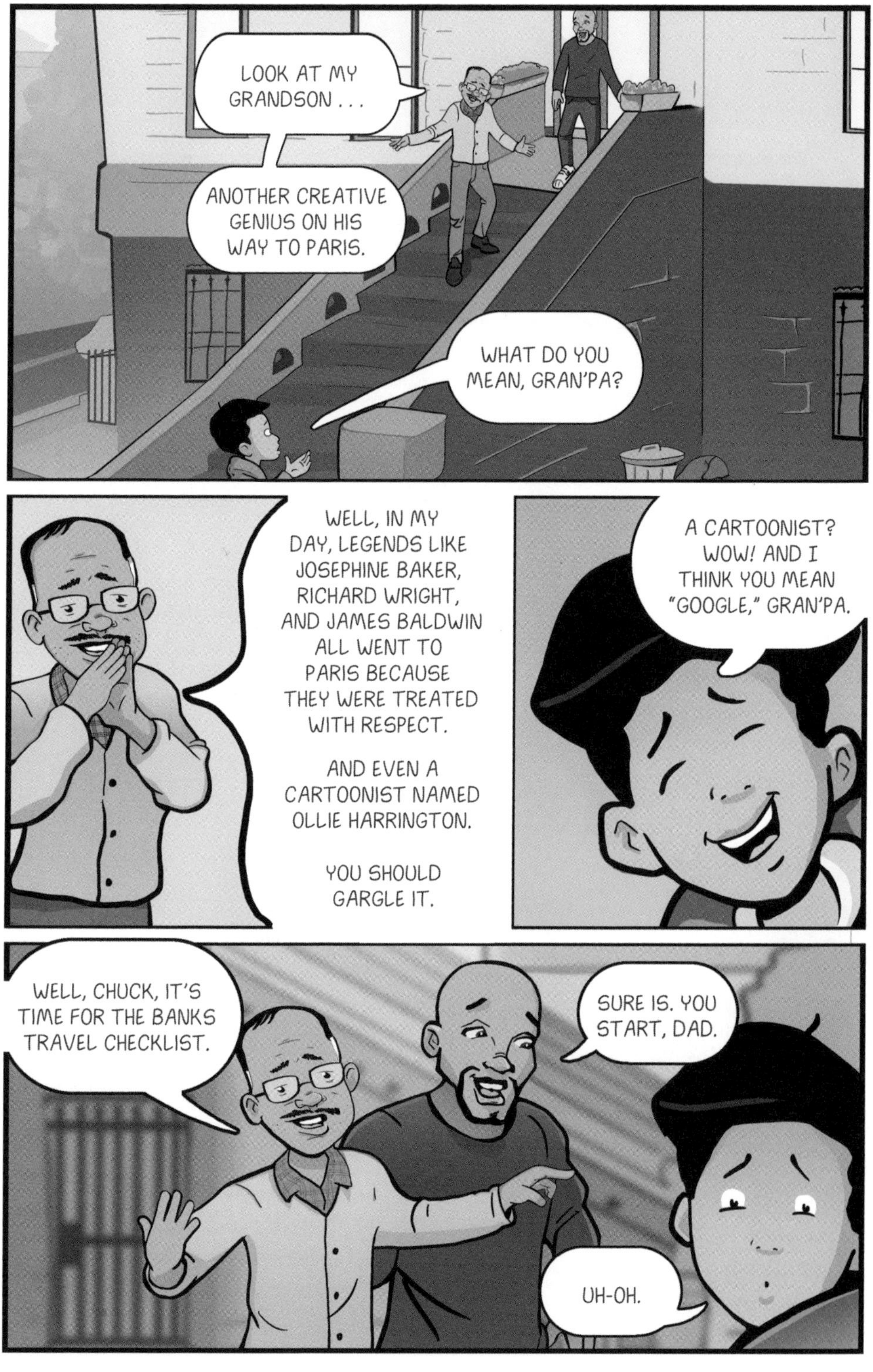
LOOK AT MY GRANDSON . . .
ANOTHER CREATIVE GENIUS ON HIS WAY TO PARIS.
WHAT DO YOU MEAN, GRAN'PA?
WELL, IN MY DAY, LEGENDS LIKE JOSEPHINE BAKER, RICHARD WRIGHT, AND JAMES BALDWIN ALL WENT TO PARIS BECAUSE THEY WERE TREATED WITH RESPECT.
AND EVEN A CARTOONIST NAMED OLLIE HARRINGTON.
YOU SHOULD GARGLE IT.
A CARTOONIST? WOW! AND I THINK YOU MEAN "GOOGLE," GRAN'PA.
WELL, CHUCK, IT'S TIME FOR THE BANKS TRAVEL CHECKLIST.
SURE IS. YOU START, DAD.
UH-OH.

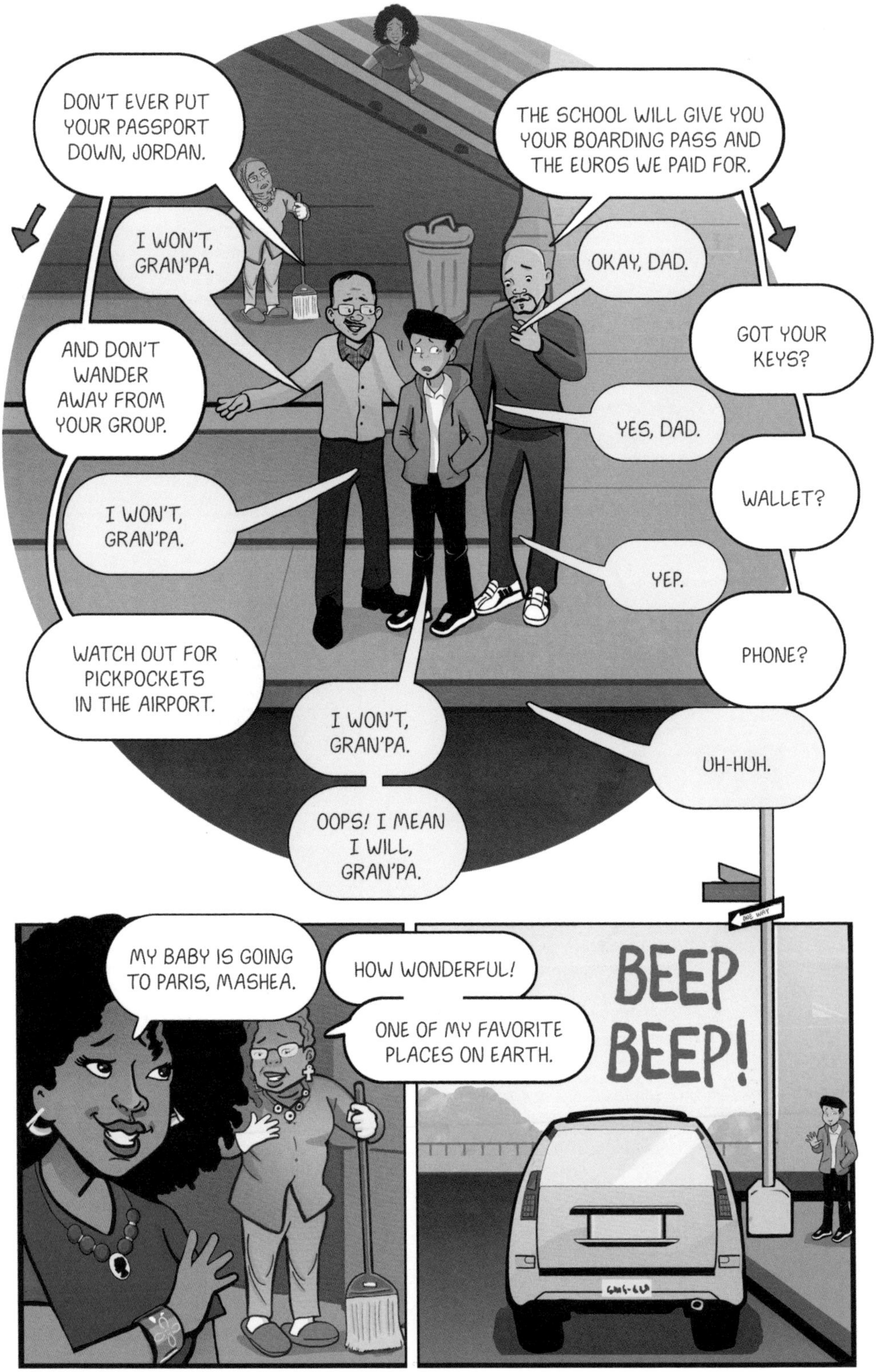
DON'T EVER PUT YOUR PASSPORT DOWN, JORDAN.
I WON'T, GRAN'PA.
AND DON'T WANDER AWAY FROM YOUR GROUP.
I WON'T, GRAN'PA.
WATCH OUT FOR PICKPOCKETS IN THE AIRPORT.
I WON'T, GRAN'PA.
OOPS! I MEAN I WILL, GRAN'PA.
THE SCHOOL WILL GIVE YOU YOUR BOARDING PASS AND THE EUROS WE PAID FOR.
OKAY, DAD.
GOT YOUR KEYS?
YES, DAD.
WALLET?
YEP.
PHONE?
UH-HUH.
MY BABY IS GOING TO PARIS, MASHEA.
HOW WONDERFUL!
ONE OF MY FAVORITE PLACES ON EARTH.
BEEP BEEP!

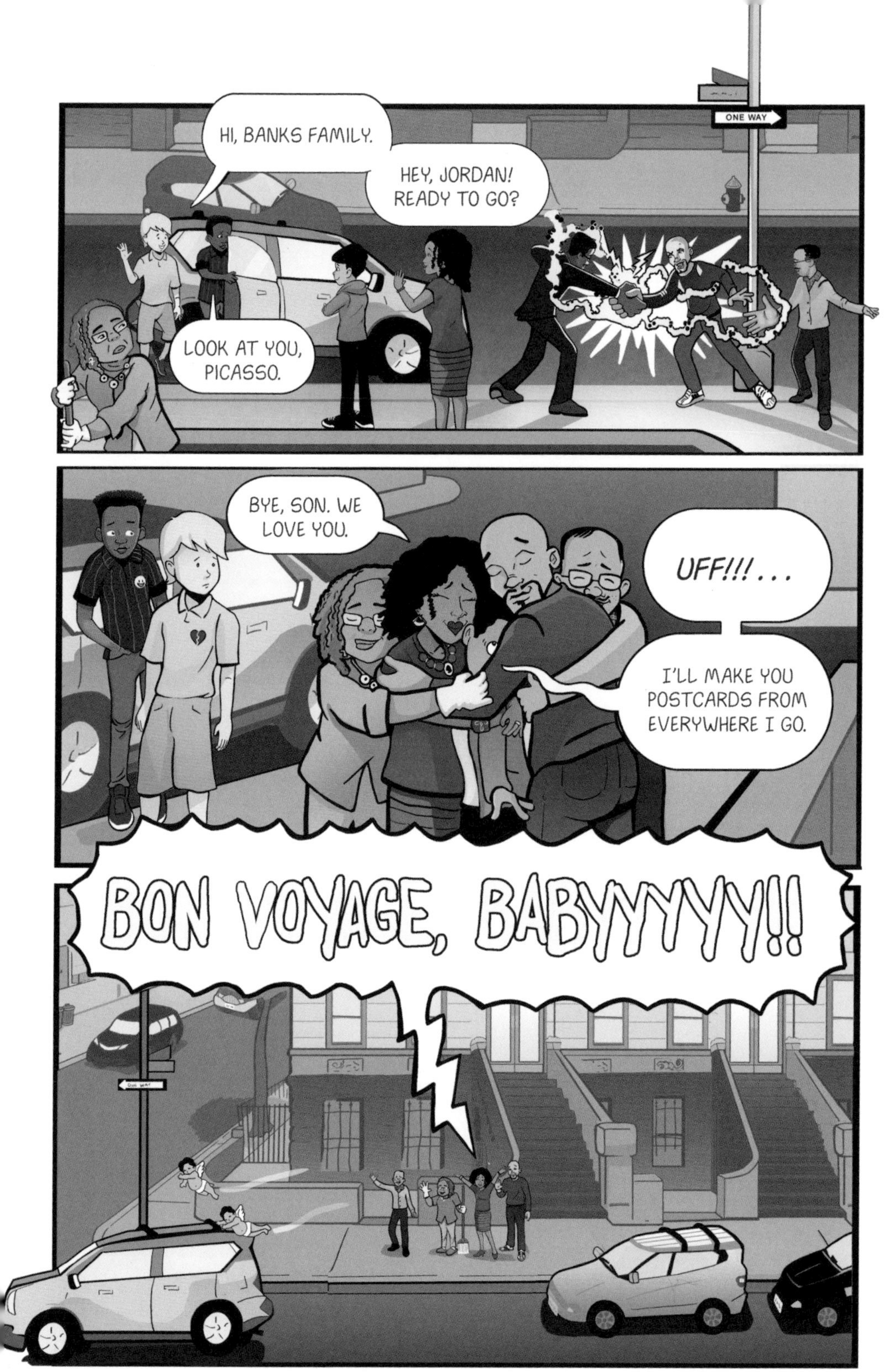
HI, BANKS FAMILY.
HEY, JORDAN! READY TO GO?
ONE WAY
LOOK AT YOU, PICASSO.
BYE, SON. WE LOVE YOU.
UFF!!! . . .
I'LL MAKE YOU POSTCARDS FROM EVERYWHERE I GO.
BON VOYAGE, BABYYYYY!!

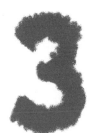

3 A Butterfly With Butterflies!

(In My Stomach!)

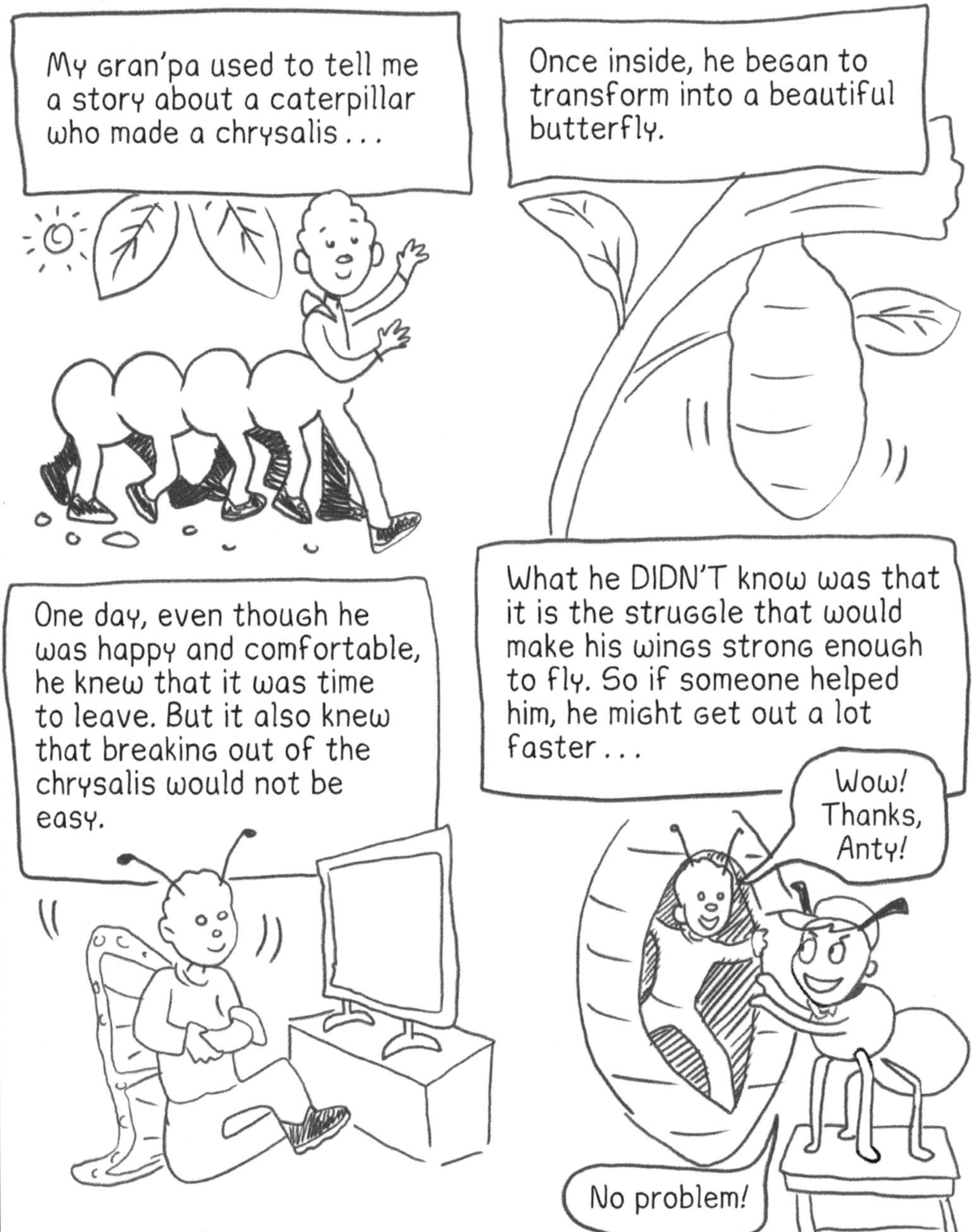
My gran'pa used to tell me a story about a caterpillar who made a chrysalis . . .
Once inside, he began to transform into a beautiful butterfly.
One day, even though he was happy and comfortable, he knew that it was time to leave. But it also knew that breaking out of the chrysalis would not be easy.
What he DIDN'T know was that it is the struggle that would make his wings strong enough to fly. So if someone helped him, he might get out a lot faster . . .
Wow! Thanks, Anty!
No problem!

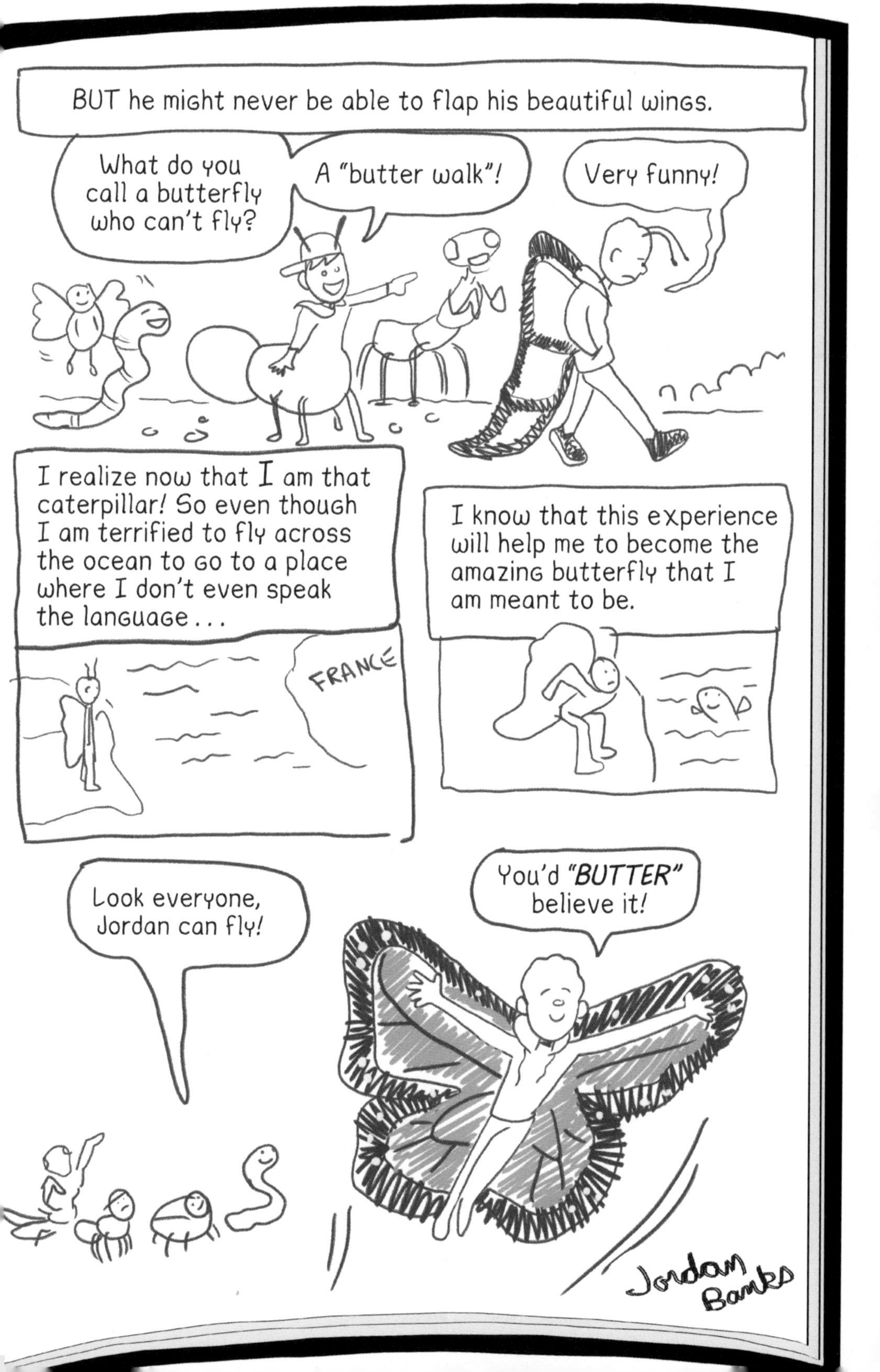

BUT he might never be able to flap his beautiful wings.
What do you call a butterfly who can't fly?
A "butter walk"!
Very funny!
I realize now that I am that caterpillar! So even though I am terrified to fly across the ocean to go to a place where I don't even speak the language . . .
FRANCE
I know that this experience will help me to become the amazing butterfly that I am meant to be.
Look everyone, Jordan can fly!
You'd *"BUTTER"* believe it!
Jordan Banks

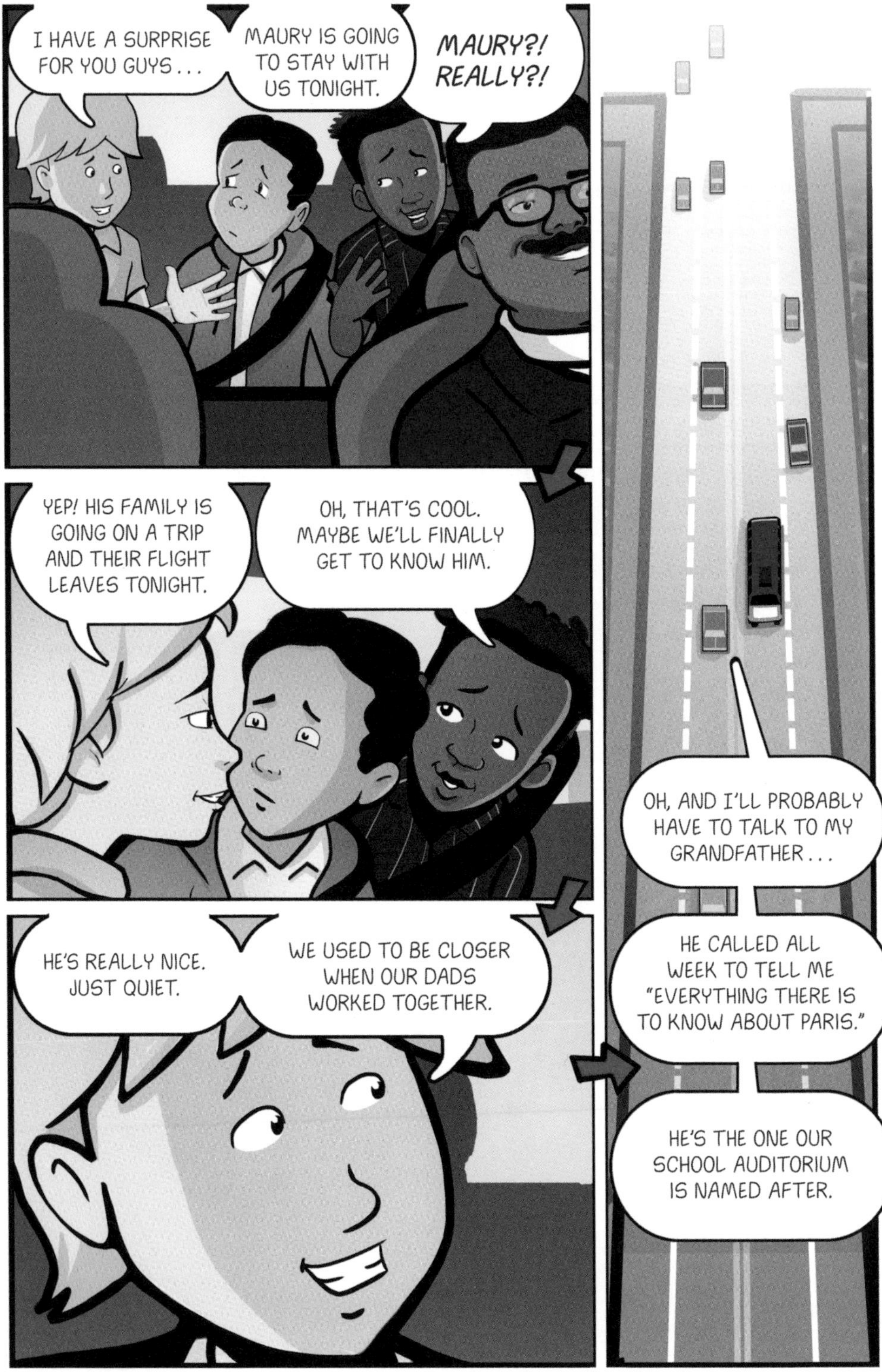
I HAVE A SURPRISE FOR YOU GUYS . . .
MAURY IS GOING TO STAY WITH US TONIGHT.
MAURY?! REALLY?!
YEP! HIS FAMILY IS GOING ON A TRIP AND THEIR FLIGHT LEAVES TONIGHT.
OH, THAT'S COOL. MAYBE WE'LL FINALLY GET TO KNOW HIM.
HE'S REALLY NICE. JUST QUIET.
WE USED TO BE CLOSER WHEN OUR DADS WORKED TOGETHER.
OH, AND I'LL PROBABLY HAVE TO TALK TO MY GRANDFATHER . . .
HE CALLED ALL WEEK TO TELL ME "EVERYTHING THERE IS TO KNOW ABOUT PARIS."
HE'S THE ONE OUR SCHOOL AUDITORIUM IS NAMED AFTER.

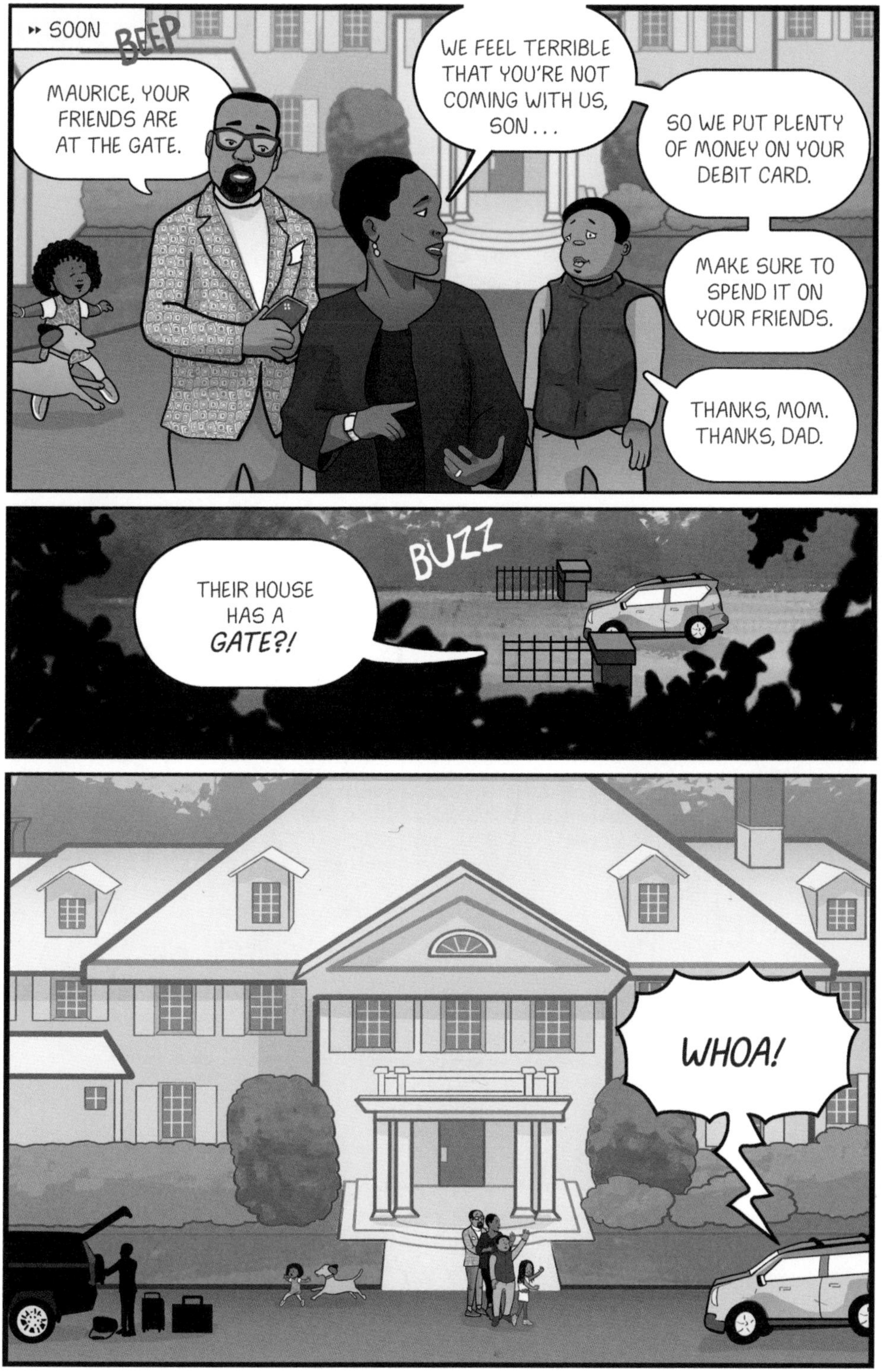
SOON
BEEP
MAURICE, YOUR FRIENDS ARE AT THE GATE.
WE FEEL TERRIBLE THAT YOU'RE NOT COMING WITH US, SON . . .
SO WE PUT PLENTY OF MONEY ON YOUR DEBIT CARD.
MAKE SURE TO SPEND IT ON YOUR FRIENDS.
THANKS, MOM. THANKS, DAD.
BUZZ
THEIR HOUSE HAS A *GATE?!*
WHOA!

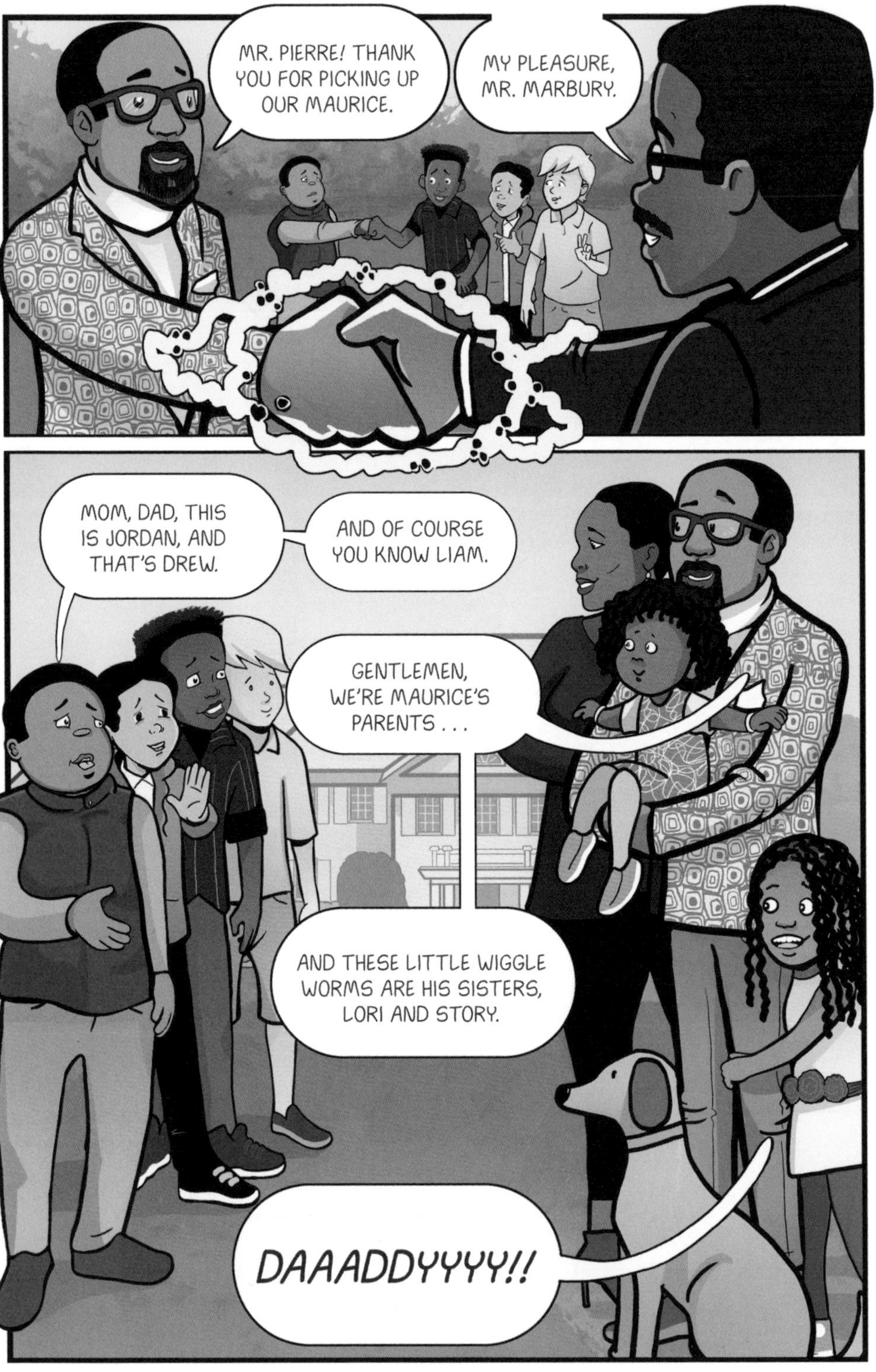
MR. PIERRE! THANK YOU FOR PICKING UP OUR MAURICE.
MY PLEASURE, MR. MARBURY.
MOM, DAD, THIS IS JORDAN, AND THAT'S DREW.
AND OF COURSE YOU KNOW LIAM.
GENTLEMEN, WE'RE MAURICE'S PARENTS . . .
AND THESE LITTLE WIGGLE WORMS ARE HIS SISTERS, LORI AND STORY.
DAAADDYYYY!!

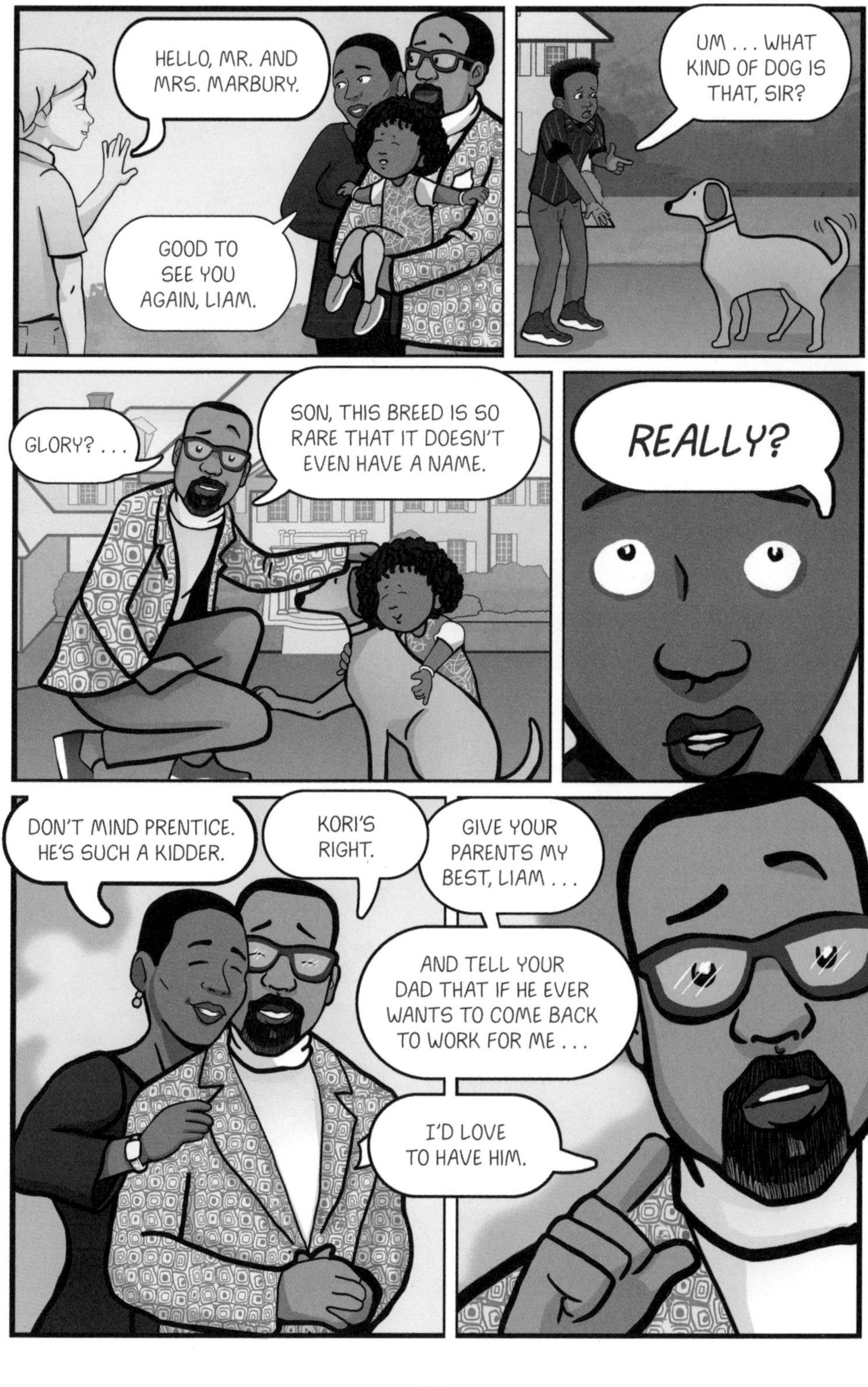
HELLO, MR. AND MRS. MARBURY.
GOOD TO SEE YOU AGAIN, LIAM.
UM . . . WHAT KIND OF DOG IS THAT, SIR?
GLORY? . . .
SON, THIS BREED IS SO RARE THAT IT DOESN'T EVEN HAVE A NAME.
REALLY?
DON'T MIND PRENTICE. HE'S SUCH A KIDDER.
KORI'S RIGHT.
GIVE YOUR PARENTS MY BEST, LIAM . . .
AND TELL YOUR DAD THAT IF HE EVER WANTS TO COME BACK TO WORK FOR ME . . .
I'D LOVE TO HAVE HIM.

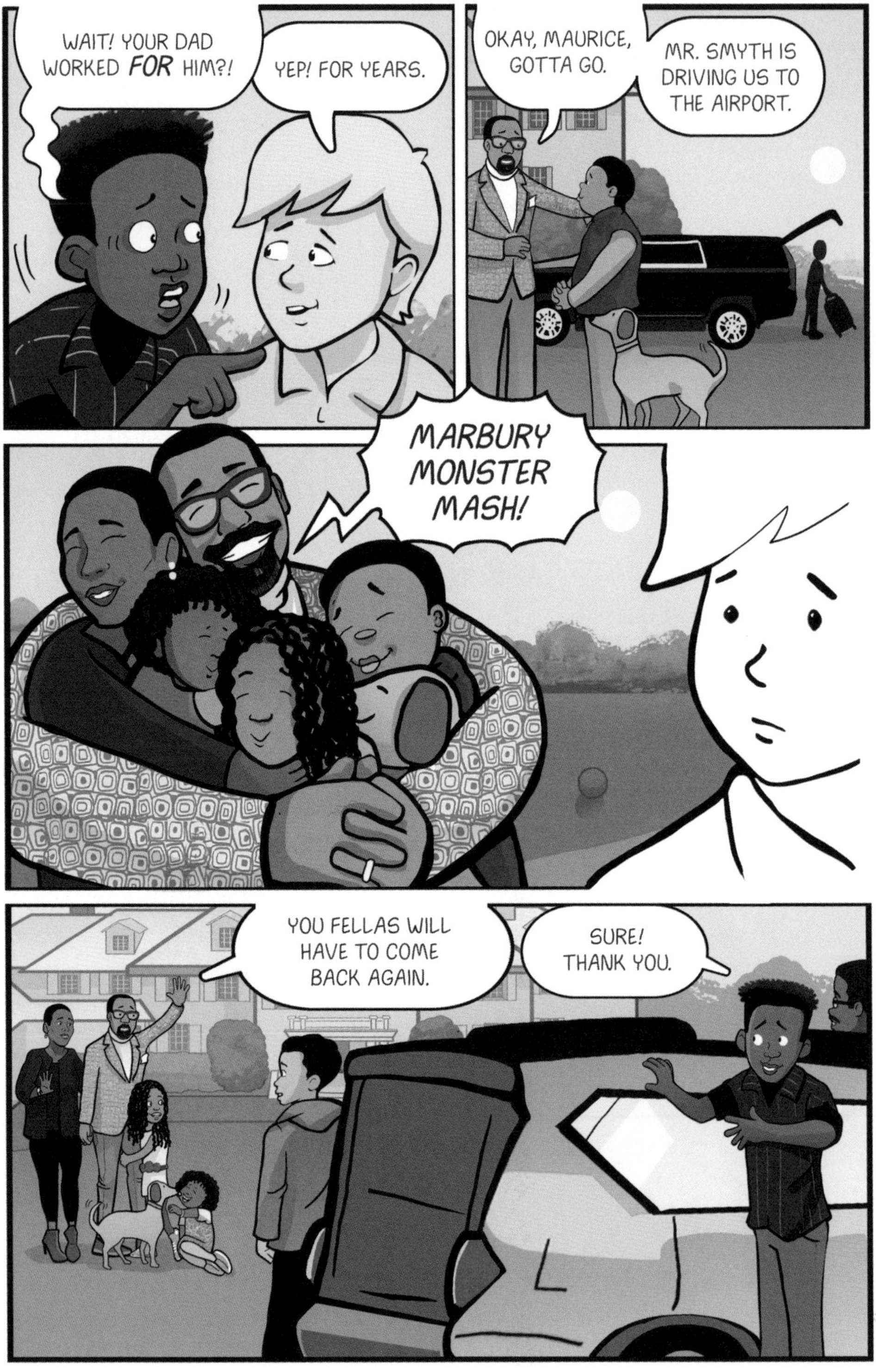
WAIT! YOUR DAD WORKED FOR HIM?!
YEP! FOR YEARS.
OKAY, MAURICE, GOTTA GO.
MR. SMYTH IS DRIVING US TO THE AIRPORT.
MARBURY MONSTER MASH!
YOU FELLAS WILL HAVE TO COME BACK AGAIN.
SURE! THANK YOU.

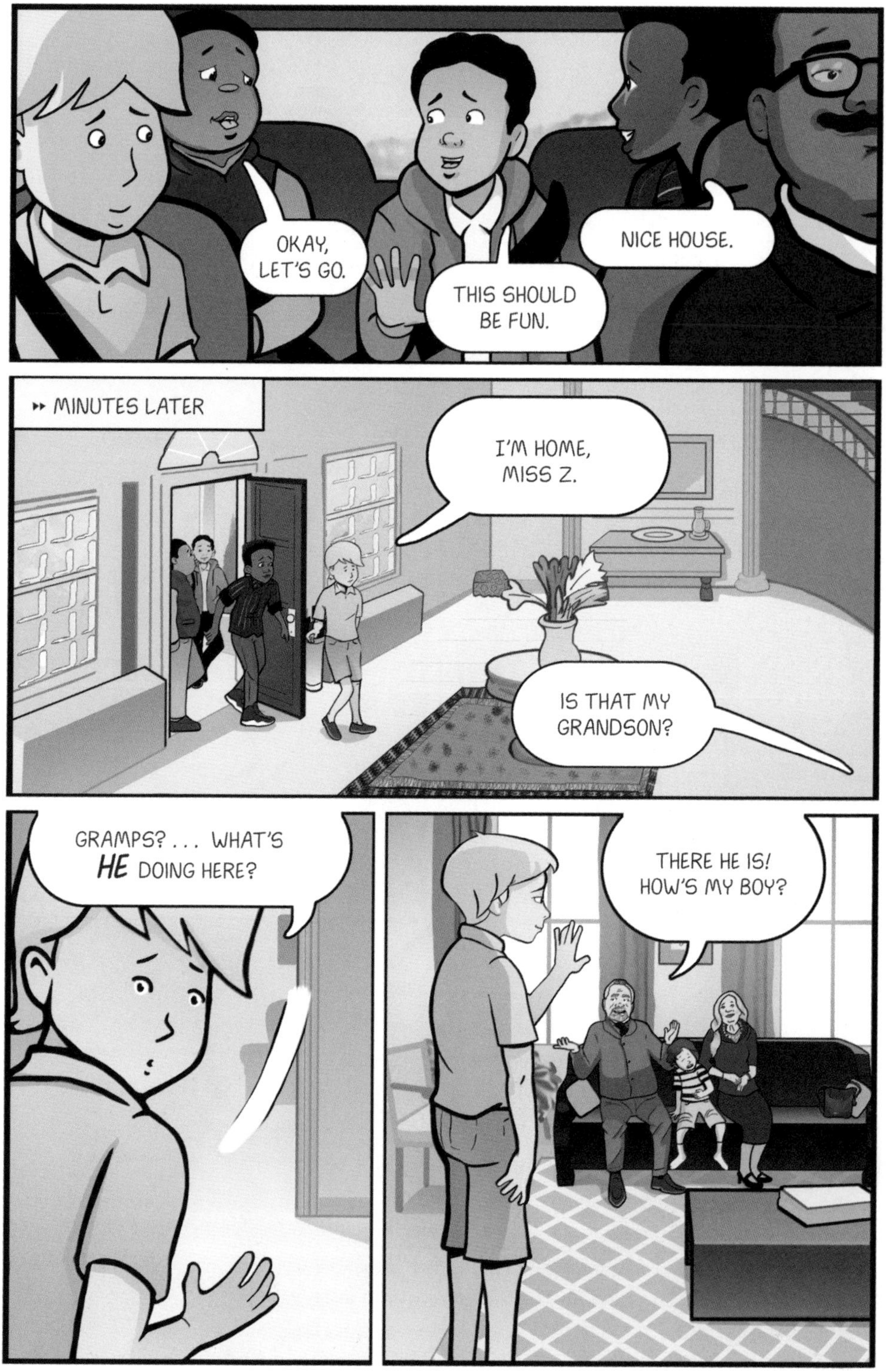
OKAY, LET'S GO.
THIS SHOULD BE FUN.
NICE HOUSE.
▸▸ MINUTES LATER
I'M HOME, MISS Z.
IS THAT MY GRANDSON?
GRAMPS? . . . WHAT'S *HE* DOING HERE?
THERE HE IS! HOW'S MY BOY?

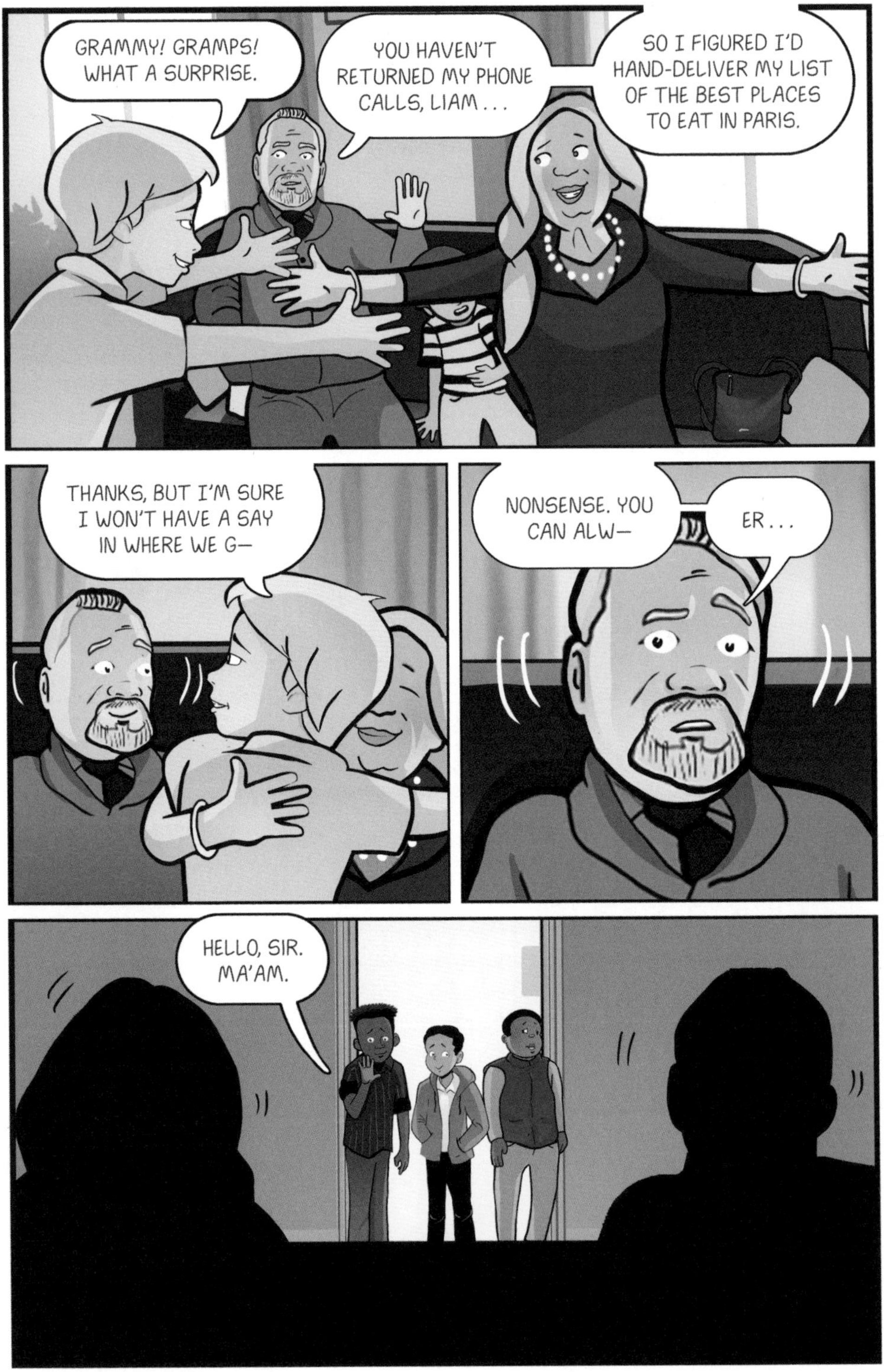
GRAMMY! GRAMPS! WHAT A SURPRISE.
YOU HAVEN'T RETURNED MY PHONE CALLS, LIAM . . .
SO I FIGURED I'D HAND-DELIVER MY LIST OF THE BEST PLACES TO EAT IN PARIS.
THANKS, BUT I'M SURE I WON'T HAVE A SAY IN WHERE WE G—
NONSENSE. YOU CAN ALW—
ER . . .
HELLO, SIR. MA'AM.

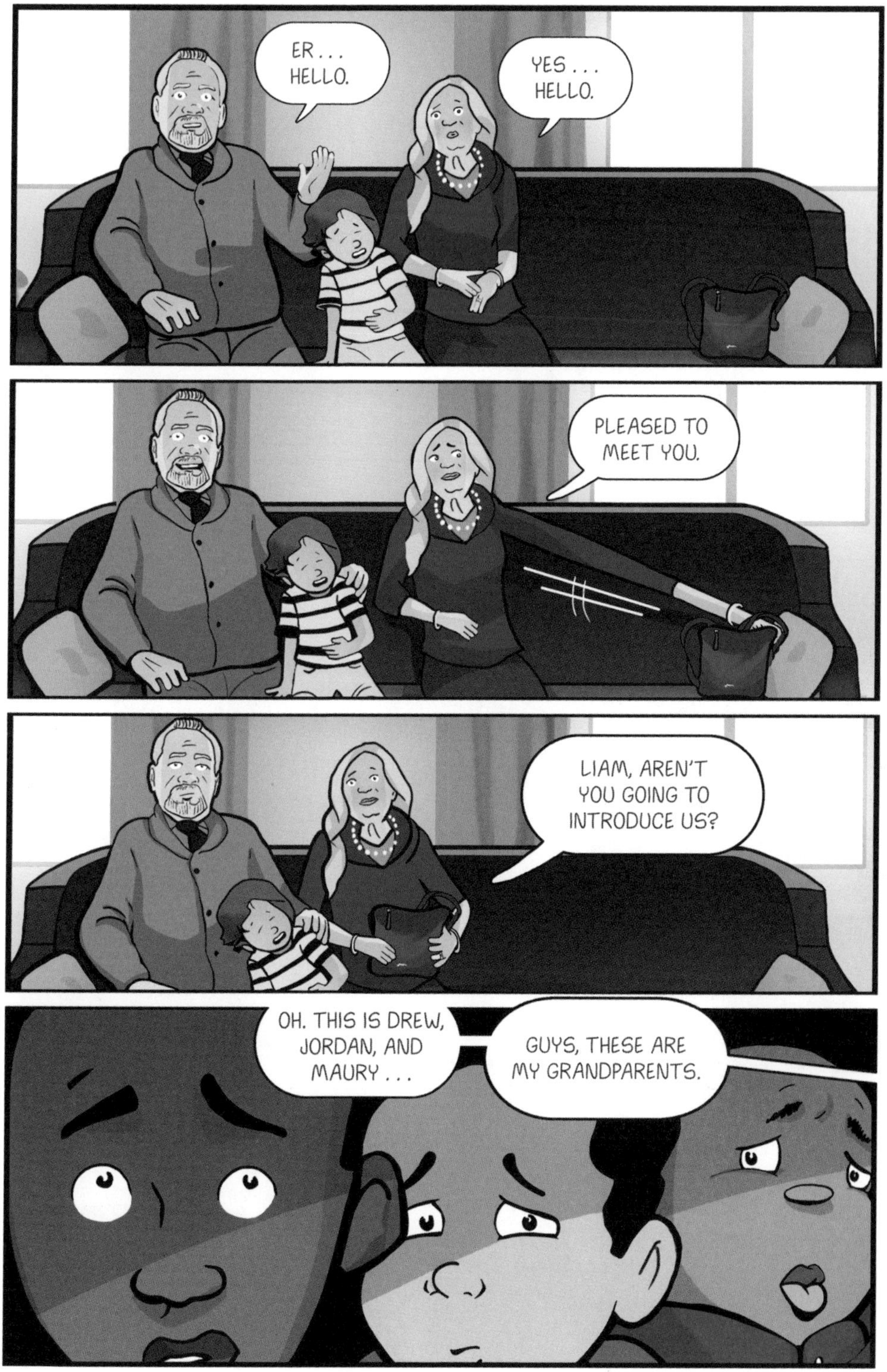
ER . . . HELLO.
YES . . . HELLO.
PLEASED TO MEET YOU.
LIAM, AREN'T YOU GOING TO INTRODUCE US?
OH. THIS IS DREW, JORDAN, AND MAURY . . .
GUYS, THESE ARE MY GRANDPARENTS.

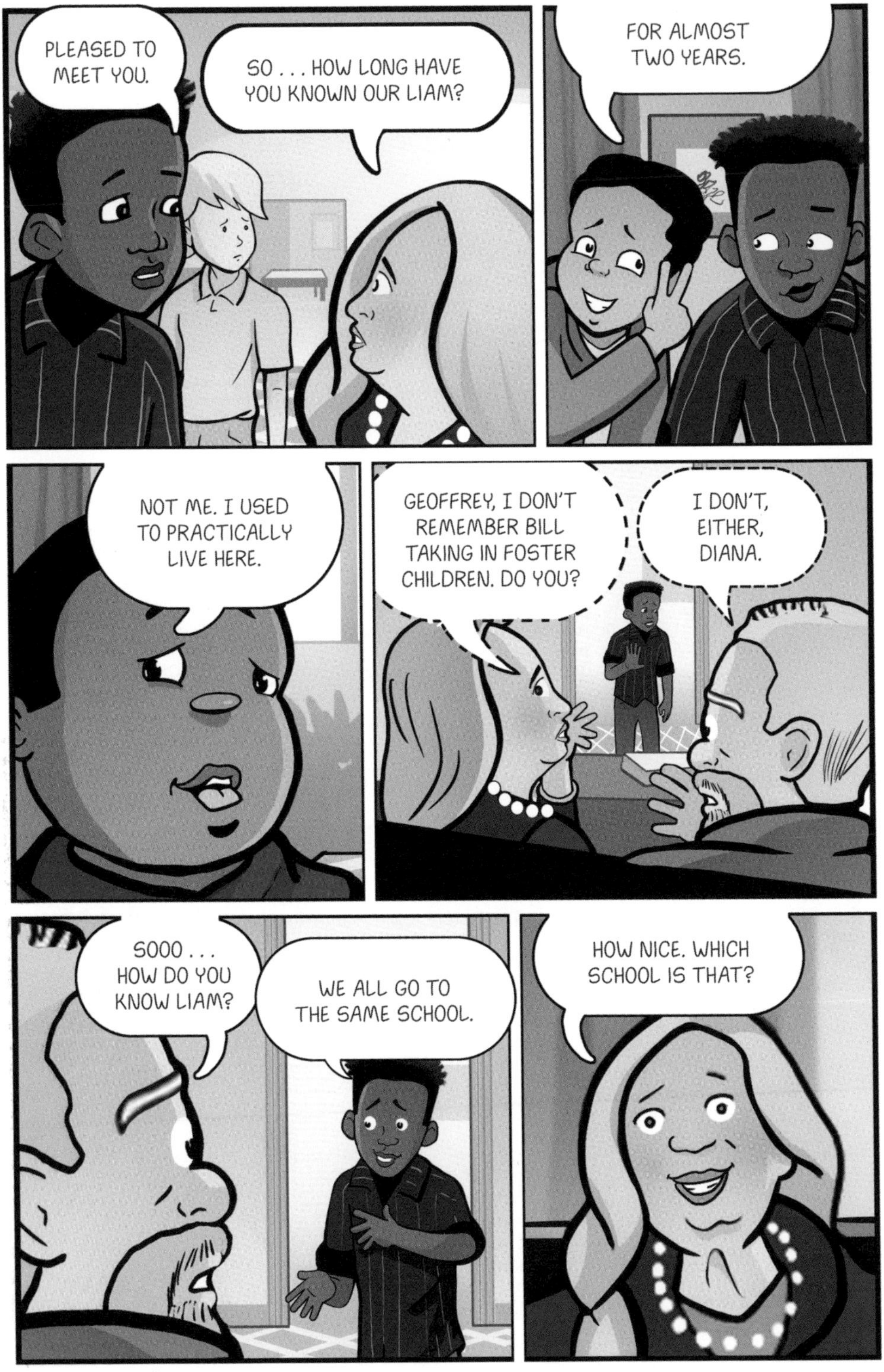
PLEASED TO MEET YOU.
SO . . . HOW LONG HAVE YOU KNOWN OUR LIAM?
FOR ALMOST TWO YEARS.
NOT ME. I USED TO PRACTICALLY LIVE HERE.
GEOFFREY, I DON'T REMEMBER BILL TAKING IN FOSTER CHILDREN. DO YOU?
I DON'T, EITHER, DIANA.
SOOO . . . HOW DO YOU KNOW LIAM?
WE ALL GO TO THE SAME SCHOOL.
HOW NICE. WHICH SCHOOL IS THAT?

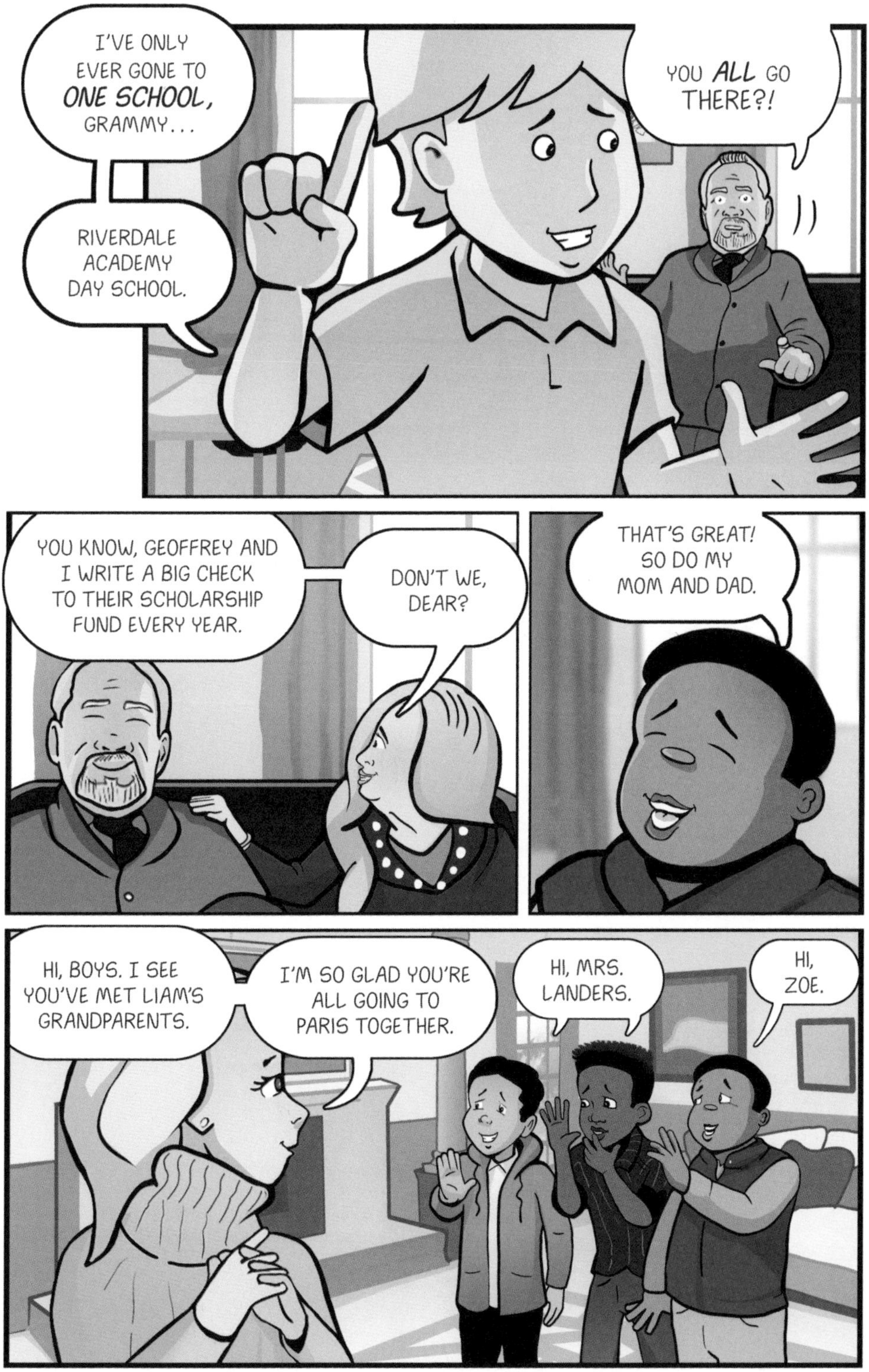
I'VE ONLY EVER GONE TO ONE SCHOOL, GRAMMY...
RIVERDALE ACADEMY DAY SCHOOL.
YOU ALL GO THERE?!
YOU KNOW, GEOFFREY AND I WRITE A BIG CHECK TO THEIR SCHOLARSHIP FUND EVERY YEAR.
DON'T WE, DEAR?
THAT'S GREAT! SO DO MY MOM AND DAD.
HI, BOYS. I SEE YOU'VE MET LIAM'S GRANDPARENTS.
I'M SO GLAD YOU'RE ALL GOING TO PARIS TOGETHER.
HI, MRS. LANDERS.
HI, ZOE.

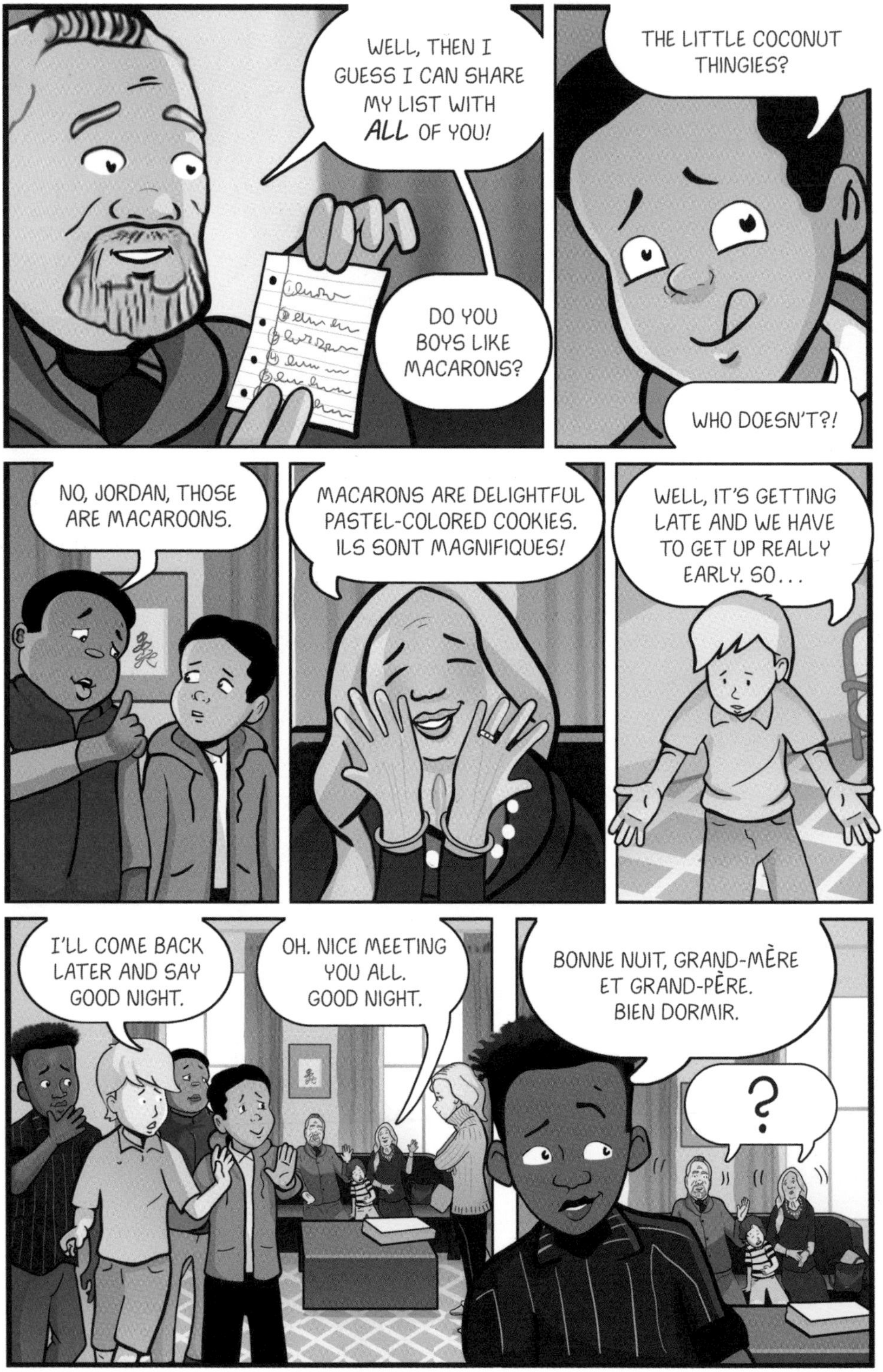
WELL, THEN I GUESS I CAN SHARE MY LIST WITH ALL OF YOU!
DO YOU BOYS LIKE MACARONS?
THE LITTLE COCONUT THINGIES?
WHO DOESN'T?!
NO, JORDAN, THOSE ARE MACAROONS.
MACARONS ARE DELIGHTFUL PASTEL-COLORED COOKIES. ILS SONT MAGNIFIQUES!
WELL, IT'S GETTING LATE AND WE HAVE TO GET UP REALLY EARLY. SO . . .
I'LL COME BACK LATER AND SAY GOOD NIGHT.
OH. NICE MEETING YOU ALL. GOOD NIGHT.
BONNE NUIT, GRAND-MÈRE ET GRAND-PÈRE. BIEN DORMIR.
?

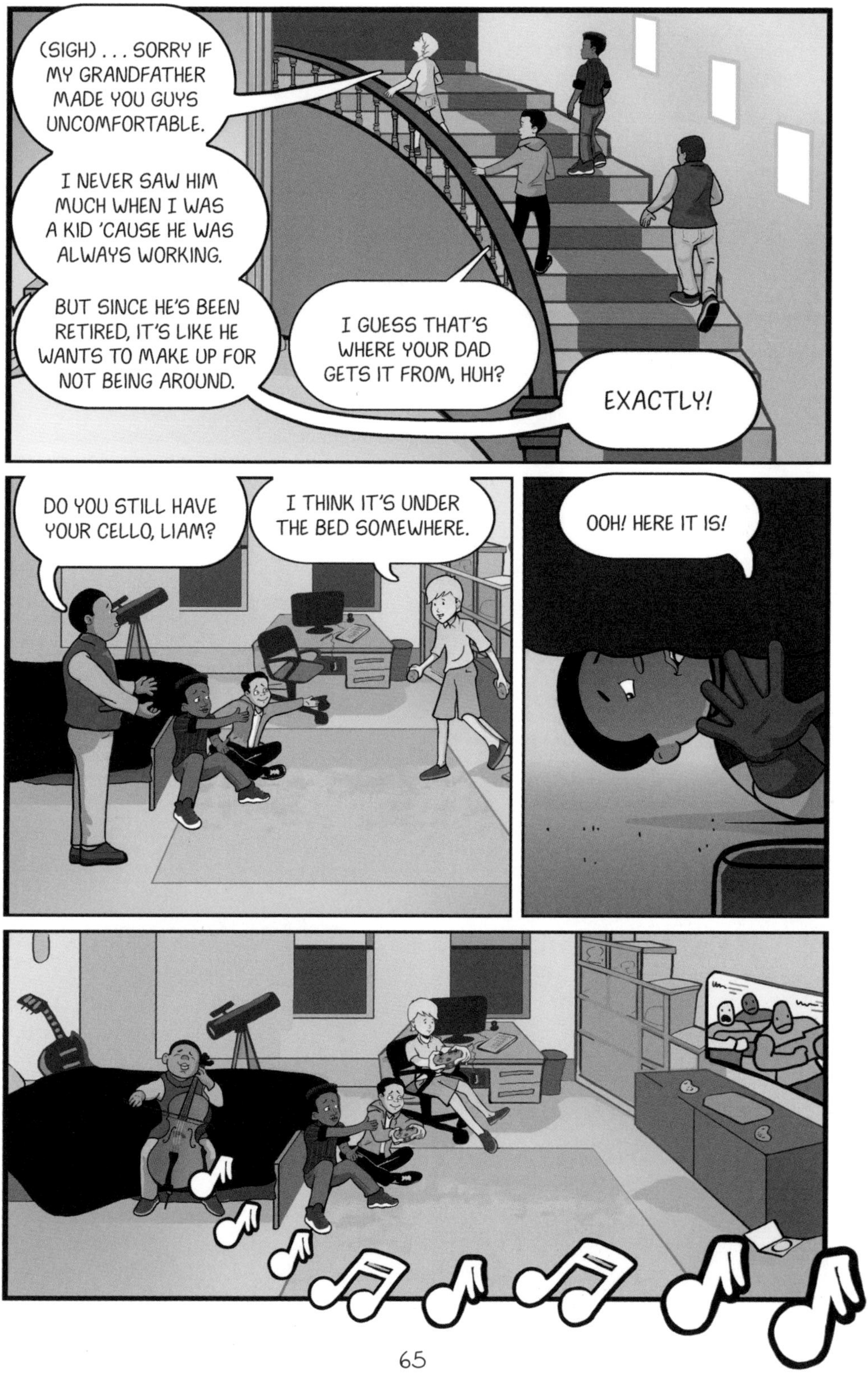
(SIGH) . . . SORRY IF MY GRANDFATHER MADE YOU GUYS UNCOMFORTABLE.
I NEVER SAW HIM MUCH WHEN I WAS A KID 'CAUSE HE WAS ALWAYS WORKING.
BUT SINCE HE'S BEEN RETIRED, IT'S LIKE HE WANTS TO MAKE UP FOR NOT BEING AROUND.
I GUESS THAT'S WHERE YOUR DAD GETS IT FROM, HUH?
EXACTLY!
DO YOU STILL HAVE YOUR CELLO, LIAM?
I THINK IT'S UNDER THE BED SOMEWHERE.
OOH! HERE IT IS!

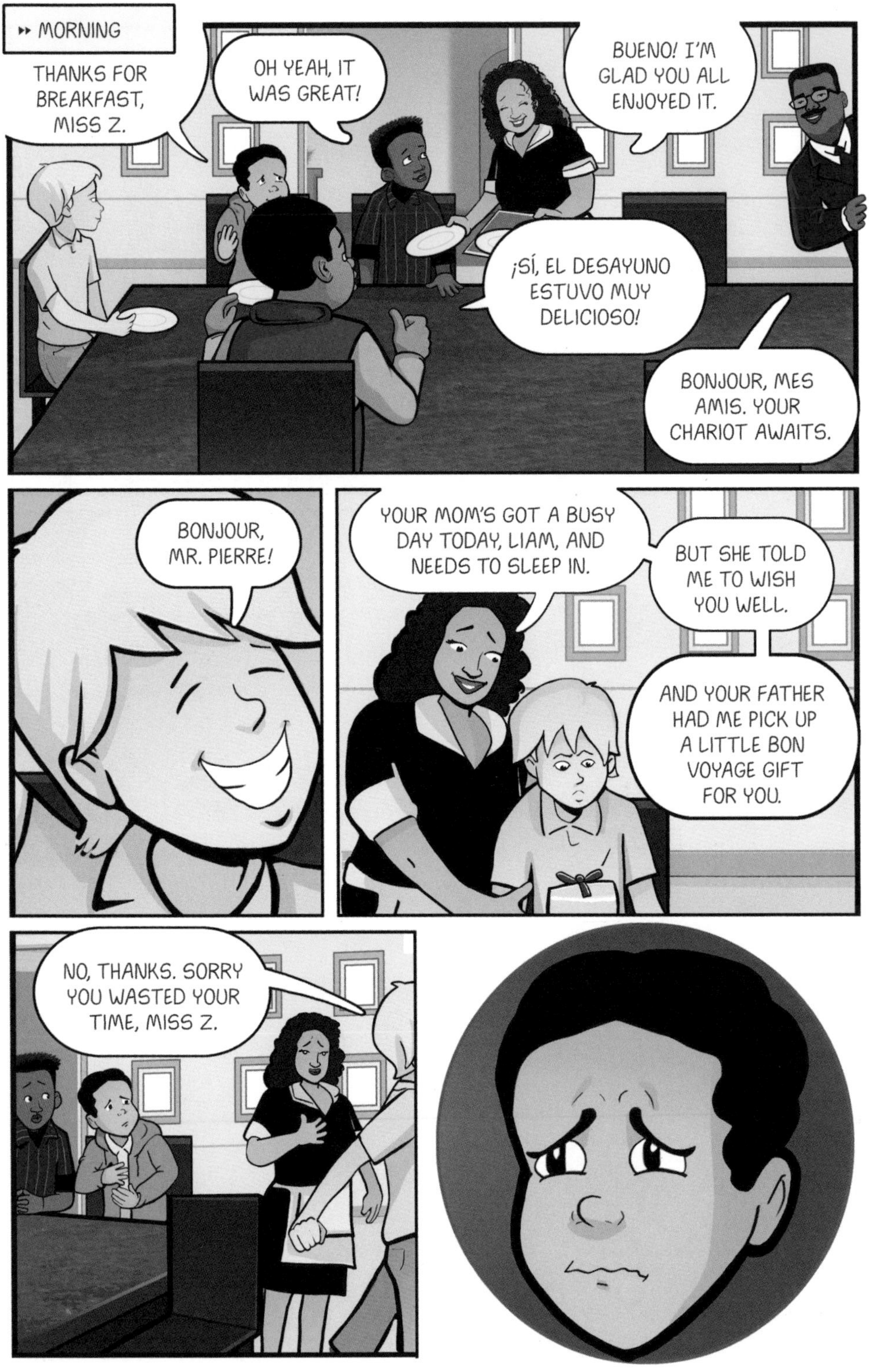
MORNING
THANKS FOR BREAKFAST, MISS Z.
OH YEAH, IT WAS GREAT!
BUENO! I'M GLAD YOU ALL ENJOYED IT.
¡SÍ, EL DESAYUNO ESTUVO MUY DELICIOSO!
BONJOUR, MES AMIS. YOUR CHARIOT AWAITS.
BONJOUR, MR. PIERRE!
YOUR MOM'S GOT A BUSY DAY TODAY, LIAM, AND NEEDS TO SLEEP IN.
BUT SHE TOLD ME TO WISH YOU WELL.
AND YOUR FATHER HAD ME PICK UP A LITTLE BON VOYAGE GIFT FOR YOU.
NO, THANKS. SORRY YOU WASTED YOUR TIME, MISS Z.

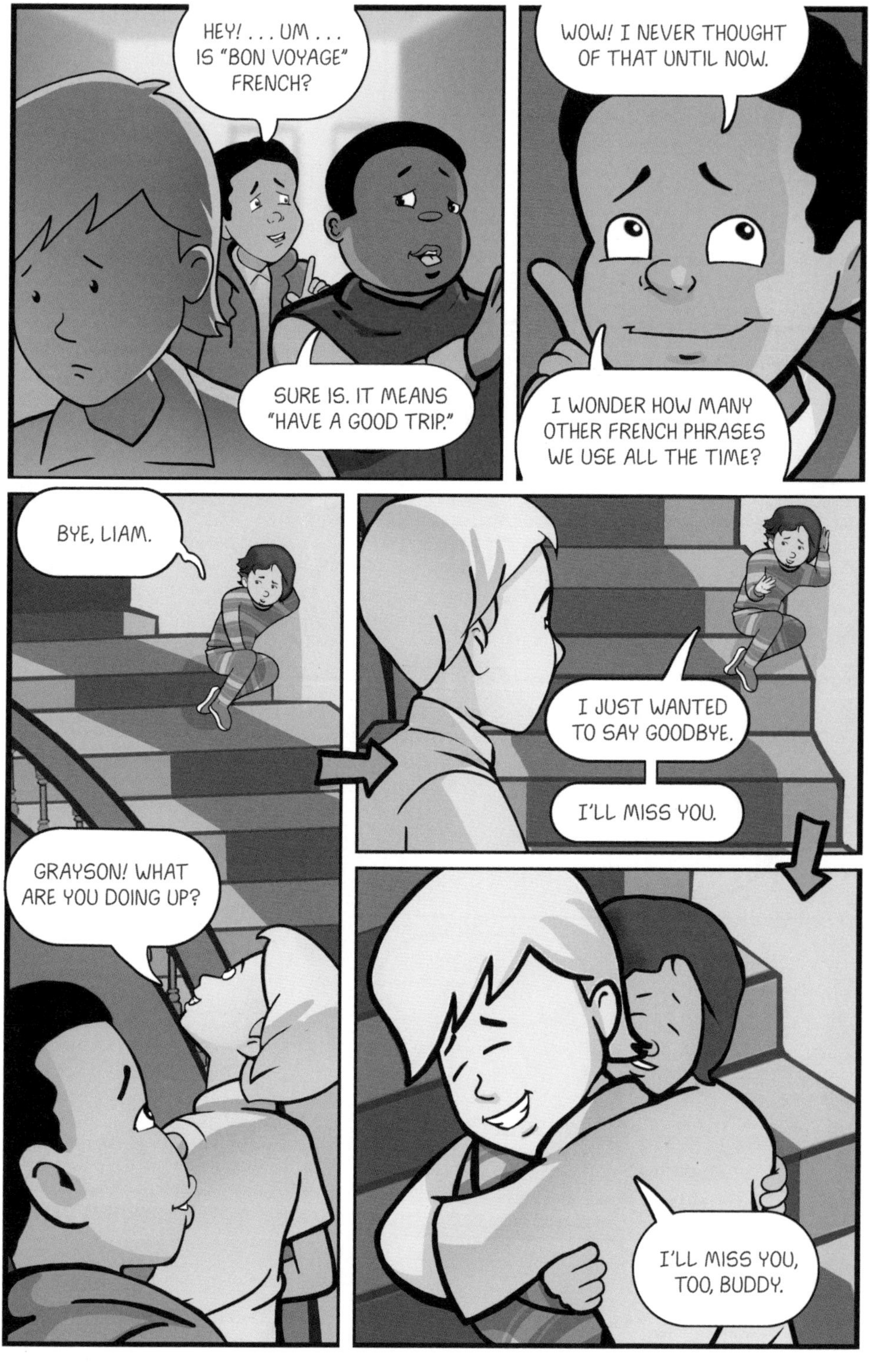
HEY! . . . UM . . . IS "BON VOYAGE" FRENCH?
SURE IS. IT MEANS "HAVE A GOOD TRIP."
WOW! I NEVER THOUGHT OF THAT UNTIL NOW.
I WONDER HOW MANY OTHER FRENCH PHRASES WE USE ALL THE TIME?
BYE, LIAM.
I JUST WANTED TO SAY GOODBYE.
I'LL MISS YOU.
GRAYSON! WHAT ARE YOU DOING UP?
I'LL MISS YOU, TOO, BUDDY.

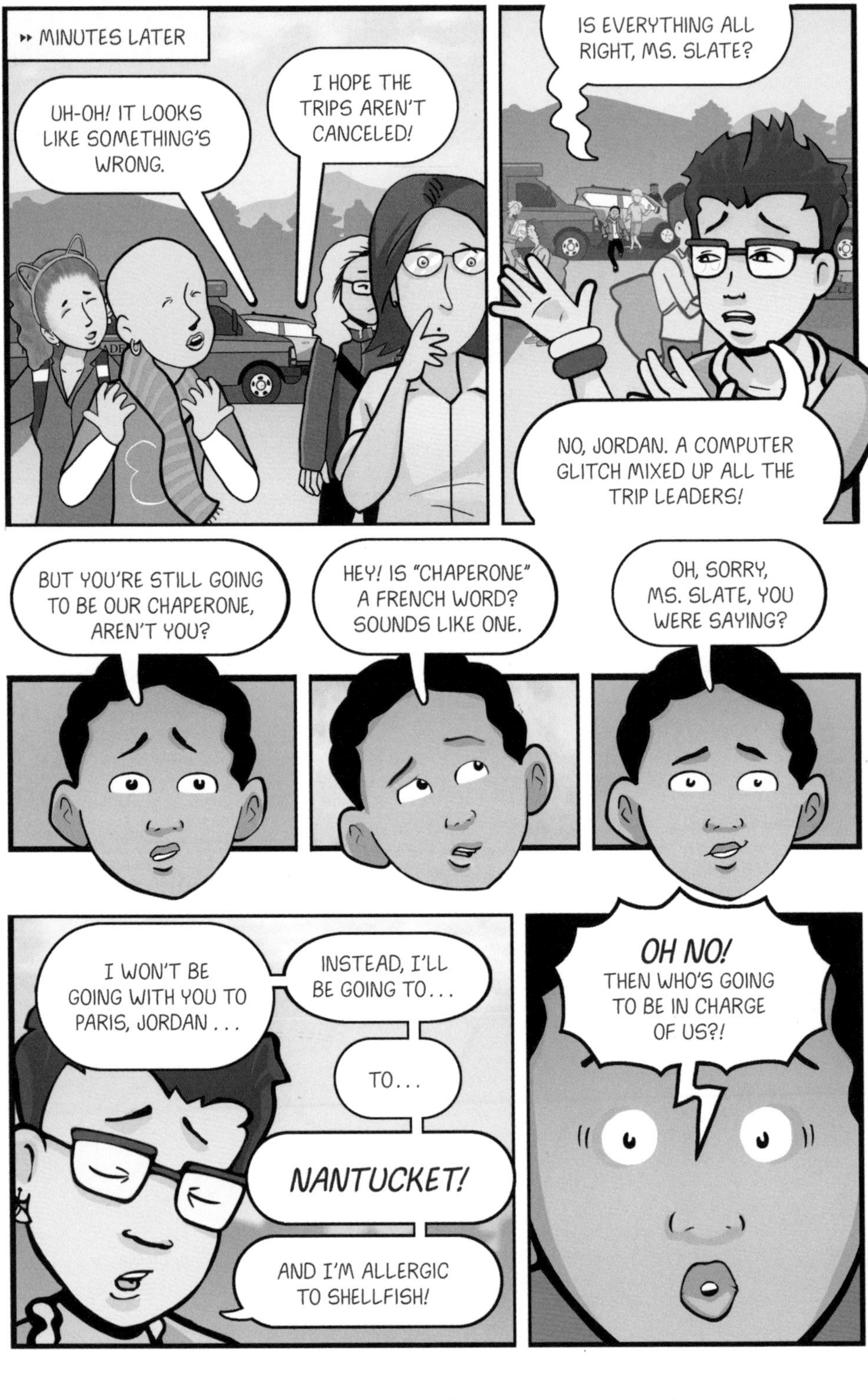
MINUTES LATER
UH-OH! IT LOOKS LIKE SOMETHING'S WRONG.
I HOPE THE TRIPS AREN'T CANCELED!
IS EVERYTHING ALL RIGHT, MS. SLATE?
NO, JORDAN. A COMPUTER GLITCH MIXED UP ALL THE TRIP LEADERS!
BUT YOU'RE STILL GOING TO BE OUR CHAPERONE, AREN'T YOU?
HEY! IS "CHAPERONE" A FRENCH WORD? SOUNDS LIKE ONE.
OH, SORRY, MS. SLATE, YOU WERE SAYING?
I WON'T BE GOING WITH YOU TO PARIS, JORDAN . . .
INSTEAD, I'LL BE GOING TO . . .
TO . . .
NANTUCKET!
AND I'M ALLERGIC TO SHELLFISH!
OH NO! THEN WHO'S GOING TO BE IN CHARGE OF US?!

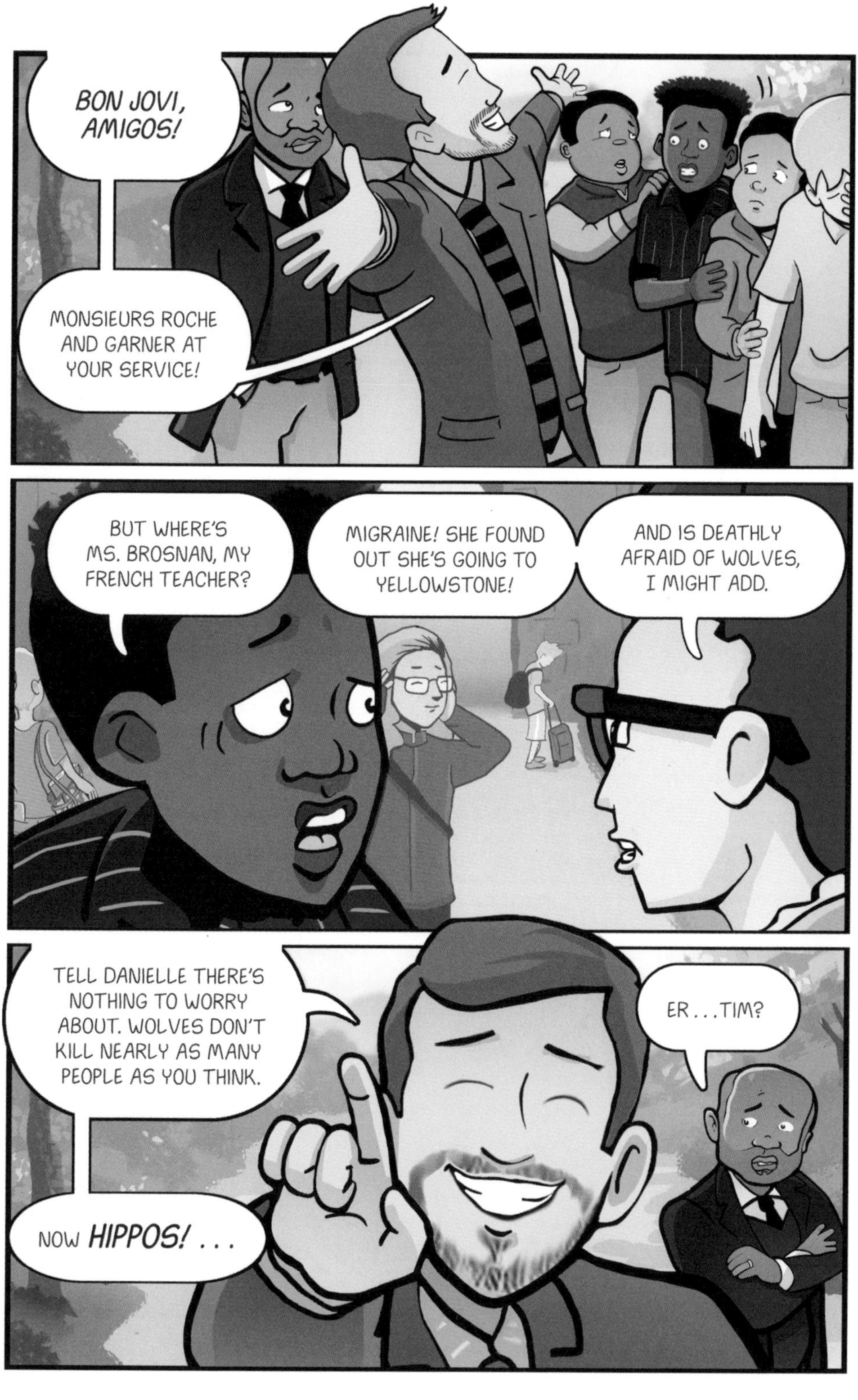
BON JOVI, AMIGOS!
MONSIEURS ROCHE AND GARNER AT YOUR SERVICE!
BUT WHERE'S MS. BROSNAN, MY FRENCH TEACHER?
MIGRAINE! SHE FOUND OUT SHE'S GOING TO YELLOWSTONE!
AND IS DEATHLY AFRAID OF WOLVES, I MIGHT ADD.
TELL DANIELLE THERE'S NOTHING TO WORRY ABOUT. WOLVES DON'T KILL NEARLY AS MANY PEOPLE AS YOU THINK.
NOW HIPPOS! . . .
ER . . . TIM?

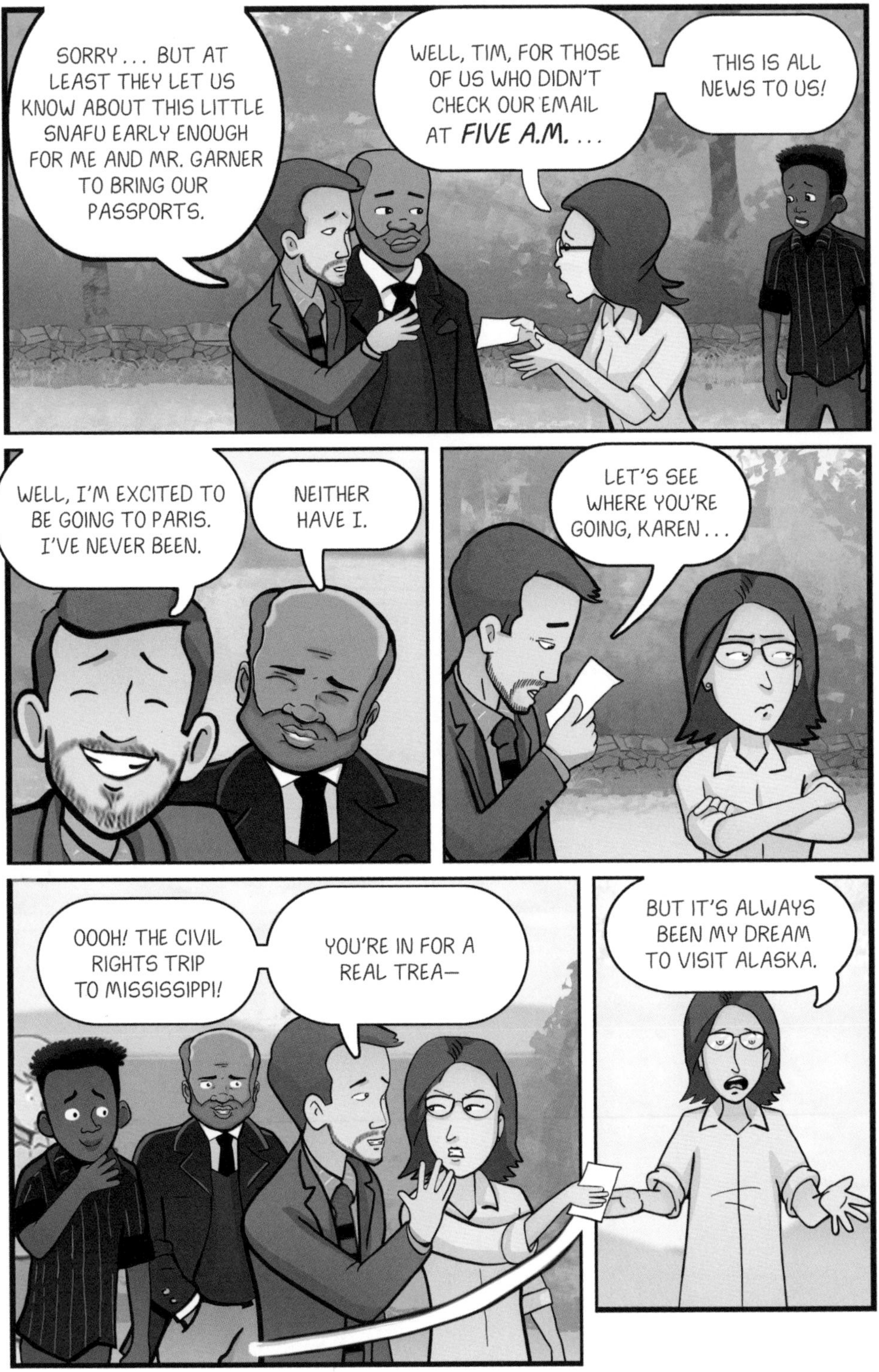
SORRY . . . BUT AT LEAST THEY LET US KNOW ABOUT THIS LITTLE SNAFU EARLY ENOUGH FOR ME AND MR. GARNER TO BRING OUR PASSPORTS.
WELL, TIM, FOR THOSE OF US WHO DIDN'T CHECK OUR EMAIL AT FIVE A.M. . . .
THIS IS ALL NEWS TO US!
WELL, I'M EXCITED TO BE GOING TO PARIS. I'VE NEVER BEEN.
NEITHER HAVE I.
LET'S SEE WHERE YOU'RE GOING, KAREN . . .
OOOH! THE CIVIL RIGHTS TRIP TO MISSISSIPPI!
YOU'RE IN FOR A REAL TREA—
BUT IT'S ALWAYS BEEN MY DREAM TO VISIT ALASKA.

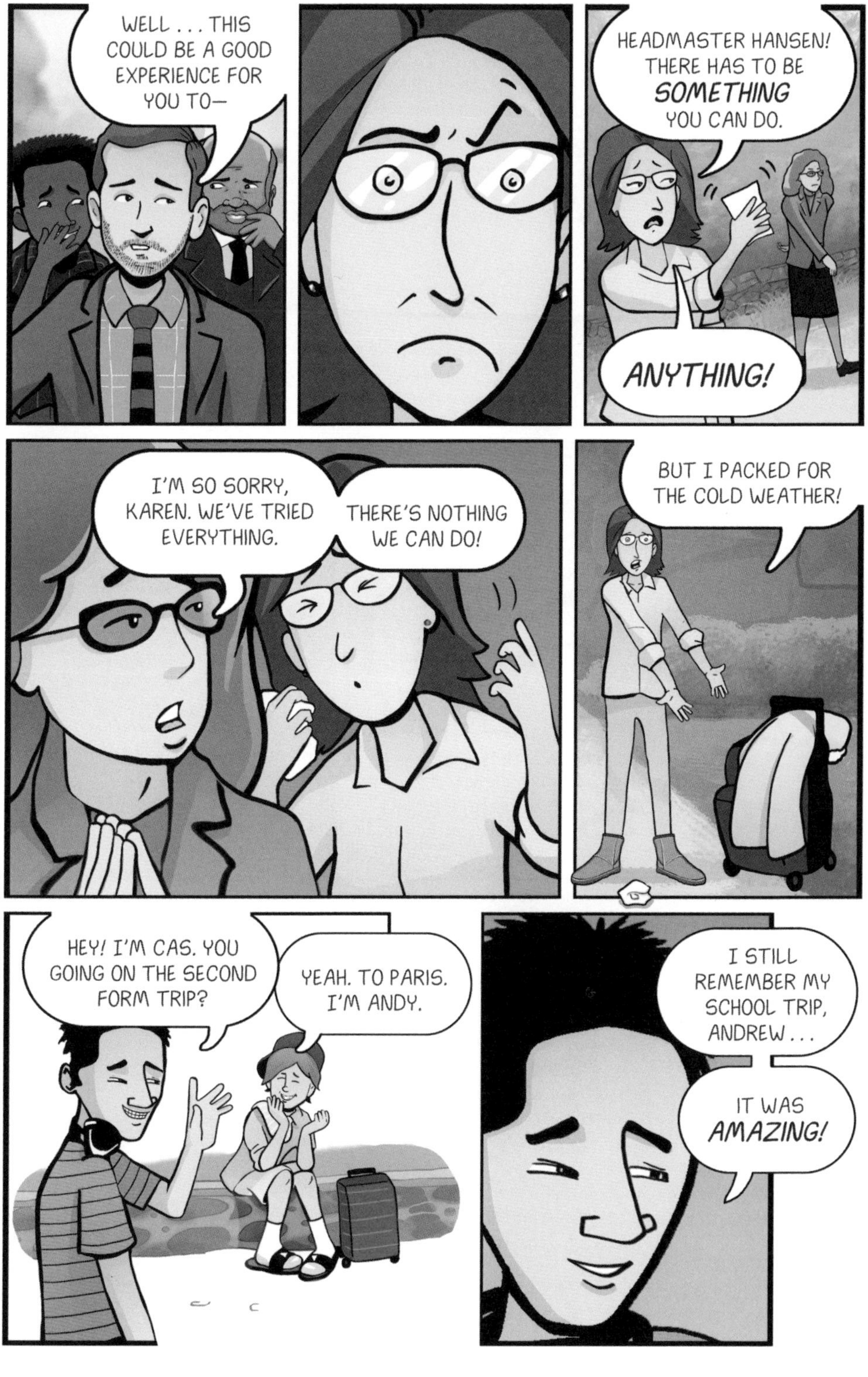
WELL . . . THIS COULD BE A GOOD EXPERIENCE FOR YOU TO—
HEADMASTER HANSEN! THERE HAS TO BE SOMETHING YOU CAN DO.
ANYTHING!
I'M SO SORRY, KAREN. WE'VE TRIED EVERYTHING.
THERE'S NOTHING WE CAN DO!
BUT I PACKED FOR THE COLD WEATHER!
HEY! I'M CAS. YOU GOING ON THE SECOND FORM TRIP?
YEAH. TO PARIS. I'M ANDY.
I STILL REMEMBER MY SCHOOL TRIP, ANDREW . . .
IT WAS AMAZING!

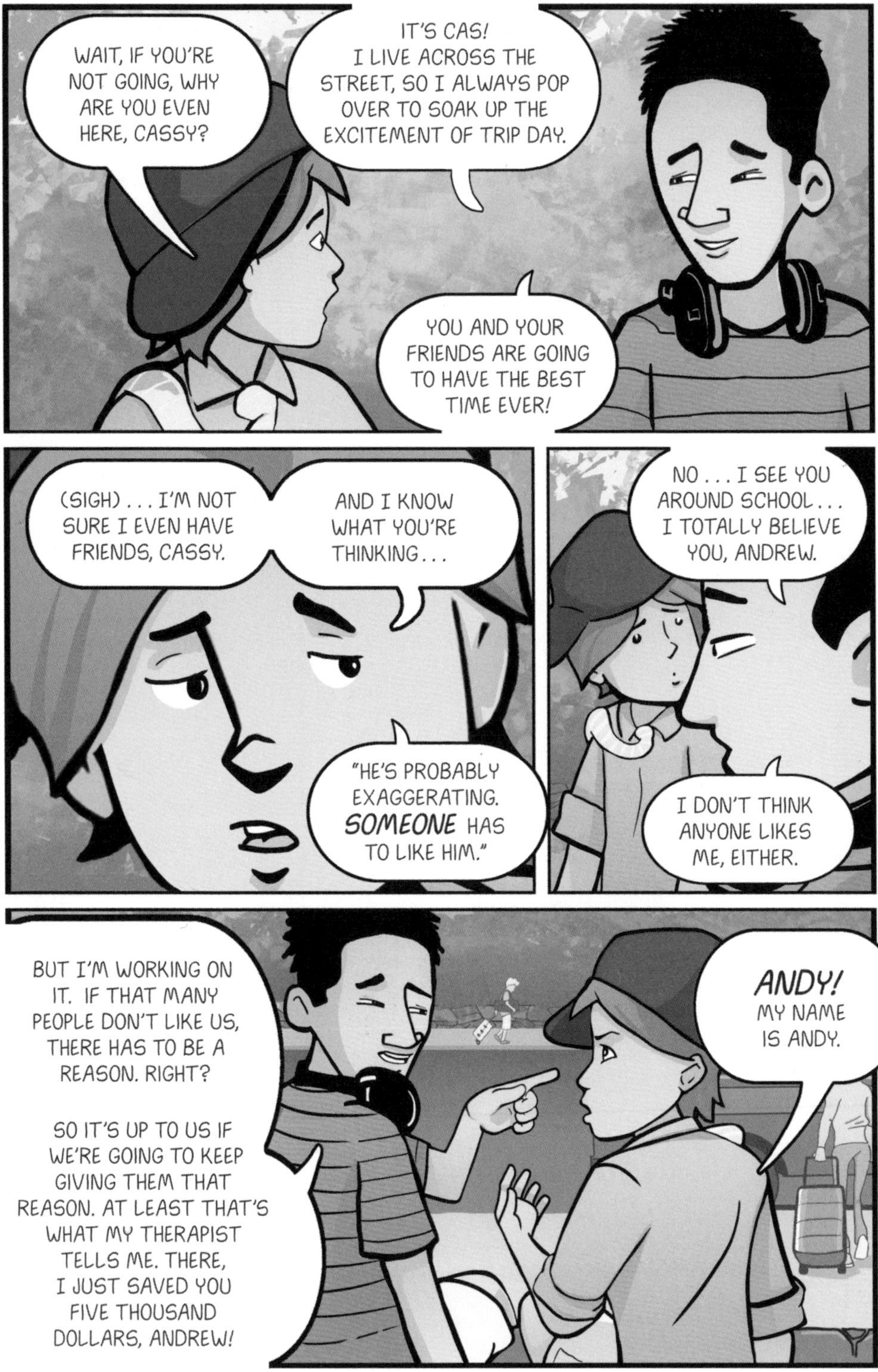

WAIT, IF YOU'RE NOT GOING, WHY ARE YOU EVEN HERE, CASSY?
IT'S CAS! I LIVE ACROSS THE STREET, SO I ALWAYS POP OVER TO SOAK UP THE EXCITEMENT OF TRIP DAY.
YOU AND YOUR FRIENDS ARE GOING TO HAVE THE BEST TIME EVER!
(SIGH) . . . I'M NOT SURE I EVEN HAVE FRIENDS, CASSY.
AND I KNOW WHAT YOU'RE THINKING . . .
"HE'S PROBABLY EXAGGERATING. *SOMEONE* HAS TO LIKE HIM."
NO . . . I SEE YOU AROUND SCHOOL . . . I TOTALLY BELIEVE YOU, ANDREW.
I DON'T THINK ANYONE LIKES ME, EITHER.
BUT I'M WORKING ON IT. IF THAT MANY PEOPLE DON'T LIKE US, THERE HAS TO BE A REASON. RIGHT?
SO IT'S UP TO US IF WE'RE GOING TO KEEP GIVING THEM THAT REASON. AT LEAST THAT'S WHAT MY THERAPIST TELLS ME. THERE, I JUST SAVED YOU FIVE THOUSAND DOLLARS, ANDREW!
ANDY! MY NAME IS ANDY.

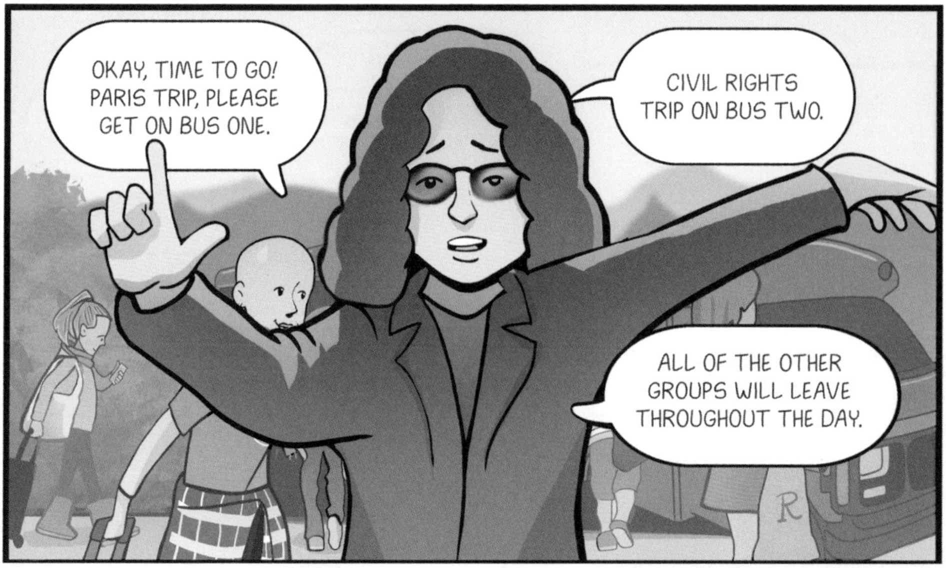
OKAY, TIME TO GO! PARIS TRIP, PLEASE GET ON BUS ONE.
CIVIL RIGHTS TRIP ON BUS TWO.
ALL OF THE OTHER GROUPS WILL LEAVE THROUGHOUT THE DAY.
R

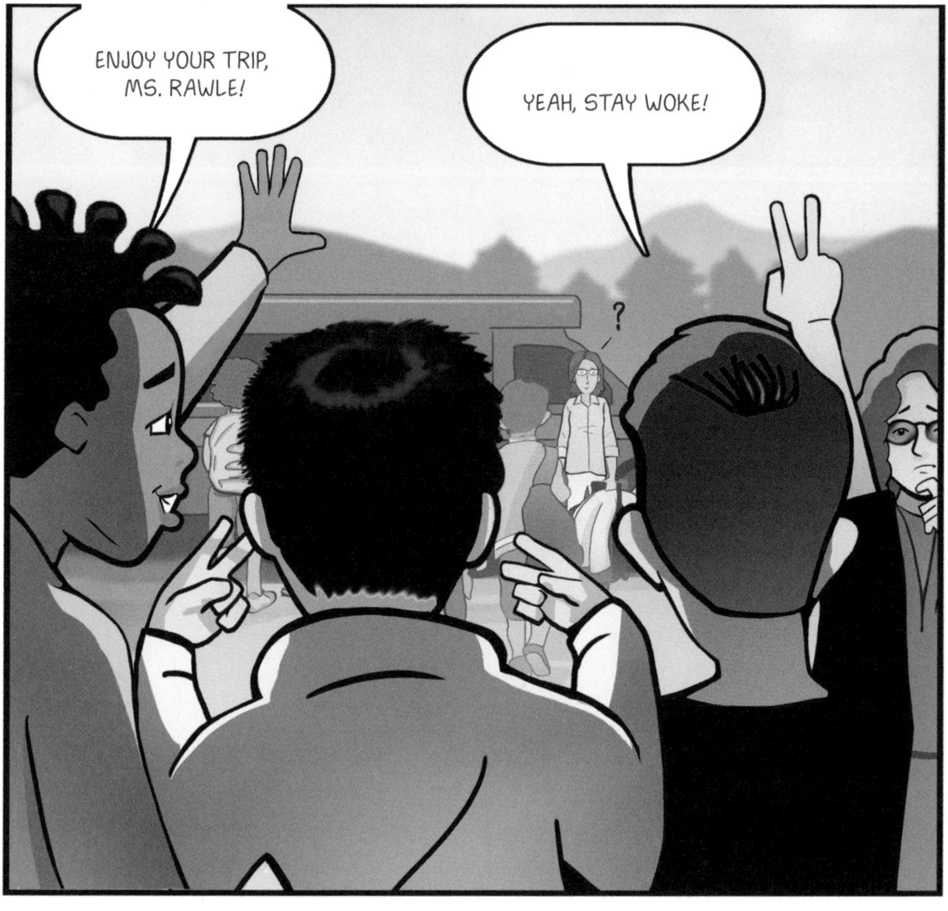
ENJOY YOUR TRIP, MS. RAWLE!
YEAH, STAY WOKE!
?

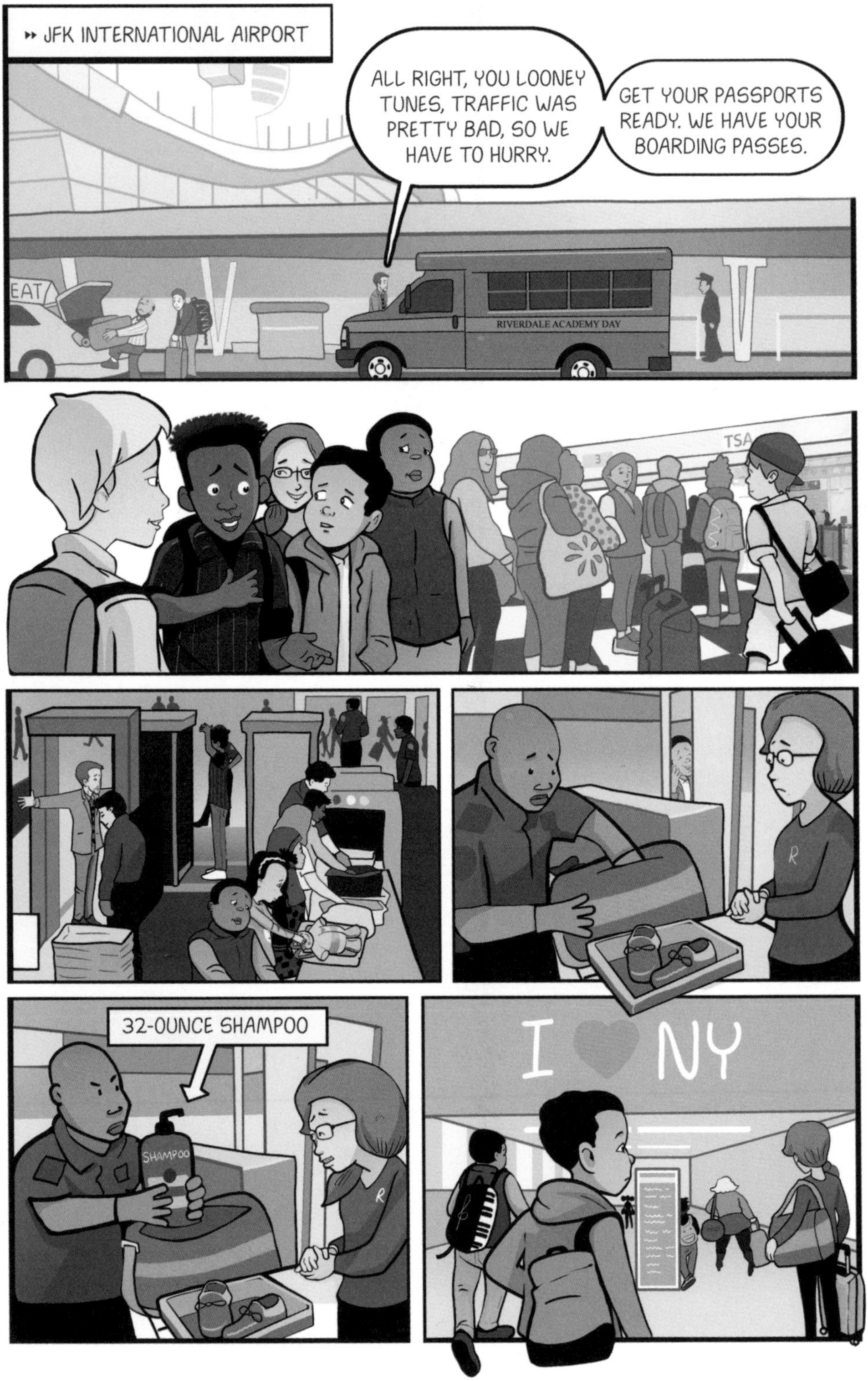
JFK INTERNATIONAL AIRPORT
ALL RIGHT, YOU LOONEY TUNES, TRAFFIC WAS PRETTY BAD, SO WE HAVE TO HURRY.
GET YOUR PASSPORTS READY. WE HAVE YOUR BOARDING PASSES.
EAT
RIVERDALE ACADEMY DAY
TSA
32-OUNCE SHAMPOO
SHAMPOO
I ♥ NY

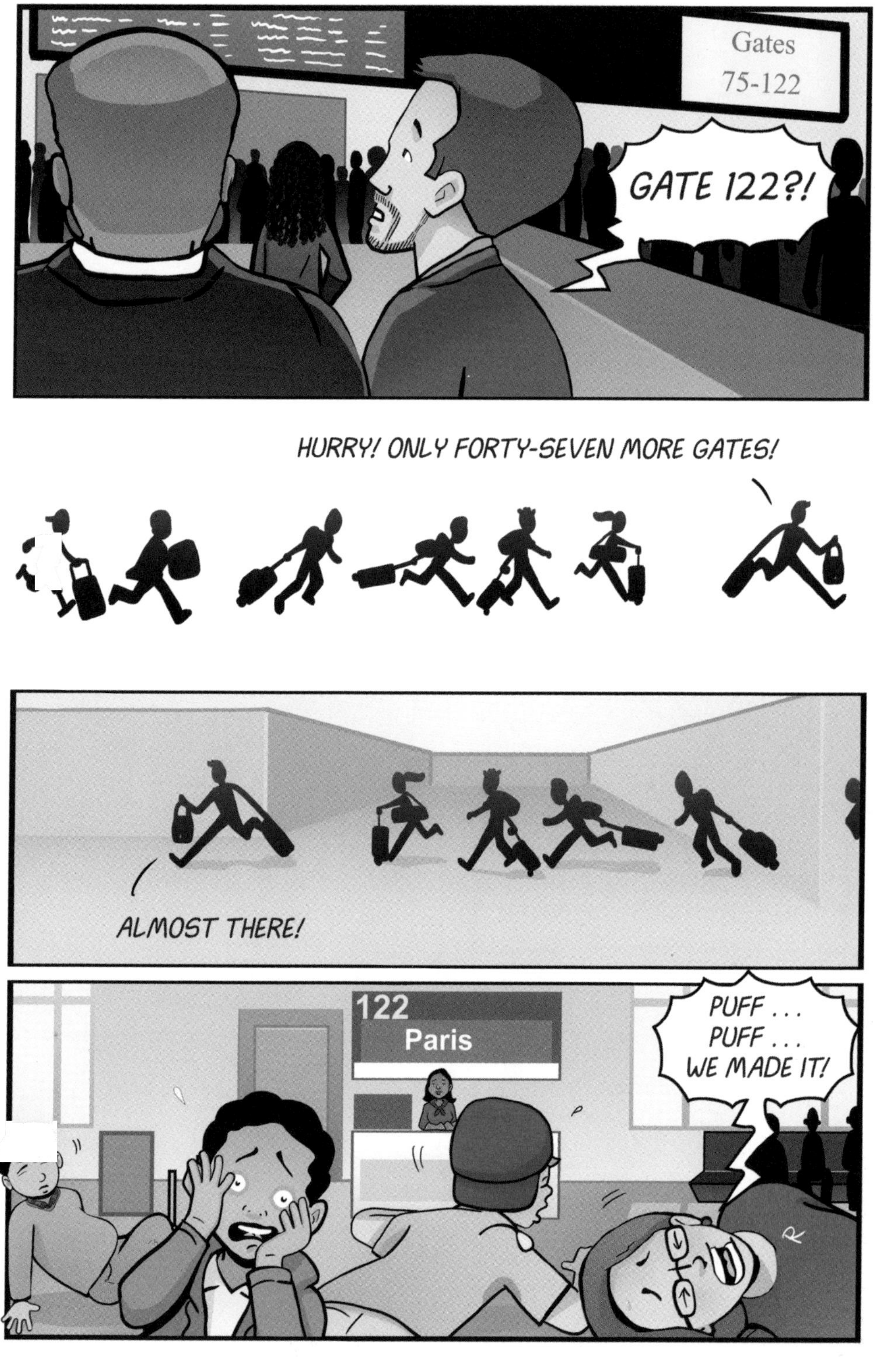
Gates
75-122
GATE 122?!
HURRY! ONLY FORTY-SEVEN MORE GATES!
ALMOST THERE!
122
Paris
PUFF . . .
PUFF . . .
WE MADE IT!

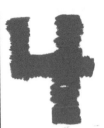

4 Airplane Etiquette

(ET-AH-KIT) The Customary Manner of Polite Behavior

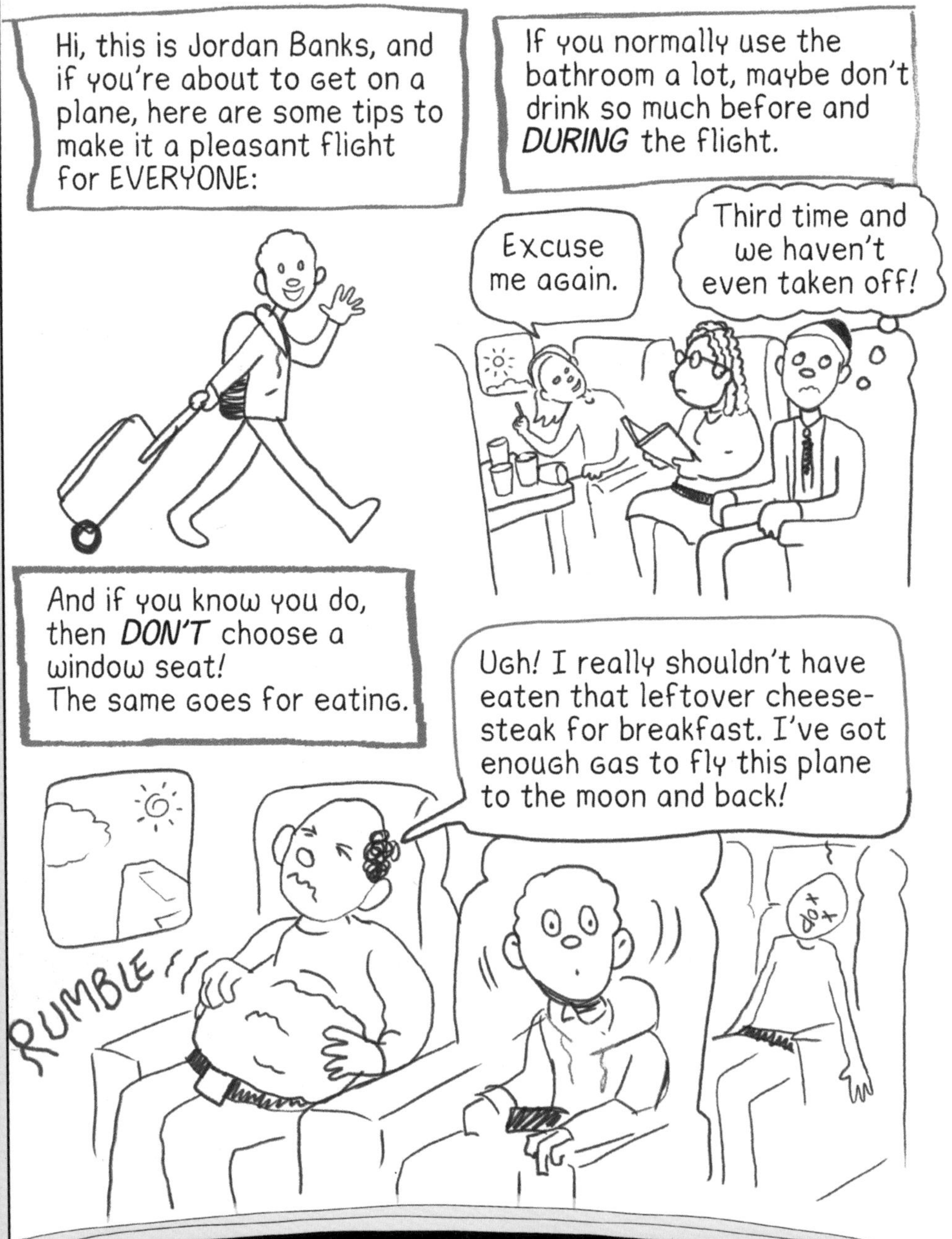
Hi, this is Jordan Banks, and if you're about to get on a plane, here are some tips to make it a pleasant flight for EVERYONE:
If you normally use the bathroom a lot, maybe don't drink so much before and *DURING* the flight.
Excuse me again.
Third time and we haven't even taken off!
And if you know you do, then *DON'T* choose a window seat! The same goes for eating.
Ugh! I really shouldn't have eaten that leftover cheese-steak for breakfast. I've got enough gas to fly this plane to the moon and back!
RUMBLE

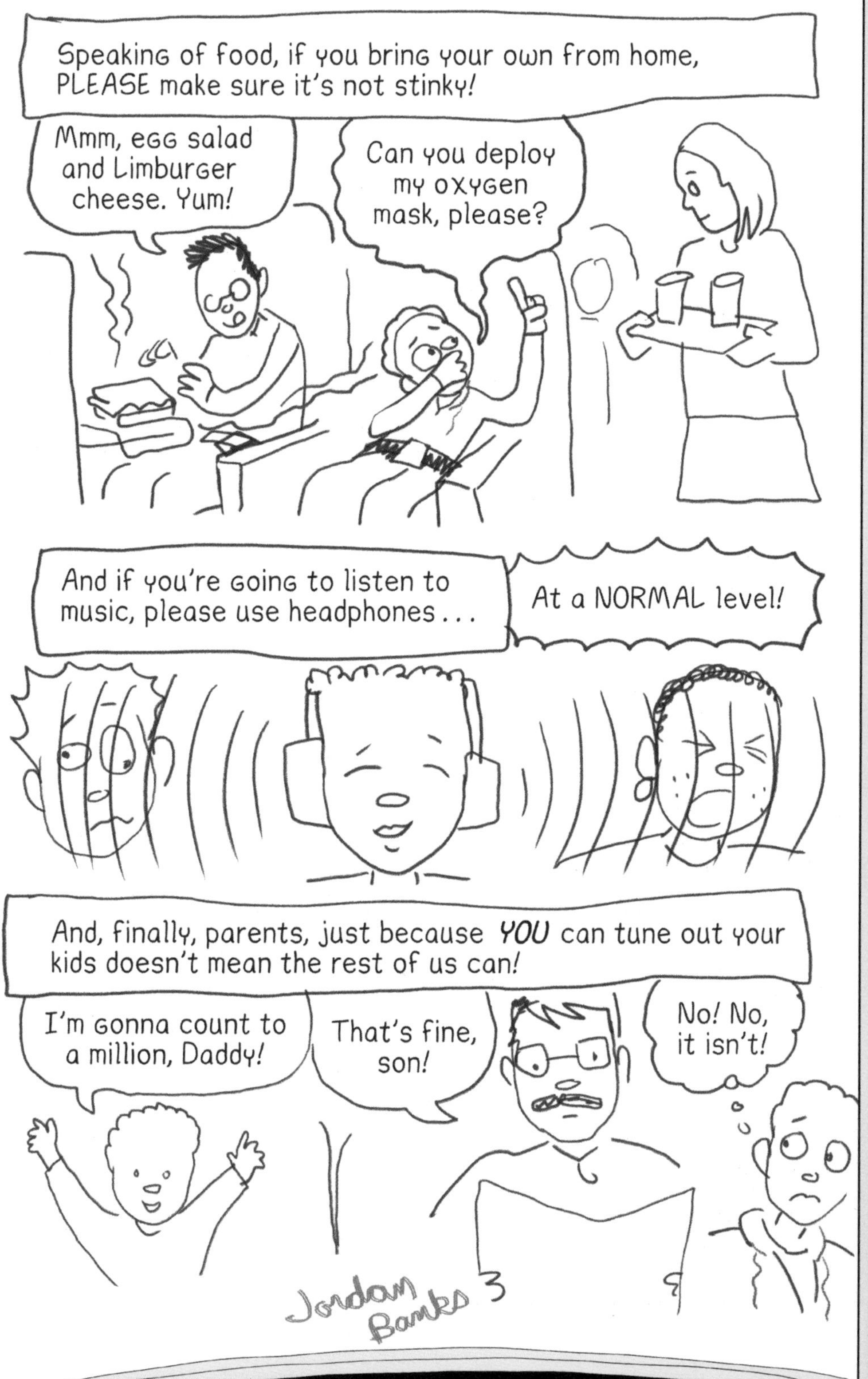
Speaking of food, if you bring your own from home, PLEASE make sure it's not stinky!
Mmm, egg salad and Limburger cheese. Yum!
Can you deploy my oxygen mask, please?
And if you're going to listen to music, please use headphones . . .
At a NORMAL level!
And, finally, parents, just because *YOU* can tune out your kids doesn't mean the rest of us can!
I'm gonna count to a million, Daddy!
That's fine, son!
No! No, it isn't!
Jordan Banks 3

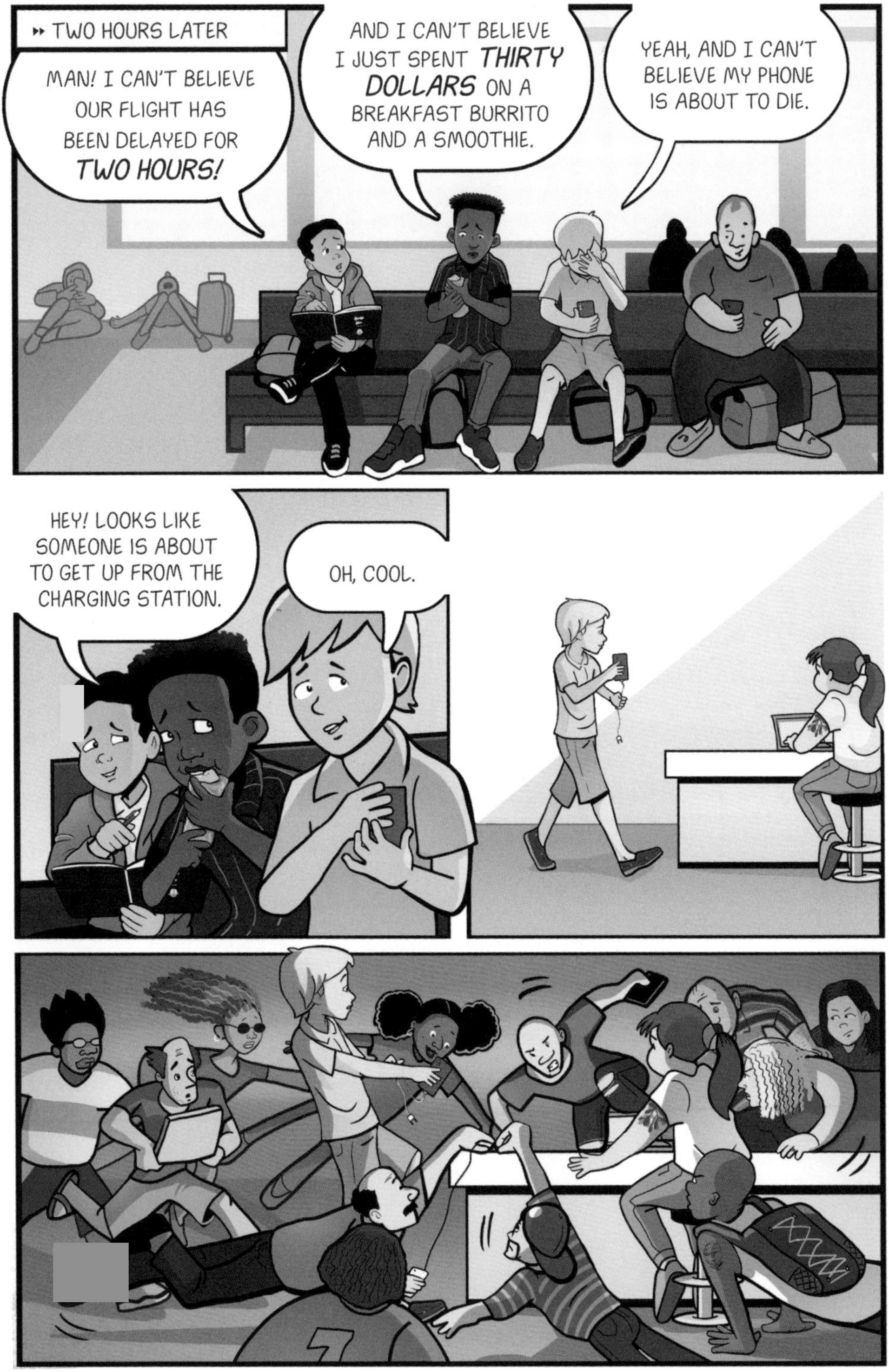

TWO HOURS LATER
MAN! I CAN'T BELIEVE OUR FLIGHT HAS BEEN DELAYED FOR TWO HOURS!
AND I CAN'T BELIEVE I JUST SPENT THIRTY DOLLARS ON A BREAKFAST BURRITO AND A SMOOTHIE.
YEAH, AND I CAN'T BELIEVE MY PHONE IS ABOUT TO DIE.
HEY! LOOKS LIKE SOMEONE IS ABOUT TO GET UP FROM THE CHARGING STATION.
OH, COOL.

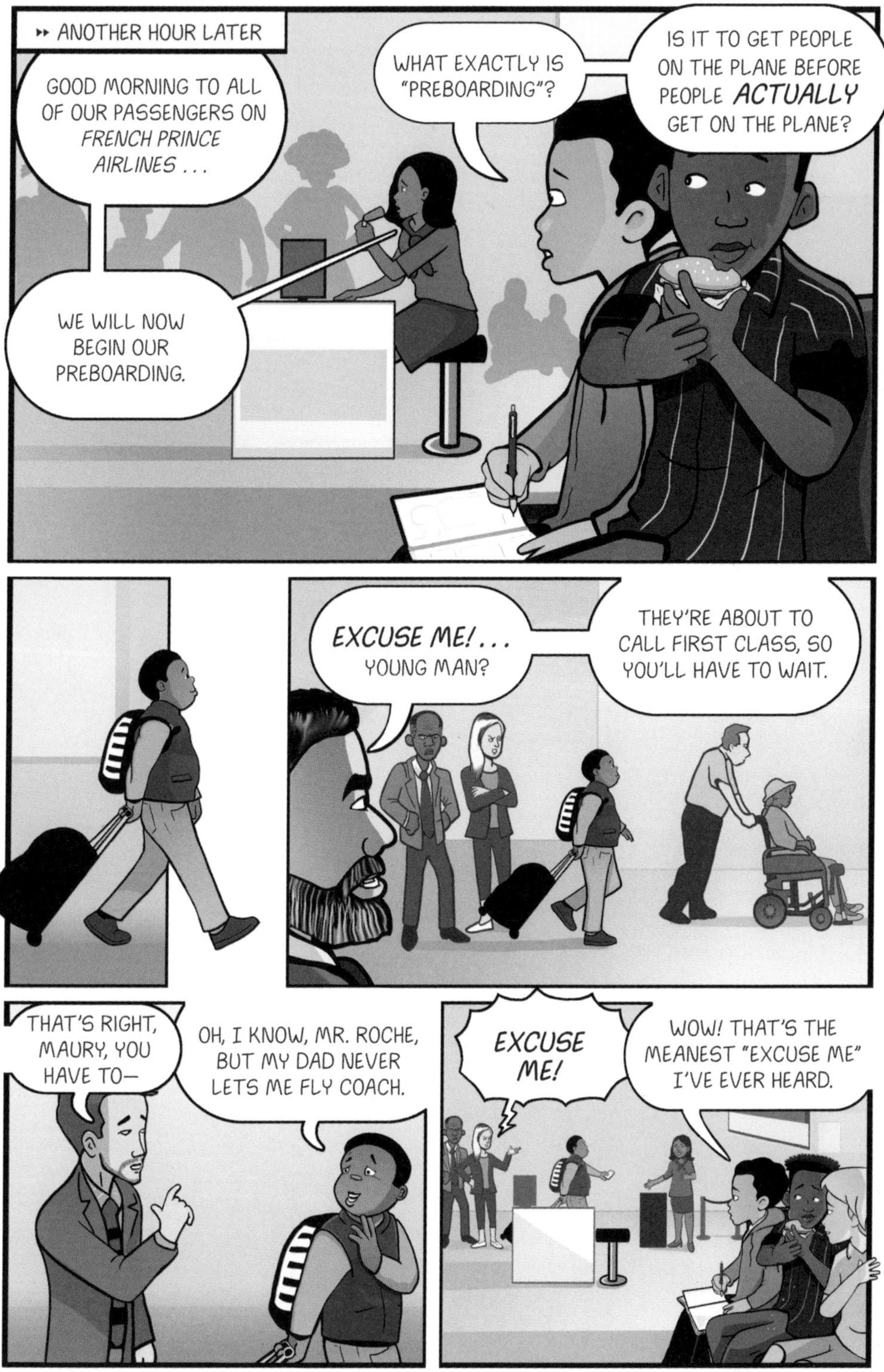
ANOTHER HOUR LATER
GOOD MORNING TO ALL OF OUR PASSENGERS ON *FRENCH PRINCE AIRLINES* . . .
WE WILL NOW BEGIN OUR PREBOARDING.
WHAT EXACTLY IS "PREBOARDING"?
IS IT TO GET PEOPLE ON THE PLANE BEFORE PEOPLE **ACTUALLY** GET ON THE PLANE?
EXCUSE ME! . . . YOUNG MAN?
THEY'RE ABOUT TO CALL FIRST CLASS, SO YOU'LL HAVE TO WAIT.
THAT'S RIGHT, MAURY, YOU HAVE TO—
OH, I KNOW, MR. ROCHE, BUT MY DAD NEVER LETS ME FLY COACH.
EXCUSE ME!
WOW! THAT'S THE MEANEST "EXCUSE ME" I'VE EVER HEARD.

That's Not What I Mean!
(Emphasis on the Word "Mean")

Just because people use nice phrases doesn't mean they're being nice. Here are some common phrases along with what they really mean, depending on the situation.

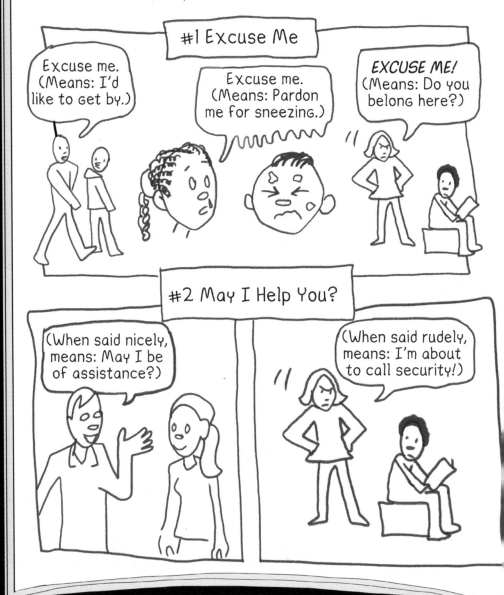

#1 Excuse Me

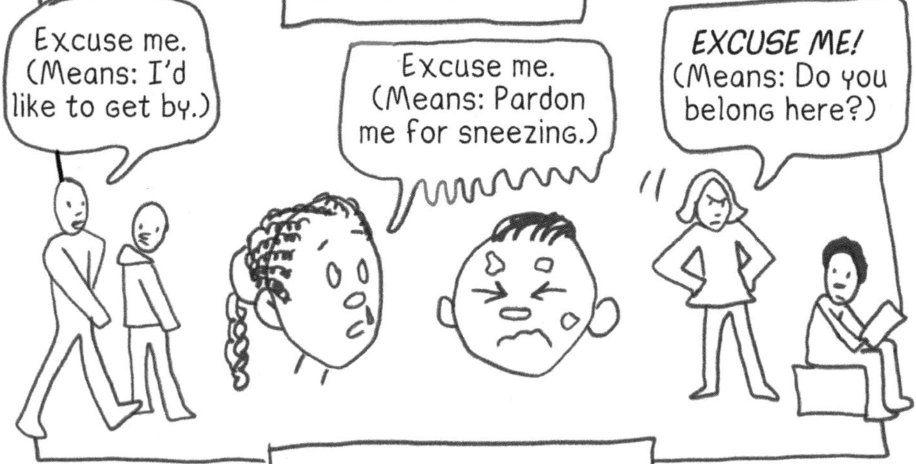
Excuse me. (Means: I'd like to get by.)
Excuse me. (Means: Pardon me for sneezing.)
EXCUSE ME! (Means: Do you belong here?)

#2 May I Help You?

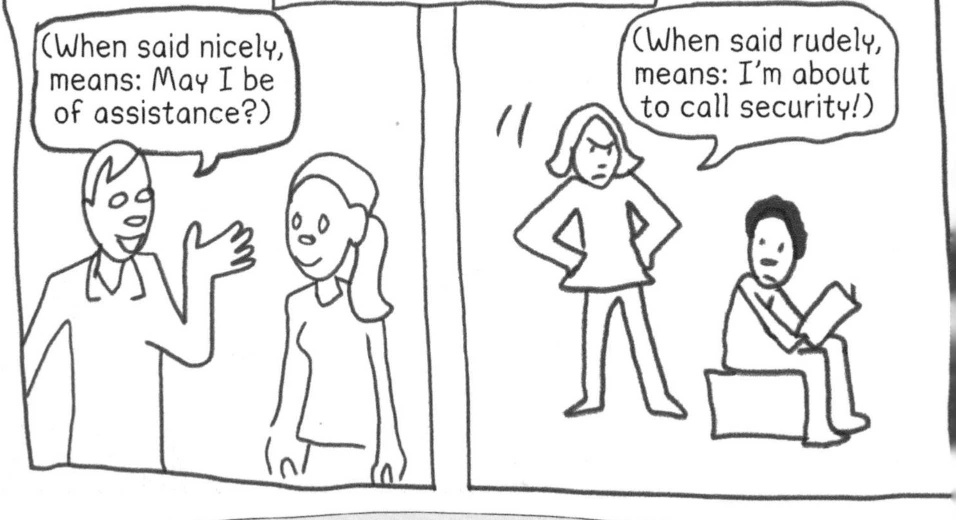
(When said nicely, means: May I be of assistance?)
(When said rudely, means: I'm about to call security!)

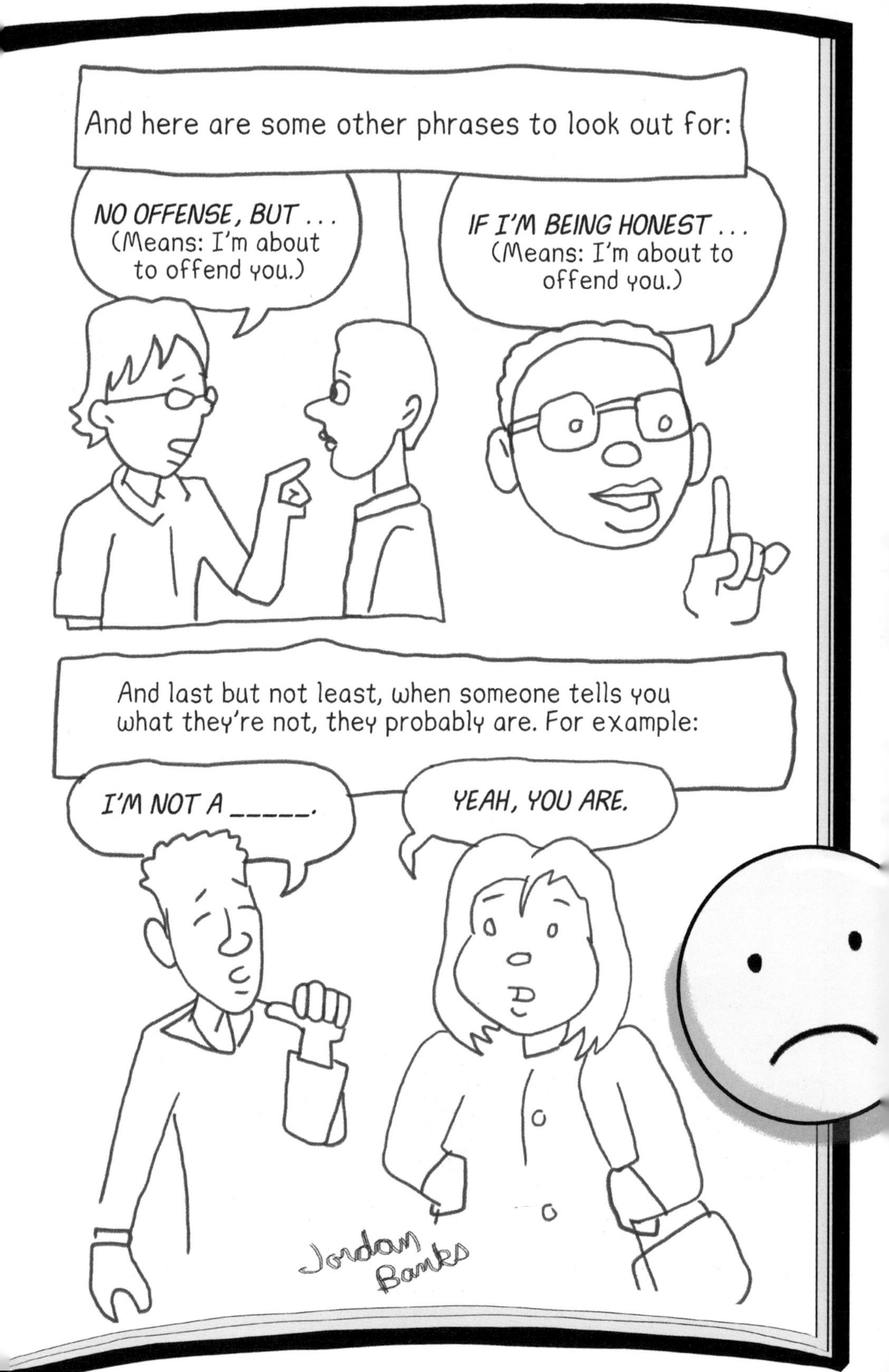
And here are some other phrases to look out for:
NO OFFENSE, BUT . . . (Means: I'm about to offend you.)
IF I'M BEING HONEST . . . (Means: I'm about to offend you.)
And last but not least, when someone tells you what they're not, they probably are. For example:
I'M NOT A _____.
YEAH, YOU ARE.
Jordan Banks

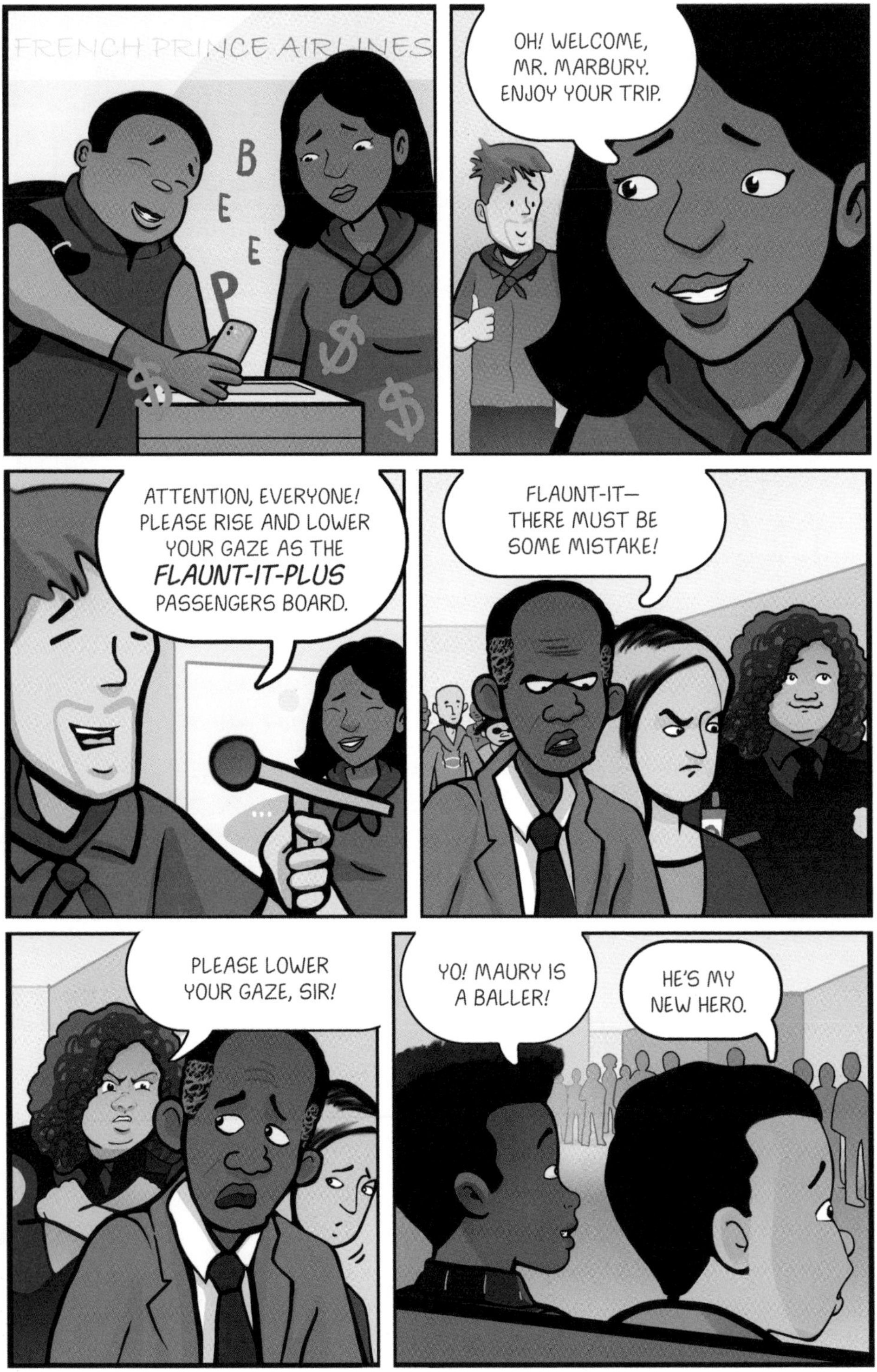
FRENCH PRINCE AIRLINES
BEEP
OH! WELCOME, MR. MARBURY. ENJOY YOUR TRIP.
ATTENTION, EVERYONE! PLEASE RISE AND LOWER YOUR GAZE AS THE *FLAUNT-IT-PLUS* PASSENGERS BOARD.
FLAUNT-IT— THERE MUST BE SOME MISTAKE!
PLEASE LOWER YOUR GAZE, SIR!
YO! MAURY IS A BALLER!
HE'S MY NEW HERO.

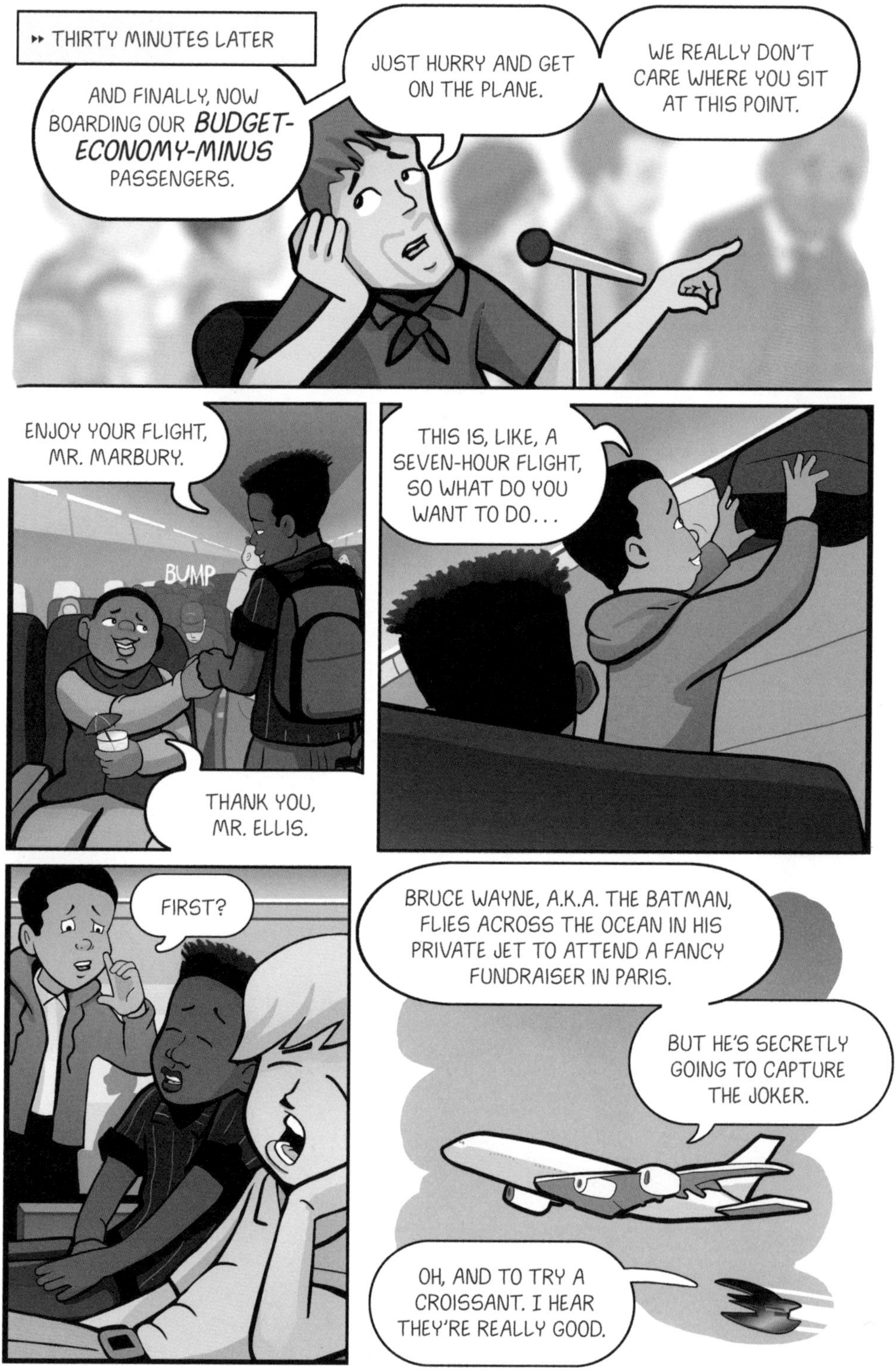

THIRTY MINUTES LATER
AND FINALLY, NOW BOARDING OUR BUDGET-ECONOMY-MINUS PASSENGERS.
JUST HURRY AND GET ON THE PLANE.
WE REALLY DON'T CARE WHERE YOU SIT AT THIS POINT.
ENJOY YOUR FLIGHT, MR. MARBURY.
BUMP
THANK YOU, MR. ELLIS.
THIS IS, LIKE, A SEVEN-HOUR FLIGHT, SO WHAT DO YOU WANT TO DO...
FIRST?
BRUCE WAYNE, A.K.A. THE BATMAN, FLIES ACROSS THE OCEAN IN HIS PRIVATE JET TO ATTEND A FANCY FUNDRAISER IN PARIS.
BUT HE'S SECRETLY GOING TO CAPTURE THE JOKER.
OH, AND TO TRY A CROISSANT. I HEAR THEY'RE REALLY GOOD.

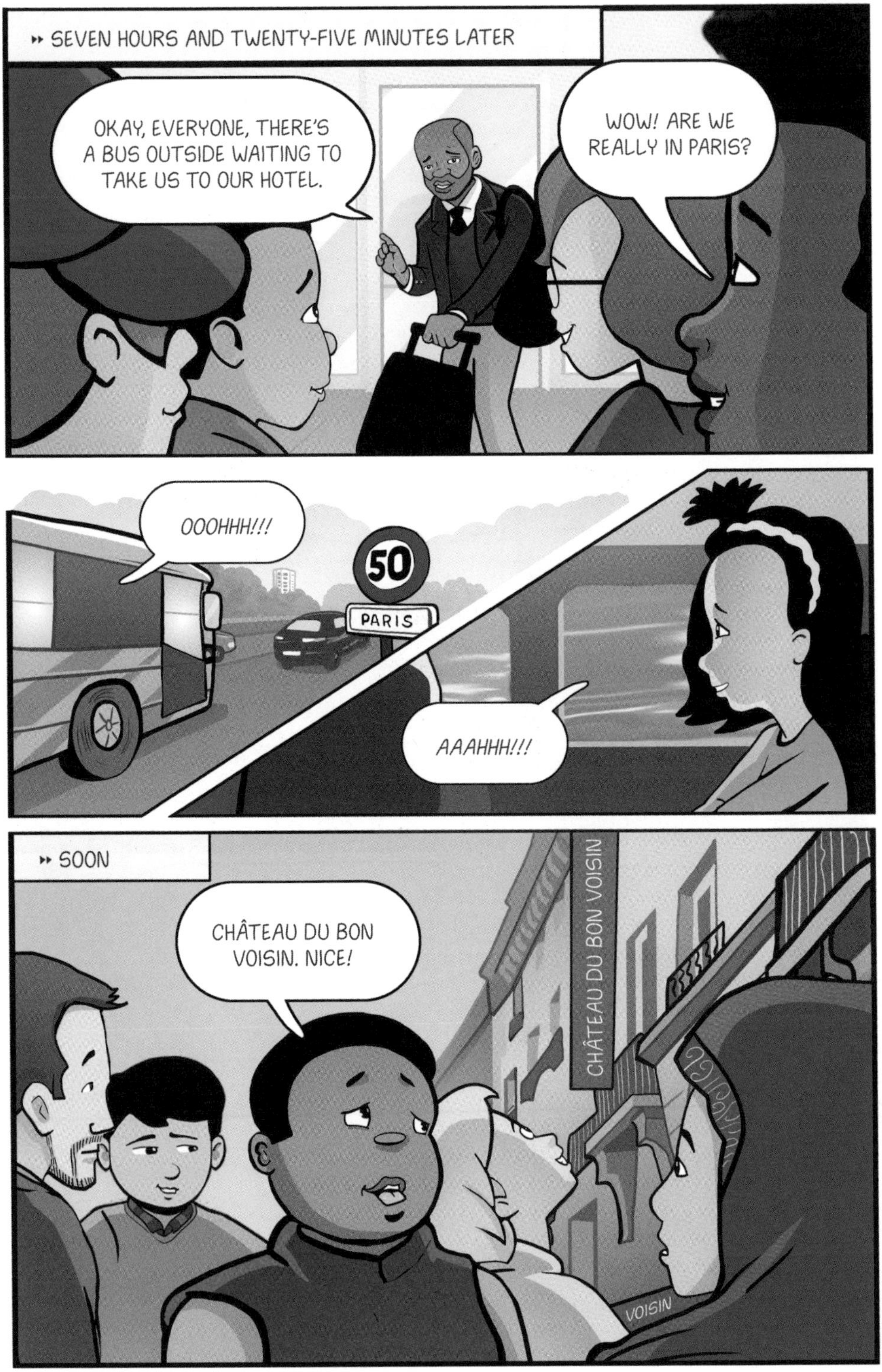
SEVEN HOURS AND TWENTY-FIVE MINUTES LATER
OKAY, EVERYONE, THERE'S A BUS OUTSIDE WAITING TO TAKE US TO OUR HOTEL.
WOW! ARE WE REALLY IN PARIS?
OOOHHH!!!
50
PARIS
AAAHHH!!!
SOON
CHÂTEAU DU BON VOISIN. NICE!
CHÂTEAU DU BON VOISIN
VOISIN

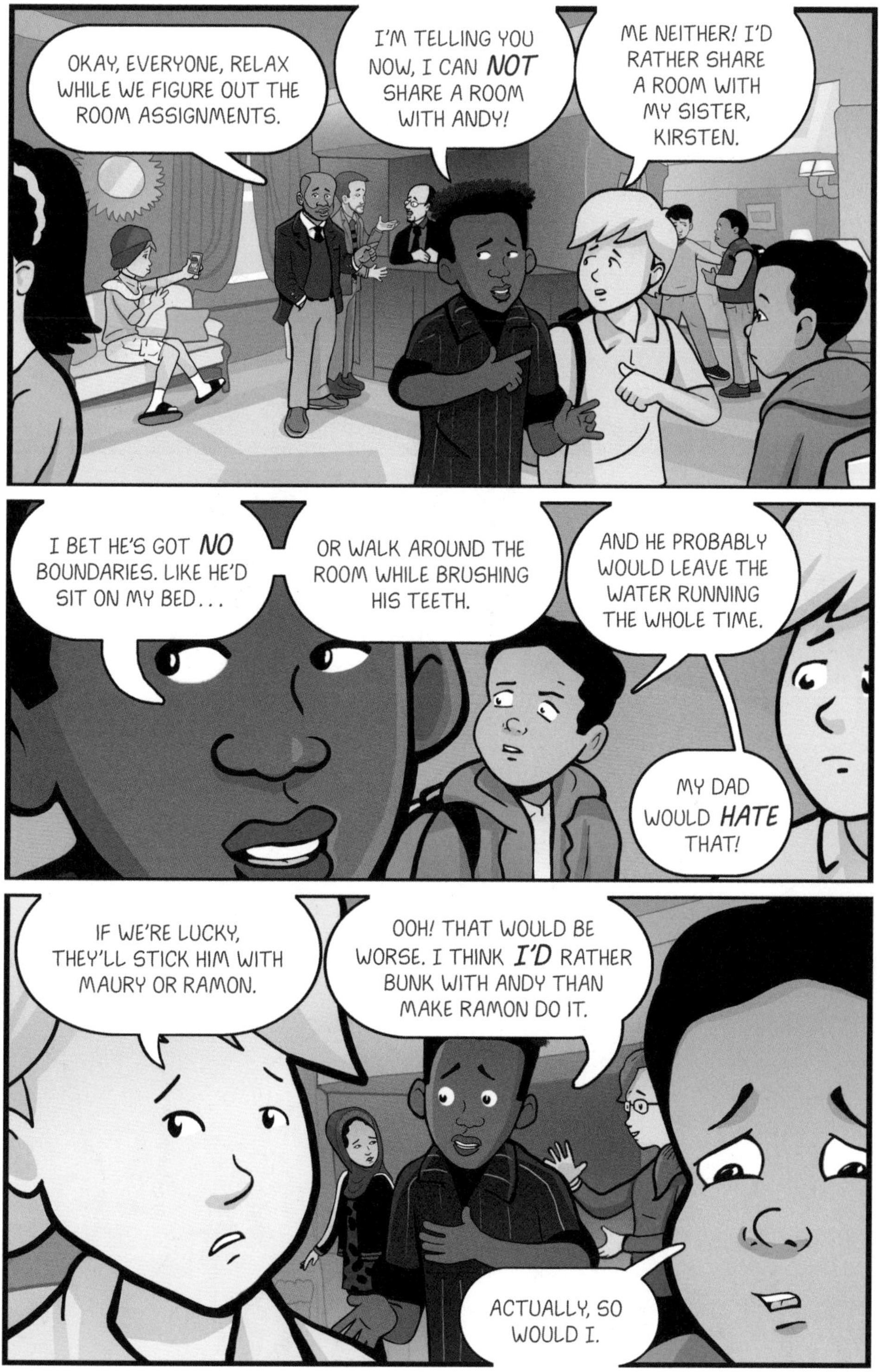
OKAY, EVERYONE, RELAX WHILE WE FIGURE OUT THE ROOM ASSIGNMENTS.
I'M TELLING YOU NOW, I CAN **NOT** SHARE A ROOM WITH ANDY!
ME NEITHER! I'D RATHER SHARE A ROOM WITH MY SISTER, KIRSTEN.
I BET HE'S GOT **NO** BOUNDARIES. LIKE HE'D SIT ON MY BED . . .
OR WALK AROUND THE ROOM WHILE BRUSHING HIS TEETH.
AND HE PROBABLY WOULD LEAVE THE WATER RUNNING THE WHOLE TIME.
MY DAD WOULD **HATE** THAT!
IF WE'RE LUCKY, THEY'LL STICK HIM WITH MAURY OR RAMON.
OOH! THAT WOULD BE WORSE. I THINK ***I'D*** RATHER BUNK WITH ANDY THAN MAKE RAMON DO IT.
ACTUALLY, SO WOULD I.

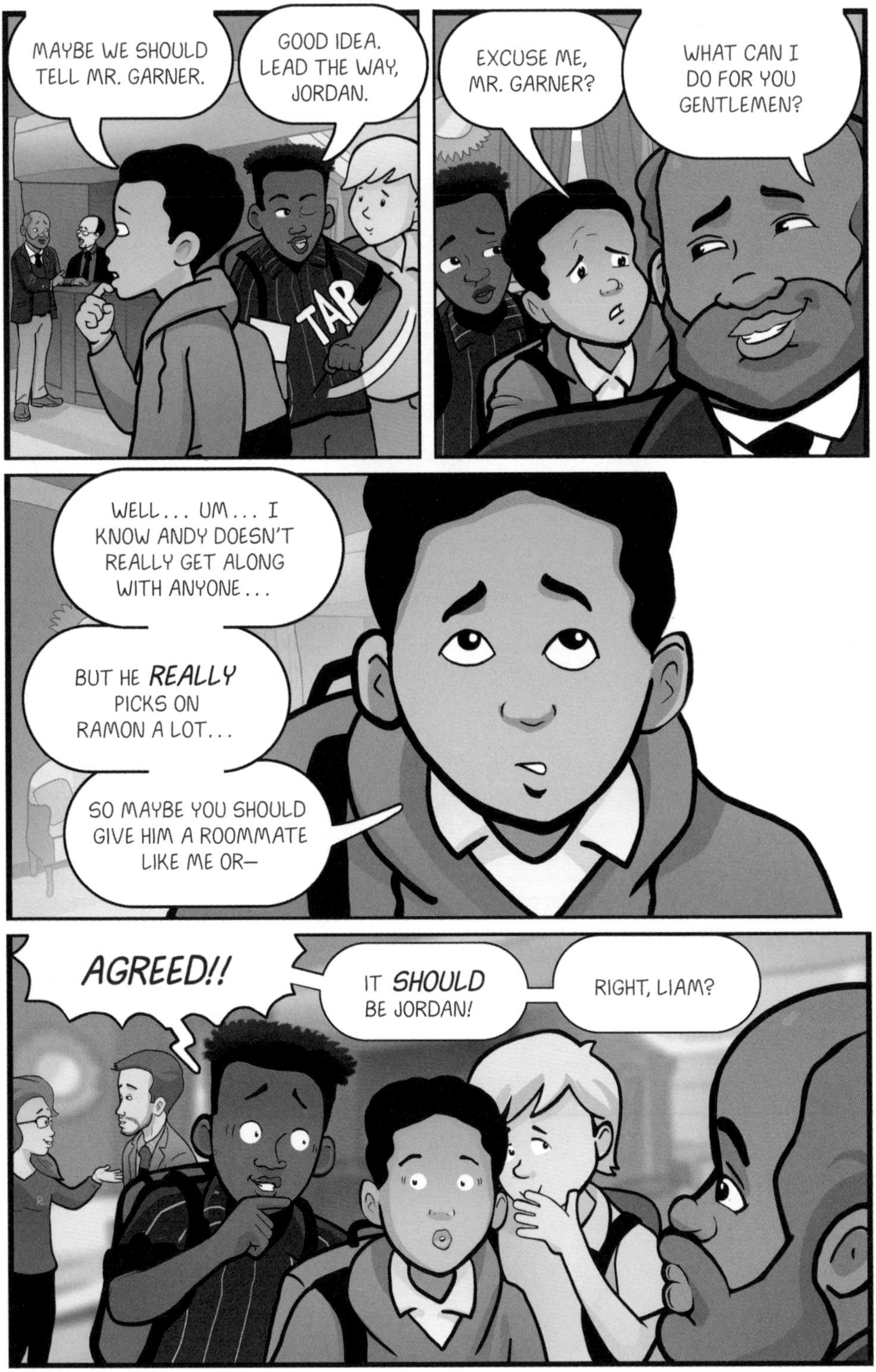
MAYBE WE SHOULD TELL MR. GARNER.
GOOD IDEA. LEAD THE WAY, JORDAN.
TAP
EXCUSE ME, MR. GARNER?
WHAT CAN I DO FOR YOU GENTLEMEN?
WELL... UM... I KNOW ANDY DOESN'T REALLY GET ALONG WITH ANYONE...
BUT HE **REALLY** PICKS ON RAMON A LOT...
SO MAYBE YOU SHOULD GIVE HIM A ROOMMATE LIKE ME OR—
AGREED!!
IT **SHOULD** BE JORDAN!
RIGHT, LIAM?

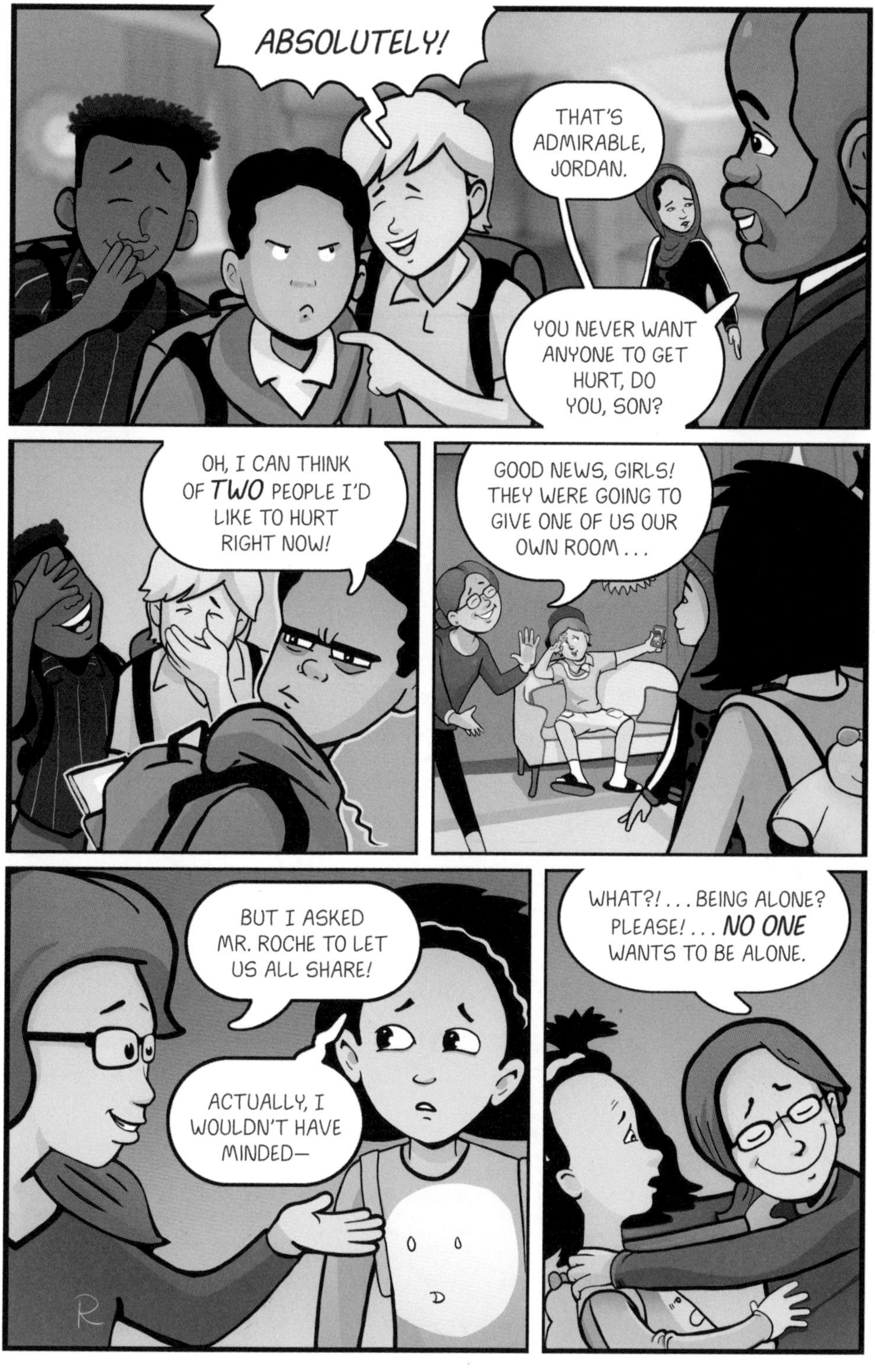
ABSOLUTELY!
THAT'S ADMIRABLE, JORDAN.
YOU NEVER WANT ANYONE TO GET HURT, DO YOU, SON?
OH, I CAN THINK OF TWO PEOPLE I'D LIKE TO HURT RIGHT NOW!
GOOD NEWS, GIRLS! THEY WERE GOING TO GIVE ONE OF US OUR OWN ROOM . . .
BUT I ASKED MR. ROCHE TO LET US ALL SHARE!
ACTUALLY, I WOULDN'T HAVE MINDED—
WHAT?! . . . BEING ALONE? PLEASE! . . . NO ONE WANTS TO BE ALONE.

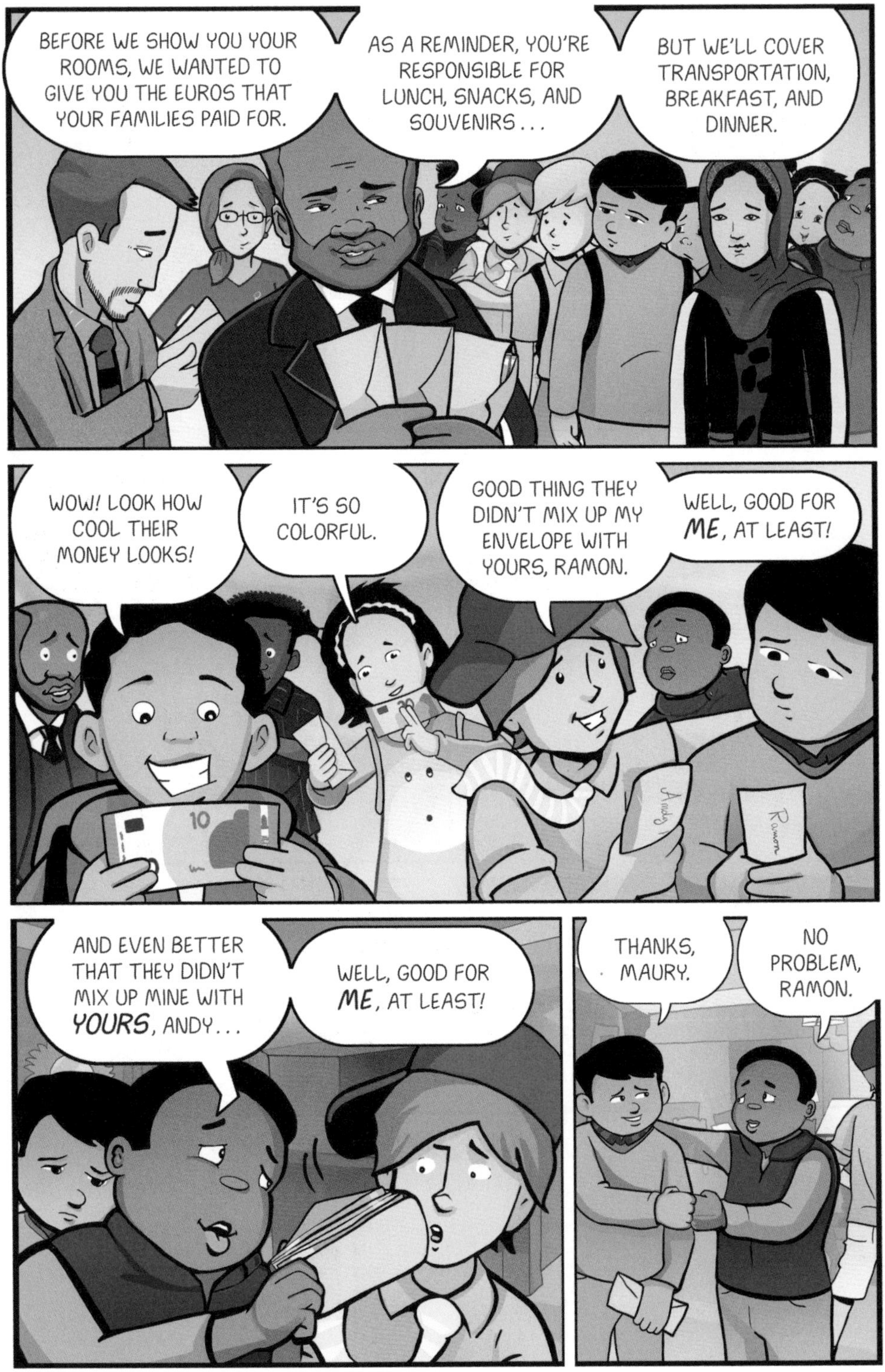
BEFORE WE SHOW YOU YOUR ROOMS, WE WANTED TO GIVE YOU THE EUROS THAT YOUR FAMILIES PAID FOR.
AS A REMINDER, YOU'RE RESPONSIBLE FOR LUNCH, SNACKS, AND SOUVENIRS . . .
BUT WE'LL COVER TRANSPORTATION, BREAKFAST, AND DINNER.
WOW! LOOK HOW COOL THEIR MONEY LOOKS!
IT'S SO COLORFUL.
GOOD THING THEY DIDN'T MIX UP MY ENVELOPE WITH YOURS, RAMON.
WELL, GOOD FOR ME, AT LEAST!
10
Andy
Ramon
AND EVEN BETTER THAT THEY DIDN'T MIX UP MINE WITH YOURS, ANDY . . .
WELL, GOOD FOR ME, AT LEAST!
THANKS, MAURY.
NO PROBLEM, RAMON.

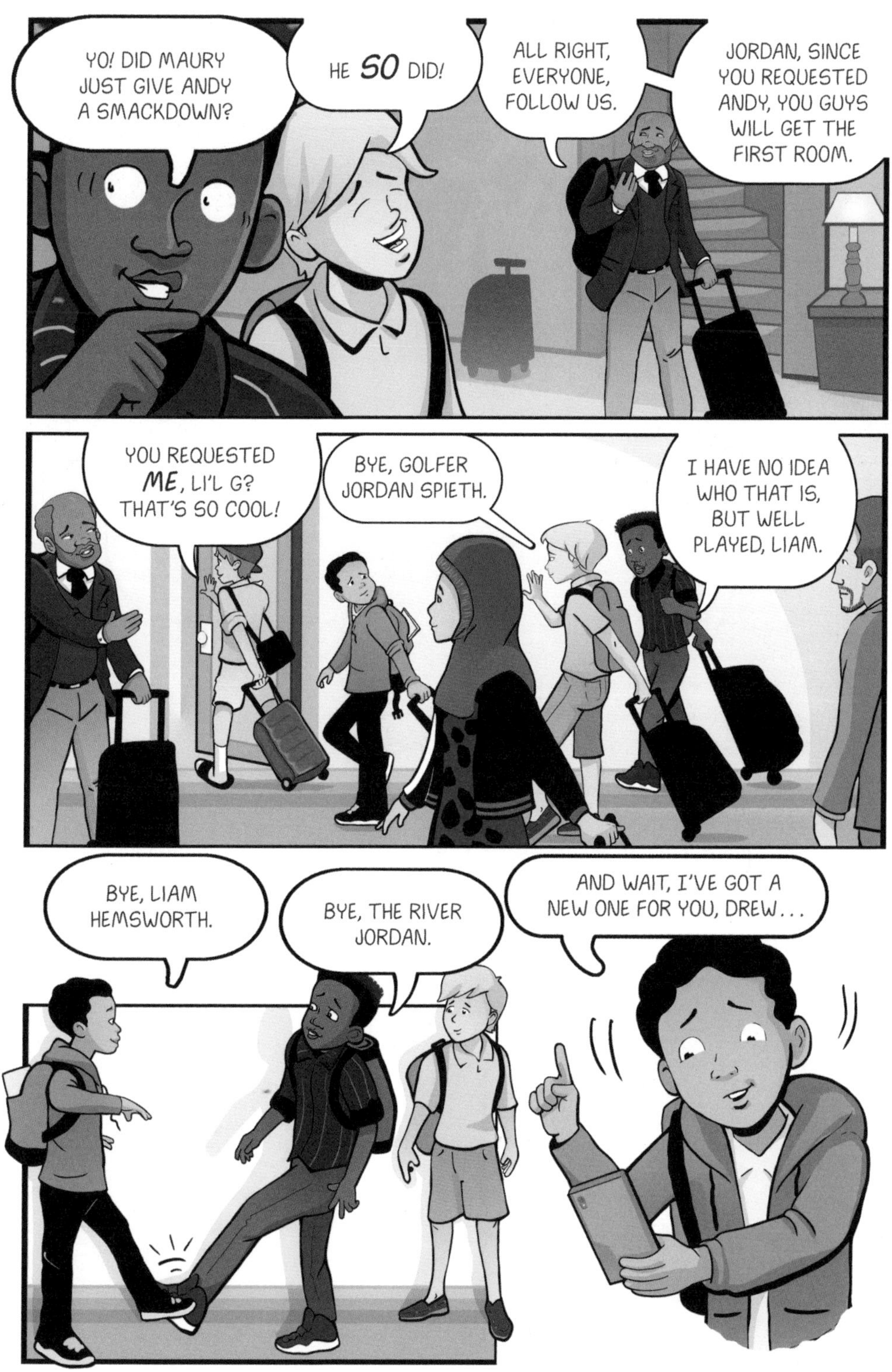
YO! DID MAURY JUST GIVE ANDY A SMACKDOWN?
HE SO DID!
ALL RIGHT, EVERYONE, FOLLOW US.
JORDAN, SINCE YOU REQUESTED ANDY, YOU GUYS WILL GET THE FIRST ROOM.
YOU REQUESTED ME, LI'L G? THAT'S SO COOL!
BYE, GOLFER JORDAN SPIETH.
I HAVE NO IDEA WHO THAT IS, BUT WELL PLAYED, LIAM.
BYE, LIAM HEMSWORTH.
BYE, THE RIVER JORDAN.
AND WAIT, I'VE GOT A NEW ONE FOR YOU, DREW...

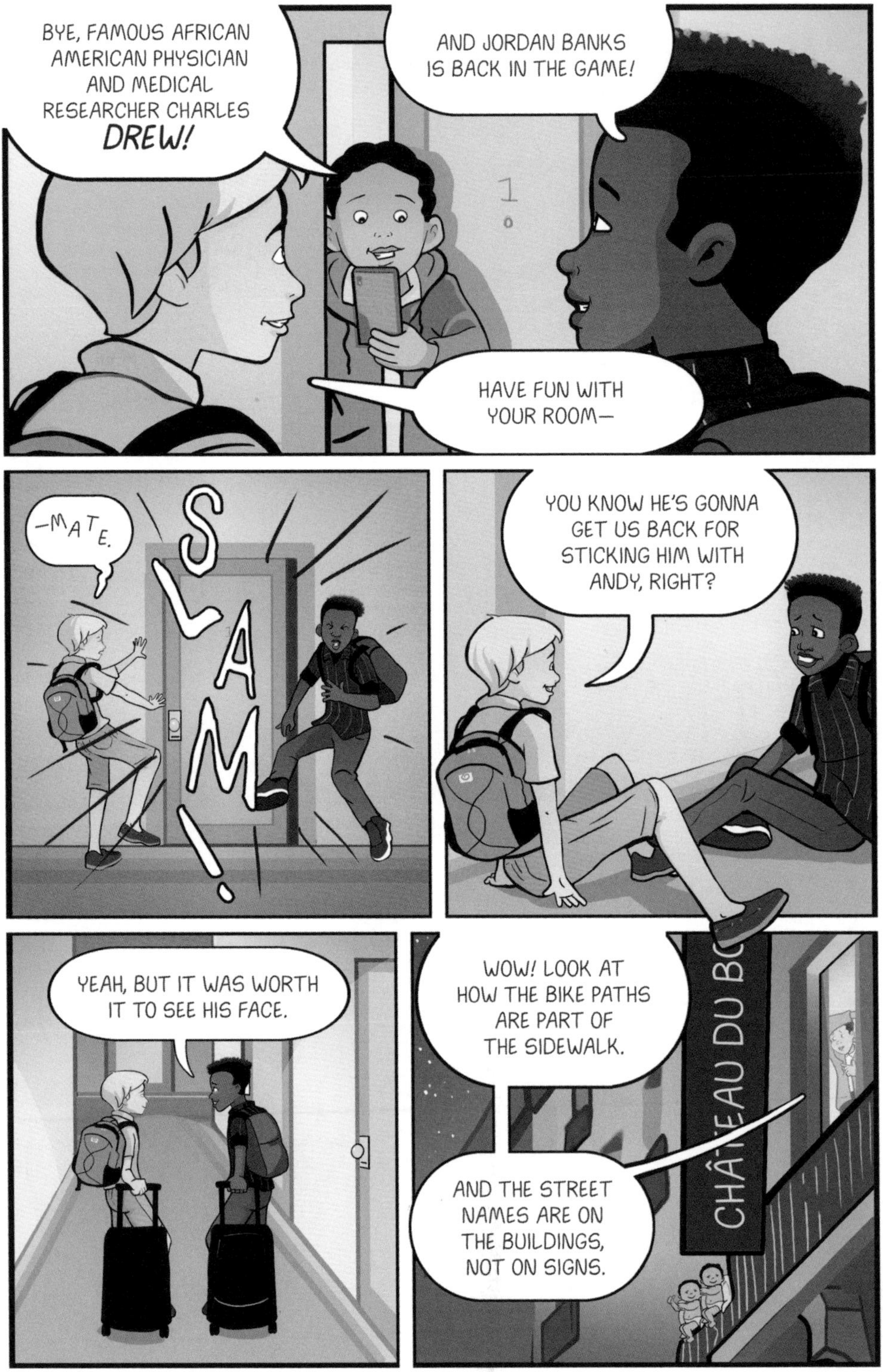
BYE, FAMOUS AFRICAN AMERICAN PHYSICIAN AND MEDICAL RESEARCHER CHARLES *DREW!*
AND JORDAN BANKS IS BACK IN THE GAME!
HAVE FUN WITH YOUR ROOM—
—MATE.
SLAM!
YOU KNOW HE'S GONNA GET US BACK FOR STICKING HIM WITH ANDY, RIGHT?
YEAH, BUT IT WAS WORTH IT TO SEE HIS FACE.
WOW! LOOK AT HOW THE BIKE PATHS ARE PART OF THE SIDEWALK.
AND THE STREET NAMES ARE ON THE BUILDINGS, NOT ON SIGNS.
CHÂTEAU DU BO

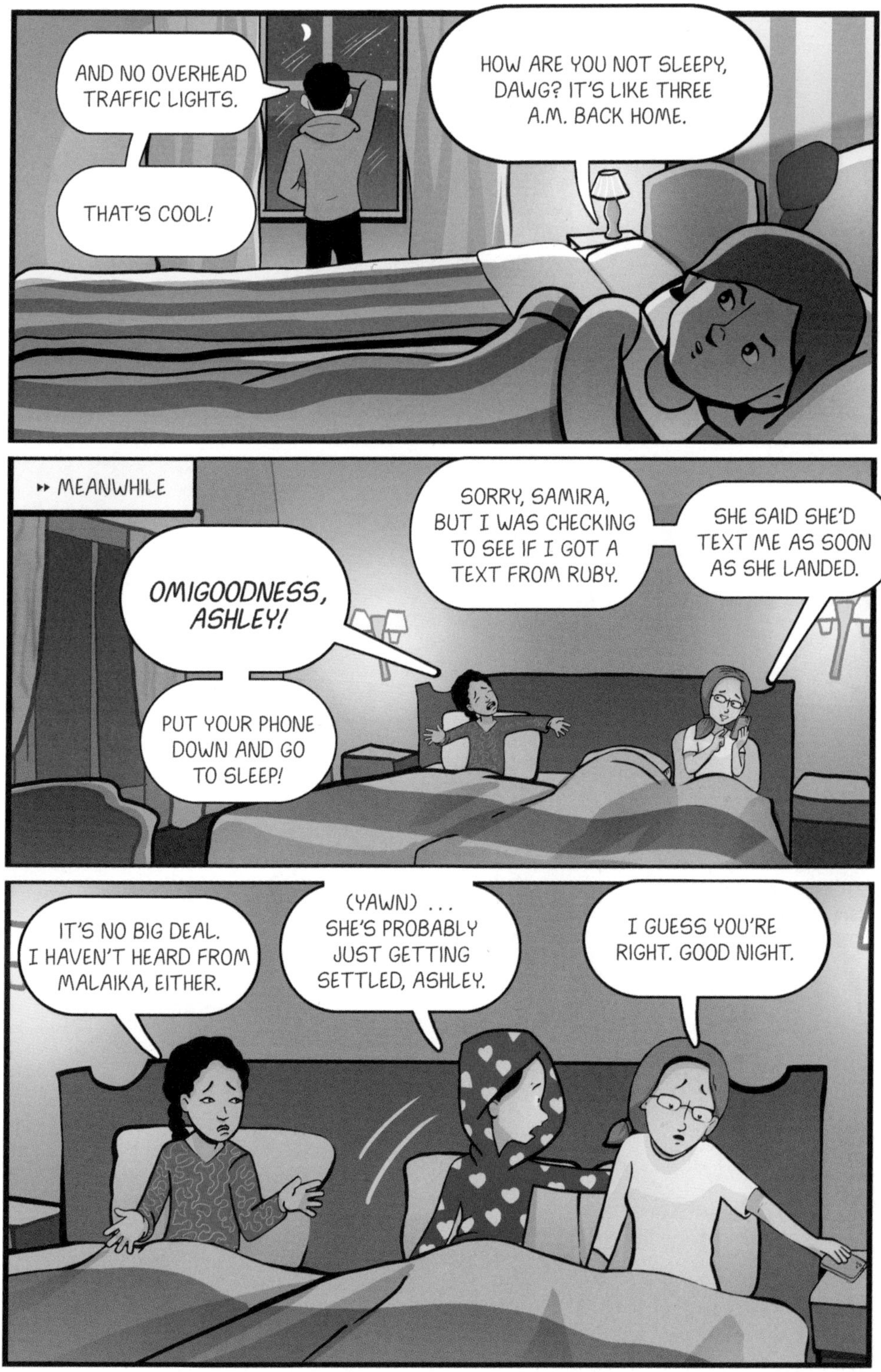
AND NO OVERHEAD TRAFFIC LIGHTS.
THAT'S COOL!
HOW ARE YOU NOT SLEEPY, DAWG? IT'S LIKE THREE A.M. BACK HOME.
MEANWHILE
OMIGOODNESS, ASHLEY!
PUT YOUR PHONE DOWN AND GO TO SLEEP!
SORRY, SAMIRA, BUT I WAS CHECKING TO SEE IF I GOT A TEXT FROM RUBY.
SHE SAID SHE'D TEXT ME AS SOON AS SHE LANDED.
IT'S NO BIG DEAL. I HAVEN'T HEARD FROM MALAIKA, EITHER.
(YAWN) . . . SHE'S PROBABLY JUST GETTING SETTLED, ASHLEY.
I GUESS YOU'RE RIGHT. GOOD NIGHT.

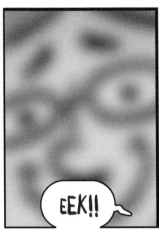

EEK!!

GOOD MORNING, ALEXANDRA. HOW DID YOU SLEEP?

ASHLEY? IS EVERYTHING ALL RIGHT?! WHAT TIME IS IT?

IT'S FIVE THIRTY.

I HEARD SAMIRA MOVING AROUND, SO I THOUGHT I'D CHECK ON YOU.

CHECK ON ME?

YOU PROBABLY MISS YOUR FRIENDS AND FAMILY SO MUCH THAT YOU'RE HAVING A HARD TIME SLEEPING. RIGHT?

ACTUALLY, I WAS SOUND ASLEEP UNTIL I FELT YOU STARING AT ME.

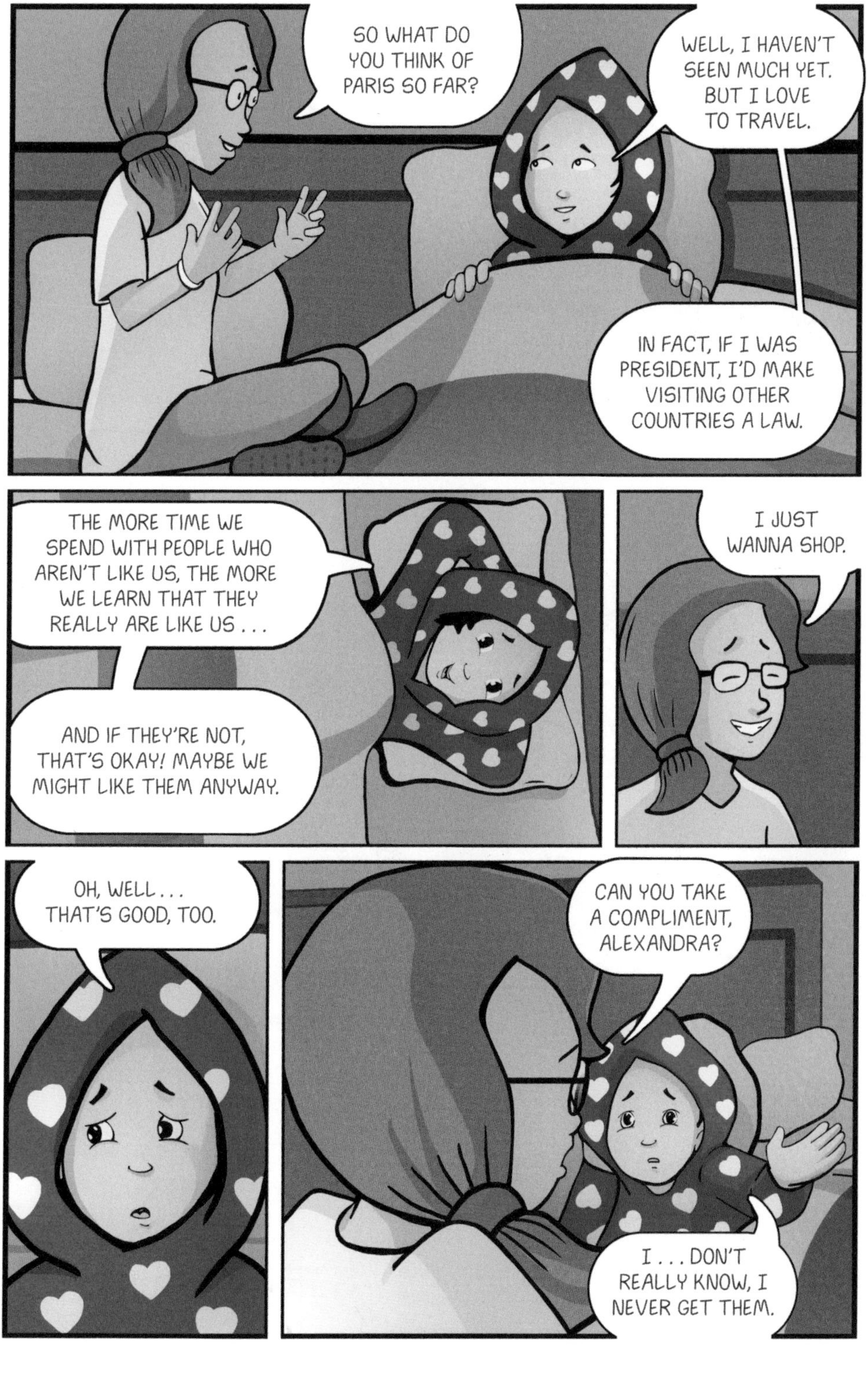
SO WHAT DO YOU THINK OF PARIS SO FAR?
WELL, I HAVEN'T SEEN MUCH YET. BUT I LOVE TO TRAVEL.
IN FACT, IF I WAS PRESIDENT, I'D MAKE VISITING OTHER COUNTRIES A LAW.
THE MORE TIME WE SPEND WITH PEOPLE WHO AREN'T LIKE US, THE MORE WE LEARN THAT THEY REALLY ARE LIKE US . . .
AND IF THEY'RE NOT, THAT'S OKAY! MAYBE WE MIGHT LIKE THEM ANYWAY.
I JUST WANNA SHOP.
OH, WELL . . . THAT'S GOOD, TOO.
CAN YOU TAKE A COMPLIMENT, ALEXANDRA?
I . . . DON'T REALLY KNOW, I NEVER GET THEM.

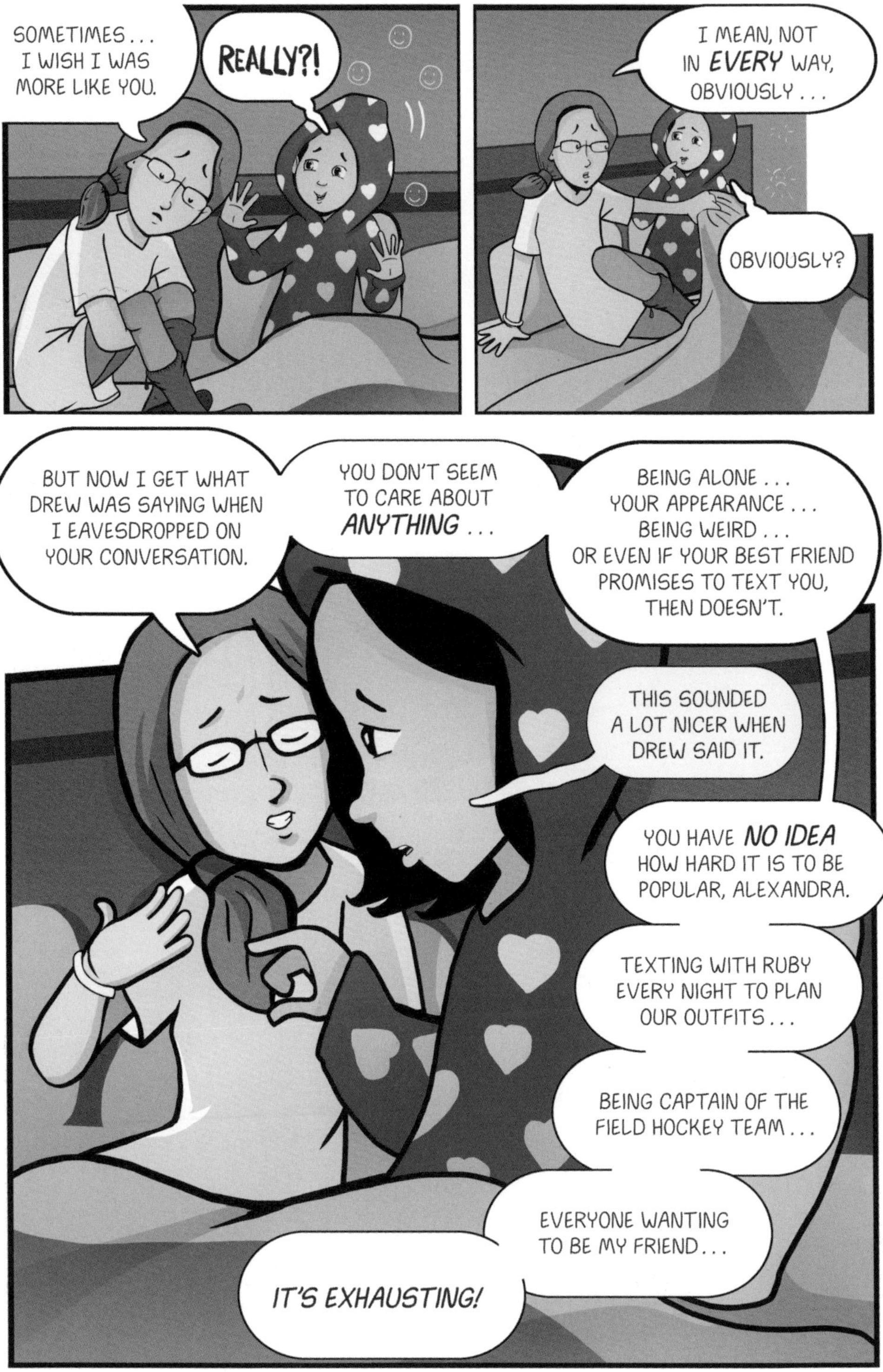
SOMETIMES . . . I WISH I WAS MORE LIKE YOU.
REALLY?!
I MEAN, NOT IN EVERY WAY, OBVIOUSLY . . .
OBVIOUSLY?
BUT NOW I GET WHAT DREW WAS SAYING WHEN I EAVESDROPPED ON YOUR CONVERSATION.
YOU DON'T SEEM TO CARE ABOUT ANYTHING . . .
BEING ALONE . . . YOUR APPEARANCE . . . BEING WEIRD . . . OR EVEN IF YOUR BEST FRIEND PROMISES TO TEXT YOU, THEN DOESN'T.
THIS SOUNDED A LOT NICER WHEN DREW SAID IT.
YOU HAVE NO IDEA HOW HARD IT IS TO BE POPULAR, ALEXANDRA.
TEXTING WITH RUBY EVERY NIGHT TO PLAN OUR OUTFITS . . .
BEING CAPTAIN OF THE FIELD HOCKEY TEAM . . .
EVERYONE WANTING TO BE MY FRIEND . . .
IT'S EXHAUSTING!

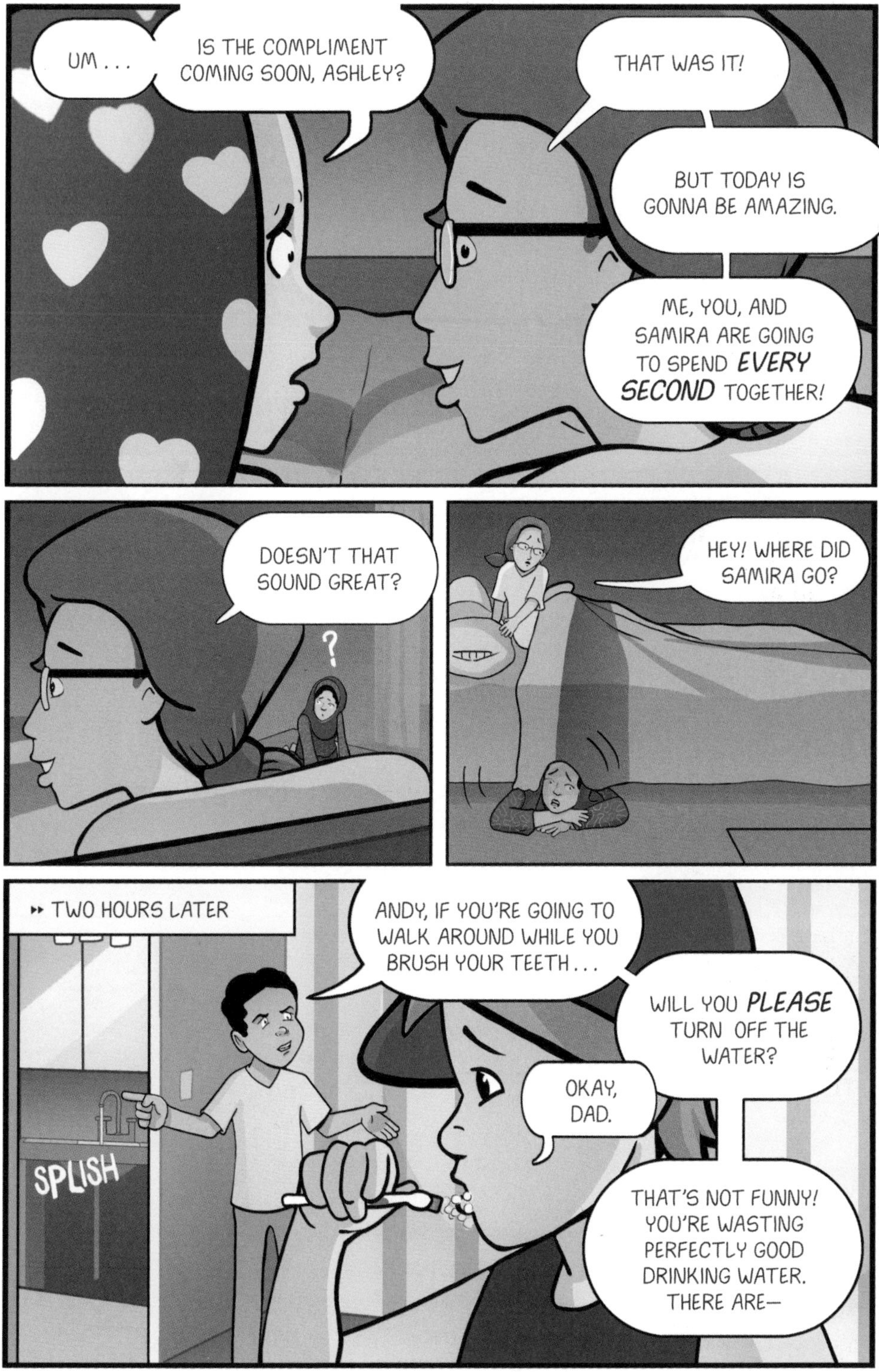
UM . . .
IS THE COMPLIMENT COMING SOON, ASHLEY?
THAT WAS IT!
BUT TODAY IS GONNA BE AMAZING.
ME, YOU, AND SAMIRA ARE GOING TO SPEND **EVERY SECOND** TOGETHER!
DOESN'T THAT SOUND GREAT?
?
HEY! WHERE DID SAMIRA GO?
TWO HOURS LATER
ANDY, IF YOU'RE GOING TO WALK AROUND WHILE YOU BRUSH YOUR TEETH . . .
WILL YOU **PLEASE** TURN OFF THE WATER?
OKAY, DAD.
THAT'S NOT FUNNY! YOU'RE WASTING PERFECTLY GOOD DRINKING WATER. THERE ARE—
SPLISH

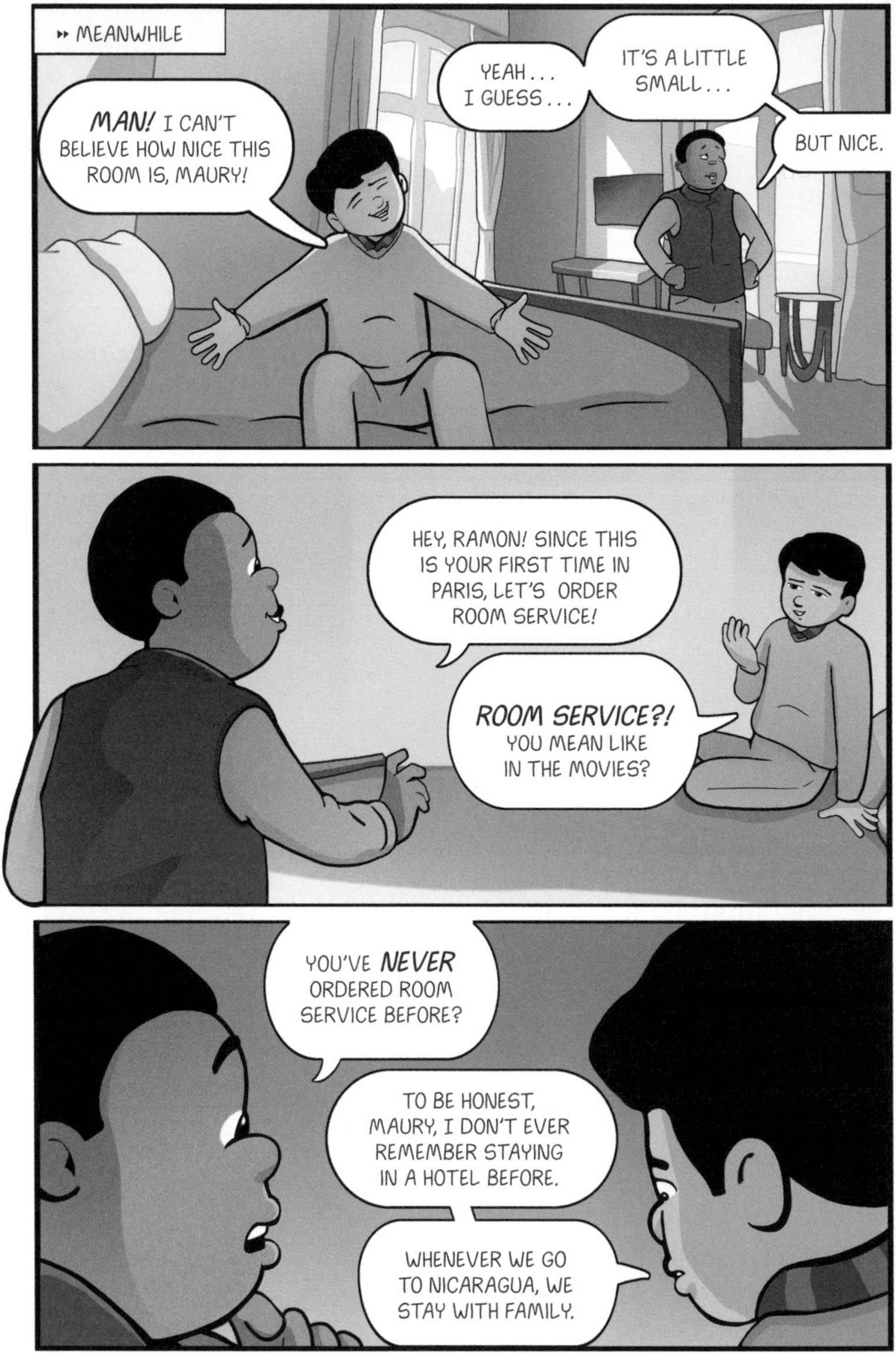
MEANWHILE
MAN! I CAN'T BELIEVE HOW NICE THIS ROOM IS, MAURY!
YEAH... I GUESS...
IT'S A LITTLE SMALL...
BUT NICE.
HEY, RAMON! SINCE THIS IS YOUR FIRST TIME IN PARIS, LET'S ORDER ROOM SERVICE!
ROOM SERVICE?! YOU MEAN LIKE IN THE MOVIES?
YOU'VE NEVER ORDERED ROOM SERVICE BEFORE?
TO BE HONEST, MAURY, I DON'T EVER REMEMBER STAYING IN A HOTEL BEFORE.
WHENEVER WE GO TO NICARAGUA, WE STAY WITH FAMILY.

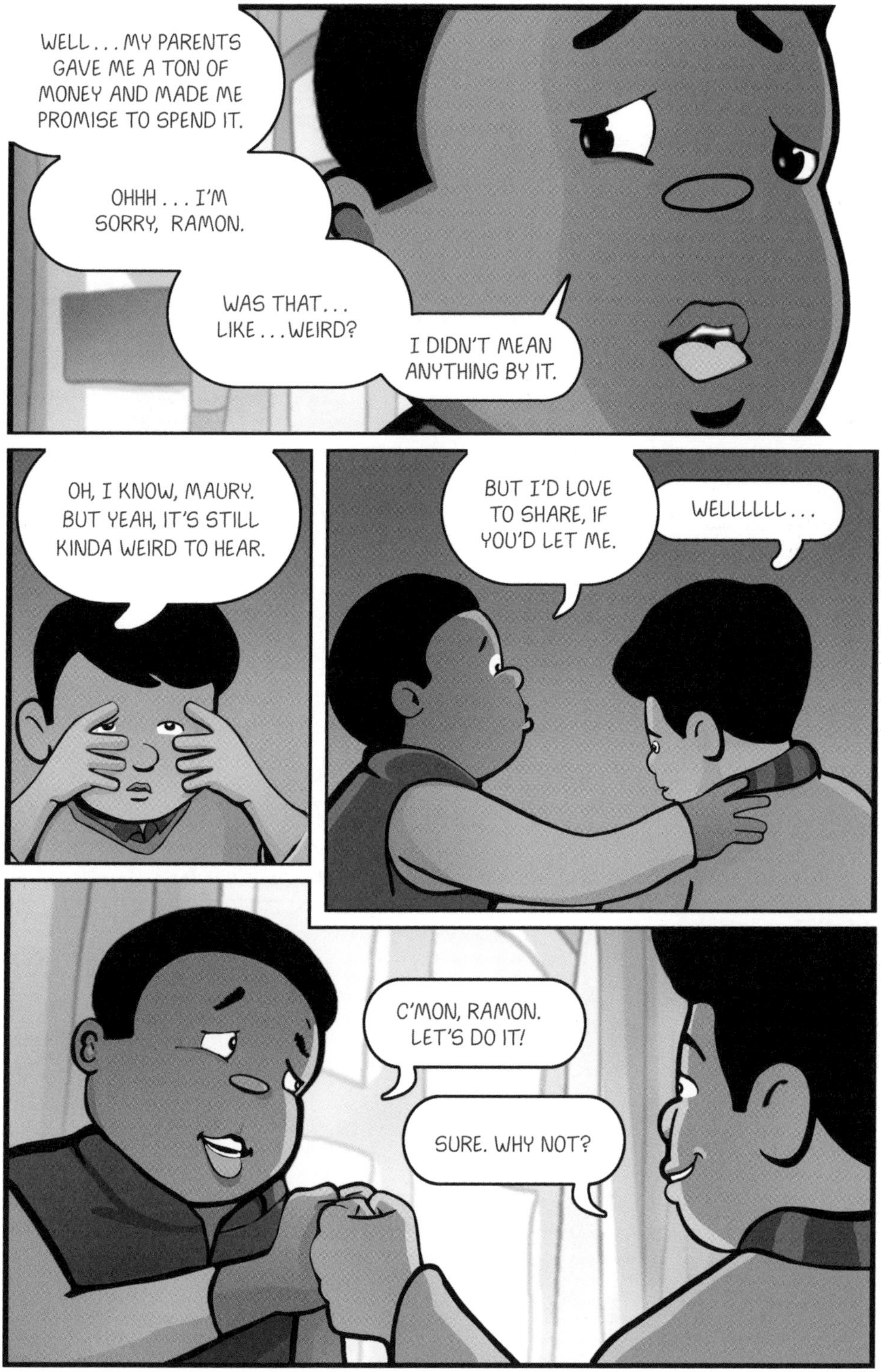
WELL . . . MY PARENTS GAVE ME A TON OF MONEY AND MADE ME PROMISE TO SPEND IT.
OHHH . . . I'M SORRY, RAMON.
WAS THAT . . . LIKE . . . WEIRD?
I DIDN'T MEAN ANYTHING BY IT.
OH, I KNOW, MAURY. BUT YEAH, IT'S STILL KINDA WEIRD TO HEAR.
BUT I'D LOVE TO SHARE, IF YOU'D LET ME.
WELLLLLL . . .
C'MON, RAMON. LET'S DO IT!
SURE. WHY NOT?

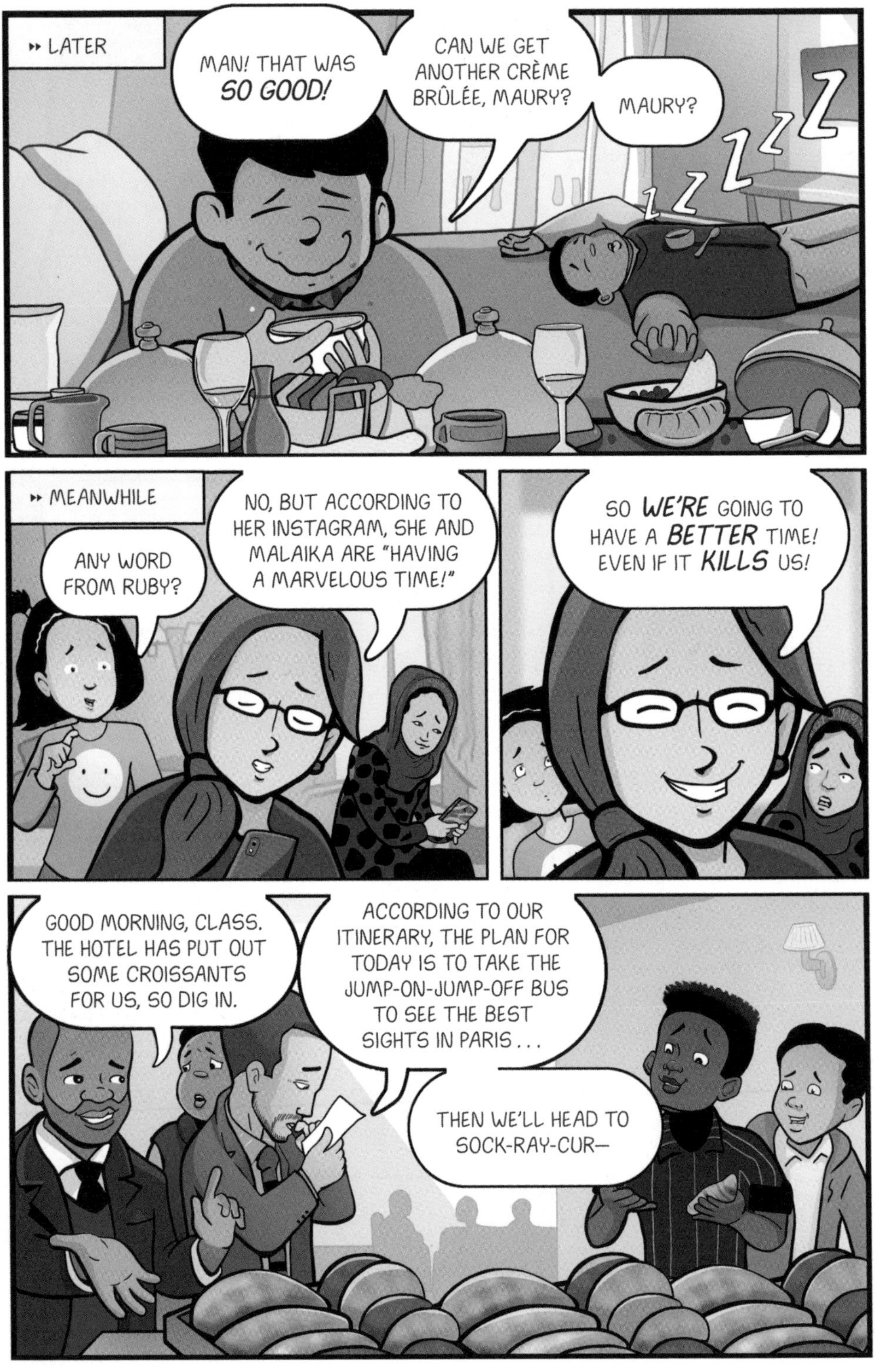
LATER
MAN! THAT WAS SO GOOD!
CAN WE GET ANOTHER CRÈME BRÛLÉE, MAURY?
MAURY?
ZZZZZZ
MEANWHILE
ANY WORD FROM RUBY?
NO, BUT ACCORDING TO HER INSTAGRAM, SHE AND MALAIKA ARE "HAVING A MARVELOUS TIME!"
SO WE'RE GOING TO HAVE A BETTER TIME! EVEN IF IT KILLS US!
GOOD MORNING, CLASS. THE HOTEL HAS PUT OUT SOME CROISSANTS FOR US, SO DIG IN.
ACCORDING TO OUR ITINERARY, THE PLAN FOR TODAY IS TO TAKE THE JUMP-ON-JUMP-OFF BUS TO SEE THE BEST SIGHTS IN PARIS . . .
THEN WE'LL HEAD TO SOCK-RAY-CUR—

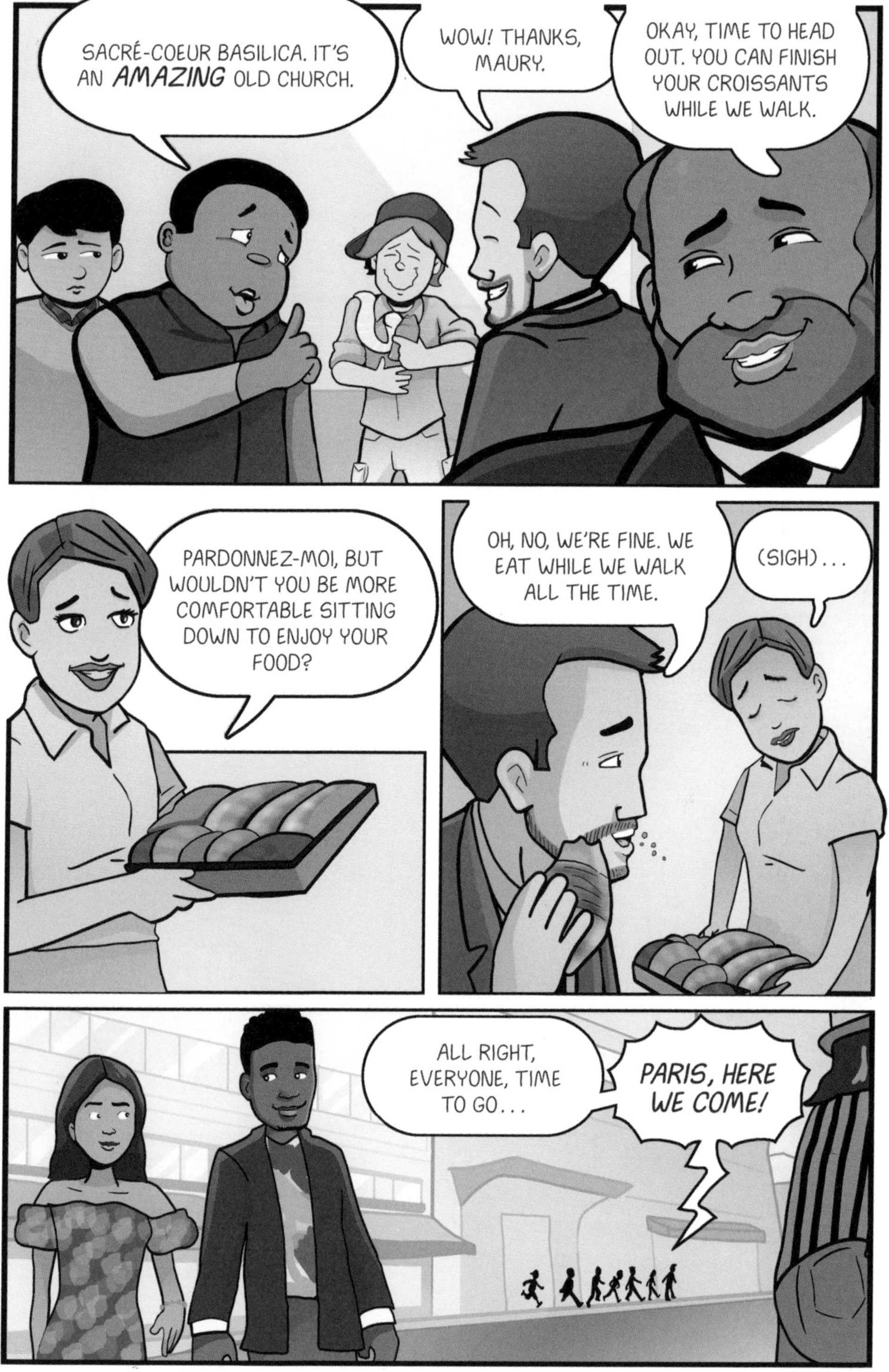

SACRÉ-COEUR BASILICA. IT'S AN *AMAZING* OLD CHURCH.
WOW! THANKS, MAURY.
OKAY, TIME TO HEAD OUT. YOU CAN FINISH YOUR CROISSANTS WHILE WE WALK.
PARDONNEZ-MOI, BUT WOULDN'T YOU BE MORE COMFORTABLE SITTING DOWN TO ENJOY YOUR FOOD?
OH, NO, WE'RE FINE. WE EAT WHILE WE WALK ALL THE TIME.
(SIGH) . . .
ALL RIGHT, EVERYONE, TIME TO GO . . .
PARIS, HERE WE COME!

5 More, More, More . . . LESS!

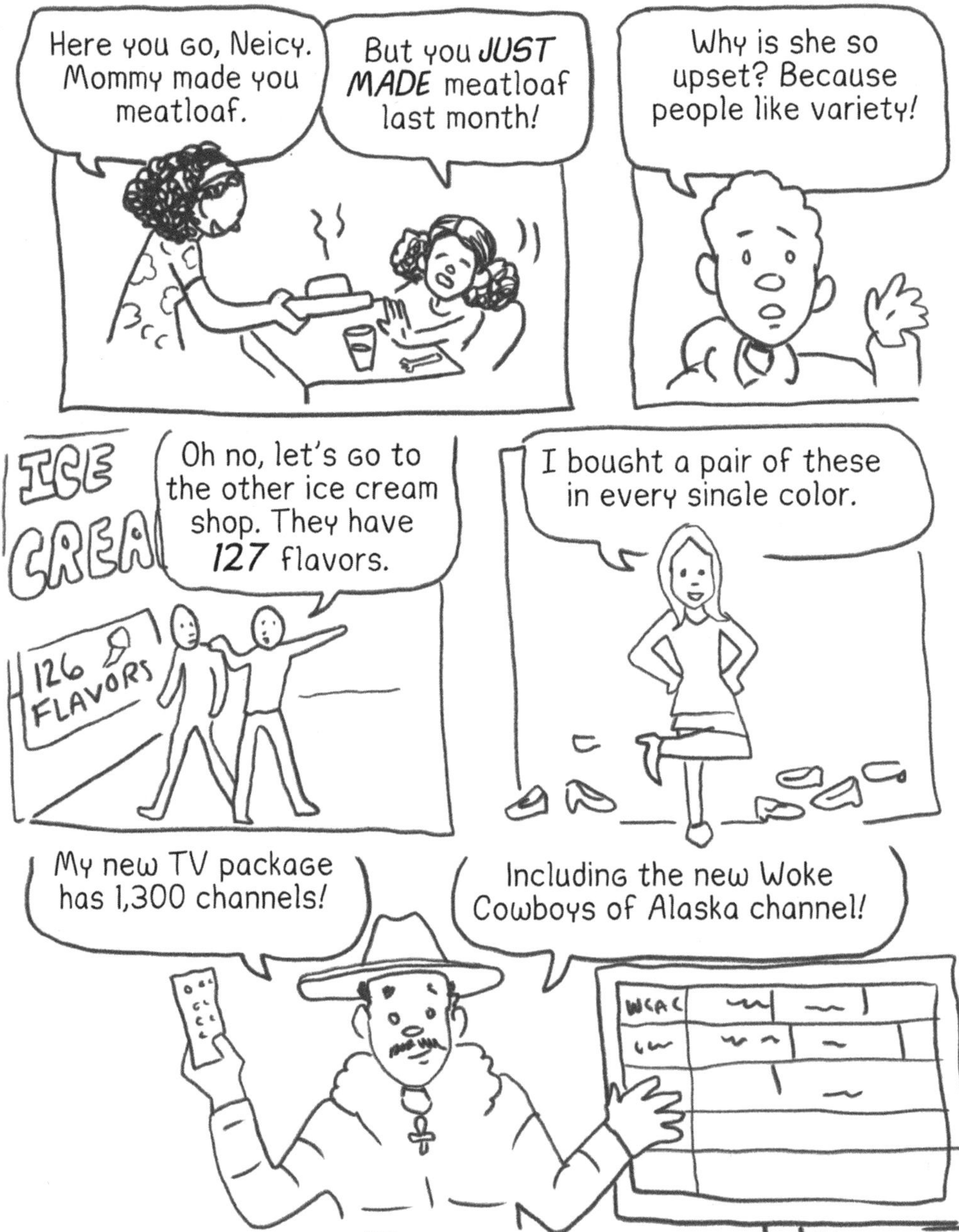

Here you go, Neicy. Mommy made you meatloaf.
But you *JUST MADE* meatloaf last month!
Why is she so upset? Because people like variety!
ICE CREA
Oh no, let's go to the other ice cream shop. They have *127* flavors.
126 FLAVORS
I bought a pair of these in every single color.
My new TV package has 1,300 channels!
Including the new Woke Cowboys of Alaska channel!

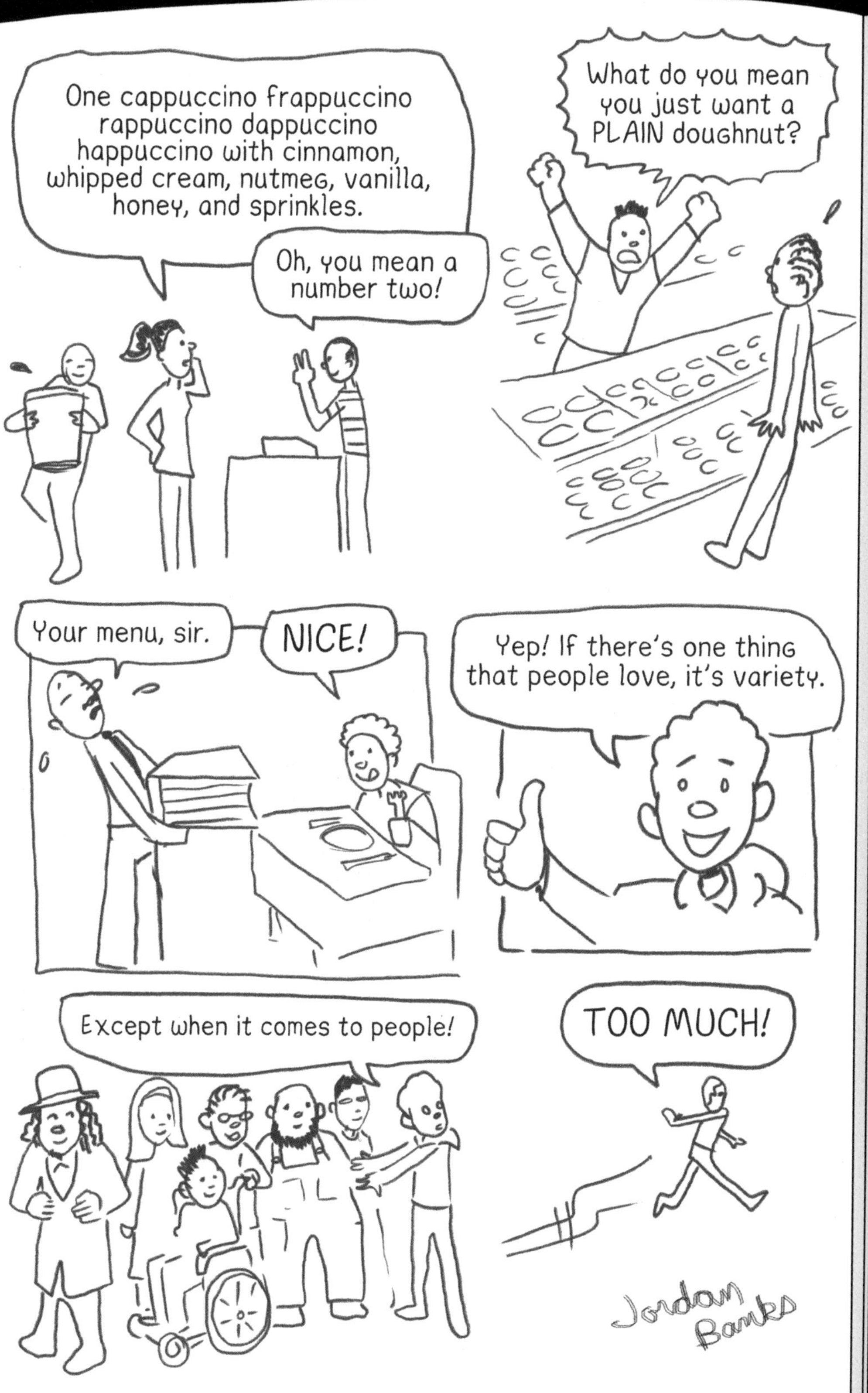
One cappuccino frappuccino rappuccino dappuccino happuccino with cinnamon, whipped cream, nutmeg, vanilla, honey, and sprinkles.
Oh, you mean a number two!
What do you mean you just want a PLAIN doughnut?
Your menu, sir.
NICE!
Yep! If there's one thing that people love, it's variety.
Except when it comes to people!
TOO MUCH!
Jordan Banks

YOU GUYS HAVE **GOT** TO WATCH TV WHEN WE GET BACK TO THE HOTEL.

ALL THE SHOWS ARE IN **FRENCH**. EVEN THE AMERICAN ONES!

I HAD SO MUCH FUN...

UNTIL MY BROTHER, KALE, CALLED TO TELL ME HE TRASHED MY ROOM AGAIN.

THAT WASN'T SO COOL.

EXCUSE ME, MR. MAURY?

YES, SAMIRA?

I ALWAYS THOUGHT THAT PARIS WAS LIKE NEW YORK. BUT THERE AREN'T A LOT OF TALL BUILDINGS. HOW COME?

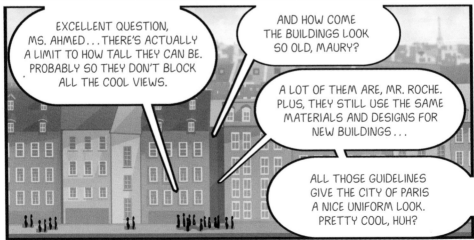

EXCELLENT QUESTION, MS. AHMED...THERE'S ACTUALLY A LIMIT TO HOW TALL THEY CAN BE. PROBABLY SO THEY DON'T BLOCK ALL THE COOL VIEWS.

AND HOW COME THE BUILDINGS LOOK SO OLD, MAURY?

A LOT OF THEM ARE, MR. ROCHE. PLUS, THEY STILL USE THE SAME MATERIALS AND DESIGNS FOR NEW BUILDINGS...

ALL THOSE GUIDELINES GIVE THE CITY OF PARIS A NICE UNIFORM LOOK. PRETTY COOL, HUH?

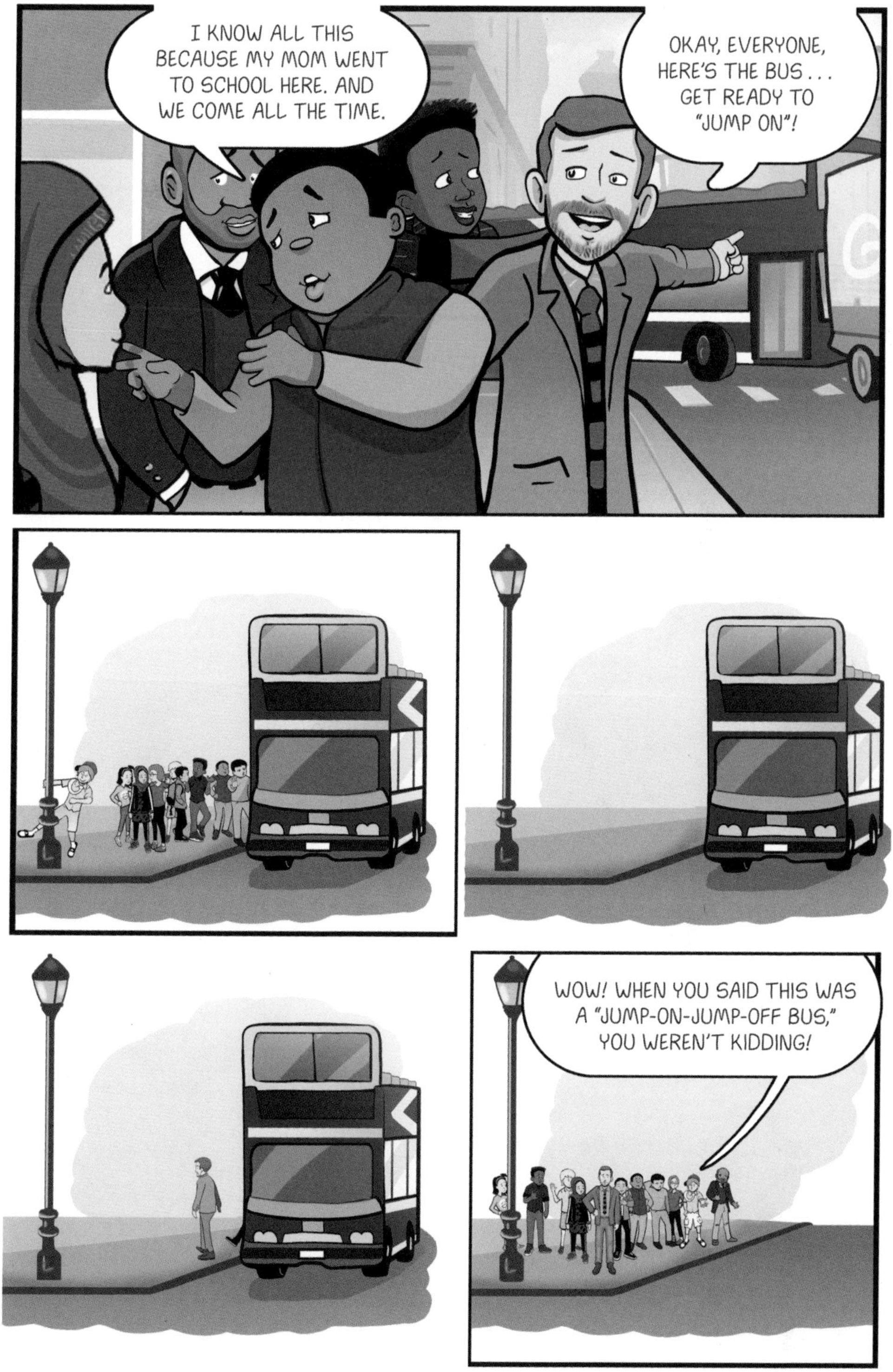
I KNOW ALL THIS BECAUSE MY MOM WENT TO SCHOOL HERE. AND WE COME ALL THE TIME.
OKAY, EVERYONE, HERE'S THE BUS . . . GET READY TO "JUMP ON"!
WOW! WHEN YOU SAID THIS WAS A "JUMP-ON-JUMP-OFF BUS," YOU WEREN'T KIDDING!

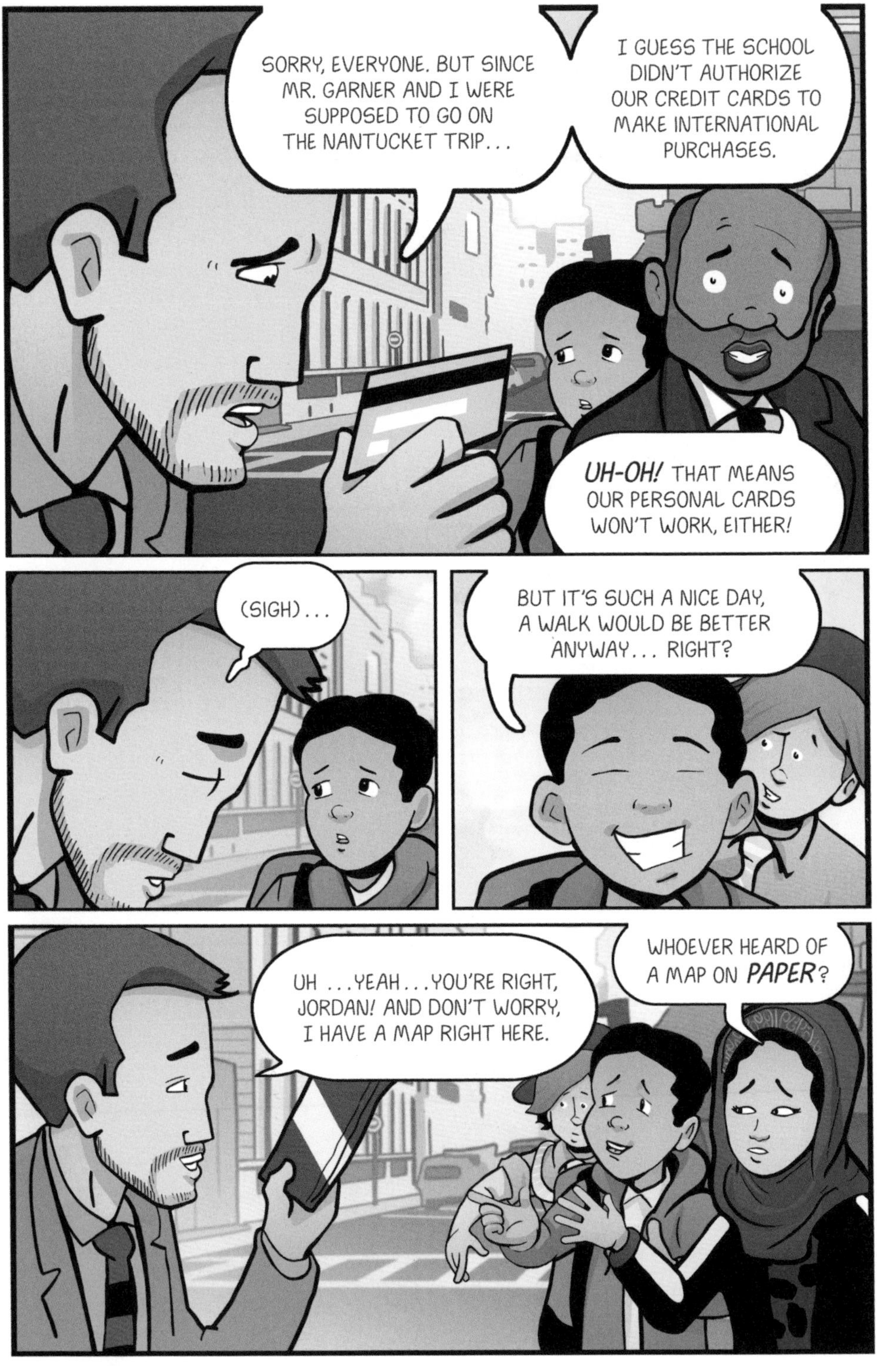
SORRY, EVERYONE. BUT SINCE MR. GARNER AND I WERE SUPPOSED TO GO ON THE NANTUCKET TRIP...
I GUESS THE SCHOOL DIDN'T AUTHORIZE OUR CREDIT CARDS TO MAKE INTERNATIONAL PURCHASES.
UH-OH! THAT MEANS OUR PERSONAL CARDS WON'T WORK, EITHER!
(SIGH)...
BUT IT'S SUCH A NICE DAY, A WALK WOULD BE BETTER ANYWAY... RIGHT?
UH ...YEAH...YOU'RE RIGHT, JORDAN! AND DON'T WORRY, I HAVE A MAP RIGHT HERE.
WHOEVER HEARD OF A MAP ON ***PAPER***?

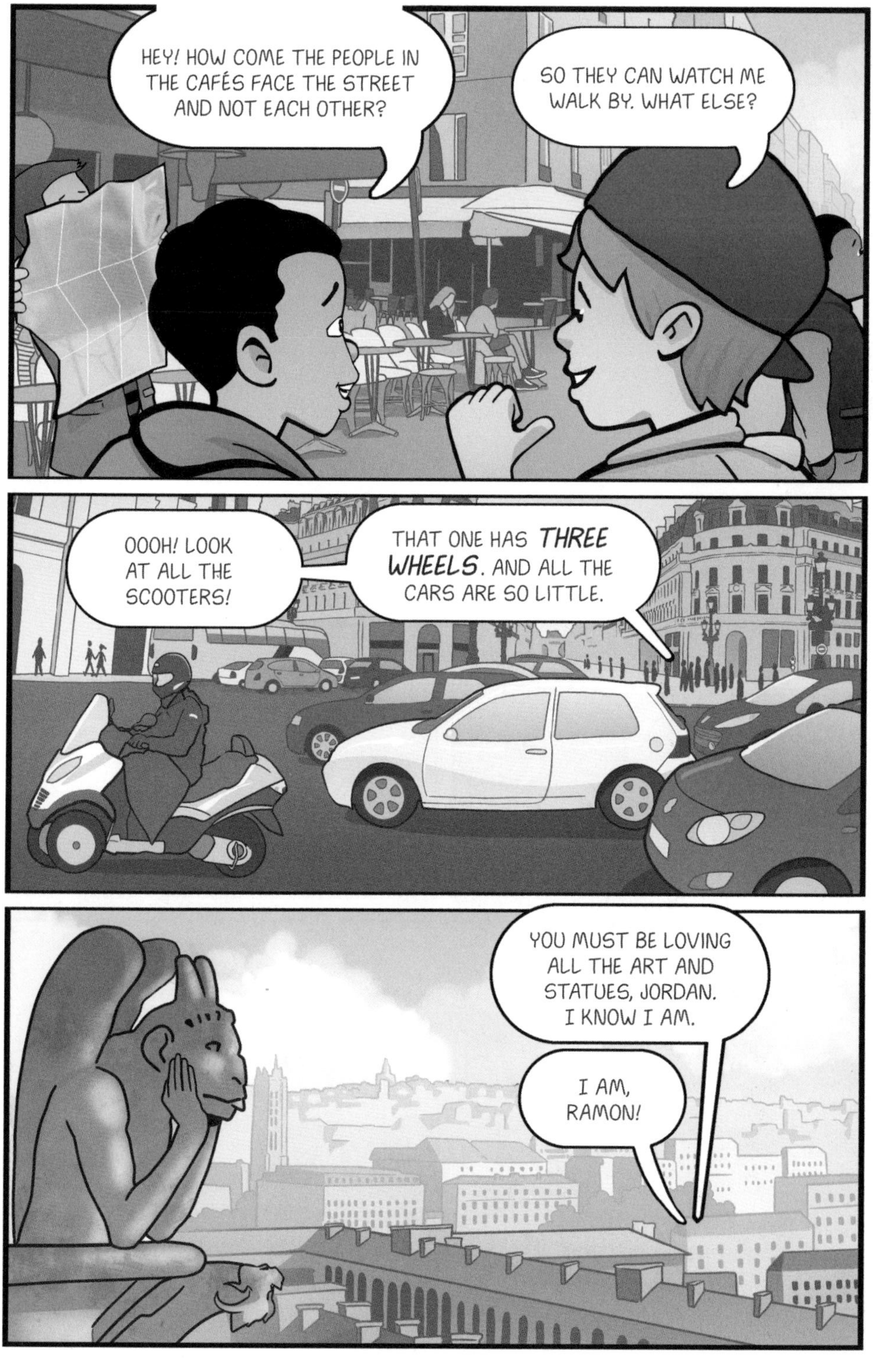
HEY! HOW COME THE PEOPLE IN THE CAFÉS FACE THE STREET AND NOT EACH OTHER?
SO THEY CAN WATCH ME WALK BY. WHAT ELSE?
OOOH! LOOK AT ALL THE SCOOTERS!
THAT ONE HAS **THREE WHEELS**. AND ALL THE CARS ARE SO LITTLE.
YOU MUST BE LOVING ALL THE ART AND STATUES, JORDAN. I KNOW I AM.
I AM, RAMON!

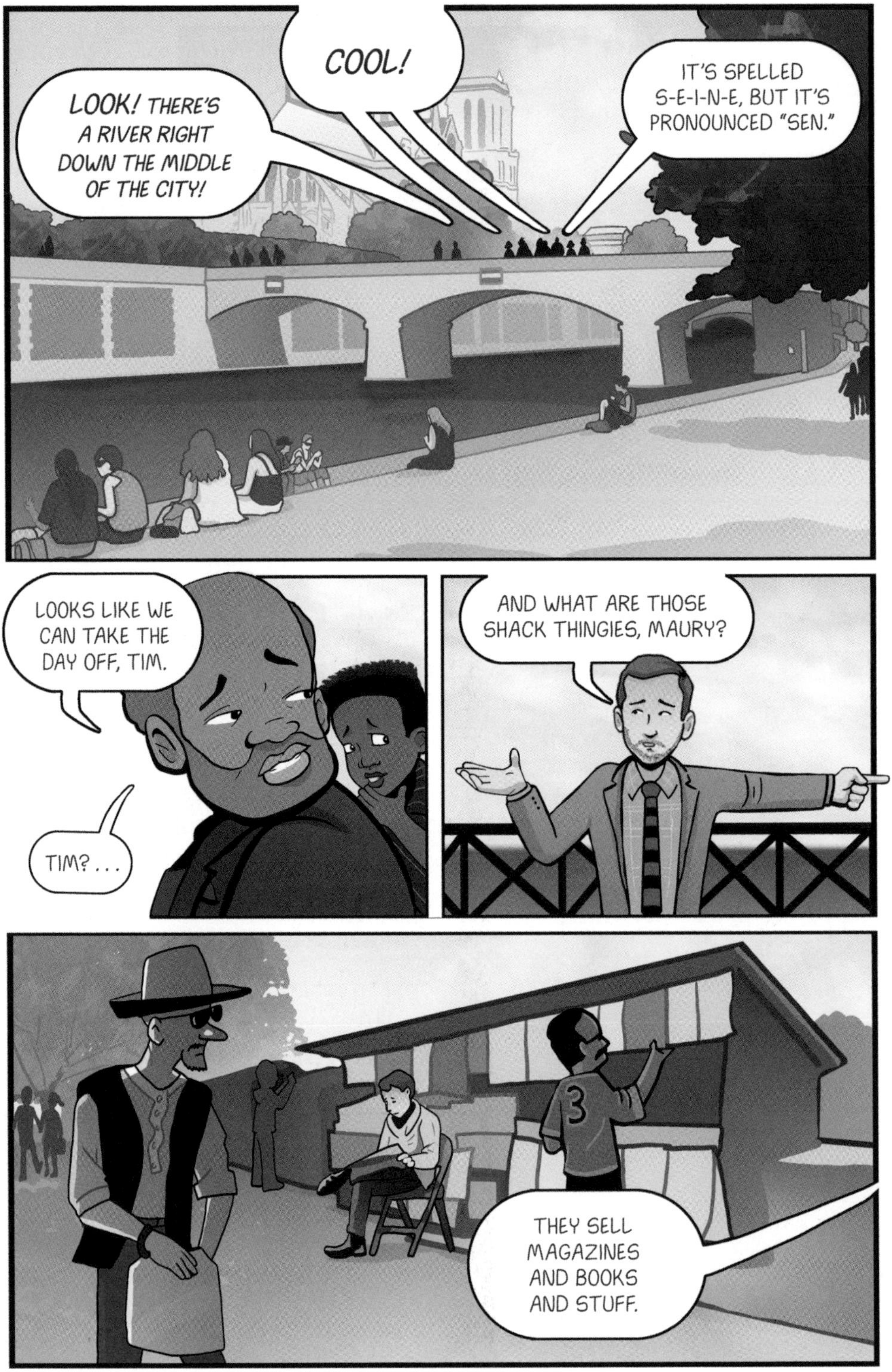
LOOK! THERE'S A RIVER RIGHT DOWN THE MIDDLE OF THE CITY!
COOL!
IT'S SPELLED S-E-I-N-E, BUT IT'S PRONOUNCED "SEN."
LOOKS LIKE WE CAN TAKE THE DAY OFF, TIM.
TIM? . . .
AND WHAT ARE THOSE SHACK THINGIES, MAURY?
THEY SELL MAGAZINES AND BOOKS AND STUFF.

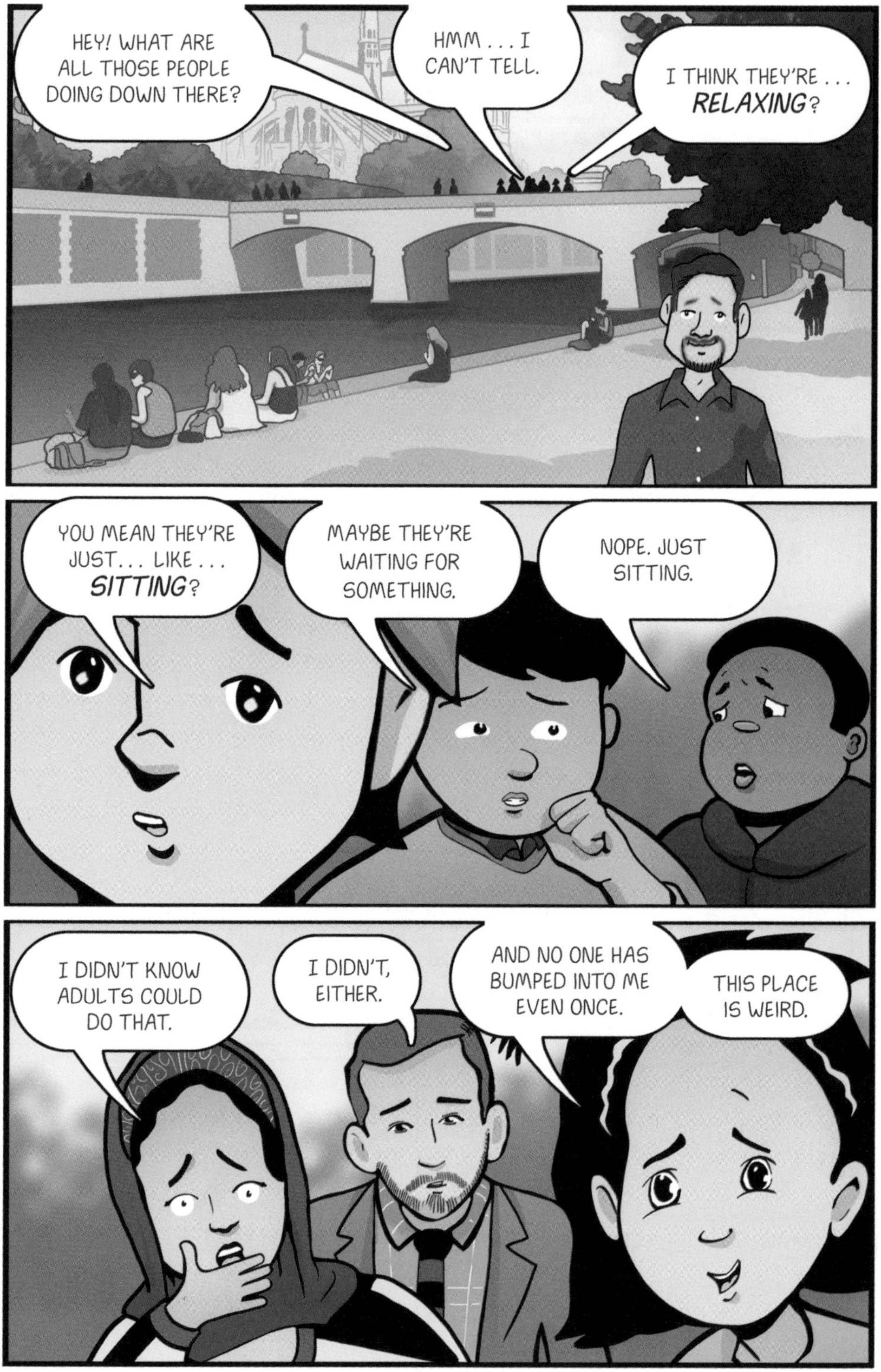
HEY! WHAT ARE ALL THOSE PEOPLE DOING DOWN THERE?
HMM . . . I CAN'T TELL.
I THINK THEY'RE . . . *RELAXING*?
YOU MEAN THEY'RE JUST . . . LIKE . . . *SITTING*?
MAYBE THEY'RE WAITING FOR SOMETHING.
NOPE. JUST SITTING.
I DIDN'T KNOW ADULTS COULD DO THAT.
I DIDN'T, EITHER.
AND NO ONE HAS BUMPED INTO ME EVEN ONCE.
THIS PLACE IS WEIRD.

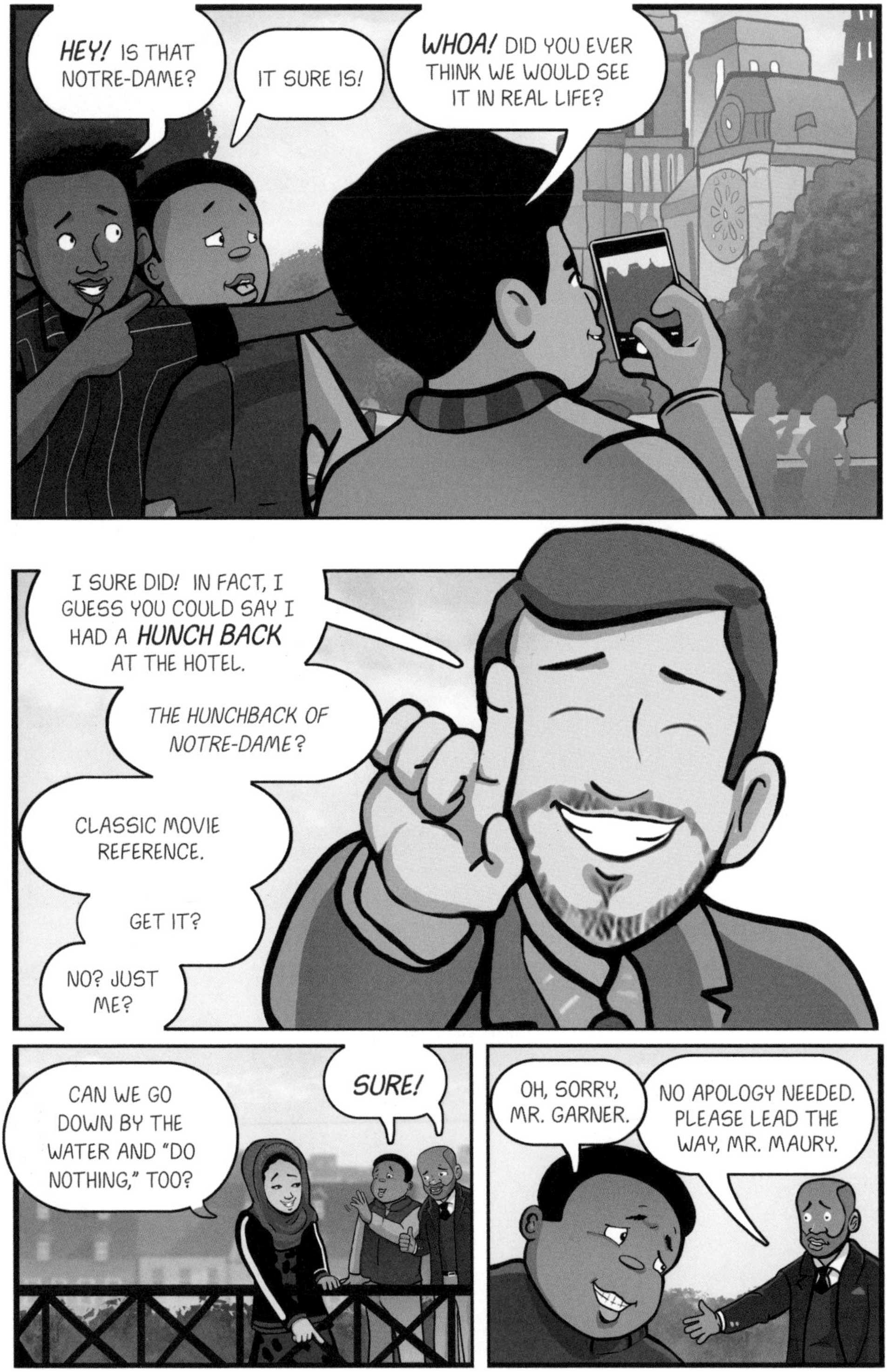
HEY! IS THAT NOTRE-DAME?
IT SURE IS!
WHOA! DID YOU EVER THINK WE WOULD SEE IT IN REAL LIFE?
I SURE DID! IN FACT, I GUESS YOU COULD SAY I HAD A HUNCH BACK AT THE HOTEL.
THE HUNCHBACK OF NOTRE-DAME?
CLASSIC MOVIE REFERENCE.
GET IT?
NO? JUST ME?
CAN WE GO DOWN BY THE WATER AND "DO NOTHING," TOO?
SURE!
OH, SORRY, MR. GARNER.
NO APOLOGY NEEDED. PLEASE LEAD THE WAY, MR. MAURY.

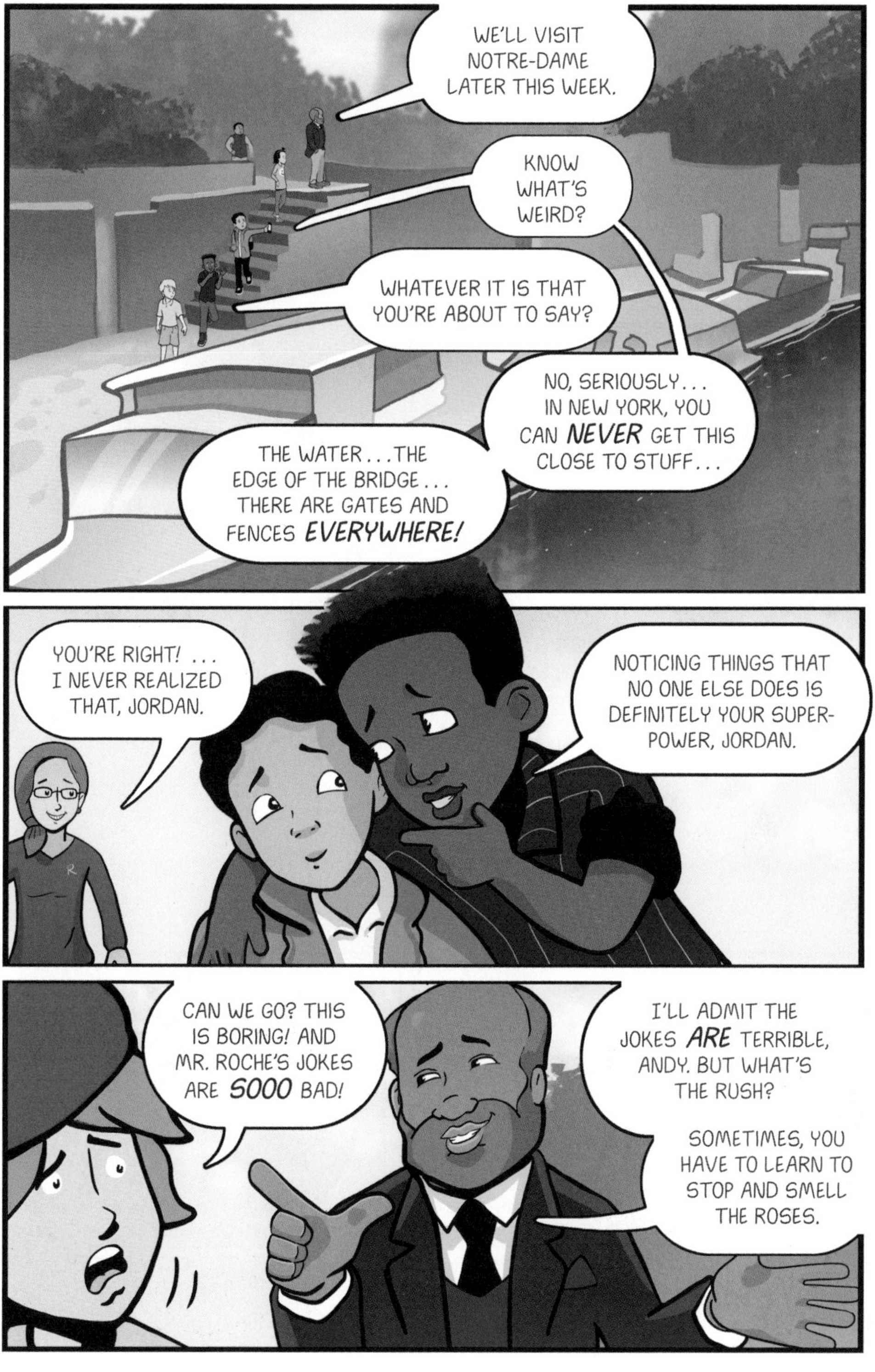
WE'LL VISIT NOTRE-DAME LATER THIS WEEK.
KNOW WHAT'S WEIRD?
WHATEVER IT IS THAT YOU'RE ABOUT TO SAY?
NO, SERIOUSLY... IN NEW YORK, YOU CAN NEVER GET THIS CLOSE TO STUFF...
THE WATER...THE EDGE OF THE BRIDGE... THERE ARE GATES AND FENCES EVERYWHERE!
YOU'RE RIGHT! ... I NEVER REALIZED THAT, JORDAN.
NOTICING THINGS THAT NO ONE ELSE DOES IS DEFINITELY YOUR SUPER-POWER, JORDAN.
CAN WE GO? THIS IS BORING! AND MR. ROCHE'S JOKES ARE SOOO BAD!
I'LL ADMIT THE JOKES ARE TERRIBLE, ANDY. BUT WHAT'S THE RUSH?
SOMETIMES, YOU HAVE TO LEARN TO STOP AND SMELL THE ROSES.

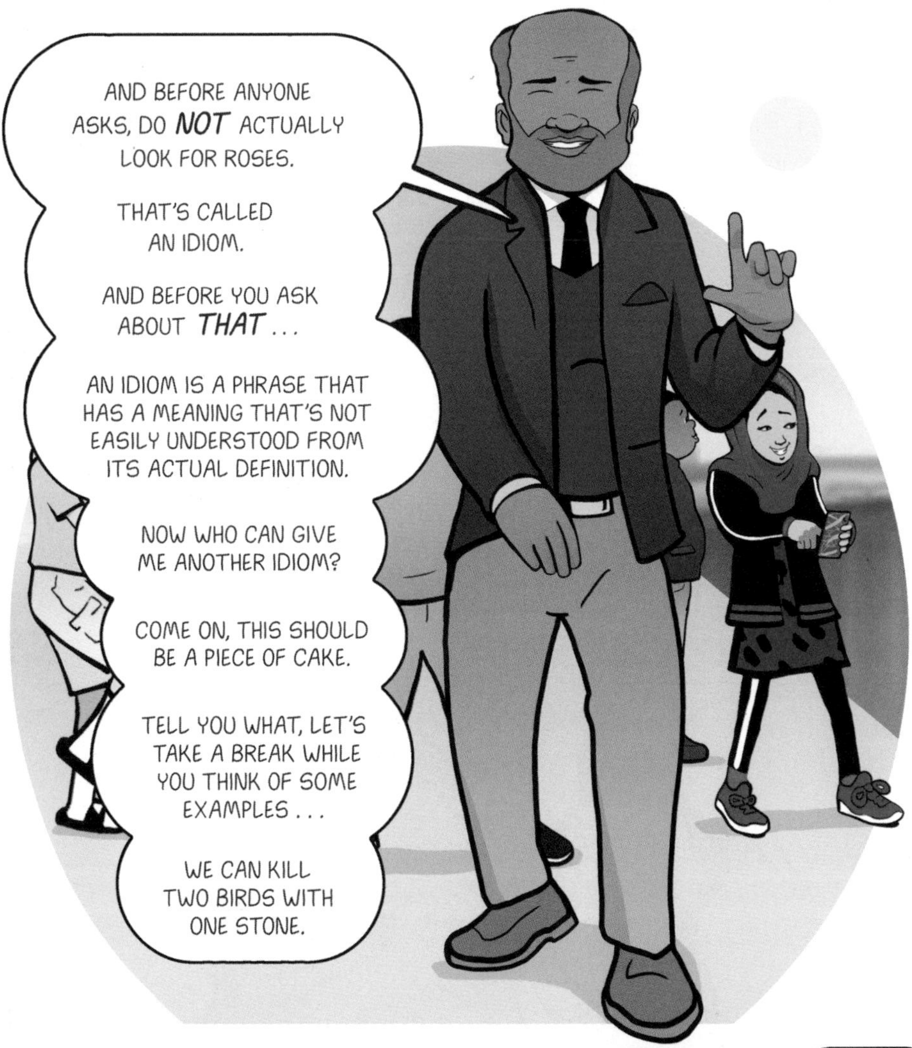
AND BEFORE ANYONE ASKS, DO NOT ACTUALLY LOOK FOR ROSES.
THAT'S CALLED AN IDIOM.
AND BEFORE YOU ASK ABOUT THAT . . .
AN IDIOM IS A PHRASE THAT HAS A MEANING THAT'S NOT EASILY UNDERSTOOD FROM ITS ACTUAL DEFINITION.
NOW WHO CAN GIVE ME ANOTHER IDIOM?
COME ON, THIS SHOULD BE A PIECE OF CAKE.
TELL YOU WHAT, LET'S TAKE A BREAK WHILE YOU THINK OF SOME EXAMPLES . . .
WE CAN KILL TWO BIRDS WITH ONE STONE.

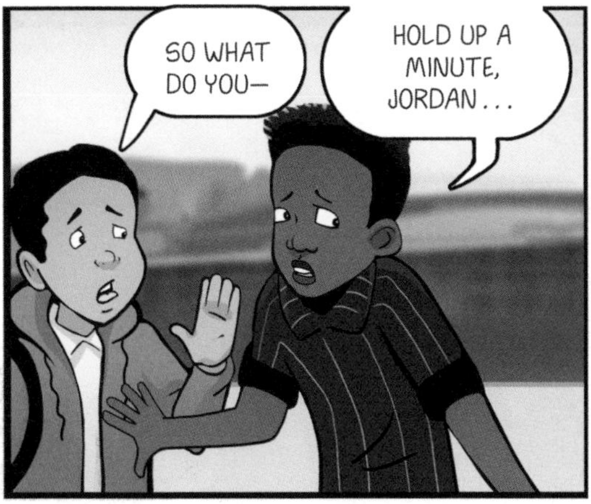
SO WHAT DO YOU—
HOLD UP A MINUTE, JORDAN . . .

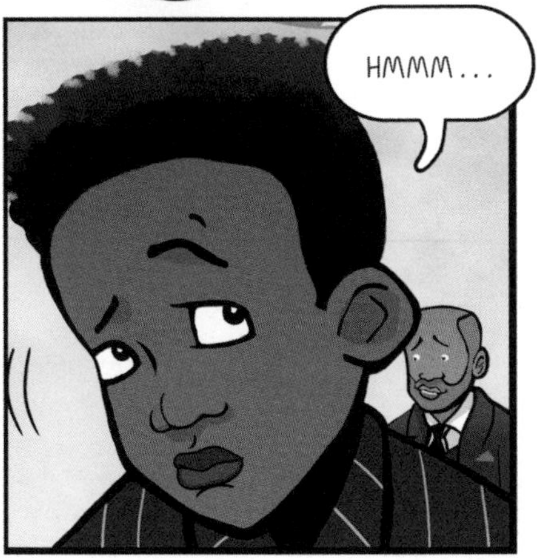
HMMM . . .

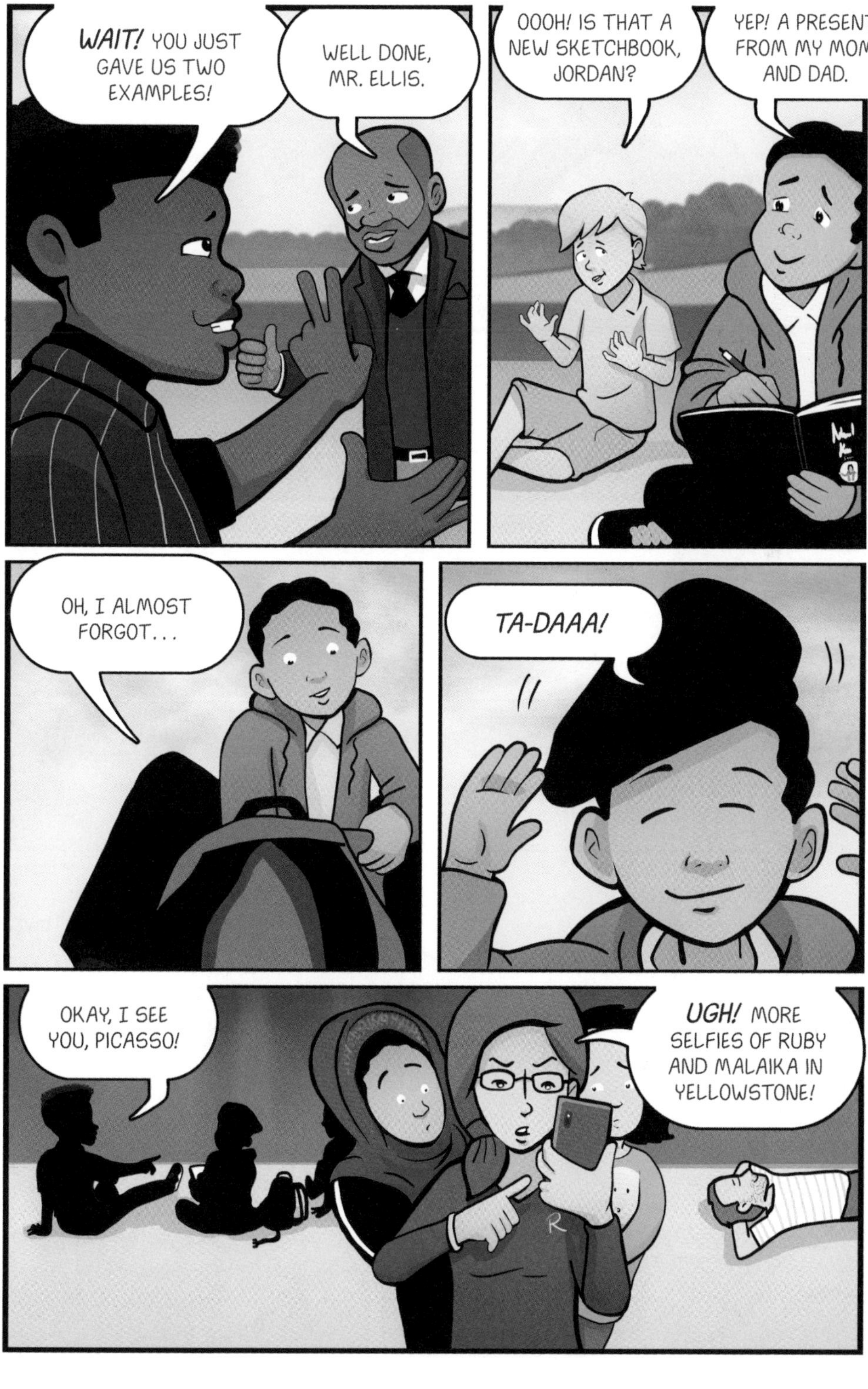
WAIT! YOU JUST GAVE US TWO EXAMPLES!
WELL DONE, MR. ELLIS.
OOOH! IS THAT A NEW SKETCHBOOK, JORDAN?
YEP! A PRESENT FROM MY MOM AND DAD.
OH, I ALMOST FORGOT...
TA-DAAA!
OKAY, I SEE YOU, PICASSO!
UGH! MORE SELFIES OF RUBY AND MALAIKA IN YELLOWSTONE!

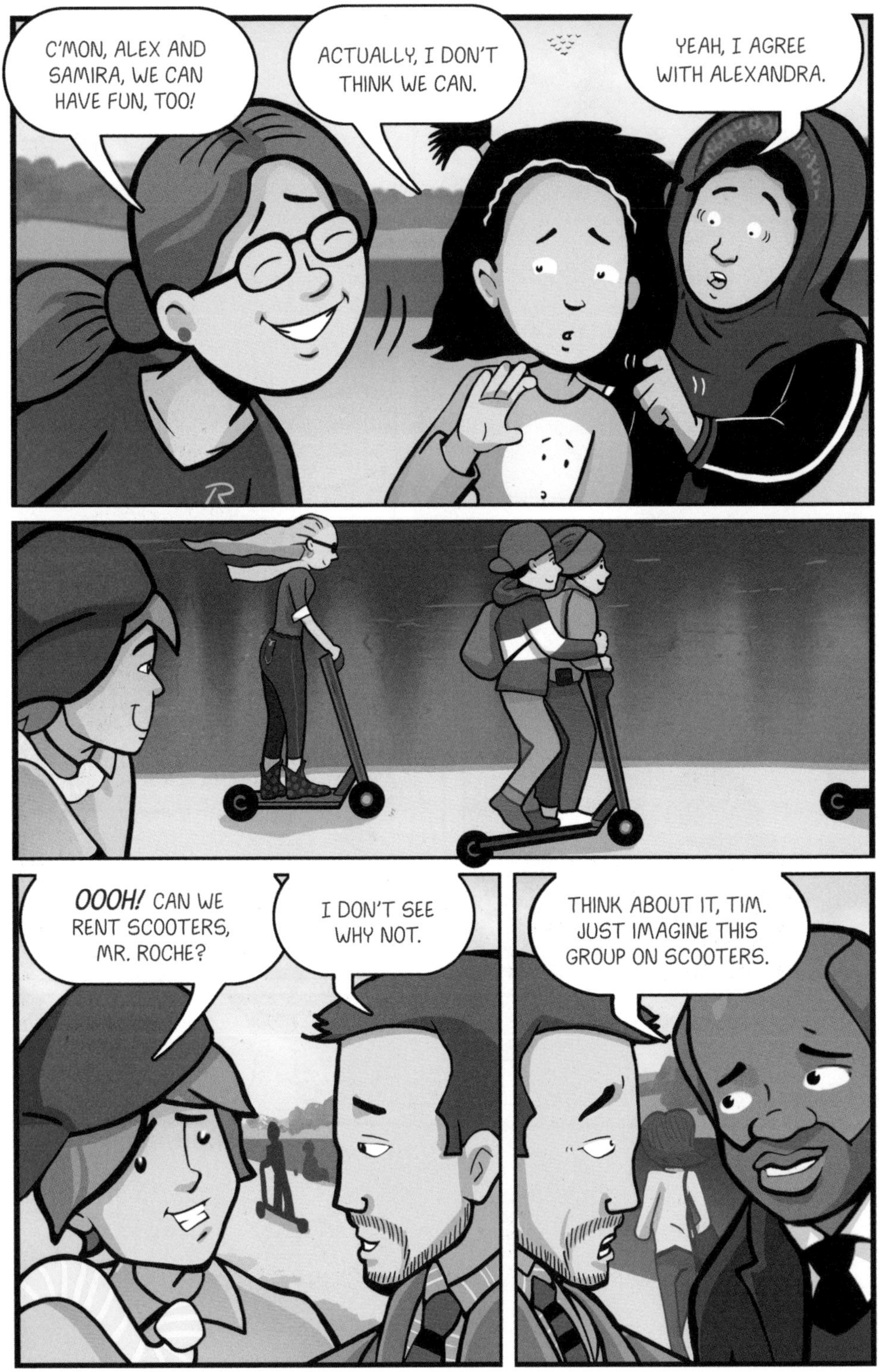
C'MON, ALEX AND SAMIRA, WE CAN HAVE FUN, TOO!
ACTUALLY, I DON'T THINK WE CAN.
YEAH, I AGREE WITH ALEXANDRA.
OOOH! CAN WE RENT SCOOTERS, MR. ROCHE?
I DON'T SEE WHY NOT.
THINK ABOUT IT, TIM. JUST IMAGINE THIS GROUP ON SCOOTERS.

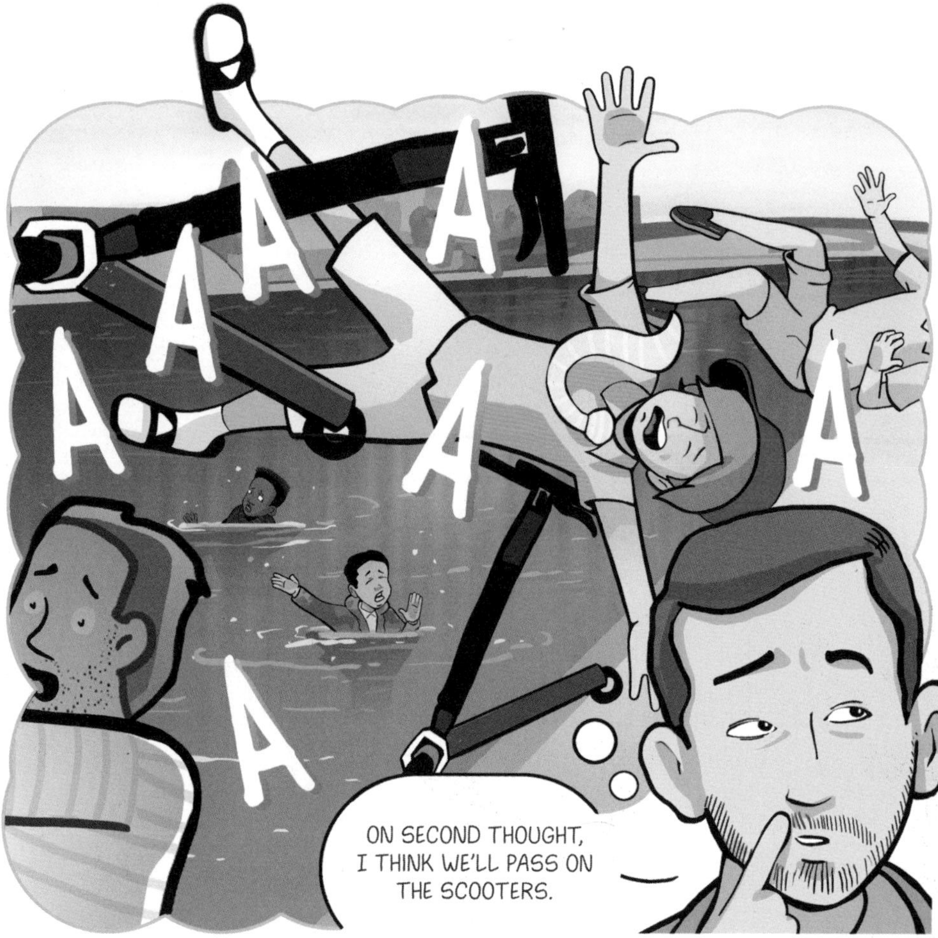

AAAAAAAAA
ON SECOND THOUGHT, I THINK WE'LL PASS ON THE SCOOTERS.

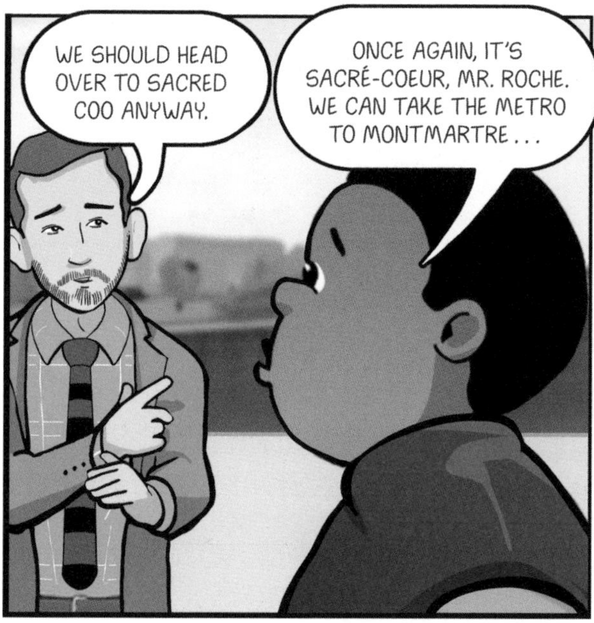

WE SHOULD HEAD OVER TO SACRED COO ANYWAY.
ONCE AGAIN, IT'S SACRÉ-COEUR, MR. ROCHE. WE CAN TAKE THE METRO TO MONTMARTRE . . .

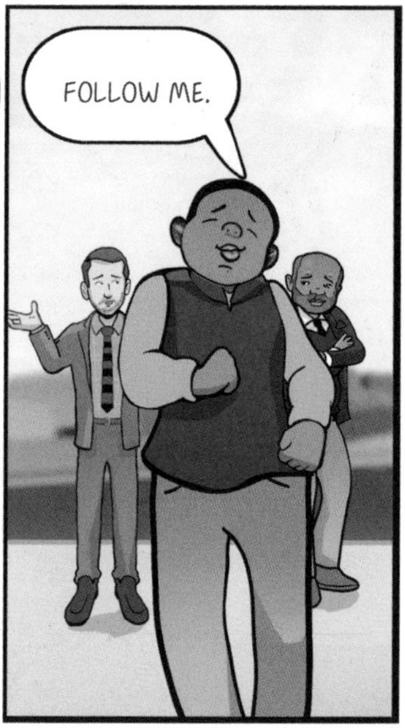

FOLLOW ME.

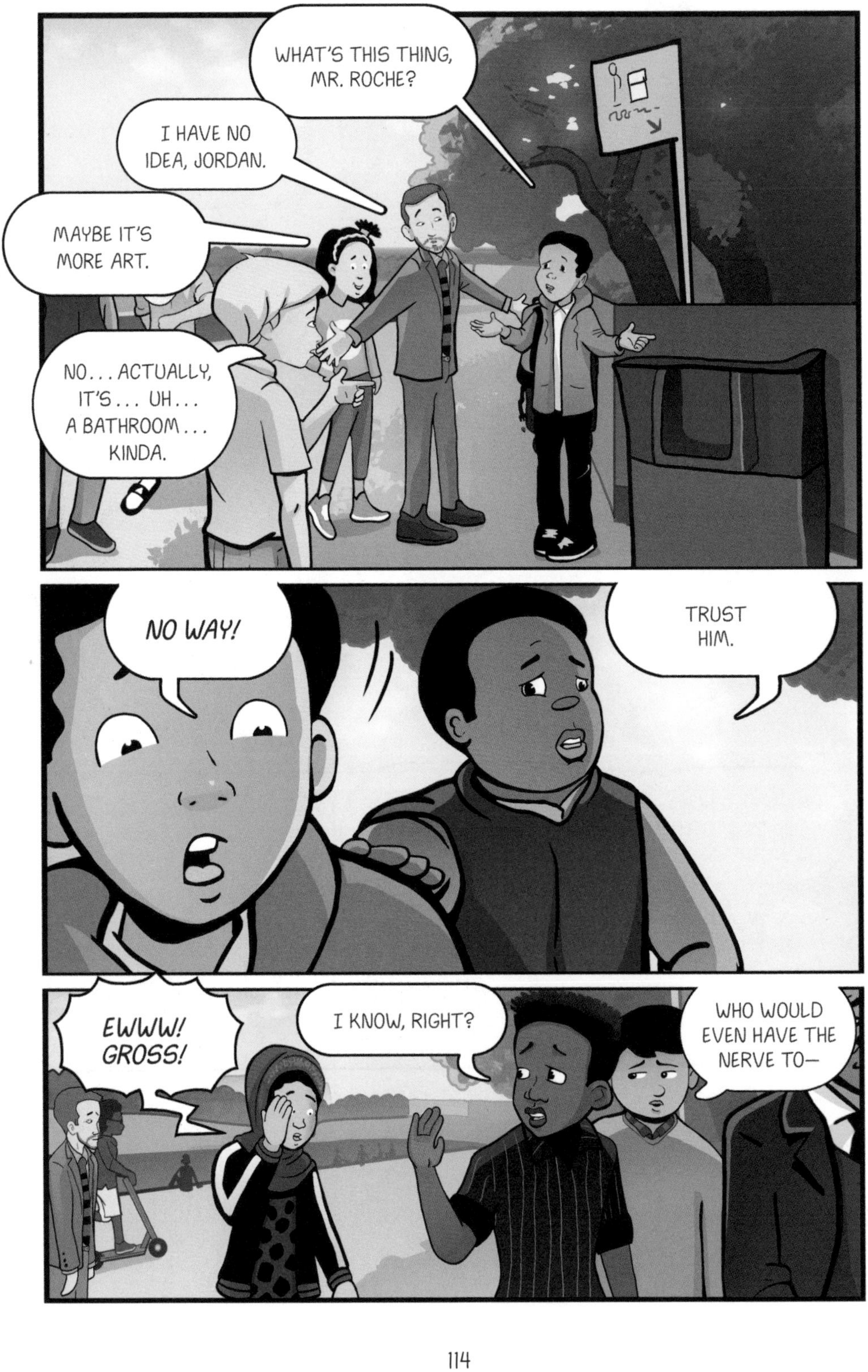

WHAT'S THIS THING, MR. ROCHE?
I HAVE NO IDEA, JORDAN.
MAYBE IT'S MORE ART.
NO... ACTUALLY, IT'S... UH... A BATHROOM... KINDA.
NO WAY!
TRUST HIM.
EWWW! GROSS!
I KNOW, RIGHT?
WHO WOULD EVEN HAVE THE NERVE TO—

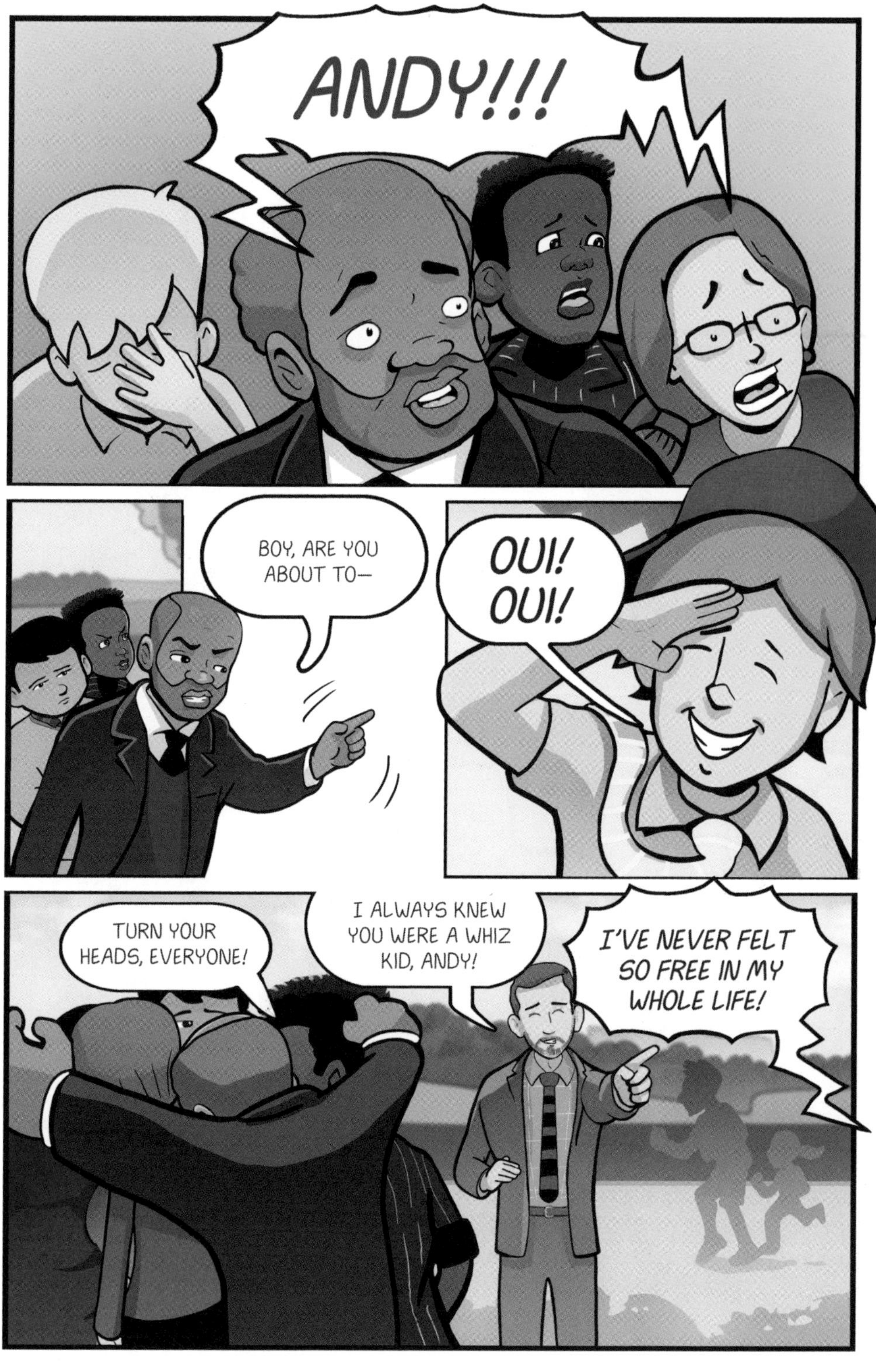
ANDY!!!
BOY, ARE YOU ABOUT TO—
OUI! OUI!
TURN YOUR HEADS, EVERYONE!
I ALWAYS KNEW YOU WERE A WHIZ KID, ANDY!
I'VE NEVER FELT SO FREE IN MY WHOLE LIFE!

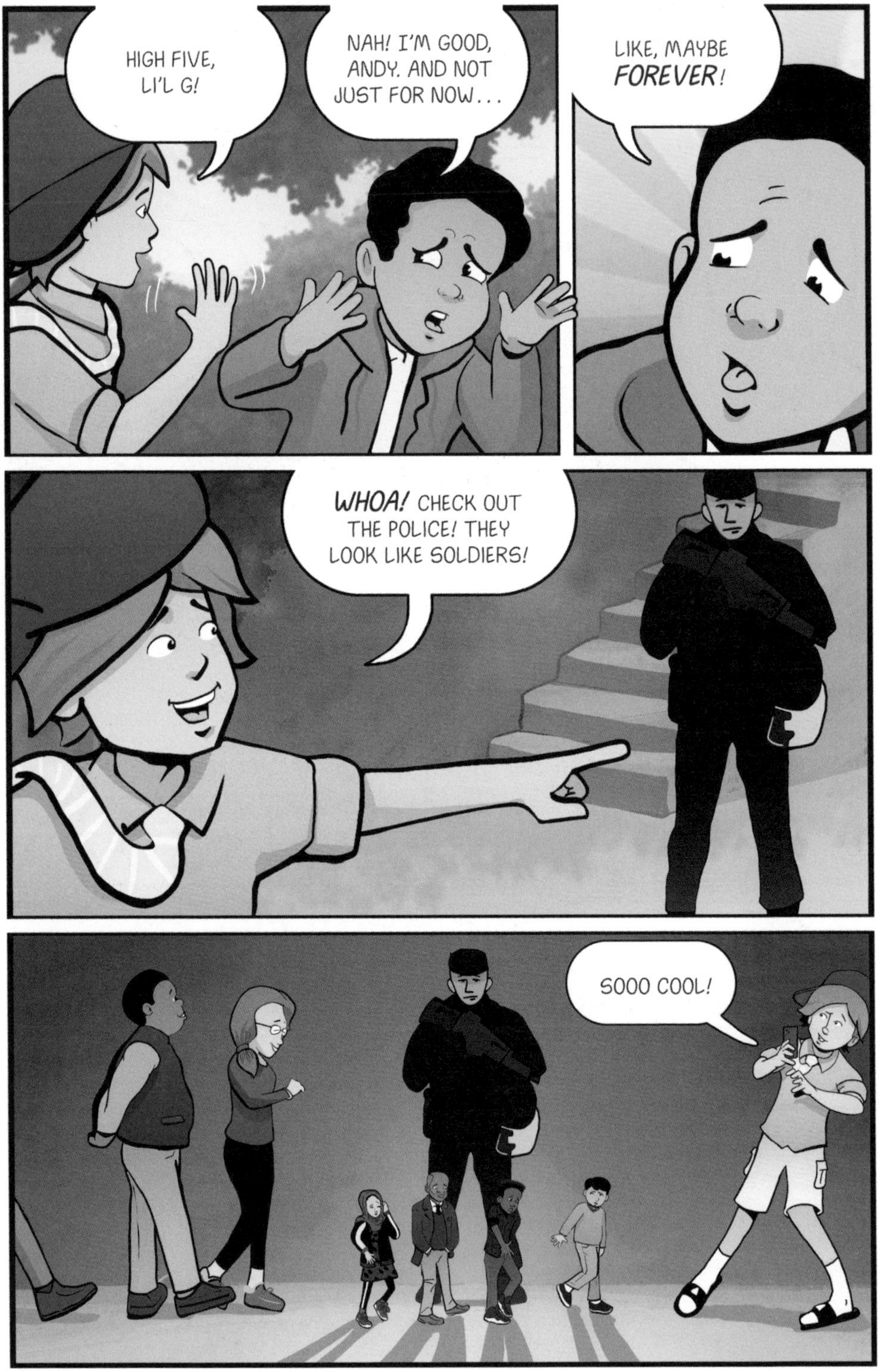
HIGH FIVE, LI'L G!
NAH! I'M GOOD, ANDY. AND NOT JUST FOR NOW . . .
LIKE, MAYBE FOREVER!
WHOA! CHECK OUT THE POLICE! THEY LOOK LIKE SOLDIERS!
SOOO COOL!

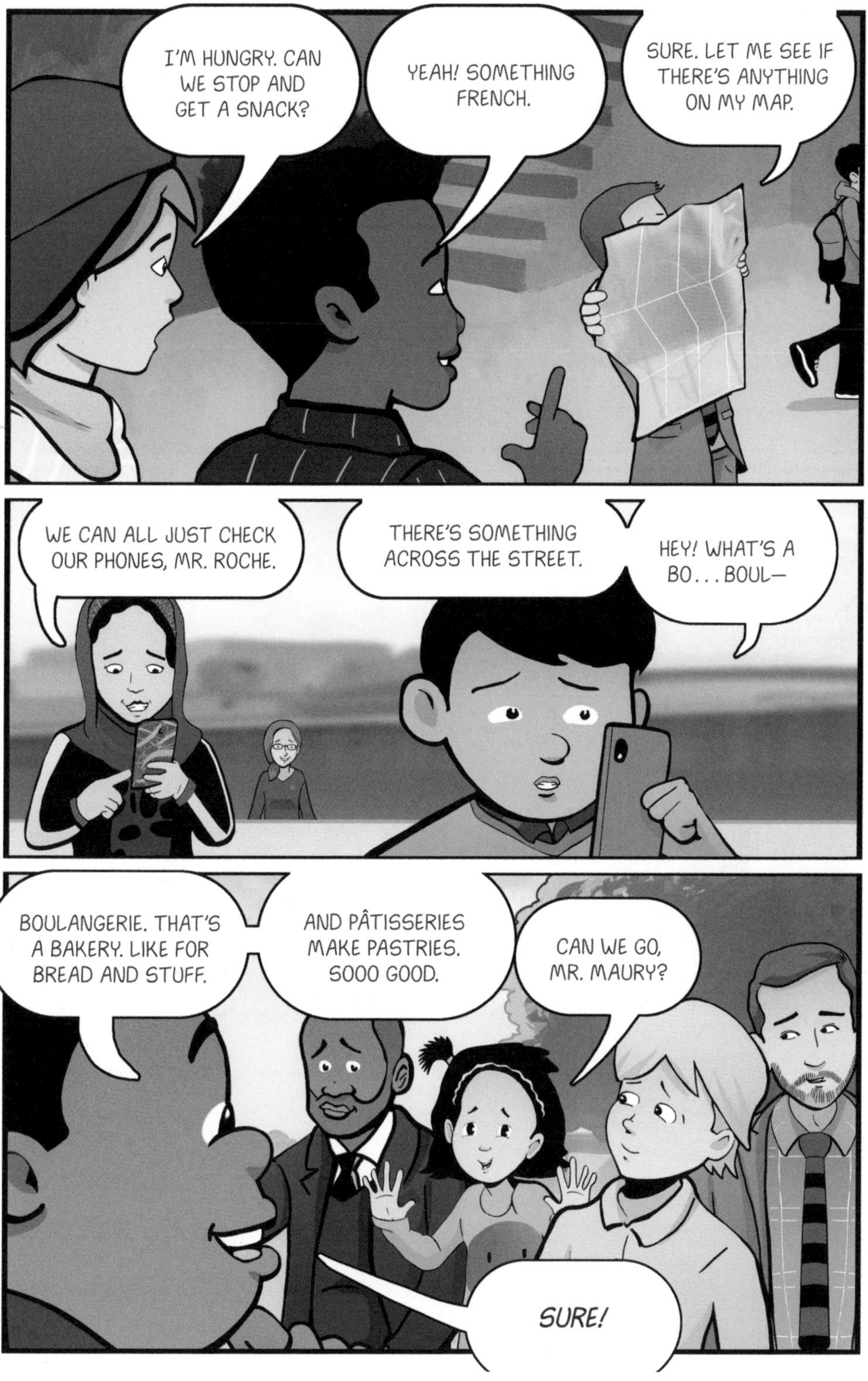
I'M HUNGRY. CAN WE STOP AND GET A SNACK?
YEAH! SOMETHING FRENCH.
SURE. LET ME SEE IF THERE'S ANYTHING ON MY MAP.
WE CAN ALL JUST CHECK OUR PHONES, MR. ROCHE.
THERE'S SOMETHING ACROSS THE STREET.
HEY! WHAT'S A BO . . . BOUL—
BOULANGERIE. THAT'S A BAKERY. LIKE FOR BREAD AND STUFF.
AND PÂTISSERIES MAKE PASTRIES. SOOO GOOD.
CAN WE GO, MR. MAURY?
SURE!

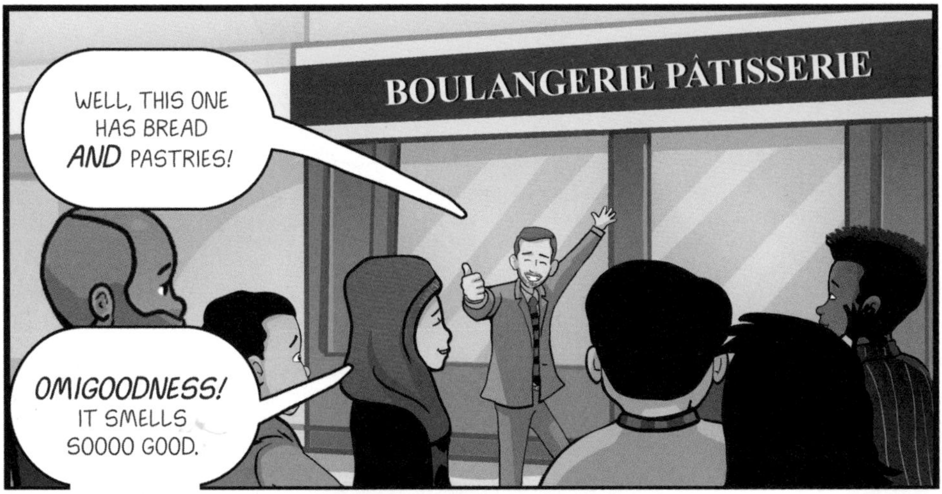
BOULANGERIE PÂTISSERIE
WELL, THIS ONE HAS BREAD **AND** PASTRIES!
OMIGOODNESS! IT SMELLS SOOOO GOOD.

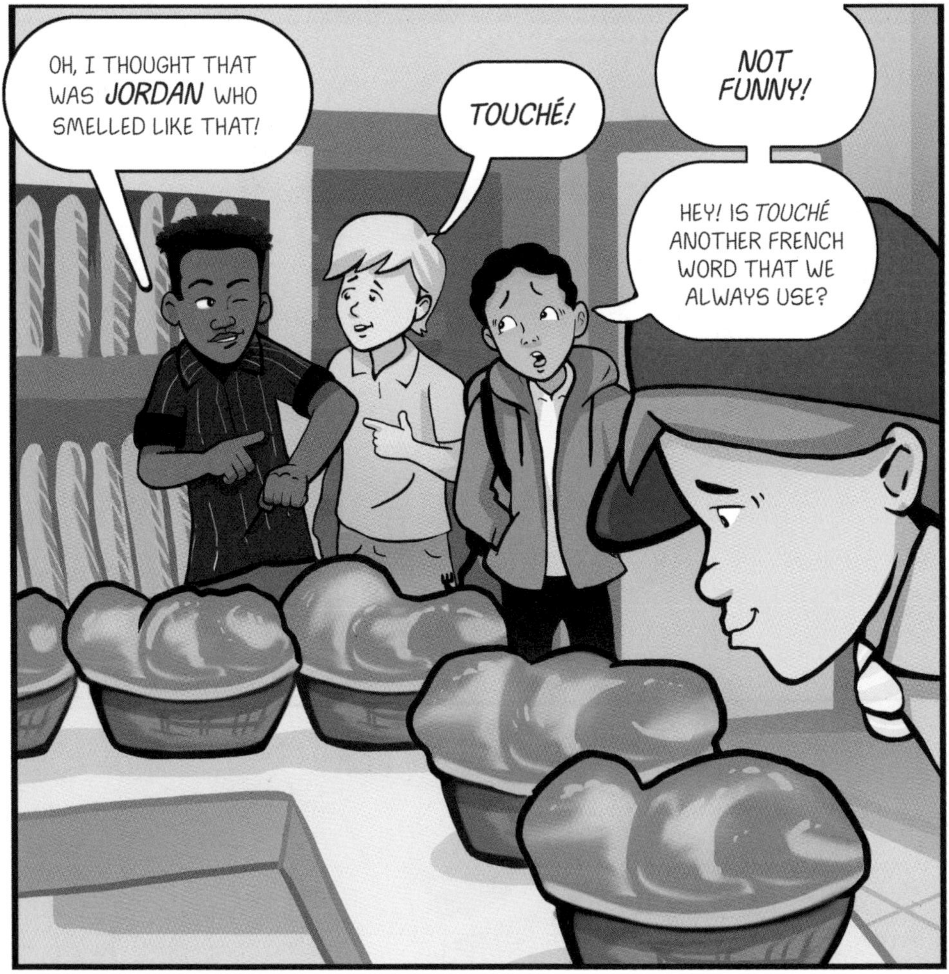
OH, I THOUGHT THAT WAS **JORDAN** WHO SMELLED LIKE THAT!
TOUCHÉ!
NOT FUNNY!
HEY! IS *TOUCHÉ* ANOTHER FRENCH WORD THAT WE ALWAYS USE?

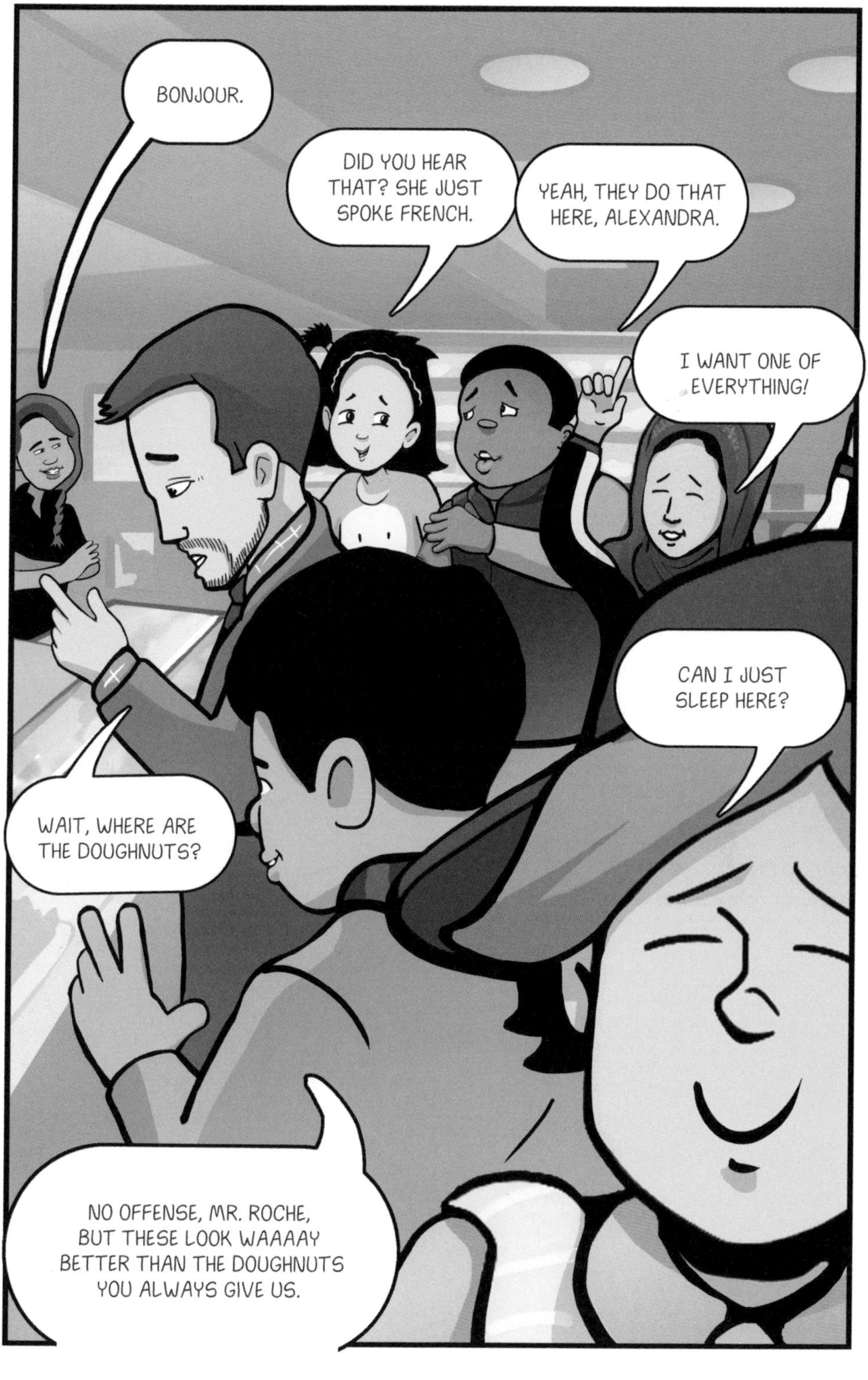
BONJOUR.
DID YOU HEAR THAT? SHE JUST SPOKE FRENCH.
YEAH, THEY DO THAT HERE, ALEXANDRA.
I WANT ONE OF EVERYTHING!
CAN I JUST SLEEP HERE?
WAIT, WHERE ARE THE DOUGHNUTS?
NO OFFENSE, MR. ROCHE, BUT THESE LOOK WAAAAY BETTER THAN THE DOUGHNUTS YOU ALWAYS GIVE US.

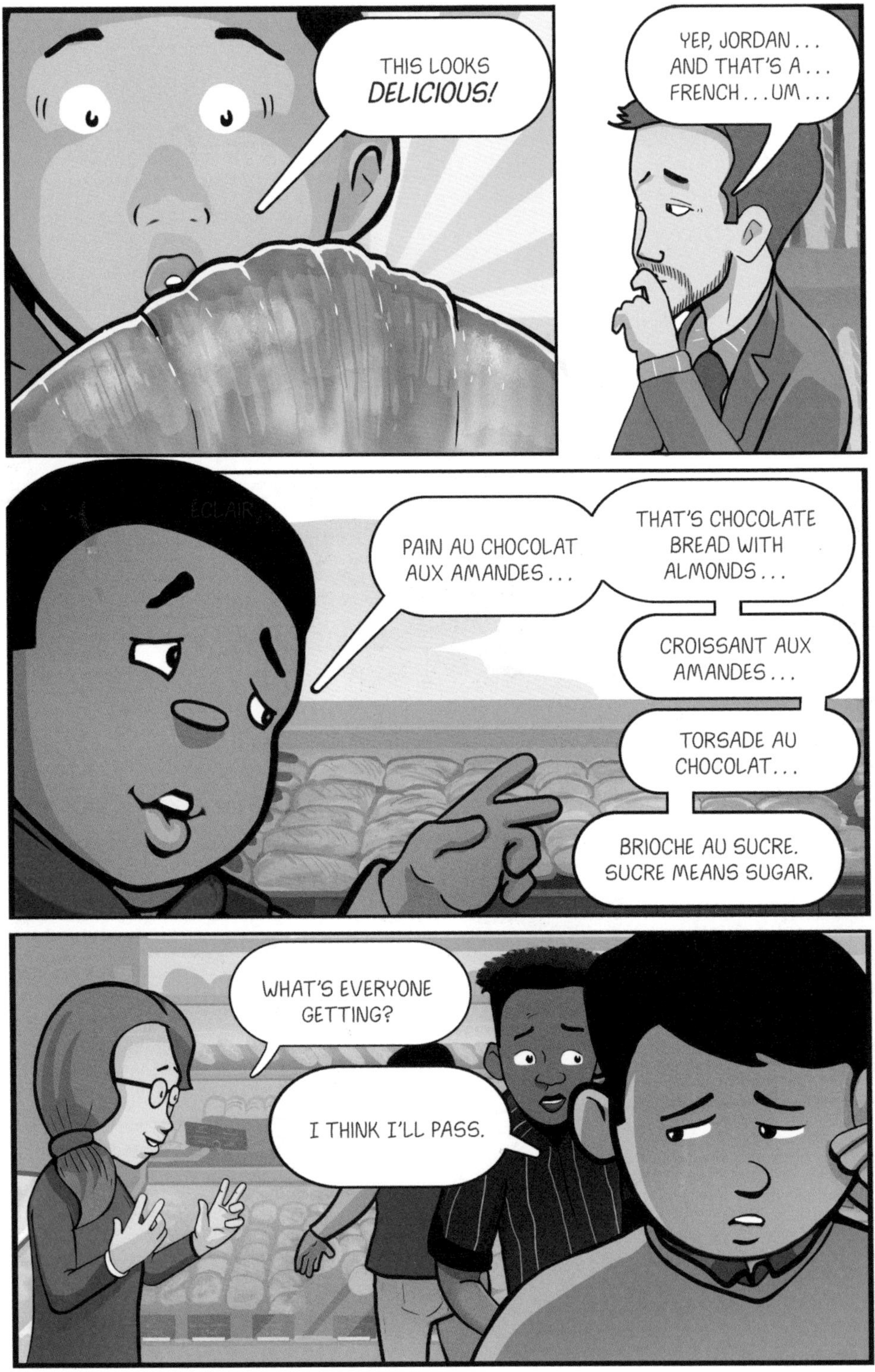
THIS LOOKS *DELICIOUS!*
YEP, JORDAN . . . AND THAT'S A . . . FRENCH . . . UM . . .
ÉCLAIR
PAIN AU CHOCOLAT AUX AMANDES . . .
THAT'S CHOCOLATE BREAD WITH ALMONDS . . .
CROISSANT AUX AMANDES . . .
TORSADE AU CHOCOLAT . . .
BRIOCHE AU SUCRE. SUCRE MEANS SUGAR.
WHAT'S EVERYONE GETTING?
I THINK I'LL PASS.

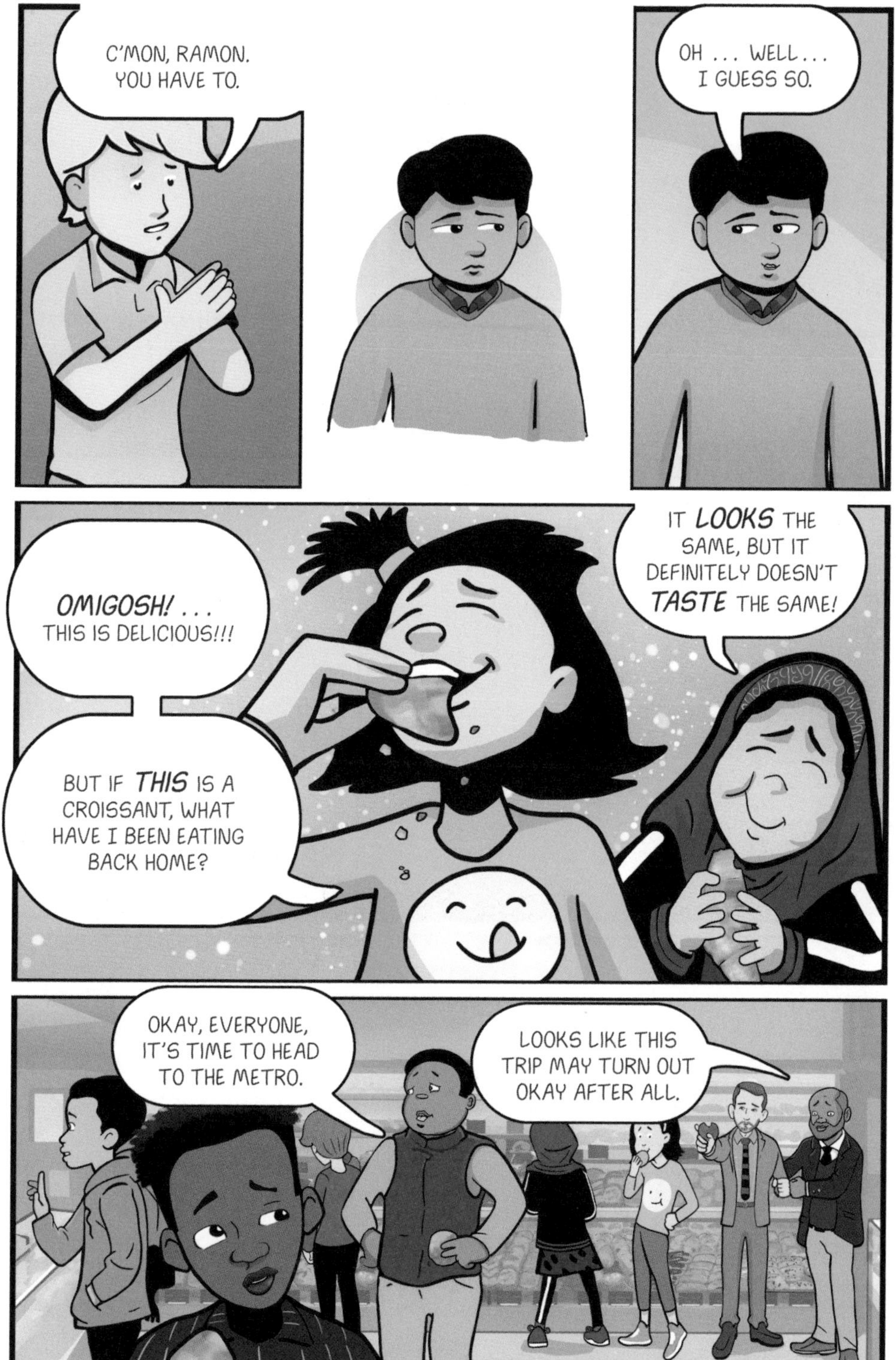
C'MON, RAMON. YOU HAVE TO.
OH . . . WELL . . . I GUESS SO.
OMIGOSH! . . . THIS IS DELICIOUS!!!
BUT IF THIS IS A CROISSANT, WHAT HAVE I BEEN EATING BACK HOME?
IT LOOKS THE SAME, BUT IT DEFINITELY DOESN'T TASTE THE SAME!
OKAY, EVERYONE, IT'S TIME TO HEAD TO THE METRO.
LOOKS LIKE THIS TRIP MAY TURN OUT OKAY AFTER ALL.

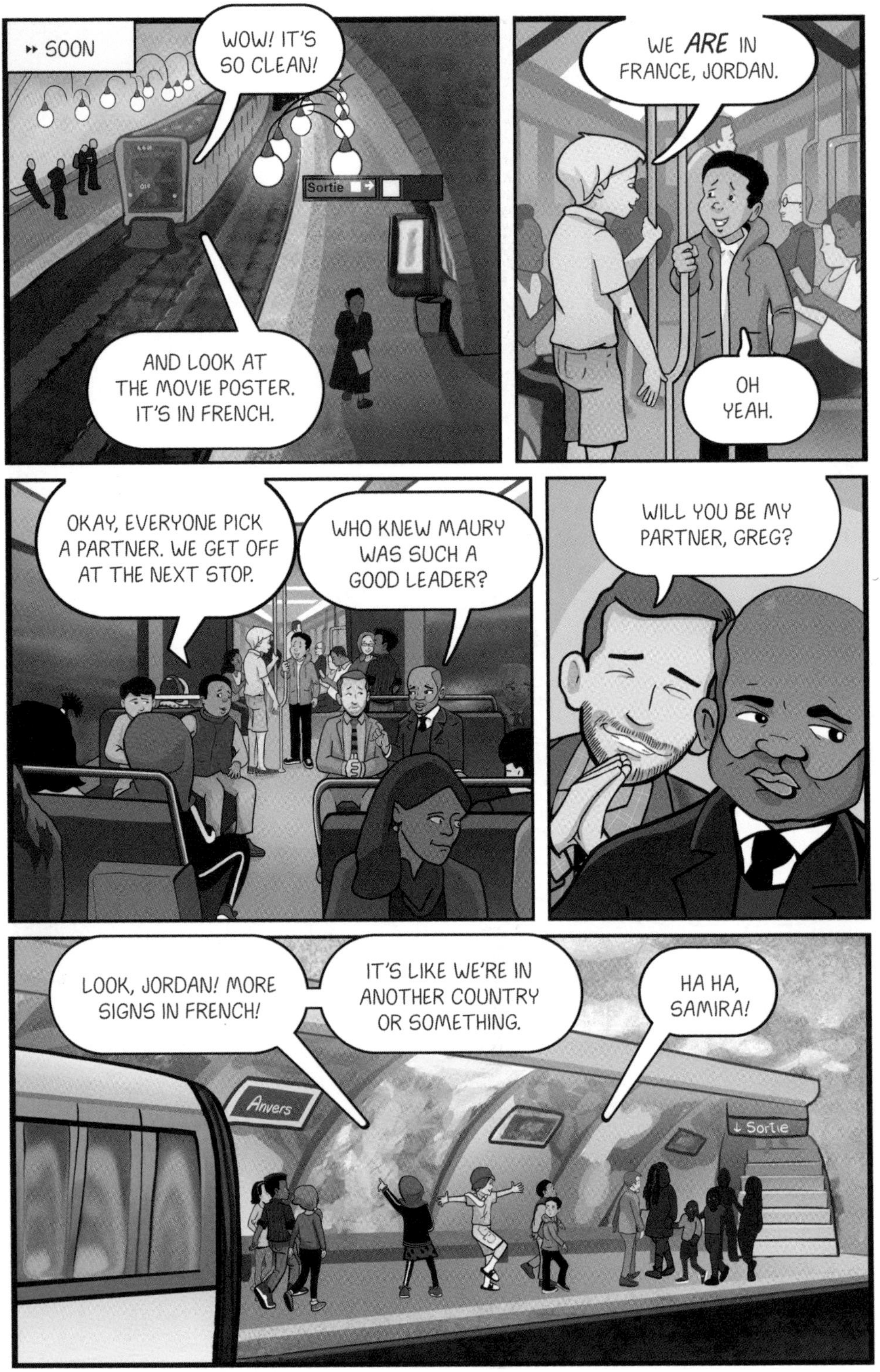
SOON
WOW! IT'S SO CLEAN!
AND LOOK AT THE MOVIE POSTER. IT'S IN FRENCH.
Sortie
WE ARE IN FRANCE, JORDAN.
OH YEAH.
OKAY, EVERYONE PICK A PARTNER. WE GET OFF AT THE NEXT STOP.
WHO KNEW MAURY WAS SUCH A GOOD LEADER?
WILL YOU BE MY PARTNER, GREG?
LOOK, JORDAN! MORE SIGNS IN FRENCH!
IT'S LIKE WE'RE IN ANOTHER COUNTRY OR SOMETHING.
HA HA, SAMIRA!
Anvers
Sortie

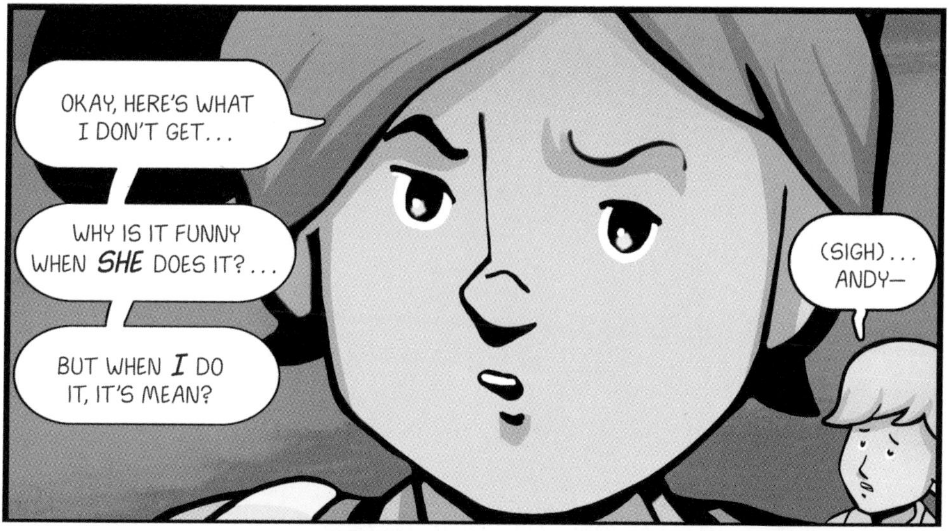
OKAY, HERE'S WHAT I DON'T GET...
WHY IS IT FUNNY WHEN SHE DOES IT?...
BUT WHEN I DO IT, IT'S MEAN?
(SIGH)... ANDY—

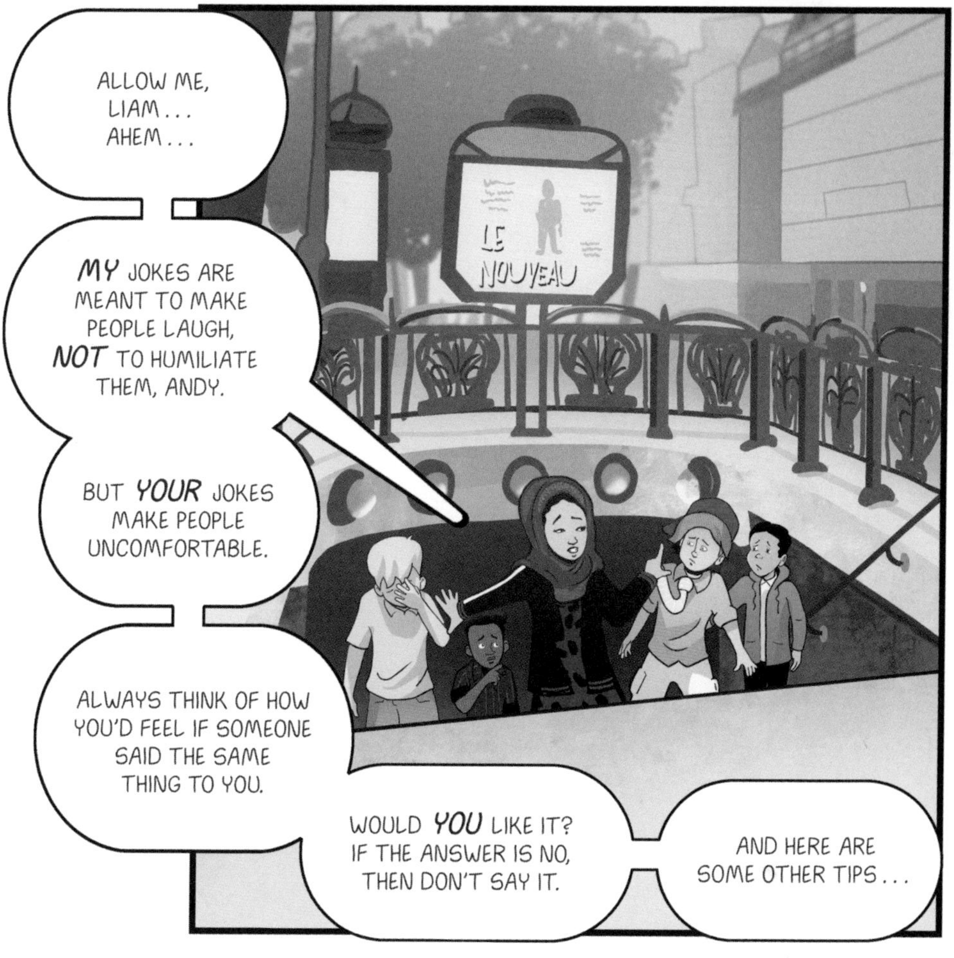
ALLOW ME, LIAM... AHEM...
MY JOKES ARE MEANT TO MAKE PEOPLE LAUGH, NOT TO HUMILIATE THEM, ANDY.
BUT YOUR JOKES MAKE PEOPLE UNCOMFORTABLE.
ALWAYS THINK OF HOW YOU'D FEEL IF SOMEONE SAID THE SAME THING TO YOU.
WOULD YOU LIKE IT? IF THE ANSWER IS NO, THEN DON'T SAY IT.
AND HERE ARE SOME OTHER TIPS...
LE NOUVEAU

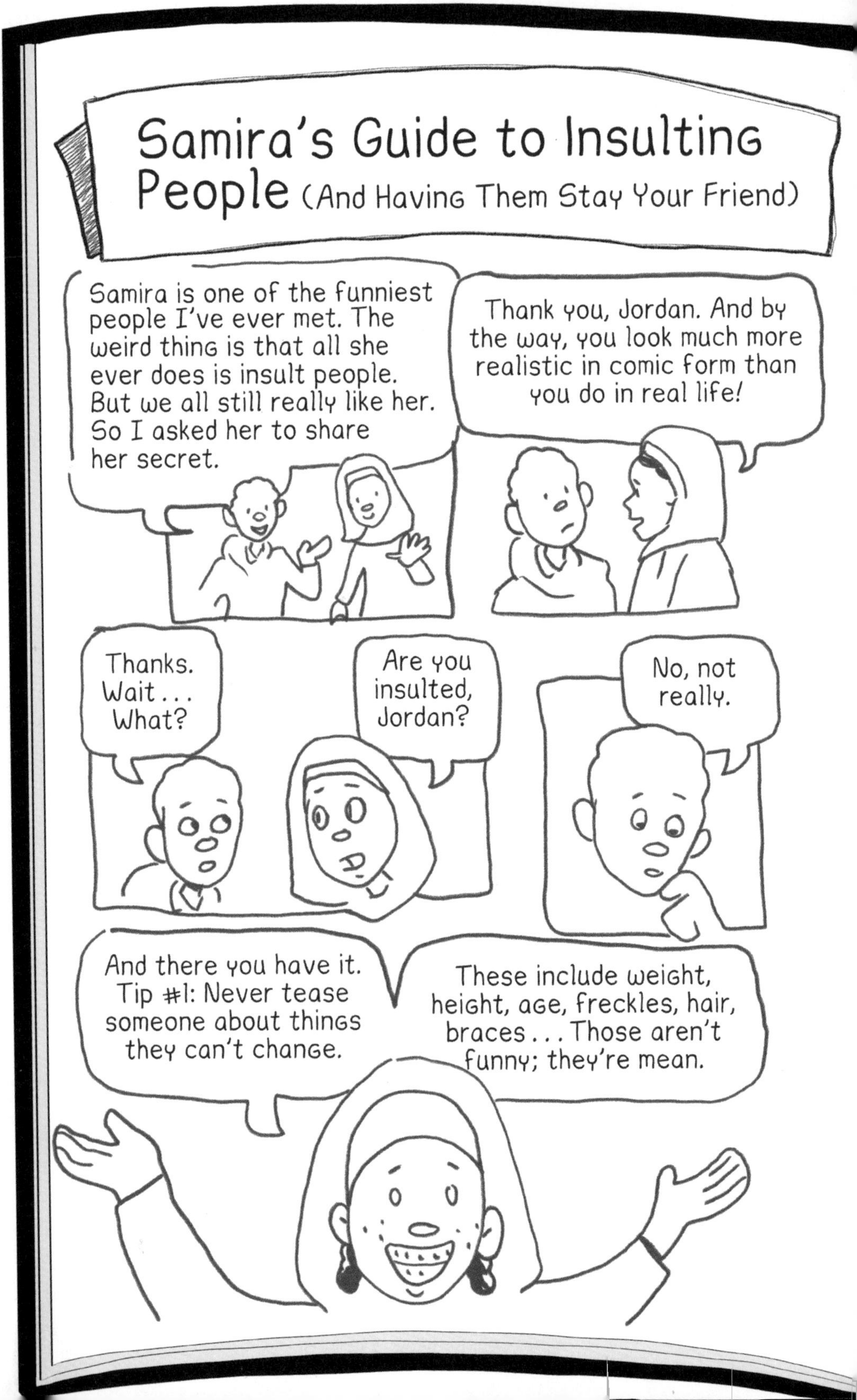
Samira's Guide to Insulting People (And Having Them Stay Your Friend)
Samira is one of the funniest people I've ever met. The weird thing is that all she ever does is insult people. But we all still really like her. So I asked her to share her secret.
Thank you, Jordan. And by the way, you look much more realistic in comic form than you do in real life!
Thanks. Wait . . . What?
Are you insulted, Jordan?
No, not really.
And there you have it. Tip #1: Never tease someone about things they can't change.
These include weight, height, age, freckles, hair, braces . . . Those aren't funny; they're mean.

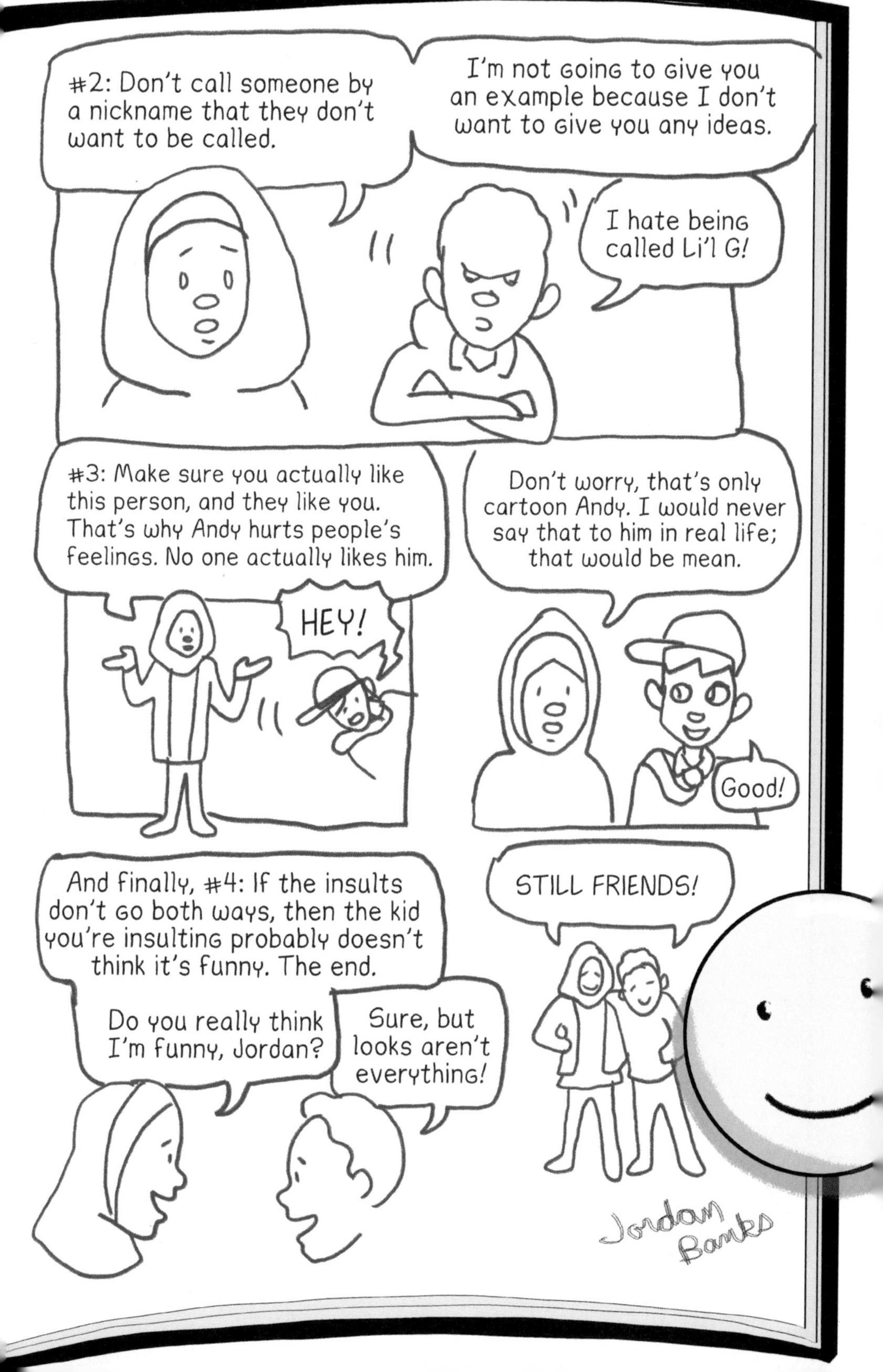
#2: Don't call someone by a nickname that they don't want to be called.
I'm not going to give you an example because I don't want to give you any ideas.
I hate being called Li'l G!
#3: Make sure you actually like this person, and they like you. That's why Andy hurts people's feelings. No one actually likes him.
HEY!
Don't worry, that's only cartoon Andy. I would never say that to him in real life; that would be mean.
Good!
And finally, #4: If the insults don't go both ways, then the kid you're insulting probably doesn't think it's funny. The end.
Do you really think I'm funny, Jordan?
Sure, but looks aren't everything!
STILL FRIENDS!
Jordan Banks

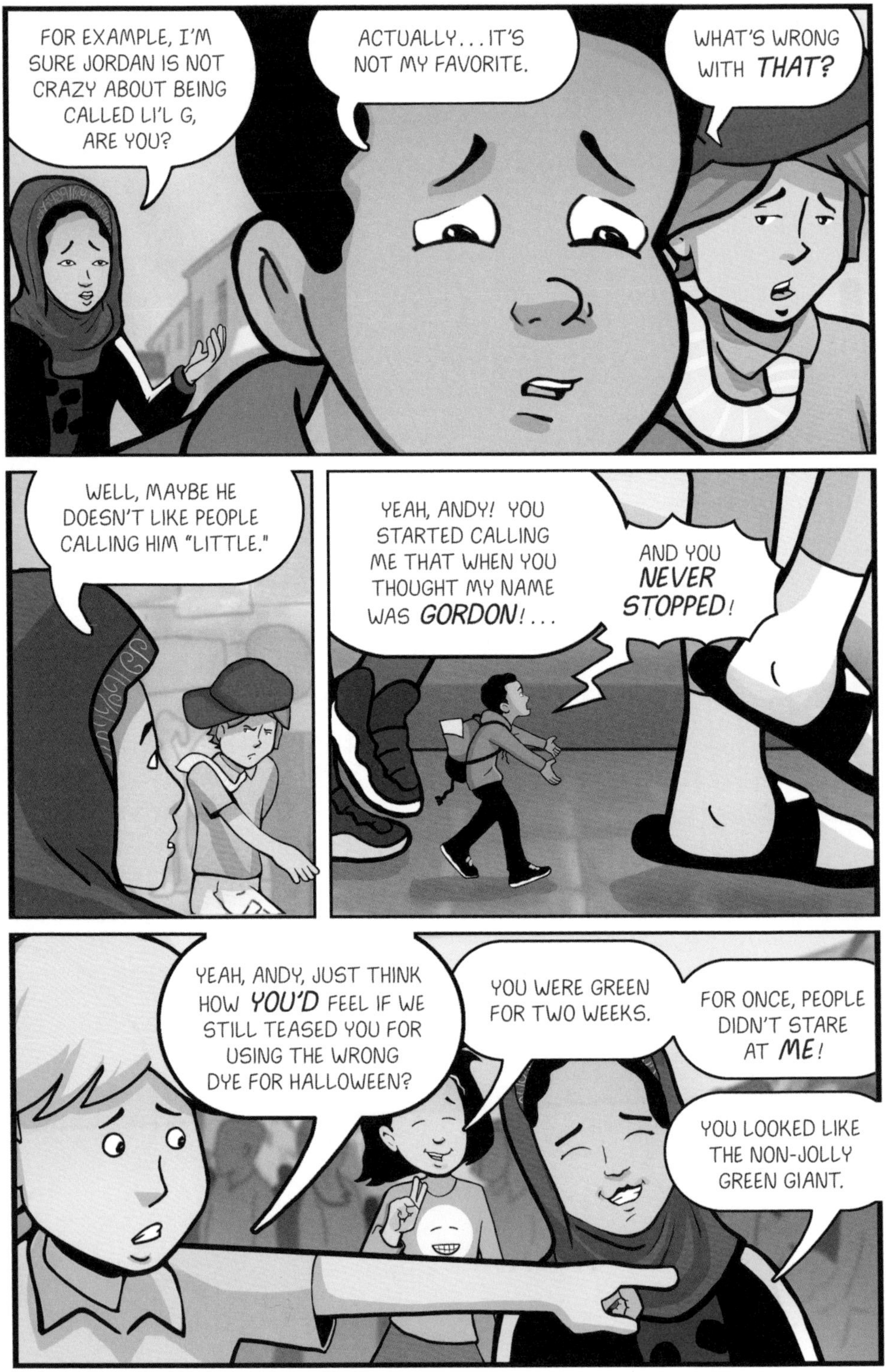
FOR EXAMPLE, I'M SURE JORDAN IS NOT CRAZY ABOUT BEING CALLED LI'L G, ARE YOU?
ACTUALLY... IT'S NOT MY FAVORITE.
WHAT'S WRONG WITH THAT?
WELL, MAYBE HE DOESN'T LIKE PEOPLE CALLING HIM "LITTLE."
YEAH, ANDY! YOU STARTED CALLING ME THAT WHEN YOU THOUGHT MY NAME WAS GORDON!...
AND YOU NEVER STOPPED!
YEAH, ANDY, JUST THINK HOW YOU'D FEEL IF WE STILL TEASED YOU FOR USING THE WRONG DYE FOR HALLOWEEN?
YOU WERE GREEN FOR TWO WEEKS.
FOR ONCE, PEOPLE DIDN'T STARE AT ME!
YOU LOOKED LIKE THE NON-JOLLY GREEN GIANT.

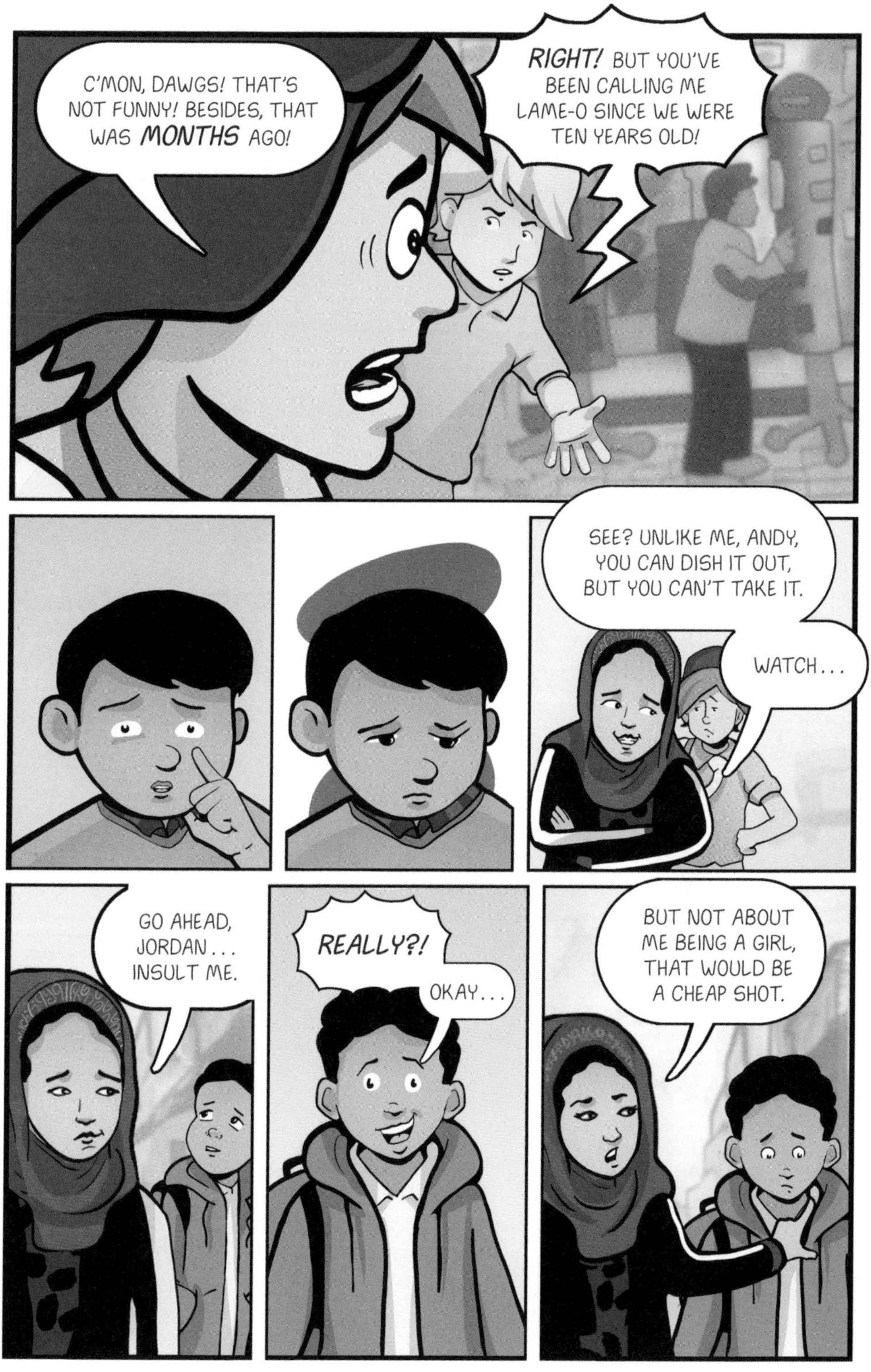
C'MON, DAWGS! THAT'S NOT FUNNY! BESIDES, THAT WAS MONTHS AGO!
RIGHT! BUT YOU'VE BEEN CALLING ME LAME-O SINCE WE WERE TEN YEARS OLD!
SEE? UNLIKE ME, ANDY, YOU CAN DISH IT OUT, BUT YOU CAN'T TAKE IT.
WATCH...
GO AHEAD, JORDAN... INSULT ME.
REALLY?!
OKAY...
BUT NOT ABOUT ME BEING A GIRL, THAT WOULD BE A CHEAP SHOT.

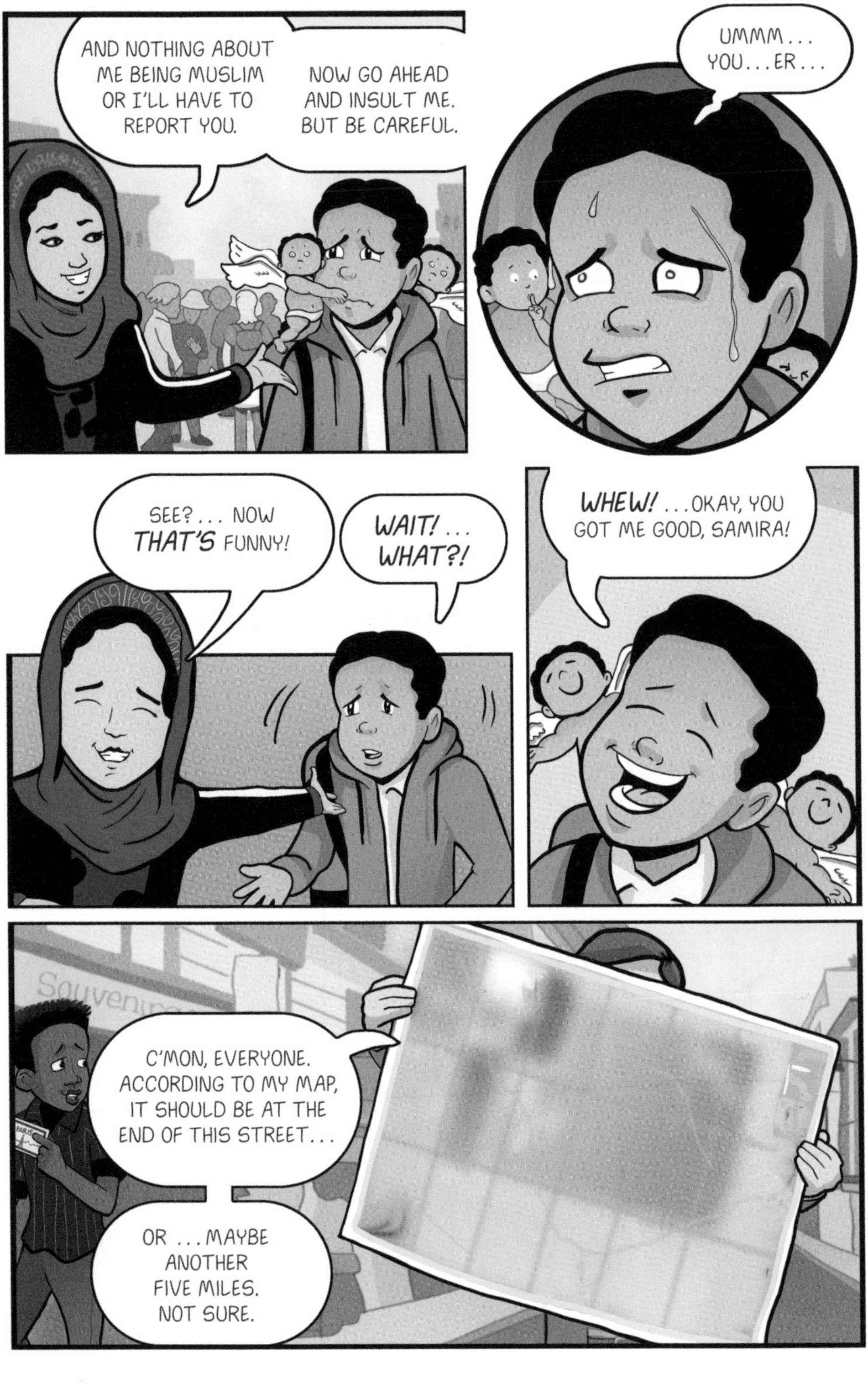
AND NOTHING ABOUT ME BEING MUSLIM OR I'LL HAVE TO REPORT YOU.
NOW GO AHEAD AND INSULT ME. BUT BE CAREFUL.
UMMM... YOU...ER...
SEE?... NOW THAT'S FUNNY!
WAIT!... WHAT?!
WHEW! ...OKAY, YOU GOT ME GOOD, SAMIRA!
Souvenirs
C'MON, EVERYONE. ACCORDING TO MY MAP, IT SHOULD BE AT THE END OF THIS STREET...
OR ...MAYBE ANOTHER FIVE MILES. NOT SURE.

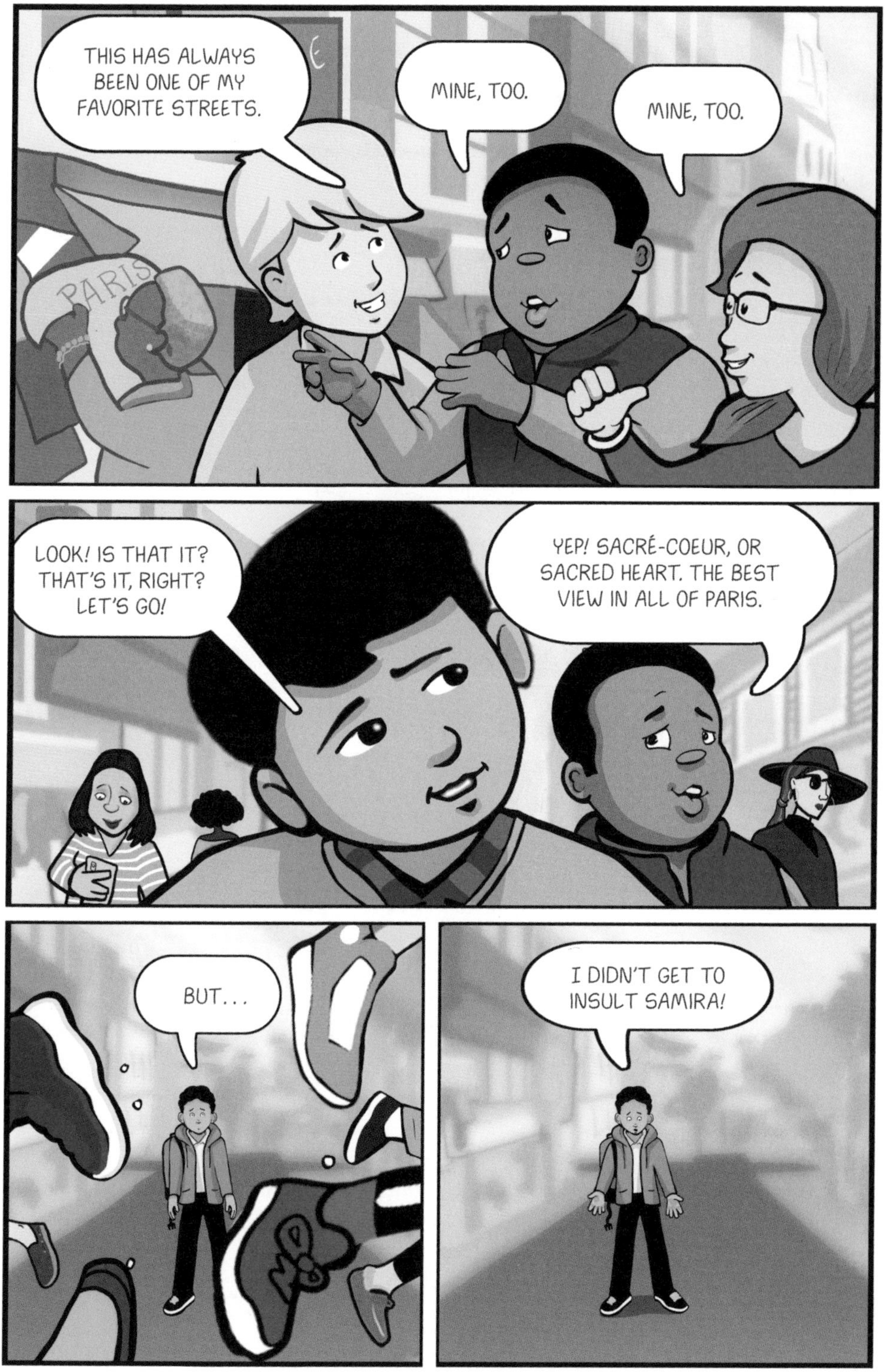
THIS HAS ALWAYS BEEN ONE OF MY FAVORITE STREETS.
MINE, TOO.
MINE, TOO.
PARIS
LOOK! IS THAT IT? THAT'S IT, RIGHT? LET'S GO!
YEP! SACRÉ-COEUR, OR SACRED HEART. THE BEST VIEW IN ALL OF PARIS.
BUT...
I DIDN'T GET TO INSULT SAMIRA!

 **6**

Goooooooals!!!

Okay, I know some kids complain that they don't have an Xbox. And others complain that they don't have the newest sneakers (or tennis shoes, depending on where you live). But the one thing that every kid SHOULD have is a dream.

And not the kind of dream you have in your sleep that doesn't make any sense.

Me being chased by giant stinky socks... AGAIN!

I mean a goal in life. And that seems to be one of the biggest differences between kids from school and my friends from around my block.

Alexandra

I want to be a child psychologist so I can help kids.

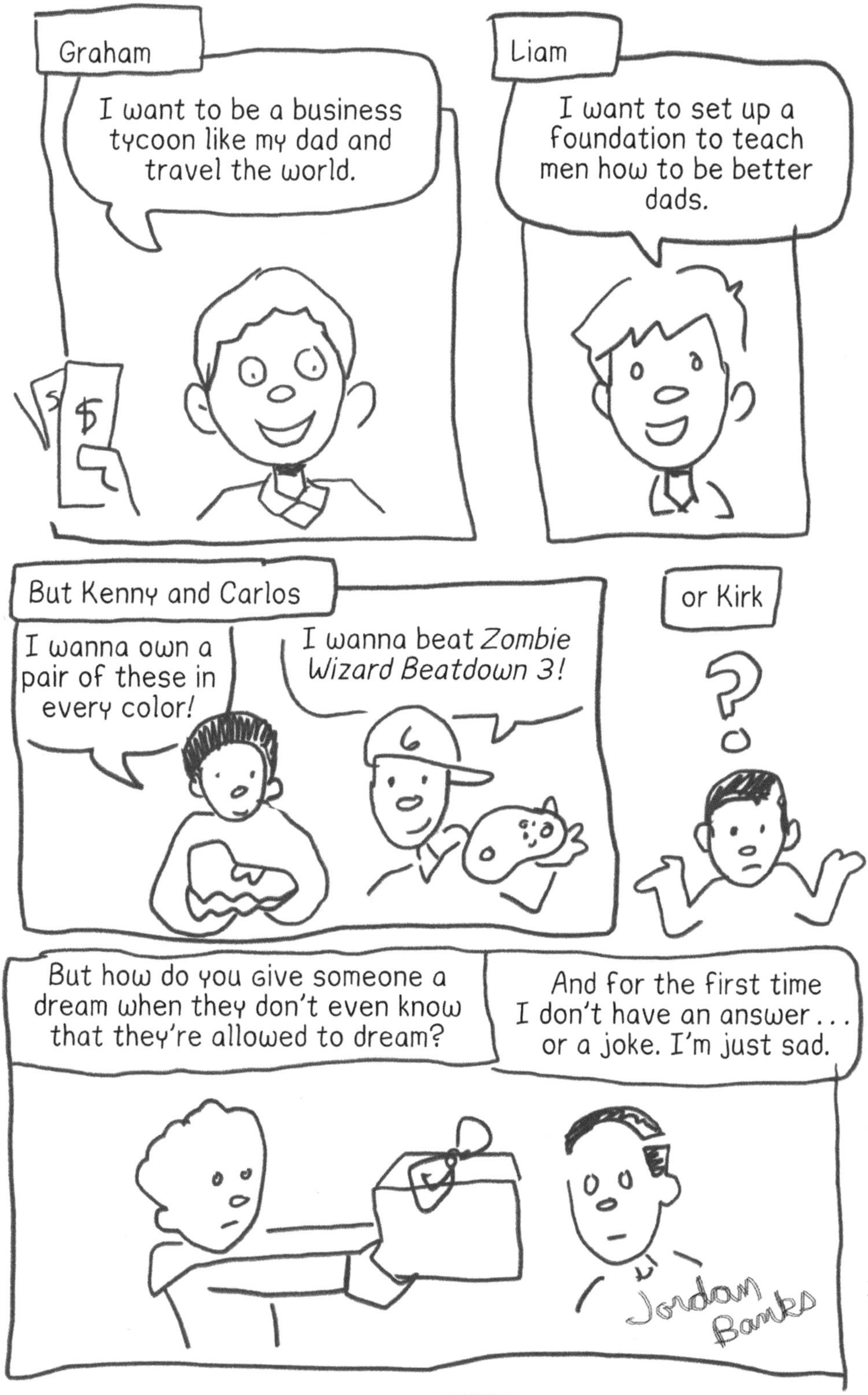
Graham
I want to be a business tycoon like my dad and travel the world.
Liam
I want to set up a foundation to teach men how to be better dads.
But Kenny and Carlos
I wanna own a pair of these in every color!
I wanna beat *Zombie Wizard Beatdown 3*!
or Kirk
?
But how do you give someone a dream when they don't even know that they're allowed to dream?
And for the first time I don't have an answer . . . or a joke. I'm just sad.
Jordan Banks

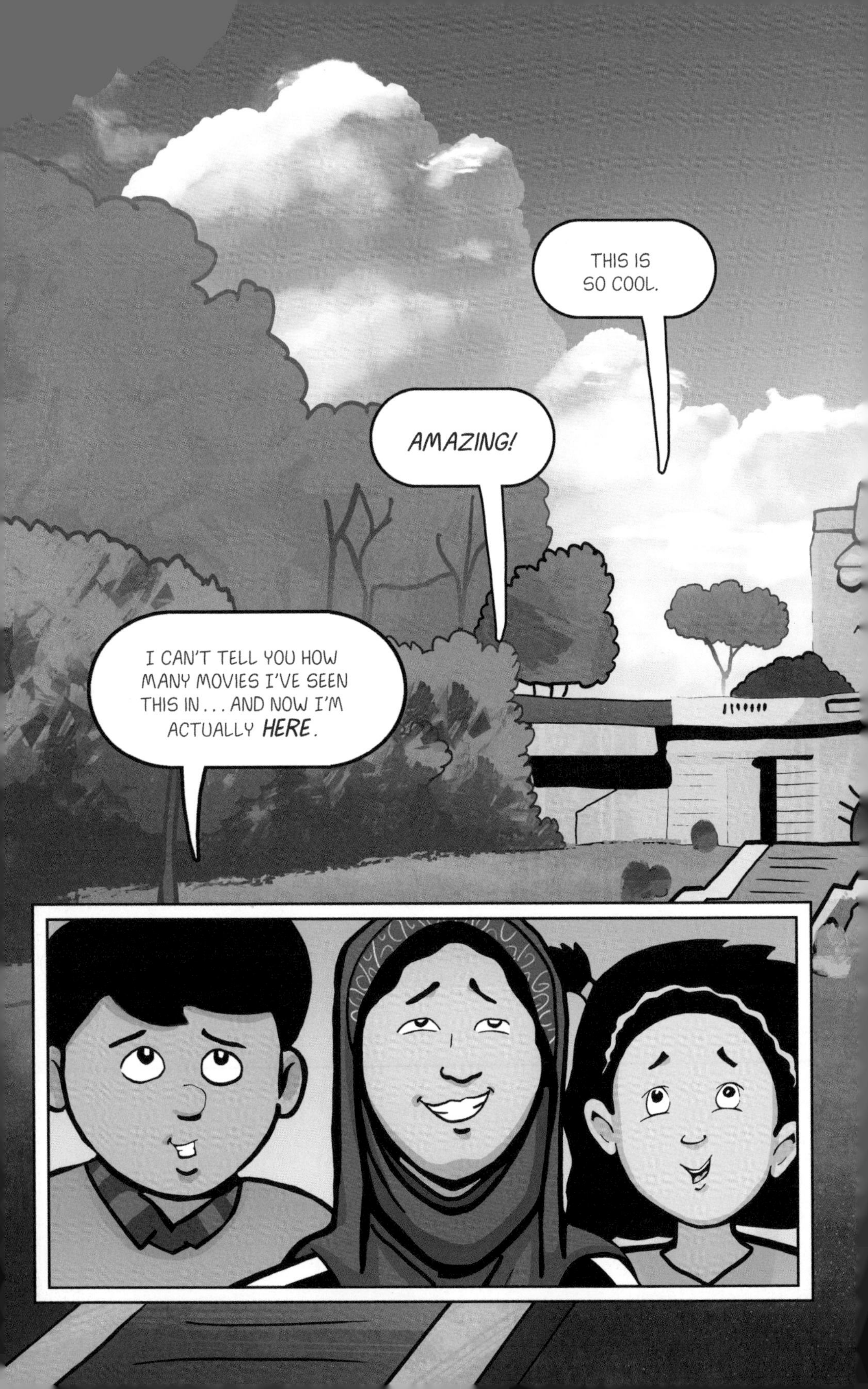
THIS IS SO COOL.
AMAZING!
I CAN'T TELL YOU HOW MANY MOVIES I'VE SEEN THIS IN . . . AND NOW I'M ACTUALLY HERE.

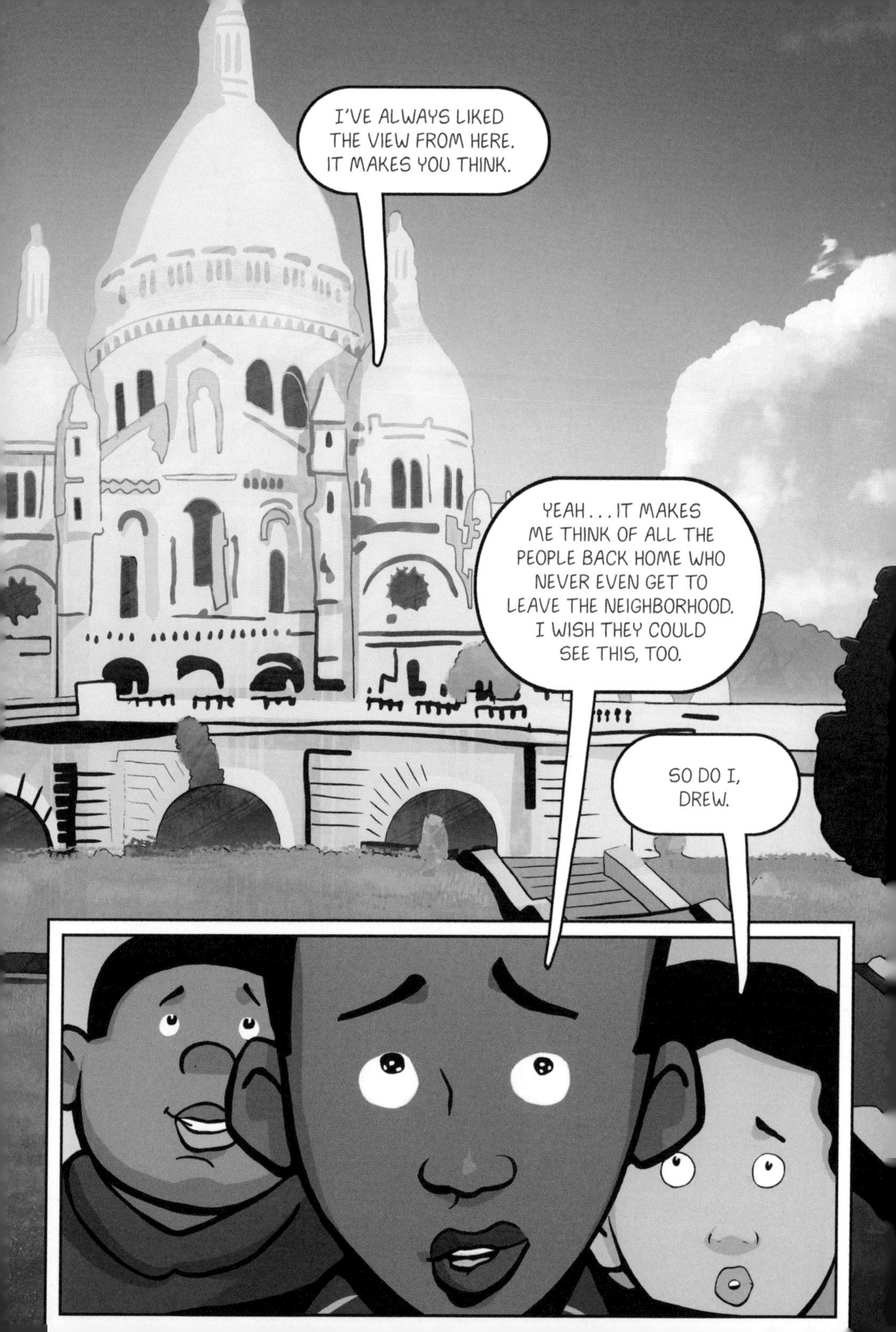
I'VE ALWAYS LIKED THE VIEW FROM HERE. IT MAKES YOU THINK.
YEAH . . . IT MAKES ME THINK OF ALL THE PEOPLE BACK HOME WHO NEVER EVEN GET TO LEAVE THE NEIGHBORHOOD. I WISH THEY COULD SEE THIS, TOO.
SO DO I, DREW.

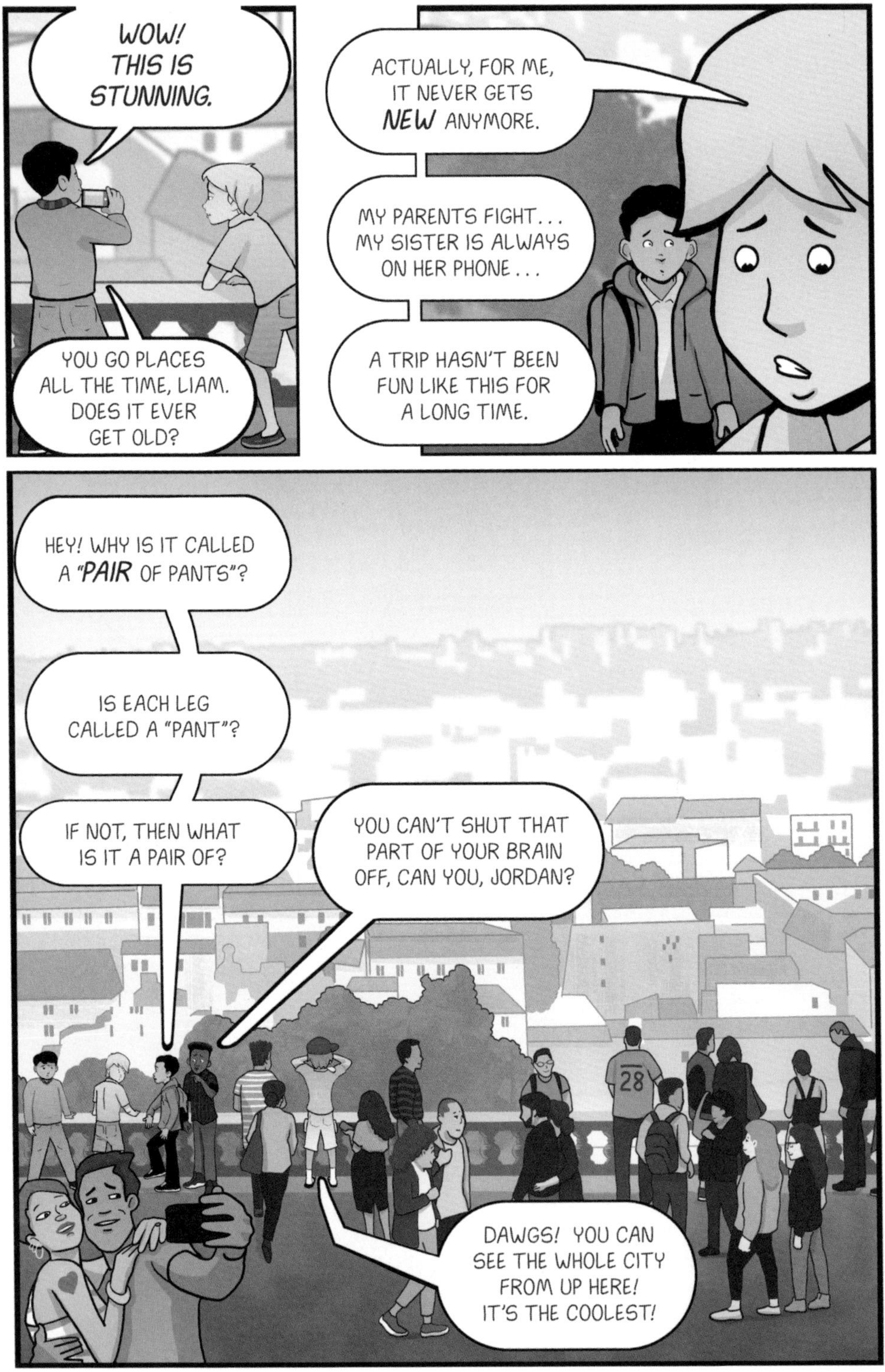
WOW! THIS IS STUNNING.
YOU GO PLACES ALL THE TIME, LIAM. DOES IT EVER GET OLD?
ACTUALLY, FOR ME, IT NEVER GETS NEW ANYMORE.
MY PARENTS FIGHT... MY SISTER IS ALWAYS ON HER PHONE...
A TRIP HASN'T BEEN FUN LIKE THIS FOR A LONG TIME.
HEY! WHY IS IT CALLED A "PAIR OF PANTS"?
IS EACH LEG CALLED A "PANT"?
IF NOT, THEN WHAT IS IT A PAIR OF?
YOU CAN'T SHUT THAT PART OF YOUR BRAIN OFF, CAN YOU, JORDAN?
28
DAWGS! YOU CAN SEE THE WHOLE CITY FROM UP HERE! IT'S THE COOLEST!

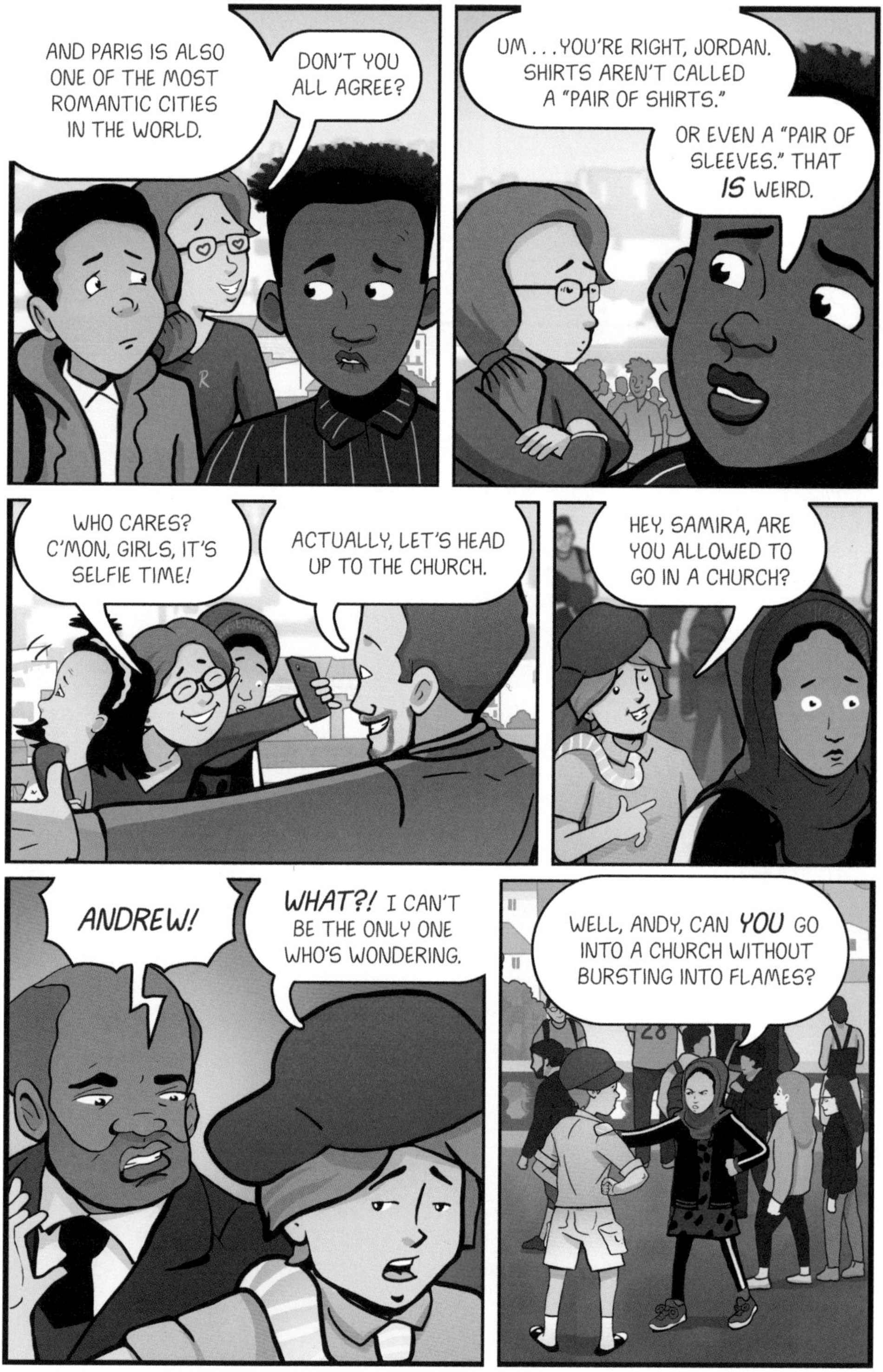

AND PARIS IS ALSO ONE OF THE MOST ROMANTIC CITIES IN THE WORLD.
DON'T YOU ALL AGREE?
UM . . . YOU'RE RIGHT, JORDAN. SHIRTS AREN'T CALLED A "PAIR OF SHIRTS."
OR EVEN A "PAIR OF SLEEVES." THAT *IS* WEIRD.
WHO CARES? C'MON, GIRLS, IT'S SELFIE TIME!
ACTUALLY, LET'S HEAD UP TO THE CHURCH.
HEY, SAMIRA, ARE YOU ALLOWED TO GO IN A CHURCH?
ANDREW!
WHAT?! I CAN'T BE THE ONLY ONE WHO'S WONDERING.
WELL, ANDY, CAN **YOU** GO INTO A CHURCH WITHOUT BURSTING INTO FLAMES?

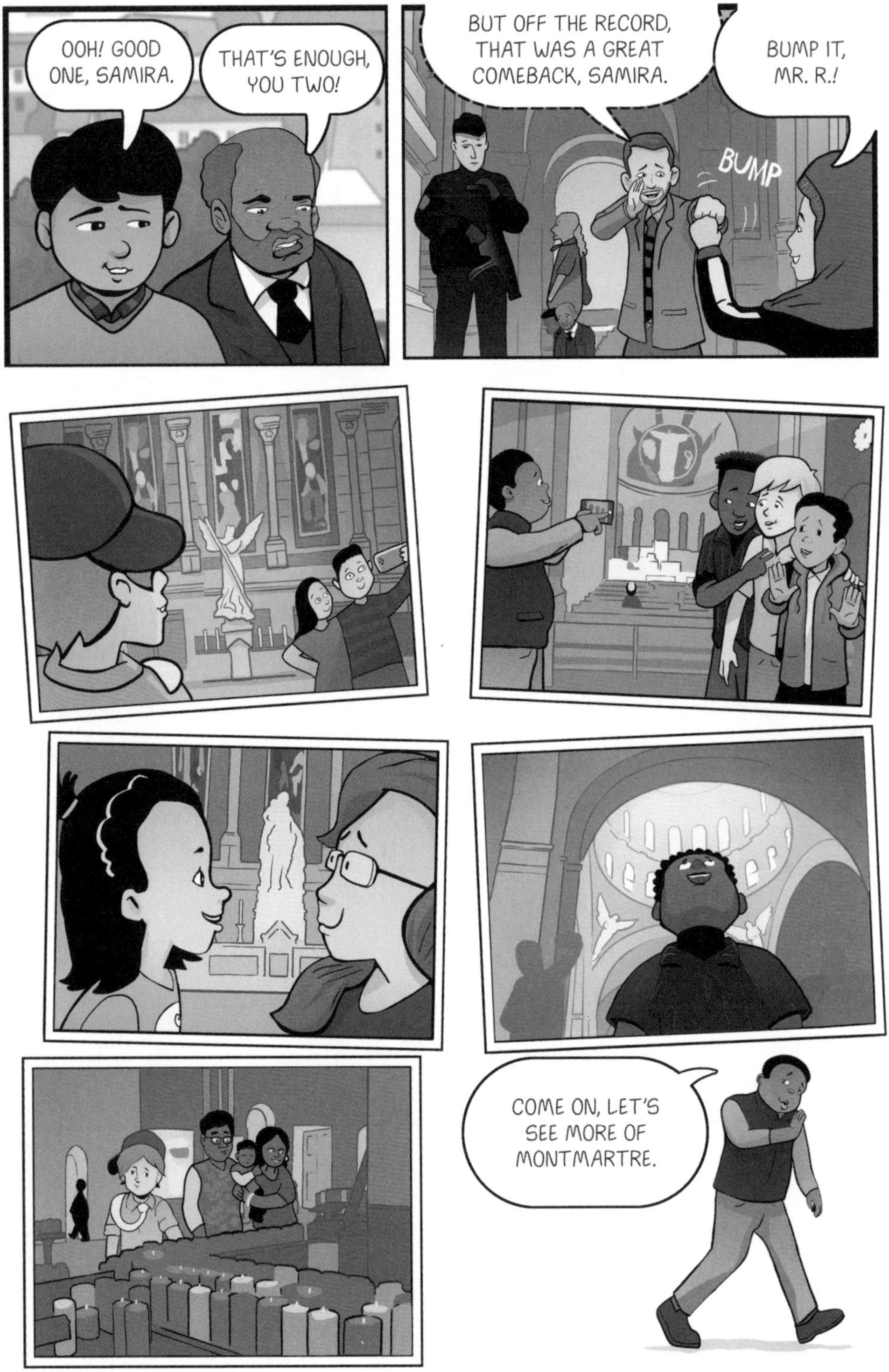
OOH! GOOD ONE, SAMIRA.
THAT'S ENOUGH, YOU TWO!
BUT OFF THE RECORD, THAT WAS A GREAT COMEBACK, SAMIRA.
BUMP IT, MR. R.!
BUMP
COME ON, LET'S SEE MORE OF MONTMARTRE.

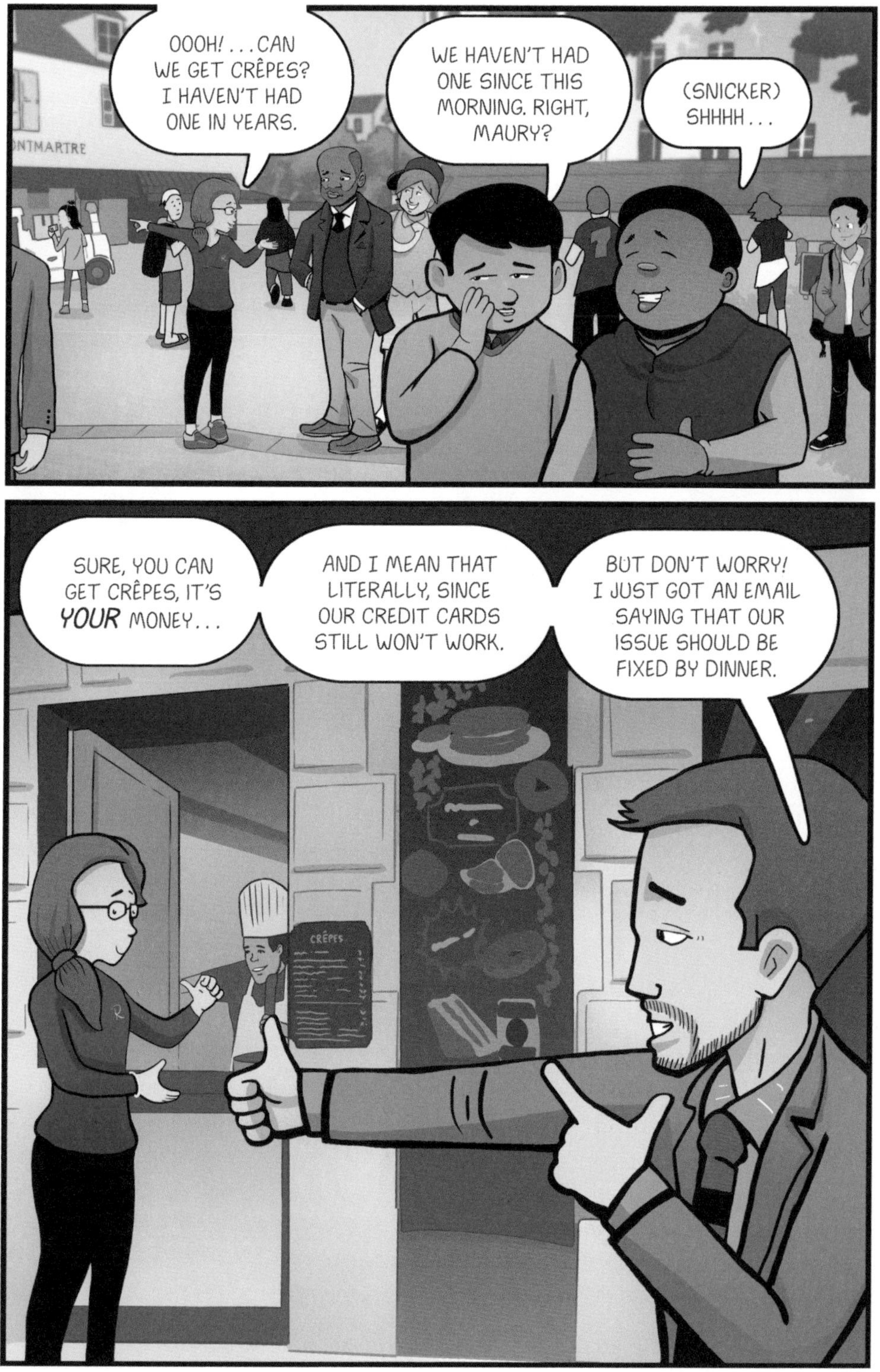
OOOH! . . . CAN WE GET CRÊPES? I HAVEN'T HAD ONE IN YEARS.
WE HAVEN'T HAD ONE SINCE THIS MORNING. RIGHT, MAURY?
(SNICKER) SHHHH . . .
NTMARTRE
SURE, YOU CAN GET CRÊPES, IT'S *YOUR* MONEY . . .
AND I MEAN THAT LITERALLY, SINCE OUR CREDIT CARDS STILL WON'T WORK.
BUT DON'T WORRY! I JUST GOT AN EMAIL SAYING THAT OUR ISSUE SHOULD BE FIXED BY DINNER.
CRÊPES

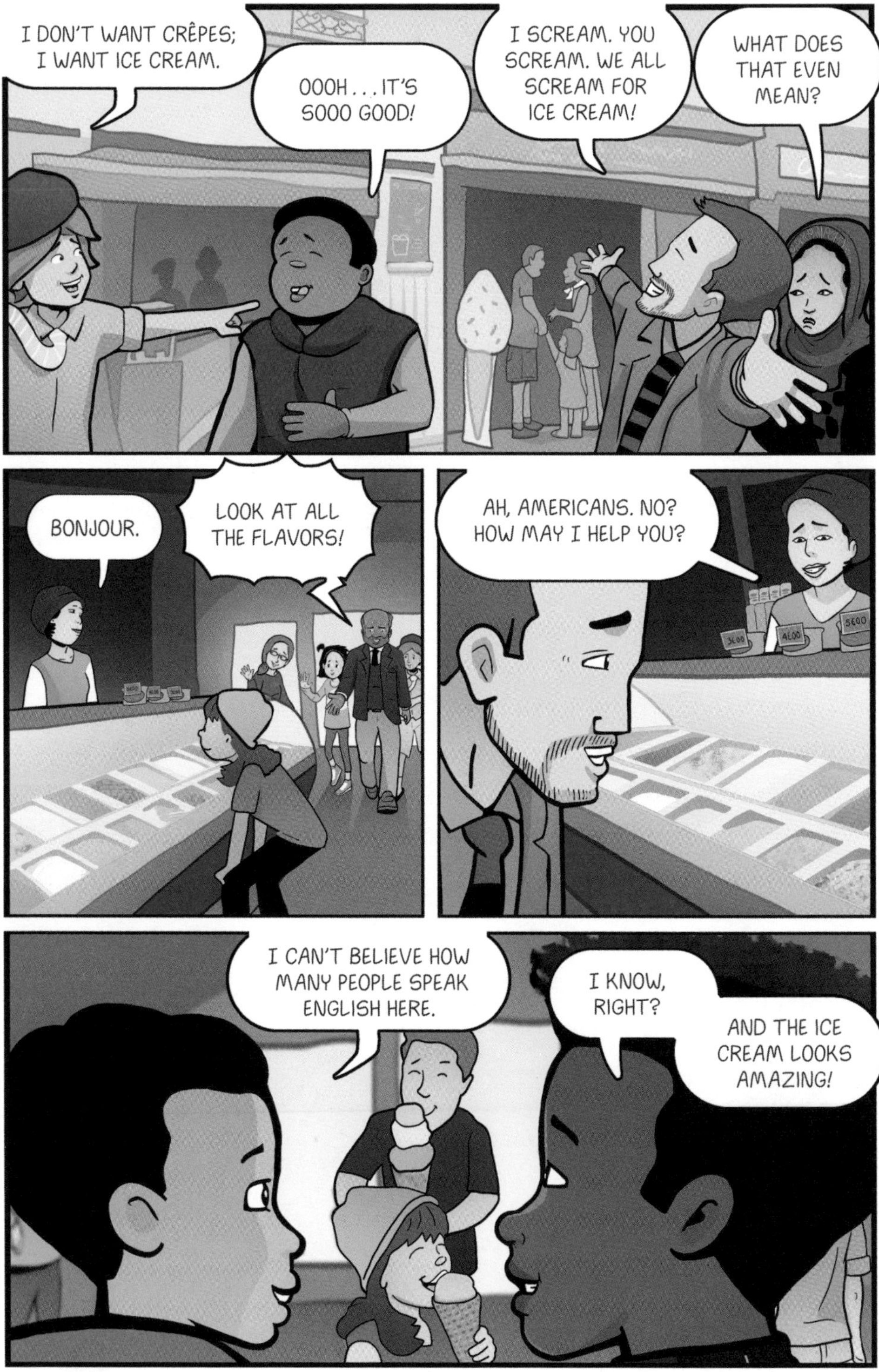
I DON'T WANT CRÊPES; I WANT ICE CREAM.
OOOH . . . IT'S SOOO GOOD!
I SCREAM. YOU SCREAM. WE ALL SCREAM FOR ICE CREAM!
WHAT DOES THAT EVEN MEAN?
BONJOUR.
LOOK AT ALL THE FLAVORS!
AH, AMERICANS. NO? HOW MAY I HELP YOU?
I CAN'T BELIEVE HOW MANY PEOPLE SPEAK ENGLISH HERE.
I KNOW, RIGHT?
AND THE ICE CREAM LOOKS AMAZING!

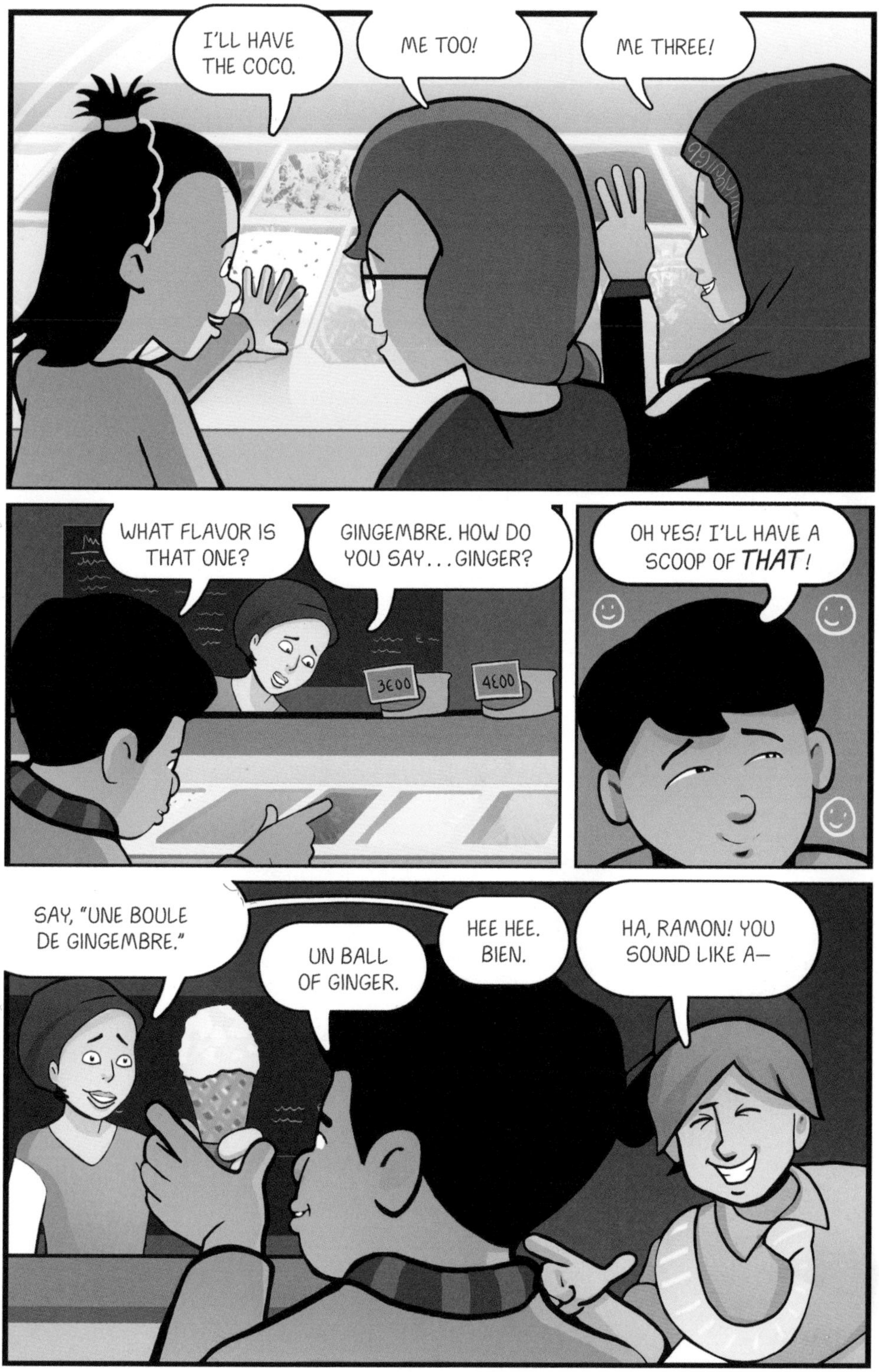
I'LL HAVE THE COCO.
ME TOO!
ME THREE!
WHAT FLAVOR IS THAT ONE?
GINGEMBRE. HOW DO YOU SAY...GINGER?
3€00
4€00
OH YES! I'LL HAVE A SCOOP OF THAT!
SAY, "UNE BOULE DE GINGEMBRE."
UN BALL OF GINGER.
HEE HEE. BIEN.
HA, RAMON! YOU SOUND LIKE A—

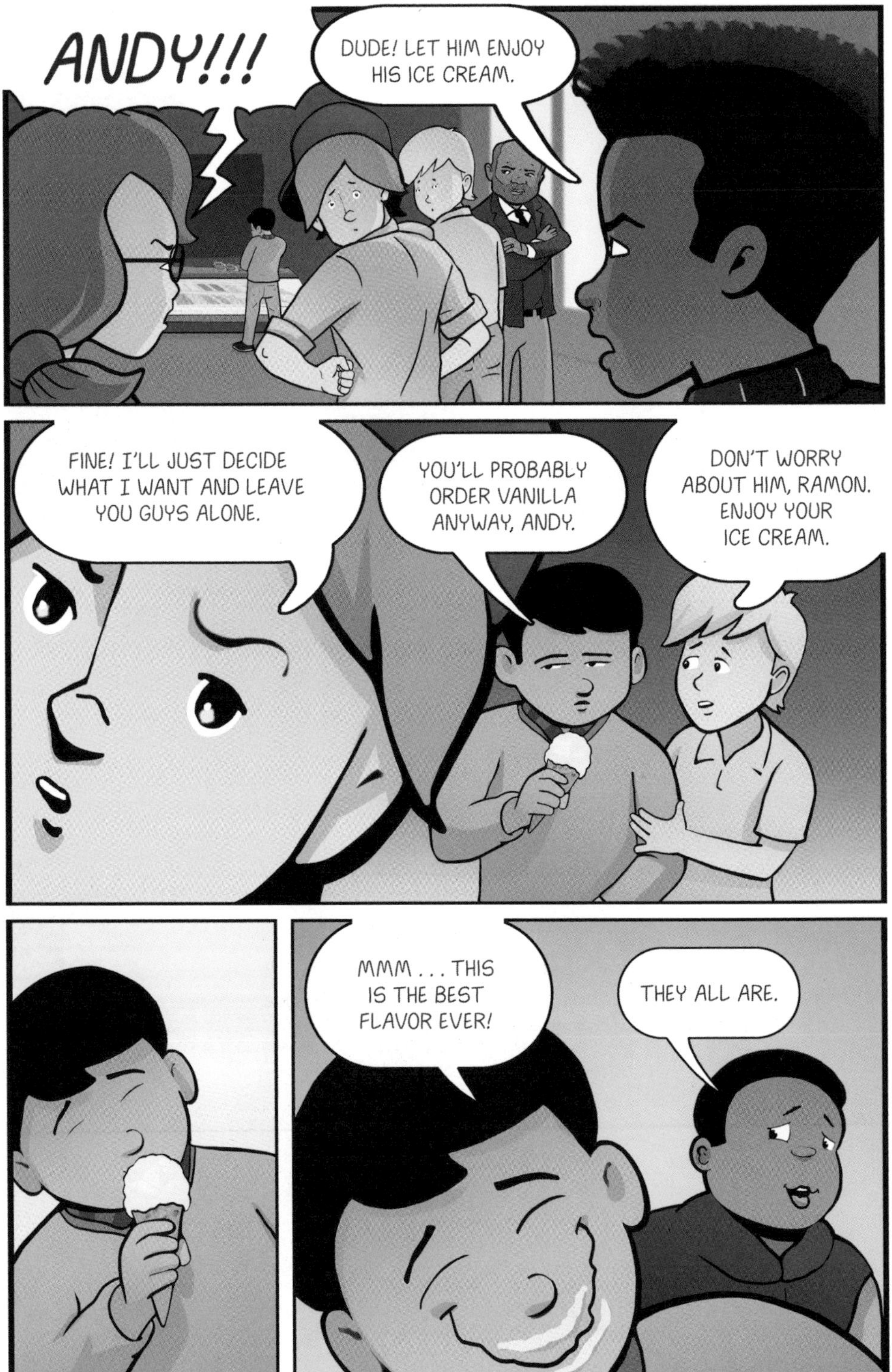
ANDY!!!
DUDE! LET HIM ENJOY HIS ICE CREAM.
FINE! I'LL JUST DECIDE WHAT I WANT AND LEAVE YOU GUYS ALONE.
YOU'LL PROBABLY ORDER VANILLA ANYWAY, ANDY.
DON'T WORRY ABOUT HIM, RAMON. ENJOY YOUR ICE CREAM.
MMM . . . THIS IS THE BEST FLAVOR EVER!
THEY ALL ARE.

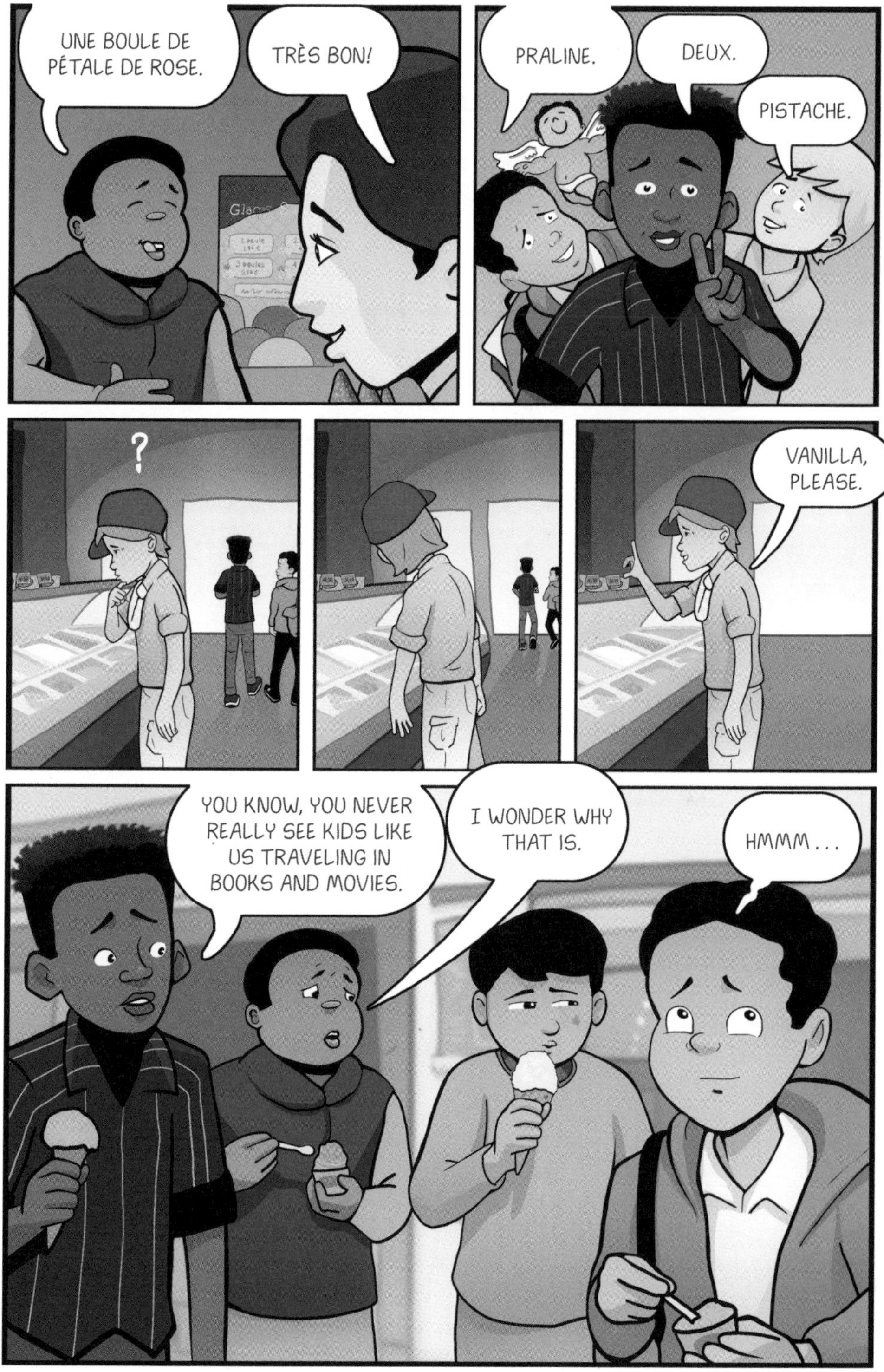
UNE BOULE DE PÉTALE DE ROSE.
TRÈS BON!
PRALINE.
DEUX.
PISTACHE.
?
VANILLA, PLEASE.
YOU KNOW, YOU NEVER REALLY SEE KIDS LIKE US TRAVELING IN BOOKS AND MOVIES.
I WONDER WHY THAT IS.
HMMM . . .

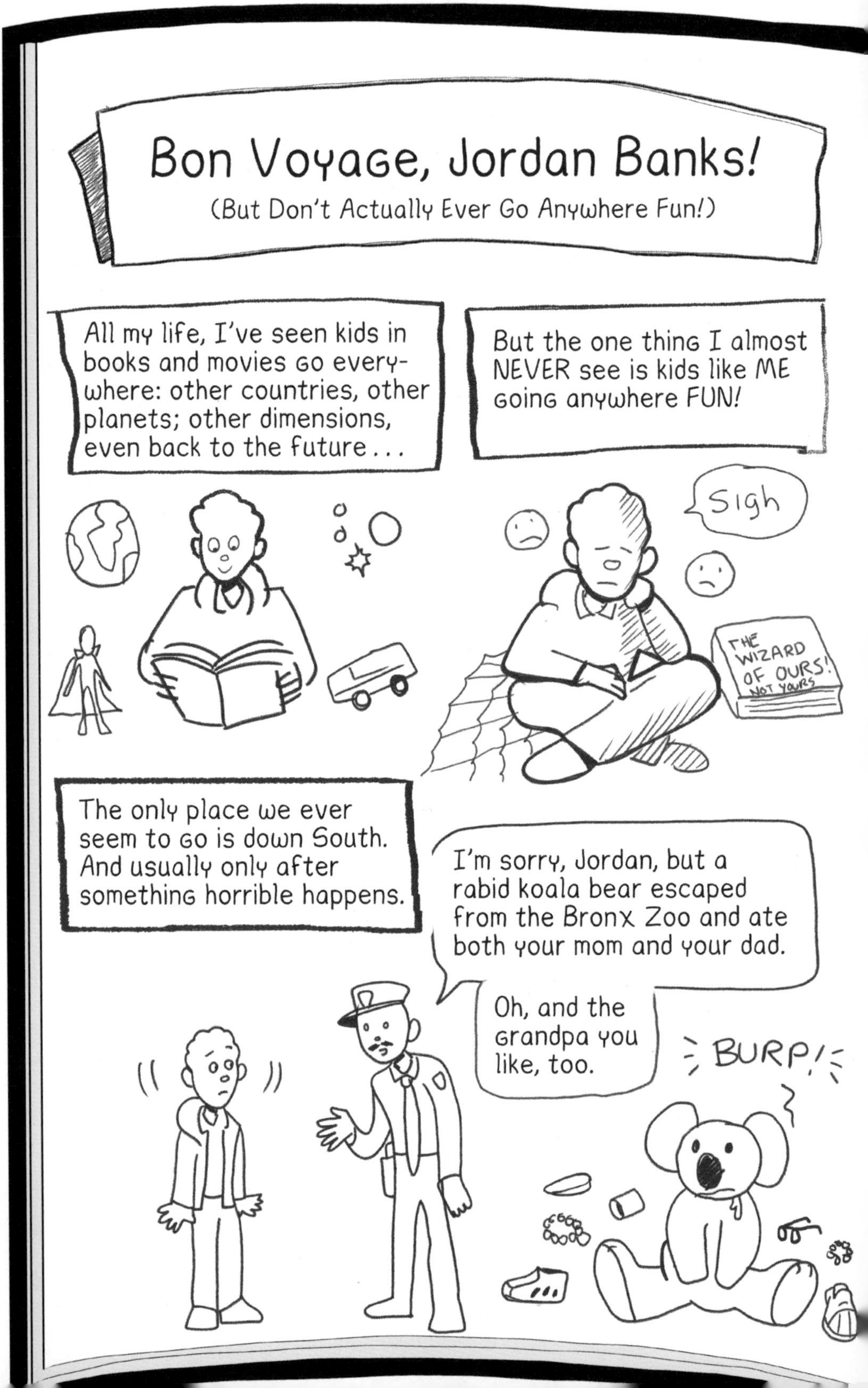
Bon Voyage, Jordan Banks!
(But Don't Actually Ever Go Anywhere Fun!)
All my life, I've seen kids in books and movies go everywhere: other countries, other planets; other dimensions, even back to the future . . .
But the one thing I almost NEVER see is kids like ME going anywhere FUN!
Sigh
THE WIZARD OF OURS! NOT YOURS
The only place we ever seem to go is down South. And usually only after something horrible happens.
I'm sorry, Jordan, but a rabid koala bear escaped from the Bronx Zoo and ate both your mom and your dad.
Oh, and the grandpa you like, too.
BURP!

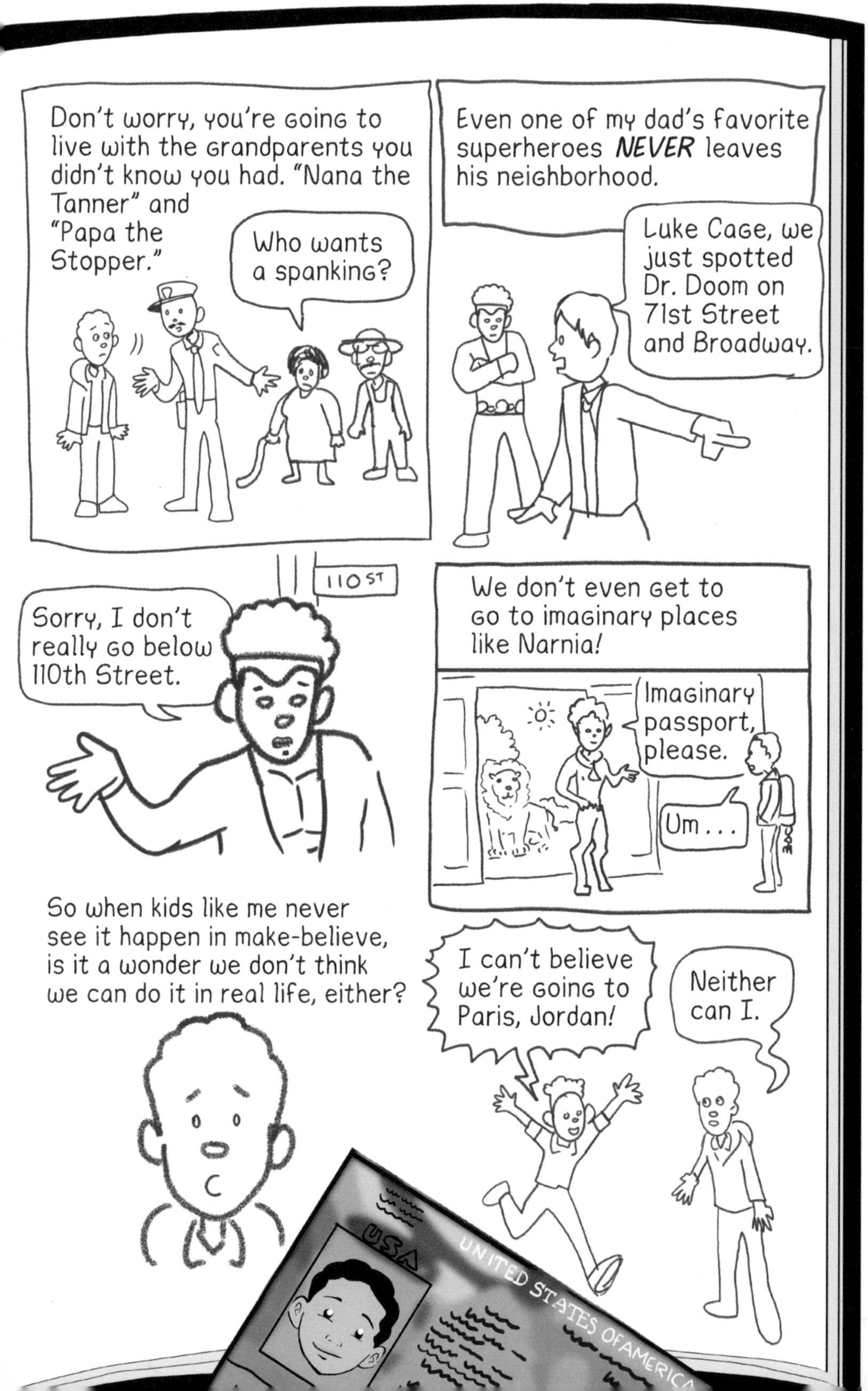

Don't worry, you're going to live with the grandparents you didn't know you had. "Nana the Tanner" and "Papa the Stopper."
Who wants a spanking?
Even one of my dad's favorite superheroes *NEVER* leaves his neighborhood.
Luke Cage, we just spotted Dr. Doom on 71st Street and Broadway.
110 ST
Sorry, I don't really go below 110th Street.
We don't even get to go to imaginary places like Narnia!
Imaginary passport, please.
Um . . .
So when kids like me never see it happen in make-believe, is it a wonder we don't think we can do it in real life, either?
I can't believe we're going to Paris, Jordan!
Neither can I.
USA
UNITED STATES OF AMERICA

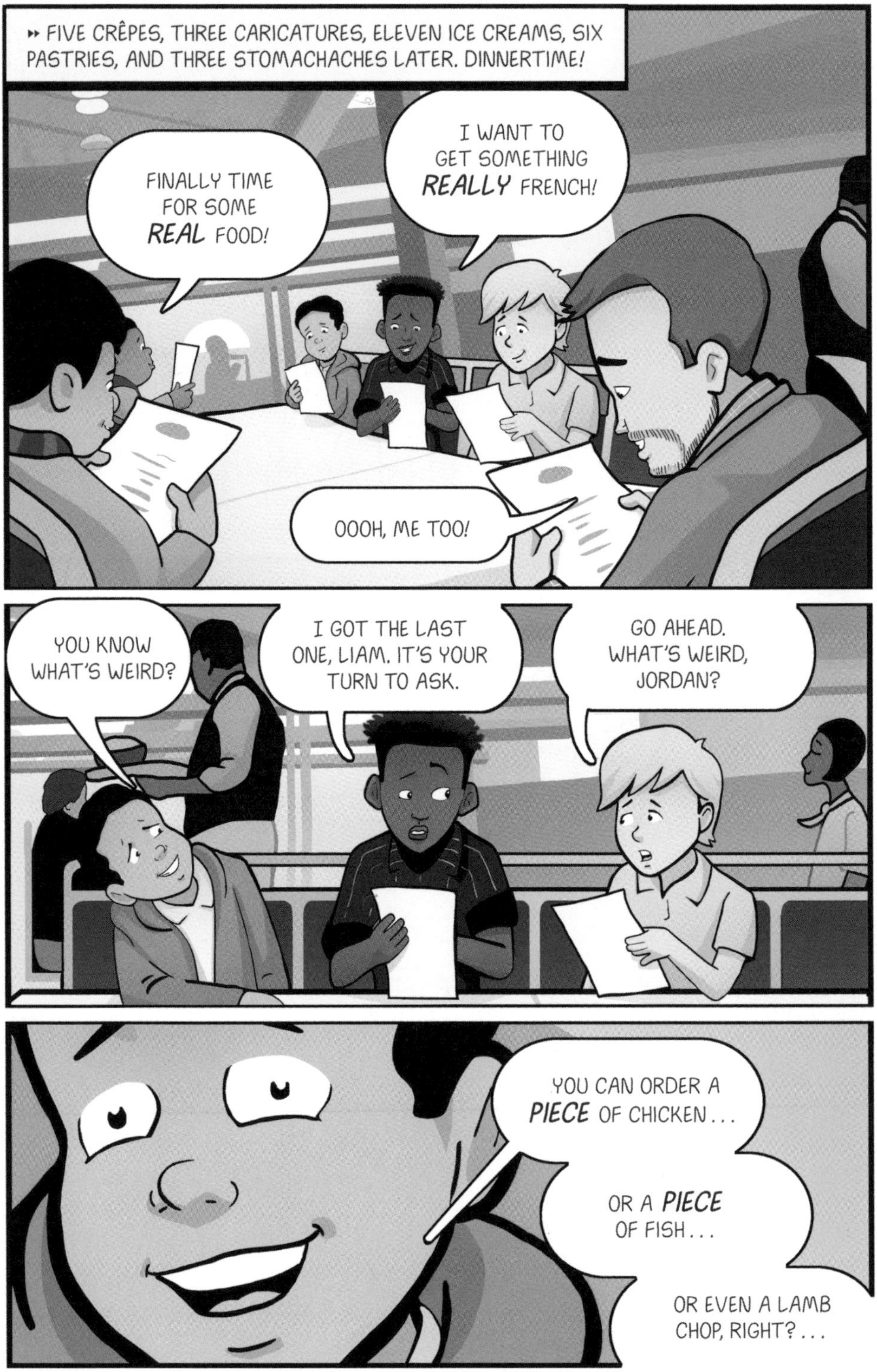

FIVE CRÊPES, THREE CARICATURES, ELEVEN ICE CREAMS, SIX PASTRIES, AND THREE STOMACHACHES LATER. DINNERTIME!
FINALLY TIME FOR SOME REAL FOOD!
I WANT TO GET SOMETHING REALLY FRENCH!
OOOH, ME TOO!
YOU KNOW WHAT'S WEIRD?
I GOT THE LAST ONE, LIAM. IT'S YOUR TURN TO ASK.
GO AHEAD. WHAT'S WEIRD, JORDAN?
YOU CAN ORDER A PIECE OF CHICKEN . . .
OR A PIECE OF FISH . . .
OR EVEN A LAMB CHOP, RIGHT? . . .

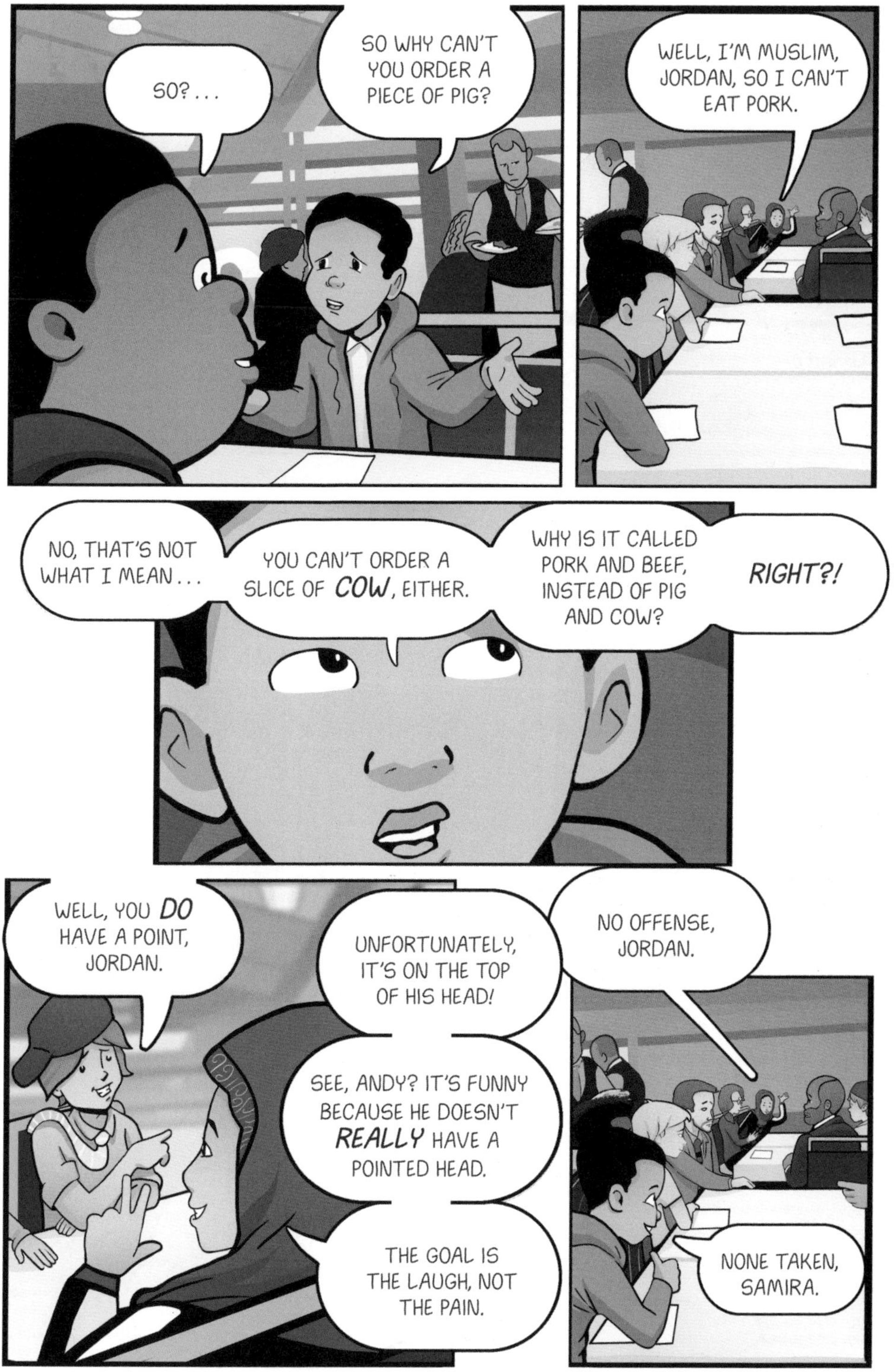
SO?...
SO WHY CAN'T YOU ORDER A PIECE OF PIG?
WELL, I'M MUSLIM, JORDAN, SO I CAN'T EAT PORK.
NO, THAT'S NOT WHAT I MEAN...
YOU CAN'T ORDER A SLICE OF COW, EITHER.
WHY IS IT CALLED PORK AND BEEF, INSTEAD OF PIG AND COW?
RIGHT?!
WELL, YOU DO HAVE A POINT, JORDAN.
UNFORTUNATELY, IT'S ON THE TOP OF HIS HEAD!
SEE, ANDY? IT'S FUNNY BECAUSE HE DOESN'T REALLY HAVE A POINTED HEAD.
THE GOAL IS THE LAUGH, NOT THE PAIN.
NO OFFENSE, JORDAN.
NONE TAKEN, SAMIRA.

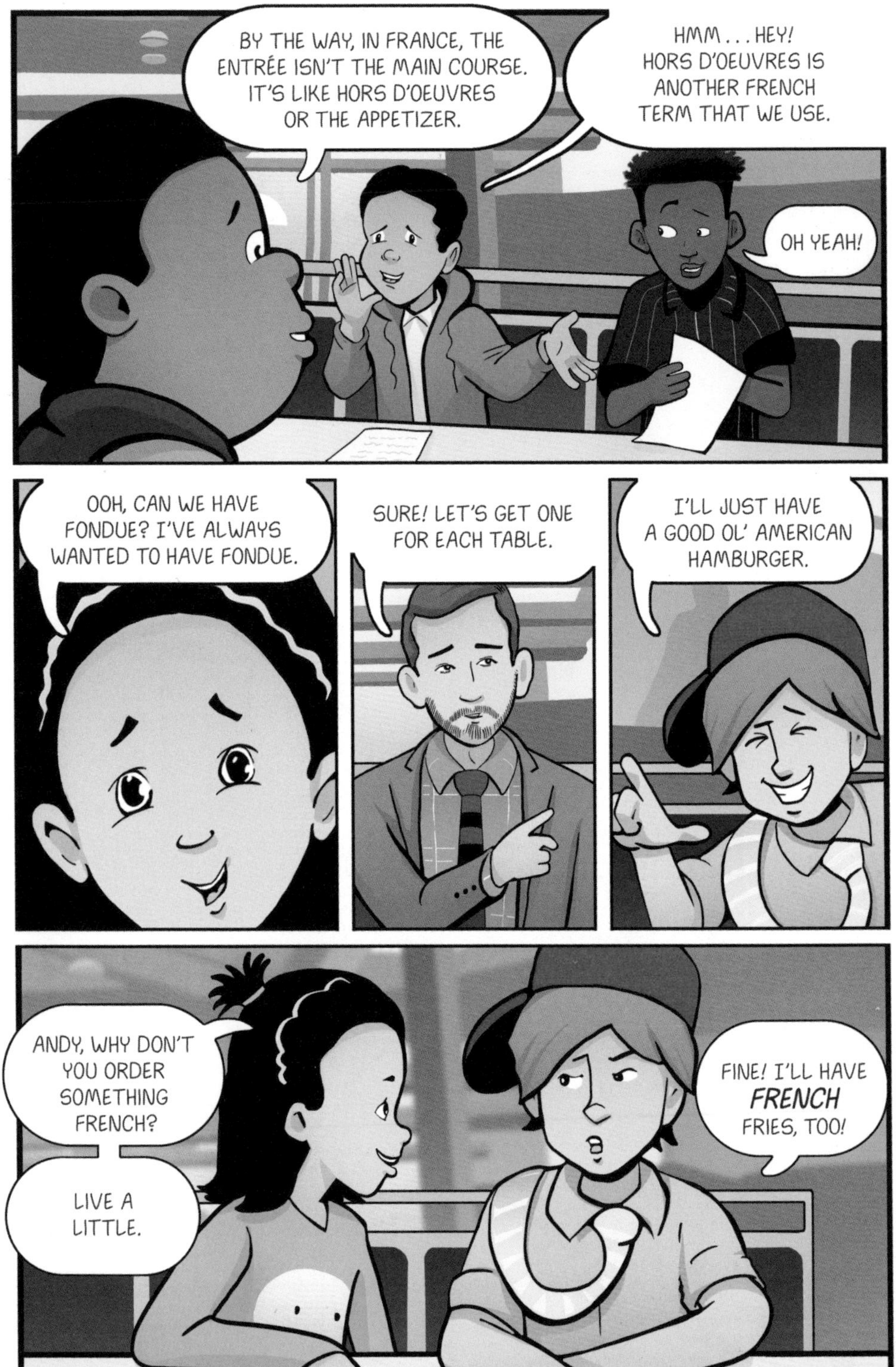
BY THE WAY, IN FRANCE, THE ENTRÉE ISN'T THE MAIN COURSE. IT'S LIKE HORS D'OEUVRES OR THE APPETIZER.
HMM . . . HEY! HORS D'OEUVRES IS ANOTHER FRENCH TERM THAT WE USE.
OH YEAH!
OOH, CAN WE HAVE FONDUE? I'VE ALWAYS WANTED TO HAVE FONDUE.
SURE! LET'S GET ONE FOR EACH TABLE.
I'LL JUST HAVE A GOOD OL' AMERICAN HAMBURGER.
ANDY, WHY DON'T YOU ORDER SOMETHING FRENCH?
LIVE A LITTLE.
FINE! I'LL HAVE ***FRENCH*** FRIES, TOO!

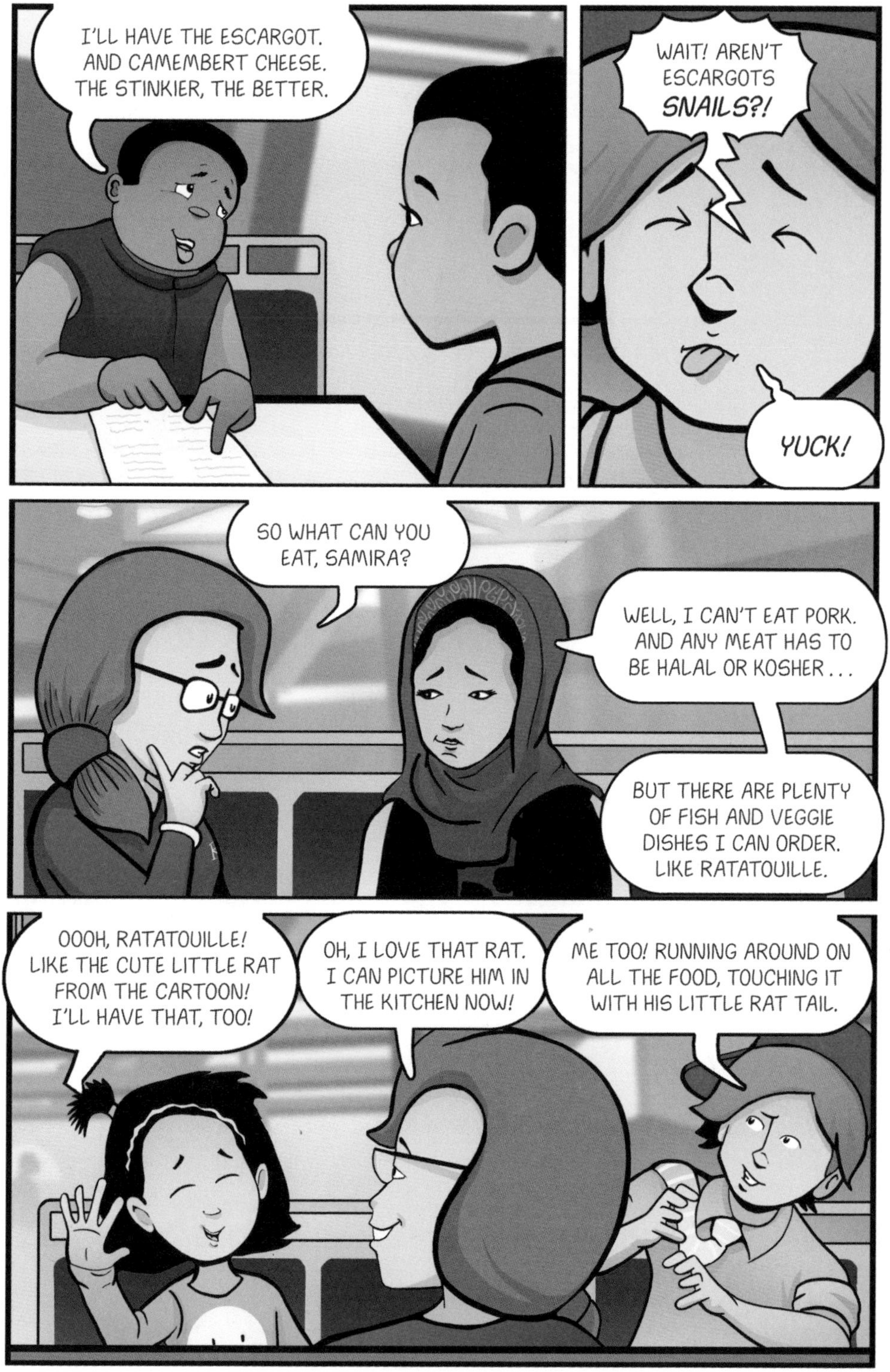
I'LL HAVE THE ESCARGOT. AND CAMEMBERT CHEESE. THE STINKIER, THE BETTER.
WAIT! AREN'T ESCARGOTS SNAILS?!
YUCK!
SO WHAT CAN YOU EAT, SAMIRA?
WELL, I CAN'T EAT PORK. AND ANY MEAT HAS TO BE HALAL OR KOSHER . . .
BUT THERE ARE PLENTY OF FISH AND VEGGIE DISHES I CAN ORDER. LIKE RATATOUILLE.
OOOH, RATATOUILLE! LIKE THE CUTE LITTLE RAT FROM THE CARTOON! I'LL HAVE THAT, TOO!
OH, I LOVE THAT RAT. I CAN PICTURE HIM IN THE KITCHEN NOW!
ME TOO! RUNNING AROUND ON ALL THE FOOD, TOUCHING IT WITH HIS LITTLE RAT TAIL.

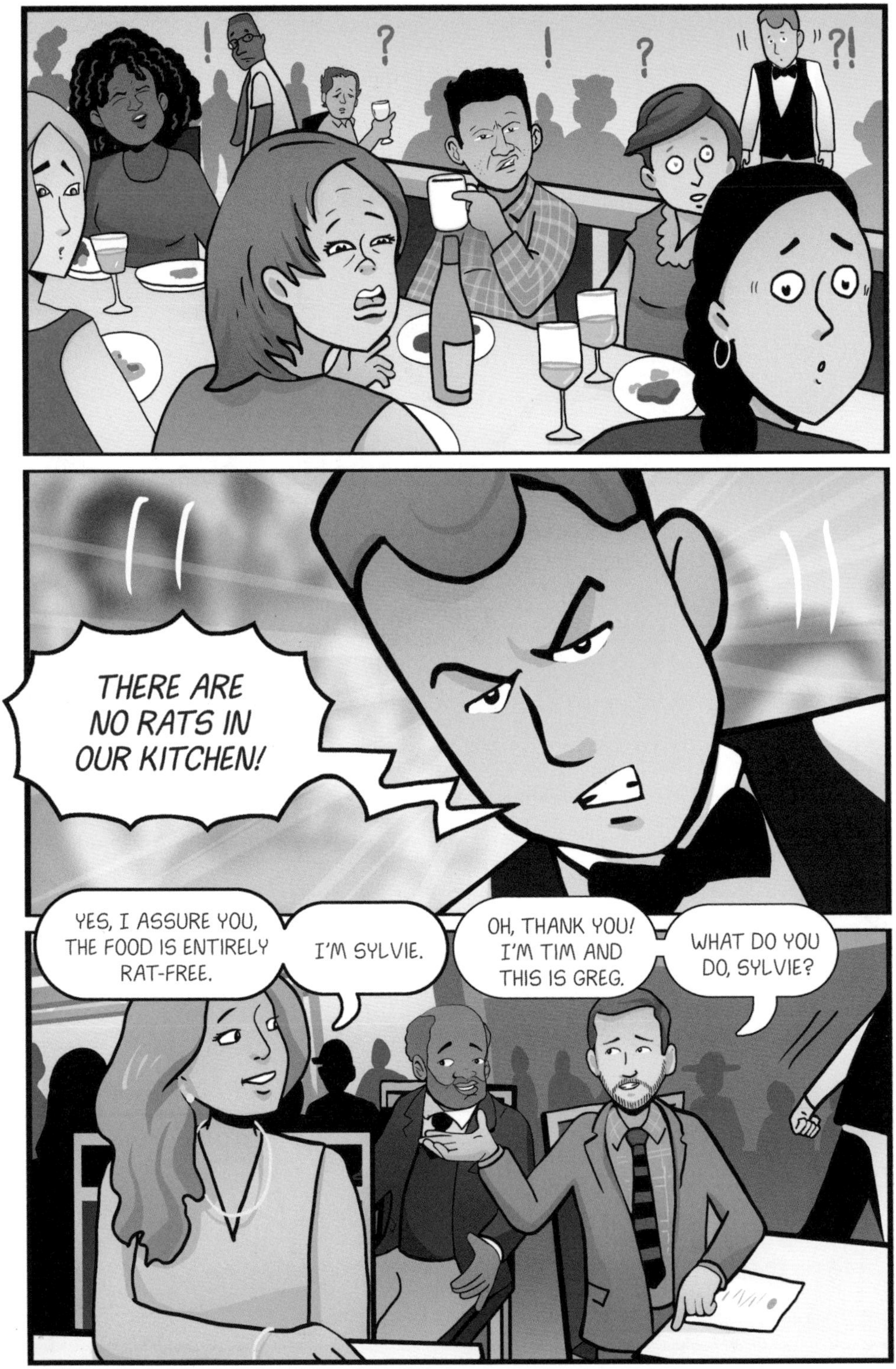

!
?
!
?
?!
THERE ARE NO RATS IN OUR KITCHEN!
YES, I ASSURE YOU, THE FOOD IS ENTIRELY RAT-FREE.
I'M SYLVIE.
OH, THANK YOU! I'M TIM AND THIS IS GREG.
WHAT DO YOU DO, SYLVIE?

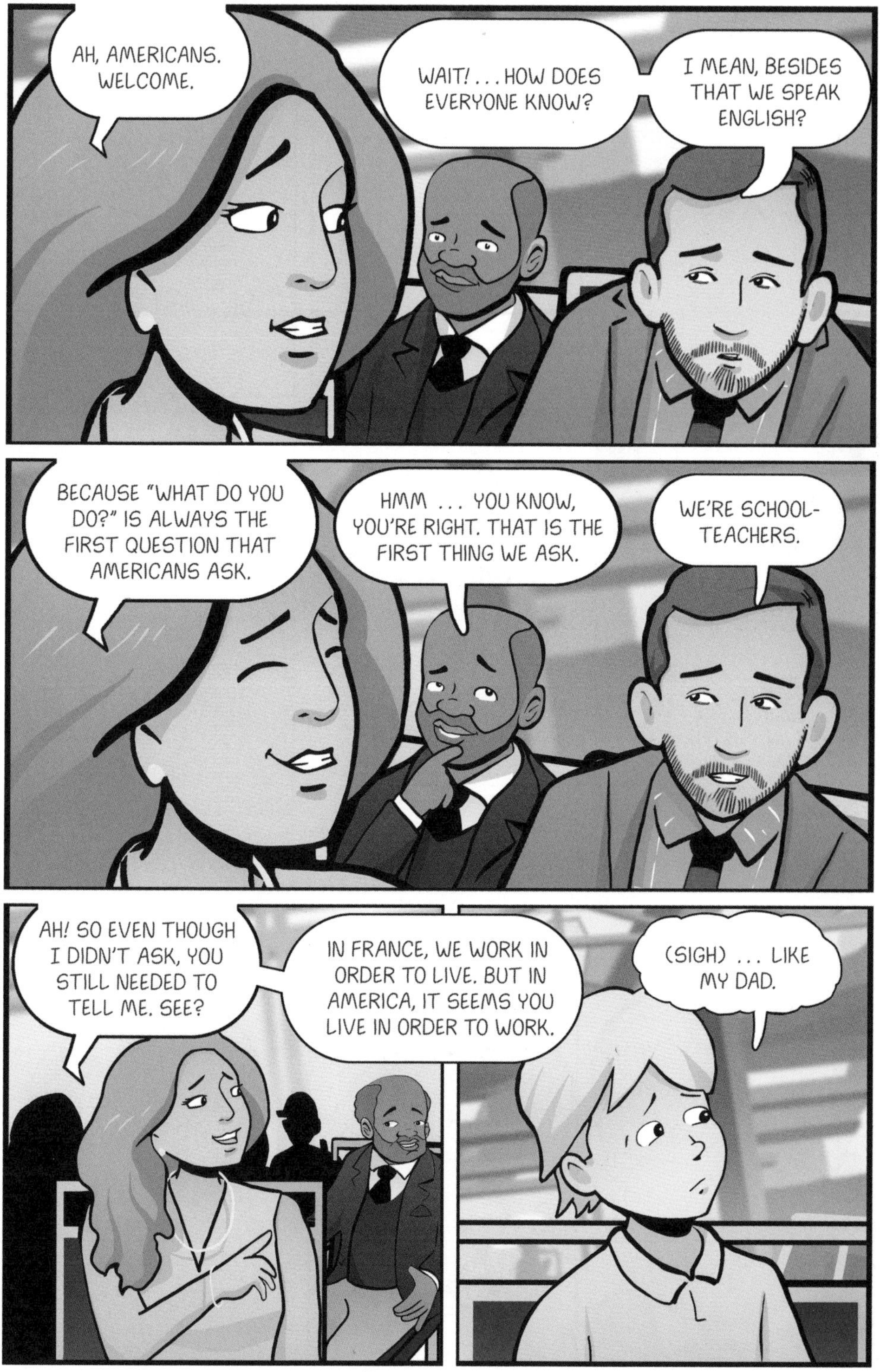
AH, AMERICANS. WELCOME.
WAIT! . . . HOW DOES EVERYONE KNOW?
I MEAN, BESIDES THAT WE SPEAK ENGLISH?
BECAUSE "WHAT DO YOU DO?" IS ALWAYS THE FIRST QUESTION THAT AMERICANS ASK.
HMM . . . YOU KNOW, YOU'RE RIGHT. THAT IS THE FIRST THING WE ASK.
WE'RE SCHOOL-TEACHERS.
AH! SO EVEN THOUGH I DIDN'T ASK, YOU STILL NEEDED TO TELL ME. SEE?
IN FRANCE, WE WORK IN ORDER TO LIVE. BUT IN AMERICA, IT SEEMS YOU LIVE IN ORDER TO WORK.
(SIGH) . . . LIKE MY DAD.

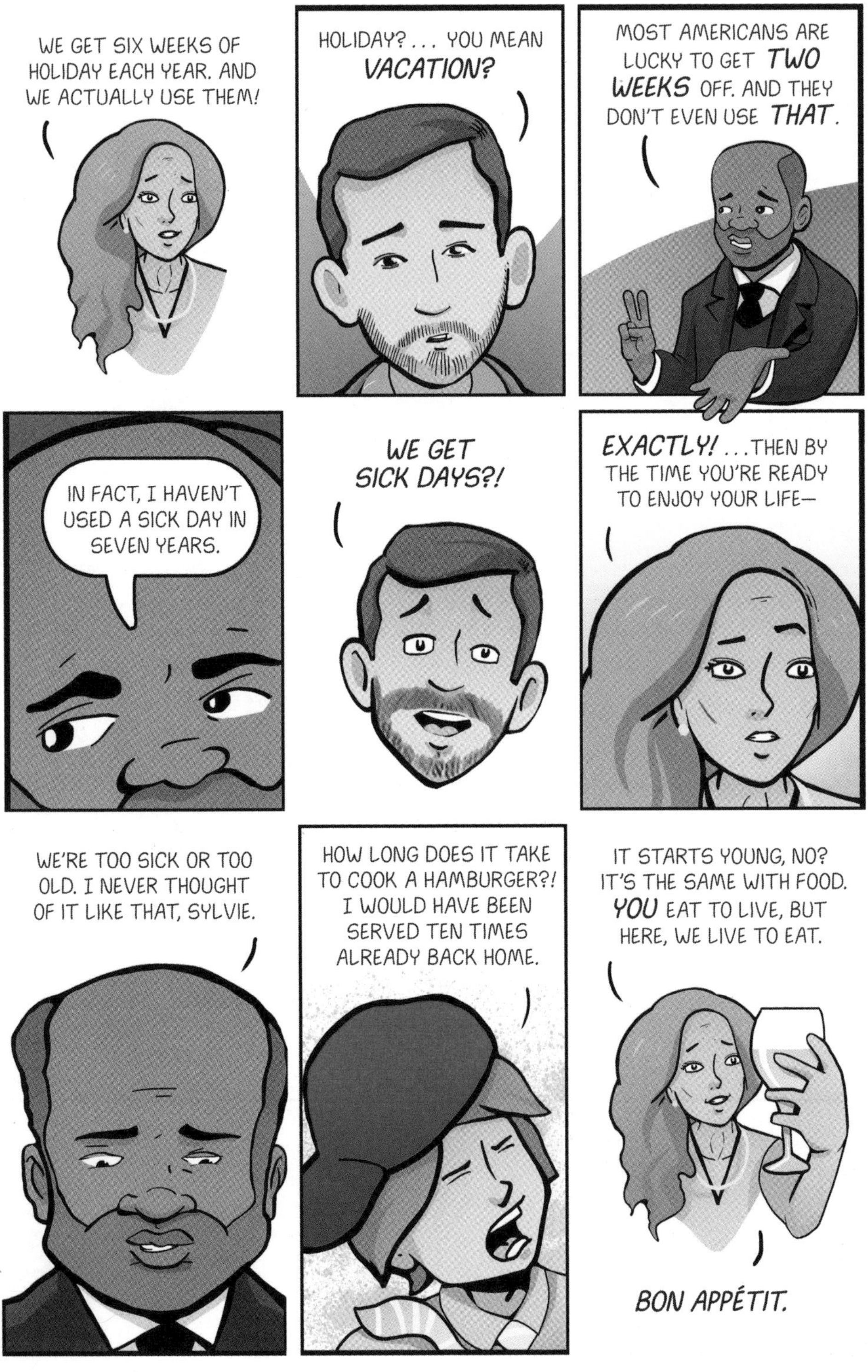
WE GET SIX WEEKS OF HOLIDAY EACH YEAR. AND WE ACTUALLY USE THEM!
HOLIDAY?... YOU MEAN VACATION?
MOST AMERICANS ARE LUCKY TO GET TWO WEEKS OFF. AND THEY DON'T EVEN USE THAT.
IN FACT, I HAVEN'T USED A SICK DAY IN SEVEN YEARS.
WE GET SICK DAYS?!
EXACTLY! ...THEN BY THE TIME YOU'RE READY TO ENJOY YOUR LIFE—
WE'RE TOO SICK OR TOO OLD. I NEVER THOUGHT OF IT LIKE THAT, SYLVIE.
HOW LONG DOES IT TAKE TO COOK A HAMBURGER?! I WOULD HAVE BEEN SERVED TEN TIMES ALREADY BACK HOME.
IT STARTS YOUNG, NO? IT'S THE SAME WITH FOOD. YOU EAT TO LIVE, BUT HERE, WE LIVE TO EAT.
BON APPÉTIT.

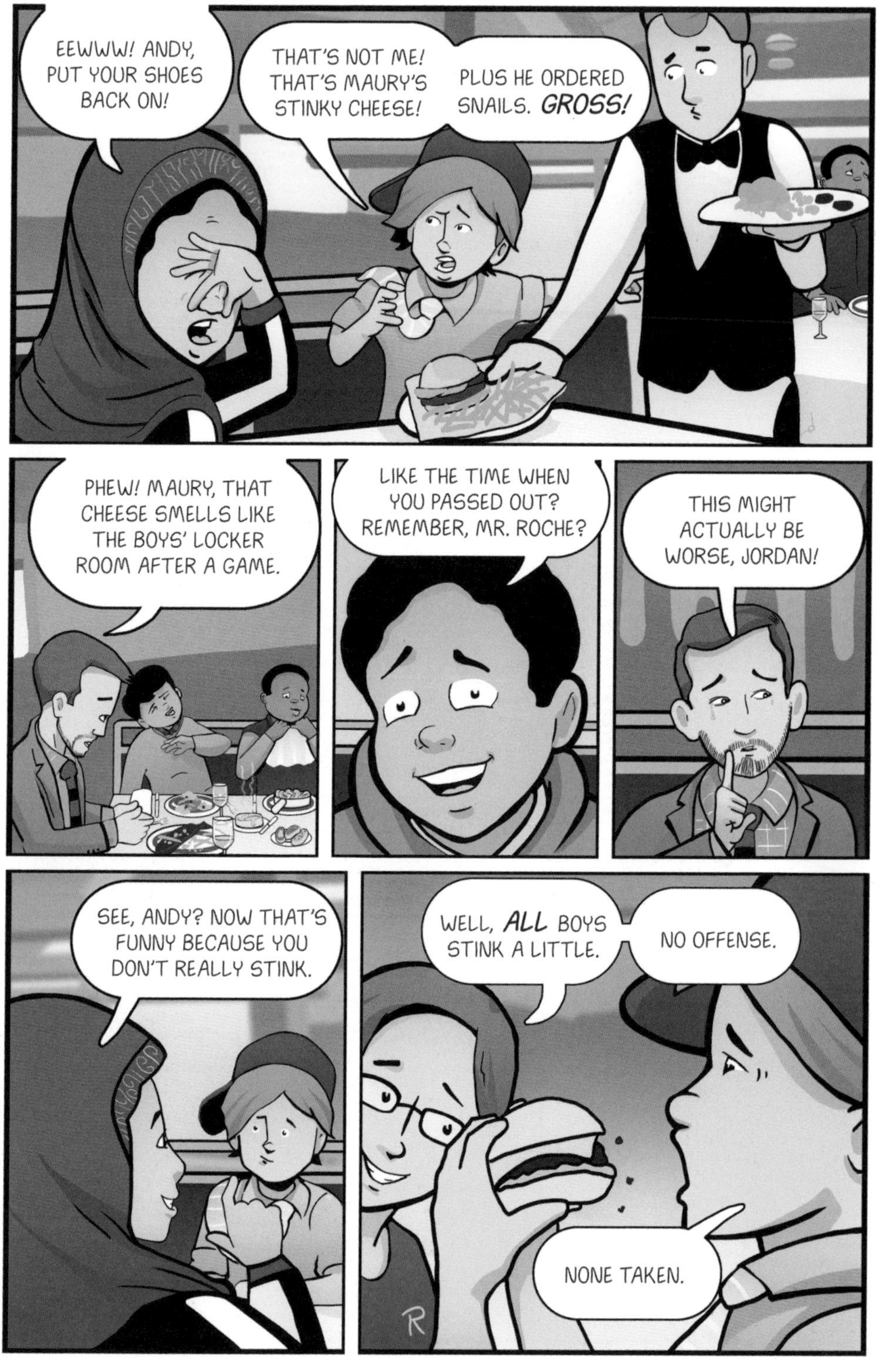
EEWWW! ANDY, PUT YOUR SHOES BACK ON!
THAT'S NOT ME! THAT'S MAURY'S STINKY CHEESE!
PLUS HE ORDERED SNAILS. *GROSS!*
PHEW! MAURY, THAT CHEESE SMELLS LIKE THE BOYS' LOCKER ROOM AFTER A GAME.
LIKE THE TIME WHEN YOU PASSED OUT? REMEMBER, MR. ROCHE?
THIS MIGHT ACTUALLY BE WORSE, JORDAN!
SEE, ANDY? NOW THAT'S FUNNY BECAUSE YOU DON'T REALLY STINK.
WELL, *ALL* BOYS STINK A LITTLE.
NO OFFENSE.
NONE TAKEN.

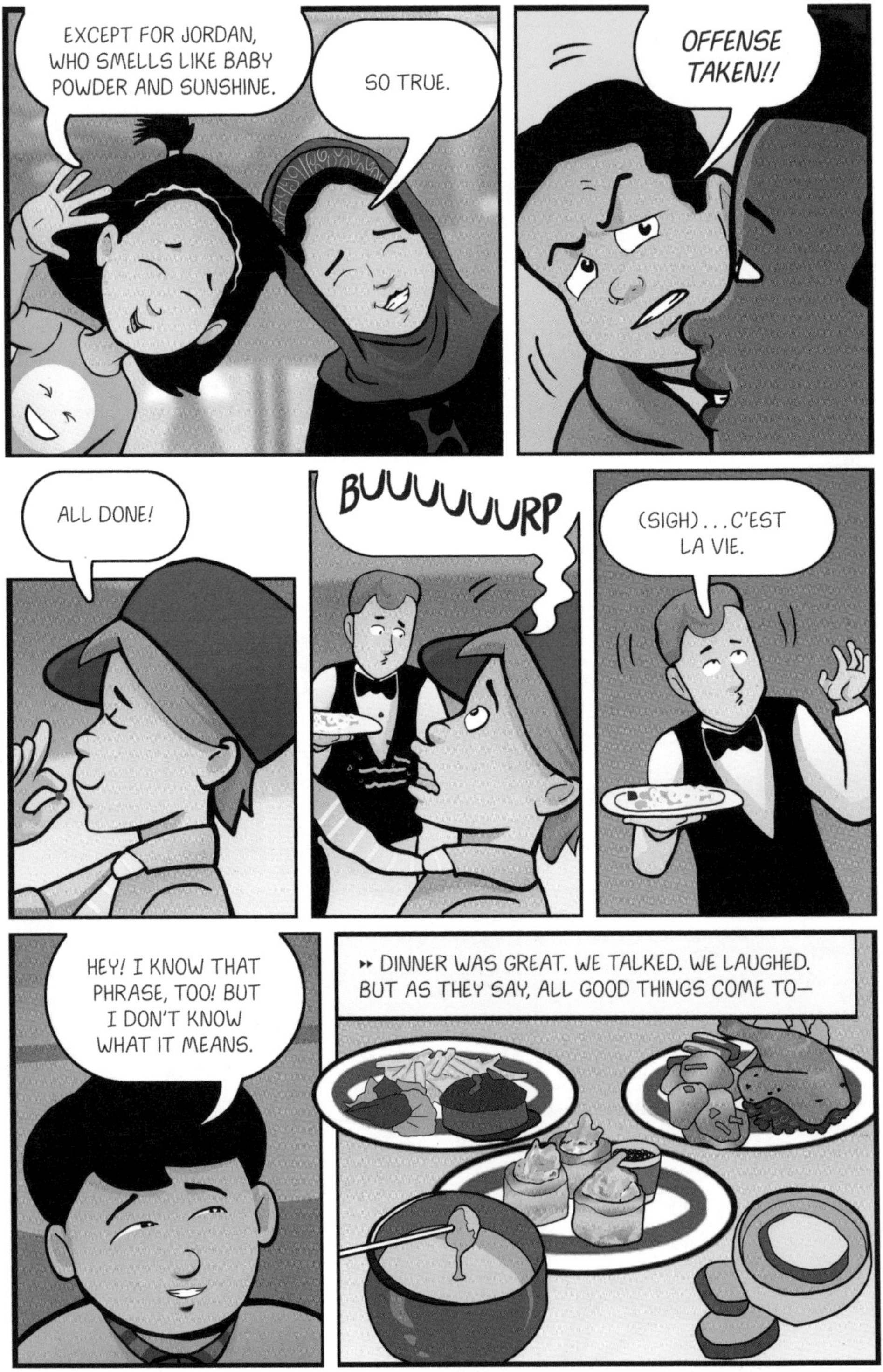
EXCEPT FOR JORDAN, WHO SMELLS LIKE BABY POWDER AND SUNSHINE.
SO TRUE.
OFFENSE TAKEN!!
ALL DONE!
BUUUUUUURP
(SIGH) . . . C'EST LA VIE.
HEY! I KNOW THAT PHRASE, TOO! BUT I DON'T KNOW WHAT IT MEANS.
▸▸ DINNER WAS GREAT. WE TALKED. WE LAUGHED. BUT AS THEY SAY, ALL GOOD THINGS COME TO—

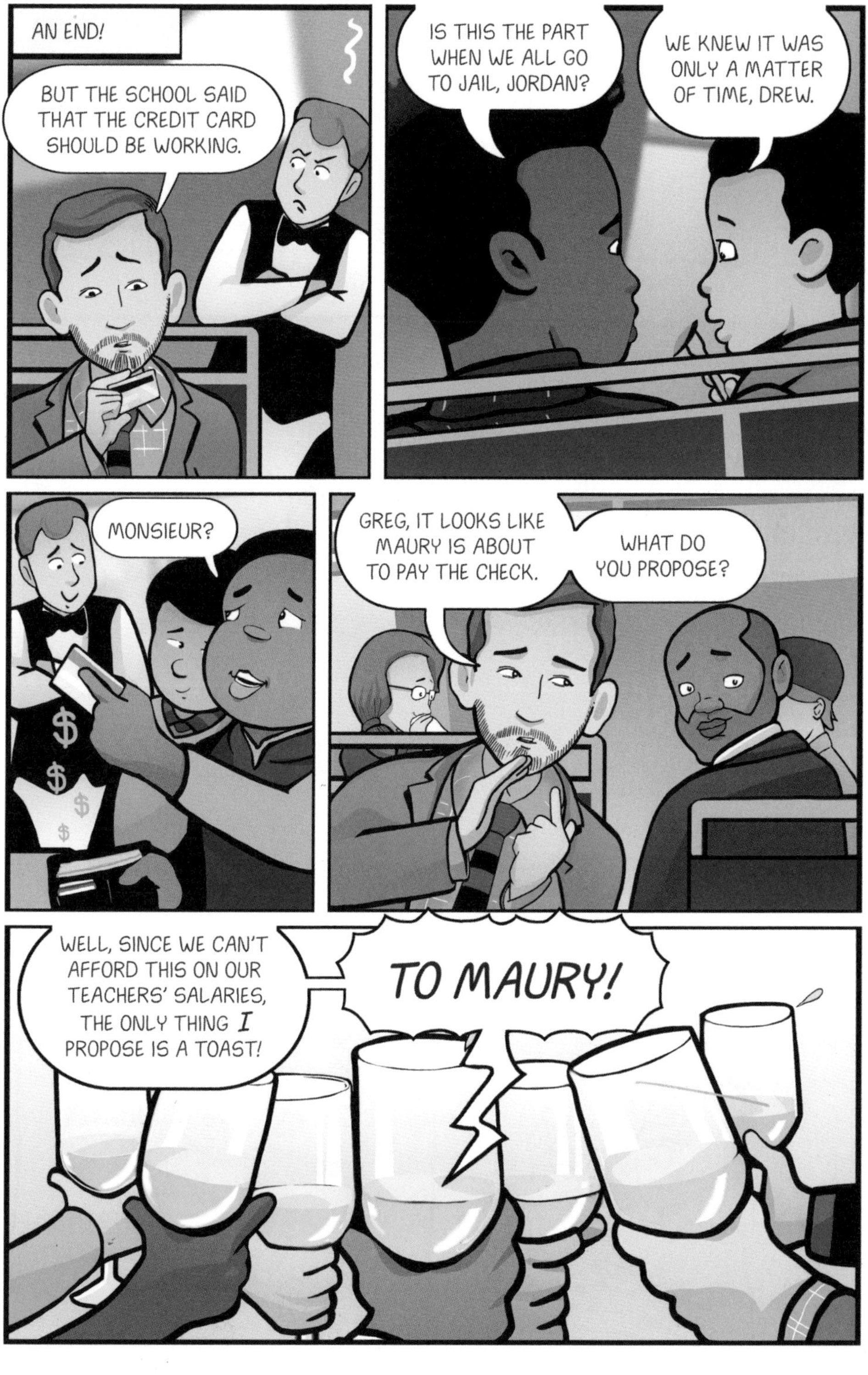
AN END!
BUT THE SCHOOL SAID THAT THE CREDIT CARD SHOULD BE WORKING.
IS THIS THE PART WHEN WE ALL GO TO JAIL, JORDAN?
WE KNEW IT WAS ONLY A MATTER OF TIME, DREW.
MONSIEUR?
GREG, IT LOOKS LIKE MAURY IS ABOUT TO PAY THE CHECK.
WHAT DO YOU PROPOSE?
WELL, SINCE WE CAN'T AFFORD THIS ON OUR TEACHERS' SALARIES, THE ONLY THING *I* PROPOSE IS A TOAST!
TO MAURY!

7 Hurry Up and Slow Down!

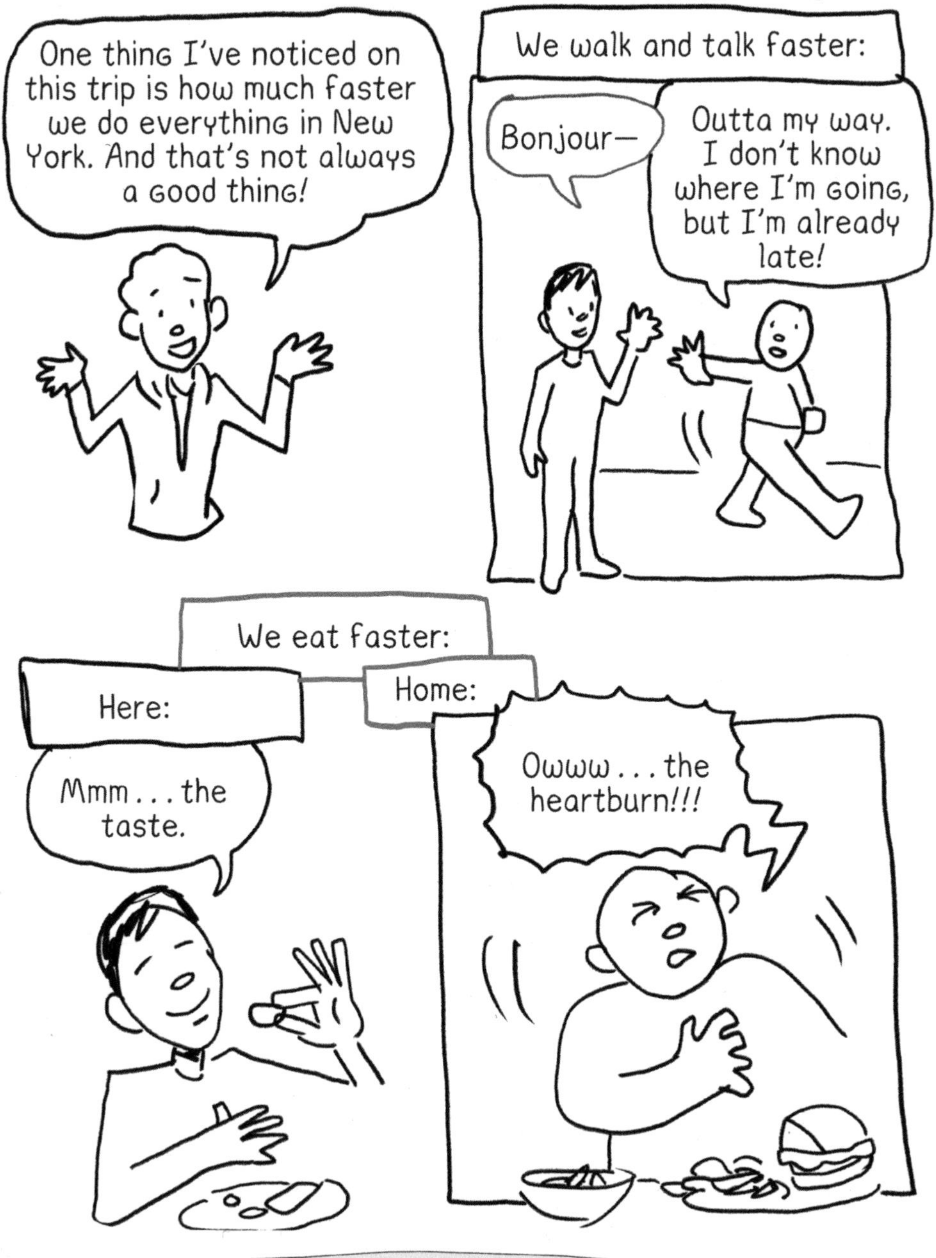
One thing I've noticed on this trip is how much faster we do everything in New York. And that's not always a good thing!
We walk and talk faster:
Bonjour—
Outta my way. I don't know where I'm going, but I'm already late!
We eat faster:
Here:
Mmm . . . the taste.
Home:
Owww . . . the heartburn!!!

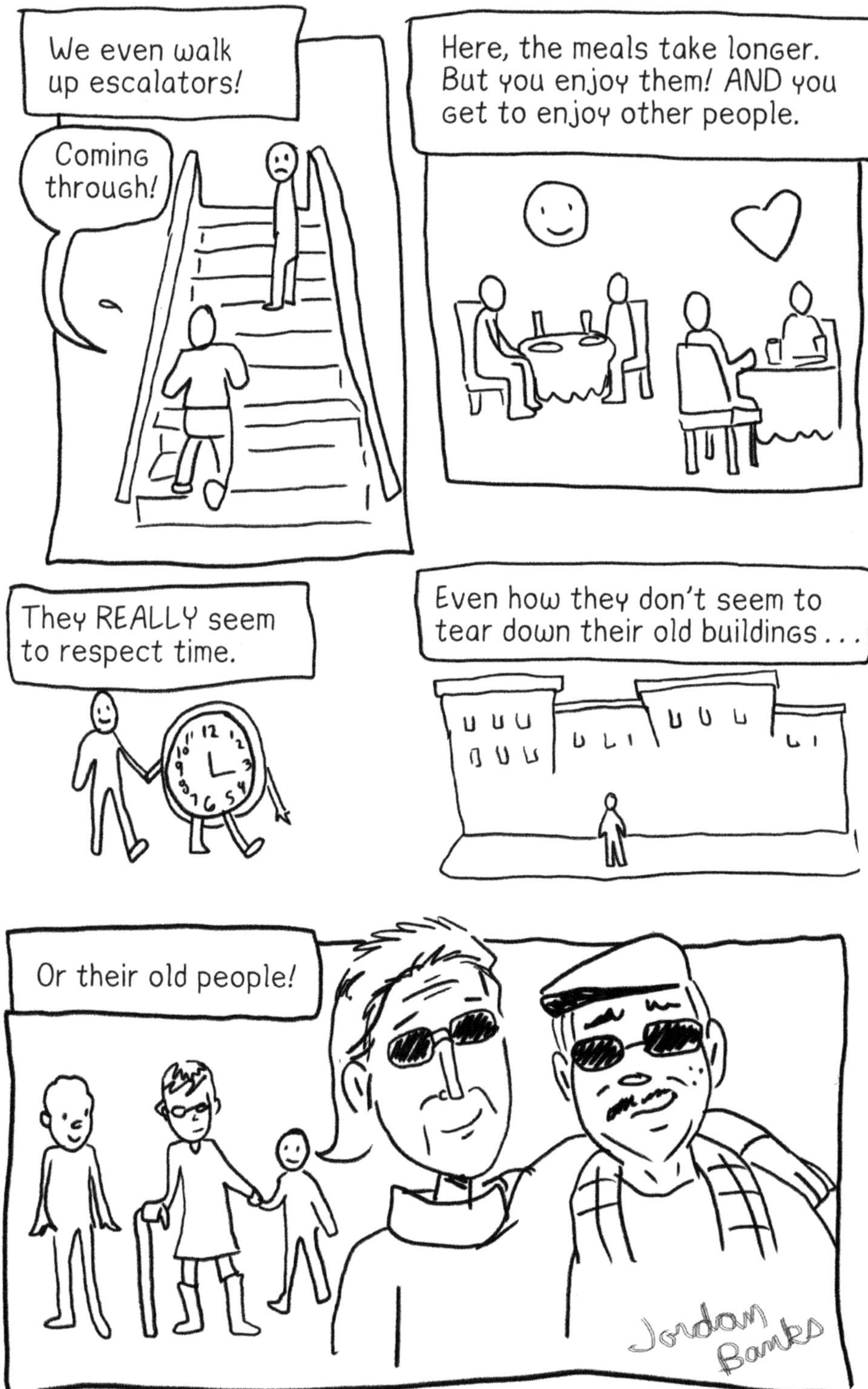
We even walk up escalators!
Coming through!
Here, the meals take longer. But you enjoy them! AND you get to enjoy other people.
They REALLY seem to respect time.
Even how they don't seem to tear down their old buildings . . .
Or their old people!
Jordan Banks

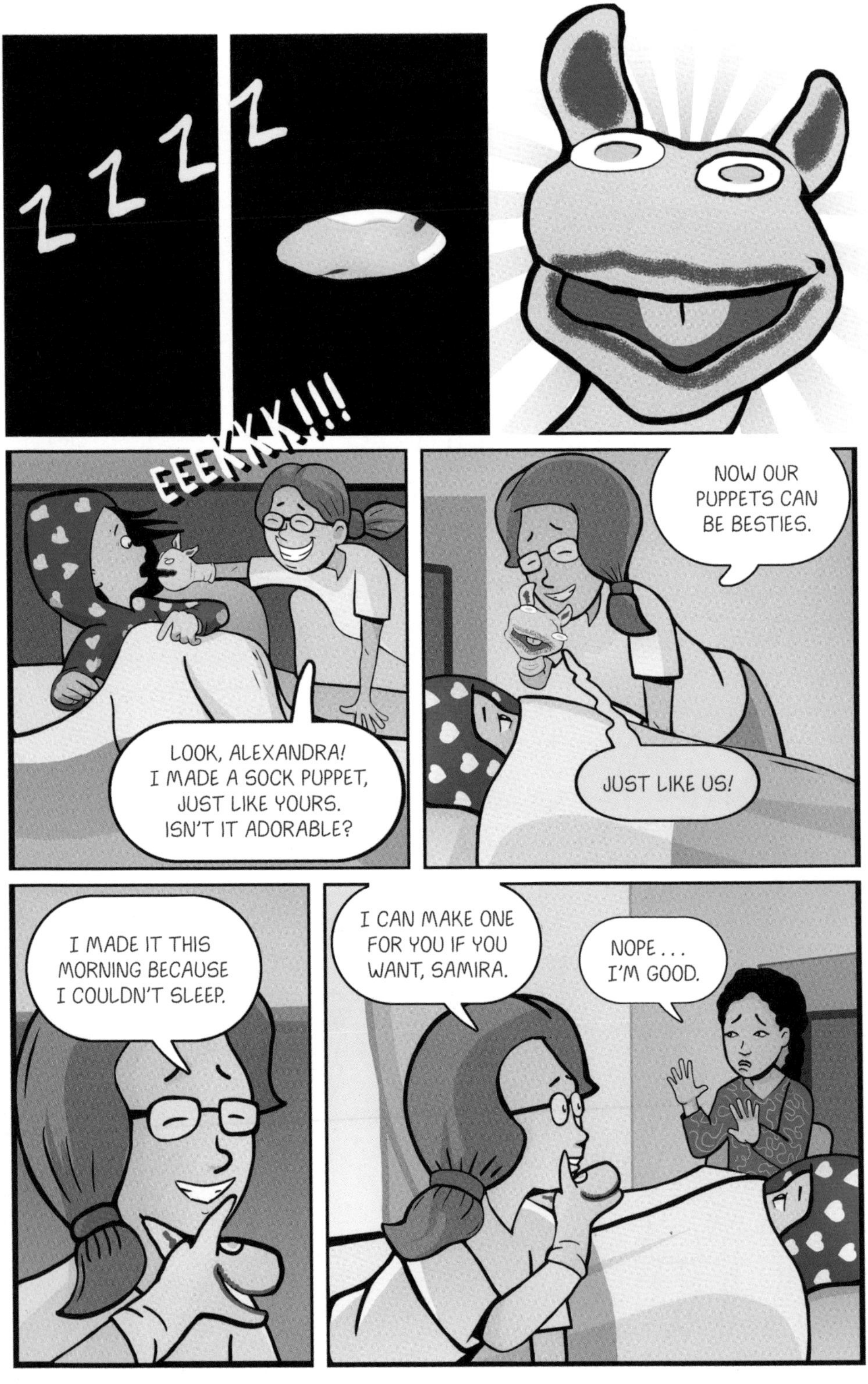
Z Z Z Z
EEEKKK!!!
LOOK, ALEXANDRA! I MADE A SOCK PUPPET, JUST LIKE YOURS. ISN'T IT ADORABLE?
NOW OUR PUPPETS CAN BE BESTIES.
JUST LIKE US!
I MADE IT THIS MORNING BECAUSE I COULDN'T SLEEP.
I CAN MAKE ONE FOR YOU IF YOU WANT, SAMIRA.
NOPE . . . I'M GOOD.

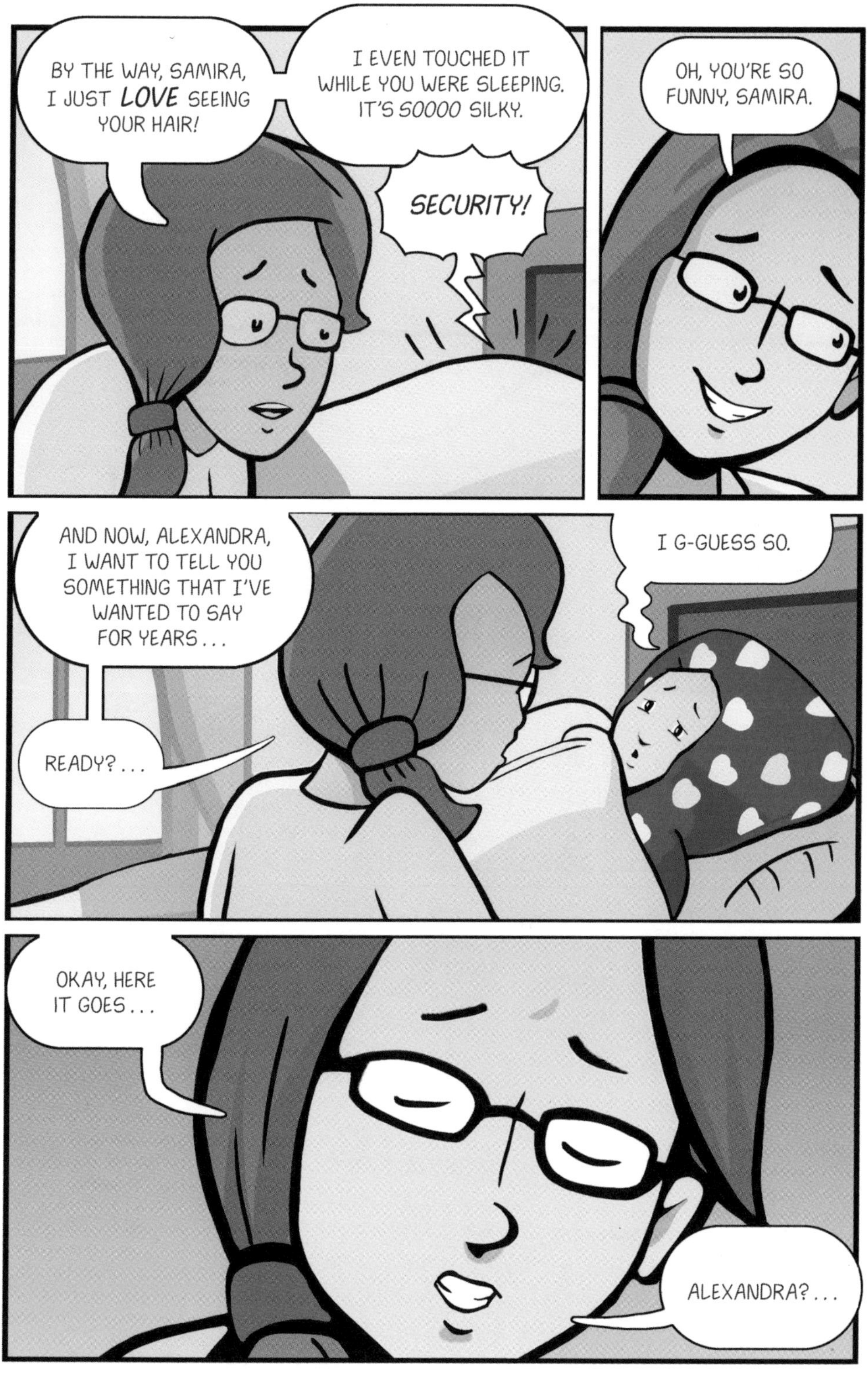
BY THE WAY, SAMIRA, I JUST LOVE SEEING YOUR HAIR!
I EVEN TOUCHED IT WHILE YOU WERE SLEEPING. IT'S SOOOO SILKY.
SECURITY!
OH, YOU'RE SO FUNNY, SAMIRA.
AND NOW, ALEXANDRA, I WANT TO TELL YOU SOMETHING THAT I'VE WANTED TO SAY FOR YEARS . . .
READY? . . .
I G-GUESS SO.
OKAY, HERE IT GOES . . .
ALEXANDRA? . . .

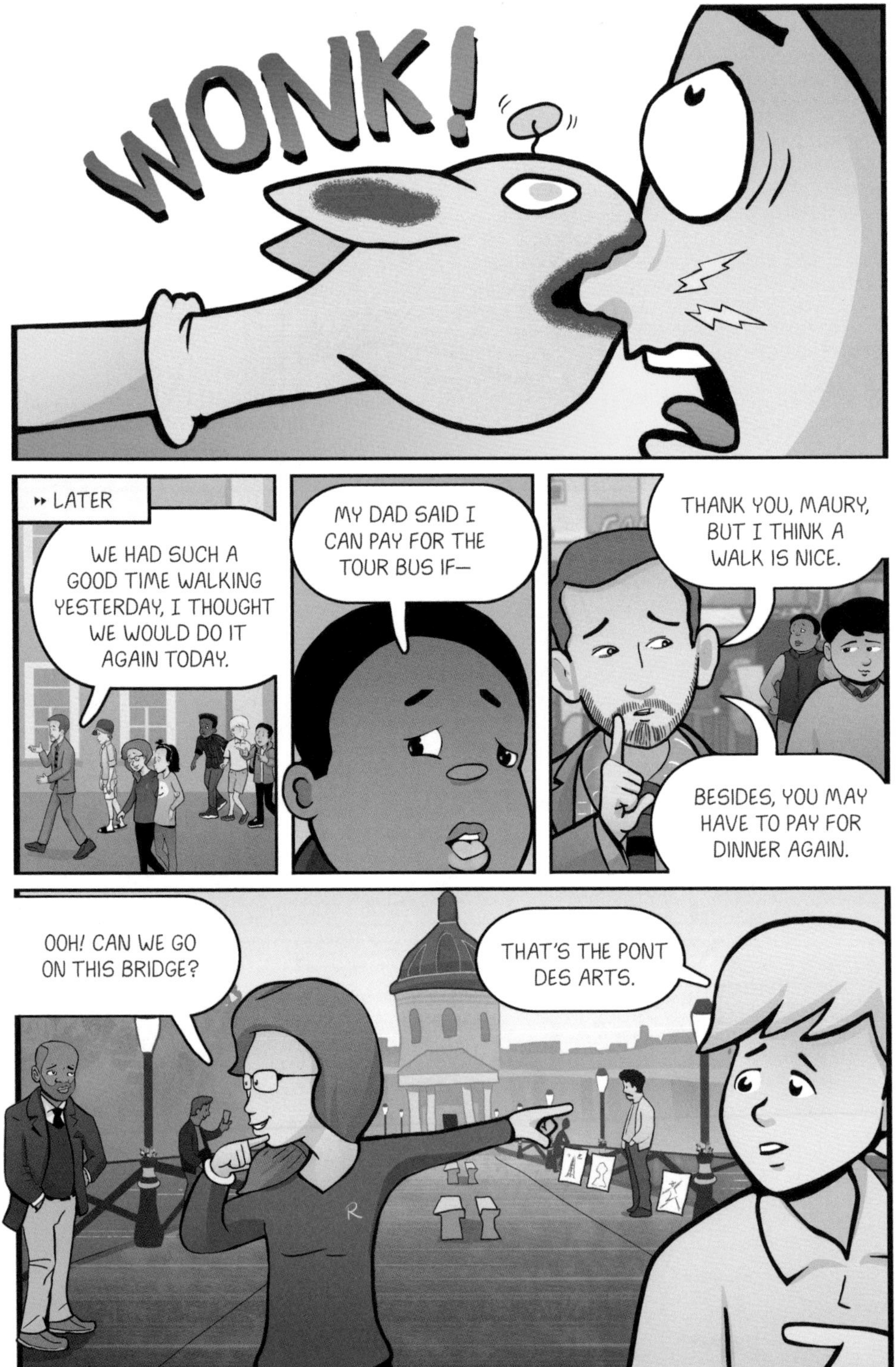
WONK!
LATER
WE HAD SUCH A GOOD TIME WALKING YESTERDAY, I THOUGHT WE WOULD DO IT AGAIN TODAY.
MY DAD SAID I CAN PAY FOR THE TOUR BUS IF—
THANK YOU, MAURY, BUT I THINK A WALK IS NICE.
BESIDES, YOU MAY HAVE TO PAY FOR DINNER AGAIN.
OOH! CAN WE GO ON THIS BRIDGE?
THAT'S THE PONT DES ARTS.

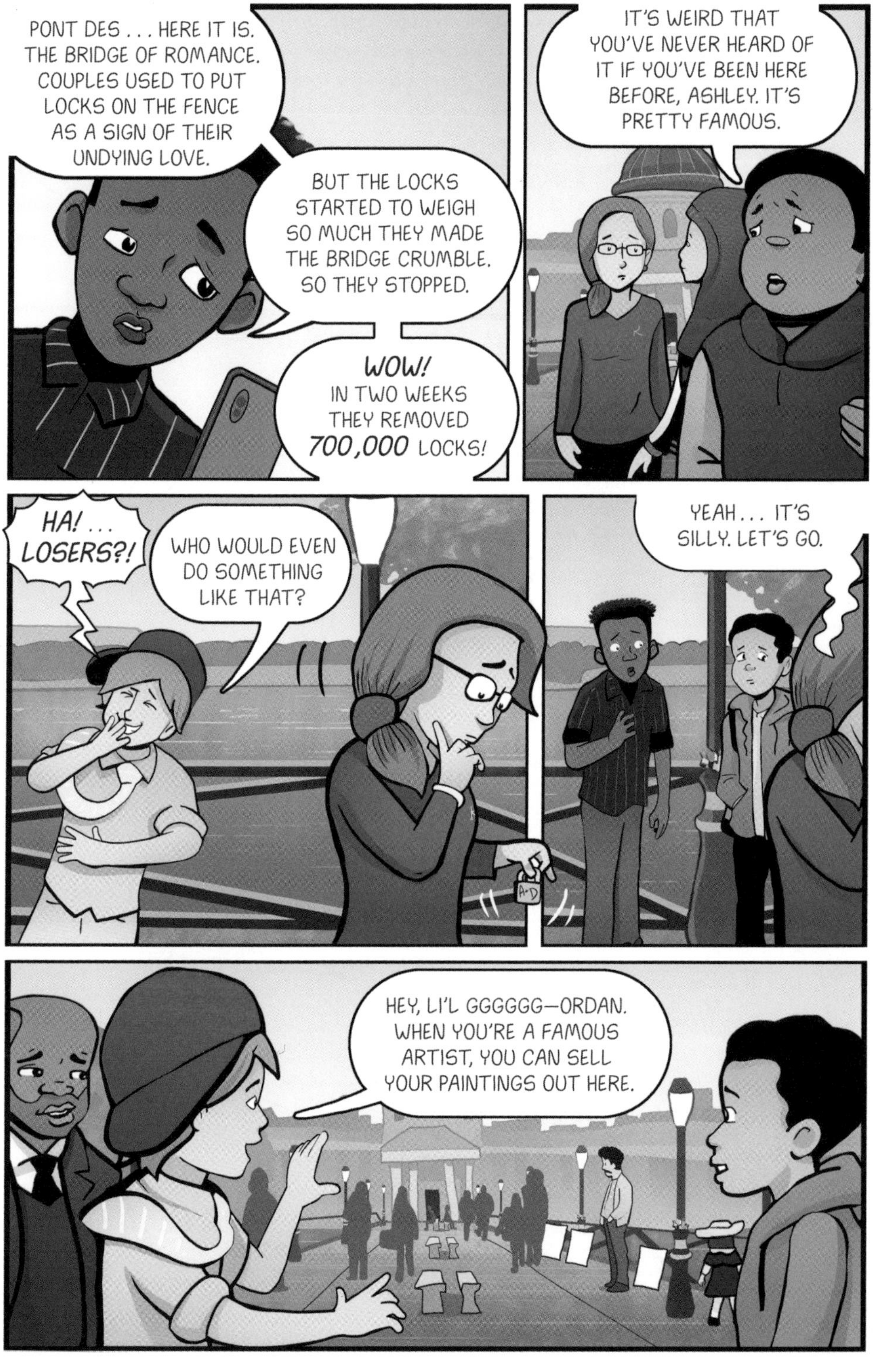
PONT DES . . . HERE IT IS. THE BRIDGE OF ROMANCE. COUPLES USED TO PUT LOCKS ON THE FENCE AS A SIGN OF THEIR UNDYING LOVE.
BUT THE LOCKS STARTED TO WEIGH SO MUCH THEY MADE THE BRIDGE CRUMBLE. SO THEY STOPPED.
WOW! IN TWO WEEKS THEY REMOVED 700,000 LOCKS!
IT'S WEIRD THAT YOU'VE NEVER HEARD OF IT IF YOU'VE BEEN HERE BEFORE, ASHLEY. IT'S PRETTY FAMOUS.
HA! . . . LOSERS?!
WHO WOULD EVEN DO SOMETHING LIKE THAT?
A+D
YEAH . . . IT'S SILLY. LET'S GO.
HEY, LI'L GGGGGG—ORDAN. WHEN YOU'RE A FAMOUS ARTIST, YOU CAN SELL YOUR PAINTINGS OUT HERE.

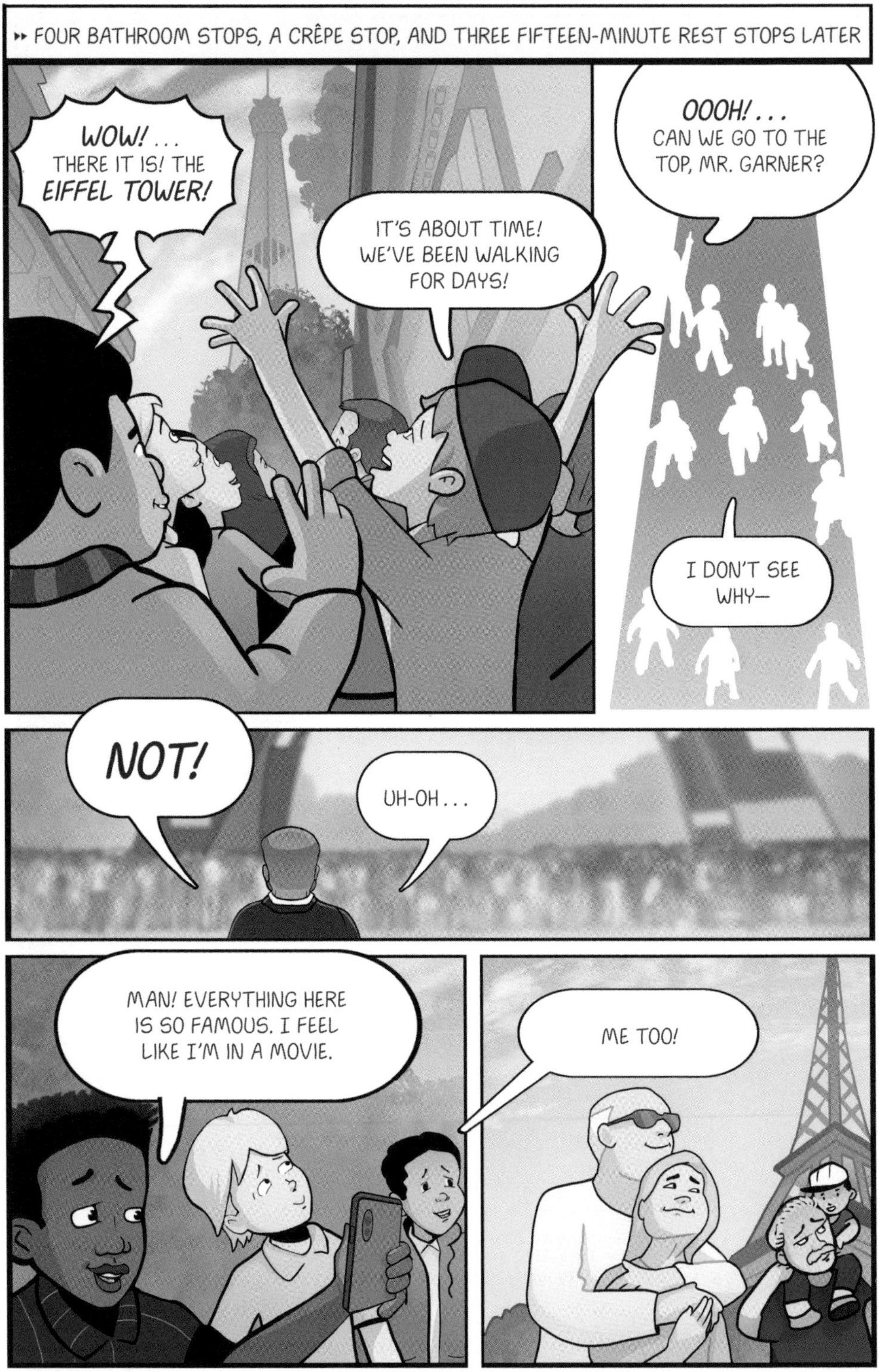
FOUR BATHROOM STOPS, A CRÊPE STOP, AND THREE FIFTEEN-MINUTE REST STOPS LATER
WOW! ... THERE IT IS! THE EIFFEL TOWER!
IT'S ABOUT TIME! WE'VE BEEN WALKING FOR DAYS!
OOOH! ... CAN WE GO TO THE TOP, MR. GARNER?
I DON'T SEE WHY—
NOT!
UH-OH ...
MAN! EVERYTHING HERE IS SO FAMOUS. I FEEL LIKE I'M IN A MOVIE.
ME TOO!

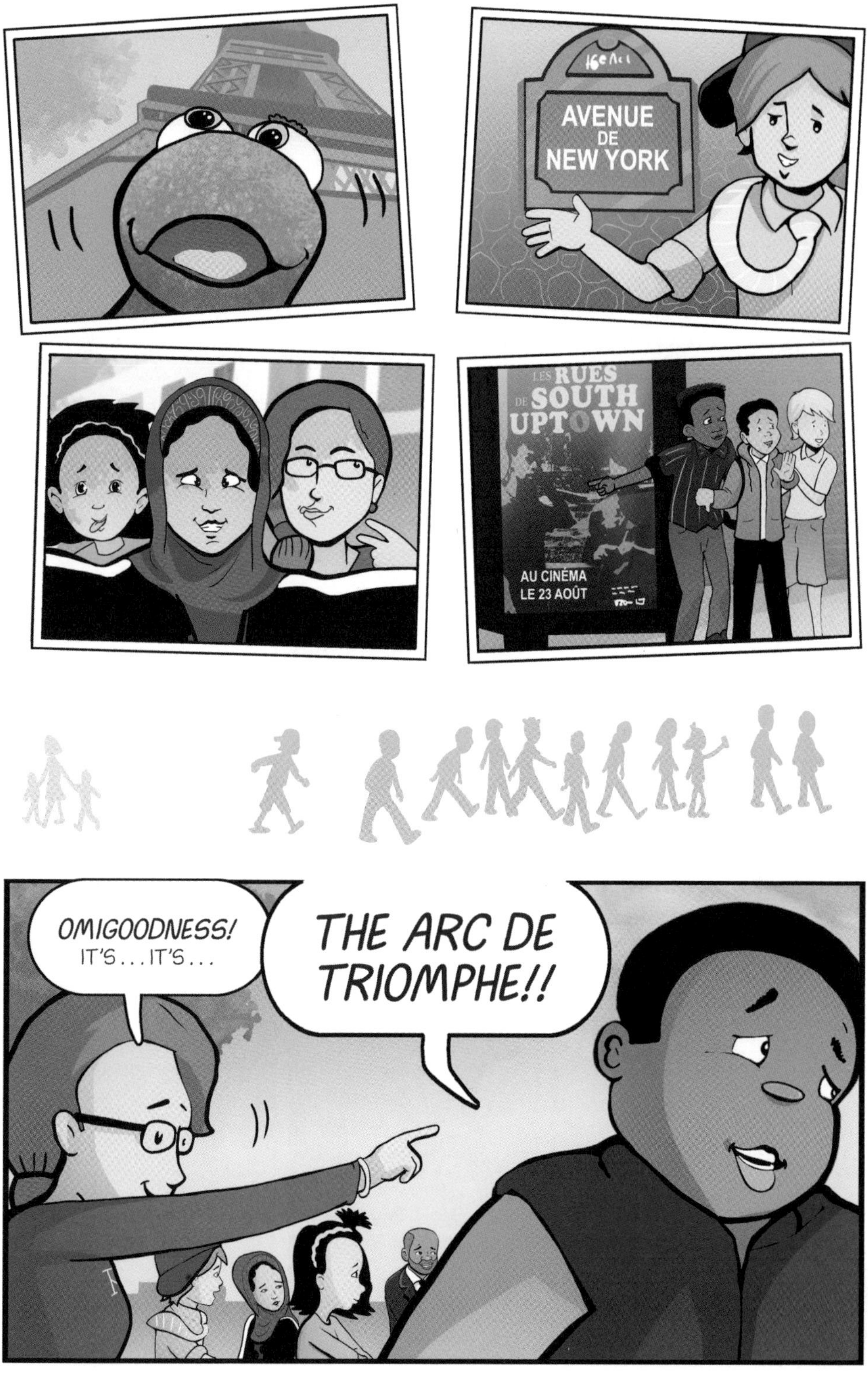
AVENUE
DE
NEW YORK
LES RUES
DE SOUTH
UPTOWN
AU CINÉMA
LE 23 AOÛT
OMIGOODNESS! IT'S . . . IT'S . . .
THE ARC DE TRIOMPHE!!

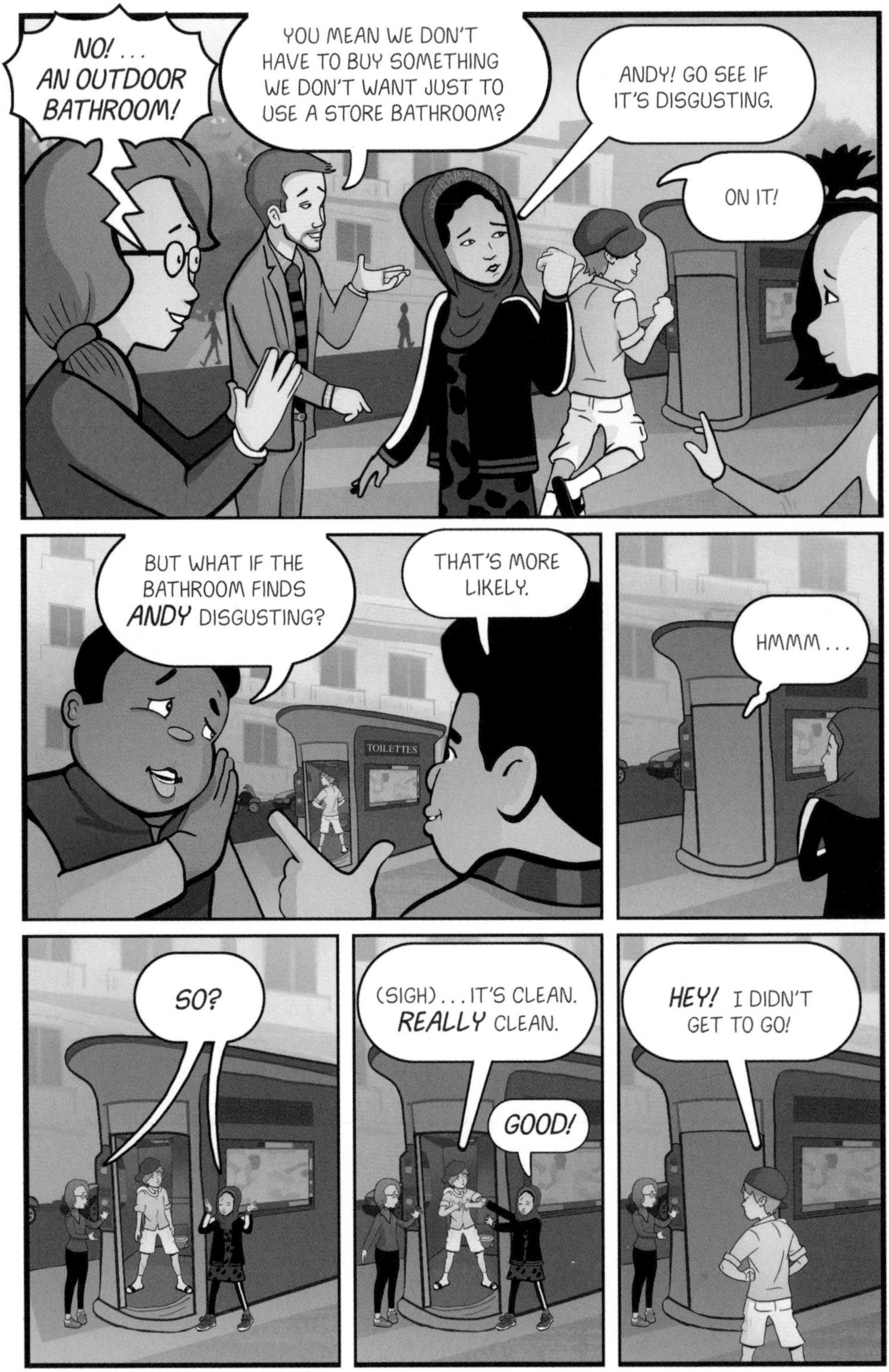
NO! . . .
AN OUTDOOR BATHROOM!
YOU MEAN WE DON'T HAVE TO BUY SOMETHING WE DON'T WANT JUST TO USE A STORE BATHROOM?
ANDY! GO SEE IF IT'S DISGUSTING.
ON IT!
BUT WHAT IF THE BATHROOM FINDS *ANDY* DISGUSTING?
THAT'S MORE LIKELY.
TOILETTES
HMMM . . .
SO?
(SIGH) . . . IT'S CLEAN. **REALLY** CLEAN.
GOOD!
HEY! I DIDN'T GET TO GO!

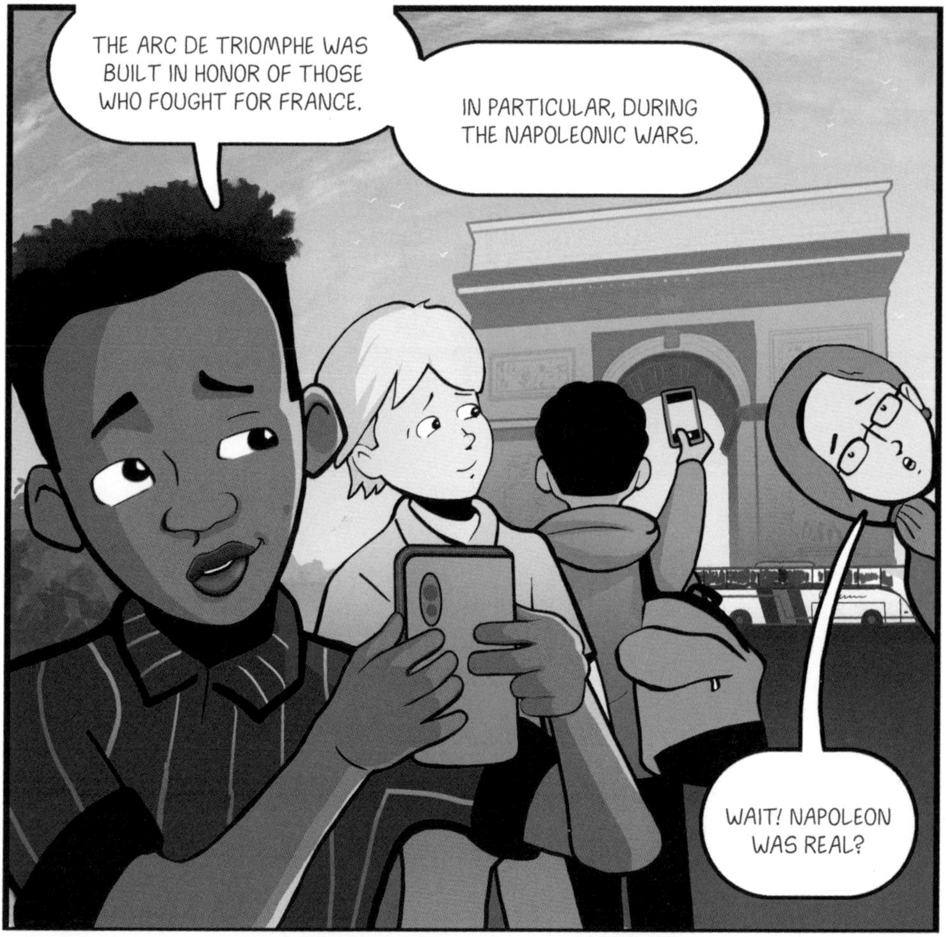
THE ARC DE TRIOMPHE WAS BUILT IN HONOR OF THOSE WHO FOUGHT FOR FRANCE.
IN PARTICULAR, DURING THE NAPOLEONIC WARS.
WAIT! NAPOLEON WAS REAL?

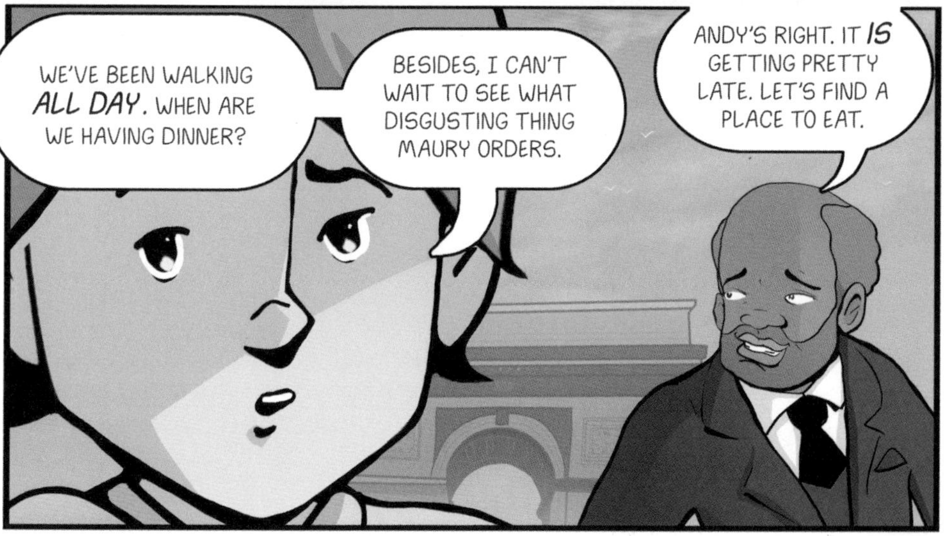
WE'VE BEEN WALKING ALL DAY. WHEN ARE WE HAVING DINNER?
BESIDES, I CAN'T WAIT TO SEE WHAT DISGUSTING THING MAURY ORDERS.
ANDY'S RIGHT. IT IS GETTING PRETTY LATE. LET'S FIND A PLACE TO EAT.

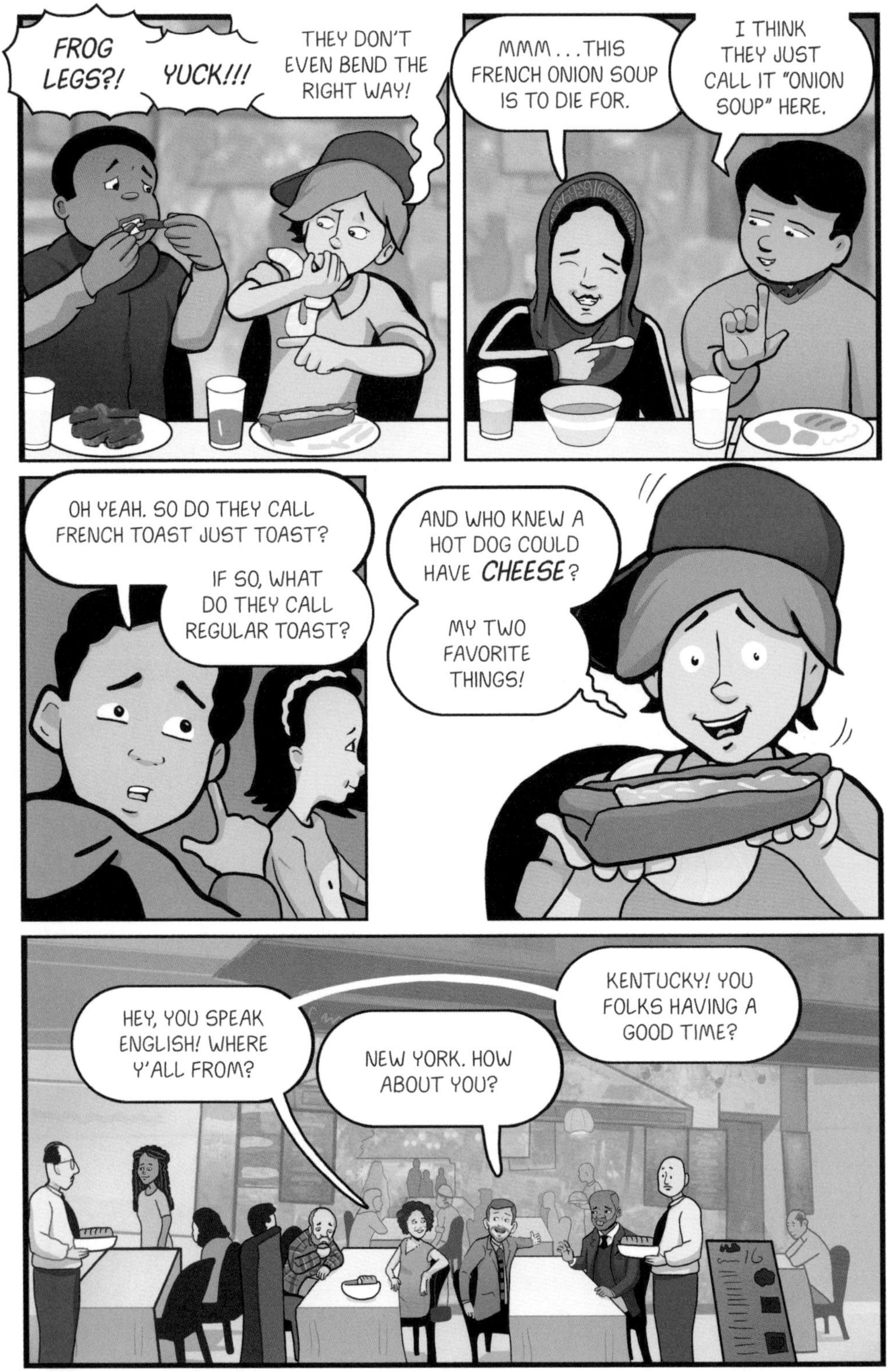
FROG LEGS?!
YUCK!!!
THEY DON'T EVEN BEND THE RIGHT WAY!
MMM . . . THIS FRENCH ONION SOUP IS TO DIE FOR.
I THINK THEY JUST CALL IT "ONION SOUP" HERE.
OH YEAH. SO DO THEY CALL FRENCH TOAST JUST TOAST?
IF SO, WHAT DO THEY CALL REGULAR TOAST?
AND WHO KNEW A HOT DOG COULD HAVE CHEESE?
MY TWO FAVORITE THINGS!
HEY, YOU SPEAK ENGLISH! WHERE Y'ALL FROM?
NEW YORK. HOW ABOUT YOU?
KENTUCKY! YOU FOLKS HAVING A GOOD TIME?

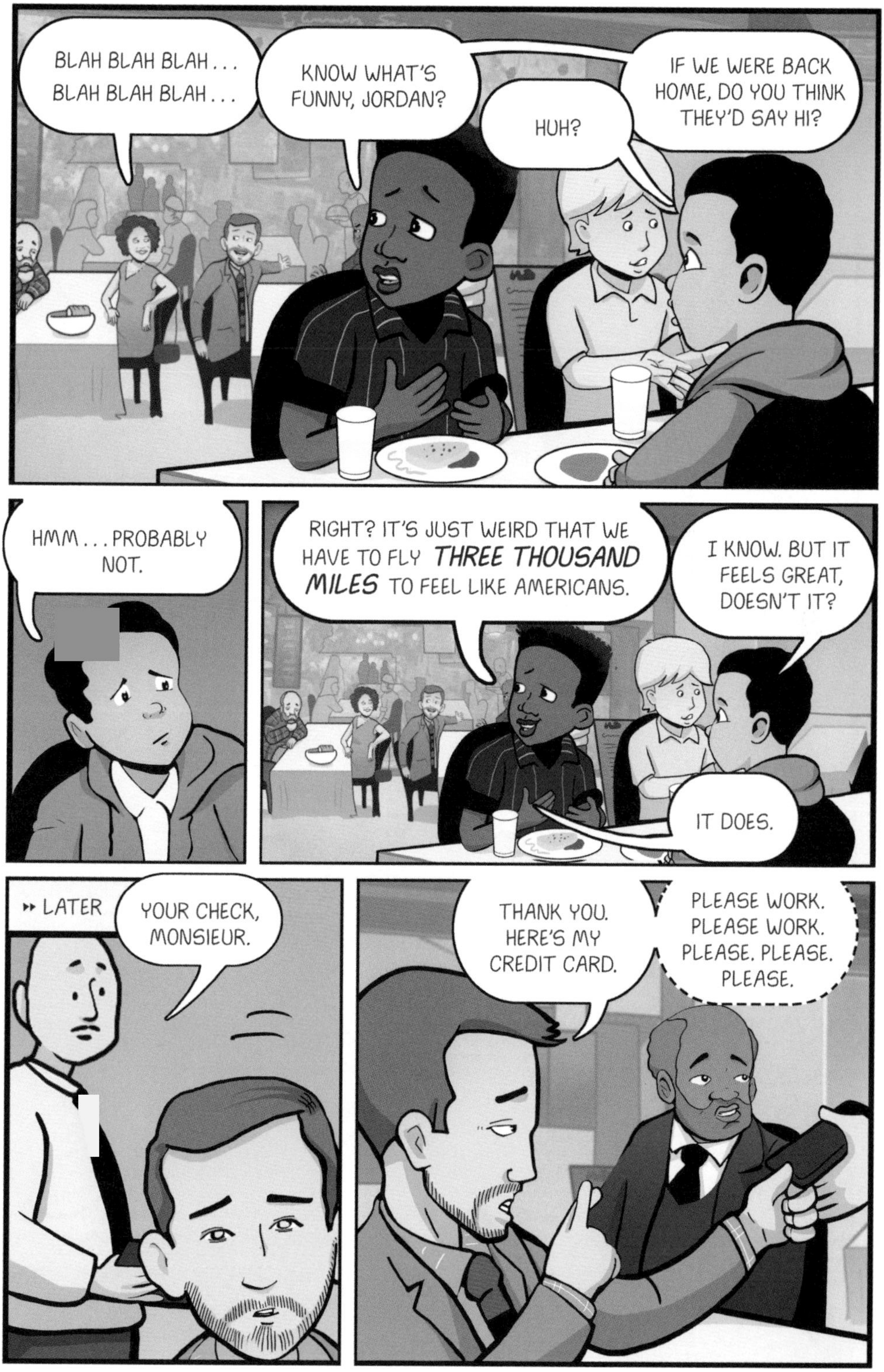
BLAH BLAH BLAH . . . BLAH BLAH BLAH . . .
KNOW WHAT'S FUNNY, JORDAN?
HUH?
IF WE WERE BACK HOME, DO YOU THINK THEY'D SAY HI?
HMM . . . PROBABLY NOT.
RIGHT? IT'S JUST WEIRD THAT WE HAVE TO FLY THREE THOUSAND MILES TO FEEL LIKE AMERICANS.
I KNOW. BUT IT FEELS GREAT, DOESN'T IT?
IT DOES.
LATER
YOUR CHECK, MONSIEUR.
THANK YOU. HERE'S MY CREDIT CARD.
PLEASE WORK. PLEASE WORK. PLEASE. PLEASE. PLEASE.

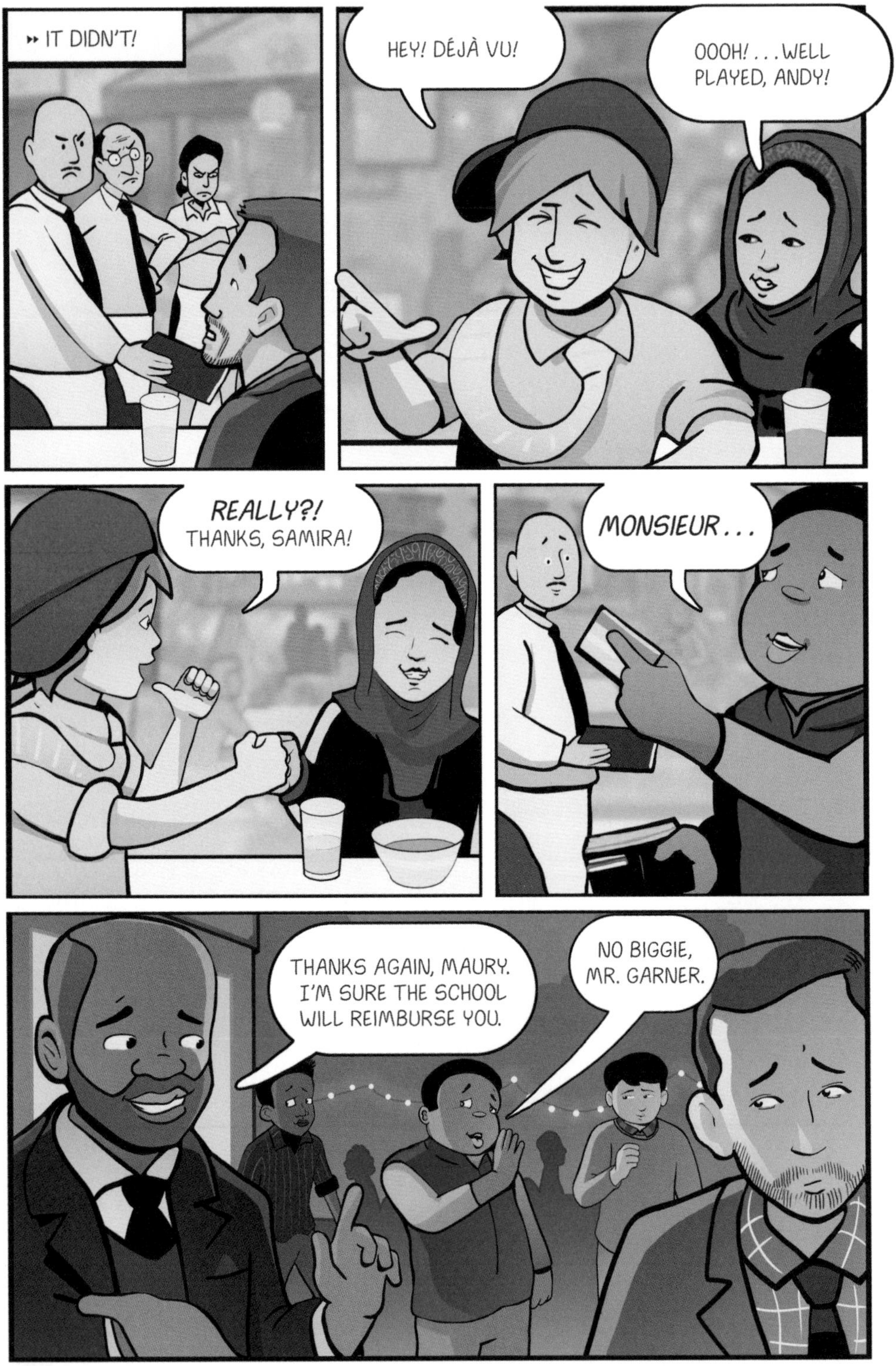
▸▸ IT DIDN'T!
HEY! DÉJÀ VU!
OOOH! . . . WELL PLAYED, ANDY!
REALLY?! THANKS, SAMIRA!
MONSIEUR . . .
THANKS AGAIN, MAURY. I'M SURE THE SCHOOL WILL REIMBURSE YOU.
NO BIGGIE, MR. GARNER.

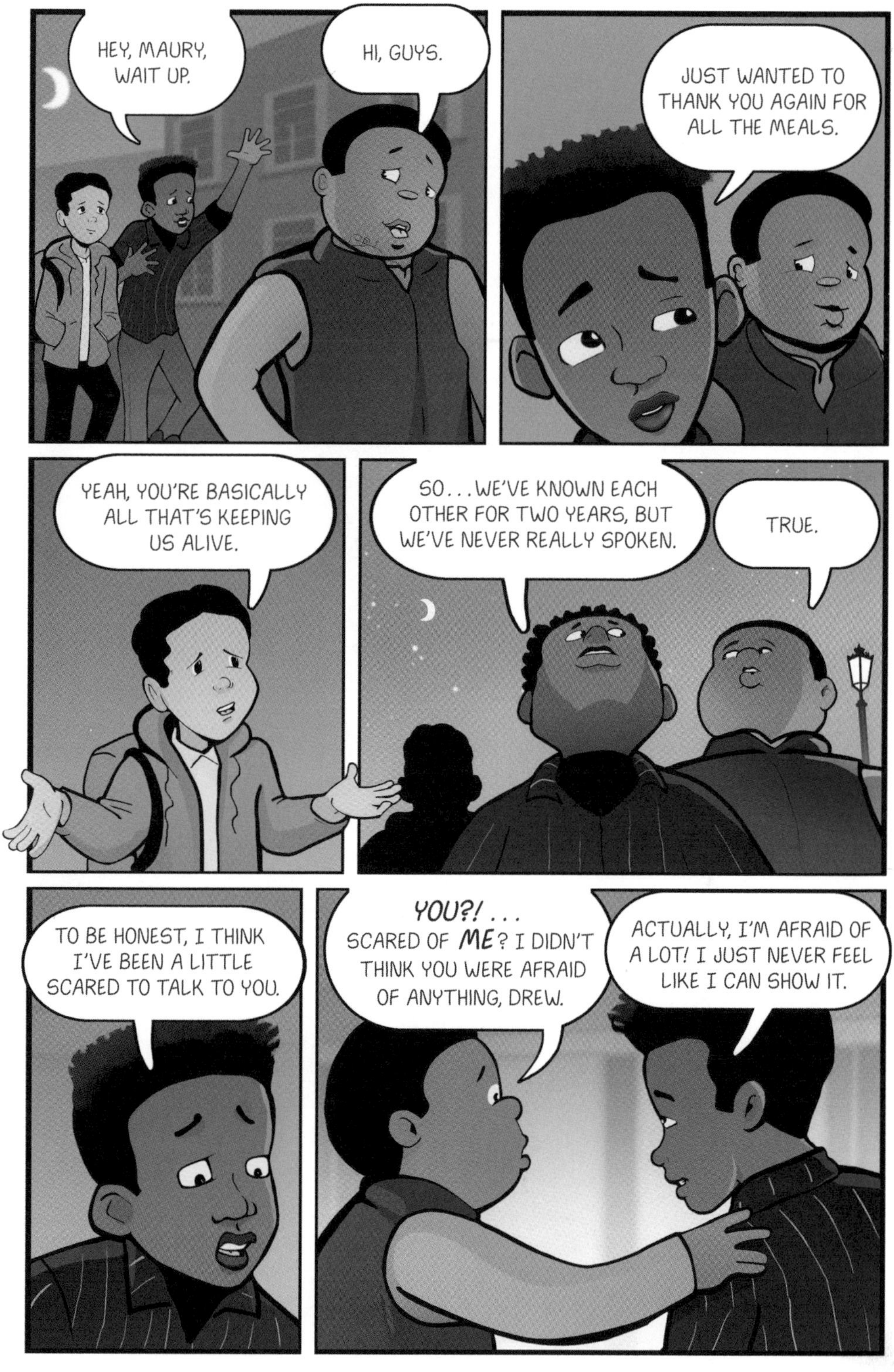
HEY, MAURY, WAIT UP.
HI, GUYS.
JUST WANTED TO THANK YOU AGAIN FOR ALL THE MEALS.
YEAH, YOU'RE BASICALLY ALL THAT'S KEEPING US ALIVE.
SO. . . WE'VE KNOWN EACH OTHER FOR TWO YEARS, BUT WE'VE NEVER REALLY SPOKEN.
TRUE.
TO BE HONEST, I THINK I'VE BEEN A LITTLE SCARED TO TALK TO YOU.
YOU?! . . . SCARED OF ME? I DIDN'T THINK YOU WERE AFRAID OF ANYTHING, DREW.
ACTUALLY, I'M AFRAID OF A LOT! I JUST NEVER FEEL LIKE I CAN SHOW IT.

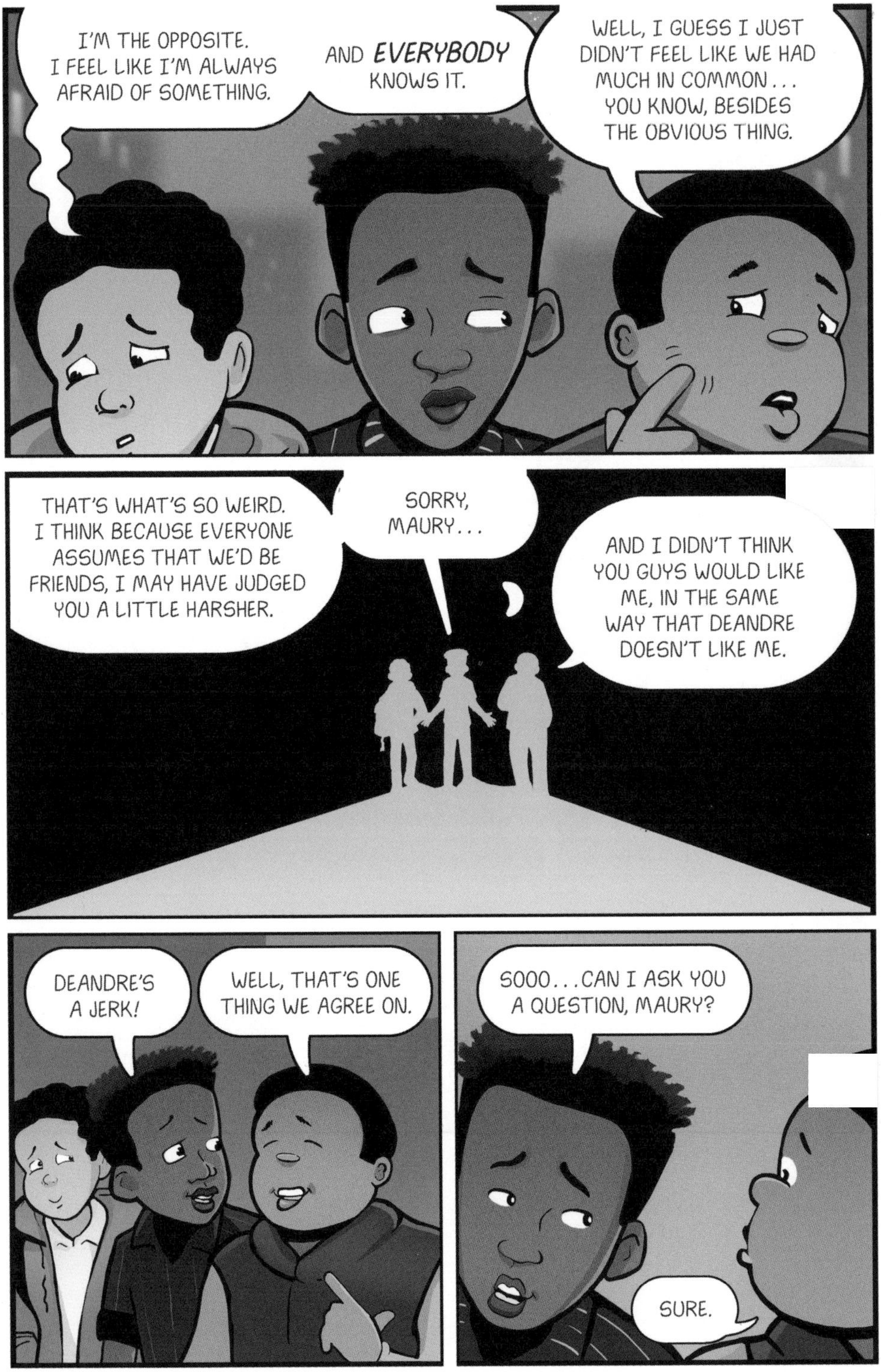
I'M THE OPPOSITE. I FEEL LIKE I'M ALWAYS AFRAID OF SOMETHING.
AND EVERYBODY KNOWS IT.
WELL, I GUESS I JUST DIDN'T FEEL LIKE WE HAD MUCH IN COMMON... YOU KNOW, BESIDES THE OBVIOUS THING.
THAT'S WHAT'S SO WEIRD. I THINK BECAUSE EVERYONE ASSUMES THAT WE'D BE FRIENDS, I MAY HAVE JUDGED YOU A LITTLE HARSHER.
SORRY, MAURY...
AND I DIDN'T THINK YOU GUYS WOULD LIKE ME, IN THE SAME WAY THAT DEANDRE DOESN'T LIKE ME.
DEANDRE'S A JERK!
WELL, THAT'S ONE THING WE AGREE ON.
SOOO...CAN I ASK YOU A QUESTION, MAURY?
SURE.

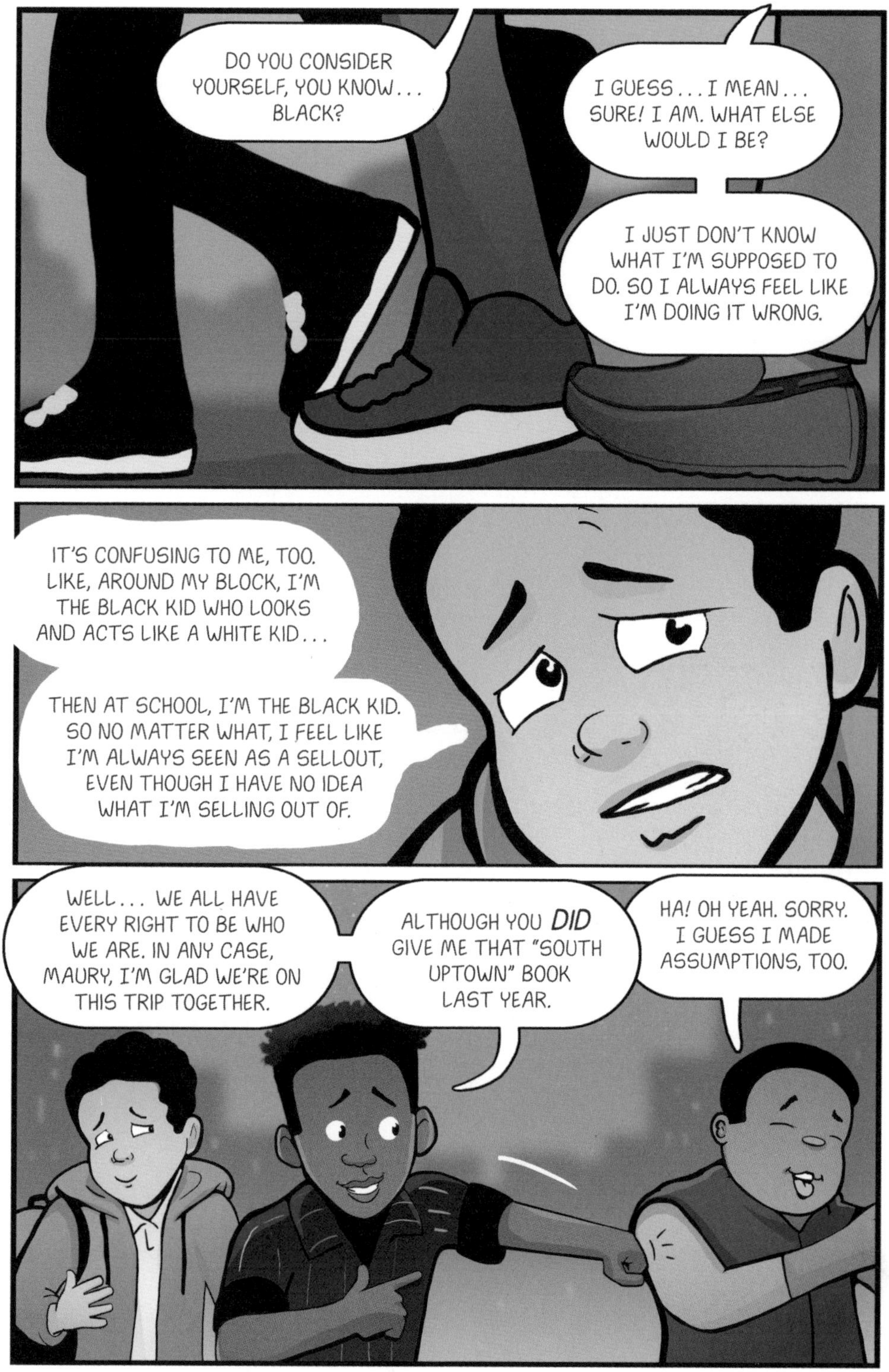
DO YOU CONSIDER YOURSELF, YOU KNOW... BLACK?
I GUESS... I MEAN... SURE! I AM. WHAT ELSE WOULD I BE?
I JUST DON'T KNOW WHAT I'M SUPPOSED TO DO. SO I ALWAYS FEEL LIKE I'M DOING IT WRONG.
IT'S CONFUSING TO ME, TOO. LIKE, AROUND MY BLOCK, I'M THE BLACK KID WHO LOOKS AND ACTS LIKE A WHITE KID...
THEN AT SCHOOL, I'M THE BLACK KID. SO NO MATTER WHAT, I FEEL LIKE I'M ALWAYS SEEN AS A SELLOUT, EVEN THOUGH I HAVE NO IDEA WHAT I'M SELLING OUT OF.
WELL... WE ALL HAVE EVERY RIGHT TO BE WHO WE ARE. IN ANY CASE, MAURY, I'M GLAD WE'RE ON THIS TRIP TOGETHER.
ALTHOUGH YOU ***DID*** GIVE ME THAT "SOUTH UPTOWN" BOOK LAST YEAR.
HA! OH YEAH. SORRY. I GUESS I MADE ASSUMPTIONS, TOO.

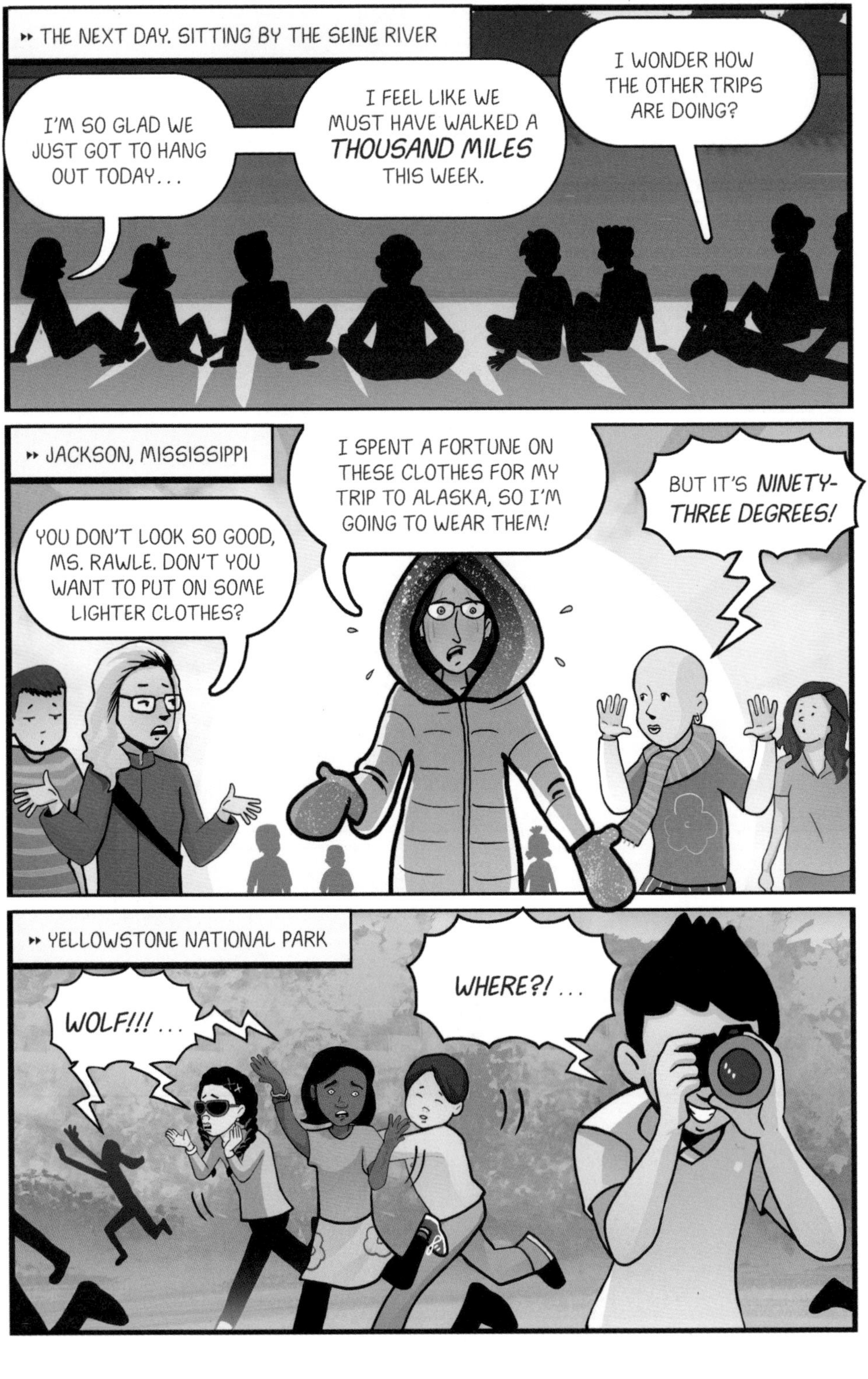
THE NEXT DAY. SITTING BY THE SEINE RIVER
I'M SO GLAD WE JUST GOT TO HANG OUT TODAY...
I FEEL LIKE WE MUST HAVE WALKED A *THOUSAND MILES* THIS WEEK.
I WONDER HOW THE OTHER TRIPS ARE DOING?
JACKSON, MISSISSIPPI
YOU DON'T LOOK SO GOOD, MS. RAWLE. DON'T YOU WANT TO PUT ON SOME LIGHTER CLOTHES?
I SPENT A FORTUNE ON THESE CLOTHES FOR MY TRIP TO ALASKA, SO I'M GOING TO WEAR THEM!
BUT IT'S *NINETY-THREE DEGREES!*
YELLOWSTONE NATIONAL PARK
WOLF!!! ...
WHERE?! ...

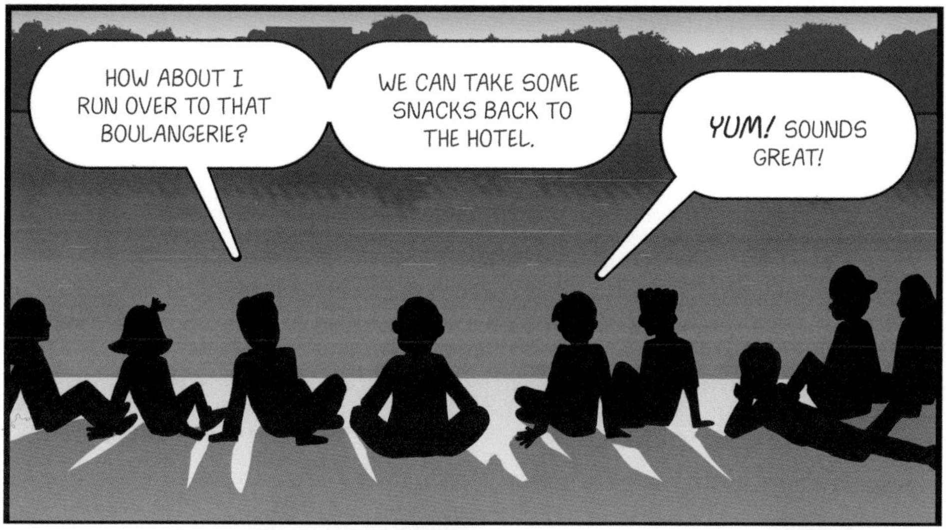
HOW ABOUT I RUN OVER TO THAT BOULANGERIE?
WE CAN TAKE SOME SNACKS BACK TO THE HOTEL.
YUM! SOUNDS GREAT!

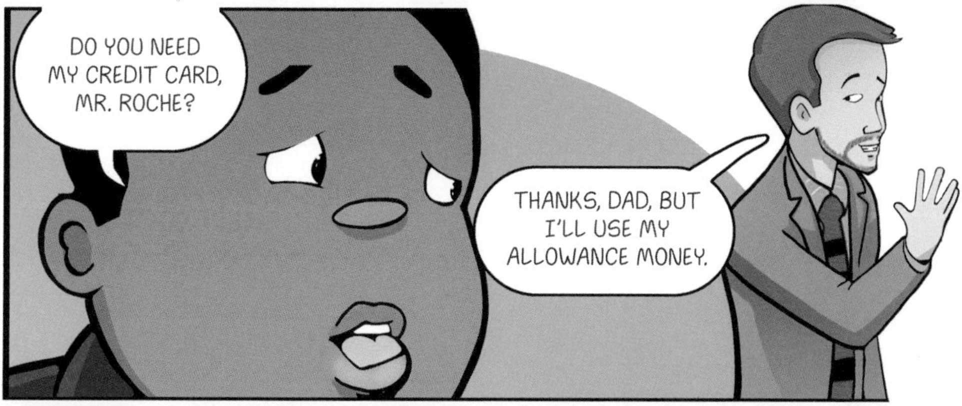
DO YOU NEED MY CREDIT CARD, MR. ROCHE?
THANKS, DAD, BUT I'LL USE MY ALLOWANCE MONEY.

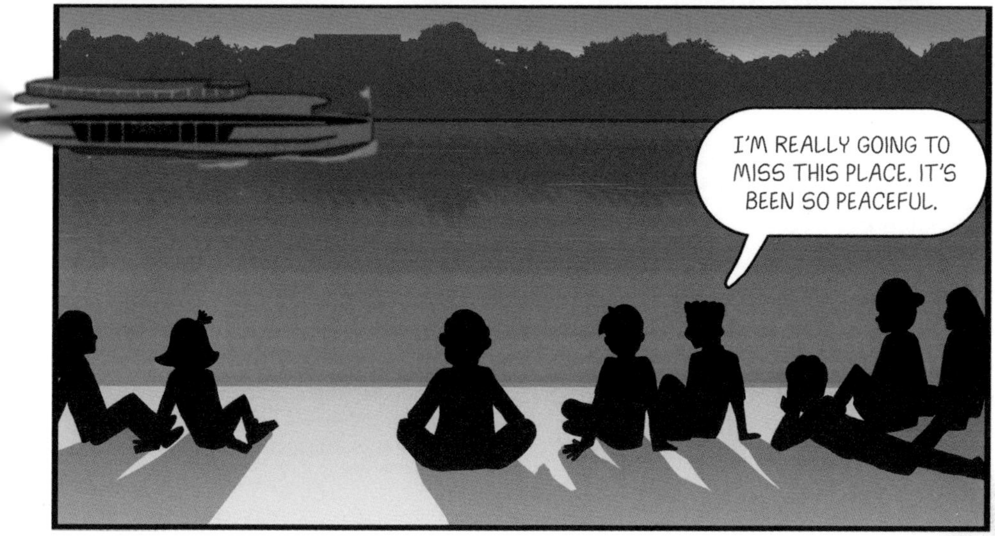
I'M REALLY GOING TO MISS THIS PLACE. IT'S BEEN SO PEACEFUL.

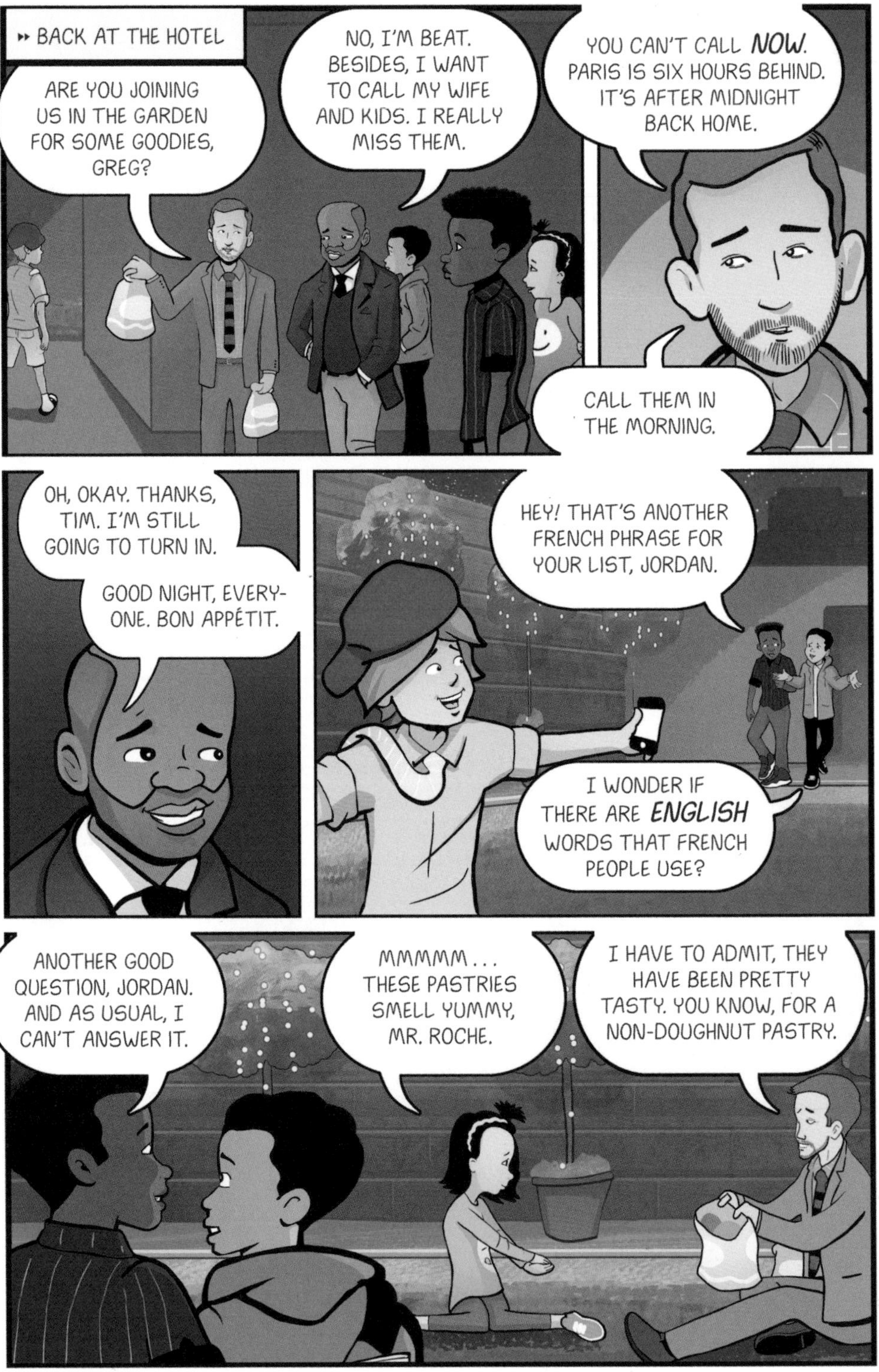
BACK AT THE HOTEL
ARE YOU JOINING US IN THE GARDEN FOR SOME GOODIES, GREG?
NO, I'M BEAT. BESIDES, I WANT TO CALL MY WIFE AND KIDS. I REALLY MISS THEM.
YOU CAN'T CALL NOW. PARIS IS SIX HOURS BEHIND. IT'S AFTER MIDNIGHT BACK HOME.
CALL THEM IN THE MORNING.
OH, OKAY. THANKS, TIM. I'M STILL GOING TO TURN IN.
GOOD NIGHT, EVERYONE. BON APPÉTIT.
HEY! THAT'S ANOTHER FRENCH PHRASE FOR YOUR LIST, JORDAN.
I WONDER IF THERE ARE ENGLISH WORDS THAT FRENCH PEOPLE USE?
ANOTHER GOOD QUESTION, JORDAN. AND AS USUAL, I CAN'T ANSWER IT.
MMMMM . . . THESE PASTRIES SMELL YUMMY, MR. ROCHE.
I HAVE TO ADMIT, THEY HAVE BEEN PRETTY TASTY. YOU KNOW, FOR A NON-DOUGHNUT PASTRY.

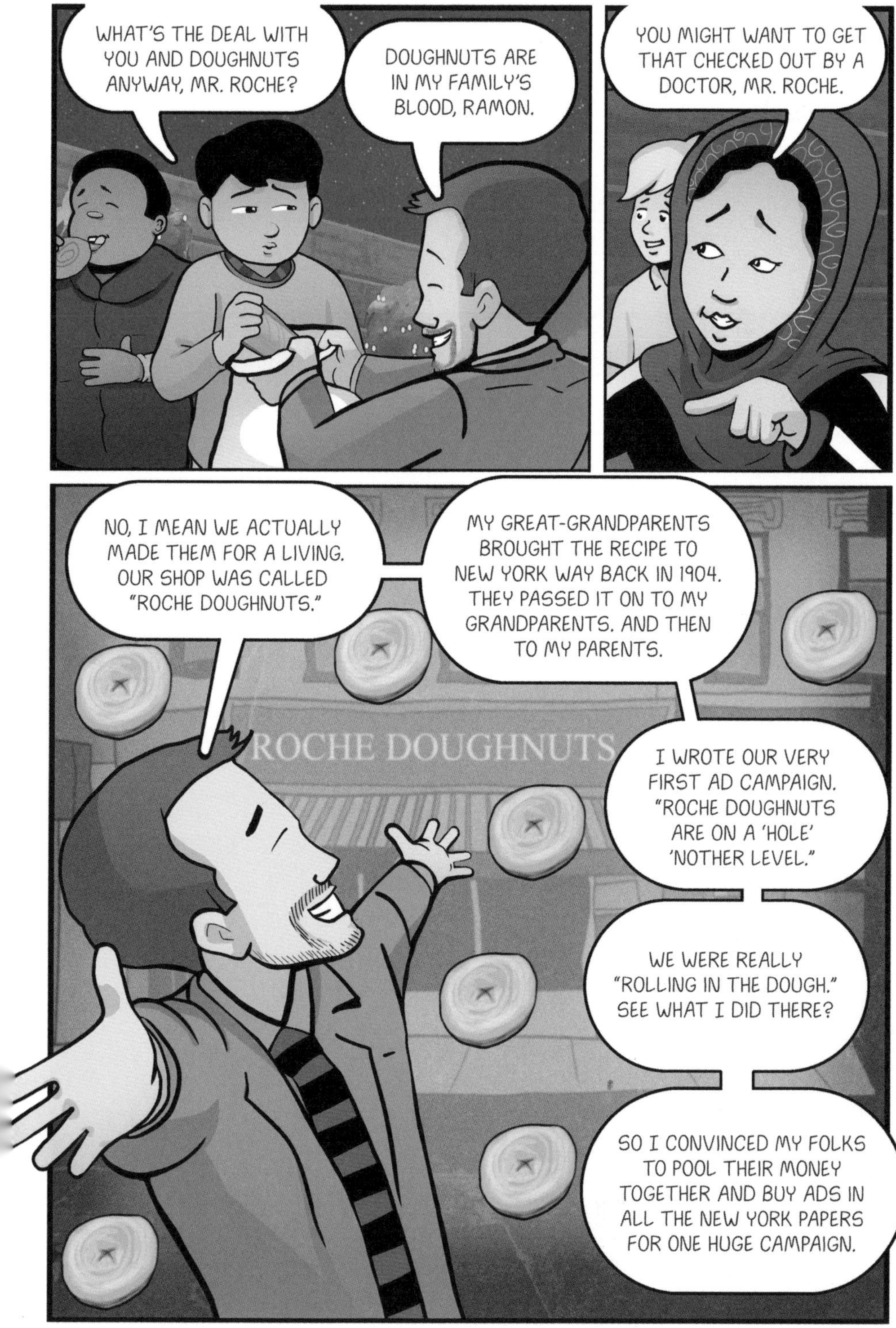
WHAT'S THE DEAL WITH YOU AND DOUGHNUTS ANYWAY, MR. ROCHE?
DOUGHNUTS ARE IN MY FAMILY'S BLOOD, RAMON.
YOU MIGHT WANT TO GET THAT CHECKED OUT BY A DOCTOR, MR. ROCHE.
NO, I MEAN WE ACTUALLY MADE THEM FOR A LIVING. OUR SHOP WAS CALLED "ROCHE DOUGHNUTS."
MY GREAT-GRANDPARENTS BROUGHT THE RECIPE TO NEW YORK WAY BACK IN 1904. THEY PASSED IT ON TO MY GRANDPARENTS. AND THEN TO MY PARENTS.
ROCHE DOUGHNUTS
I WROTE OUR VERY FIRST AD CAMPAIGN. "ROCHE DOUGHNUTS ARE ON A 'HOLE' 'NOTHER LEVEL."
WE WERE REALLY "ROLLING IN THE DOUGH." SEE WHAT I DID THERE?
SO I CONVINCED MY FOLKS TO POOL THEIR MONEY TOGETHER AND BUY ADS IN ALL THE NEW YORK PAPERS FOR ONE HUGE CAMPAIGN.

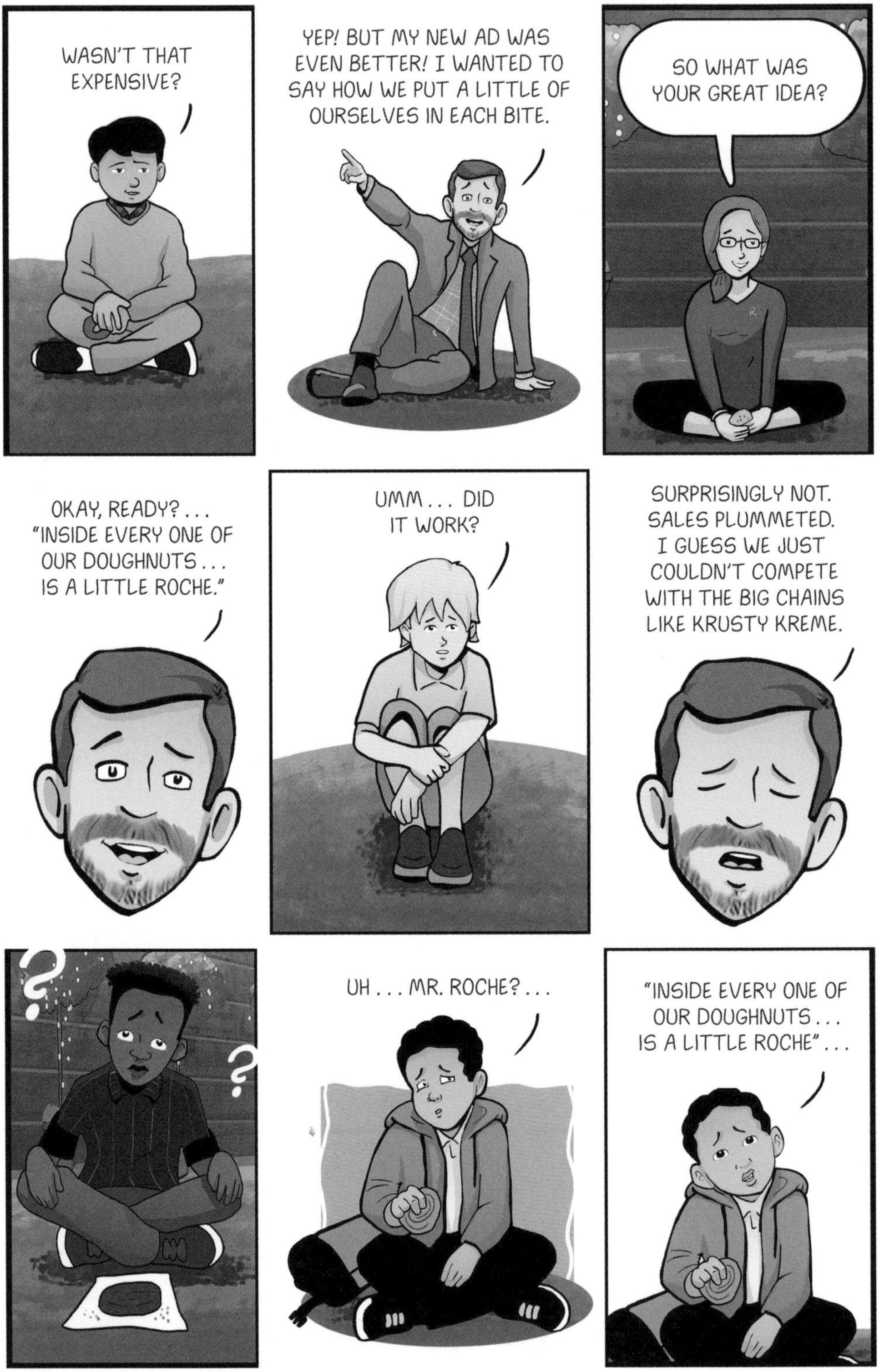
WASN'T THAT EXPENSIVE?
YEP! BUT MY NEW AD WAS EVEN BETTER! I WANTED TO SAY HOW WE PUT A LITTLE OF OURSELVES IN EACH BITE.
SO WHAT WAS YOUR GREAT IDEA?
OKAY, READY? . . . "INSIDE EVERY ONE OF OUR DOUGHNUTS . . . IS A LITTLE ROCHE."
UMM . . . DID IT WORK?
SURPRISINGLY NOT. SALES PLUMMETED. I GUESS WE JUST COULDN'T COMPETE WITH THE BIG CHAINS LIKE KRUSTY KREME.
UH . . . MR. ROCHE? . . .
"INSIDE EVERY ONE OF OUR DOUGHNUTS . . . IS A LITTLE ROCHE" . . .

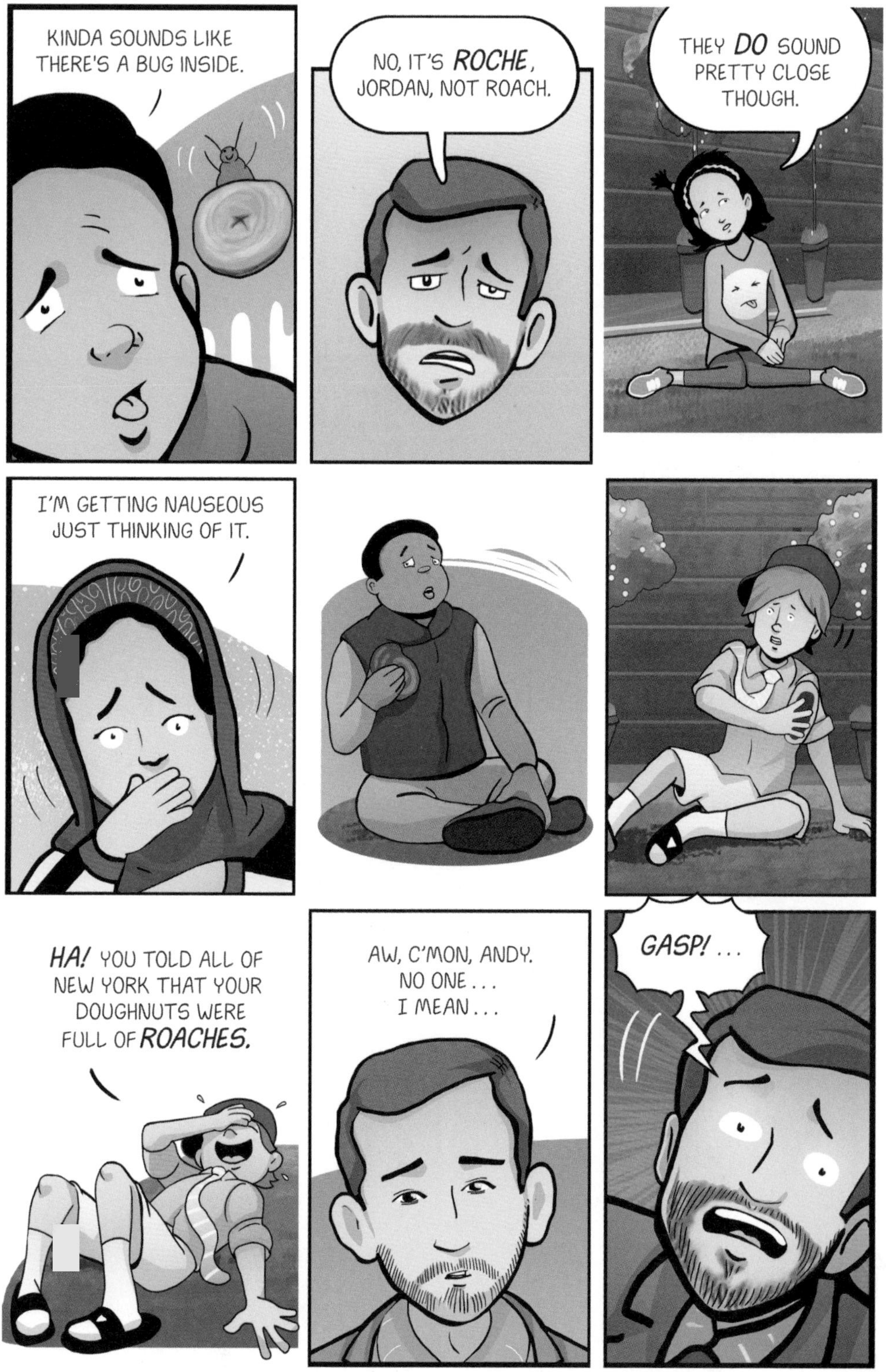
KINDA SOUNDS LIKE THERE'S A BUG INSIDE.
NO, IT'S ROCHE, JORDAN, NOT ROACH.
THEY DO SOUND PRETTY CLOSE THOUGH.
I'M GETTING NAUSEOUS JUST THINKING OF IT.
HA! YOU TOLD ALL OF NEW YORK THAT YOUR DOUGHNUTS WERE FULL OF ROACHES.
AW, C'MON, ANDY. NO ONE . . . I MEAN . . .
GASP! . . .

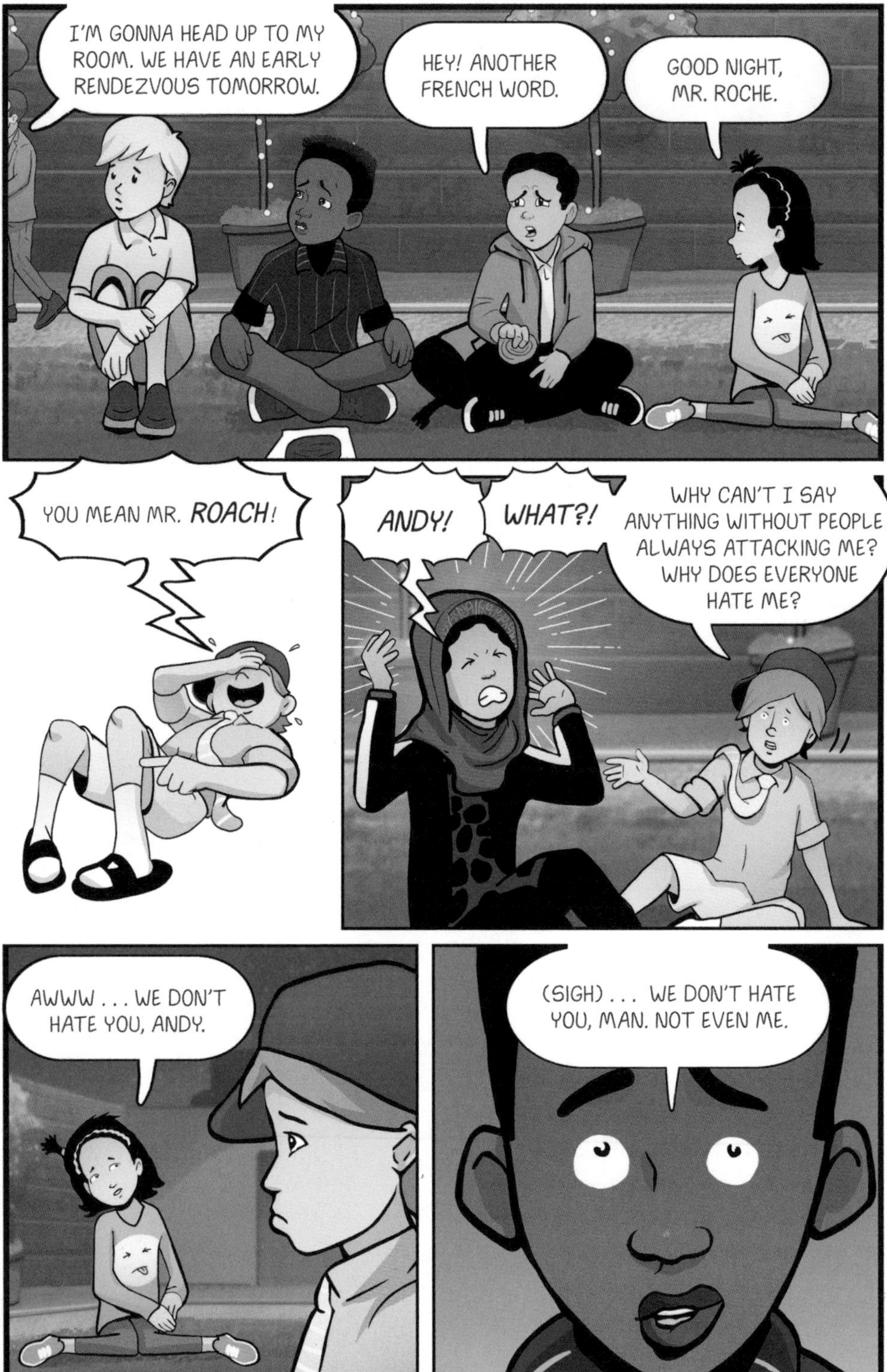
I'M GONNA HEAD UP TO MY ROOM. WE HAVE AN EARLY RENDEZVOUS TOMORROW.
HEY! ANOTHER FRENCH WORD.
GOOD NIGHT, MR. ROCHE.
YOU MEAN MR. ROACH!
ANDY!
WHAT?!
WHY CAN'T I SAY ANYTHING WITHOUT PEOPLE ALWAYS ATTACKING ME? WHY DOES EVERYONE HATE ME?
AWWW . . . WE DON'T HATE YOU, ANDY.
(SIGH) . . . WE DON'T HATE YOU, MAN. NOT EVEN ME.

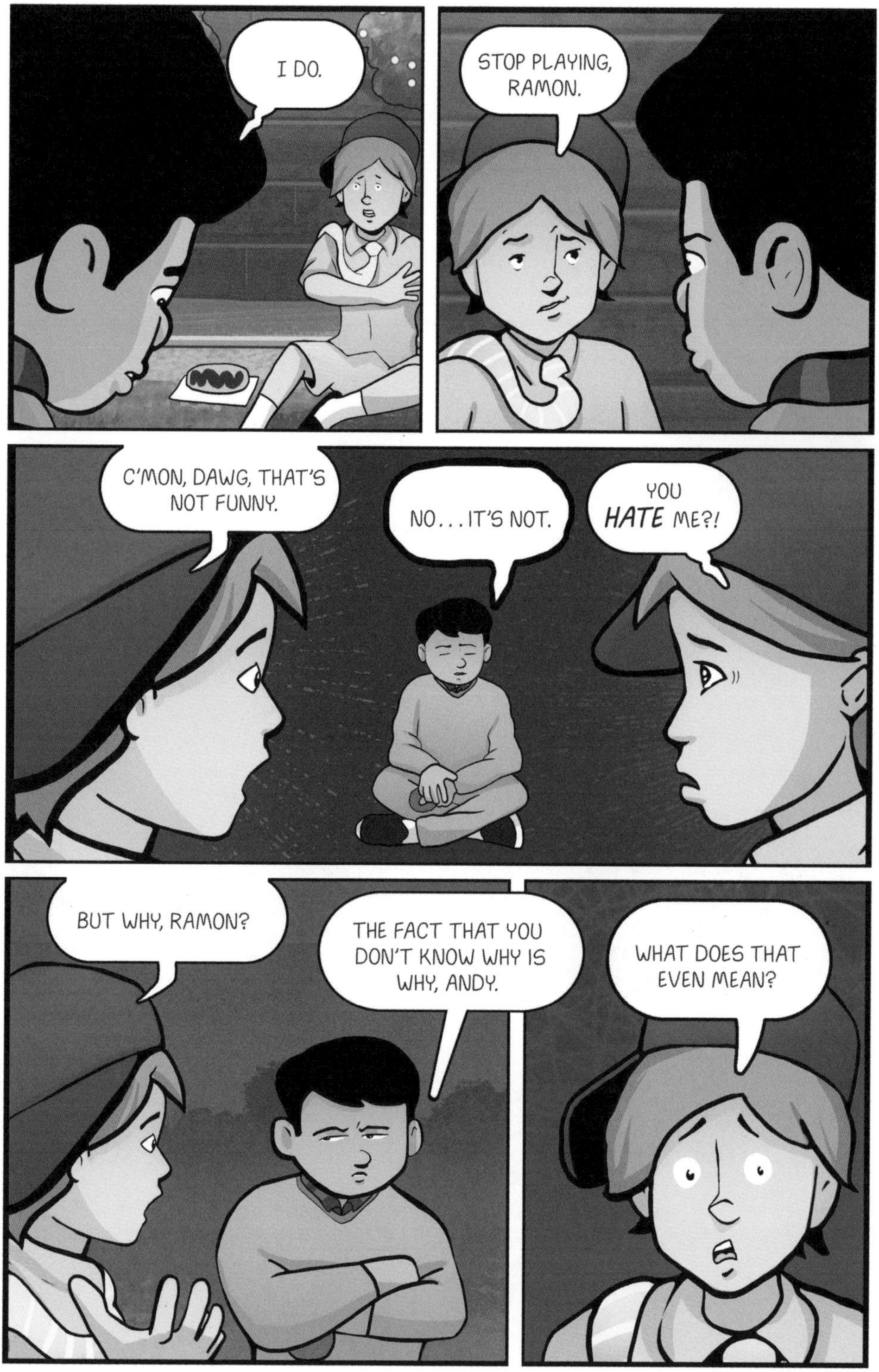

I DO.
STOP PLAYING, RAMON.
C'MON, DAWG, THAT'S NOT FUNNY.
NO... IT'S NOT.
YOU HATE ME?!
BUT WHY, RAMON?
THE FACT THAT YOU DON'T KNOW WHY IS WHY, ANDY.
WHAT DOES THAT EVEN MEAN?

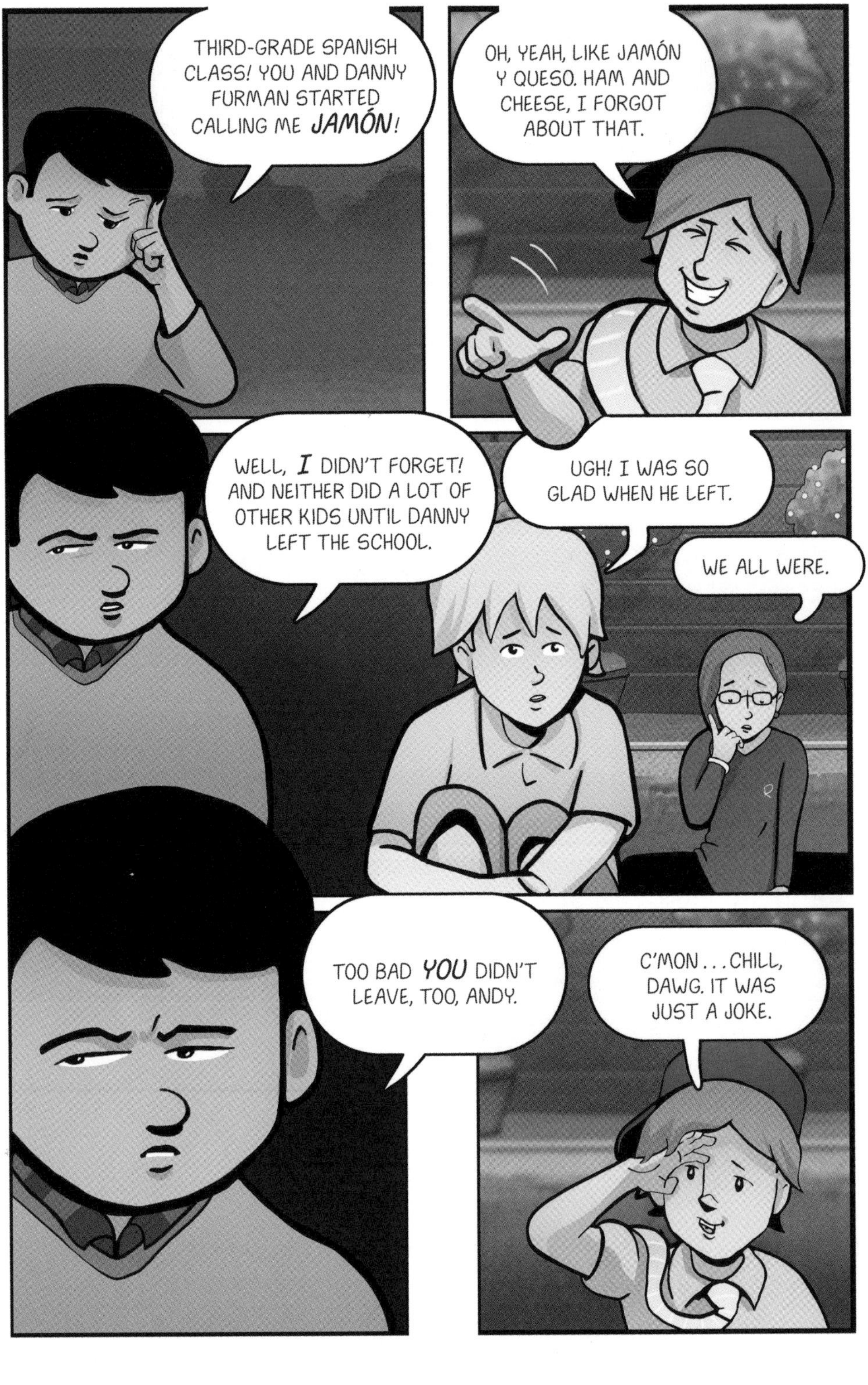
THIRD-GRADE SPANISH CLASS! YOU AND DANNY FURMAN STARTED CALLING ME JAMÓN!
OH, YEAH, LIKE JAMÓN Y QUESO. HAM AND CHEESE, I FORGOT ABOUT THAT.
WELL, I DIDN'T FORGET! AND NEITHER DID A LOT OF OTHER KIDS UNTIL DANNY LEFT THE SCHOOL.
UGH! I WAS SO GLAD WHEN HE LEFT.
WE ALL WERE.
TOO BAD YOU DIDN'T LEAVE, TOO, ANDY.
C'MON . . . CHILL, DAWG. IT WAS JUST A JOKE.

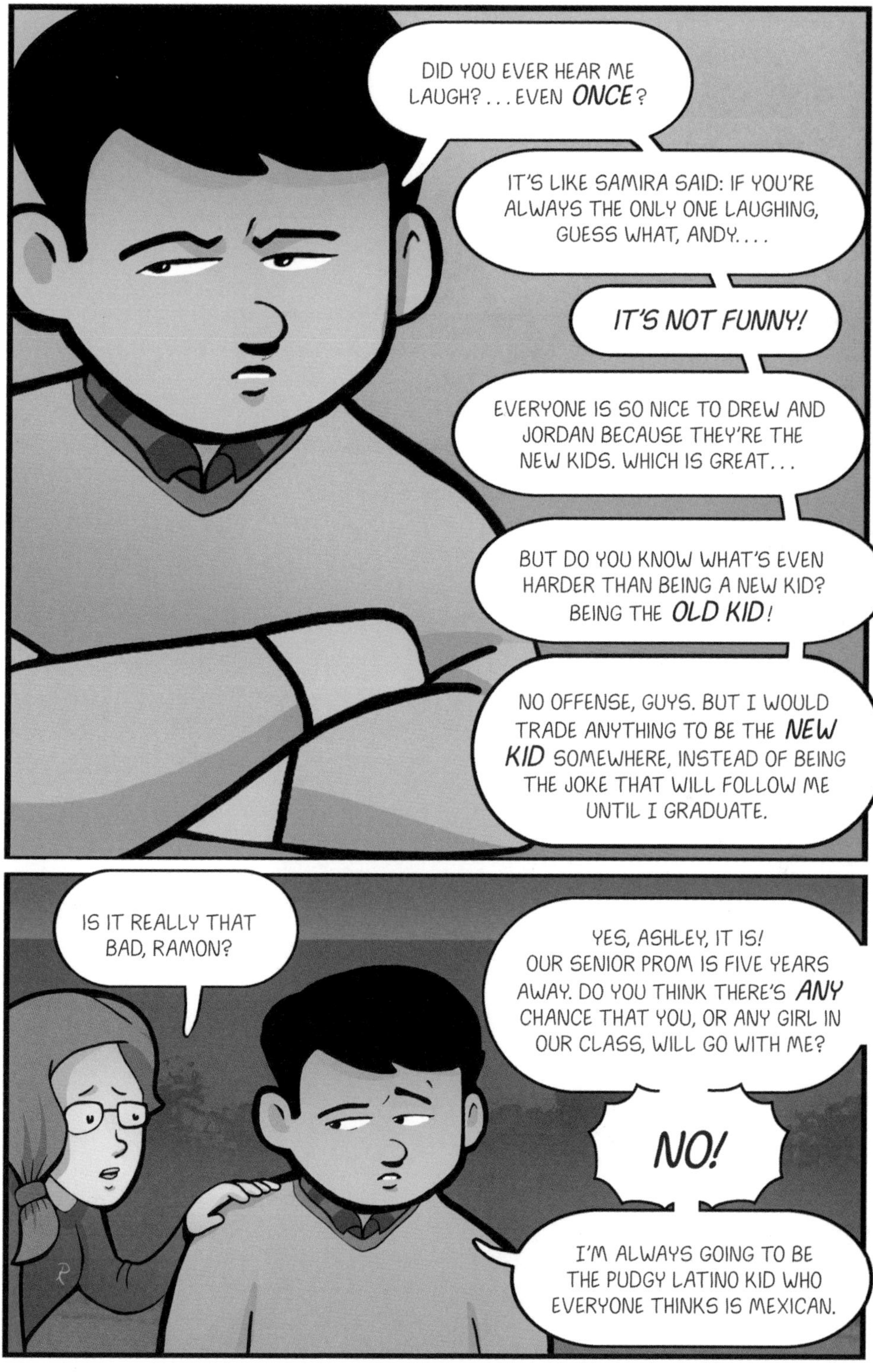

DID YOU EVER HEAR ME LAUGH? . . . EVEN ONCE?
IT'S LIKE SAMIRA SAID: IF YOU'RE ALWAYS THE ONLY ONE LAUGHING, GUESS WHAT, ANDY. . . .
IT'S NOT FUNNY!
EVERYONE IS SO NICE TO DREW AND JORDAN BECAUSE THEY'RE THE NEW KIDS. WHICH IS GREAT. . .
BUT DO YOU KNOW WHAT'S EVEN HARDER THAN BEING A NEW KID? BEING THE OLD KID!
NO OFFENSE, GUYS. BUT I WOULD TRADE ANYTHING TO BE THE NEW KID SOMEWHERE, INSTEAD OF BEING THE JOKE THAT WILL FOLLOW ME UNTIL I GRADUATE.
IS IT REALLY THAT BAD, RAMON?
YES, ASHLEY, IT IS! OUR SENIOR PROM IS FIVE YEARS AWAY. DO YOU THINK THERE'S ANY CHANCE THAT YOU, OR ANY GIRL IN OUR CLASS, WILL GO WITH ME?
NO!
I'M ALWAYS GOING TO BE THE PUDGY LATINO KID WHO EVERYONE THINKS IS MEXICAN.

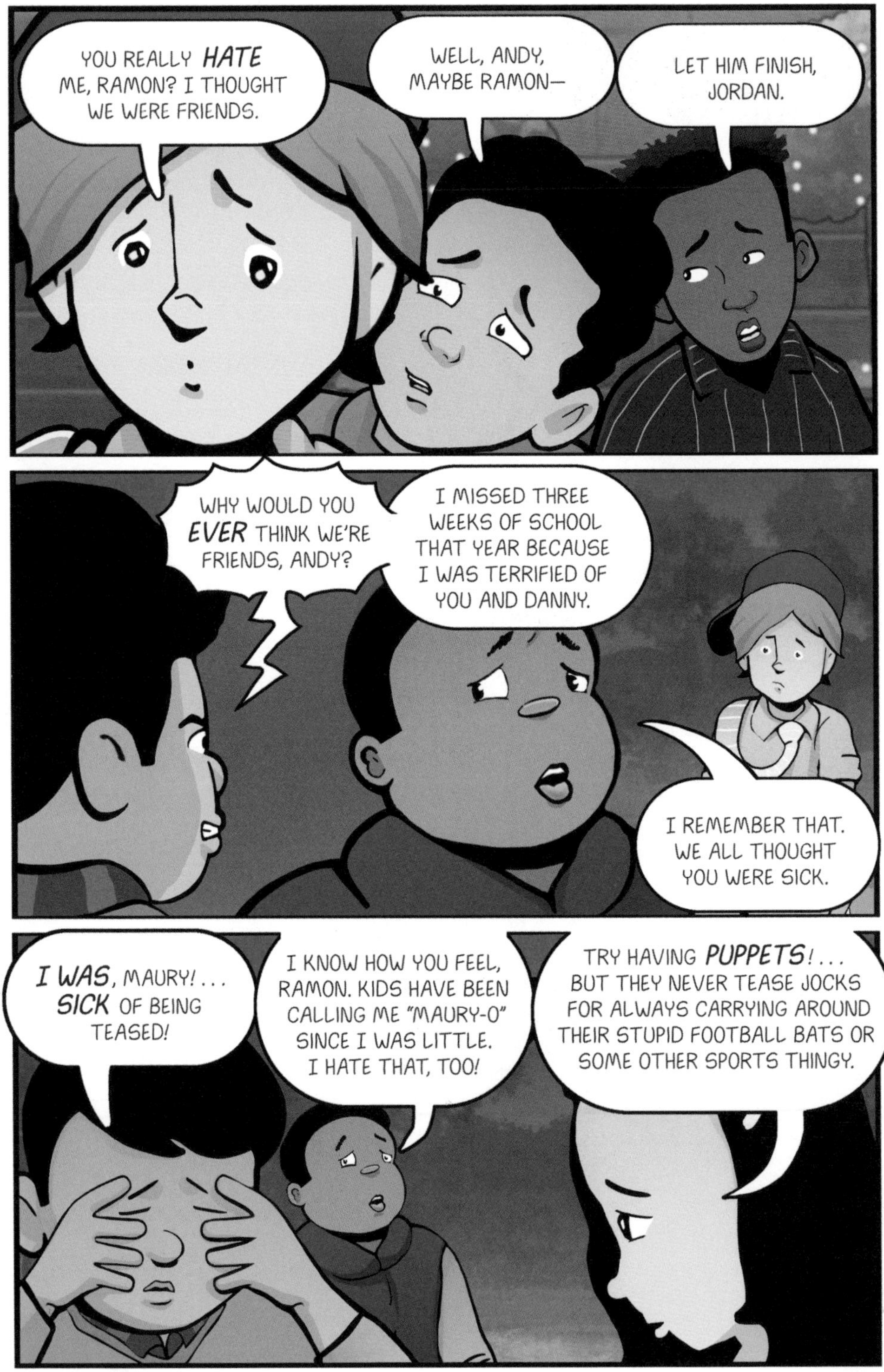
YOU REALLY HATE ME, RAMON? I THOUGHT WE WERE FRIENDS.
WELL, ANDY, MAYBE RAMON—
LET HIM FINISH, JORDAN.
WHY WOULD YOU EVER THINK WE'RE FRIENDS, ANDY?
I MISSED THREE WEEKS OF SCHOOL THAT YEAR BECAUSE I WAS TERRIFIED OF YOU AND DANNY.
I REMEMBER THAT. WE ALL THOUGHT YOU WERE SICK.
I WAS, MAURY!... SICK OF BEING TEASED!
I KNOW HOW YOU FEEL, RAMON. KIDS HAVE BEEN CALLING ME "MAURY-O" SINCE I WAS LITTLE. I HATE THAT, TOO!
TRY HAVING PUPPETS!... BUT THEY NEVER TEASE JOCKS FOR ALWAYS CARRYING AROUND THEIR STUPID FOOTBALL BATS OR SOME OTHER SPORTS THINGY.

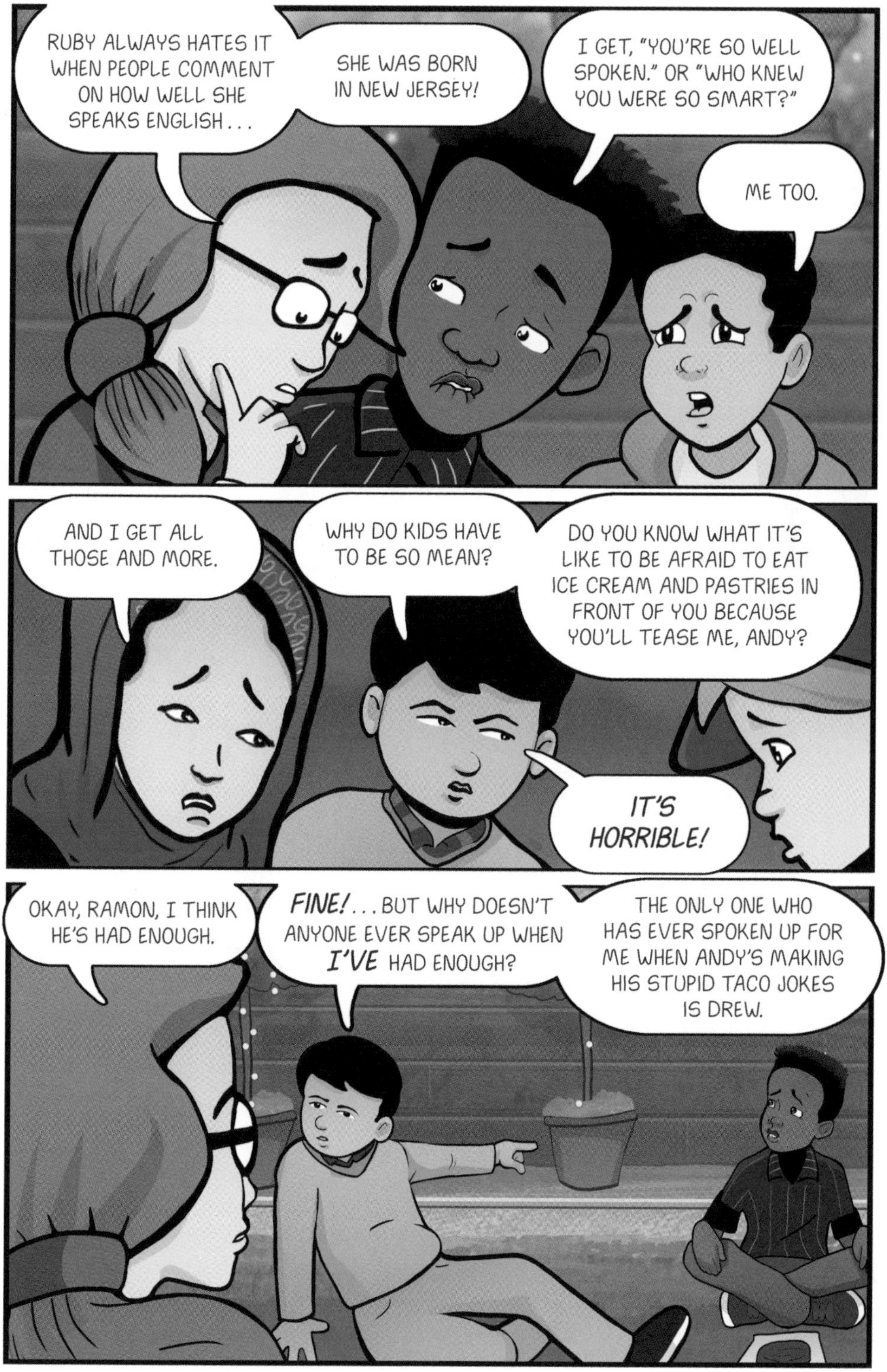
RUBY ALWAYS HATES IT WHEN PEOPLE COMMENT ON HOW WELL SHE SPEAKS ENGLISH . . .
SHE WAS BORN IN NEW JERSEY!
I GET, "YOU'RE SO WELL SPOKEN." OR "WHO KNEW YOU WERE SO SMART?"
ME TOO.
AND I GET ALL THOSE AND MORE.
WHY DO KIDS HAVE TO BE SO MEAN?
DO YOU KNOW WHAT IT'S LIKE TO BE AFRAID TO EAT ICE CREAM AND PASTRIES IN FRONT OF YOU BECAUSE YOU'LL TEASE ME, ANDY?
IT'S HORRIBLE!
OKAY, RAMON, I THINK HE'S HAD ENOUGH.
FINE! . . . BUT WHY DOESN'T ANYONE EVER SPEAK UP WHEN I'VE HAD ENOUGH?
THE ONLY ONE WHO HAS EVER SPOKEN UP FOR ME WHEN ANDY'S MAKING HIS STUPID TACO JOKES IS DREW.

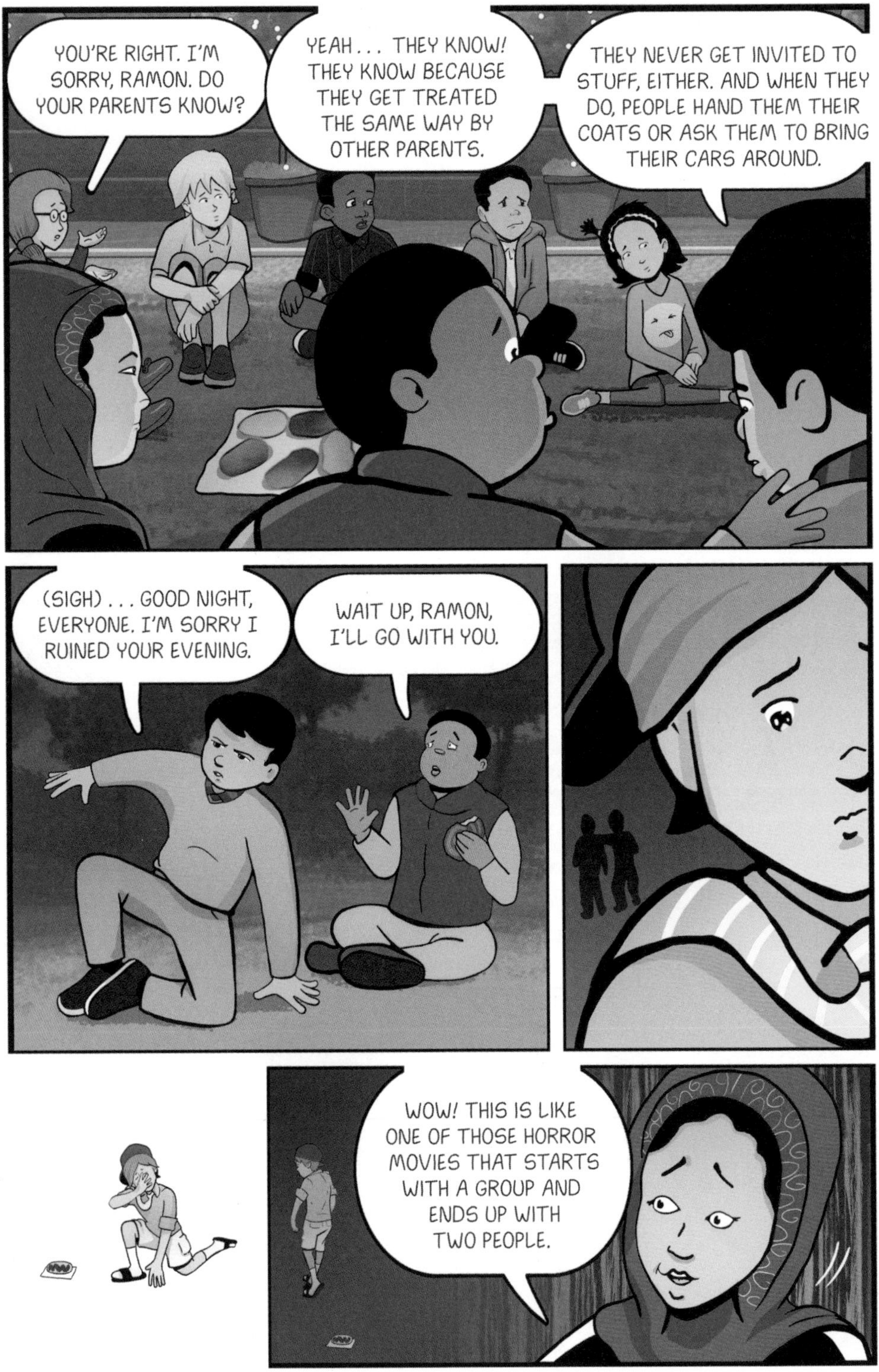
YOU'RE RIGHT. I'M SORRY, RAMON. DO YOUR PARENTS KNOW?
YEAH . . . THEY KNOW! THEY KNOW BECAUSE THEY GET TREATED THE SAME WAY BY OTHER PARENTS.
THEY NEVER GET INVITED TO STUFF, EITHER. AND WHEN THEY DO, PEOPLE HAND THEM THEIR COATS OR ASK THEM TO BRING THEIR CARS AROUND.
(SIGH) . . . GOOD NIGHT, EVERYONE. I'M SORRY I RUINED YOUR EVENING.
WAIT UP, RAMON, I'LL GO WITH YOU.
WOW! THIS IS LIKE ONE OF THOSE HORROR MOVIES THAT STARTS WITH A GROUP AND ENDS UP WITH TWO PEOPLE.

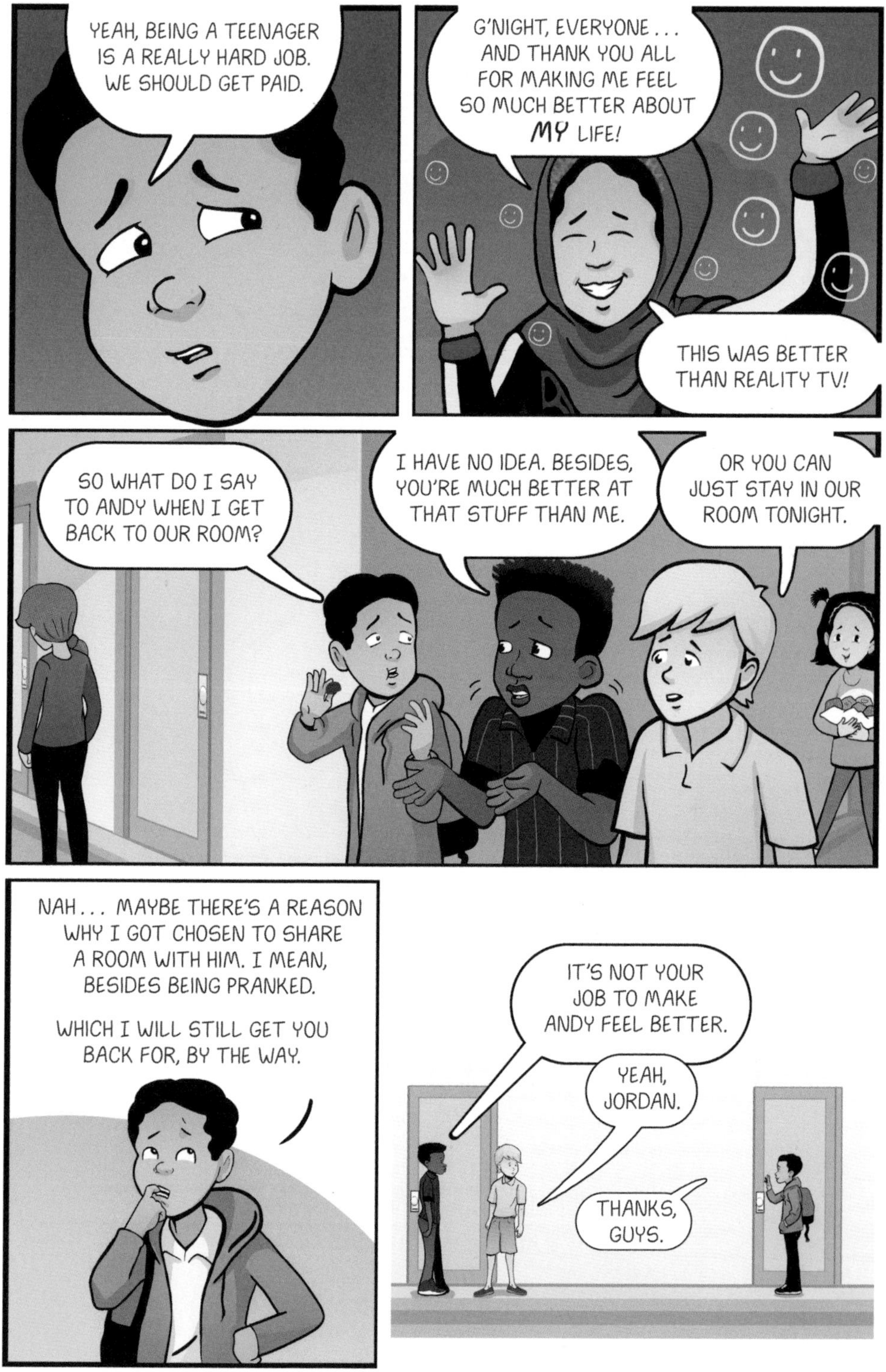
YEAH, BEING A TEENAGER IS A REALLY HARD JOB. WE SHOULD GET PAID.
G'NIGHT, EVERYONE . . . AND THANK YOU ALL FOR MAKING ME FEEL SO MUCH BETTER ABOUT MY LIFE!
THIS WAS BETTER THAN REALITY TV!
SO WHAT DO I SAY TO ANDY WHEN I GET BACK TO OUR ROOM?
I HAVE NO IDEA. BESIDES, YOU'RE MUCH BETTER AT THAT STUFF THAN ME.
OR YOU CAN JUST STAY IN OUR ROOM TONIGHT.
NAH . . . MAYBE THERE'S A REASON WHY I GOT CHOSEN TO SHARE A ROOM WITH HIM. I MEAN, BESIDES BEING PRANKED.
WHICH I WILL STILL GET YOU BACK FOR, BY THE WAY.
IT'S NOT YOUR JOB TO MAKE ANDY FEEL BETTER.
YEAH, JORDAN.
THANKS, GUYS.

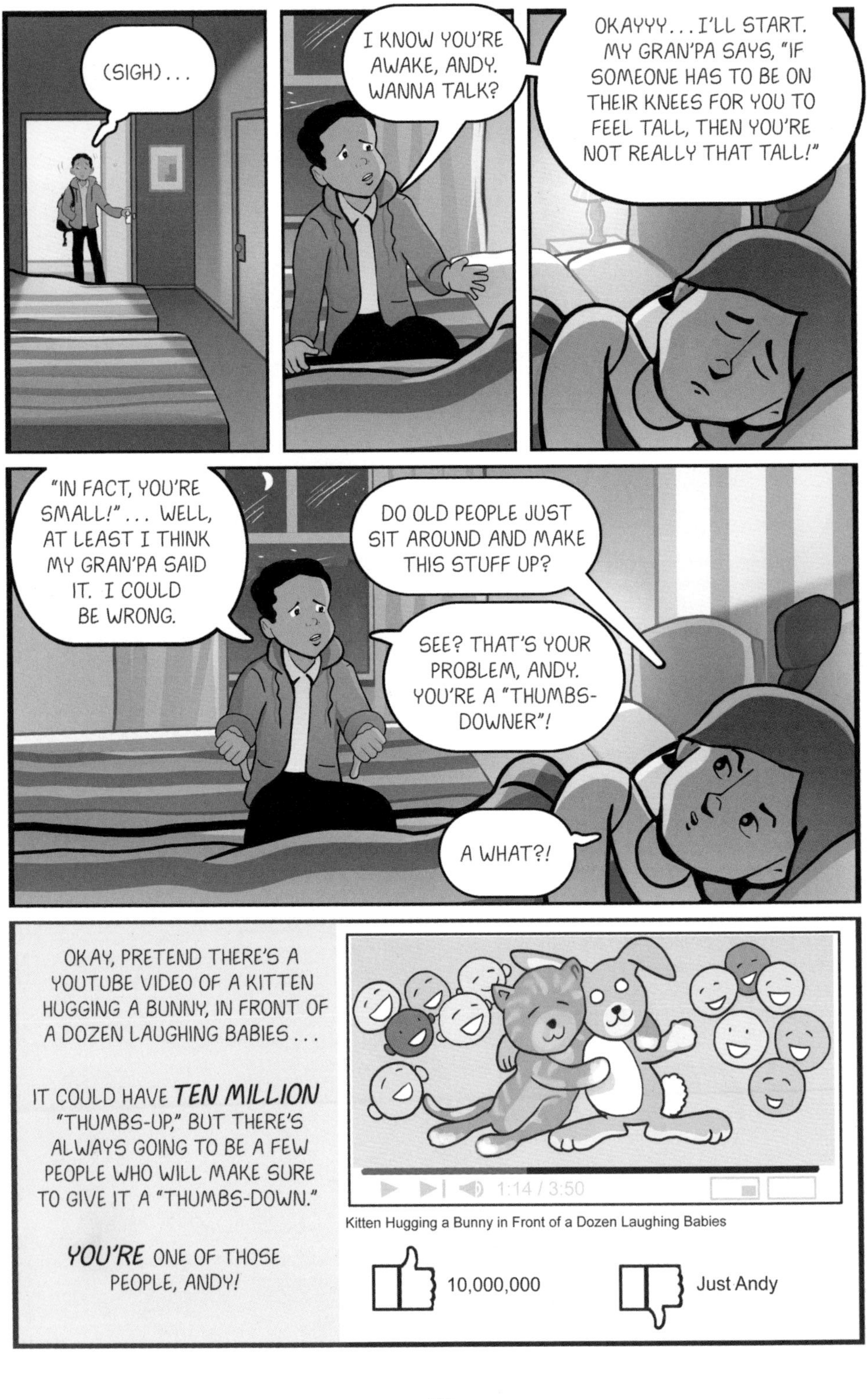
(SIGH)...
I KNOW YOU'RE AWAKE, ANDY. WANNA TALK?
OKAYYY... I'LL START. MY GRAN'PA SAYS, "IF SOMEONE HAS TO BE ON THEIR KNEES FOR YOU TO FEEL TALL, THEN YOU'RE NOT REALLY THAT TALL!"
"IN FACT, YOU'RE SMALL!"... WELL, AT LEAST I THINK MY GRAN'PA SAID IT. I COULD BE WRONG.
DO OLD PEOPLE JUST SIT AROUND AND MAKE THIS STUFF UP?
SEE? THAT'S YOUR PROBLEM, ANDY. YOU'RE A "THUMBS-DOWNER"!
A WHAT?!
OKAY, PRETEND THERE'S A YOUTUBE VIDEO OF A KITTEN HUGGING A BUNNY, IN FRONT OF A DOZEN LAUGHING BABIES...
IT COULD HAVE ***TEN MILLION*** "THUMBS-UP," BUT THERE'S ALWAYS GOING TO BE A FEW PEOPLE WHO WILL MAKE SURE TO GIVE IT A "THUMBS-DOWN."
YOU'RE ONE OF THOSE PEOPLE, ANDY!
1:14 / 3:50
Kitten Hugging a Bunny in Front of a Dozen Laughing Babies
10,000,000
Just Andy

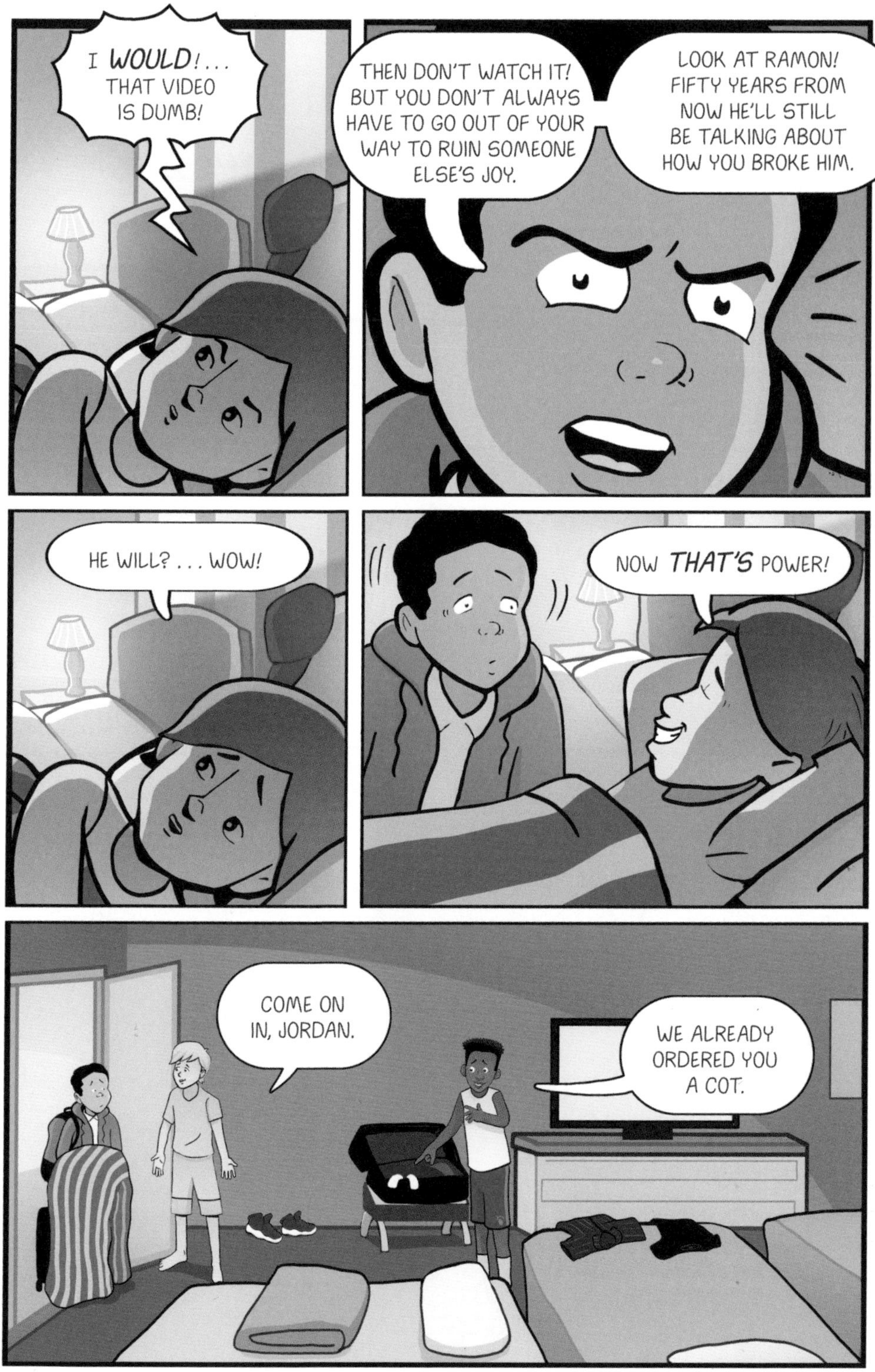
I WOULD!... THAT VIDEO IS DUMB!
THEN DON'T WATCH IT! BUT YOU DON'T ALWAYS HAVE TO GO OUT OF YOUR WAY TO RUIN SOMEONE ELSE'S JOY.
LOOK AT RAMON! FIFTY YEARS FROM NOW HE'LL STILL BE TALKING ABOUT HOW YOU BROKE HIM.
HE WILL?... WOW!
NOW THAT'S POWER!
COME ON IN, JORDAN.
WE ALREADY ORDERED YOU A COT.

8 Attack of the Thumbs-Downers!

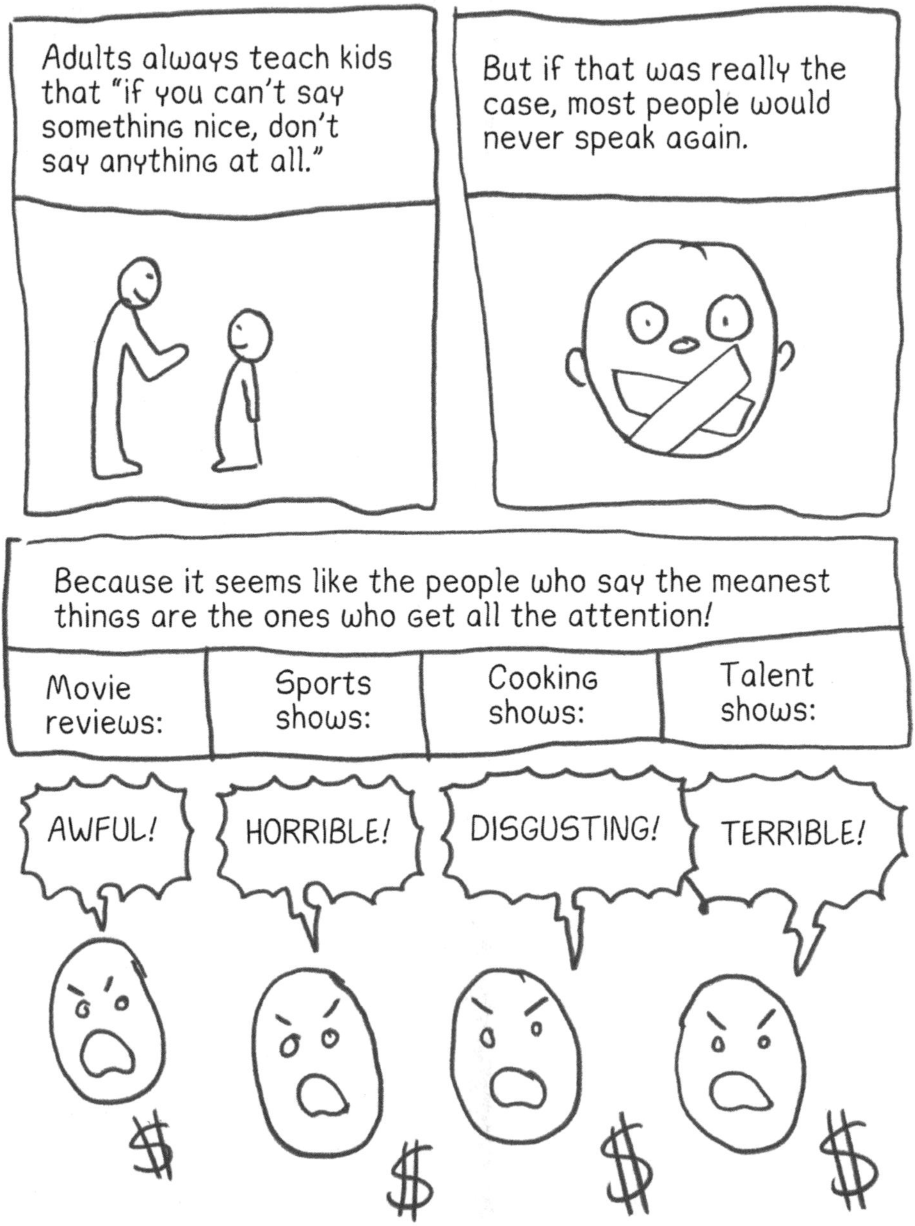
Adults always teach kids that "if you can't say something nice, don't say anything at all."
But if that was really the case, most people would never speak again.
Because it seems like the people who say the meanest things are the ones who get all the attention!
Movie reviews:
Sports shows:
Cooking shows:
Talent shows:
AWFUL!
HORRIBLE!
DISGUSTING!
TERRIBLE!
$
$
$
$

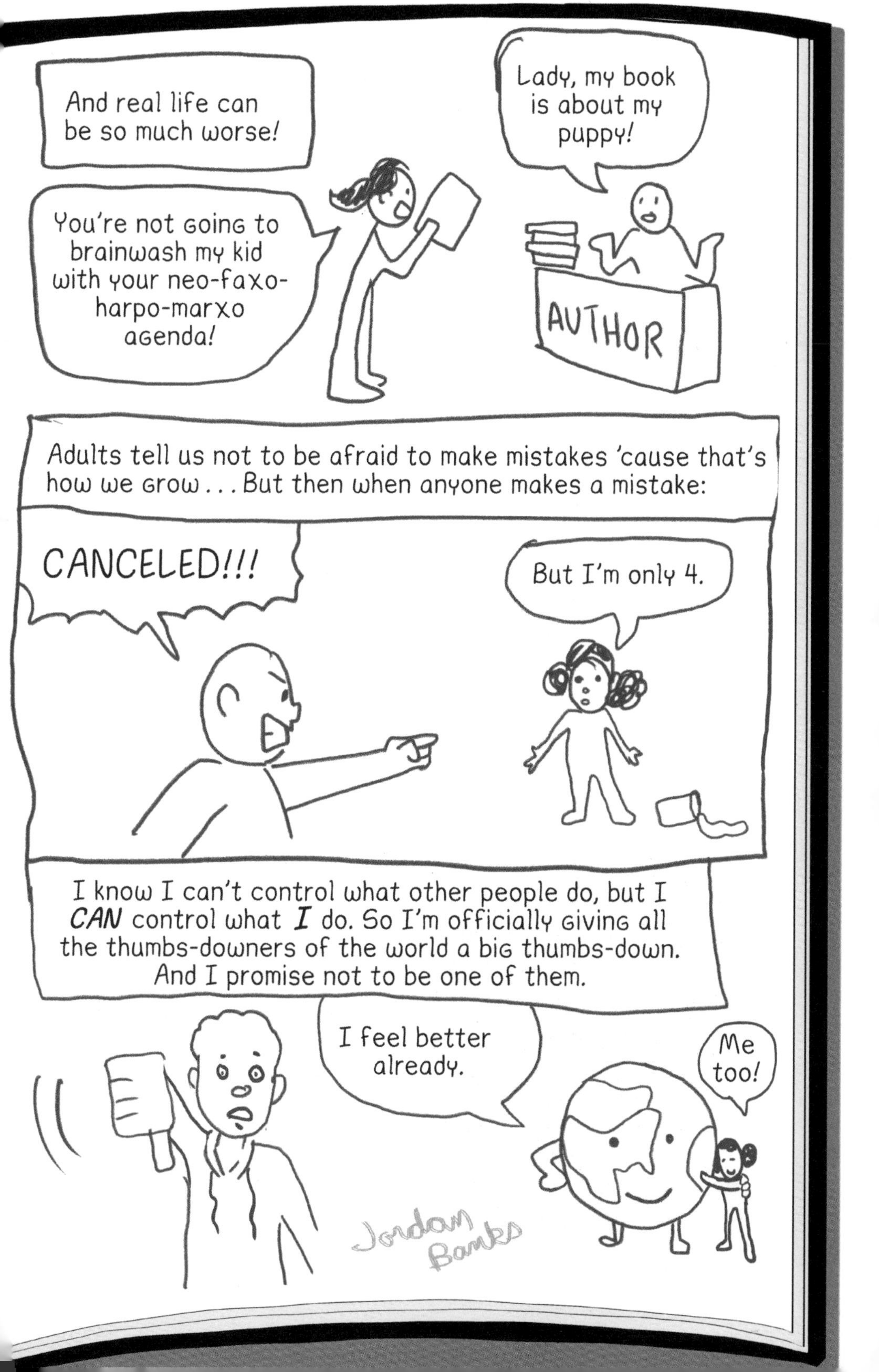
And real life can be so much worse!
You're not going to brainwash my kid with your neo-faxo-harpo-marxo agenda!
Lady, my book is about my puppy!
AUTHOR
Adults tell us not to be afraid to make mistakes 'cause that's how we grow . . . But then when anyone makes a mistake:
CANCELED!!!
But I'm only 4.
I know I can't control what other people do, but I *CAN* control what *I* do. So I'm officially giving all the thumbs-downers of the world a big thumbs-down. And I promise not to be one of them.
I feel better already.
Me too!
Jordan Banks

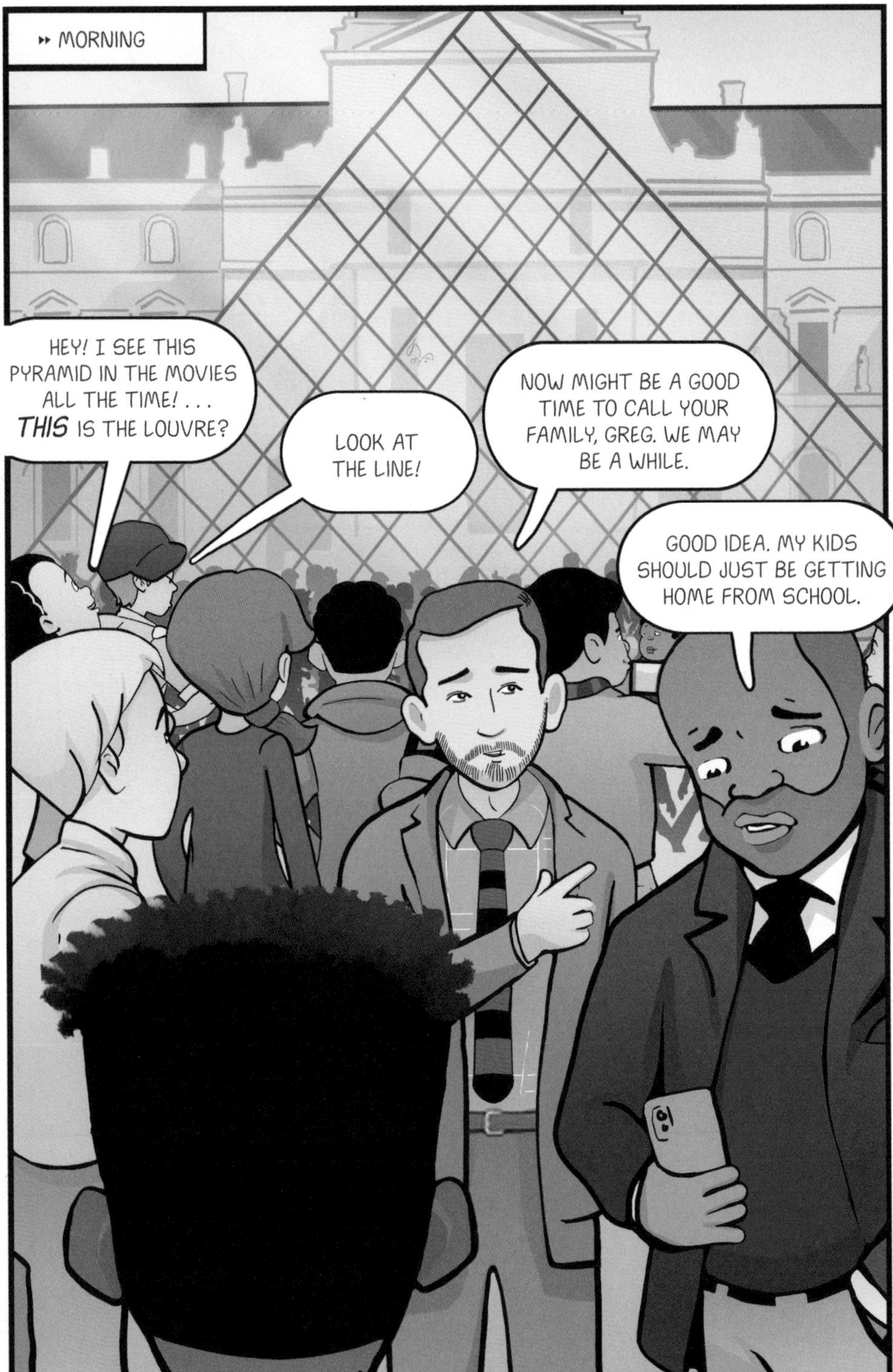
MORNING
HEY! I SEE THIS PYRAMID IN THE MOVIES ALL THE TIME! . . . THIS IS THE LOUVRE?
LOOK AT THE LINE!
NOW MIGHT BE A GOOD TIME TO CALL YOUR FAMILY, GREG. WE MAY BE A WHILE.
GOOD IDEA. MY KIDS SHOULD JUST BE GETTING HOME FROM SCHOOL.

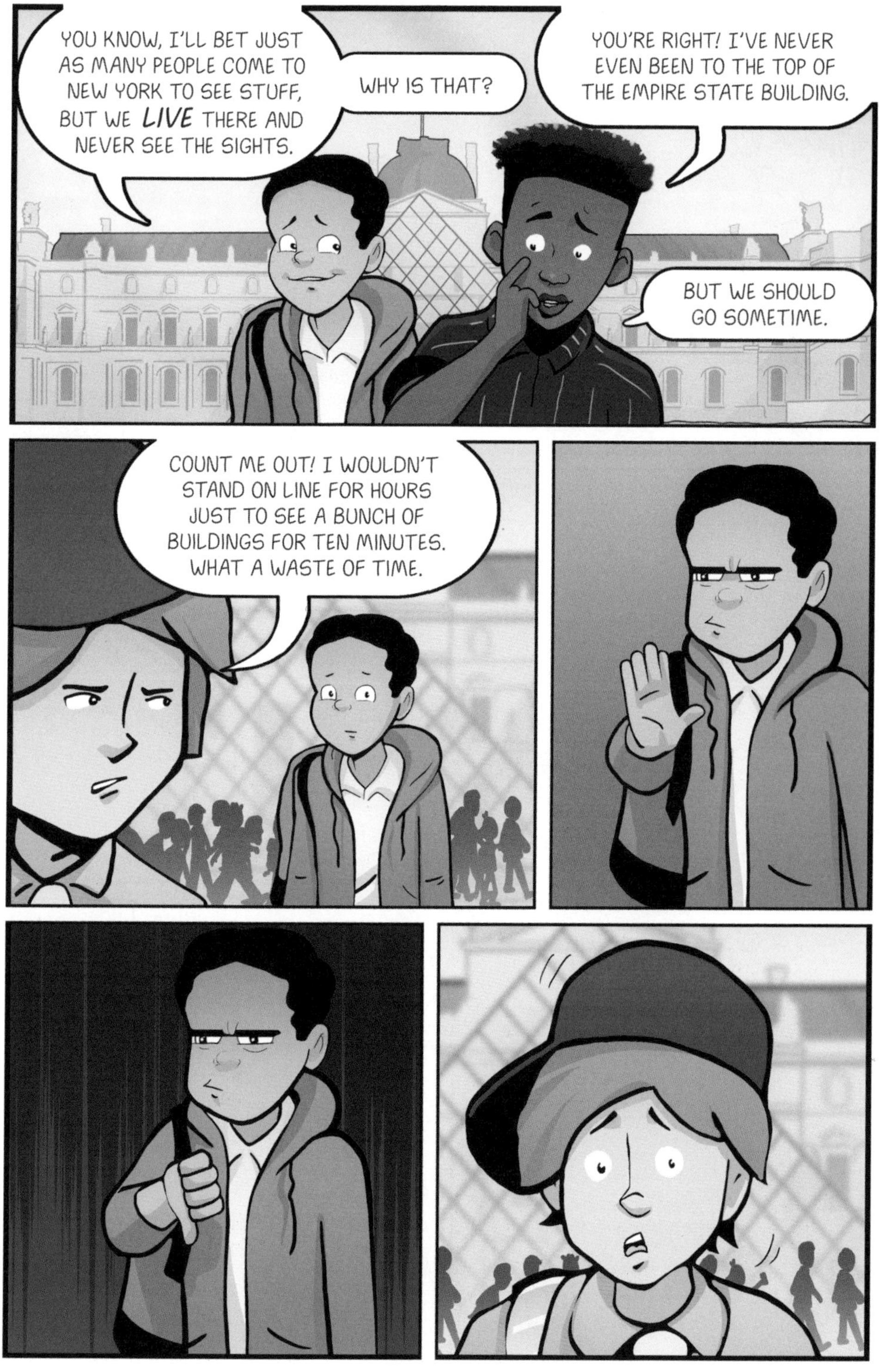
YOU KNOW, I'LL BET JUST AS MANY PEOPLE COME TO NEW YORK TO SEE STUFF, BUT WE *LIVE* THERE AND NEVER SEE THE SIGHTS.
WHY IS THAT?
YOU'RE RIGHT! I'VE NEVER EVEN BEEN TO THE TOP OF THE EMPIRE STATE BUILDING.
BUT WE SHOULD GO SOMETIME.
COUNT ME OUT! I WOULDN'T STAND ON LINE FOR HOURS JUST TO SEE A BUNCH OF BUILDINGS FOR TEN MINUTES. WHAT A WASTE OF TIME.

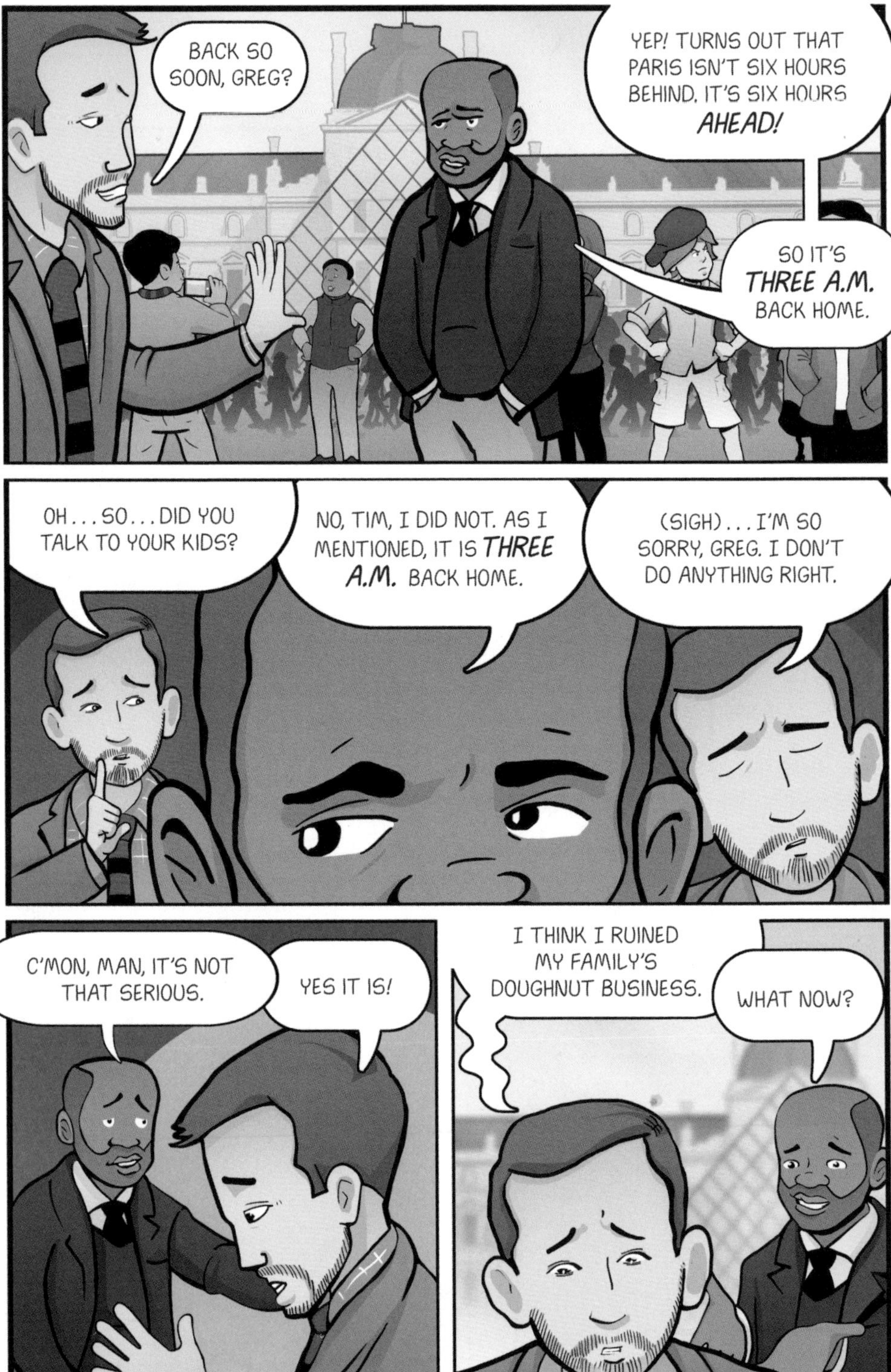
BACK SO SOON, GREG?
YEP! TURNS OUT THAT PARIS ISN'T SIX HOURS BEHIND, IT'S SIX HOURS AHEAD!
SO IT'S THREE A.M. BACK HOME.
OH . . . SO . . . DID YOU TALK TO YOUR KIDS?
NO, TIM, I DID NOT. AS I MENTIONED, IT IS THREE A.M. BACK HOME.
(SIGH) . . . I'M SO SORRY, GREG. I DON'T DO ANYTHING RIGHT.
C'MON, MAN, IT'S NOT THAT SERIOUS.
YES IT IS!
I THINK I RUINED MY FAMILY'S DOUGHNUT BUSINESS.
WHAT NOW?

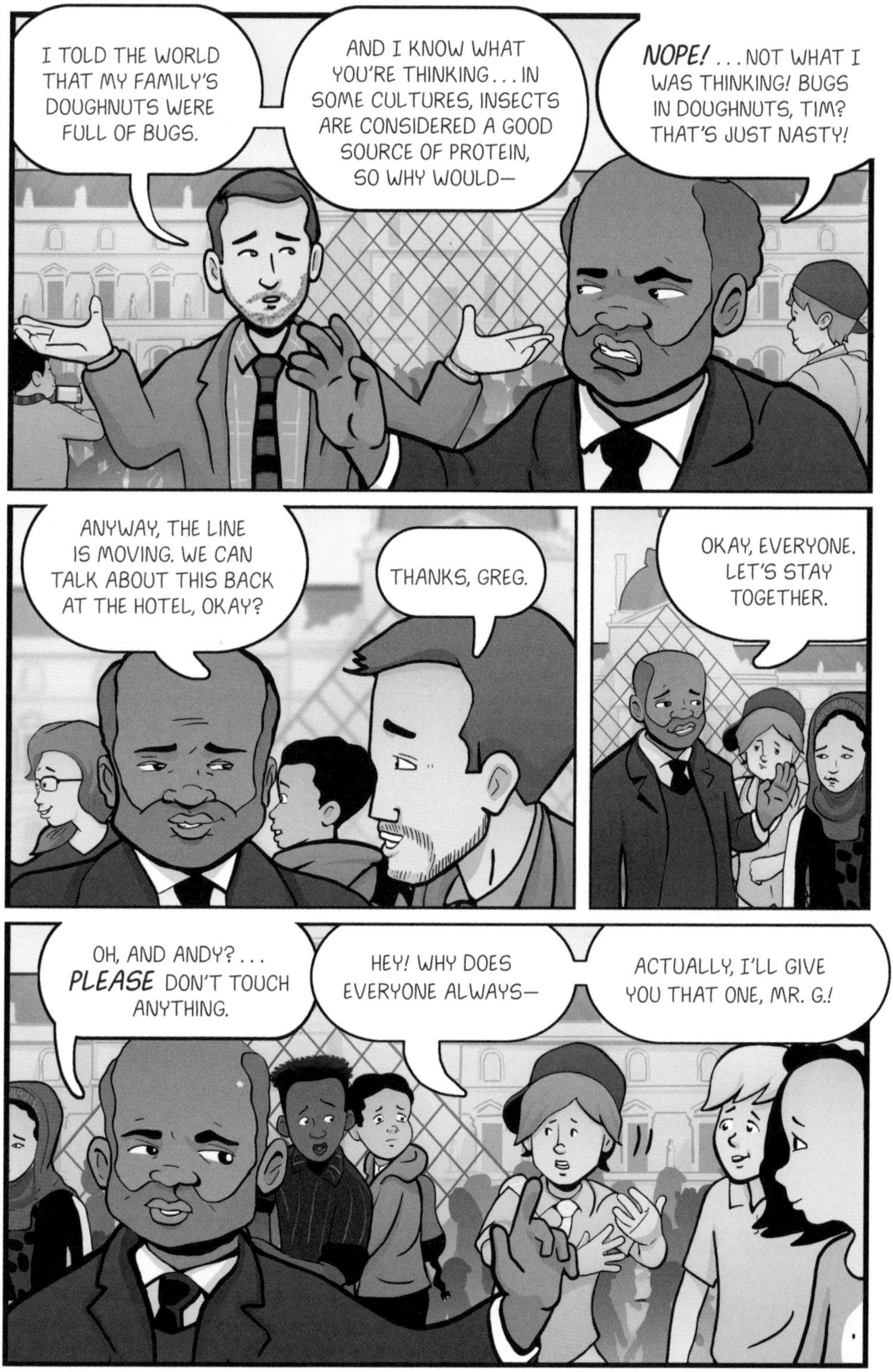

I TOLD THE WORLD THAT MY FAMILY'S DOUGHNUTS WERE FULL OF BUGS.
AND I KNOW WHAT YOU'RE THINKING . . . IN SOME CULTURES, INSECTS ARE CONSIDERED A GOOD SOURCE OF PROTEIN, SO WHY WOULD—
NOPE! . . . NOT WHAT I WAS THINKING! BUGS IN DOUGHNUTS, TIM? THAT'S JUST NASTY!
ANYWAY, THE LINE IS MOVING. WE CAN TALK ABOUT THIS BACK AT THE HOTEL, OKAY?
THANKS, GREG.
OKAY, EVERYONE. LET'S STAY TOGETHER.
OH, AND ANDY? . . . PLEASE DON'T TOUCH ANYTHING.
HEY! WHY DOES EVERYONE ALWAYS—
ACTUALLY, I'LL GIVE YOU THAT ONE, MR. G.!

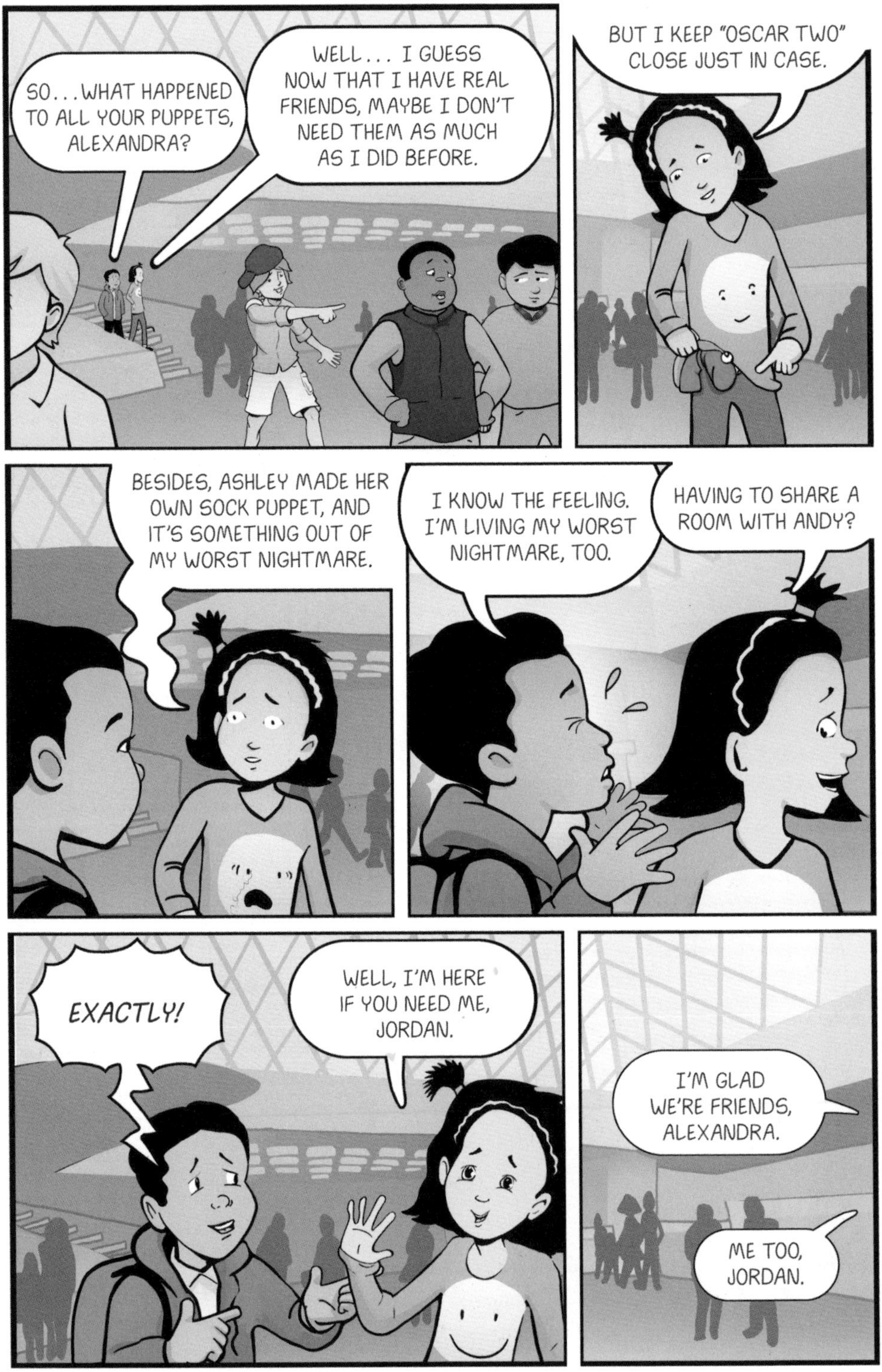
SO...WHAT HAPPENED TO ALL YOUR PUPPETS, ALEXANDRA?
WELL... I GUESS NOW THAT I HAVE REAL FRIENDS, MAYBE I DON'T NEED THEM AS MUCH AS I DID BEFORE.
BUT I KEEP "OSCAR TWO" CLOSE JUST IN CASE.
BESIDES, ASHLEY MADE HER OWN SOCK PUPPET, AND IT'S SOMETHING OUT OF MY WORST NIGHTMARE.
I KNOW THE FEELING. I'M LIVING MY WORST NIGHTMARE, TOO.
HAVING TO SHARE A ROOM WITH ANDY?
EXACTLY!
WELL, I'M HERE IF YOU NEED ME, JORDAN.
I'M GLAD WE'RE FRIENDS, ALEXANDRA.
ME TOO, JORDAN.

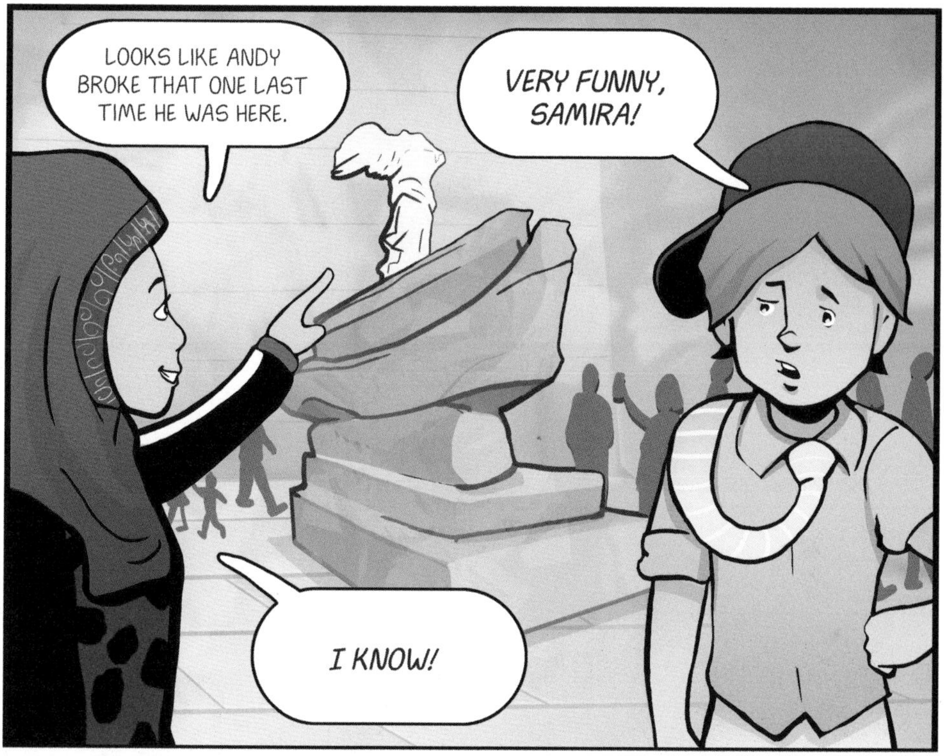
LOOKS LIKE ANDY BROKE THAT ONE LAST TIME HE WAS HERE.
VERY FUNNY, SAMIRA!
I KNOW!

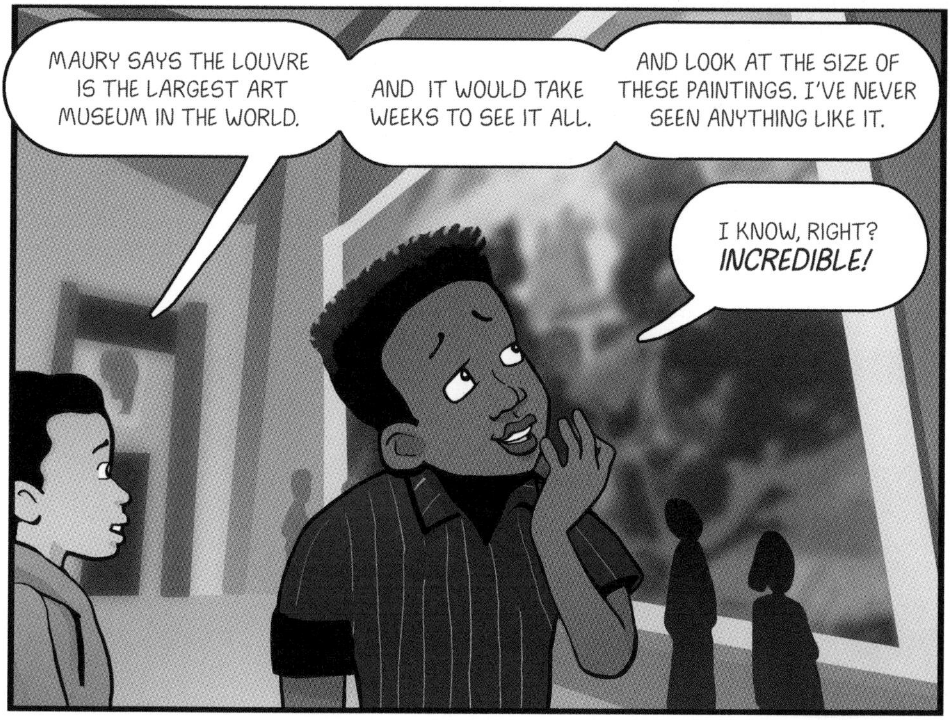
MAURY SAYS THE LOUVRE IS THE LARGEST ART MUSEUM IN THE WORLD.
AND IT WOULD TAKE WEEKS TO SEE IT ALL.
AND LOOK AT THE SIZE OF THESE PAINTINGS. I'VE NEVER SEEN ANYTHING LIKE IT.
I KNOW, RIGHT? INCREDIBLE!

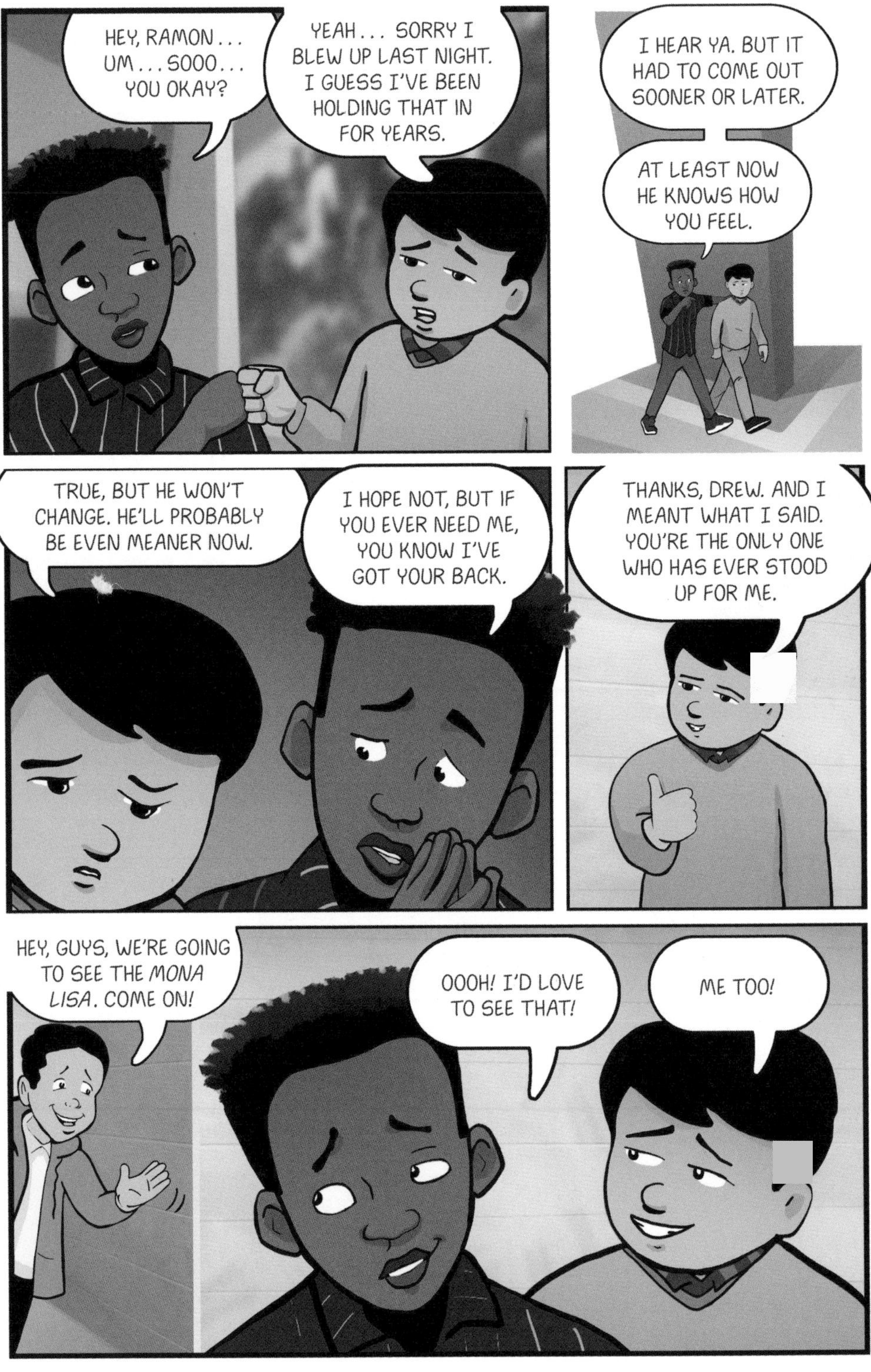
HEY, RAMON . . . UM . . . SOOO . . . YOU OKAY?
YEAH . . . SORRY I BLEW UP LAST NIGHT. I GUESS I'VE BEEN HOLDING THAT IN FOR YEARS.
I HEAR YA. BUT IT HAD TO COME OUT SOONER OR LATER.
AT LEAST NOW HE KNOWS HOW YOU FEEL.
TRUE, BUT HE WON'T CHANGE. HE'LL PROBABLY BE EVEN MEANER NOW.
I HOPE NOT, BUT IF YOU EVER NEED ME, YOU KNOW I'VE GOT YOUR BACK.
THANKS, DREW. AND I MEANT WHAT I SAID. YOU'RE THE ONLY ONE WHO HAS EVER STOOD UP FOR ME.
HEY, GUYS, WE'RE GOING TO SEE THE *MONA LISA*. COME ON!
OOOH! I'D LOVE TO SEE THAT!
ME TOO!

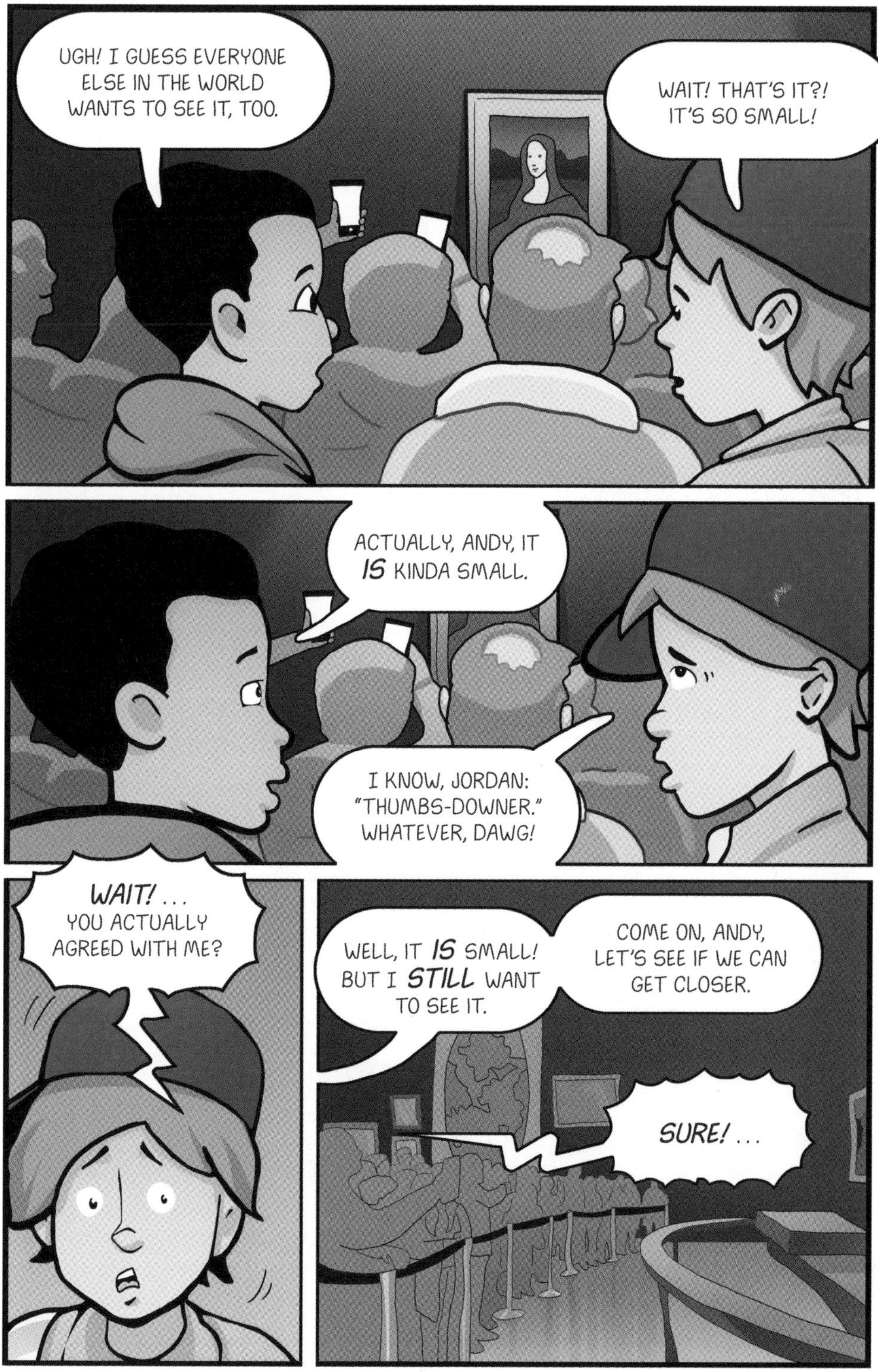
UGH! I GUESS EVERYONE ELSE IN THE WORLD WANTS TO SEE IT, TOO.
WAIT! THAT'S IT?! IT'S SO SMALL!
ACTUALLY, ANDY, IT **IS** KINDA SMALL.
I KNOW, JORDAN: "THUMBS-DOWNER." WHATEVER, DAWG!
WAIT! . . . YOU ACTUALLY AGREED WITH ME?
WELL, IT **IS** SMALL! BUT I **STILL** WANT TO SEE IT.
COME ON, ANDY, LET'S SEE IF WE CAN GET CLOSER.
SURE! . . .

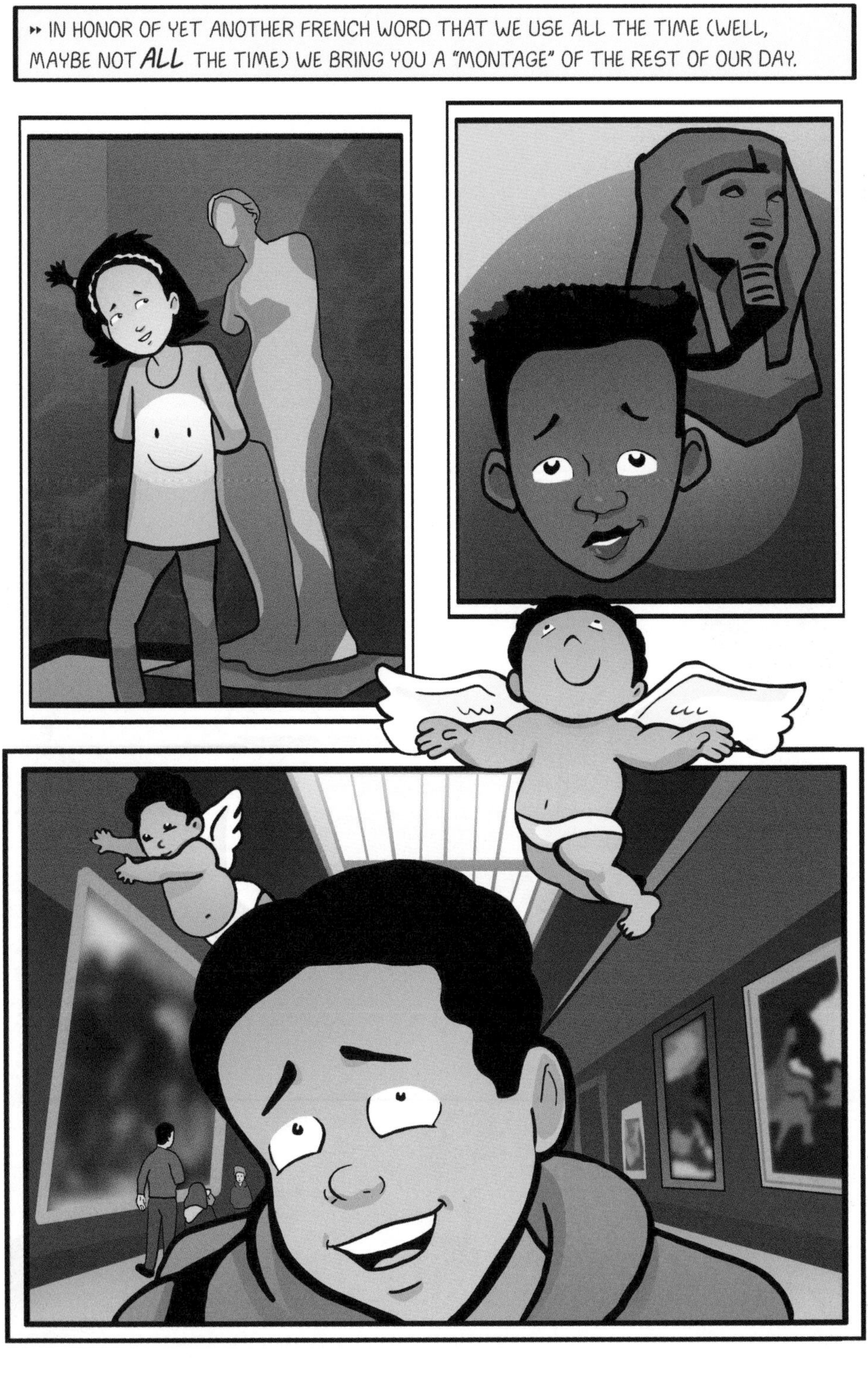
▸▸ IN HONOR OF YET ANOTHER FRENCH WORD THAT WE USE ALL THE TIME (WELL, MAYBE NOT **ALL** THE TIME) WE BRING YOU A "MONTAGE" OF THE REST OF OUR DAY.

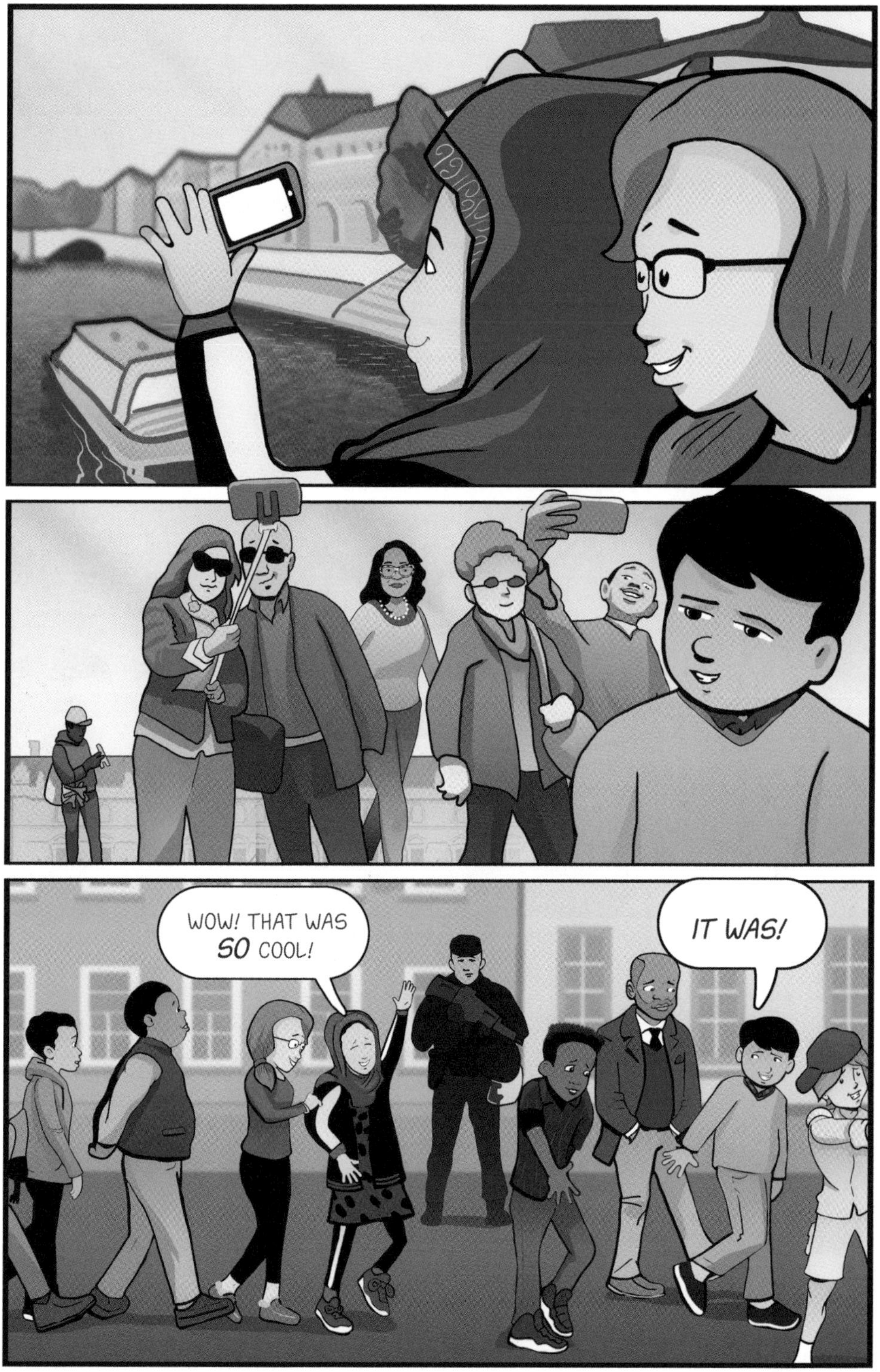
WOW! THAT WAS SO COOL!
IT WAS!

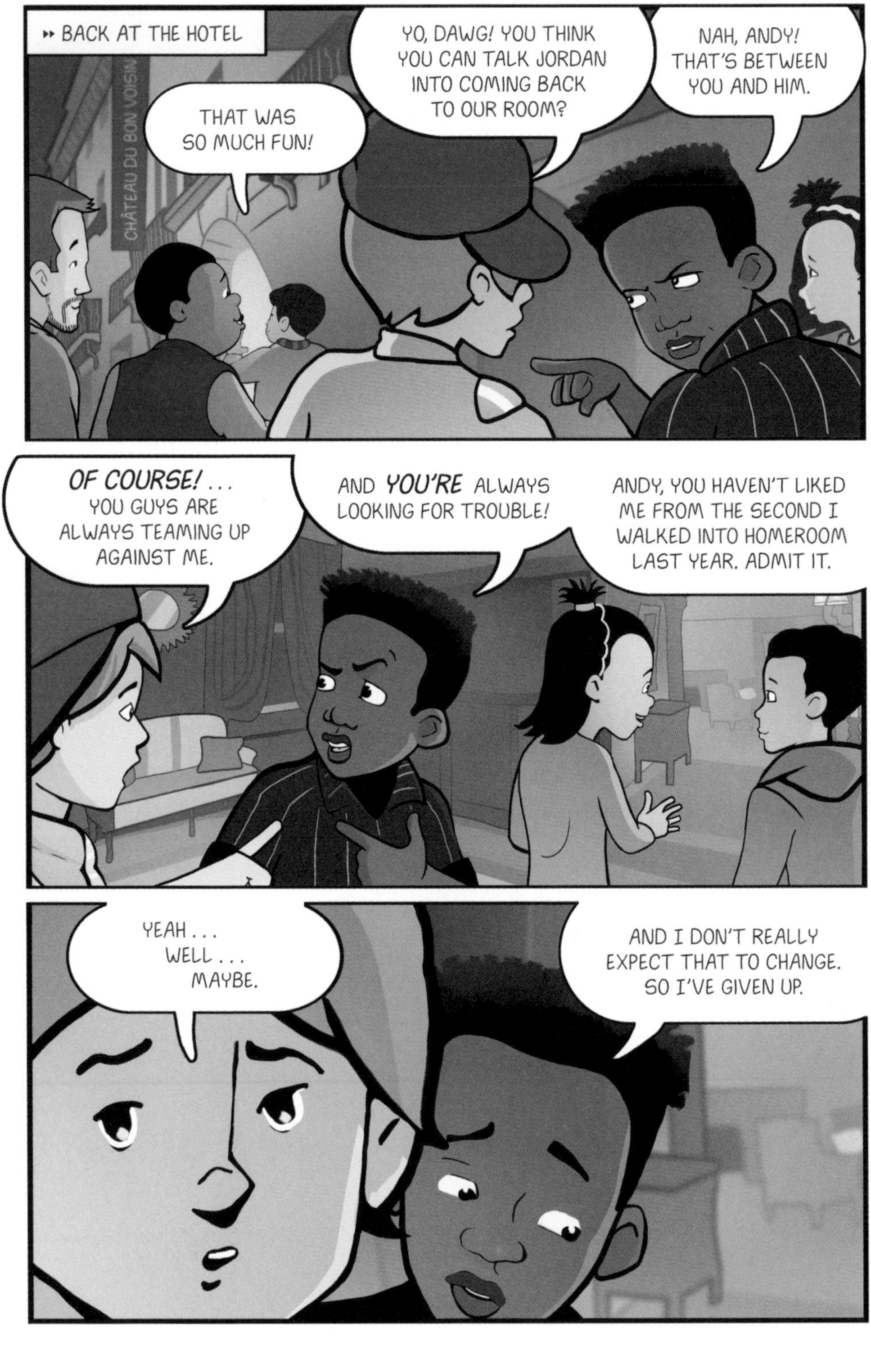
BACK AT THE HOTEL
CHÂTEAU DU BON VOISIN
THAT WAS SO MUCH FUN!
YO, DAWG! YOU THINK YOU CAN TALK JORDAN INTO COMING BACK TO OUR ROOM?
NAH, ANDY! THAT'S BETWEEN YOU AND HIM.
OF COURSE! . . . YOU GUYS ARE ALWAYS TEAMING UP AGAINST ME.
AND YOU'RE ALWAYS LOOKING FOR TROUBLE!
ANDY, YOU HAVEN'T LIKED ME FROM THE SECOND I WALKED INTO HOMEROOM LAST YEAR. ADMIT IT.
YEAH . . . WELL . . . MAYBE.
AND I DON'T REALLY EXPECT THAT TO CHANGE. SO I'VE GIVEN UP.

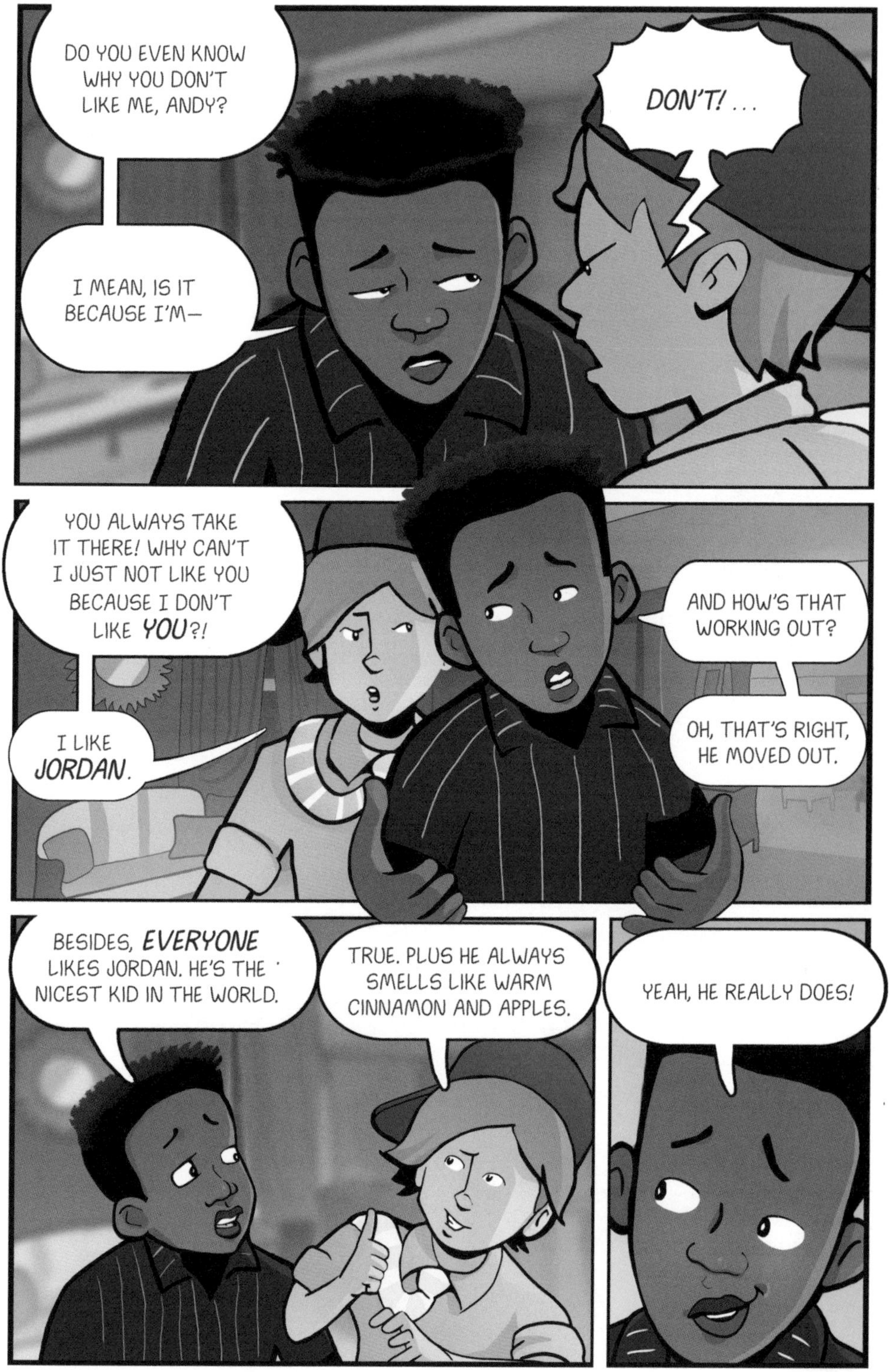
DO YOU EVEN KNOW WHY YOU DON'T LIKE ME, ANDY?
DON'T! . . .
I MEAN, IS IT BECAUSE I'M—
YOU ALWAYS TAKE IT THERE! WHY CAN'T I JUST NOT LIKE YOU BECAUSE I DON'T LIKE **YOU**?!
I LIKE **JORDAN**.
AND HOW'S THAT WORKING OUT?
OH, THAT'S RIGHT, HE MOVED OUT.
BESIDES, **EVERYONE** LIKES JORDAN. HE'S THE NICEST KID IN THE WORLD.
TRUE. PLUS HE ALWAYS SMELLS LIKE WARM CINNAMON AND APPLES.
YEAH, HE REALLY DOES!

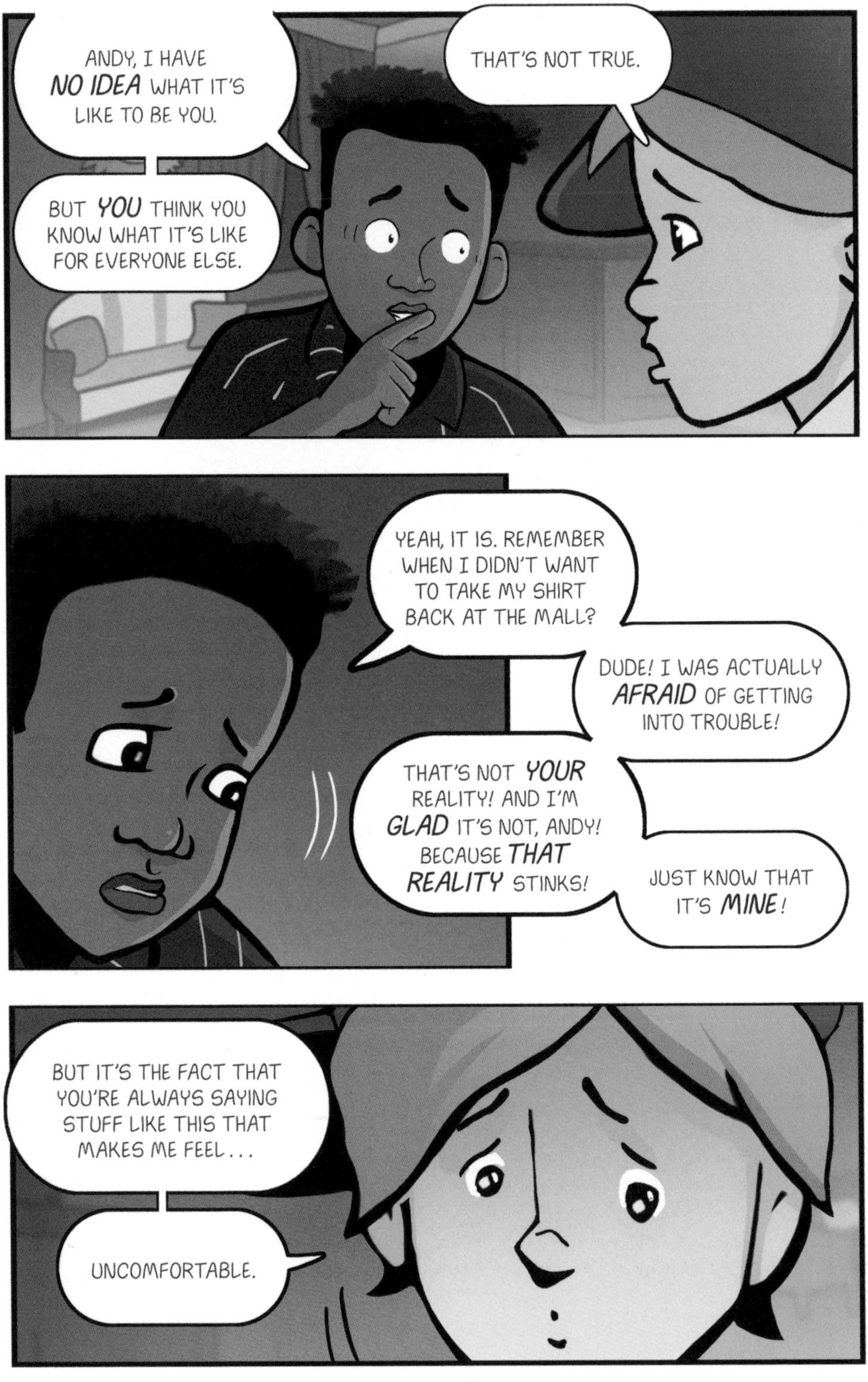
ANDY, I HAVE NO IDEA WHAT IT'S LIKE TO BE YOU.
BUT YOU THINK YOU KNOW WHAT IT'S LIKE FOR EVERYONE ELSE.
THAT'S NOT TRUE.
YEAH, IT IS. REMEMBER WHEN I DIDN'T WANT TO TAKE MY SHIRT BACK AT THE MALL?
DUDE! I WAS ACTUALLY AFRAID OF GETTING INTO TROUBLE!
THAT'S NOT YOUR REALITY! AND I'M GLAD IT'S NOT, ANDY! BECAUSE THAT REALITY STINKS!
JUST KNOW THAT IT'S MINE!
BUT IT'S THE FACT THAT YOU'RE ALWAYS SAYING STUFF LIKE THIS THAT MAKES ME FEEL . . .
UNCOMFORTABLE.

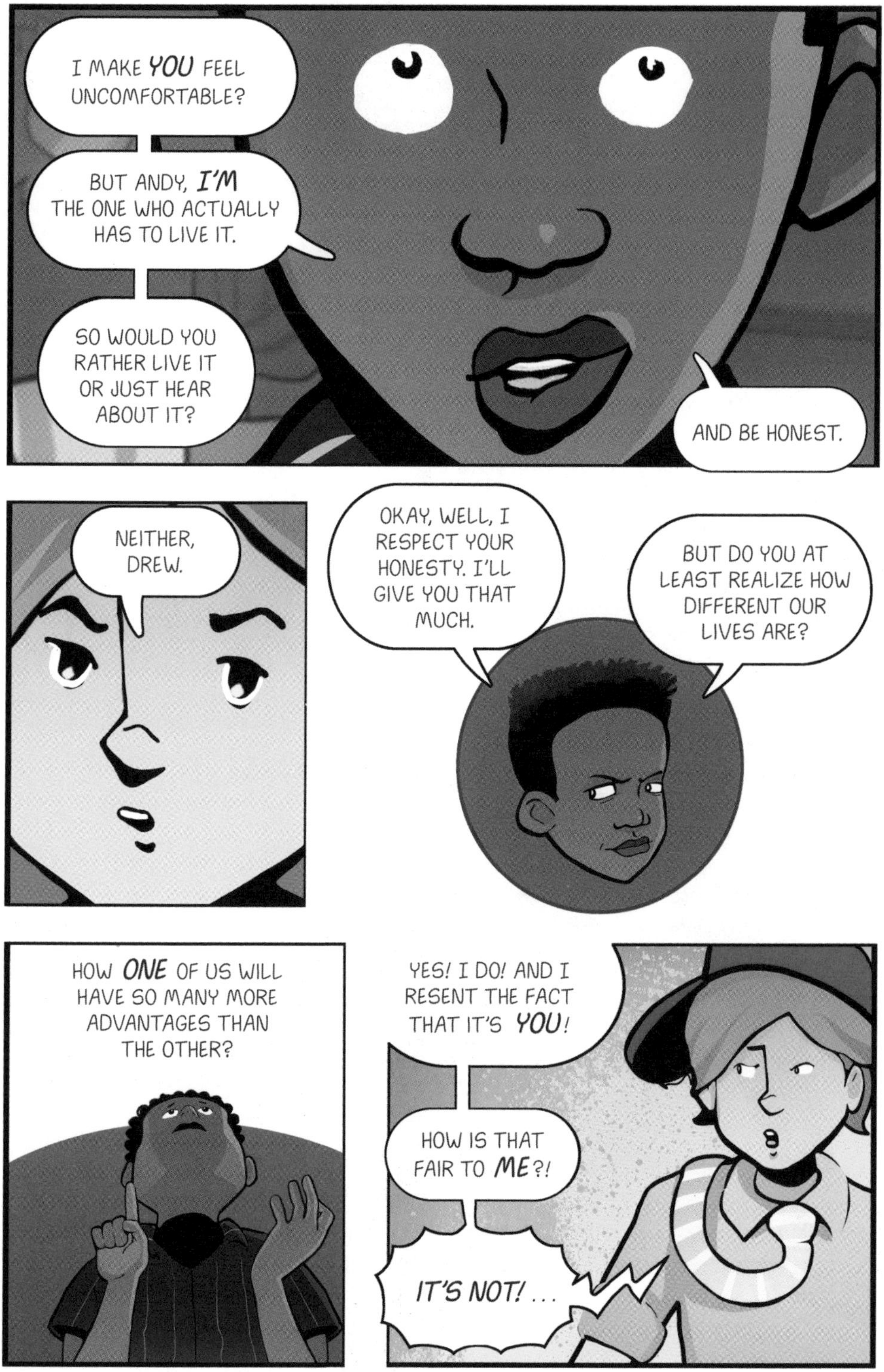
I MAKE YOU FEEL UNCOMFORTABLE?
BUT ANDY, I'M THE ONE WHO ACTUALLY HAS TO LIVE IT.
SO WOULD YOU RATHER LIVE IT OR JUST HEAR ABOUT IT?
AND BE HONEST.
NEITHER, DREW.
OKAY, WELL, I RESPECT YOUR HONESTY. I'LL GIVE YOU THAT MUCH.
BUT DO YOU AT LEAST REALIZE HOW DIFFERENT OUR LIVES ARE?
HOW ONE OF US WILL HAVE SO MANY MORE ADVANTAGES THAN THE OTHER?
YES! I DO! AND I RESENT THE FACT THAT IT'S YOU!
HOW IS THAT FAIR TO ME?!
IT'S NOT! . . .

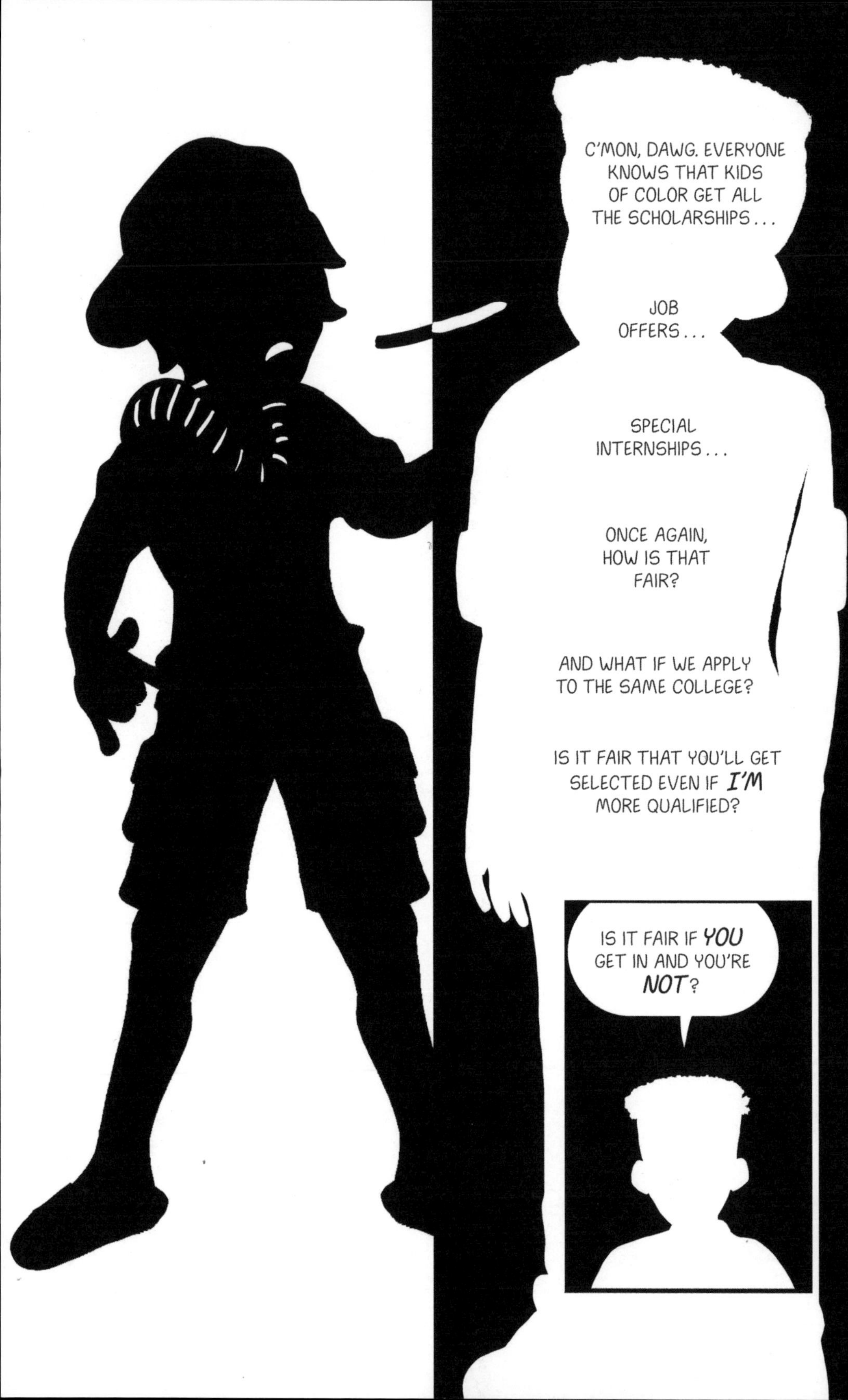
C'MON, DAWG. EVERYONE KNOWS THAT KIDS OF COLOR GET ALL THE SCHOLARSHIPS . . .
JOB OFFERS . . .
SPECIAL INTERNSHIPS . . .
ONCE AGAIN, HOW IS THAT FAIR?
AND WHAT IF WE APPLY TO THE SAME COLLEGE?
IS IT FAIR THAT YOU'LL GET SELECTED EVEN IF *I'M* MORE QUALIFIED?
IS IT FAIR IF ***YOU*** GET IN AND YOU'RE ***NOT***?

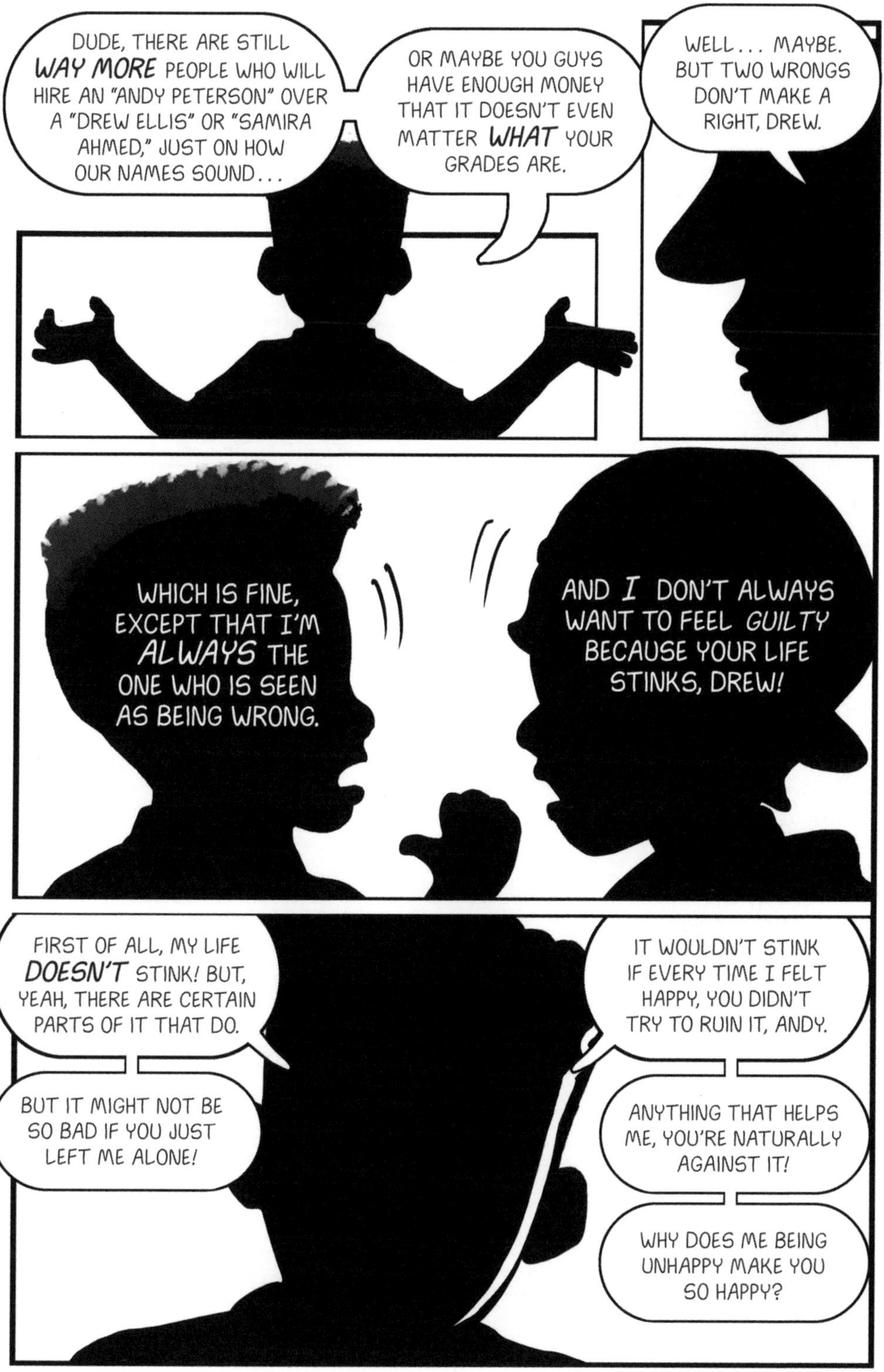
DUDE, THERE ARE STILL WAY MORE PEOPLE WHO WILL HIRE AN "ANDY PETERSON" OVER A "DREW ELLIS" OR "SAMIRA AHMED," JUST ON HOW OUR NAMES SOUND...
OR MAYBE YOU GUYS HAVE ENOUGH MONEY THAT IT DOESN'T EVEN MATTER WHAT YOUR GRADES ARE.
WELL... MAYBE. BUT TWO WRONGS DON'T MAKE A RIGHT, DREW.
WHICH IS FINE, EXCEPT THAT I'M ALWAYS THE ONE WHO IS SEEN AS BEING WRONG.
AND I DON'T ALWAYS WANT TO FEEL GUILTY BECAUSE YOUR LIFE STINKS, DREW!
FIRST OF ALL, MY LIFE DOESN'T STINK! BUT, YEAH, THERE ARE CERTAIN PARTS OF IT THAT DO.
BUT IT MIGHT NOT BE SO BAD IF YOU JUST LEFT ME ALONE!
IT WOULDN'T STINK IF EVERY TIME I FELT HAPPY, YOU DIDN'T TRY TO RUIN IT, ANDY.
ANYTHING THAT HELPS ME, YOU'RE NATURALLY AGAINST IT!
WHY DOES ME BEING UNHAPPY MAKE YOU SO HAPPY?

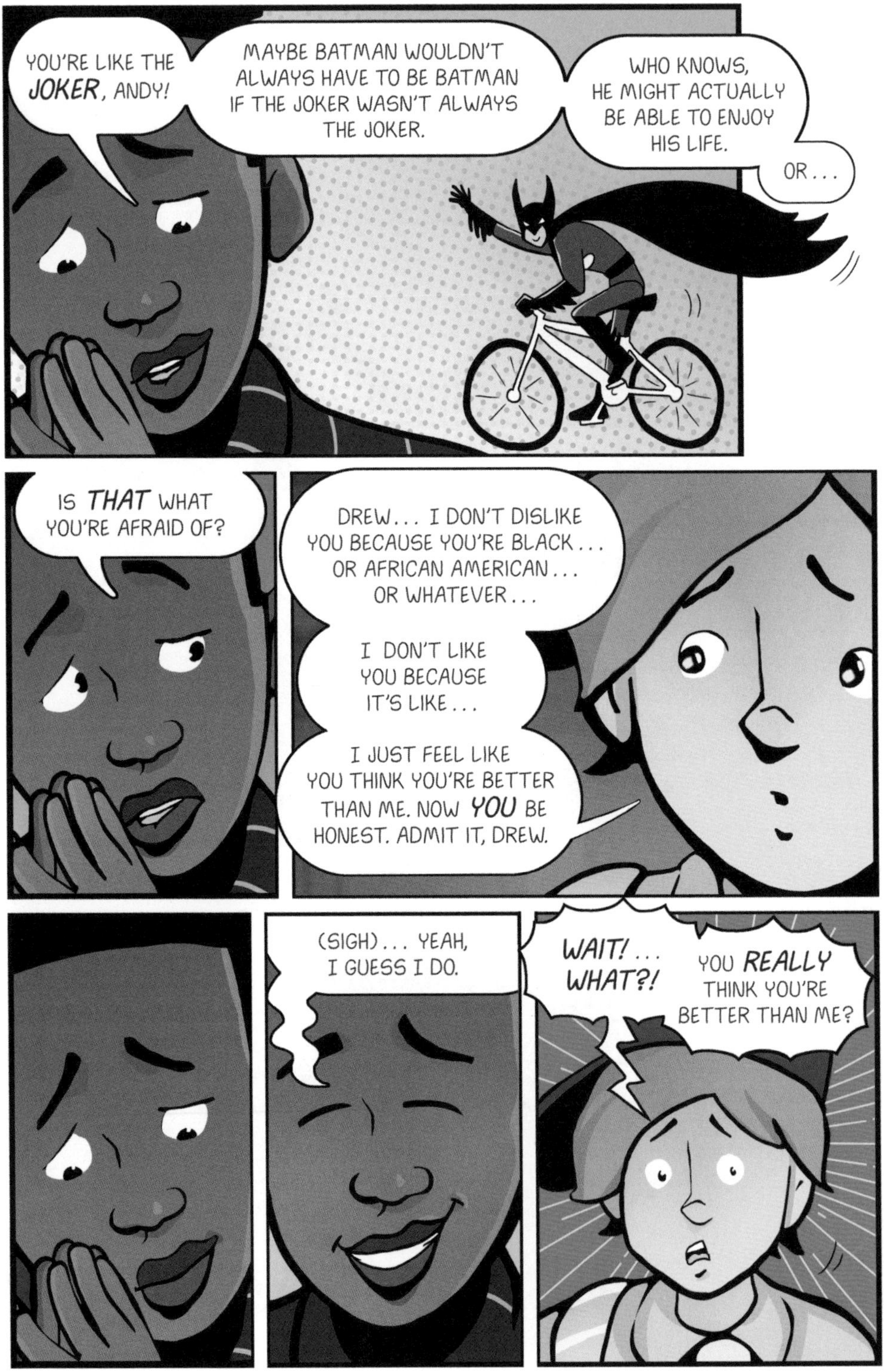

YOU'RE LIKE THE *JOKER*, ANDY!
MAYBE BATMAN WOULDN'T ALWAYS HAVE TO BE BATMAN IF THE JOKER WASN'T ALWAYS THE JOKER.
WHO KNOWS, HE MIGHT ACTUALLY BE ABLE TO ENJOY HIS LIFE.
OR . . .
IS *THAT* WHAT YOU'RE AFRAID OF?
DREW . . . I DON'T DISLIKE YOU BECAUSE YOU'RE BLACK . . . OR AFRICAN AMERICAN . . . OR WHATEVER . . .
I DON'T LIKE YOU BECAUSE IT'S LIKE . . .
I JUST FEEL LIKE YOU THINK YOU'RE BETTER THAN ME. NOW *YOU* BE HONEST. ADMIT IT, DREW.
(SIGH) . . . YEAH, I GUESS I DO.
WAIT! . . . *WHAT?!*
YOU *REALLY* THINK YOU'RE BETTER THAN ME?

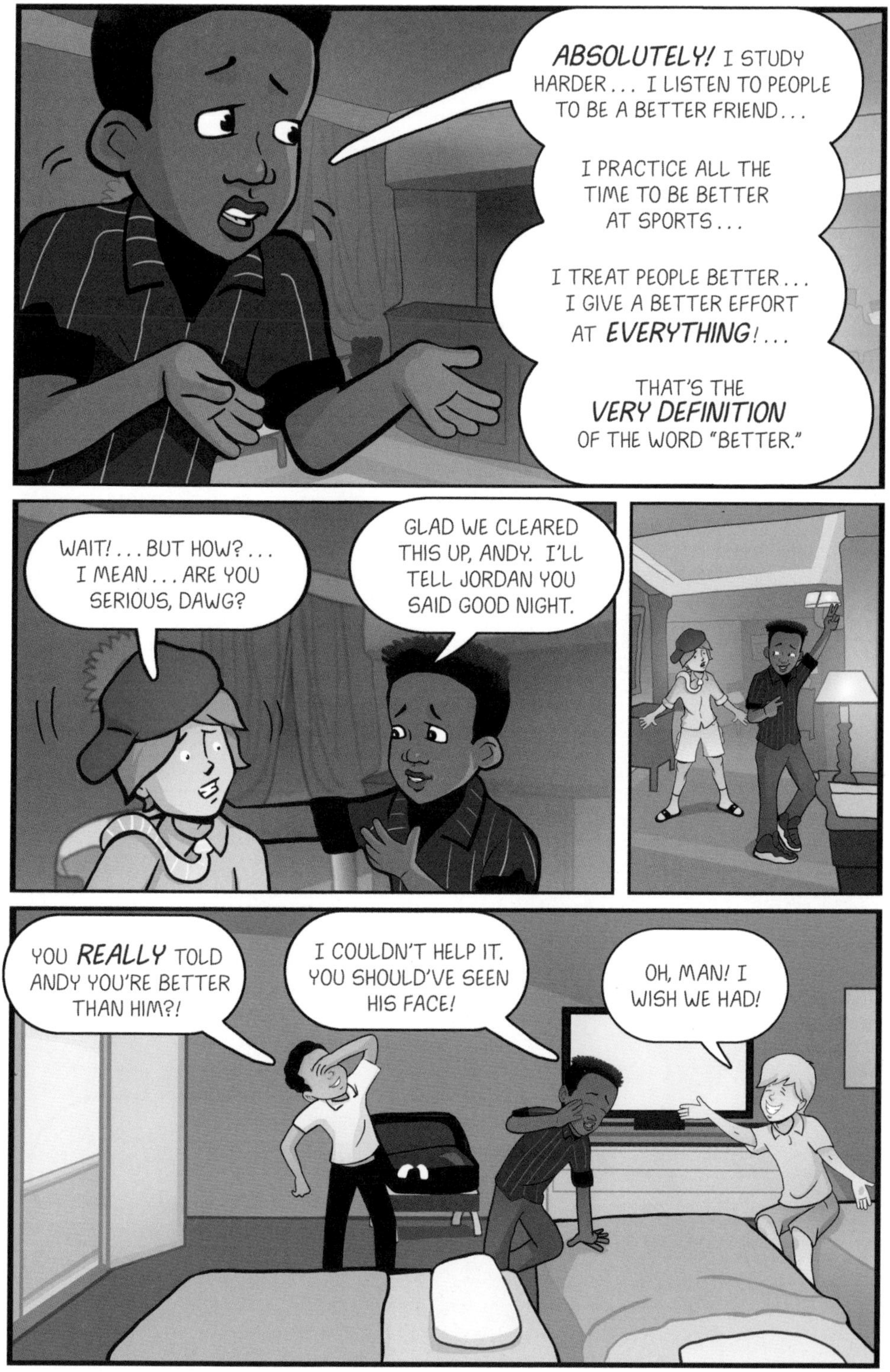
ABSOLUTELY! I STUDY HARDER . . . I LISTEN TO PEOPLE TO BE A BETTER FRIEND . . .
I PRACTICE ALL THE TIME TO BE BETTER AT SPORTS . . .
I TREAT PEOPLE BETTER . . . I GIVE A BETTER EFFORT AT EVERYTHING! . . .
THAT'S THE VERY DEFINITION OF THE WORD "BETTER."
WAIT! . . . BUT HOW? . . . I MEAN . . . ARE YOU SERIOUS, DAWG?
GLAD WE CLEARED THIS UP, ANDY. I'LL TELL JORDAN YOU SAID GOOD NIGHT.
YOU REALLY TOLD ANDY YOU'RE BETTER THAN HIM?!
I COULDN'T HELP IT. YOU SHOULD'VE SEEN HIS FACE!
OH, MAN! I WISH WE HAD!

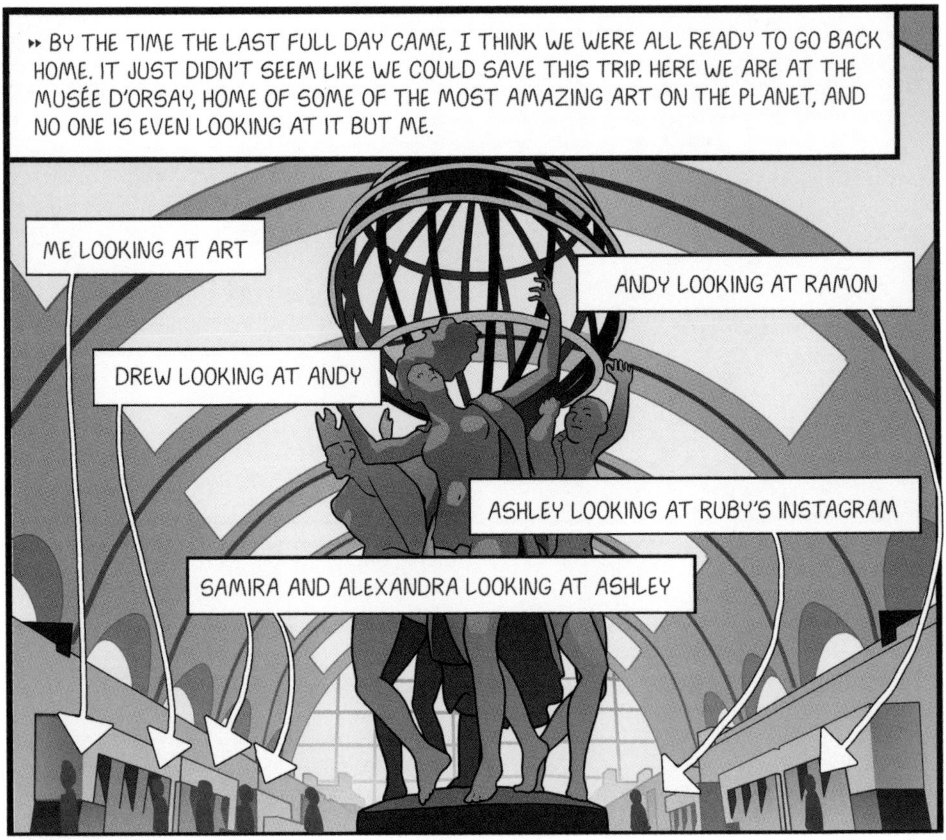
BY THE TIME THE LAST FULL DAY CAME, I THINK WE WERE ALL READY TO GO BACK HOME. IT JUST DIDN'T SEEM LIKE WE COULD SAVE THIS TRIP. HERE WE ARE AT THE MUSÉE D'ORSAY, HOME OF SOME OF THE MOST AMAZING ART ON THE PLANET, AND NO ONE IS EVEN LOOKING AT IT BUT ME.
ME LOOKING AT ART
ANDY LOOKING AT RAMON
DREW LOOKING AT ANDY
ASHLEY LOOKING AT RUBY'S INSTAGRAM
SAMIRA AND ALEXANDRA LOOKING AT ASHLEY

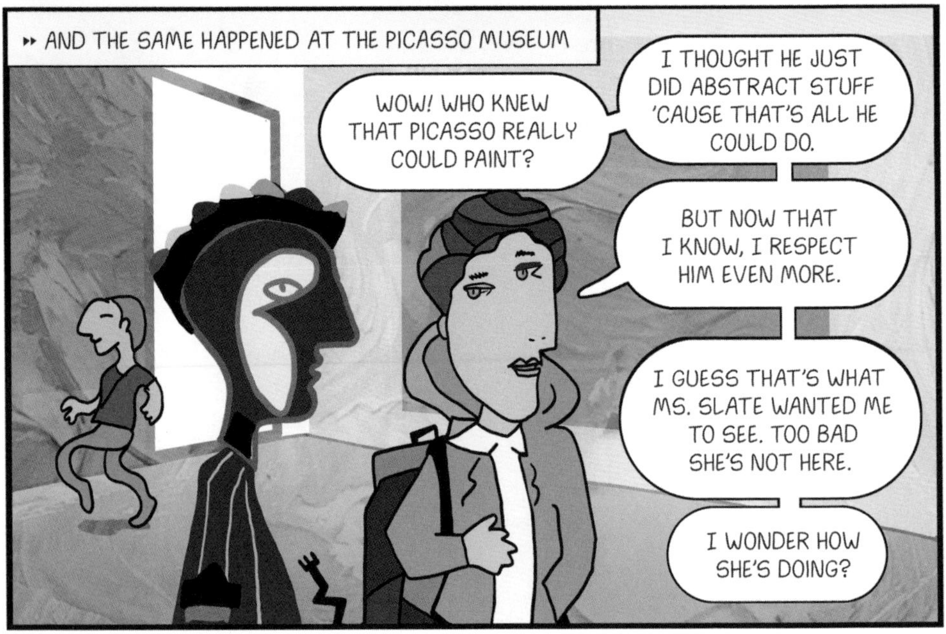
AND THE SAME HAPPENED AT THE PICASSO MUSEUM
WOW! WHO KNEW THAT PICASSO REALLY COULD PAINT?
I THOUGHT HE JUST DID ABSTRACT STUFF 'CAUSE THAT'S ALL HE COULD DO.
BUT NOW THAT I KNOW, I RESPECT HIM EVEN MORE.
I GUESS THAT'S WHAT MS. SLATE WANTED ME TO SEE. TOO BAD SHE'S NOT HERE.
I WONDER HOW SHE'S DOING?

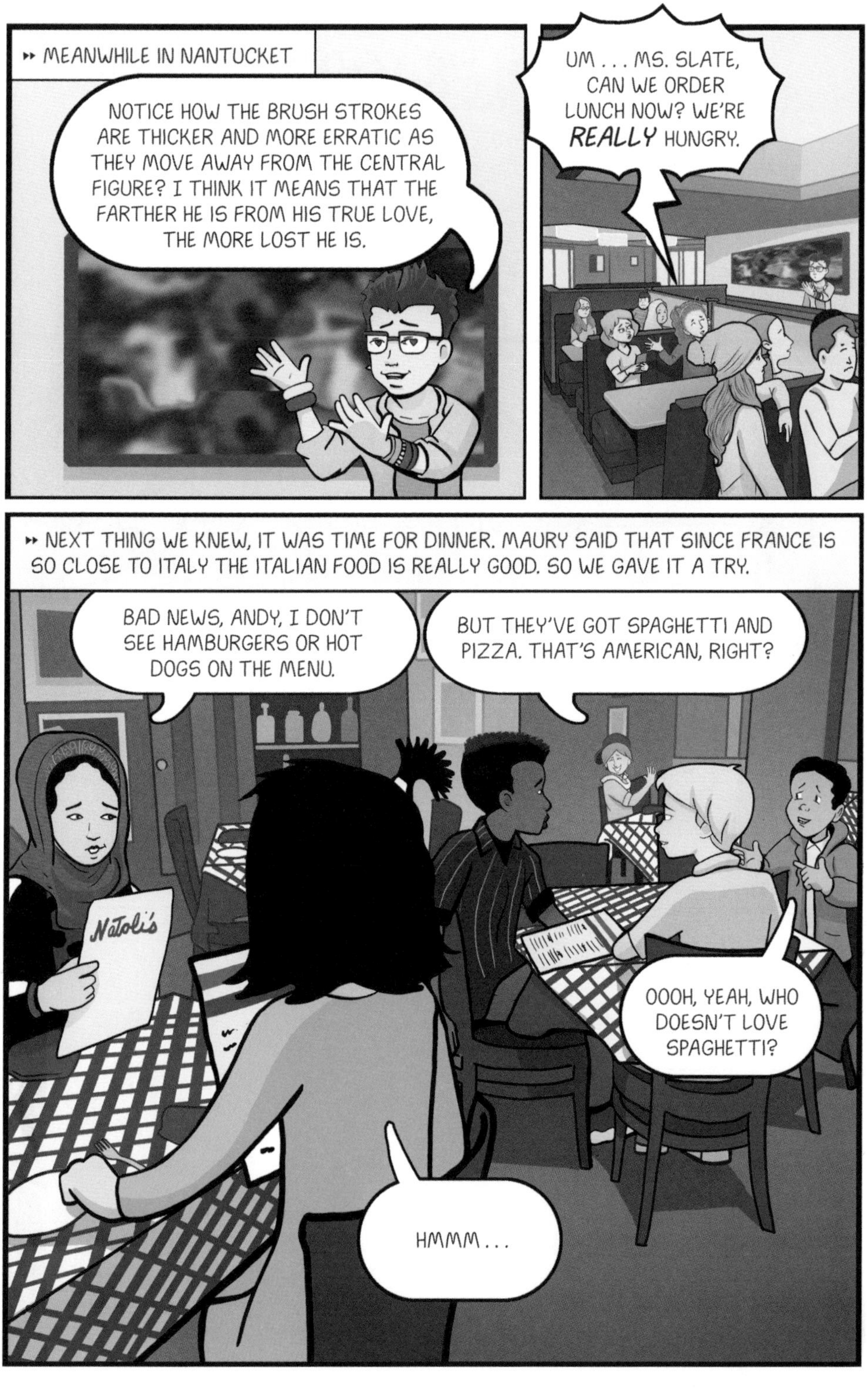

MEANWHILE IN NANTUCKET
NOTICE HOW THE BRUSH STROKES ARE THICKER AND MORE ERRATIC AS THEY MOVE AWAY FROM THE CENTRAL FIGURE? I THINK IT MEANS THAT THE FARTHER HE IS FROM HIS TRUE LOVE, THE MORE LOST HE IS.
UM . . . MS. SLATE, CAN WE ORDER LUNCH NOW? WE'RE *REALLY* HUNGRY.
NEXT THING WE KNEW, IT WAS TIME FOR DINNER. MAURY SAID THAT SINCE FRANCE IS SO CLOSE TO ITALY THE ITALIAN FOOD IS REALLY GOOD. SO WE GAVE IT A TRY.
BAD NEWS, ANDY, I DON'T SEE HAMBURGERS OR HOT DOGS ON THE MENU.
BUT THEY'VE GOT SPAGHETTI AND PIZZA. THAT'S AMERICAN, RIGHT?
Natoli's
OOOH, YEAH, WHO DOESN'T LOVE SPAGHETTI?
HMMM . . .

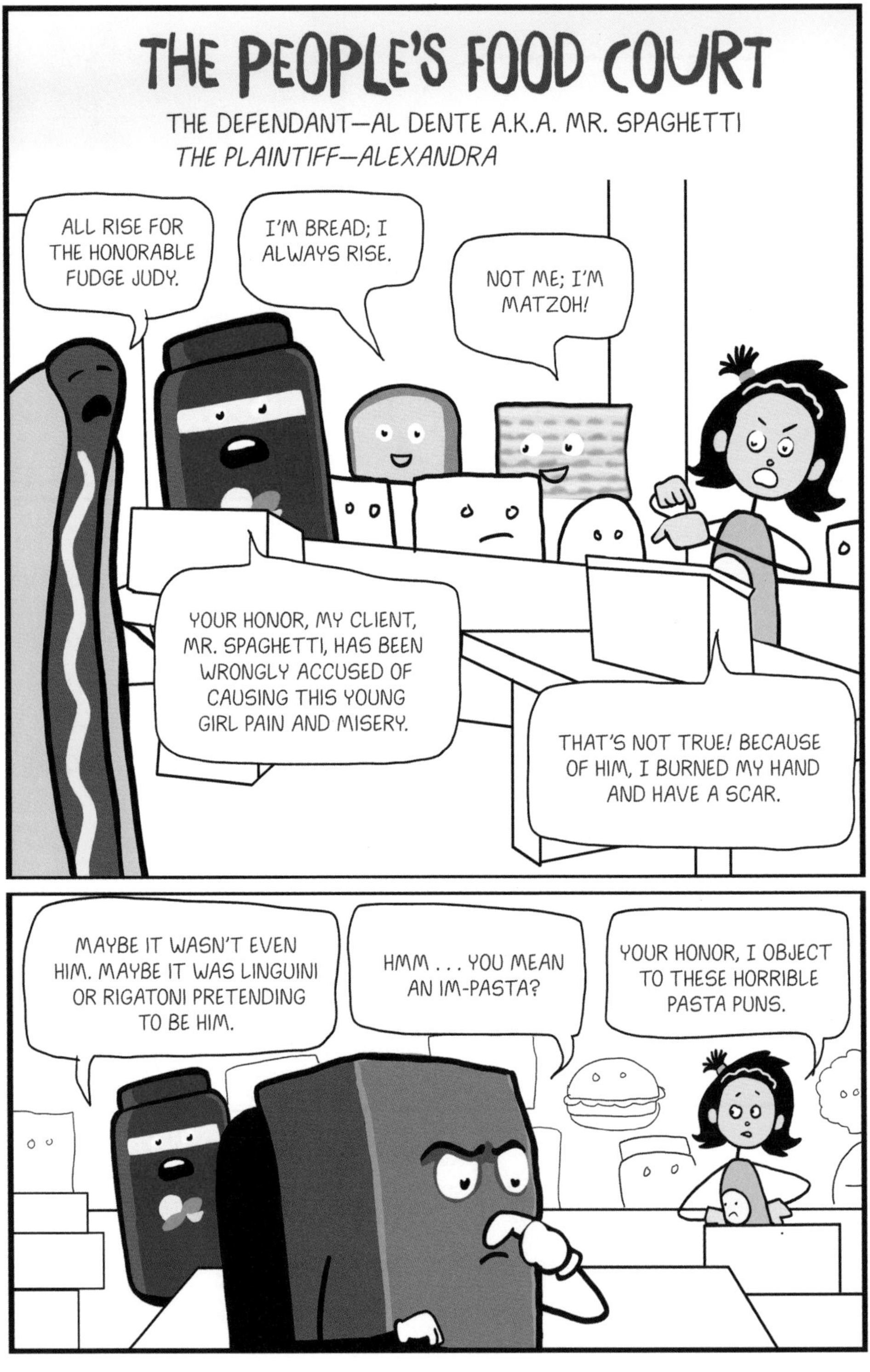
THE PEOPLE'S FOOD COURT
THE DEFENDANT—AL DENTE A.K.A. MR. SPAGHETTI
THE PLAINTIFF—ALEXANDRA
ALL RISE FOR THE HONORABLE FUDGE JUDY.
I'M BREAD; I ALWAYS RISE.
NOT ME; I'M MATZOH!
YOUR HONOR, MY CLIENT, MR. SPAGHETTI, HAS BEEN WRONGLY ACCUSED OF CAUSING THIS YOUNG GIRL PAIN AND MISERY.
THAT'S NOT TRUE! BECAUSE OF HIM, I BURNED MY HAND AND HAVE A SCAR.
MAYBE IT WASN'T EVEN HIM. MAYBE IT WAS LINGUINI OR RIGATONI PRETENDING TO BE HIM.
HMM . . . YOU MEAN AN IM-PASTA?
YOUR HONOR, I OBJECT TO THESE HORRIBLE PASTA PUNS.

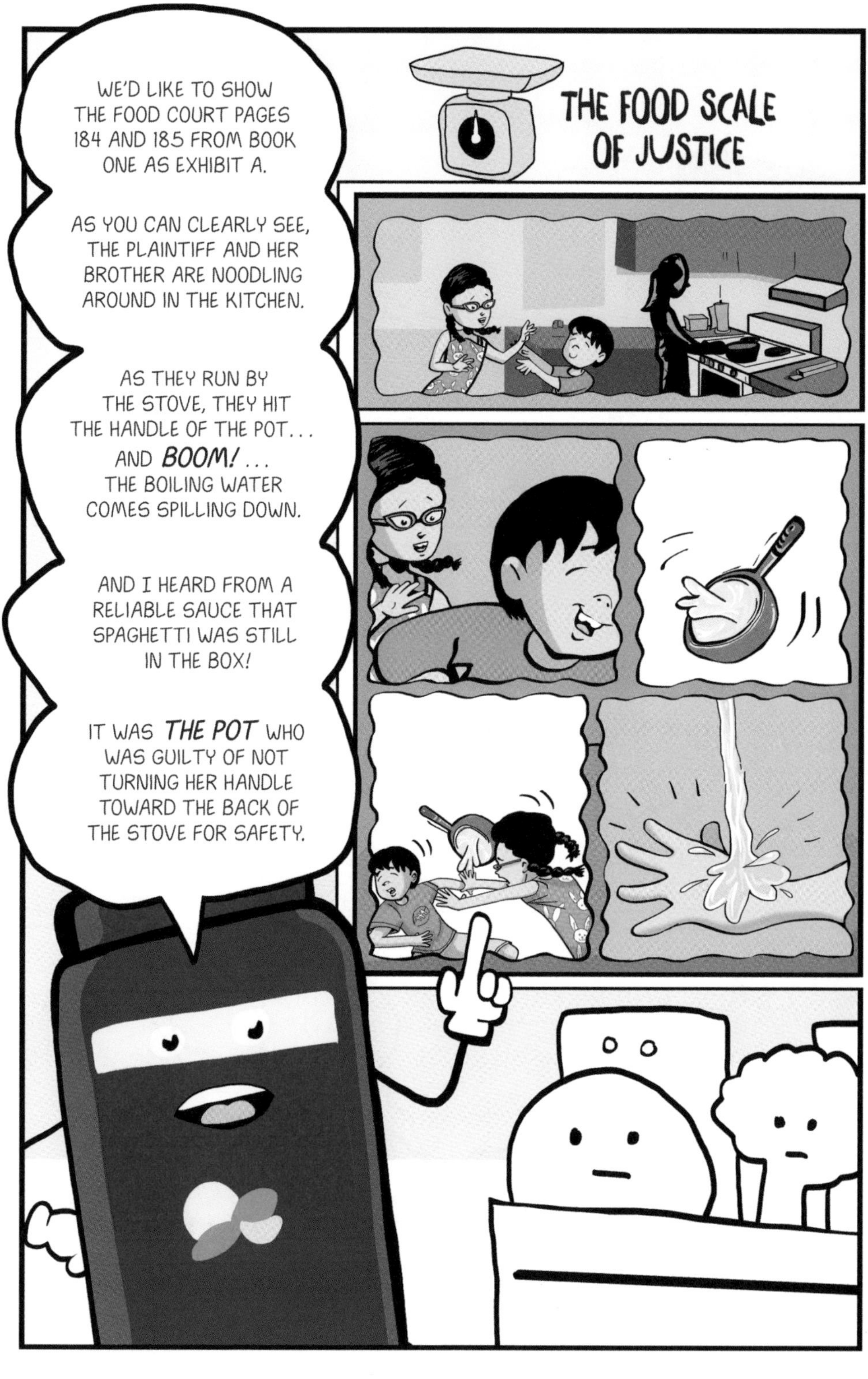
WE'D LIKE TO SHOW THE FOOD COURT PAGES 184 AND 185 FROM BOOK ONE AS EXHIBIT A.
AS YOU CAN CLEARLY SEE, THE PLAINTIFF AND HER BROTHER ARE NOODLING AROUND IN THE KITCHEN.
AS THEY RUN BY THE STOVE, THEY HIT THE HANDLE OF THE POT... AND BOOM!... THE BOILING WATER COMES SPILLING DOWN.
AND I HEARD FROM A RELIABLE SAUCE THAT SPAGHETTI WAS STILL IN THE BOX!
IT WAS THE POT WHO WAS GUILTY OF NOT TURNING HER HANDLE TOWARD THE BACK OF THE STOVE FOR SAFETY.
THE FOOD SCALE OF JUSTICE

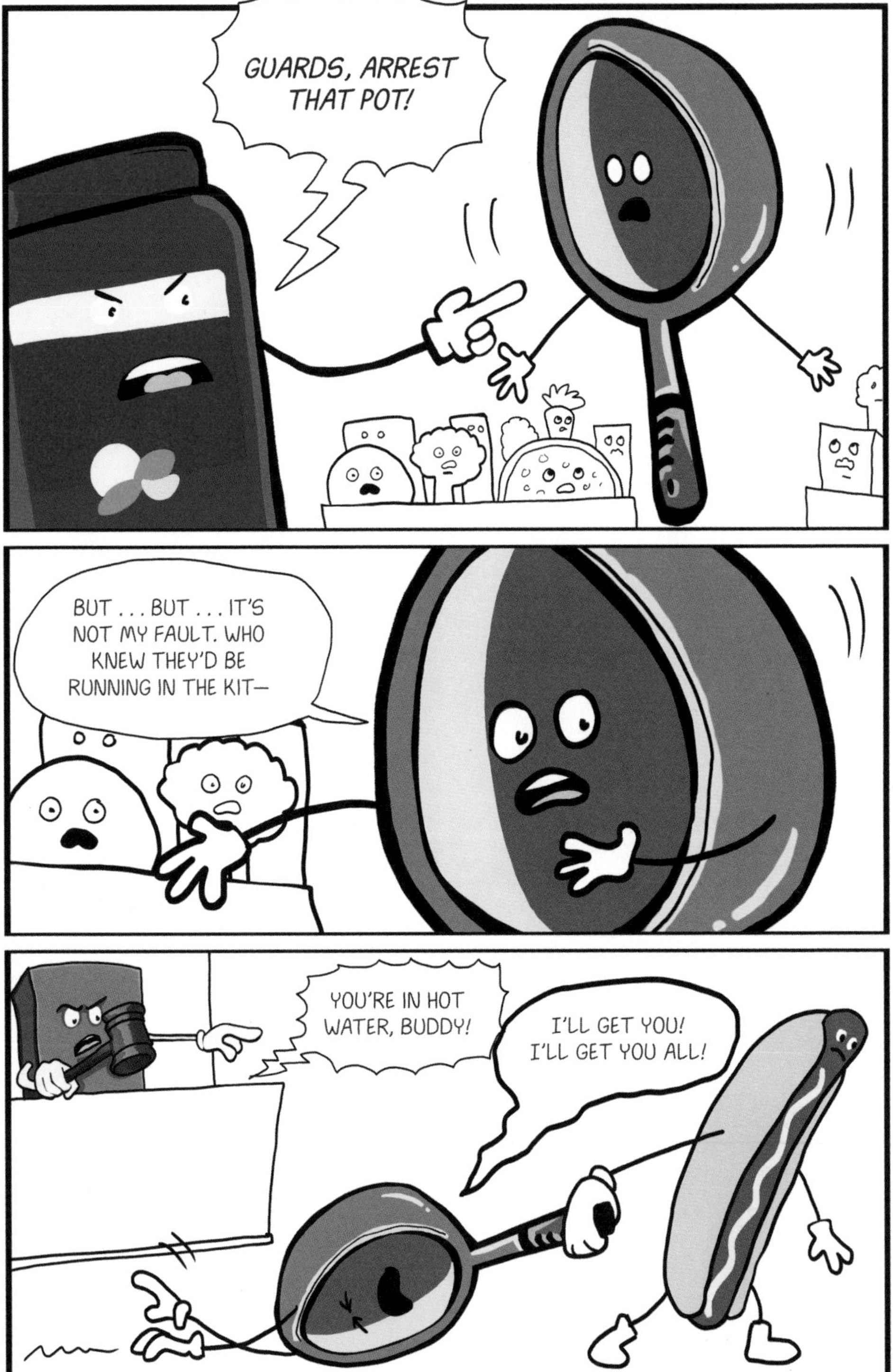
GUARDS, ARREST THAT POT!
BUT . . . BUT . . . IT'S NOT MY FAULT. WHO KNEW THEY'D BE RUNNING IN THE KIT—
YOU'RE IN HOT WATER, BUDDY!
I'LL GET YOU! I'LL GET YOU ALL!

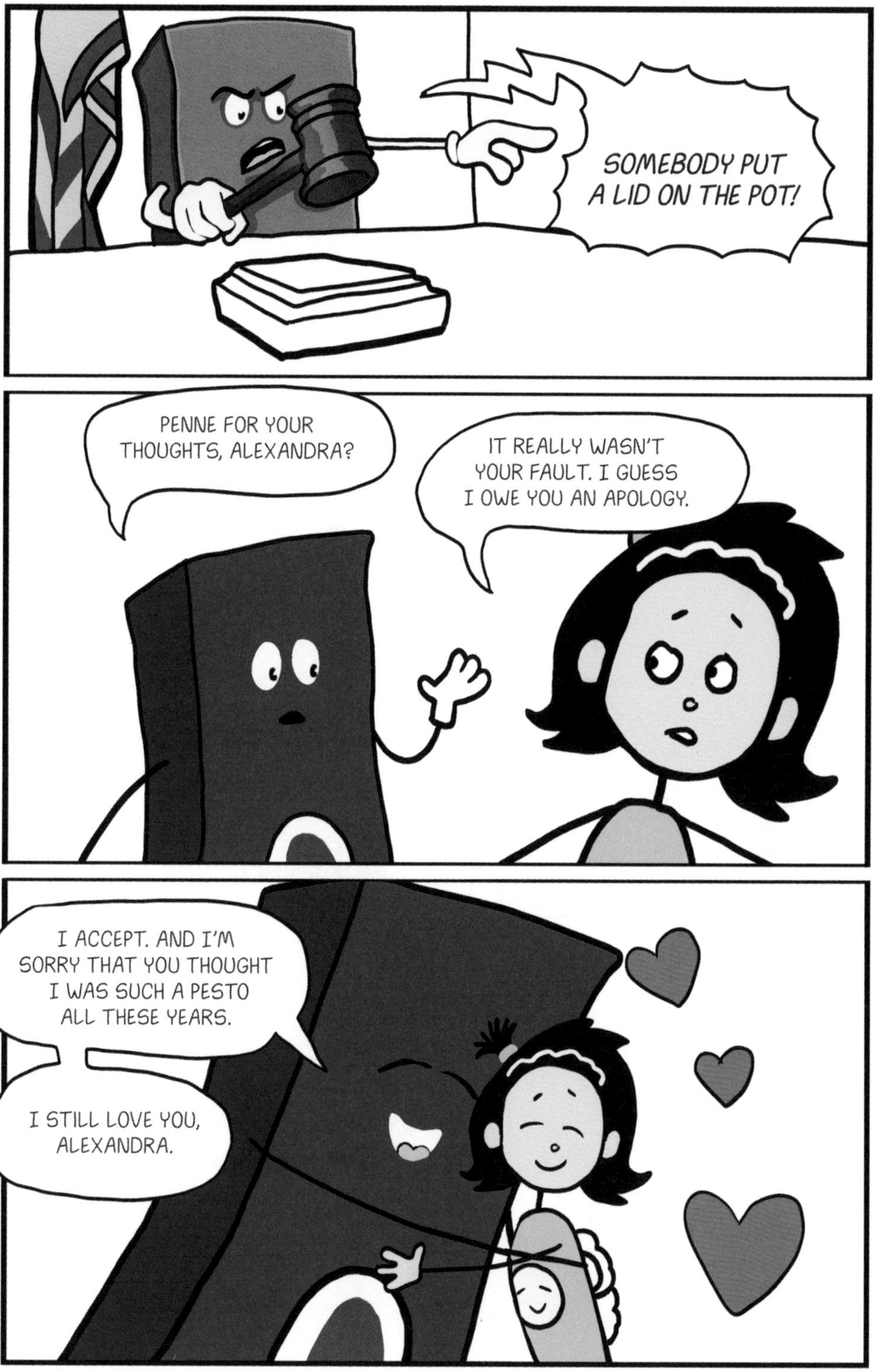
SOMEBODY PUT A LID ON THE POT!
PENNE FOR YOUR THOUGHTS, ALEXANDRA?
IT REALLY WASN'T YOUR FAULT. I GUESS I OWE YOU AN APOLOGY.
I ACCEPT. AND I'M SORRY THAT YOU THOUGHT I WAS SUCH A PESTO ALL THESE YEARS.
I STILL LOVE YOU, ALEXANDRA.

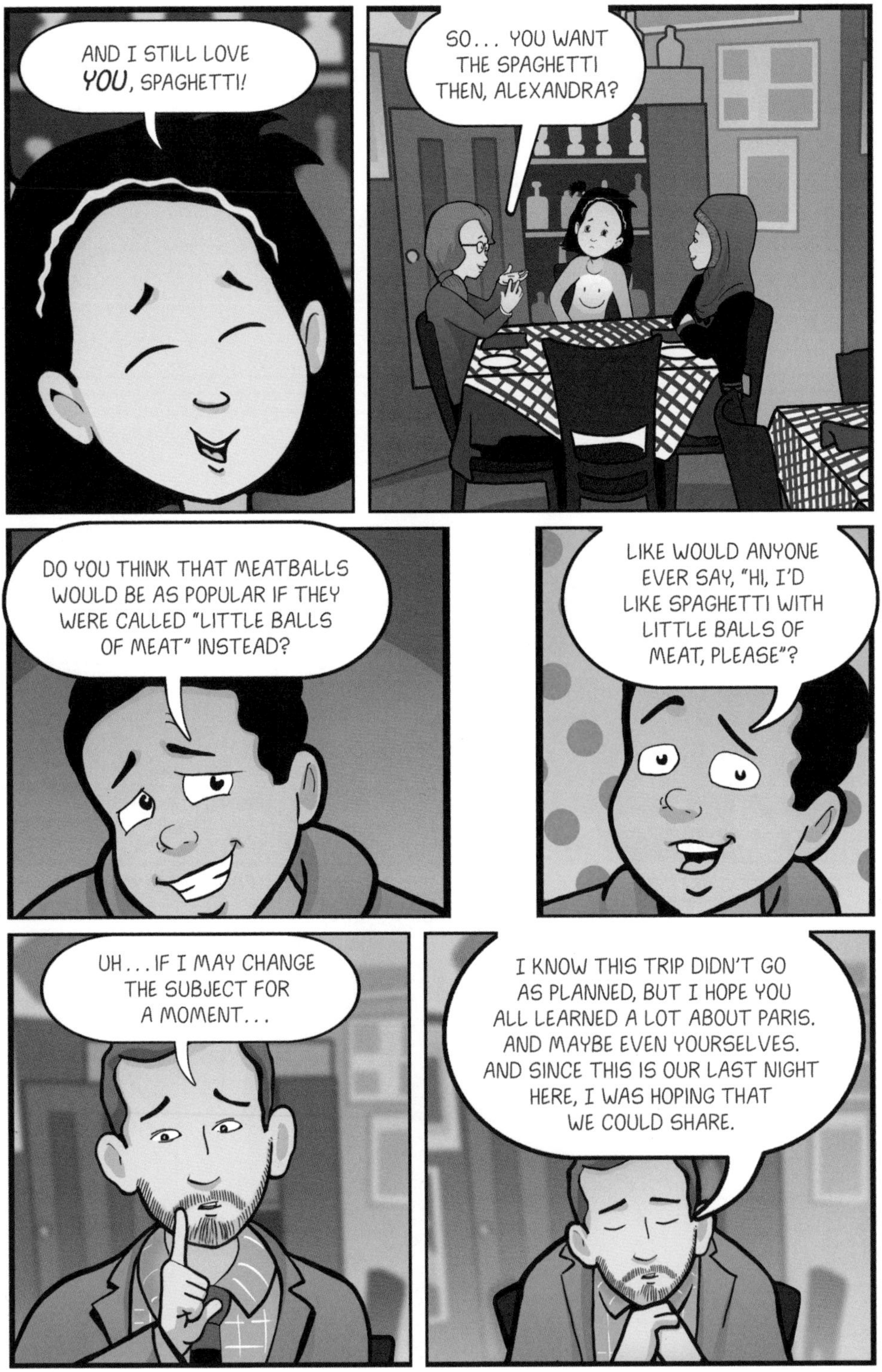
AND I STILL LOVE YOU, SPAGHETTI!
SO... YOU WANT THE SPAGHETTI THEN, ALEXANDRA?
DO YOU THINK THAT MEATBALLS WOULD BE AS POPULAR IF THEY WERE CALLED "LITTLE BALLS OF MEAT" INSTEAD?
LIKE WOULD ANYONE EVER SAY, "HI, I'D LIKE SPAGHETTI WITH LITTLE BALLS OF MEAT, PLEASE"?
UH... IF I MAY CHANGE THE SUBJECT FOR A MOMENT...
I KNOW THIS TRIP DIDN'T GO AS PLANNED, BUT I HOPE YOU ALL LEARNED A LOT ABOUT PARIS. AND MAYBE EVEN YOURSELVES. AND SINCE THIS IS OUR LAST NIGHT HERE, I WAS HOPING THAT WE COULD SHARE.

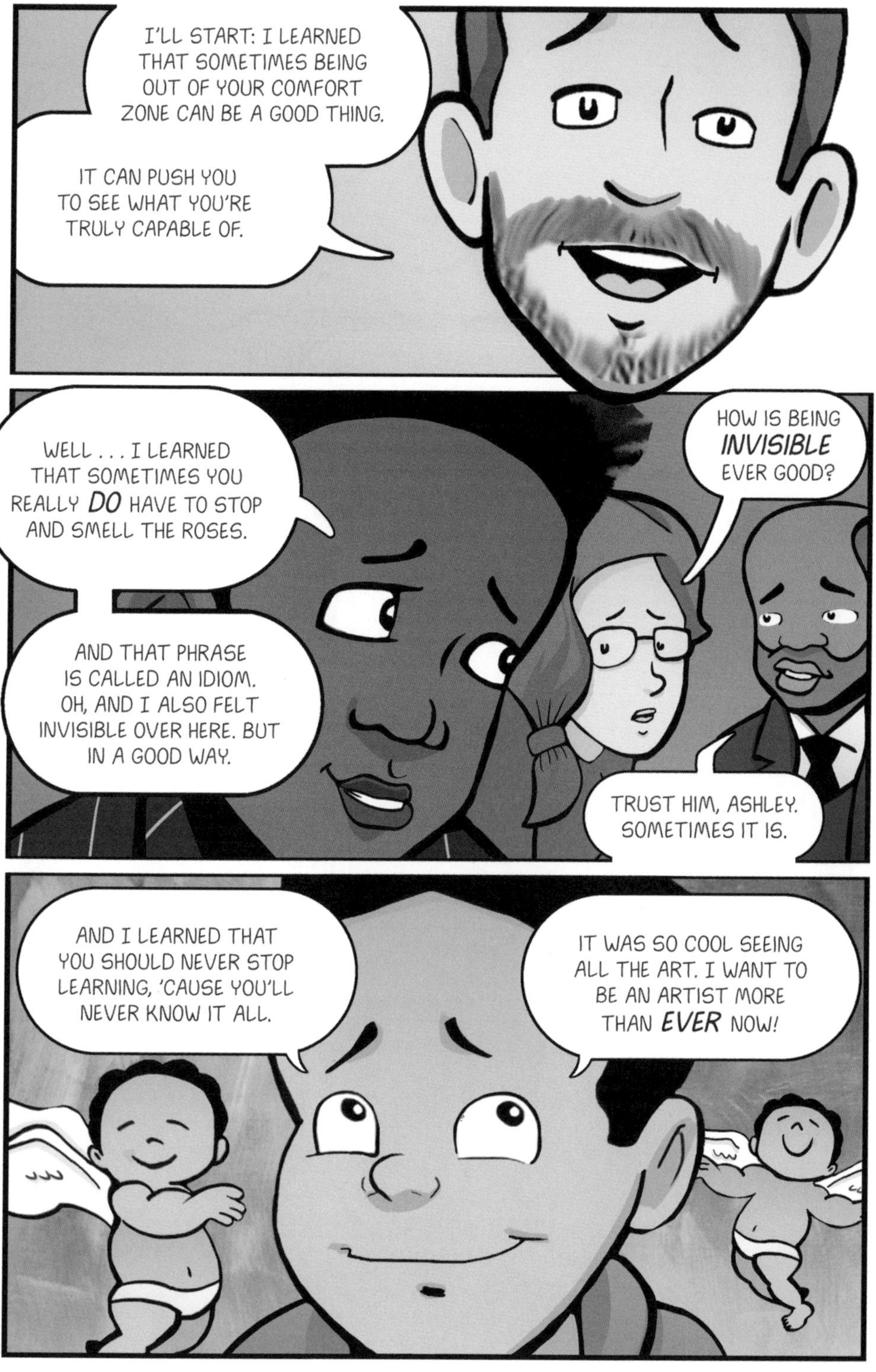
I'LL START: I LEARNED THAT SOMETIMES BEING OUT OF YOUR COMFORT ZONE CAN BE A GOOD THING.
IT CAN PUSH YOU TO SEE WHAT YOU'RE TRULY CAPABLE OF.
WELL . . . I LEARNED THAT SOMETIMES YOU REALLY *DO* HAVE TO STOP AND SMELL THE ROSES.
AND THAT PHRASE IS CALLED AN IDIOM. OH, AND I ALSO FELT INVISIBLE OVER HERE. BUT IN A GOOD WAY.
HOW IS BEING *INVISIBLE* EVER GOOD?
TRUST HIM, ASHLEY. SOMETIMES IT IS.
AND I LEARNED THAT YOU SHOULD NEVER STOP LEARNING, 'CAUSE YOU'LL NEVER KNOW IT ALL.
IT WAS SO COOL SEEING ALL THE ART. I WANT TO BE AN ARTIST MORE THAN *EVER* NOW!

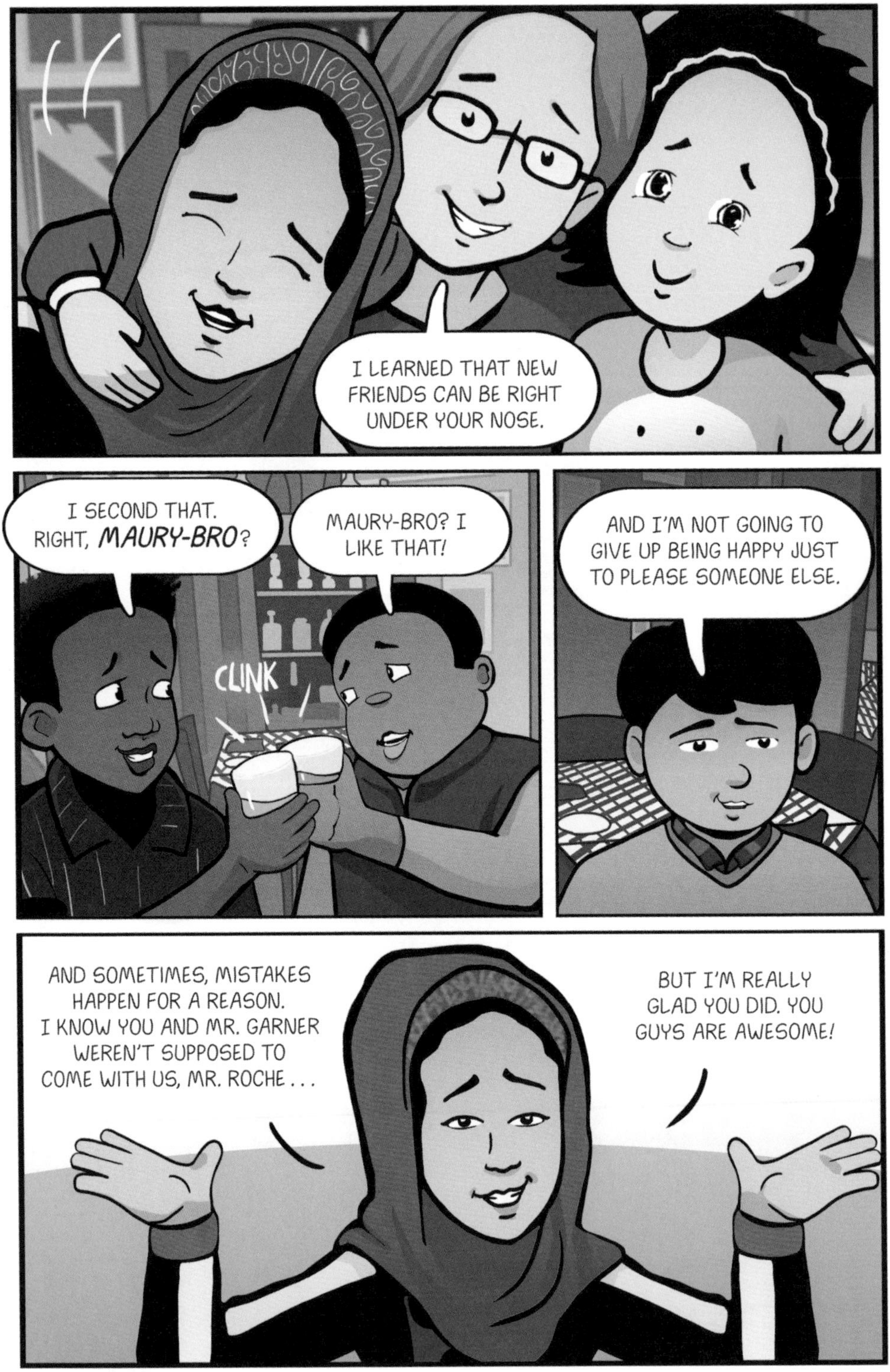
I LEARNED THAT NEW FRIENDS CAN BE RIGHT UNDER YOUR NOSE.
I SECOND THAT. RIGHT, *MAURY-BRO*?
MAURY-BRO? I LIKE THAT!
CLINK
AND I'M NOT GOING TO GIVE UP BEING HAPPY JUST TO PLEASE SOMEONE ELSE.
AND SOMETIMES, MISTAKES HAPPEN FOR A REASON. I KNOW YOU AND MR. GARNER WEREN'T SUPPOSED TO COME WITH US, MR. ROCHE . . .
BUT I'M REALLY GLAD YOU DID. YOU GUYS ARE AWESOME!

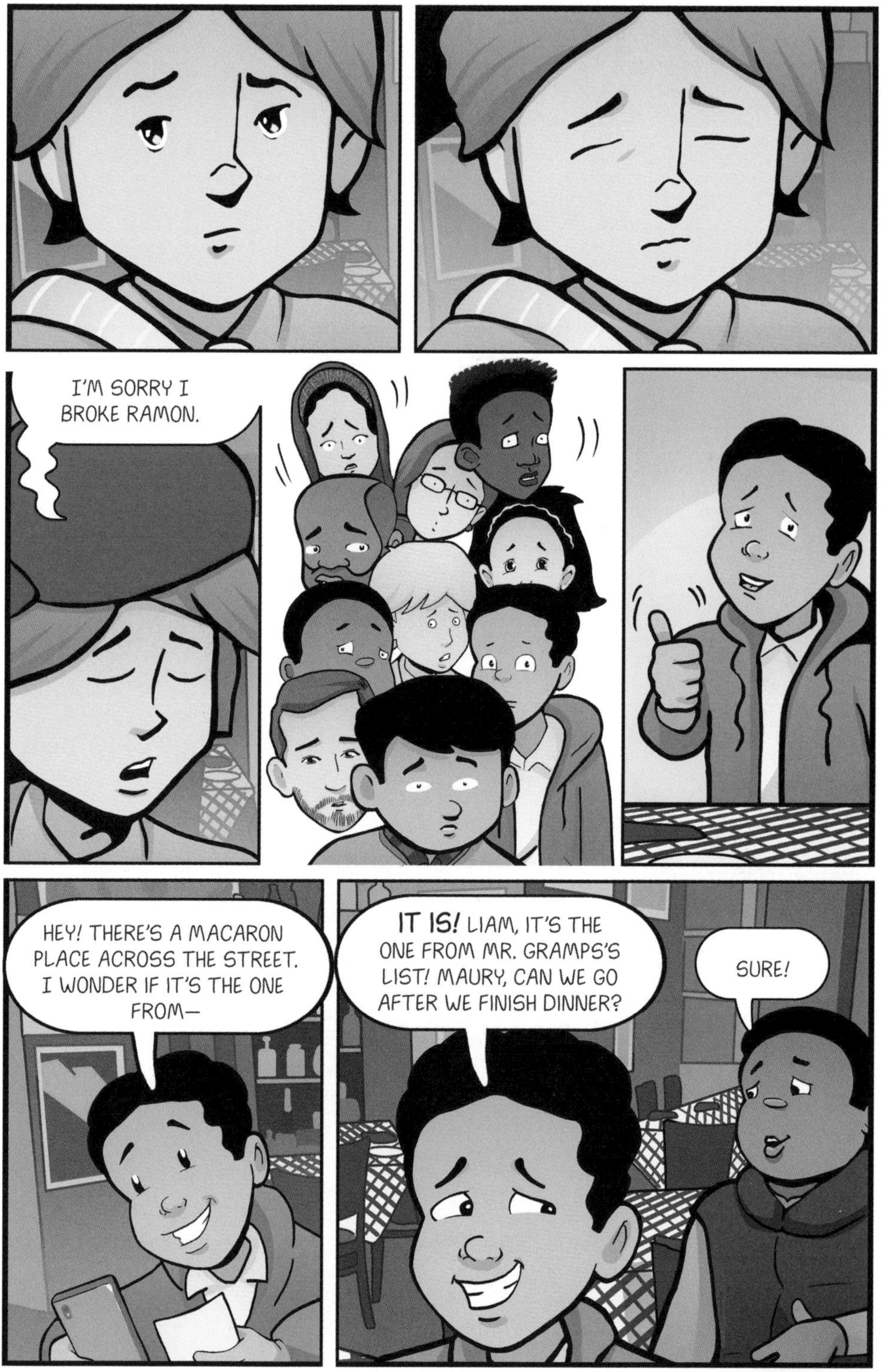
I'M SORRY I BROKE RAMON.
HEY! THERE'S A MACARON PLACE ACROSS THE STREET. I WONDER IF IT'S THE ONE FROM—
IT IS! LIAM, IT'S THE ONE FROM MR. GRAMPS'S LIST! MAURY, CAN WE GO AFTER WE FINISH DINNER?
SURE!

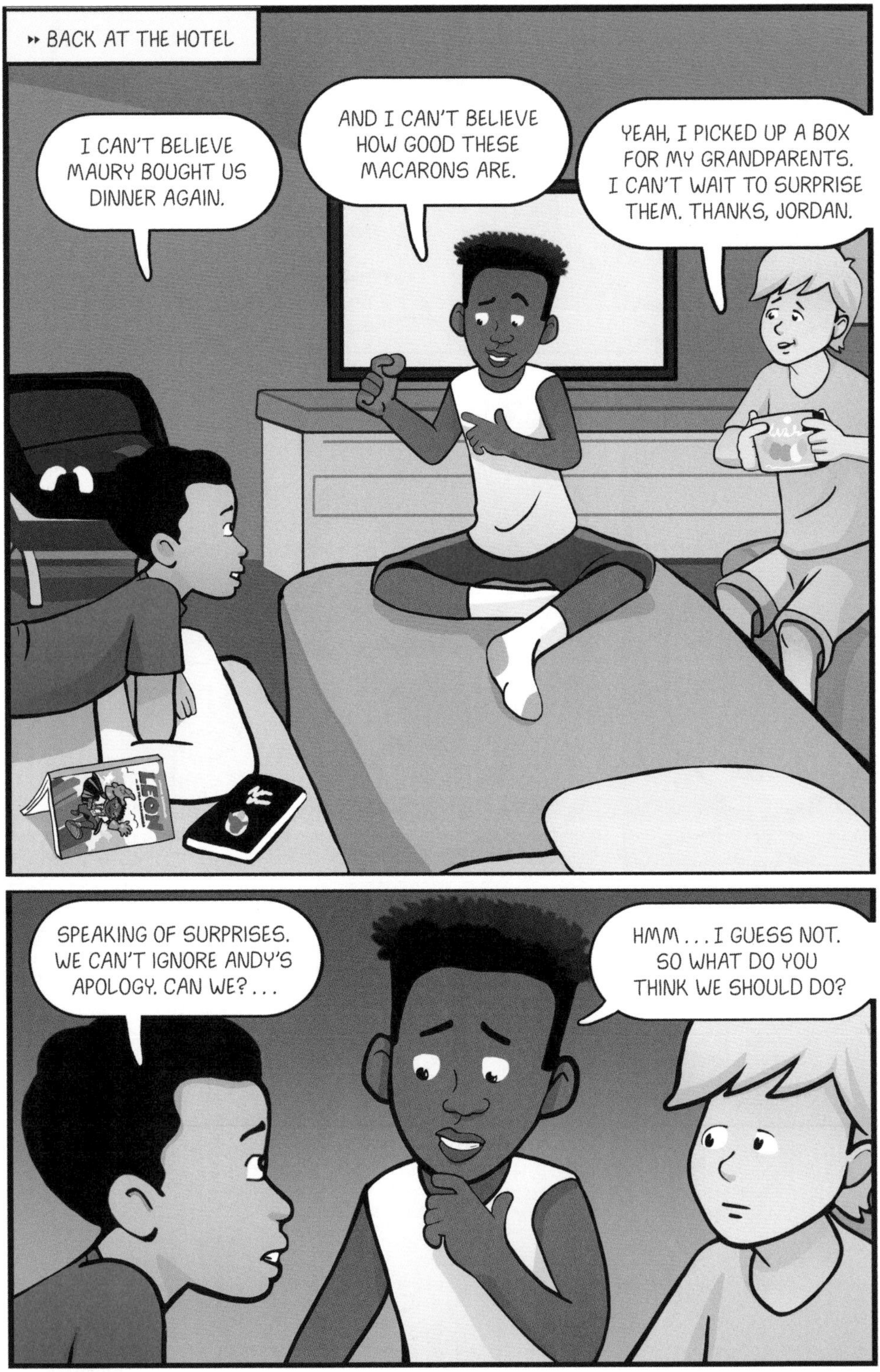
BACK AT THE HOTEL
I CAN'T BELIEVE MAURY BOUGHT US DINNER AGAIN.
AND I CAN'T BELIEVE HOW GOOD THESE MACARONS ARE.
YEAH, I PICKED UP A BOX FOR MY GRANDPARENTS. I CAN'T WAIT TO SURPRISE THEM. THANKS, JORDAN.
LEON
SPEAKING OF SURPRISES. WE CAN'T IGNORE ANDY'S APOLOGY. CAN WE? . . .
HMM . . . I GUESS NOT. SO WHAT DO YOU THINK WE SHOULD DO?

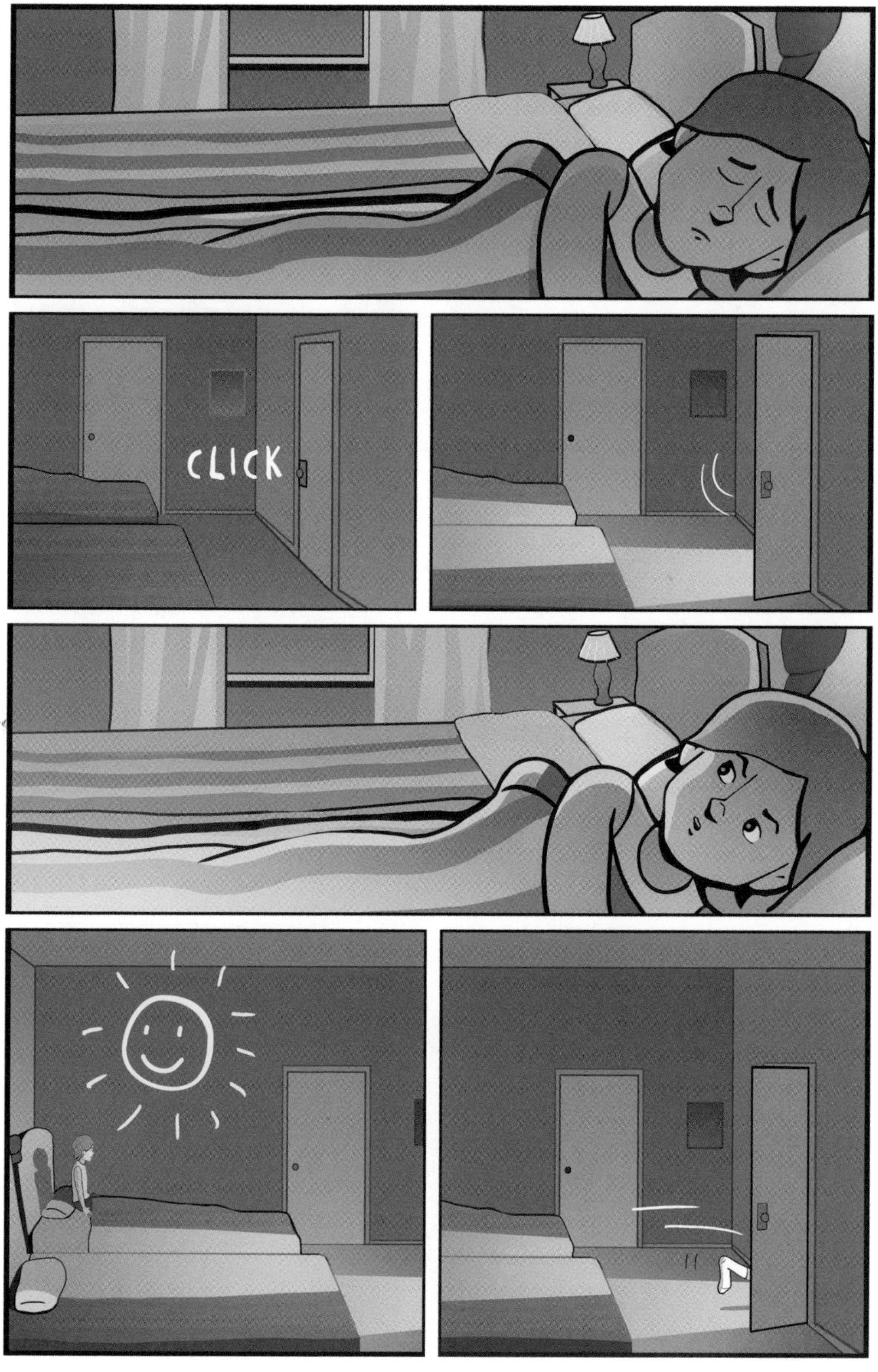
CLICK

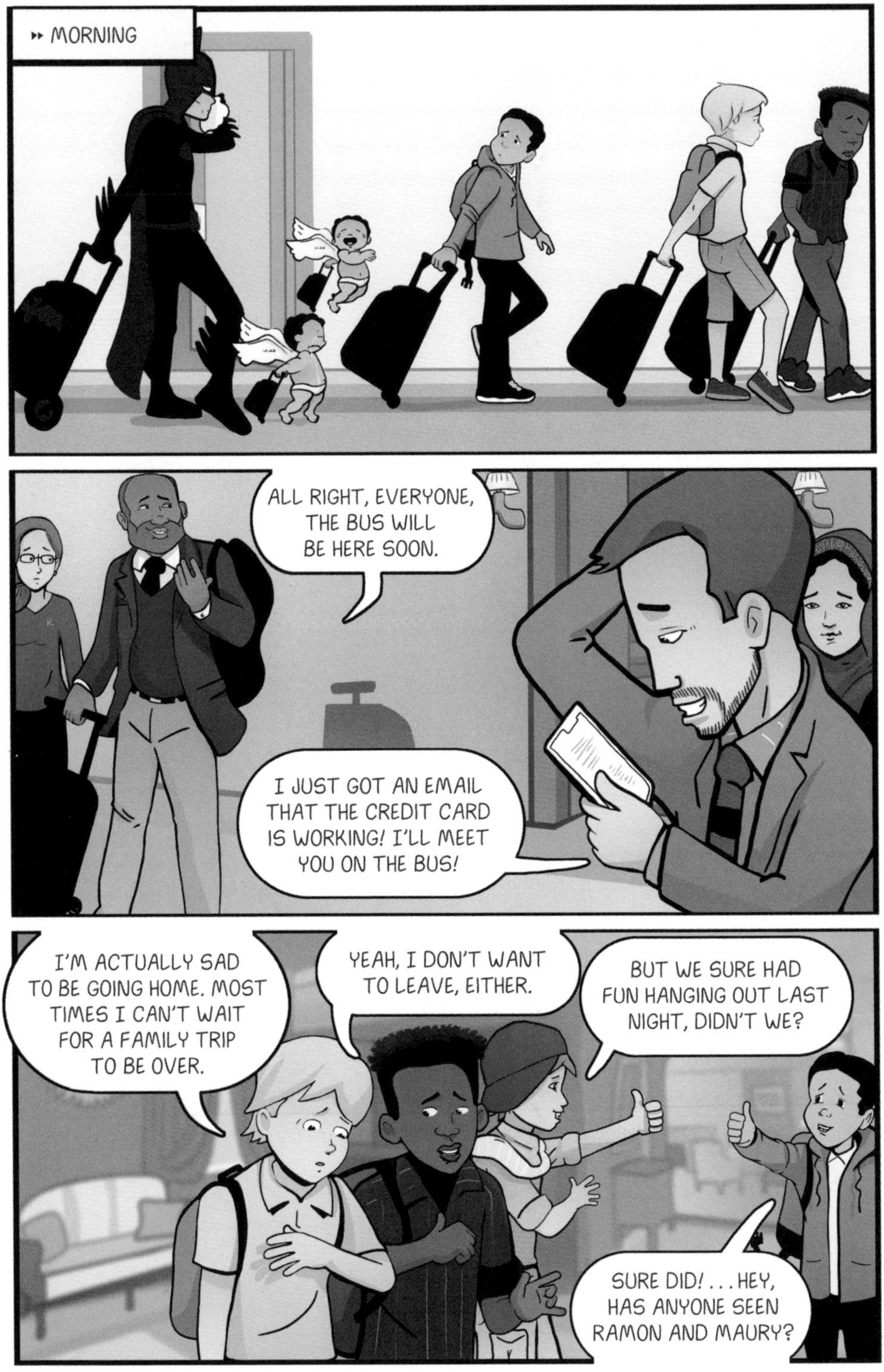
MORNING
ALL RIGHT, EVERYONE, THE BUS WILL BE HERE SOON.
I JUST GOT AN EMAIL THAT THE CREDIT CARD IS WORKING! I'LL MEET YOU ON THE BUS!
I'M ACTUALLY SAD TO BE GOING HOME. MOST TIMES I CAN'T WAIT FOR A FAMILY TRIP TO BE OVER.
YEAH, I DON'T WANT TO LEAVE, EITHER.
BUT WE SURE HAD FUN HANGING OUT LAST NIGHT, DIDN'T WE?
SURE DID! . . . HEY, HAS ANYONE SEEN RAMON AND MAURY?

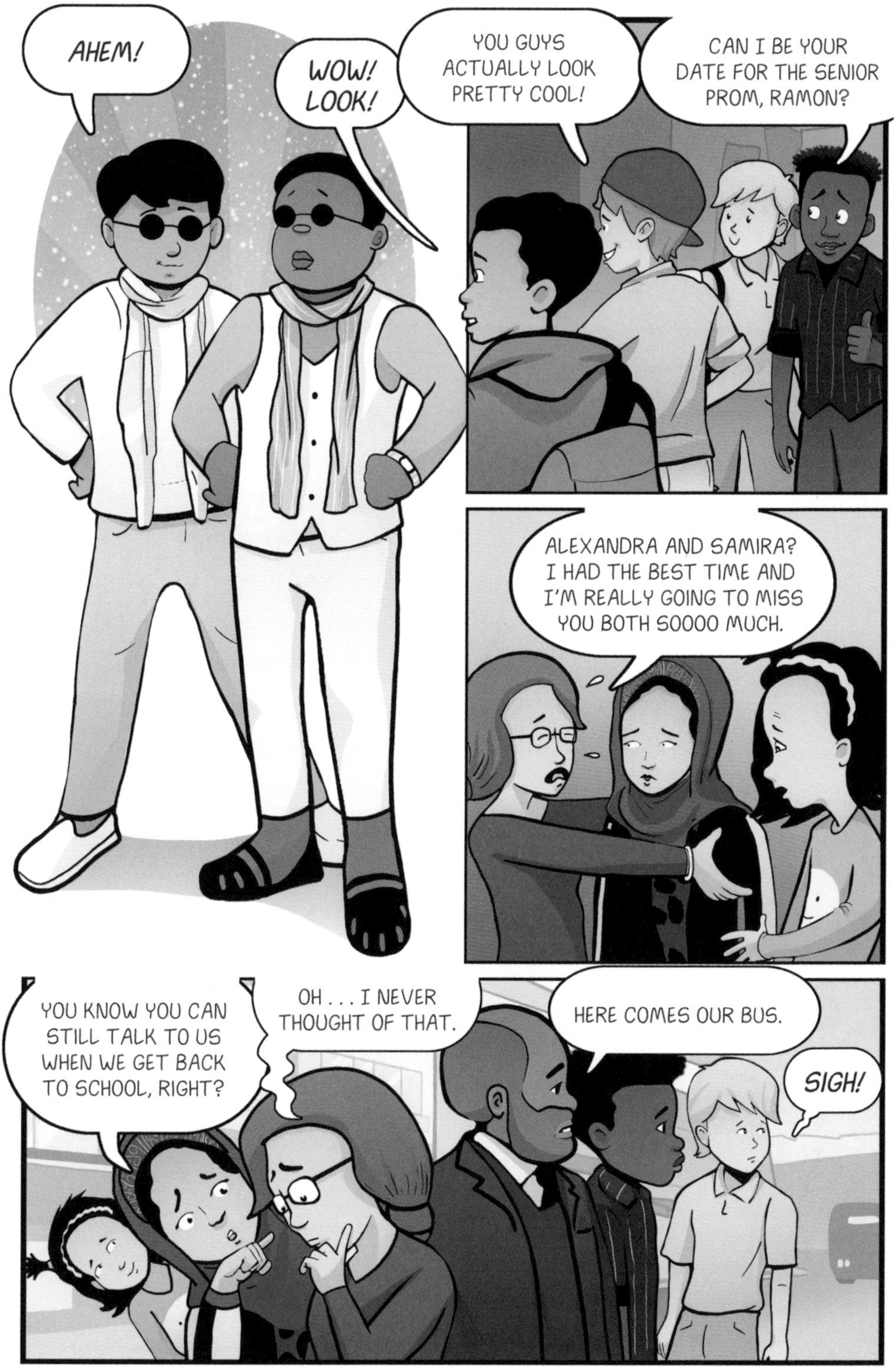
AHEM!
WOW! LOOK!
YOU GUYS ACTUALLY LOOK PRETTY COOL!
CAN I BE YOUR DATE FOR THE SENIOR PROM, RAMON?
ALEXANDRA AND SAMIRA? I HAD THE BEST TIME AND I'M REALLY GOING TO MISS YOU BOTH SOOOO MUCH.
YOU KNOW YOU CAN STILL TALK TO US WHEN WE GET BACK TO SCHOOL, RIGHT?
OH . . . I NEVER THOUGHT OF THAT.
HERE COMES OUR BUS.
SIGH!

9 Band Together!

(Or Is It "Banned" Together?)

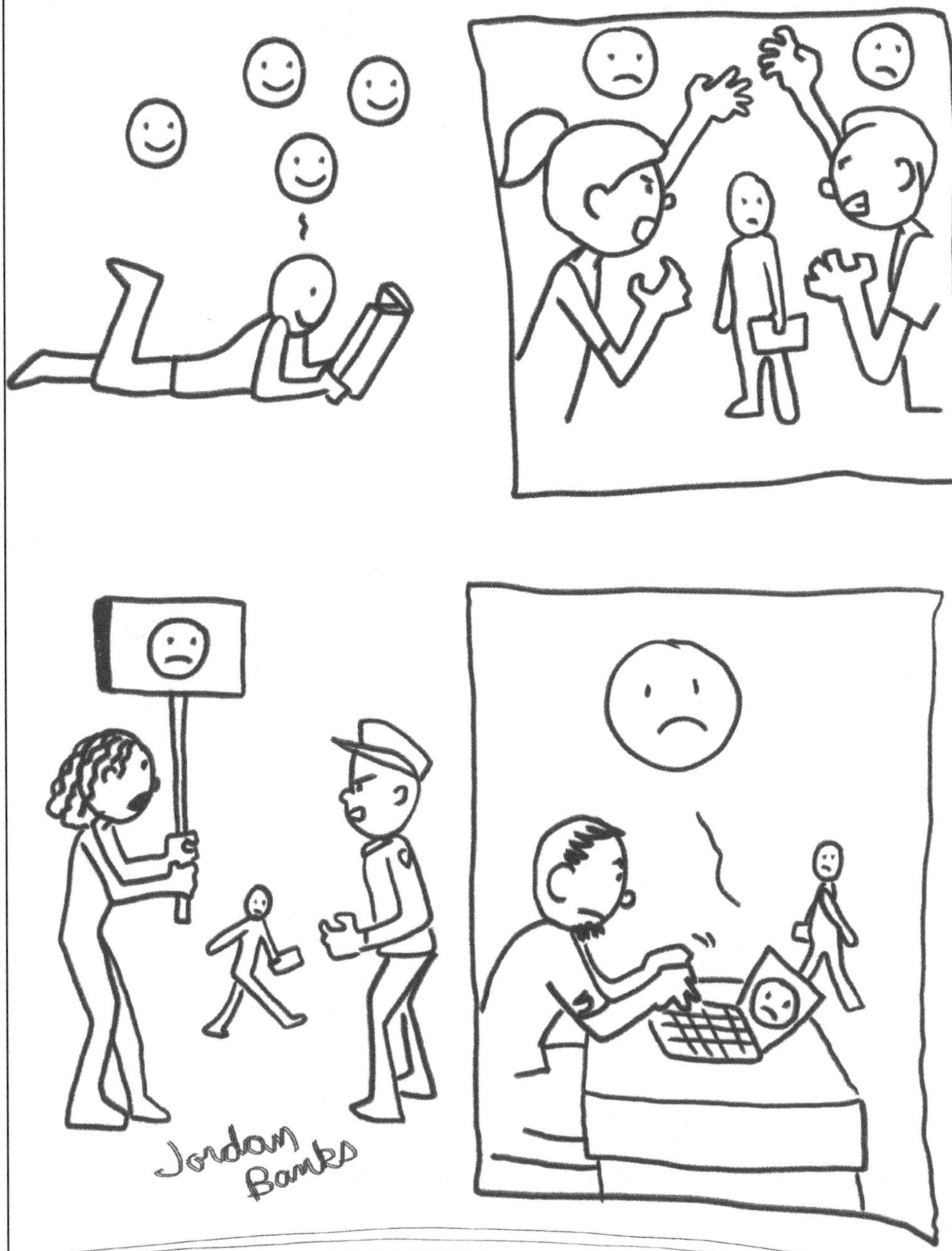
Jordan Banks

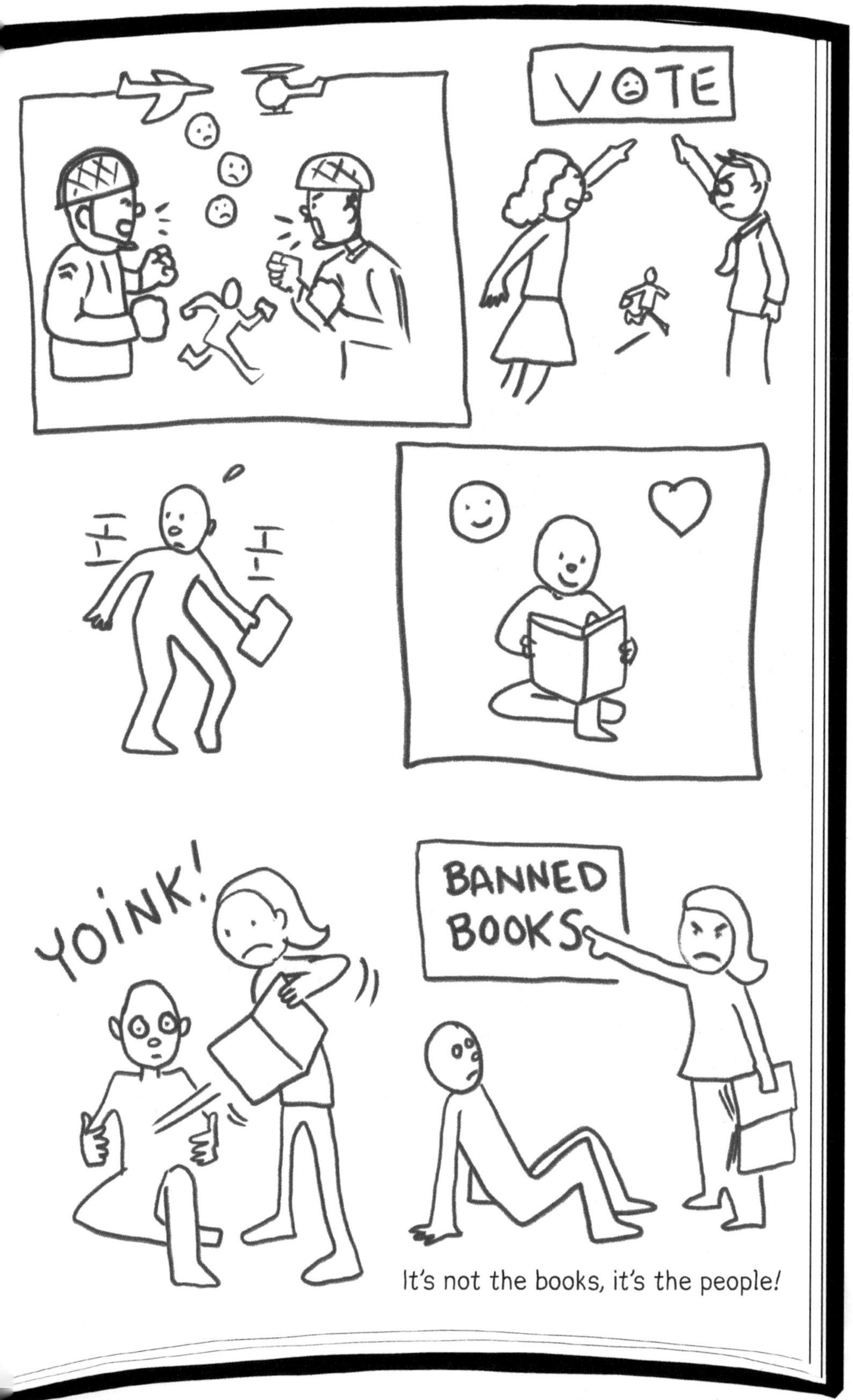
VOTE
YOINK!
BANNED BOOKS
It's not the books, it's the people!

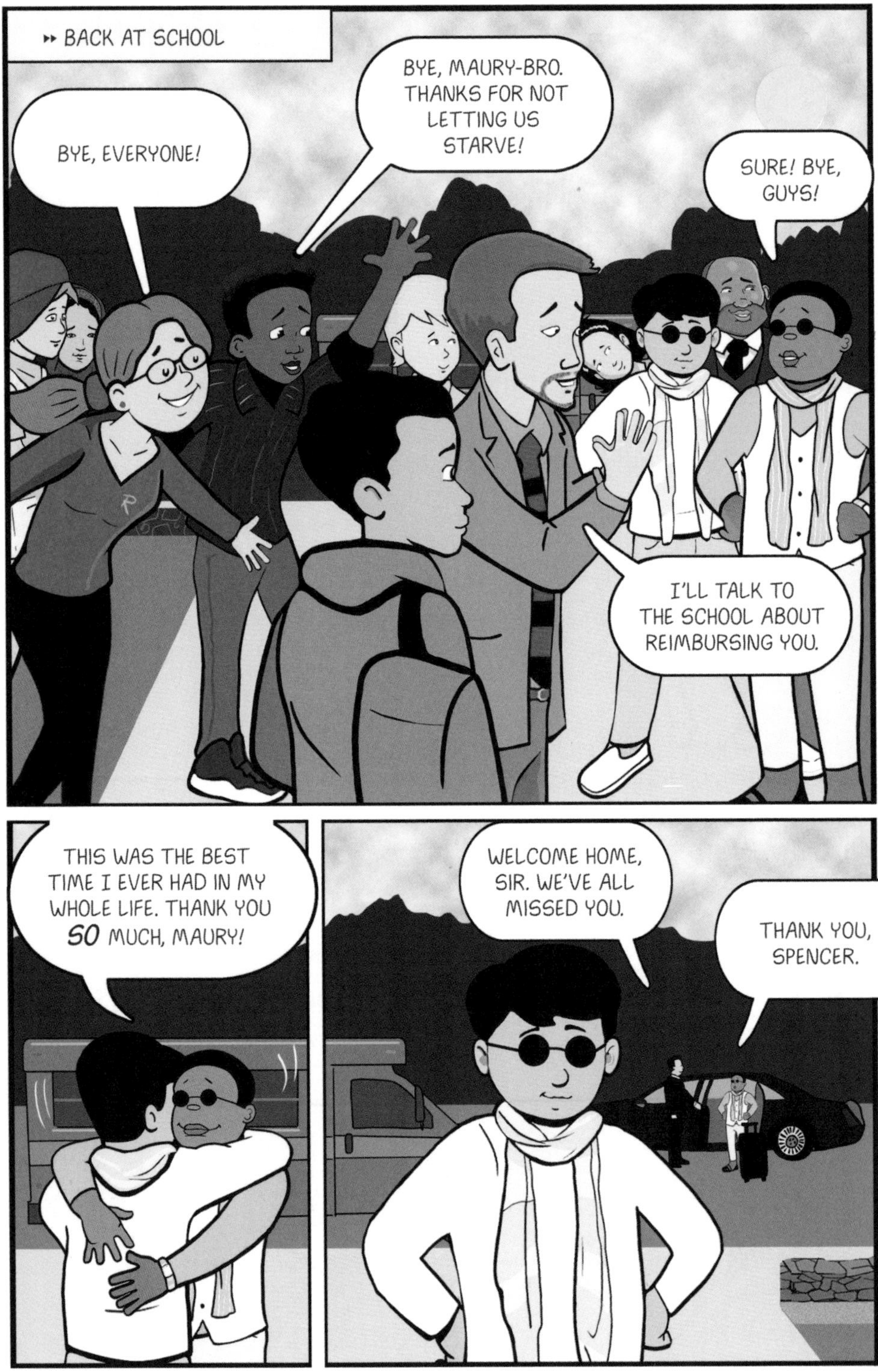
BACK AT SCHOOL
BYE, EVERYONE!
BYE, MAURY-BRO. THANKS FOR NOT LETTING US STARVE!
SURE! BYE, GUYS!
I'LL TALK TO THE SCHOOL ABOUT REIMBURSING YOU.
THIS WAS THE BEST TIME I EVER HAD IN MY WHOLE LIFE. THANK YOU SO MUCH, MAURY!
WELCOME HOME, SIR. WE'VE ALL MISSED YOU.
THANK YOU, SPENCER.

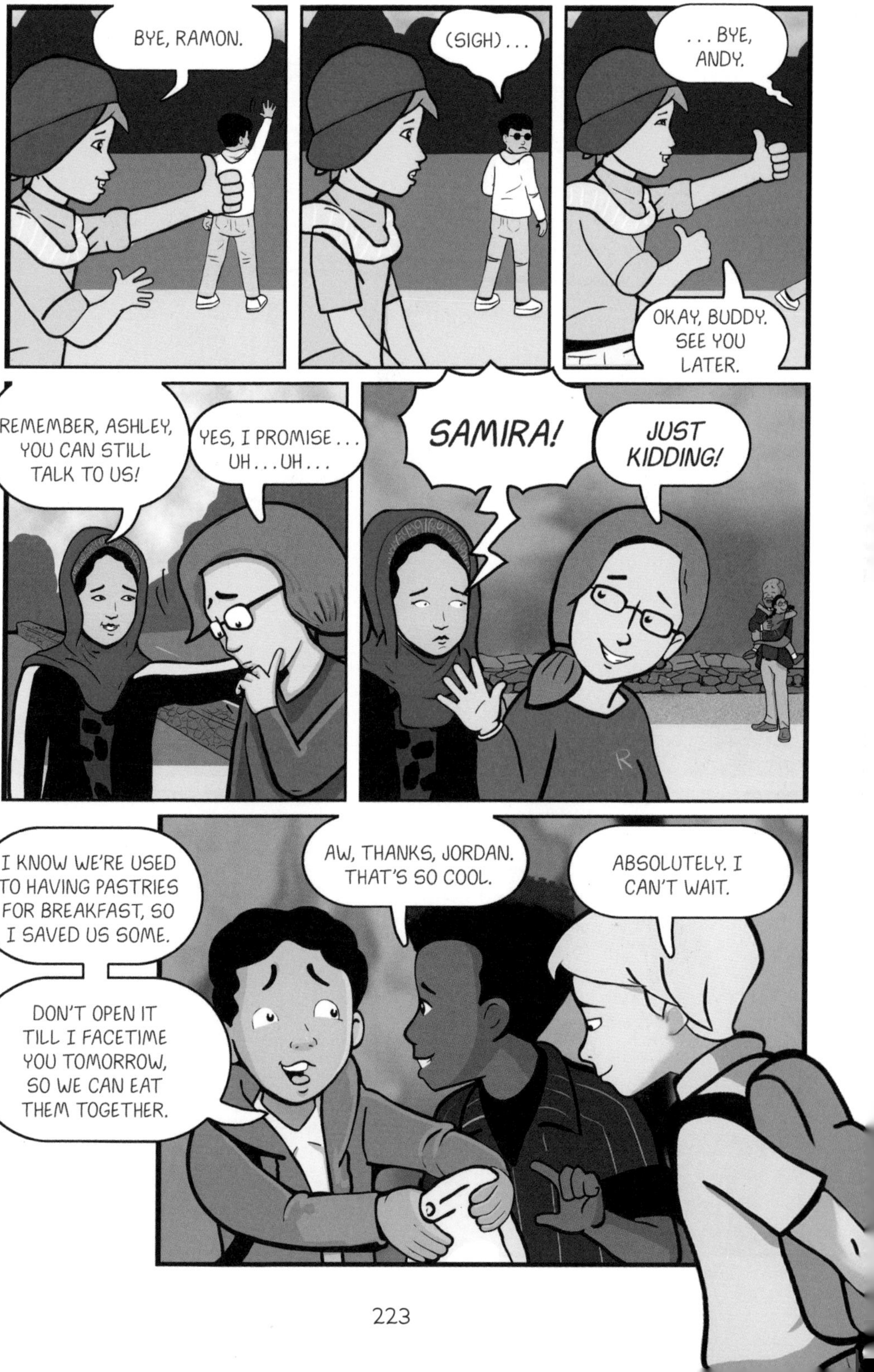
BYE, RAMON.
(SIGH) . . .
. . . BYE, ANDY.
OKAY, BUDDY. SEE YOU LATER.
REMEMBER, ASHLEY, YOU CAN STILL TALK TO US!
YES, I PROMISE . . . UH . . . UH . . .
SAMIRA!
JUST KIDDING!
I KNOW WE'RE USED TO HAVING PASTRIES FOR BREAKFAST, SO I SAVED US SOME.
DON'T OPEN IT TILL I FACETIME YOU TOMORROW, SO WE CAN EAT THEM TOGETHER.
AW, THANKS, JORDAN. THAT'S SO COOL.
ABSOLUTELY. I CAN'T WAIT.

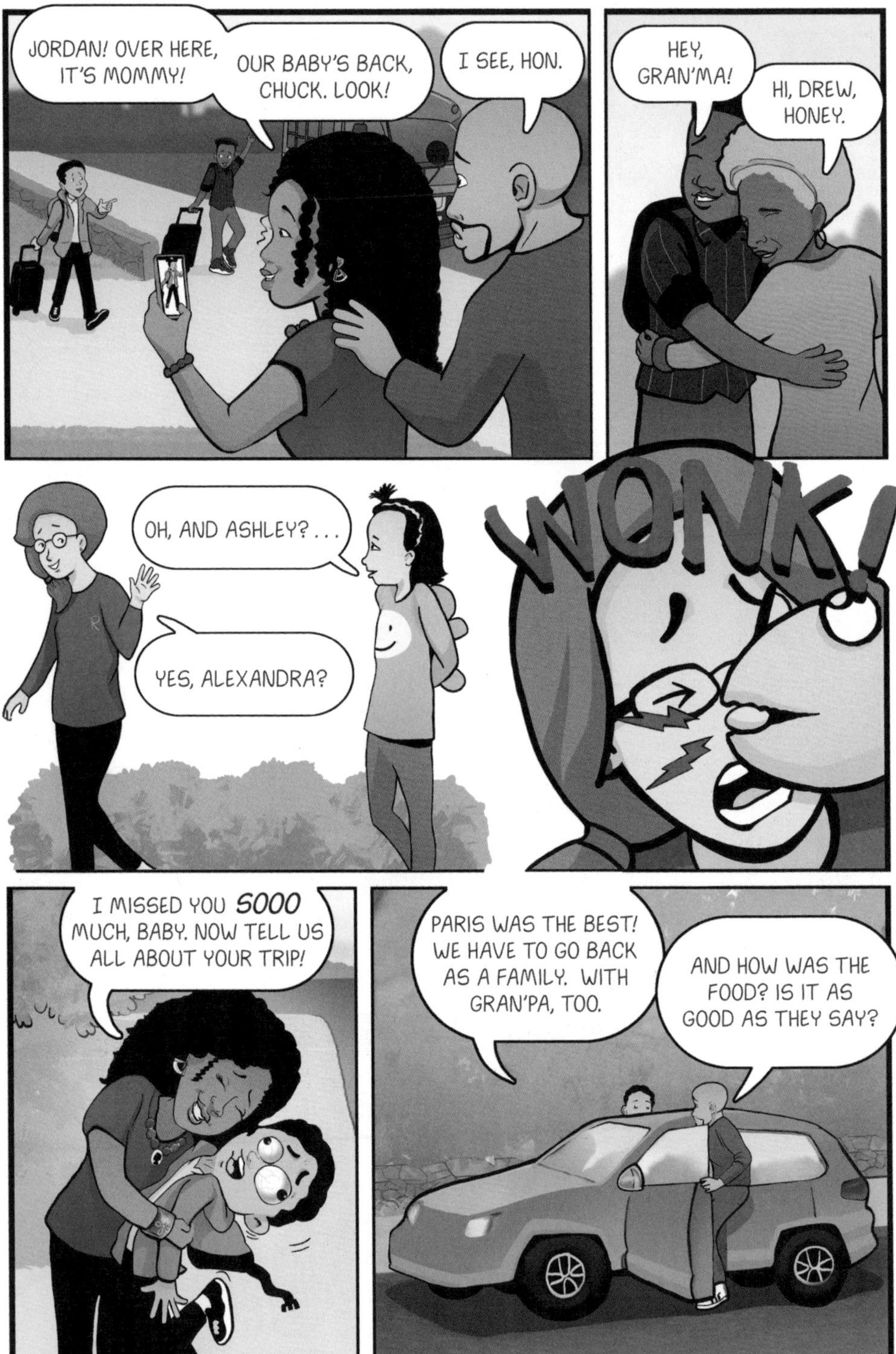
JORDAN! OVER HERE, IT'S MOMMY!
OUR BABY'S BACK, CHUCK. LOOK!
I SEE, HON.
HEY, GRAN'MA!
HI, DREW, HONEY.
OH, AND ASHLEY? . . .
YES, ALEXANDRA?
WONK!
I MISSED YOU SOOO MUCH, BABY. NOW TELL US ALL ABOUT YOUR TRIP!
PARIS WAS THE BEST! WE HAVE TO GO BACK AS A FAMILY. WITH GRAN'PA, TOO.
AND HOW WAS THE FOOD? IS IT AS GOOD AS THEY SAY?

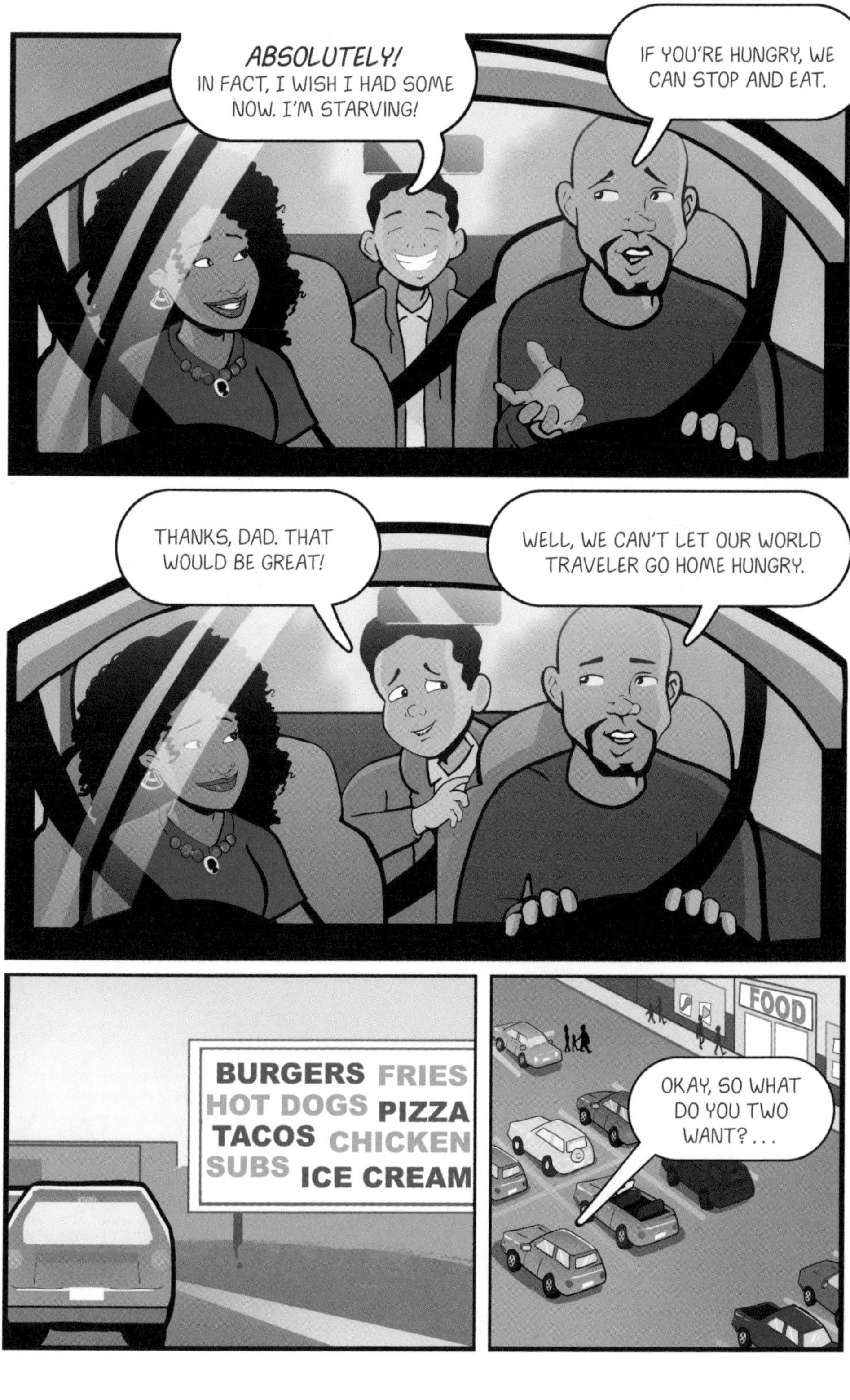
ABSOLUTELY! IN FACT, I WISH I HAD SOME NOW. I'M STARVING!
IF YOU'RE HUNGRY, WE CAN STOP AND EAT.
THANKS, DAD. THAT WOULD BE GREAT!
WELL, WE CAN'T LET OUR WORLD TRAVELER GO HOME HUNGRY.
BURGERS FRIES HOT DOGS PIZZA TACOS CHICKEN SUBS ICE CREAM
FOOD
OKAY, SO WHAT DO YOU TWO WANT? . . .

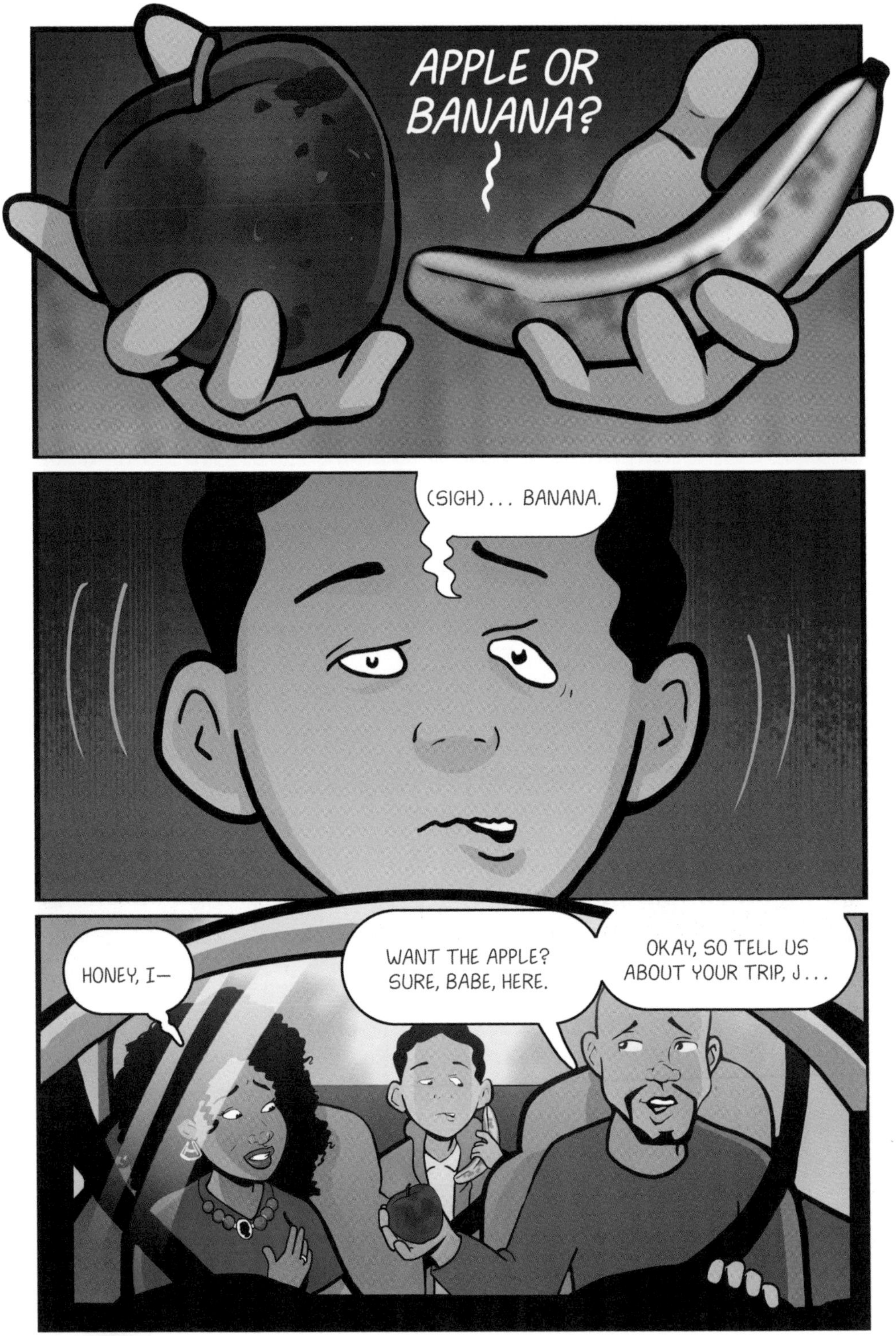
APPLE OR BANANA?
(SIGH)... BANANA.
HONEY, I—
WANT THE APPLE? SURE, BABE, HERE.
OKAY, SO TELL US ABOUT YOUR TRIP, J...

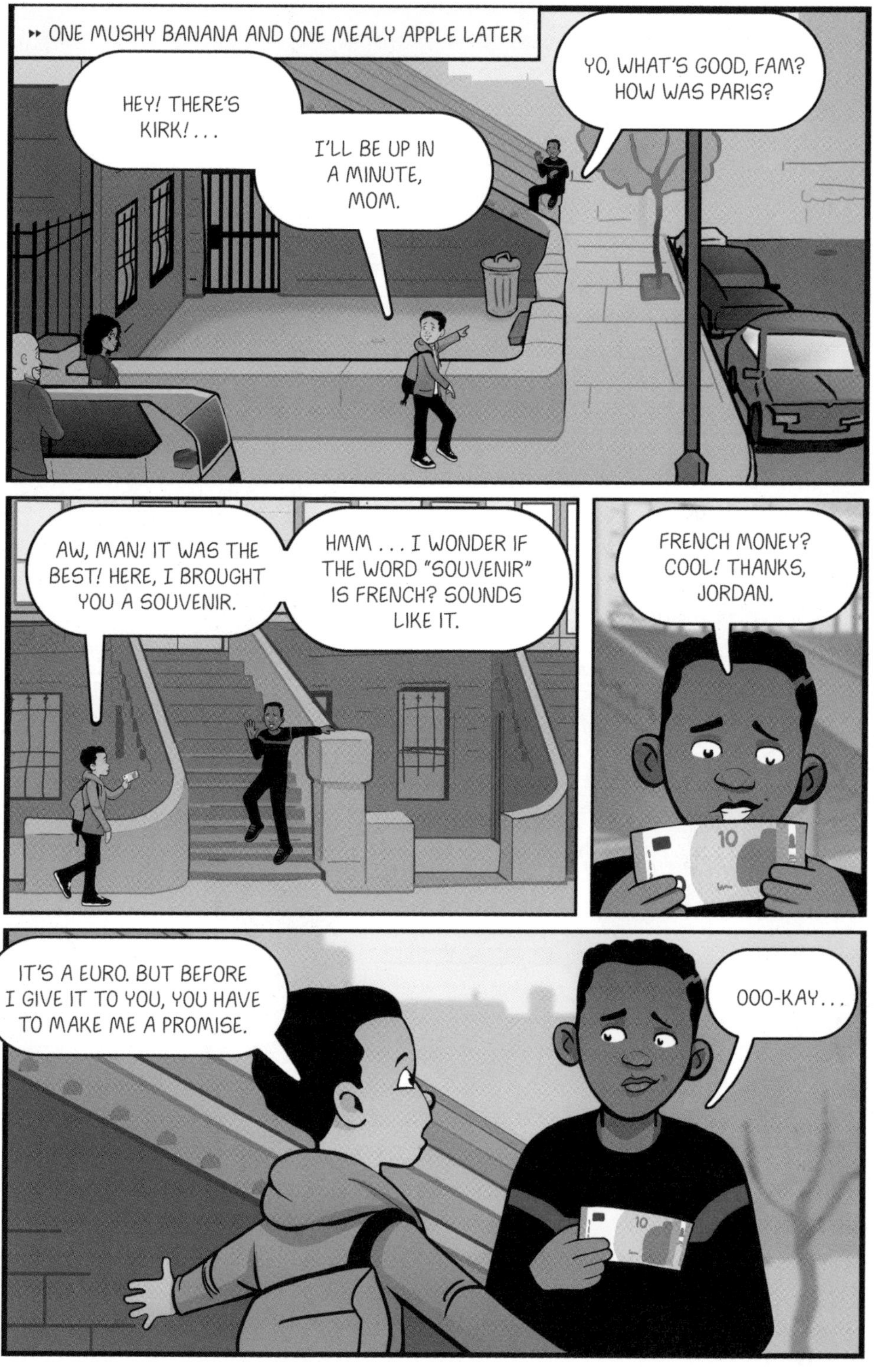
ONE MUSHY BANANA AND ONE MEALY APPLE LATER
HEY! THERE'S KIRK! . . .
I'LL BE UP IN A MINUTE, MOM.
YO, WHAT'S GOOD, FAM? HOW WAS PARIS?
AW, MAN! IT WAS THE BEST! HERE, I BROUGHT YOU A SOUVENIR.
HMM . . . I WONDER IF THE WORD "SOUVENIR" IS FRENCH? SOUNDS LIKE IT.
FRENCH MONEY? COOL! THANKS, JORDAN.
10
IT'S A EURO. BUT BEFORE I GIVE IT TO YOU, YOU HAVE TO MAKE ME A PROMISE.
OOO-KAY . . .

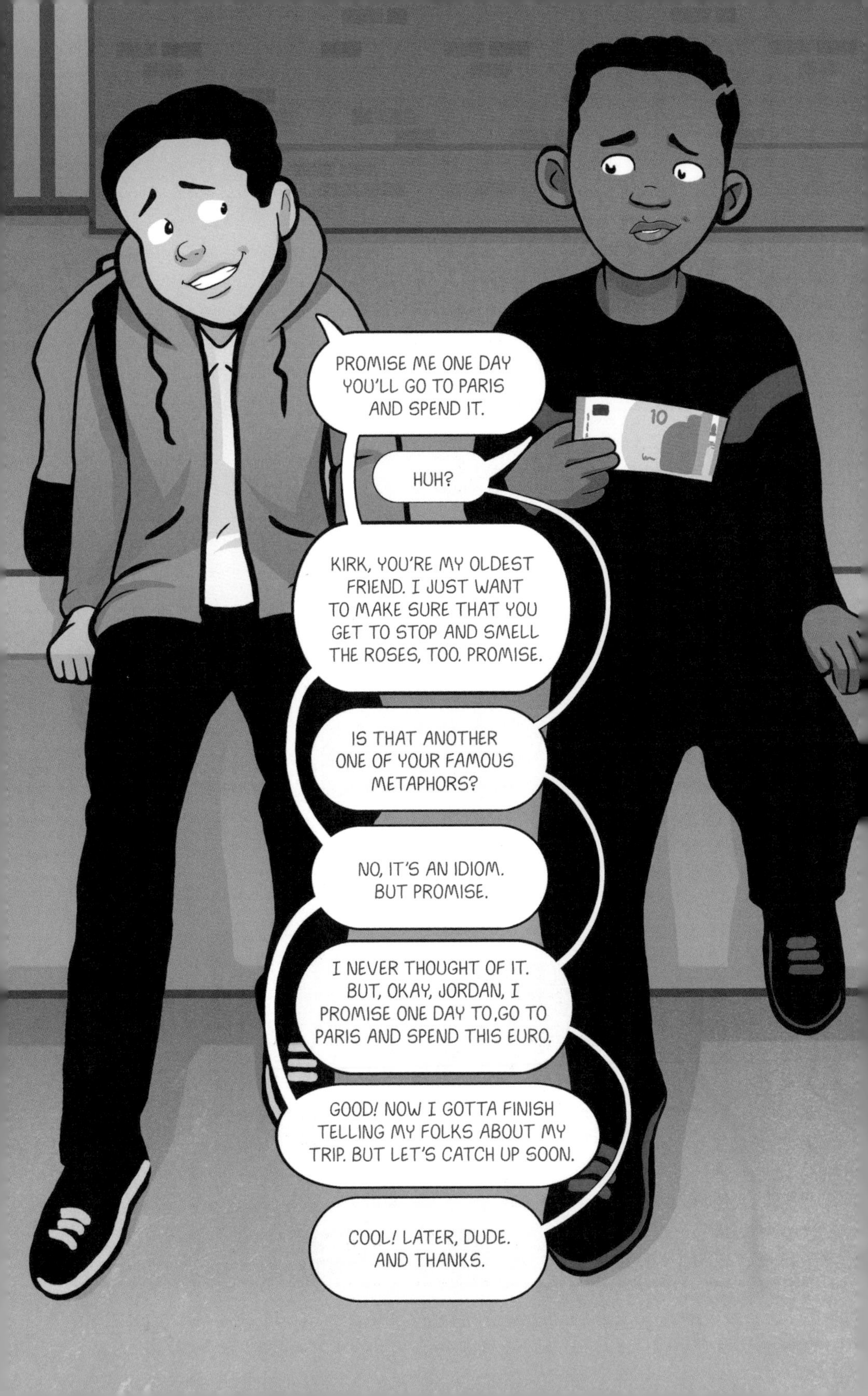
PROMISE ME ONE DAY YOU'LL GO TO PARIS AND SPEND IT.
HUH?
KIRK, YOU'RE MY OLDEST FRIEND. I JUST WANT TO MAKE SURE THAT YOU GET TO STOP AND SMELL THE ROSES, TOO. PROMISE.
IS THAT ANOTHER ONE OF YOUR FAMOUS METAPHORS?
NO, IT'S AN IDIOM. BUT PROMISE.
I NEVER THOUGHT OF IT. BUT, OKAY, JORDAN, I PROMISE ONE DAY TO GO TO PARIS AND SPEND THIS EURO.
GOOD! NOW I GOTTA FINISH TELLING MY FOLKS ABOUT MY TRIP. BUT LET'S CATCH UP SOON.
COOL! LATER, DUDE. AND THANKS.

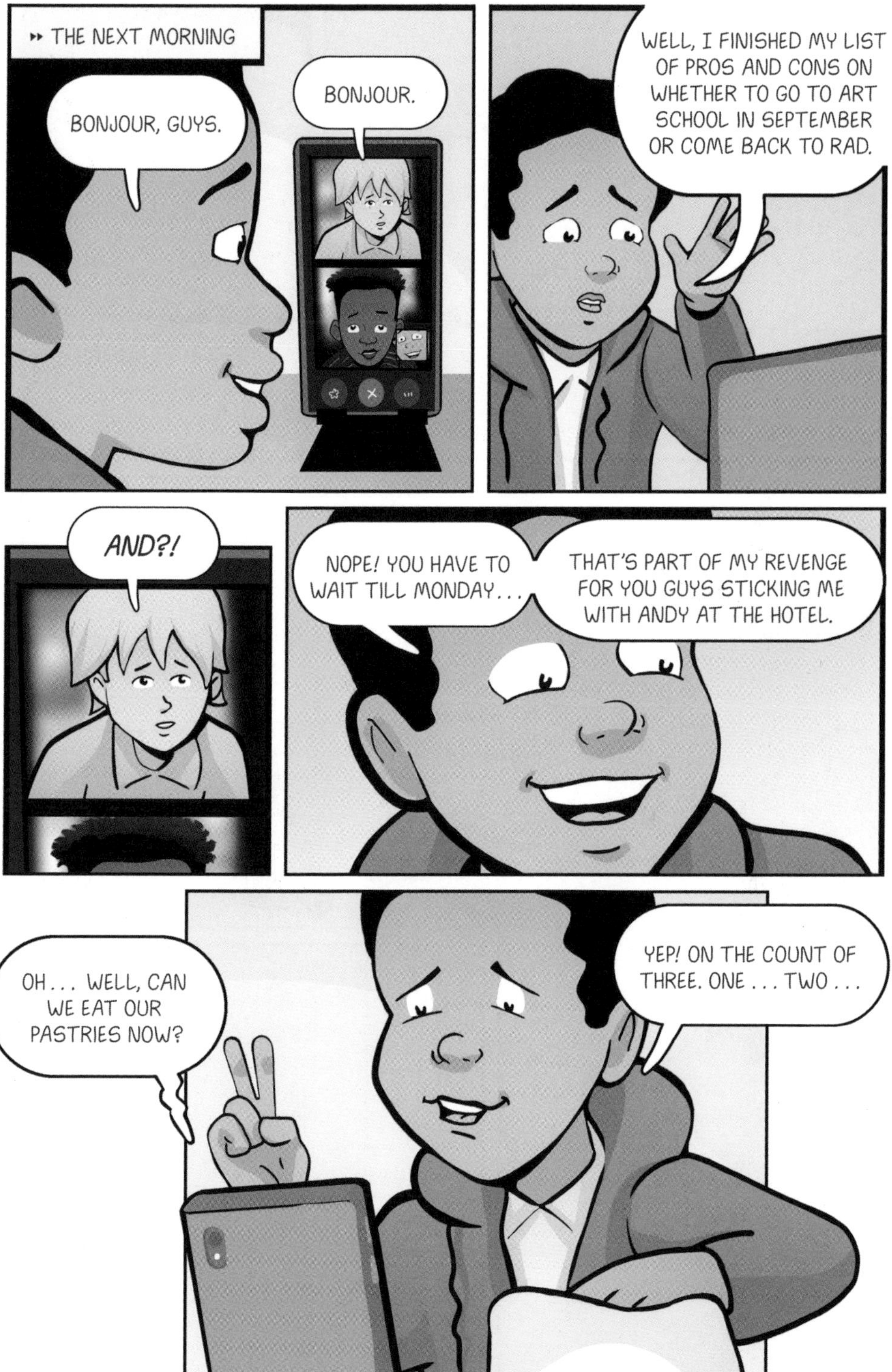
THE NEXT MORNING
BONJOUR, GUYS.
BONJOUR.
WELL, I FINISHED MY LIST OF PROS AND CONS ON WHETHER TO GO TO ART SCHOOL IN SEPTEMBER OR COME BACK TO RAD.
AND?!
NOPE! YOU HAVE TO WAIT TILL MONDAY . . .
THAT'S PART OF MY REVENGE FOR YOU GUYS STICKING ME WITH ANDY AT THE HOTEL.
OH . . . WELL, CAN WE EAT OUR PASTRIES NOW?
YEP! ON THE COUNT OF THREE. ONE . . . TWO . . .

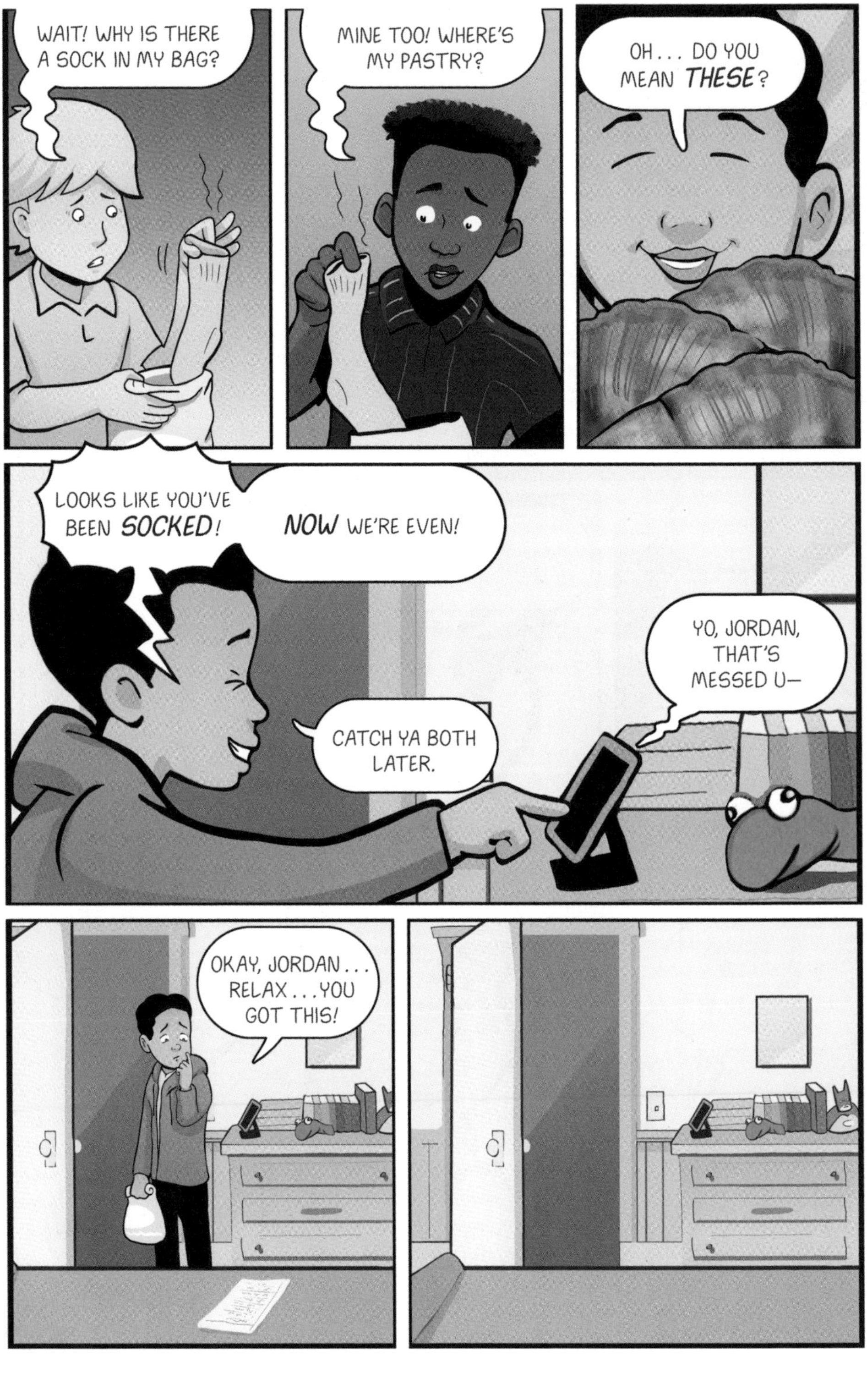
WAIT! WHY IS THERE A SOCK IN MY BAG?
MINE TOO! WHERE'S MY PASTRY?
OH . . . DO YOU MEAN THESE?
LOOKS LIKE YOU'VE BEEN SOCKED!
NOW WE'RE EVEN!
YO, JORDAN, THAT'S MESSED U—
CATCH YA BOTH LATER.
OKAY, JORDAN . . . RELAX . . . YOU GOT THIS!

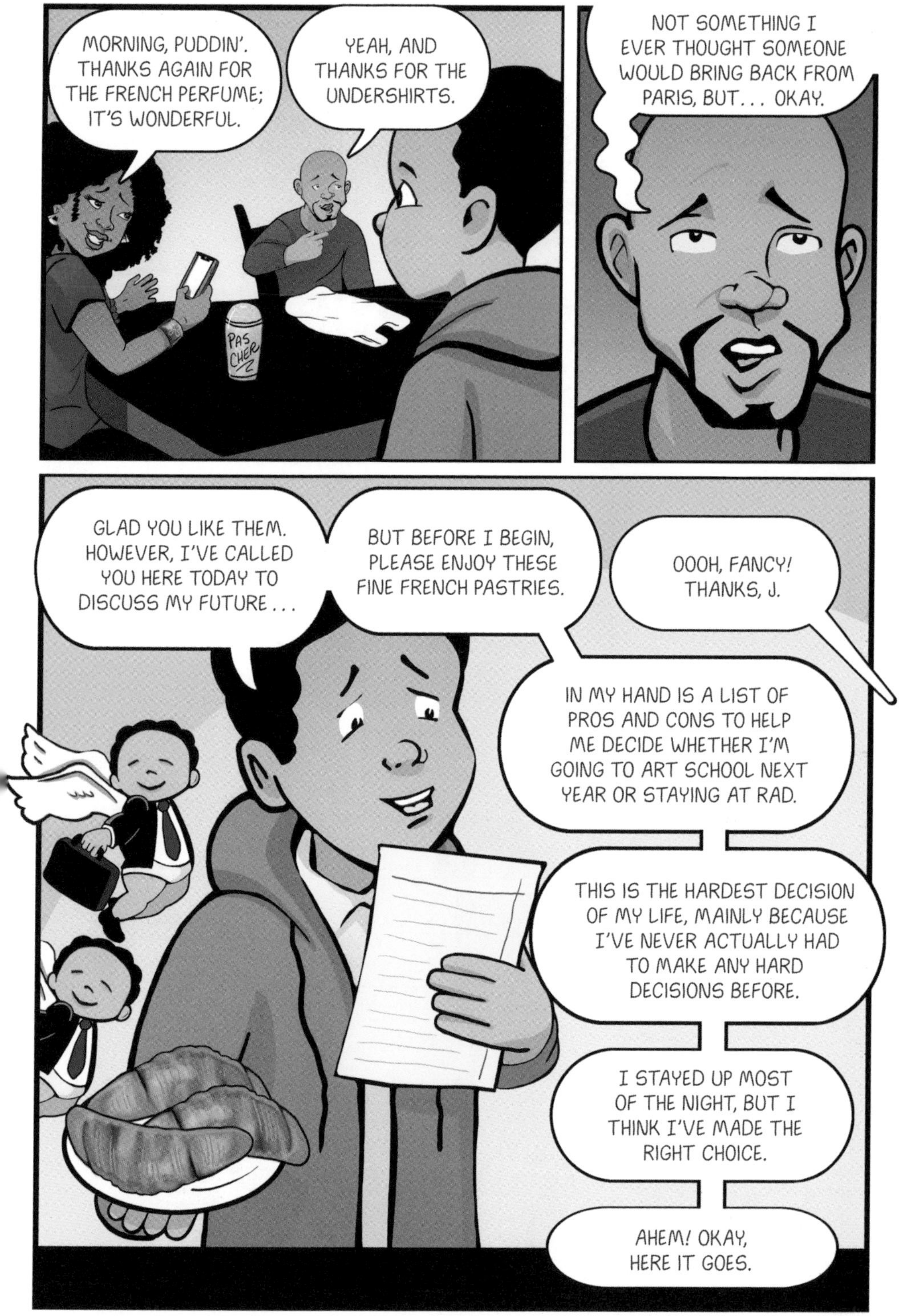
MORNING, PUDDIN'. THANKS AGAIN FOR THE FRENCH PERFUME; IT'S WONDERFUL.
YEAH, AND THANKS FOR THE UNDERSHIRTS.
PAS CHER
NOT SOMETHING I EVER THOUGHT SOMEONE WOULD BRING BACK FROM PARIS, BUT... OKAY.
GLAD YOU LIKE THEM. HOWEVER, I'VE CALLED YOU HERE TODAY TO DISCUSS MY FUTURE...
BUT BEFORE I BEGIN, PLEASE ENJOY THESE FINE FRENCH PASTRIES.
OOOH, FANCY! THANKS, J.
IN MY HAND IS A LIST OF PROS AND CONS TO HELP ME DECIDE WHETHER I'M GOING TO ART SCHOOL NEXT YEAR OR STAYING AT RAD.
THIS IS THE HARDEST DECISION OF MY LIFE, MAINLY BECAUSE I'VE NEVER ACTUALLY HAD TO MAKE ANY HARD DECISIONS BEFORE.
I STAYED UP MOST OF THE NIGHT, BUT I THINK I'VE MADE THE RIGHT CHOICE.
AHEM! OKAY, HERE IT GOES.

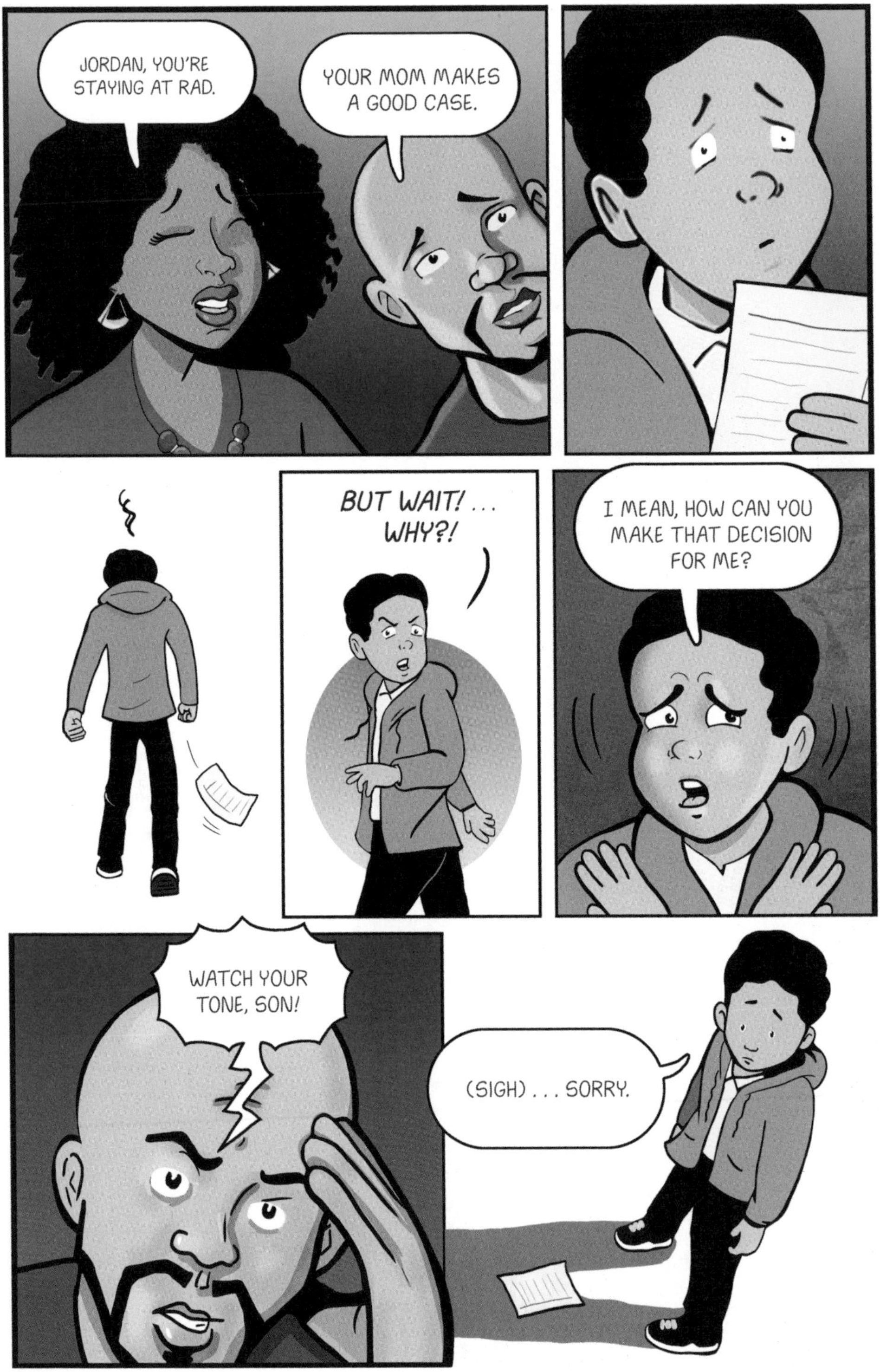
JORDAN, YOU'RE STAYING AT RAD.
YOUR MOM MAKES A GOOD CASE.
BUT WAIT! . . . WHY?!
I MEAN, HOW CAN YOU MAKE THAT DECISION FOR ME?
WATCH YOUR TONE, SON!
(SIGH) . . . SORRY.

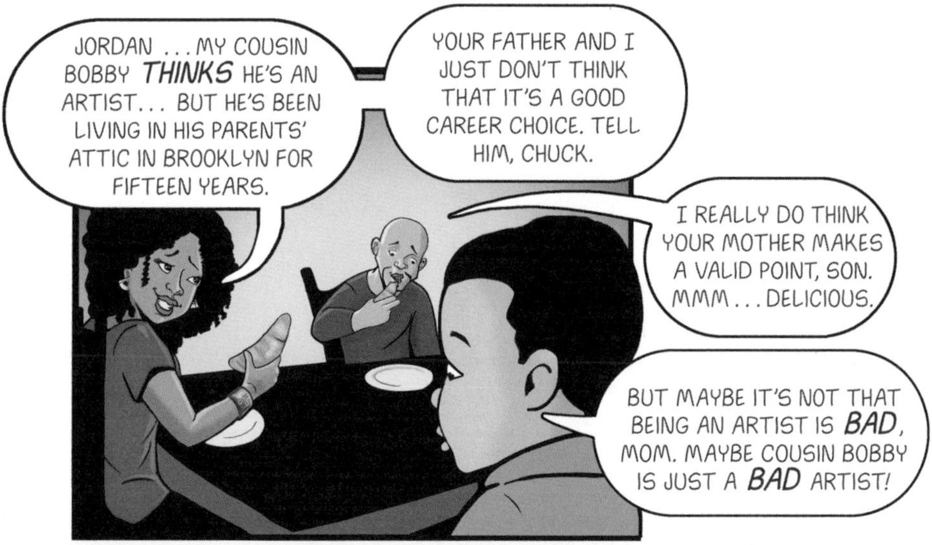
JORDAN . . . MY COUSIN BOBBY THINKS HE'S AN ARTIST . . . BUT HE'S BEEN LIVING IN HIS PARENTS' ATTIC IN BROOKLYN FOR FIFTEEN YEARS.
YOUR FATHER AND I JUST DON'T THINK THAT IT'S A GOOD CAREER CHOICE. TELL HIM, CHUCK.
I REALLY DO THINK YOUR MOTHER MAKES A VALID POINT, SON. MMM . . . DELICIOUS.
BUT MAYBE IT'S NOT THAT BEING AN ARTIST IS BAD, MOM. MAYBE COUSIN BOBBY IS JUST A BAD ARTIST!

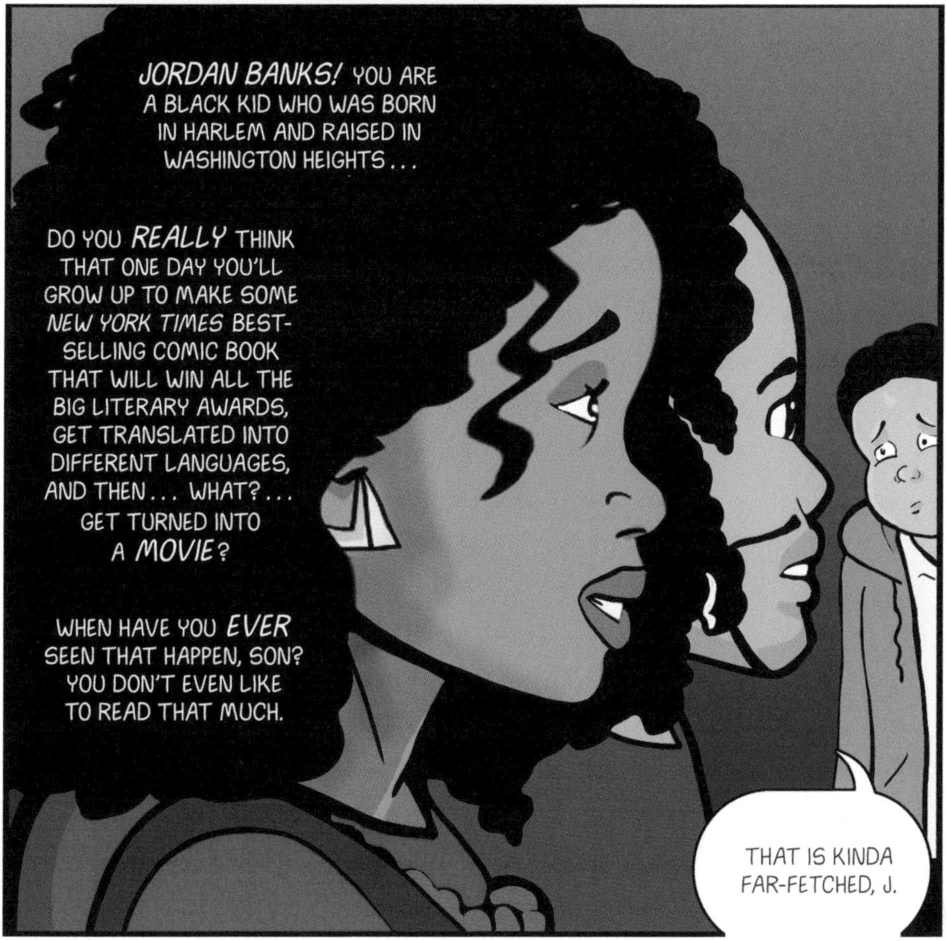
JORDAN BANKS! YOU ARE A BLACK KID WHO WAS BORN IN HARLEM AND RAISED IN WASHINGTON HEIGHTS . . .
DO YOU REALLY THINK THAT ONE DAY YOU'LL GROW UP TO MAKE SOME NEW YORK TIMES BEST-SELLING COMIC BOOK THAT WILL WIN ALL THE BIG LITERARY AWARDS, GET TRANSLATED INTO DIFFERENT LANGUAGES, AND THEN . . . WHAT? . . . GET TURNED INTO A MOVIE?
WHEN HAVE YOU EVER SEEN THAT HAPPEN, SON? YOU DON'T EVEN LIKE TO READ THAT MUCH.
THAT IS KINDA FAR-FETCHED, J.

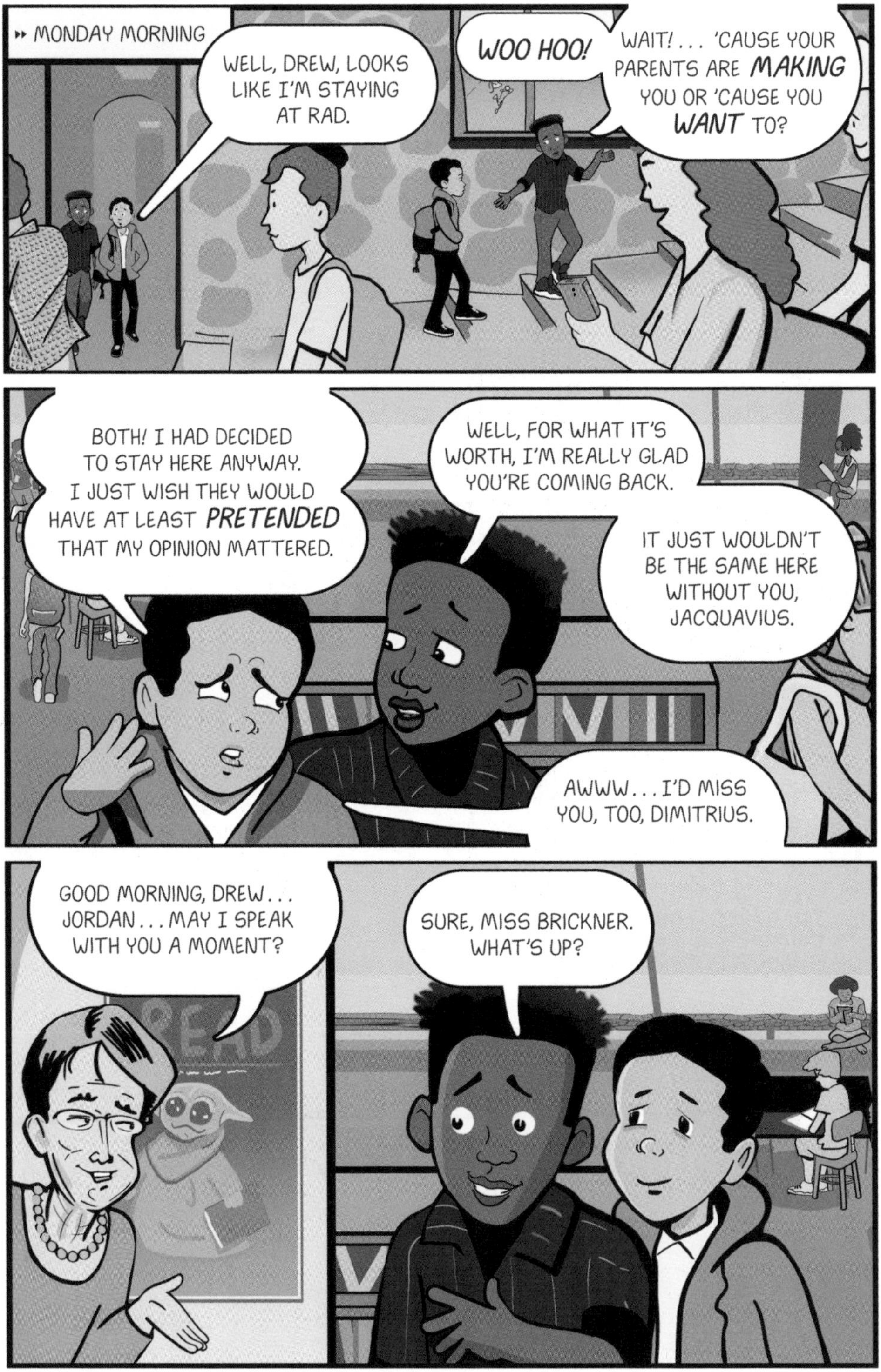
MONDAY MORNING
WELL, DREW, LOOKS LIKE I'M STAYING AT RAD.
WOO HOO!
WAIT! . . . 'CAUSE YOUR PARENTS ARE *MAKING* YOU OR 'CAUSE YOU *WANT* TO?
BOTH! I HAD DECIDED TO STAY HERE ANYWAY. I JUST WISH THEY WOULD HAVE AT LEAST *PRETENDED* THAT MY OPINION MATTERED.
WELL, FOR WHAT IT'S WORTH, I'M REALLY GLAD YOU'RE COMING BACK.
IT JUST WOULDN'T BE THE SAME HERE WITHOUT YOU, JACQUAVIUS.
AWWW . . . I'D MISS YOU, TOO, DIMITRIUS.
GOOD MORNING, DREW . . . JORDAN . . . MAY I SPEAK WITH YOU A MOMENT?
SURE, MISS BRICKNER. WHAT'S UP?
READ

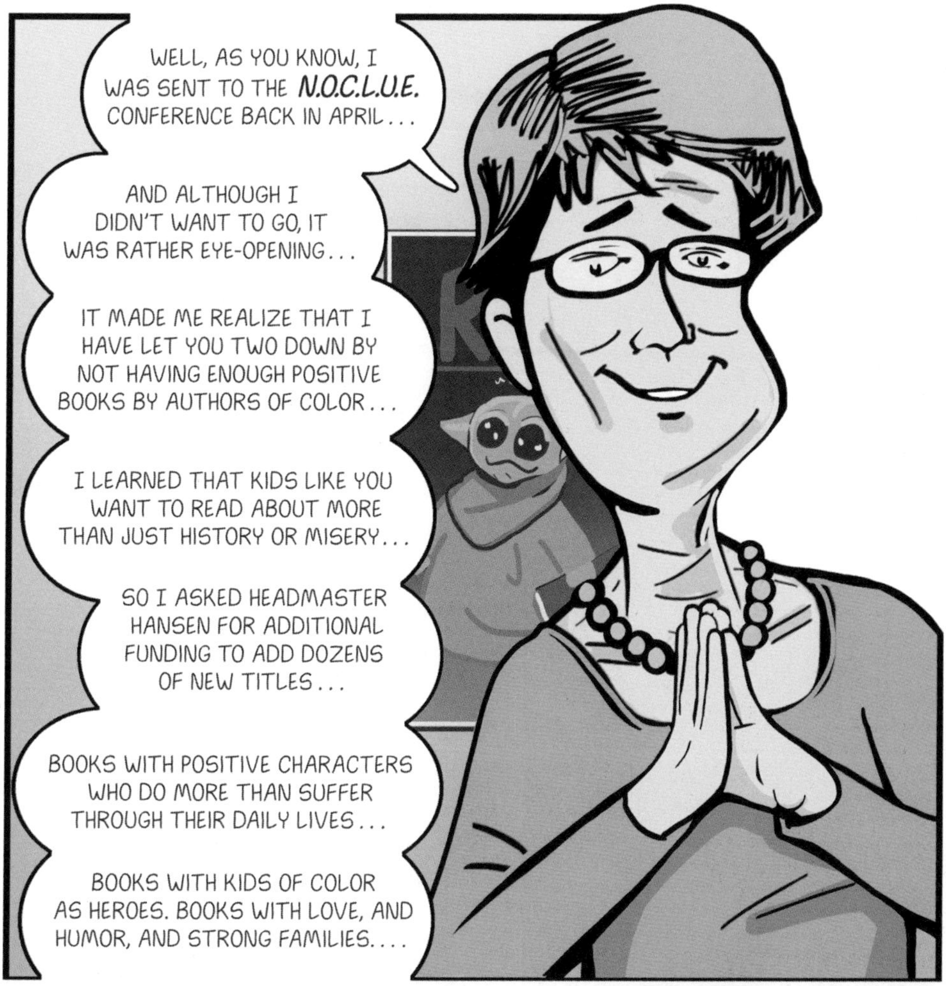
WELL, AS YOU KNOW, I WAS SENT TO THE N.O.C.L.U.E. CONFERENCE BACK IN APRIL . . .
AND ALTHOUGH I DIDN'T WANT TO GO, IT WAS RATHER EYE-OPENING . . .
IT MADE ME REALIZE THAT I HAVE LET YOU TWO DOWN BY NOT HAVING ENOUGH POSITIVE BOOKS BY AUTHORS OF COLOR . . .
I LEARNED THAT KIDS LIKE YOU WANT TO READ ABOUT MORE THAN JUST HISTORY OR MISERY . . .
SO I ASKED HEADMASTER HANSEN FOR ADDITIONAL FUNDING TO ADD DOZENS OF NEW TITLES . . .
BOOKS WITH POSITIVE CHARACTERS WHO DO MORE THAN SUFFER THROUGH THEIR DAILY LIVES . . .
BOOKS WITH KIDS OF COLOR AS HEROES. BOOKS WITH LOVE, AND HUMOR, AND STRONG FAMILIES. . . .

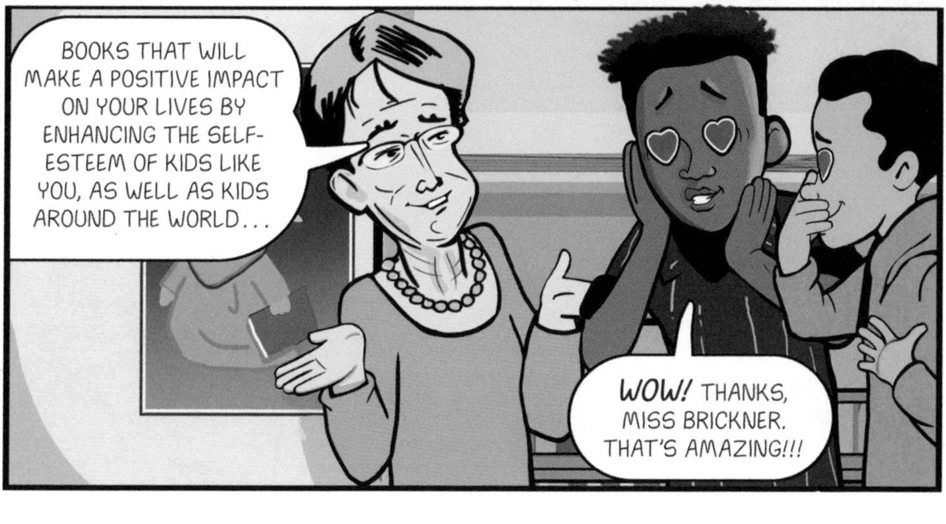
BOOKS THAT WILL MAKE A POSITIVE IMPACT ON YOUR LIVES BY ENHANCING THE SELF-ESTEEM OF KIDS LIKE YOU, AS WELL AS KIDS AROUND THE WORLD . . .
WOW! THANKS, MISS BRICKNER. THAT'S AMAZING!!!

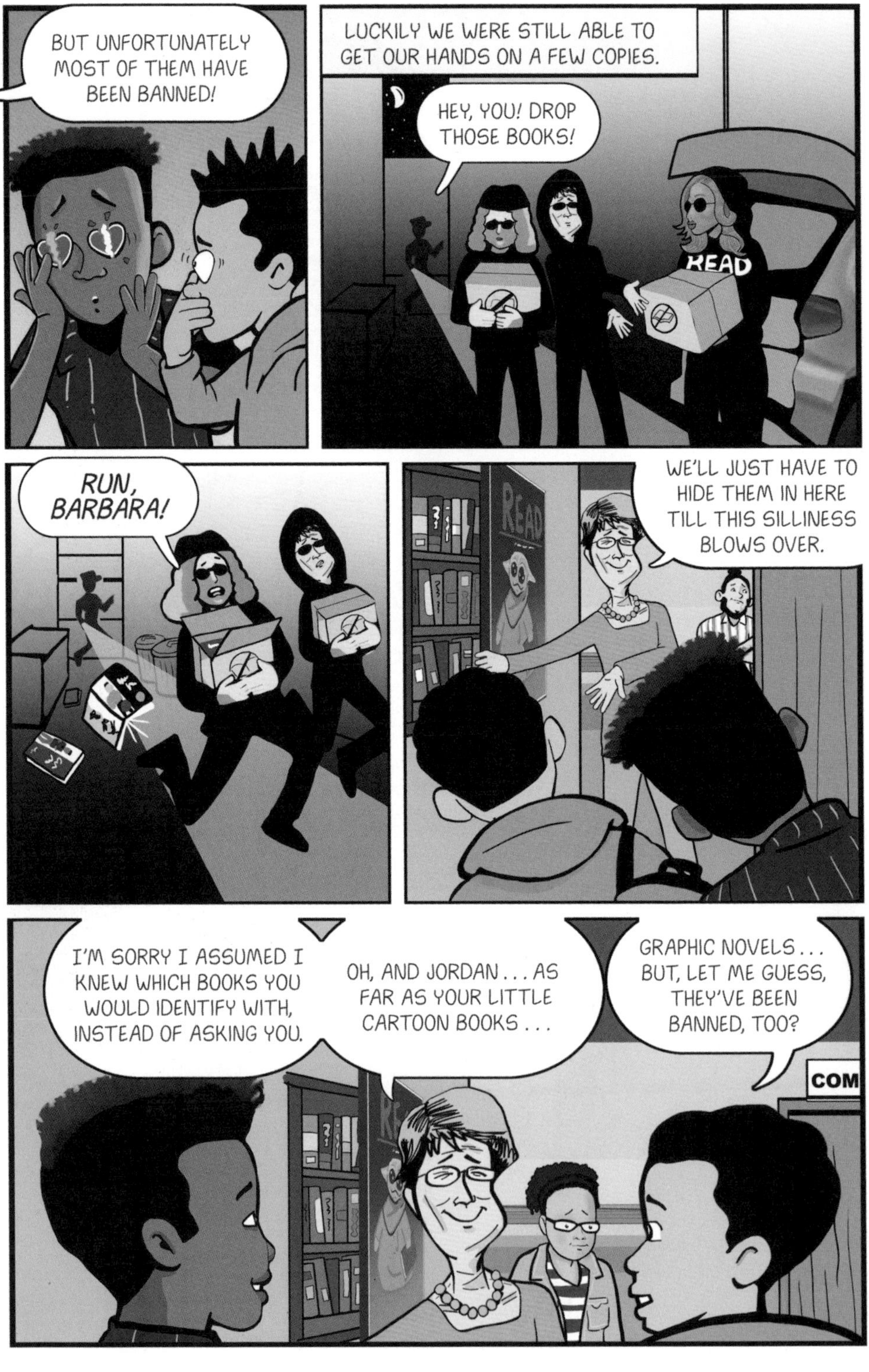
BUT UNFORTUNATELY MOST OF THEM HAVE BEEN BANNED!
LUCKILY WE WERE STILL ABLE TO GET OUR HANDS ON A FEW COPIES.
HEY, YOU! DROP THOSE BOOKS!
READ
RUN, BARBARA!
WE'LL JUST HAVE TO HIDE THEM IN HERE TILL THIS SILLINESS BLOWS OVER.
READ
I'M SORRY I ASSUMED I KNEW WHICH BOOKS YOU WOULD IDENTIFY WITH, INSTEAD OF ASKING YOU.
OH, AND JORDAN . . . AS FAR AS YOUR LITTLE CARTOON BOOKS . . .
GRAPHIC NOVELS . . . BUT, LET ME GUESS, THEY'VE BEEN BANNED, TOO?
COM

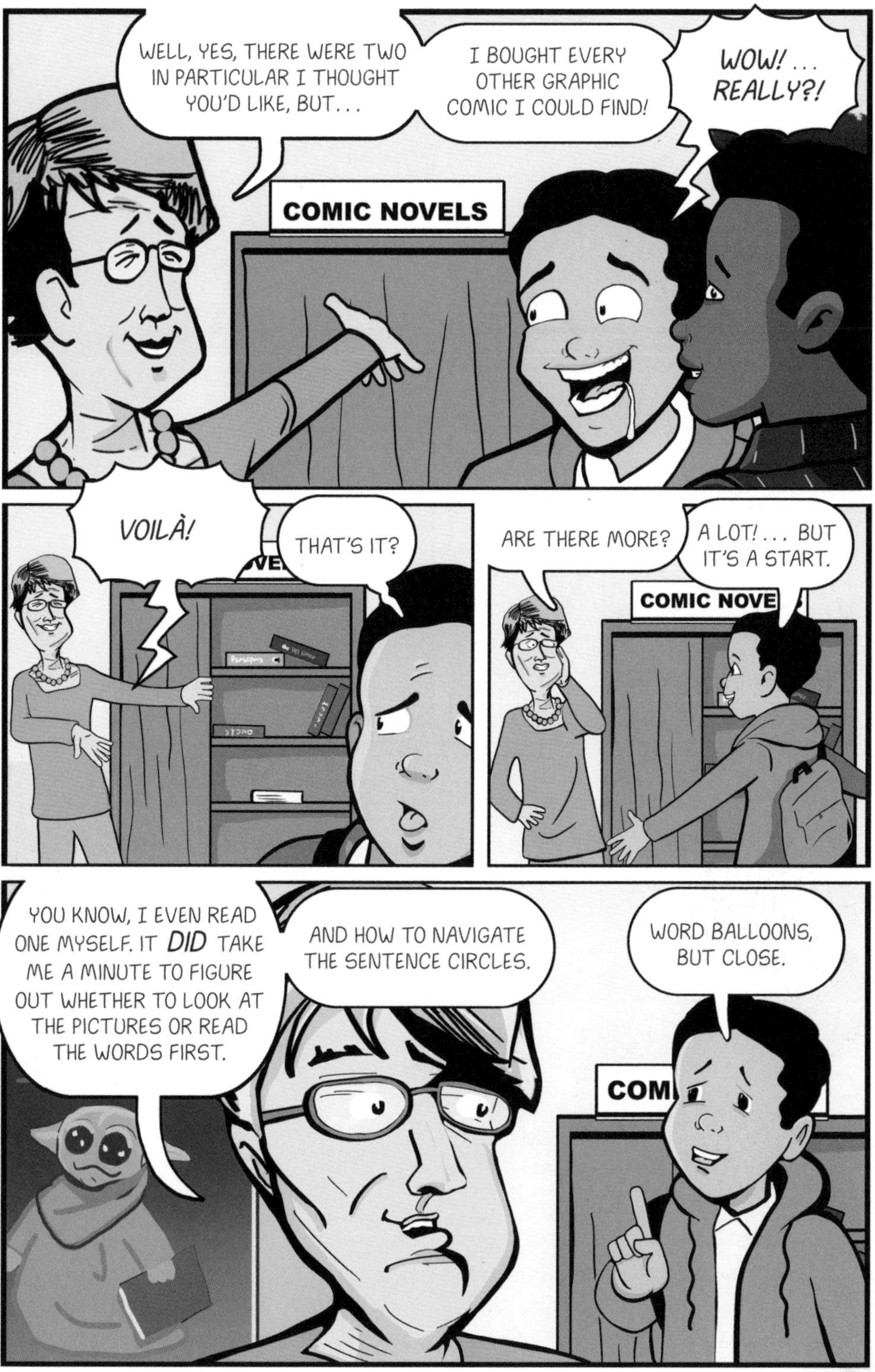
WELL, YES, THERE WERE TWO IN PARTICULAR I THOUGHT YOU'D LIKE, BUT...
I BOUGHT EVERY OTHER GRAPHIC COMIC I COULD FIND!
WOW! ... REALLY?!
COMIC NOVELS
VOILÀ!
THAT'S IT?
ARE THERE MORE?
A LOT! ... BUT IT'S A START.
COMIC NOVE
YOU KNOW, I EVEN READ ONE MYSELF. IT DID TAKE ME A MINUTE TO FIGURE OUT WHETHER TO LOOK AT THE PICTURES OR READ THE WORDS FIRST.
AND HOW TO NAVIGATE THE SENTENCE CIRCLES.
WORD BALLOONS, BUT CLOSE.
COM

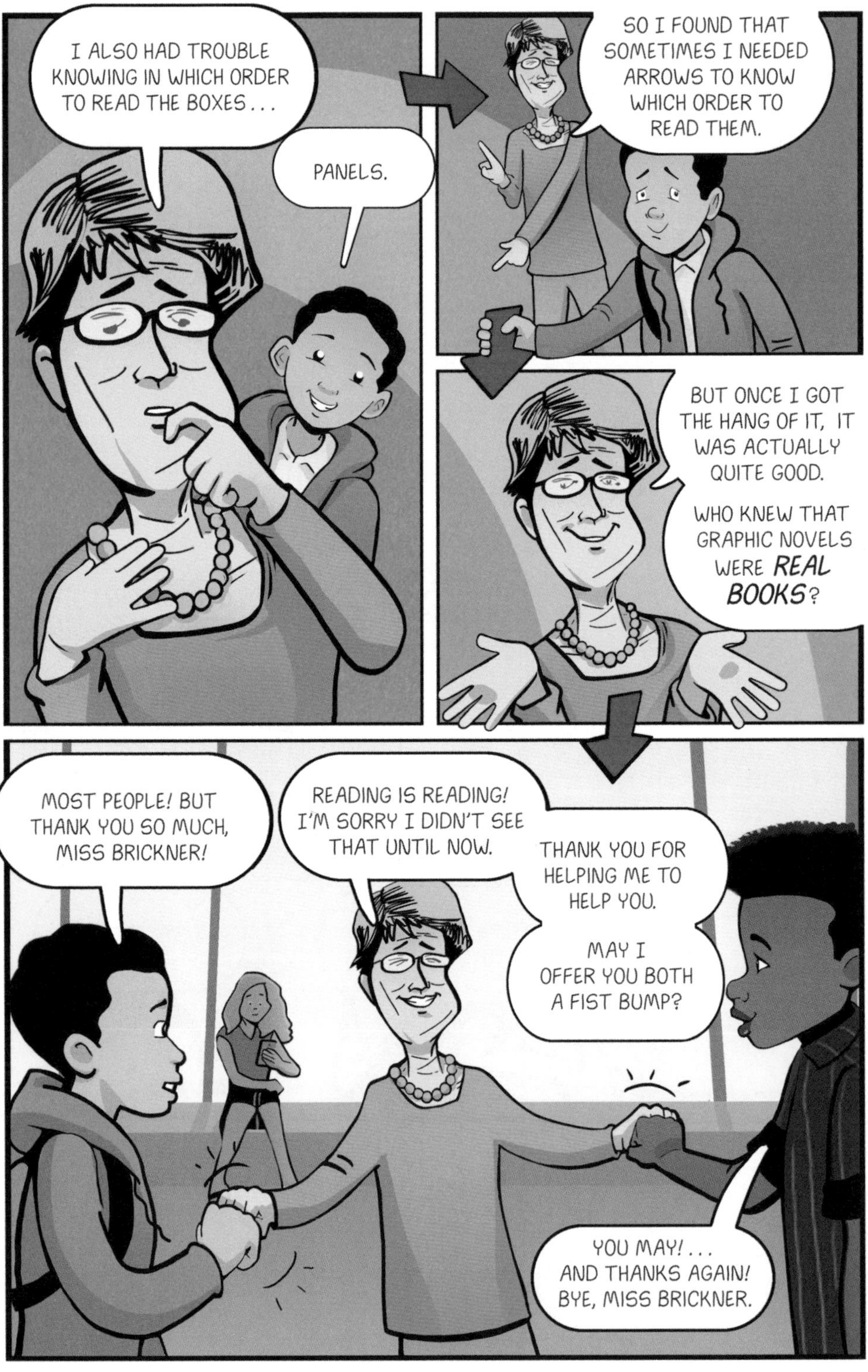
I ALSO HAD TROUBLE KNOWING IN WHICH ORDER TO READ THE BOXES . . .
PANELS.
SO I FOUND THAT SOMETIMES I NEEDED ARROWS TO KNOW WHICH ORDER TO READ THEM.
BUT ONCE I GOT THE HANG OF IT, IT WAS ACTUALLY QUITE GOOD.
WHO KNEW THAT GRAPHIC NOVELS WERE REAL BOOKS?
MOST PEOPLE! BUT THANK YOU SO MUCH, MISS BRICKNER!
READING IS READING! I'M SORRY I DIDN'T SEE THAT UNTIL NOW.
THANK YOU FOR HELPING ME TO HELP YOU.
MAY I OFFER YOU BOTH A FIST BUMP?
YOU MAY! . . . AND THANKS AGAIN! BYE, MISS BRICKNER.

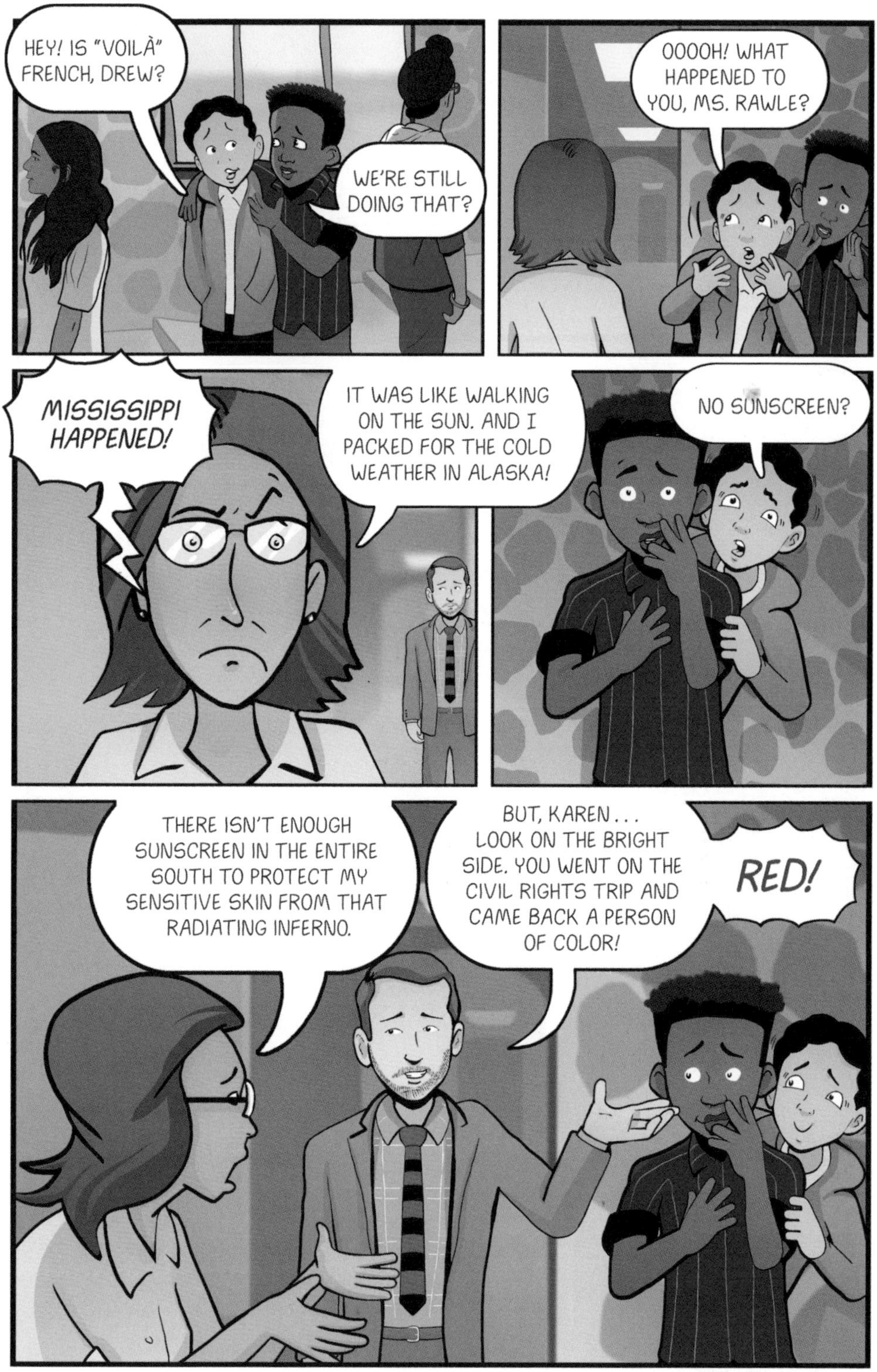
HEY! IS "VOILÀ" FRENCH, DREW?
WE'RE STILL DOING THAT?
OOOOH! WHAT HAPPENED TO YOU, MS. RAWLE?
MISSISSIPPI HAPPENED!
IT WAS LIKE WALKING ON THE SUN. AND I PACKED FOR THE COLD WEATHER IN ALASKA!
NO SUNSCREEN?
THERE ISN'T ENOUGH SUNSCREEN IN THE ENTIRE SOUTH TO PROTECT MY SENSITIVE SKIN FROM THAT RADIATING INFERNO.
BUT, KAREN . . . LOOK ON THE BRIGHT SIDE. YOU WENT ON THE CIVIL RIGHTS TRIP AND CAME BACK A PERSON OF COLOR!
RED!

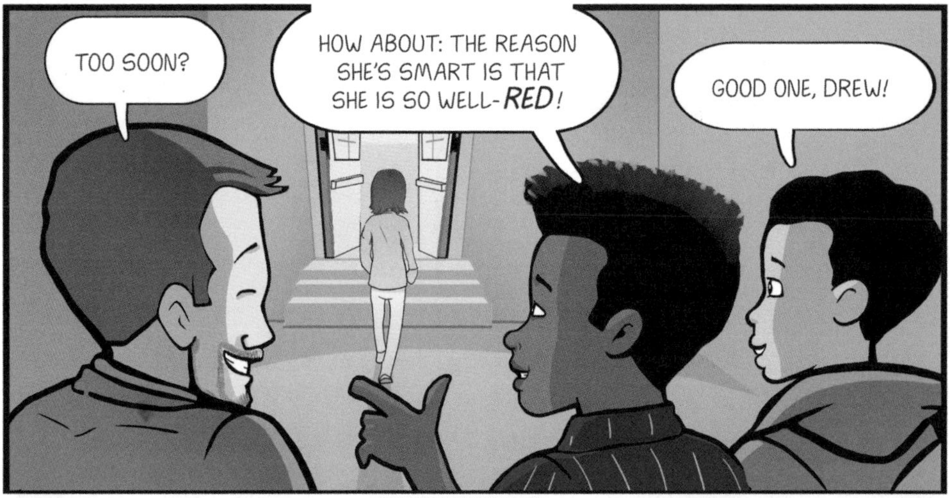
TOO SOON?
HOW ABOUT: THE REASON SHE'S SMART IS THAT SHE IS SO WELL-**RED**!
GOOD ONE, DREW!

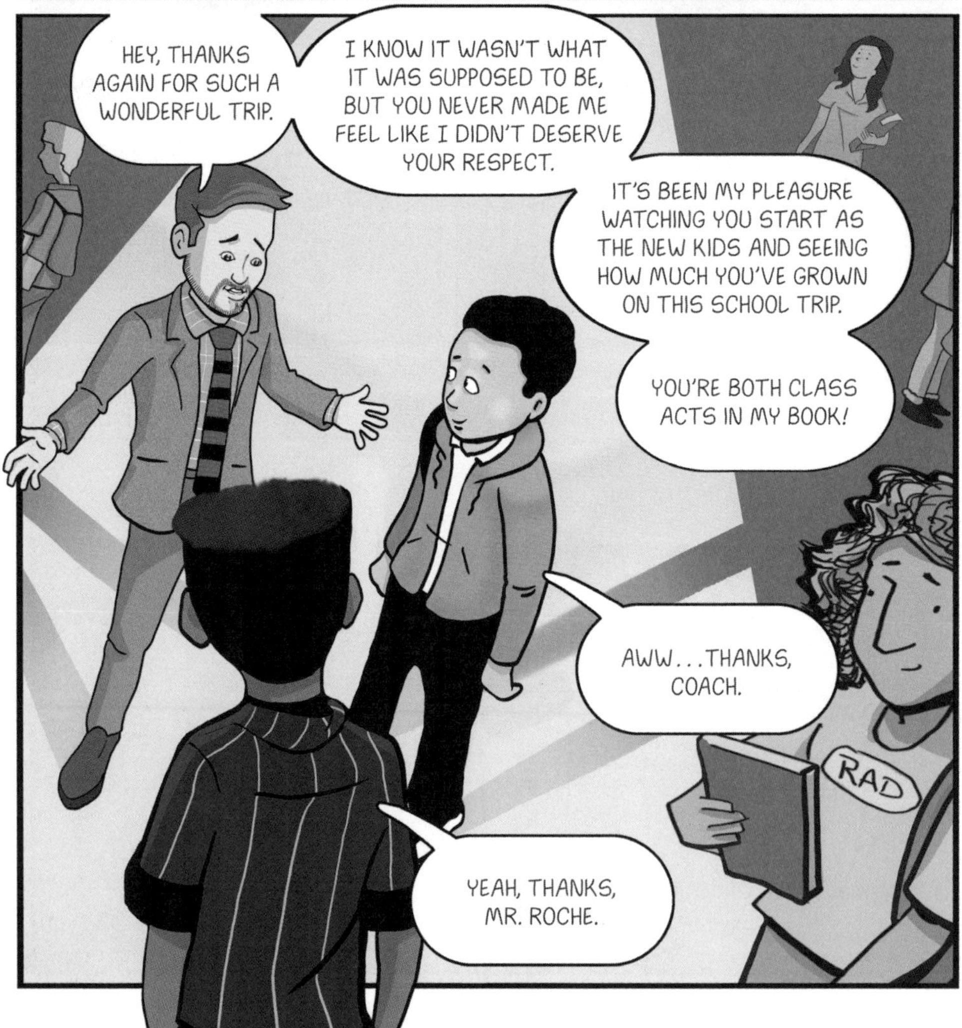
HEY, THANKS AGAIN FOR SUCH A WONDERFUL TRIP.
I KNOW IT WASN'T WHAT IT WAS SUPPOSED TO BE, BUT YOU NEVER MADE ME FEEL LIKE I DIDN'T DESERVE YOUR RESPECT.
IT'S BEEN MY PLEASURE WATCHING YOU START AS THE NEW KIDS AND SEEING HOW MUCH YOU'VE GROWN ON THIS SCHOOL TRIP.
YOU'RE BOTH CLASS ACTS IN MY BOOK!
AWW...THANKS, COACH.
YEAH, THANKS, MR. ROCHE.
RAD

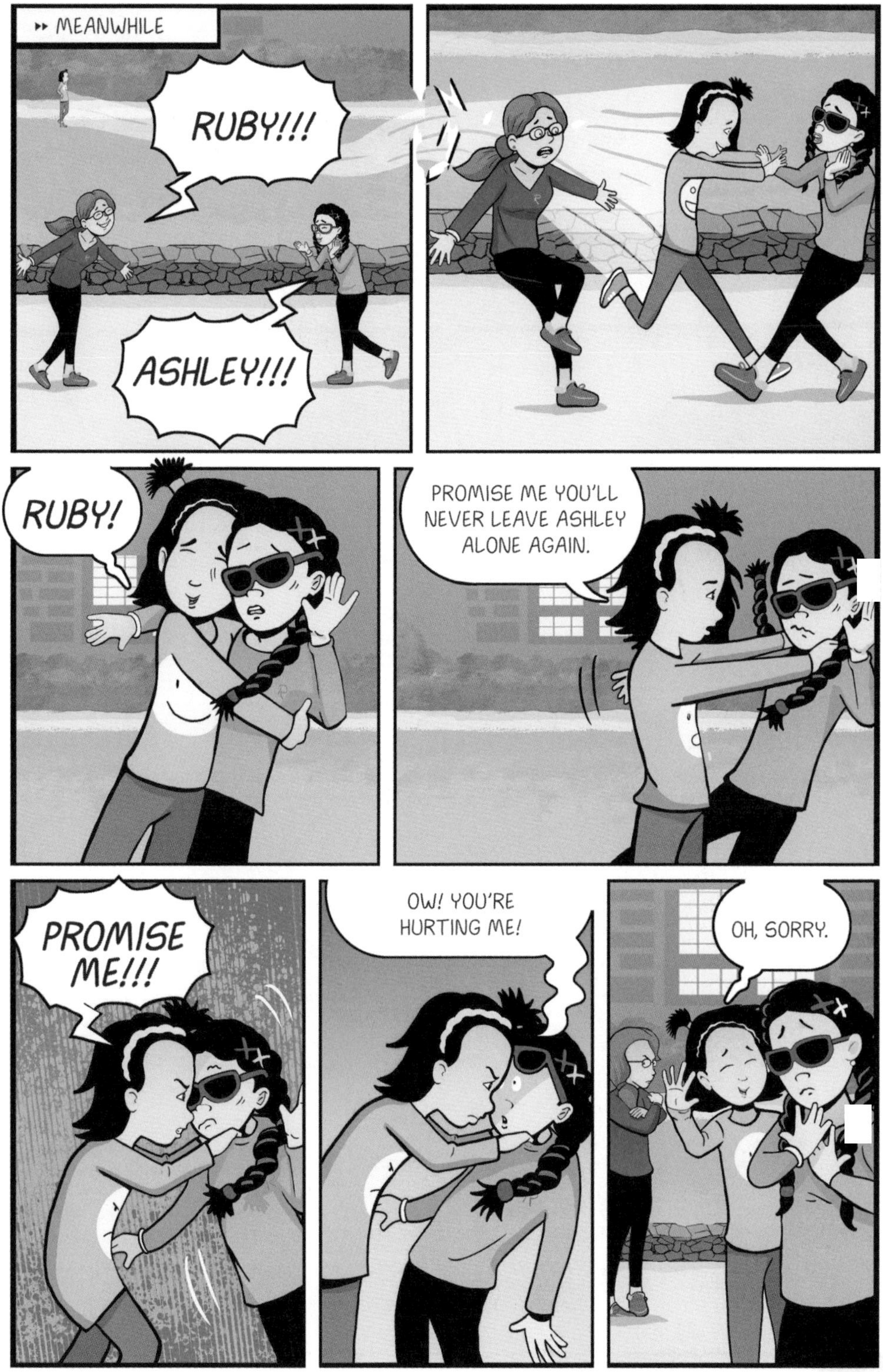
MEANWHILE
RUBY!!!
ASHLEY!!!
RUBY!
PROMISE ME YOU'LL NEVER LEAVE ASHLEY ALONE AGAIN.
PROMISE ME!!!
OW! YOU'RE HURTING ME!
OH, SORRY.

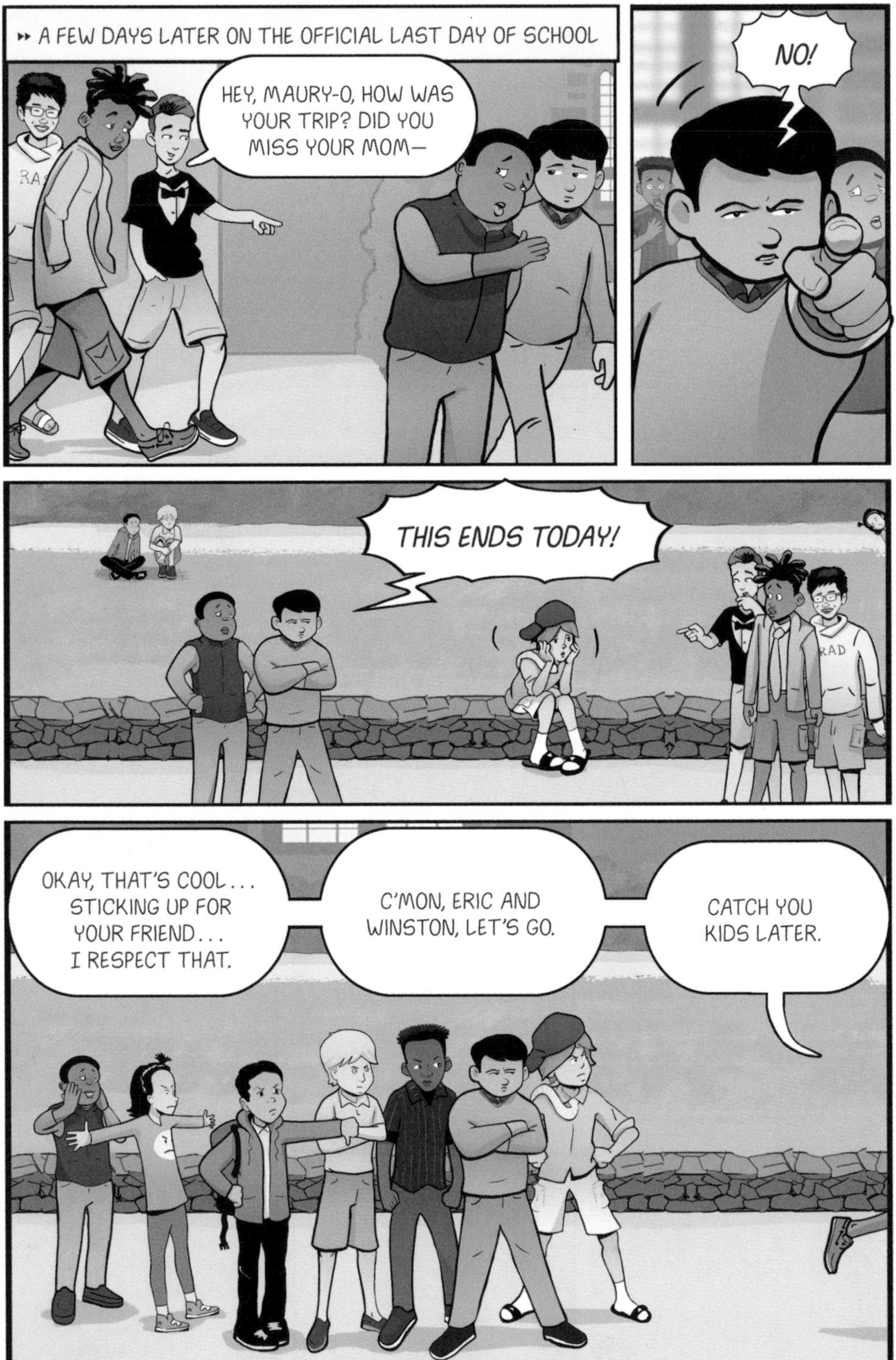

A FEW DAYS LATER ON THE OFFICIAL LAST DAY OF SCHOOL
HEY, MAURY-O, HOW WAS YOUR TRIP? DID YOU MISS YOUR MOM—
NO!
THIS ENDS TODAY!
OKAY, THAT'S COOL... STICKING UP FOR YOUR FRIEND... I RESPECT THAT.
C'MON, ERIC AND WINSTON, LET'S GO.
CATCH YOU KIDS LATER.

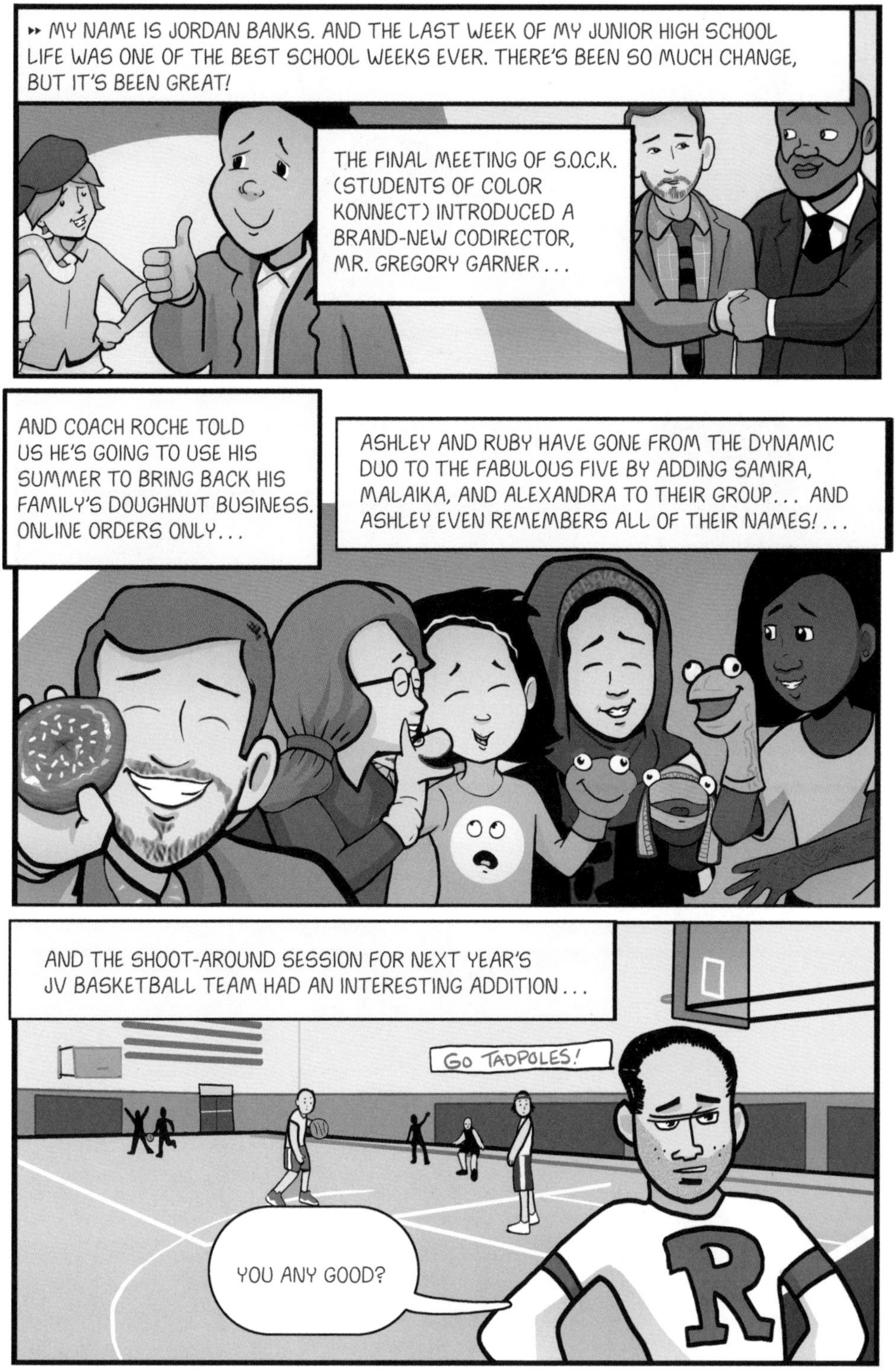
▸▸ MY NAME IS JORDAN BANKS. AND THE LAST WEEK OF MY JUNIOR HIGH SCHOOL LIFE WAS ONE OF THE BEST SCHOOL WEEKS EVER. THERE'S BEEN SO MUCH CHANGE, BUT IT'S BEEN GREAT!
THE FINAL MEETING OF S.O.C.K. (STUDENTS OF COLOR KONNECT) INTRODUCED A BRAND-NEW CODIRECTOR, MR. GREGORY GARNER . . .
AND COACH ROCHE TOLD US HE'S GOING TO USE HIS SUMMER TO BRING BACK HIS FAMILY'S DOUGHNUT BUSINESS. ONLINE ORDERS ONLY . . .
ASHLEY AND RUBY HAVE GONE FROM THE DYNAMIC DUO TO THE FABULOUS FIVE BY ADDING SAMIRA, MALAIKA, AND ALEXANDRA TO THEIR GROUP . . . AND ASHLEY EVEN REMEMBERS ALL OF THEIR NAMES! . . .
AND THE SHOOT-AROUND SESSION FOR NEXT YEAR'S JV BASKETBALL TEAM HAD AN INTERESTING ADDITION . . .
GO TADPOLES!
YOU ANY GOOD?

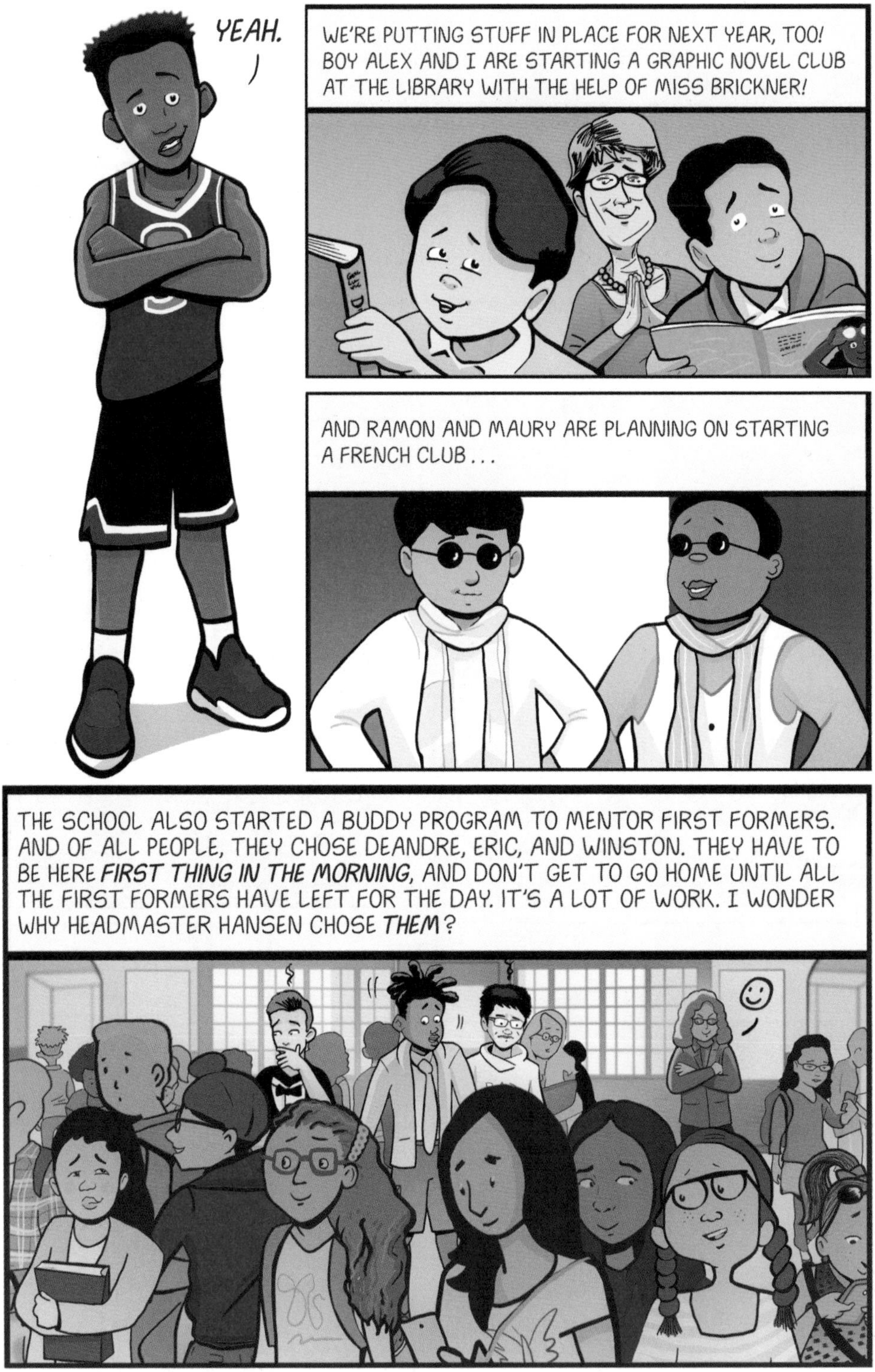
YEAH.
WE'RE PUTTING STUFF IN PLACE FOR NEXT YEAR, TOO! BOY ALEX AND I ARE STARTING A GRAPHIC NOVEL CLUB AT THE LIBRARY WITH THE HELP OF MISS BRICKNER!
AND RAMON AND MAURY ARE PLANNING ON STARTING A FRENCH CLUB . . .
THE SCHOOL ALSO STARTED A BUDDY PROGRAM TO MENTOR FIRST FORMERS. AND OF ALL PEOPLE, THEY CHOSE DEANDRE, ERIC, AND WINSTON. THEY HAVE TO BE HERE *FIRST THING IN THE MORNING*, AND DON'T GET TO GO HOME UNTIL ALL THE FIRST FORMERS HAVE LEFT FOR THE DAY. IT'S A LOT OF WORK. I WONDER WHY HEADMASTER HANSEN CHOSE ***THEM***?

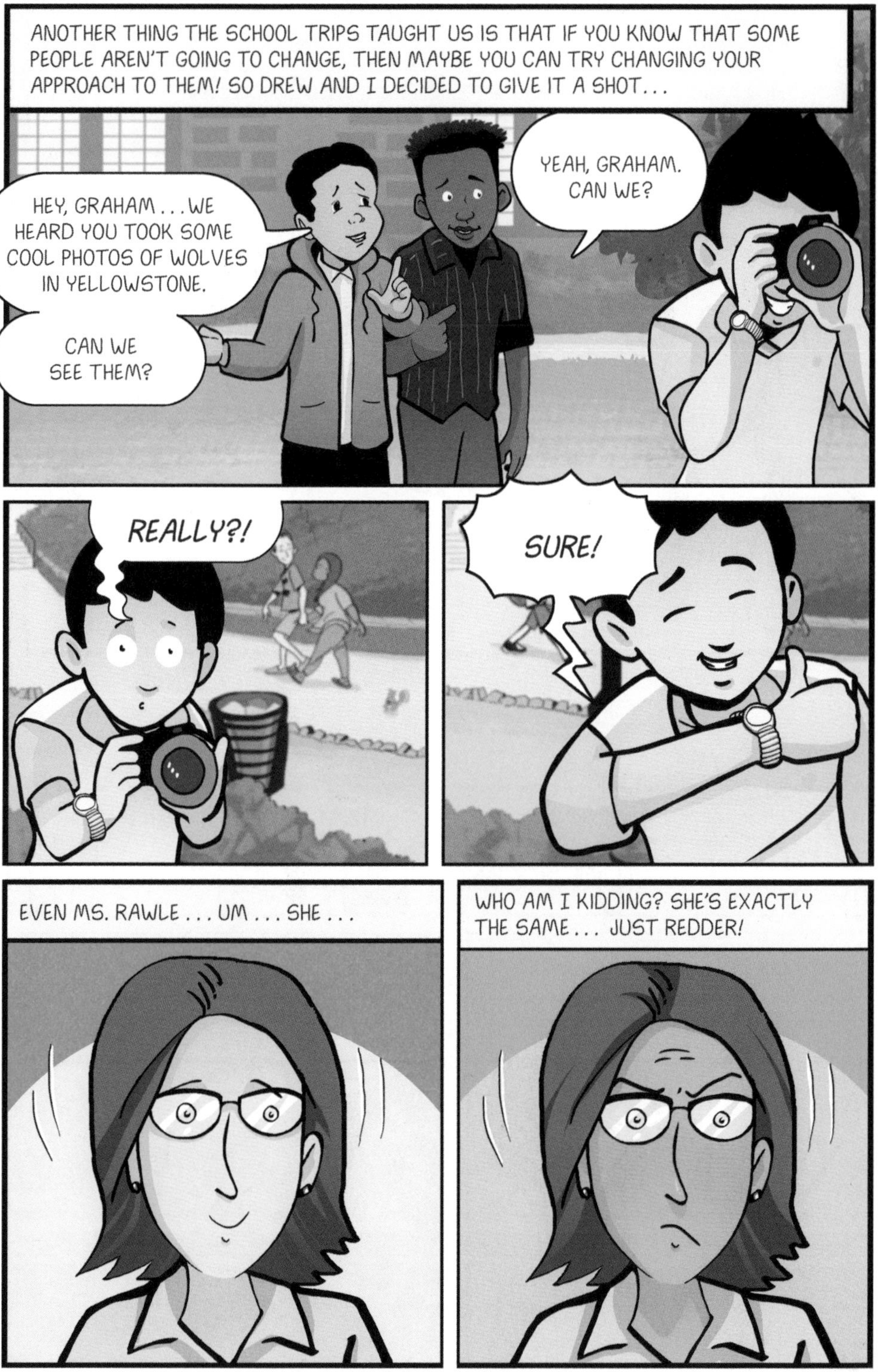

ANOTHER THING THE SCHOOL TRIPS TAUGHT US IS THAT IF YOU KNOW THAT SOME PEOPLE AREN'T GOING TO CHANGE, THEN MAYBE YOU CAN TRY CHANGING YOUR APPROACH TO THEM! SO DREW AND I DECIDED TO GIVE IT A SHOT...
HEY, GRAHAM... WE HEARD YOU TOOK SOME COOL PHOTOS OF WOLVES IN YELLOWSTONE.
CAN WE SEE THEM?
YEAH, GRAHAM. CAN WE?
REALLY?!
SURE!
EVEN MS. RAWLE... UM... SHE...
WHO AM I KIDDING? SHE'S EXACTLY THE SAME... JUST REDDER!

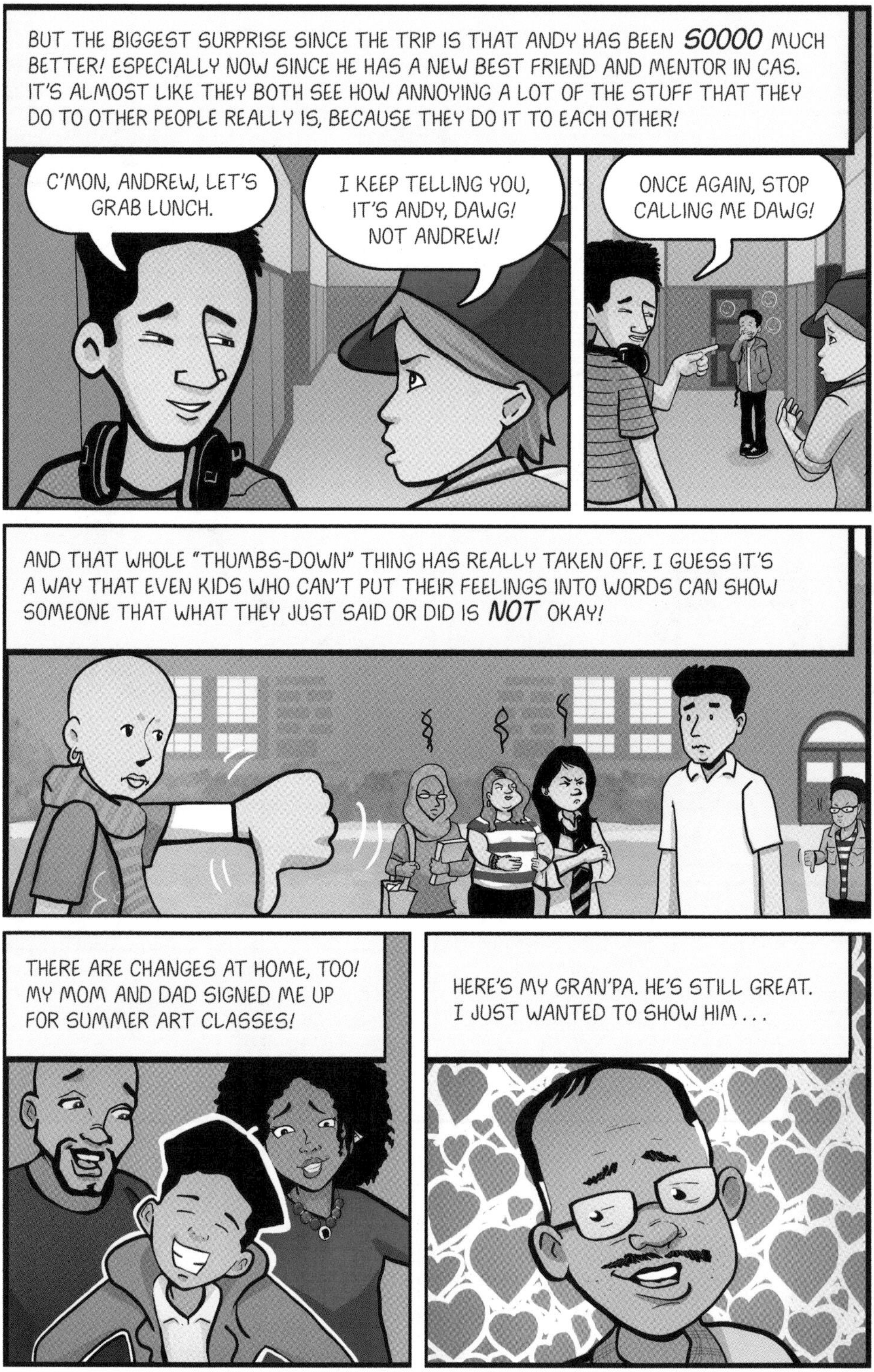
BUT THE BIGGEST SURPRISE SINCE THE TRIP IS THAT ANDY HAS BEEN SOOOO MUCH BETTER! ESPECIALLY NOW SINCE HE HAS A NEW BEST FRIEND AND MENTOR IN CAS. IT'S ALMOST LIKE THEY BOTH SEE HOW ANNOYING A LOT OF THE STUFF THAT THEY DO TO OTHER PEOPLE REALLY IS, BECAUSE THEY DO IT TO EACH OTHER!
C'MON, ANDREW, LET'S GRAB LUNCH.
I KEEP TELLING YOU, IT'S ANDY, DAWG! NOT ANDREW!
ONCE AGAIN, STOP CALLING ME DAWG!
AND THAT WHOLE "THUMBS-DOWN" THING HAS REALLY TAKEN OFF. I GUESS IT'S A WAY THAT EVEN KIDS WHO CAN'T PUT THEIR FEELINGS INTO WORDS CAN SHOW SOMEONE THAT WHAT THEY JUST SAID OR DID IS NOT OKAY!
THERE ARE CHANGES AT HOME, TOO! MY MOM AND DAD SIGNED ME UP FOR SUMMER ART CLASSES!
HERE'S MY GRAN'PA. HE'S STILL GREAT. I JUST WANTED TO SHOW HIM . . .

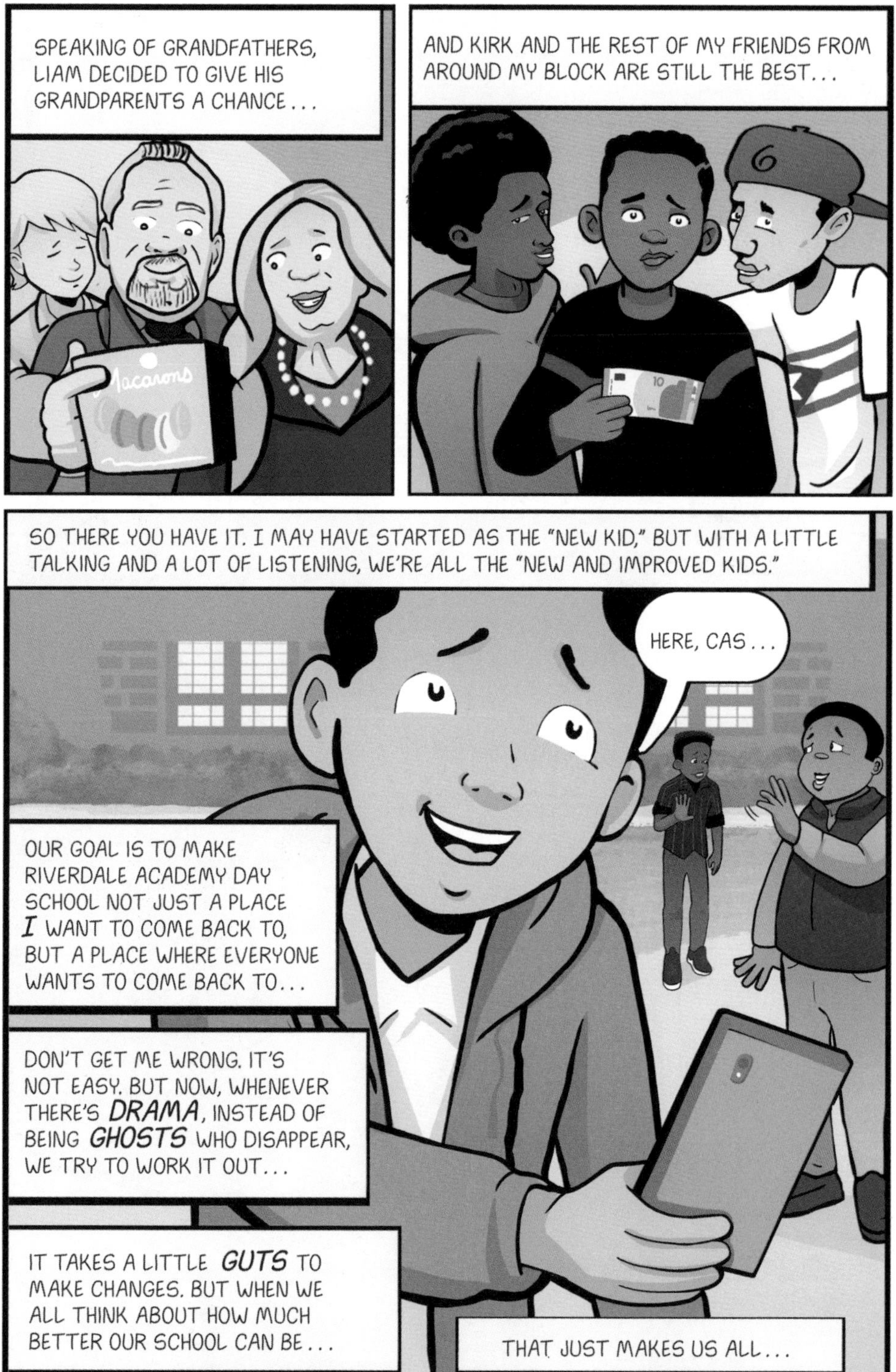
SPEAKING OF GRANDFATHERS, LIAM DECIDED TO GIVE HIS GRANDPARENTS A CHANCE...
Macarons
AND KIRK AND THE REST OF MY FRIENDS FROM AROUND MY BLOCK ARE STILL THE BEST...
SO THERE YOU HAVE IT. I MAY HAVE STARTED AS THE "NEW KID," BUT WITH A LITTLE TALKING AND A LOT OF LISTENING, WE'RE ALL THE "NEW AND IMPROVED KIDS."
HERE, CAS...
OUR GOAL IS TO MAKE RIVERDALE ACADEMY DAY SCHOOL NOT JUST A PLACE *I* WANT TO COME BACK TO, BUT A PLACE WHERE EVERYONE WANTS TO COME BACK TO...
DON'T GET ME WRONG. IT'S NOT EASY. BUT NOW, WHENEVER THERE'S **DRAMA**, INSTEAD OF BEING **GHOSTS** WHO DISAPPEAR, WE TRY TO WORK IT OUT...
IT TAKES A LITTLE **GUTS** TO MAKE CHANGES. BUT WHEN WE ALL THINK ABOUT HOW MUCH BETTER OUR SCHOOL CAN BE...
THAT JUST MAKES US ALL...

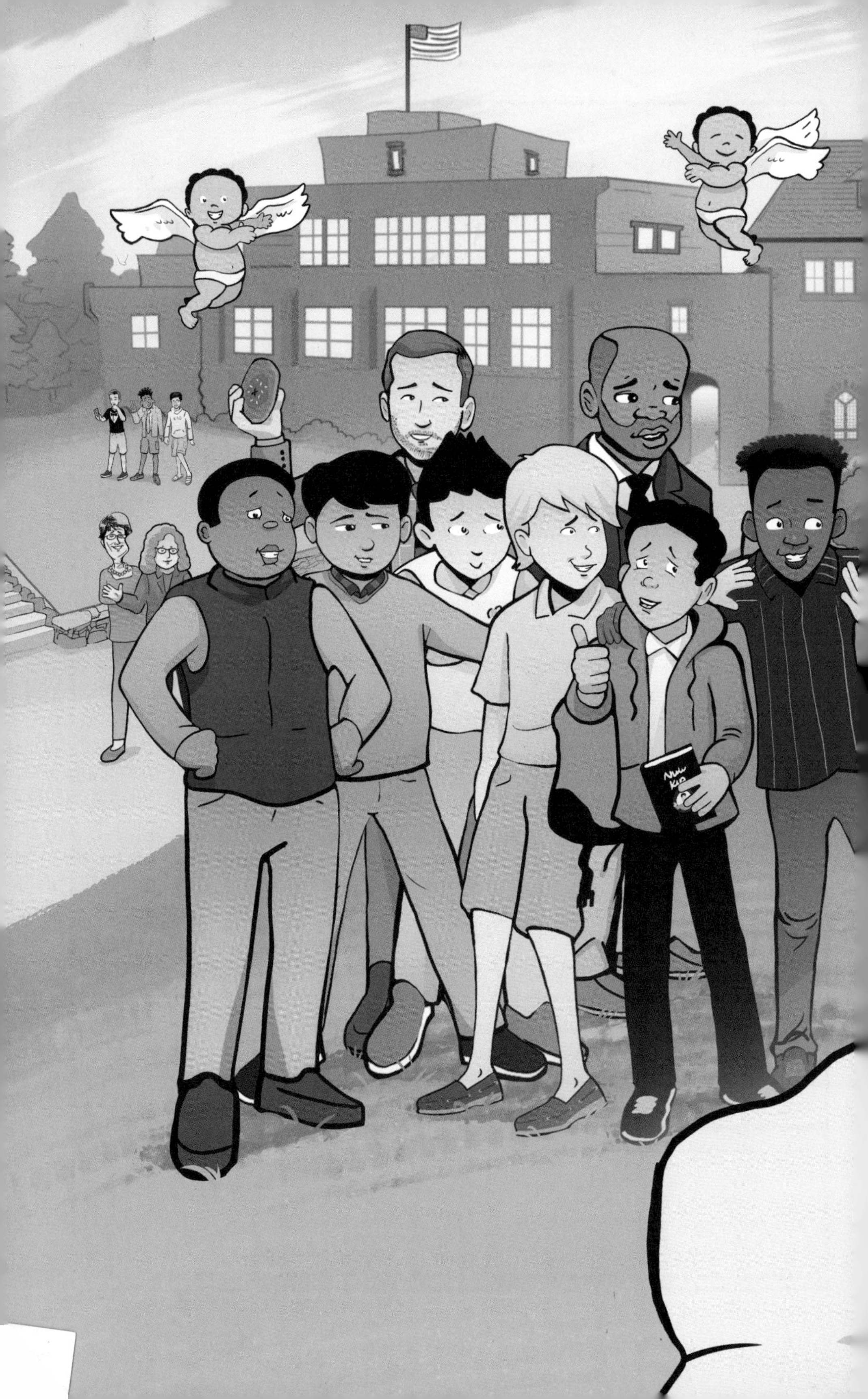

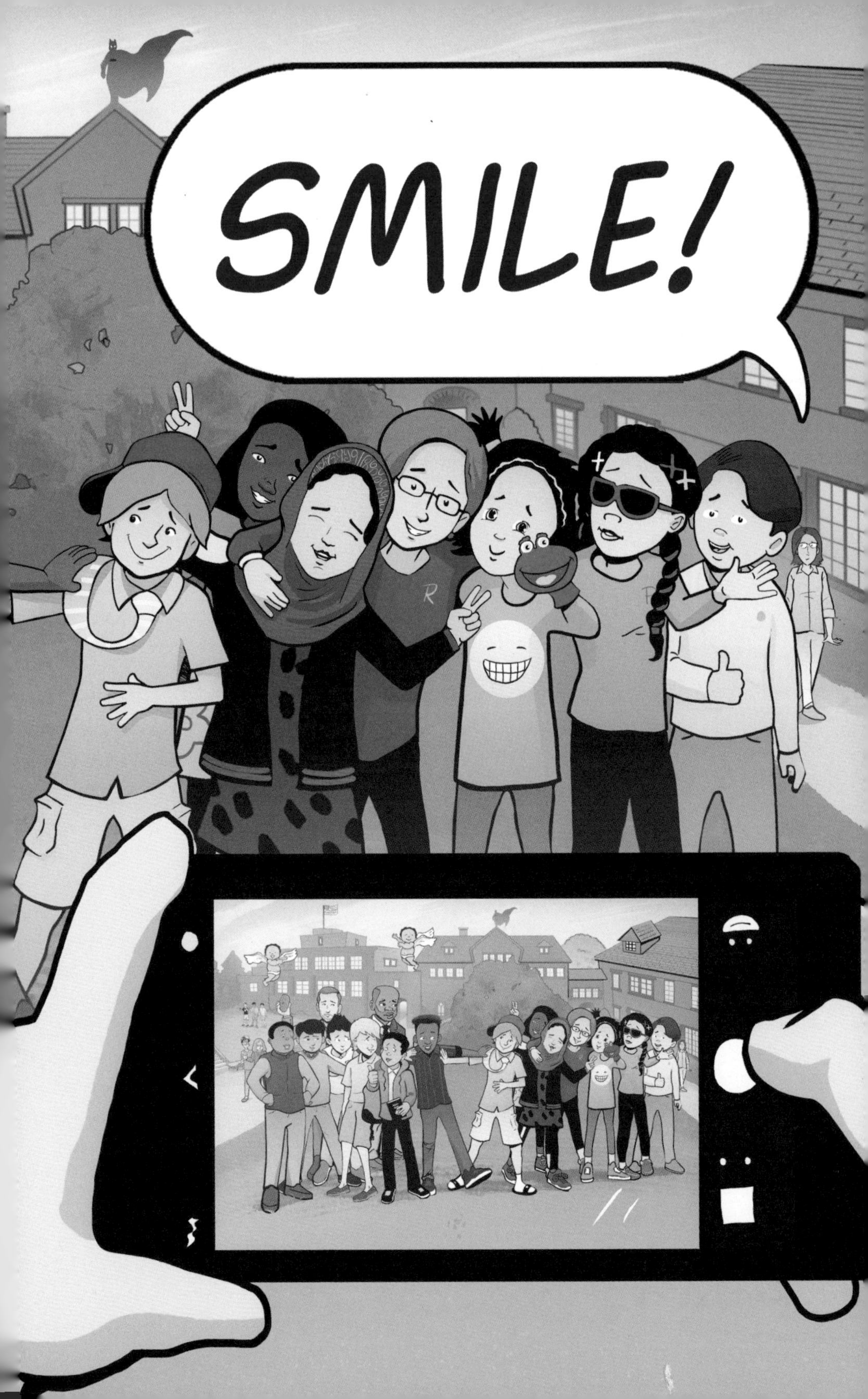
SMILE!

All I have ever wanted to do was to make the books that I wish I had when I was a kid. To show kids of color in new and positive ways. Like traveling to Paris! And that is why this book is so important to me. But there would be no *School Trip* without my first two books.

In January 2017, I signed with HarperCollins to do a graphic novel called *New Kid* and my life has never been the same. A mere three years later, it became the first graphic novel ever to win the John Newbery Medal for the most outstanding contribution to children's literature, the Kirkus Prize for Young Readers' Literature, and the Coretta Scott King Author Award for the most outstanding work by an African American writer.

In October 2020, *New Kid* was joined by its companion book, *Class Act*, which was welcomed with six starred reviews and quickly also became a #1 *New York Times* bestseller.
Since then, I have seen *New Kid* listed as one of the most influential children's books of all time, as well as one of the most banned and challenged. I have also seen my books read by fans all over the world as they have been translated into more than a dozen languages.

But I couldn't have done it without the support of some incredible people. Thank you to the supertalented Der-shing Helmer for bringing my colors to life! And to my art assistant, John-Raymond De Bard, for making my workload a little easier.

Thank you to Suzanne Murphy, Rosemary Brosnan, and my amazing team at Quill Tree Books.

A huge thank-you to my agent, Judy Hansen, who has stood with me from the very beginning to help bring *New Kid*, *Class Act*, and *School Trip* to life.

Thank you to my fans: The kids. The teachers. The librarians. The parents. The book groups. The reviewers. The bloggers. The publications. And the award committees who have shown my books so much love.

And last but not least, to my sons, Jay and Aren, for always supporting their dad. And to my wife, Denise, for keeping me company during my eighteen-hour workdays.

BRANDON
HARRUP
CHARLES

BH